PETER LOVESEY OMNIBUS

Bloodhounds

Diamond Dust

PETER LOVESEY OMNIBUS

Bloodhounds
Diamond Dust

PETER LOVESEY

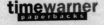

A *Time Warner* Paperback

This omnibus edition first published in Great Britain by
Time Warner Paperbacks in 2004
Peter Lovesey Omnibus Copyright © Peter Lovesey 2004

Previously published separately:
Bloodhounds first published in Great Britain in 1996
by Little, Brown and Company
Published by Warner Books in 1997
Reprinted 1998
Reprinted by Time Warner Paperbacks in 2003
Copyright © Peter Lovesey 1996

Diamond Dust first published in Great Britain in 2002
by Little, Brown
Published by Time Warner Paperbacks in 2003
Copyright © Peter Lovesey 2002

The moral right of the author has been asserted.

A CIP catalogue record for this book
is available from the British Library.

ISBN 0 7515 3626 1

Printed and bound in Great Britain by
Clays Ltd, St Ives plc

Time Warner Paperbacks
An imprint of
Time Warner Books UK
Brettenham House
Lancaster Place
London WC2E 7EN

www.TimeWarnerBooks.co.uk

Bloodhounds

THE FIRST RIDDLE

The Challenge

ONE

Detective Superintendent Peter Diamond was suffering in the rear seat of a police car scorching towards Bath along the Keynsham bypass with the headlamps on full beam, blue light pulsing and siren wailing.

'You want to look out for idiot drivers,' he shouted to his driver.

'Everyone can hear us coming, sir.'

'Yes, but they don't all do what you expect.' If this went on much longer, his heels would make holes in the carpet. He was only aboard because he'd been giving evidence in court at Bristol and happened to ask the driver for a lift back to Bath. The emergency call had come over the car radio soon after they drove off. Sheer bad luck. 'You said this one is a bank.'

'Yes, sir.'

'Do you have a bank account, son?'

'Yes, sir.'

'At this branch?'

'No, sir.'

'Well, then.'

'It's an emergency call.'

'It happens all the time,' Diamond told him, still competing with the siren. 'Some poor chump goes into the red and the manager bites his leg off. They're sharks. They send you a letter telling you you're two pounds overdrawn and then slap on a ten-pound charge for sending it.'

The conversation didn't develop. The siren defeated it. Diamond tried not to look at the dizzying blur of green that

3

was all he could see of the trees beside the road. Only that morning, sitting in court, he had seriously thought police work in Bath was a doddle. When they approached the roundabout that linked Bath Road and Broadmead Lane he closed his eyes.

They came to a screeching halt outside a branch bank on the A4 in Saltford.

'Looks like we're the first,' Diamond said without a trace of pleasure in the achievement. 'Who's that wally in the doorway, do your reckon – one of ours, or one of theirs?'

The man was wearing a grey pinstripe three-piece and waving to the police car, so the balance of probability was that he was friendly. He came over while Diamond was still in the act of levering his large body out.

'Routledge,' the pinstriped gent introduced himself. The voice had a fruity quality, a definite hint of the plum. 'Chief clerk.' He actually offered to shake hands – as if Diamond had called to open an account. 'You got here very quickly.'

'What's the state of play?'

'Well, the manager, Mr Bellini, is dead.'

'*Dead?*'

'Shot through the head,' the chief clerk said in the clipped, matter-of-fact tone of a British actor suppressing his emotion in a film about the war.

'You mean that? Is the gunman still in there?'

'Er, no.'

'Any witnesses?'

'Witnesses? No, it happened in Mr Bellini's office.'

'People must have heard the shot,' said Diamond.

'Oh, that's for sure.'

'And seen the man come out.'

Routledge gave the matter serious thought. 'I don't think they could have done. You'll have to ask them. I think they ducked behind the counters.'

Diamond's brain was grinding through the information he'd been given. 'If no one saw the gunman come

4

out, how do you know he isn't in there still, with Mr Bellini?'

Routledge gave a shrug and a self-effacing smile. 'Well, as a matter of fact, officer, I shot him myself. Forgive me for speaking plainly. Mr Bellini was a total plonker.'

TWO

The Church of St Michael with St Paul, built just before Queen Victoria came to the throne, stands at the point where Broad Street meets Walcot Street, close to the Podium and the Post Office. The writer John Haddon in his *Portrait of Bath* described it as 'a good eye-stopper', a summing-up that is difficult to better. The spire is one of the tallest in the city. The south front, necessarily slender because of the tapered piece of ground it occupies, is said to have been inspired by Salisbury Cathedral. Unhappily Salisbury Cathedral doesn't sit well in the centre of Bath. Narrow lancet windows, buttresses and pinnacles do not blend easily with Georgian or mock-Georgian pediments and columns. The nicest thing that has happened to St Michael's in recent years is that the stone-cleaners were called in. A century and a half of grime has been removed and now the colour of the building matches adjacent buildings even if the architecture does not.

At ten to eight on a rainy October evening a woman in a yellow PVC raincoat approached from Broad Street, taking care to block her view of most of the building with her umbrella. The scale of St Michael's intimidated Shirley-Ann Miller. She was not a church-goer. The only time she had braved the inside of a church in the past ten years was for a Nigel Kennedy recital at Christchurch during the Festival some years back. The adolescent crush she'd had on the punk violinist had lasted well into her twenties. This evening she was drawn by another enthusiasm and it had to be a strong

6

pull to get her here, for the meeting was to take place in the crypt.

The main doors to the church were locked. Shirley-Ann toured the outside searching for another entrance, doubts growing as to whether she had been misinformed. On the Walcot Street side she found a set of descending steps behind railings. She took off her glasses and wiped them dry, looking for some kind of notice. At the bottom of the steps was an arch-topped door that definitely led under floor level. She released the catch on the umbrella and gave it a shake, took a deep breath and stepped down.

Prepared for flagstones, cobwebs and tombs, she was reassured to find that the way into the crypt was clean and well-lit. There were doors leading off a short corridor and she could hear voices from the room at the end.

She always felt nervous meeting people for the first time, but that had to be overcome. She pushed open the glass door to her right and stepped inside. It was like a private health centre, warm, light and carpeted, with not a coffin in sight. The cream-coloured walls had travel posters. Everything was so immaculate that she was concerned about marking the oatmeal carpet with her wet shoes.

The man and woman she had overheard stopped speaking and stared at her. To Shirley-Ann in her jittery state, the woman appeared a dragon empress, sixtyish, with a broad, powdered face with emerald-green eye-shadow that toned with her peacock-blue high-necked oriental dress. Jade ear-rings. Heavily varnished nails. The rest of her was more European: permed blonde hair and fleshy orange lips pursed in disdain.

The man was as awesome in his way as the woman. His black beard looked as if it came from a joke-shop; it didn't match the silver hair on his head. Shirley-Ann found herself wondering if the beard was attached to his red-framed glasses, and if the whole thing lifted off in one piece.

Since neither of these people spoke, she introduced herself.

They just stared back, so she felt compelled to announce, 'I do hope I'm not in the wrong place. Are you the Bloodhounds of Bath?'

How toe-curling it sounded.

The man didn't answer directly, but said, 'Do you want to become a member, then?'

'I was told there might be room for me. I adore detective stories.'

'I wouldn't admit to that if I were you,' he cautioned her as if he were giving legal advice. 'Some of the group won't be at all happy with such an admission. We have to define our tastes most scrupulously. You would be better advised – if you must give anything away at this stage – to say that you are a student of the crime novel, wouldn't she, Miss Chilmark?'

The dragon empress twitched her mouth and said nothing.

The man went on, 'The term *crime novel* embraces so much more than the old-fashioned detective story.' He took a measured look at the stone pillars of the crypt. 'We're a broad church here.'

Shirley-Ann realised that this last remark was meant to be witty. She managed a semi-stifled laugh, and then said, 'I didn't mean just detective stories.'

'What did you mean?' he asked.

She was beginning to think she had made a ghastly mistake coming here. 'I said the first thing that came into my head.'

'Not always wise. Should we call you Miss, Mrs or Ms?'

'I'd prefer you to use my first name, if that's all right.'

'Perfectly all right with me,' the man said in a more friendly tone. 'I'm known to everyone as Milo. I don't much care for my surname. It's Motion and I was called deplorable things at prep school. On the other hand, Miss Chilmark is always addressed as . . . Miss Chilmark.'

Miss Chilmark explained in a voice that might have announced the programmes in the early days of television, 'There have been Chilmarks in the West Country for seven hundred years. I'm not ashamed of my surname.'

'How many are there in the group?' Shirley-Ann asked. It had to be asked. If there weren't any others, she wasn't staying.

'The Bloodhounds? We're down to six. Seven, if you join,' Milo informed her. 'We've had a goodly number over the years, but they don't all persevere. Some die, some leave the district and some are out of their depth. Are you well informed about the genre?'

'The what?'

'The crime fiction genre. What do you read?'

'Oh, just about everything,' said Shirley-Ann, not wishing anyone to think she was out of her depth. She felt marginally more comfortable knowing that there were other Bloodhounds than these two. 'I devour them. I've been through everything in the library and I have to go round charity shops for more. I'm always looking for new titles.'

'Yes, but what are they? Whodunits? Police procedurals? Psychological thrillers?'

'All of those, all the time. Plus courtroom dramas, private eyes, espionage, historicals.'

'And you like them all?' asked Milo dubiously.

'I read them all, even the dreadful ones. It's a compulsion, I think. I like them better if they're well written, of course.'

'It sounds as if you could contribute something to the group,' he said.

'Why not?' she said generously. 'I have hundreds to spare.'

Milo felt the beard as if to check that it was still attached and said, 'I meant a contribution of opinions, not books. We're not all so catholic in our reading. We tend to specialise.'

Miss Chilmark was moved to say, 'Personally, I require some intellectual challenge, and I don't mean an impossible plot set in a country house between the wars. Have you read *The Name of the Rose*, by Umberto Eco?'

9

Shirley-Ann nodded.

She wasn't given time to say any more.

'A masterly book,' Miss Chilmark enthused. 'Full of wonderful things. Such atmosphere. Such learning. What a brilliant concept, placing a murder mystery in a medieval monastery. And the mystery – so intriguing that you don't want it to end! A map, a labyrinth, a distorting mirror and brilliant deductions. Of course everyone else has climbed on the bandwagon since. These stories that you see everywhere, about the monk in Shrewsbury—'

'Brother Cadfael?' said Shirley-Ann.

'That's the one. Transparently inspired by Eco's great work.'

'I think you could be mistaken there,' Shirley-Ann gently pointed out. 'The first Cadfael book, *A Morbid Taste for Bones*, appeared some years before *The Name of the Rose*. I know, because I read it when I was recovering from my appendix operation, in 1977. *The Name of the Rose* came out in 1983, the year I got a frozen shoulder.'

'That can be agony,' said Milo.

'Oh, but I'm sure it was available in the Italian,' said Miss Chilmark with a superior smile.

'I should check your facts before you take her on,' Milo muttered.

Shirley-Ann said no more about Brother Cadfael, but she had privately vowed to find the truth of it at the first opportunity.

There was a timely interruption. Another of the Blood-hounds came in, unfastened the silk scarf from her head – it looked like a Liberty design – and shook her hair. Blonde and short, this was hair of the springy, loose-curled kind that needed no combing to look neatly groomed.

Shirley-Ann's hand automatically moved to her own head to tidy the crow's nest she knew was there. Hers would never co-operate.

Milo introduced the newcomer. 'This is Jessica, our expert on the female investigator. Give her a chance and she'll reel off all their names.'

'Lovely!' Shirley-Ann was relieved to discover that the Bloodhounds weren't all over sixty. 'Let me try some. V.I. Warshawski, Kinsey Mullhone, Sharon McCone, Jenny Cain.'

'Let's hear it for the Brits,' countered Jessica with a wide smile. 'Cordelia Gray, Jemima Shore, Anna Lee, Penny Wanawake, Kate . . . Kate . . . Val McDermid's character, em . . . Oh, what's my brain doing?'

'Kate Brannigan,' Shirley-Ann said almost apologetically.

'You read McDermid?'

'She reads everything, apparently,' said Milo without spite. 'She's going to keep us very well informed. I'm extremely wary of disclosing my special interest in such company.'

The remark, and the arch way it was said, caused Shirley-Ann to wonder if Milo was gay.

Jessica removed her black Burberry raincoat and dropped it on a table at the side of the room. She was dressed dramatically in a black top and leggings with a white satin sash. 'Where's the chair?'

Milo looked puzzled, and no wonder, since ten padded chairs were arranged in a circle in the centre of the room.

'Chairperson,' Jessica explained. 'Polly.'

'Late for once,' said Milo. 'And so is Rupert.'

'Rupert is always late,' said Miss Chilmark. 'I'm quite willing to take the chair for the time being if you wish to begin.' She strutted across to the circle and sat down.

'That one would love to take over,' Milo confided to Shirley-Ann. 'It's her ambition.'

Jessica said, 'Let's give Polly a few more minutes. She'll be all flustered if she thinks she held us up.'

'Which is why we should start, in my opinion,' said Miss Chilmark from the circle.

No one else moved to join her, and that seemed to settle the matter.

Jessica asked nobody in particular, 'Is Sid here? Oh, yes.'

11

To Shirley-Ann's amazement a man in a fawn raincoat confirmed his presence by stepping into view from behind a pillar and lifting a hand in a gesture that might have been intended as a friendly wave, except that the outstretched fingers and the startled eyes behind them suggested Sid was warding off a banshee attack. He must have been in the crypt before she arrived. He said nothing, no one took any more notice and Shirley-Ann felt rather embarrassed for him.

'You must be local. Am I right?' Jessica enquired of Shirley-Ann in the charmingly assertive tone cultivated English women use to show that they ignore certain things.

'We have a flat in Russell Street,' Shirley-Ann answered. 'That is, Bert – my partner – has the flat. We've been together almost six months. He's local, born and bred in Bath. I'm afraid I'm not. I only arrived in the city last year.'

'Don't apologise for that, my dear,' said Jessica.

'Well, I do feel slightly ashamed among people who have been here for years. You see, I work with one of the bus companies, on their tours.'

'You're a guide, and you only came last year!' said Jessica with a peal of laughter. 'Good luck to you. Where are you from? You sound like a Londoner.'

'Islington, originally.'

'And your partner's a Bathonian. Well, you'll get all the gossip on the city from him, I expect. What does he do?' She was drawing out the information in a way no one could object to.

'Bert? He works at the Sports and Leisure Centre. He's often out in the evenings, so the Bloodhounds would fit in quite nicely for me – if you'll have me. Who runs it?'

Milo pitched in. 'We're totally informal,' he claimed, though the evidence so far suggested otherwise. 'Two or three of us – that is to say, Polly Wycherley, Tom Parry-Morgan (now dead, poor fellow) and I – discovered a mutual interest in crime fiction through a dinner at the

12

Pump Room a few years back, when the writer P.D. James was one of the speakers. We happened to be sharing a table, you see. Polly is one of life's organisers, as you will discover, and she made sure that we all met again. Periodically we've been traced to our lair by other Bloodhounds.'

'That's how you join,' added Jessica.

'Now I understand the name,' said Shirley-Ann. 'And is there a fee?'

'We chip in enough to cover the hire of the room,' said Milo. 'We used to meet in pubs at the beginning, but some of the ladies decided a meeting room would be more civilised.'

'That isn't true,' Miss Chilmark called across from the chair. 'We were asked to meet somewhere else after Rupert misbehaved himself in the Roman Bar at the Francis.'

'We could have gone to another pub,' said Milo.

'You know it would have been the same story.'

The information-gathering had not been entirely one-sided. Shirley-Ann did some mental addition and realised that she now knew something about all the Bloodhounds. Six, Milo had said. Three women: Polly, the Chair, famous for her organising skills, but liable to be flustered if late; the Eco devotee, Miss Chilmark, ambitious to take over; and Jessica, the expert on the female private eyes. She was grateful for Jessica. And the men: Milo, probably a civil servant by his pedantic manner, and possibly gay; Sid, who hid; and Rupert, who misbehaved in pubs. Good thing she hadn't come here to look for male companionship.

'Rupert's all right,' Jessica told her. 'I think it's mostly role-play with him. He claims to have met all sorts of famous people. But he stops us from getting too stuffy and parochial. He's deeply into what he calls "Crime Noir" – authors like James Ellroy and Jonathan Kellerman.'

'Will he be coming tonight?'

'I expect so, but not before we start. He likes to make an entrance.'

13

Shirley-Ann wasn't yet convinced that she would tolerate Rupert as blithely as Jessica did.

A voice from the door said, 'So sorry, everyone. What will you think of me? I dropped my car keys down a drain and I've been trying to hook them up for the past twenty minutes.' It had to be Polly Wycherley, and the poor dear was flushed with the experience, or her embarrassment. Her breathing sounded asthmatic. She raised the average age of the group closer to sixty, but there was a reassuring softness and mobility in her features. Short, chunky, silver-haired and wearing a pale green Dannimac coat, she was Shirley-Ann's idea of a favourite aunt.

'Did you get them back?' Milo asked.

'Yes – thanks to a kind-hearted taxi-driver who saw me on my knees by the side of the road. It happens quite often, apparently. Not to me, I mean.' Dimples of amusement appeared in her cheeks. 'I could tell you what to do if it happens to you, but I've wasted enough time already. Listen everyone, I've got to wash my hands. Why don't you begin without me?'

'Good suggestion,' said Miss Chilmark. 'Sit down, ladies and gentlemen.'

'We can wait a few more minutes,' said Jessica quickly.

'Yes, let's wait,' Milo chipped in.

Miss Chilmark's eyes narrowed, but she said no more.

'What's the programme tonight?' Shirley-Ann asked Milo.

'I'm not sure. We leave that up to Polly. We're not too rigid about the way we run it. One thing you should be prepared for: we take turns to talk about a book we enjoyed recently.'

'Don't you dare mention *The Name of the Rose*,' murmured Jessica.

'I hope I don't have to go through some initiation rite.'

Milo's eyes sparkled. 'A secret ceremony?'

Jessica said, 'Black candles and a skull? What's that club

14

that writers belong to? The Detection Club.'

Polly reappeared and there was a general move towards the circle of chairs. The Bloodhounds didn't look as if they went in for secret ceremonies.

THREE

'Come in, Peter, we're waiting with bated breath,' said the
Assistant Chief Constable.

'What for, sir?'

'You don't know?'

With distrust, Diamond eyed the amused faces around
the oval table in the conference room. This was the
evening when the ACC's monthly meeting of high fliers
took place upstairs in the 'eagle's nest' in Bath Central
Police Station.

'For the story of your latest arrest. How you nicked the
Saltford bank clerk.'

'Am I being ever so gently sent up?'

'Good Lord, no. We want to share in your satisfaction.
You let it be known in no uncertain terms that a decent
murder hadn't come your way since you were reinstated
as head of the squad. Now this falls into your lap.'

'I wouldn't call it a decent murder,' said Diamond. 'Two
little men in a bank. One gets on the other's wick, so he
shoots him. It isn't worth the paperwork.'

'Has he confessed?'

'In seventeen pages – so far.'

The ACC commented, 'That *is* some paperwork. It isn't
so straightforward, then.'

'He has a list of grievances going back six years.'

Several sets of eyes met in amusement across the table.
No one said it, but Diamond was well known for having
grievances of his own and one of them was the amount
of form-filling in modern police work.

'Where did he get the gun?' someone asked.

'Right between the eyes,' said Diamond.

'I meant where—'

'We haven't got to that yet. About page twenty-five, I should think.'

'Don't despair, Peter,' said the ACC – a relative newcomer who hadn't really earned the right to call anyone by his first name yet. 'Keep taking the statement. Your bank clerk may turn out to have been a serial murderer.'

Polite smiles all round.

Diamond shook his head and said, 'A good old-fashioned mystery will do me. I don't ask for bodies at every turn. Just one will do if it presents a challenge. Is that too much to ask in Bath?'

'Any time you feel like giving up . . .' murmured John Wigfull, head of the murder squad until Diamond's recall. Wigfull now functioned as head of CID operations and he wasn't a happy man either.

The ACC sensed that it was time to get down to business, and for the next hour Wigfull, rather than Diamond, was in the hot seat. The main item on the agenda was crime prevention and Wigfull had taken over Operation Bumblebee, the publicity campaign against burglary. It was a new baby for him, but he'd done his homework and he managed to talk convincingly about the reduction in the crime figures. 'It's an outstanding success however you measure it, sir,' he summed up. 'And of course all the break-ins reported go straight into the hive.'

'The what?' said the ACC.

'The hive, sir. The computer system operated by the Bumblebee team. We analyse the results and decide on initiatives to sting the villains.'

'So computer technology has a major role here?' said the ACC, worthily trying to head off a veritable swarm of bee references.

Diamond stifled a yawn. He wasn't in sympathy with computers any more than he was with bee-based PR campaigns. His thoughts turned to poetry, of all things.

17

This was totally unlike him. He hadn't read a line of verse in years. Yet a phrase mugged up years ago for a school exam was stirring in his memory. What the devil was it? An illustration of some figure of speech?

The discussion of Operation Bumblebee persisted for another twenty minutes. Everyone else around the table seemed to feel it was a chance to make an impression on the new boss, and the squirm factor steadily increased, with talk of getting the buzz on burglars and how the entire station was humming.

Then that elusive phrase surfaced clear and sonorous in Diamond's mind. He spoke it aloud. 'The murmur of innumerable bees.'

The room went silent.

'Onomatopoeia.'

'I suppose it is time we brought this to a close,' the ACC said, after a long, baffled stare at Diamond.

FOUR

In the crypt, the Bloodhounds were in full cry.

'The puzzle is the thing,' Milo Motion bayed. 'The challenge of the puzzle. Without that, there's nothing.'

'You said it!' Jessica rounded on him. 'There's nothing in those books except the puzzle, and if the puzzle's no good you feel cheated at the end. Most of those so-called classic detective stories are flawed. Agatha Christie went to preposterous lengths to mystify her readers and she's reckoned to be the best of them. Take the plot of *The Mousetrap.*'

'Better not,' Polly Wycherley gently cautioned her. 'Just in case any of us hasn't seen the play.'

Jessica jerked her head towards Polly in annoyance, and the flounce of the blonde curls drew an envious sigh from Shirley-Ann. 'Have a heart, Polly,' Jessica said. 'How can we have a serious discussion if we aren't allowed to analyse the plots?'

The reason why Polly was everyone's choice as chairman was made clear. She explained evenly, but with a distinct note of authority, 'Jessica, dear, we all love discussing crime stories, or we wouldn't be here, but another reason for coming is to get recommendations from each other of marvellous books we haven't read. Don't let's rob any book of its mystery.'

'I deliberately mentioned *The Mousetrap* because it isn't a book,' Jessica pointed out.

'Yes, and we appreciate your restraint, but just in case some of us haven't seen the play . . .'

'Is that a ruling from the chair?'

'No, we don't go in for rules,' Polly said serenely. 'If you want to criticise the puzzle story in general terms, my dear, I'm positive that you can do it, and still make the points you wish to.'

'All right,' offered Jessica. 'What I'm saying without mentioning any titles—'

'Thank you, dear,' murmured Polly.

'—is that in order to mystify people, *really* fox them, I mean, writers were forced into concocting story-lines that were just plain silly, like one very well known whodunit in which the person who tells the story is revealed as the killer in the last chapter.'

'The last chapter but two, if my memory serves me right,' put in Shirley-Ann.

Jessica widened her eyes. 'I can see we're going to have to watch what we say in future.'

Shirley-Ann felt herself reddening and was relieved when Jessica softened the remark with a smile.

Milo was not smiling. 'What's wrong with the narrator doing it?'

'Because that's a trick,' said Jessica. 'A piece of literary sleight-of-hand. She had to go to absurd lengths to make it work. I mean, the writer did. This is so difficult, Polly.'

'It didn't trouble me,' said Milo. 'And it didn't trouble millions of other people, judged by the success of the book you're talking about. It's still in print after seventy years.'

'Is that how long ago it was written?' said Polly, dangerously close to offending the principle she had recommended a second or two before. But it seemed she was only steering the discussion in a less adversarial direction. Her piloting couldn't be faulted.

Miss Chilmark, the dragon empress, had been silent up to now. 'There's really no reason why a puzzle story shouldn't have other merits,' she waded in. 'I can think of a work with a wonderful, intricate puzzle that is intellectually pleasing as well as theologically instructive. A novel of character, with a respect for history . . .'

'Any guesses? I never got past page forty-two,' murmured Jessica, unheard by Miss Chilmark, who continued to rhapsodise on the merits of *The Name of the Rose* until she was interrupted by the barking of a dog.

'This will be Rupert,' Jessica informed Shirley-Ann.

'With a dog?'

'The dog isn't the problem,' said Milo.

As it turned out, Milo was mistaken. The dog was a problem. Everyone looked towards the door and a large brown mongrel, perhaps a cross between a setter and a German shepherd, stepped in and sniffed the air. It had a thick, wavy coat gleaming from the drenching it had got and it trotted directly to the centre of the circle and shook itself vigorously. Everyone was spattered. There were shrieks of outrage and the meeting broke up in disorder. A chair was overturned and Polly's handbag tipped upside down. The dog, excited by the commotion, rolled on its back, got up and barked some more.

Miss Chilmark cried, 'Somebody take it outside. My dress is ruined.'

The owner appeared, a tall, thin, staring man in a black leather jacket, dark blue corduroys and a black beret, and rapped out a command.

'Marlowe, heel!'

The dog wagged its tail, gave another shimmy and distributed more moisture.

'It takes no notice of you whatsoever,' Miss Chilmark complained. 'You ought to have it on a leash. Or, better still, leave it at home.'

'That's a flint-hearted attitude, if I may say so, madam,' Rupert replied in an accent redolent of one of the better public schools. 'Coming here is the high point of Marlowe's week. He's merely doing what dogs do to dry themselves.'

Milo said, 'And what about all the other things dogs

21

do? Are we going to be treated to those? I can't bear the suspense.'

'What have you got against dumb animals?' said Rupert. 'How would you like to sit here in a sopping wet coat?'

'How would you like it if I sent you the dry-cleaning bill?' Miss Chilmark riposted.

'Call yourselves Bloodhounds and you panic when a real dog turns up,' Rupert said with a grin that displayed more gaps than teeth.

Polly Wycherley judged this as the proper moment to restore order. 'Why don't we all go back to our seats? Then Marlowe ought to settle down. He's usually no trouble.'

'The chairs are wet,' Miss Chilmark objected. 'I refuse to sit on a wet chair.'

A cloth was produced, the seats were wiped, and the meeting resumed with Marlowe in disgrace, anchored by a lead to his master's chair-leg, and forced to lie outside the circle.

Shirley-Ann was intrigued that Rupert could appear so indifferent to the chaos he and his dog had just inflicted. He sat between Polly and Milo in a relaxed attitude with legs crossed and his left hand cupping his chin. It was a face without much flesh, dominated by a beak of a nose and dark, deep-set, alert eyes overlapped by the front edge of the black beret.

Polly said, 'We were having quite a fruitful discussion about the predominance of the puzzle in the classic detective novel.'

'Tiresome, isn't it?' Rupert took up the challenge at once. 'Totally unconnected with the real world. All those eccentric detectives – snobbish lords and little old ladies and Belgian refugees looking for unconsidered clues. Absolute codswallop. In the whole history of crime in this country, real crime, I defy you to name one murder that was solved by a private detective. You can't.' His owlish eyes scanned the circle. 'You can't.'

22

'That doesn't put me off,' Milo gamely answered. 'I don't want my reading too close to real life.'

'Or real death,' said Jessica.

'Exactly.' But Milo had missed the point.

Rupert laughed and displayed even more gum. He was quite a ruin, but extremely watchable. 'Fairy stories for grown-ups.'

'Why not?' said Milo. 'I like a little magic, even if it turns out to have been a trick.'

Shirley-Ann chimed in, 'That goes for me, too.'

Rupert gave her a pained look. 'Another one suffering from arrested development. Hell's teeth, I'm seriously outnumbered now.'

Polly sounded a lighter note. 'When some of us heard P.D. James at the Pump Room a few years ago, she said she must have had the mind of a crime writer even as a child, because when she first heard the nursery rhyme about Humpty Dumpty, her thought was "Did he fall, or was he pushed?"'

Even Rupert smiled, and then went straight on to the offensive again. 'And they all live happily ever after?' he pressed them. 'Is that what you want from your reading?'

'A sense of order restored, anyway,' said Shirley-Ann. 'Is that the same thing?'

Milo remarked, 'I like the loose ends tidied up.'

'So that you can sleep easy, knowing that all's right with the world,' Rupert summed up with heavy irony. 'Do you people ever read the crime statistics? Do you know what the clear-up rate is? Has any of you ever had your house burgled?'

'Yes.'

Heads turned abruptly, for it was Sid who had spoken. He was so inconspicuous that even a single word was quite a bombshell. Having let it fall, he lowered his eyes again, as if the flat cap resting on his knees had become more interesting than anything else in the room.

Shirley-Ann was intrigued to know what Sid was doing

in a discussion group like this if he was so reluctant to join in. He plainly didn't wish to say any more. He avoided eye contact. His posture, his whole behaviour, seemed to ask the others to ignore him, and that was what she herself had done up to now. She prided herself on being observant, so Sid obviously had a special talent for self-effacement. Not to be defeated, she regarded him minutely. Probably in his early forties, she guessed, with a more powerful physique than his bowed shoulders suggested. Slightly hooded blue-grey eyes, of which she had seen only glimpses, so her power of observation was not so faulty after all. Small, even teeth. Nothing in his looks could justify such shyness. Perhaps he felt out of his element socially. The clothes didn't give obvious clues, except that they were what you expected a man twenty years older to wear. A white shirt and black tie under the raincoat. Was he an undertaker, perhaps? Not a policeman, for heaven's sake? Dark blue trousers, probably part of a suit. Black, well-polished laced-up shoes. The working man's raincoat that he wouldn't be shedding, however warm the surroundings. And the flat cap on his knees. You poor, pathetic bloke, Shirley-Ann summed up. You're not enjoying this one bit, so why are you here?

Rupert had been slightly thrown by Sid's observation. 'The point I was about to make – I think – is that the sort of thing you people enjoy doesn't deserve to be called a crime novel. The only crime novelists worthy of the name are writers you've probably never heard of, let alone read. Ellroy, Vachss, Raymond – the ones bold enough to lift stones and show us the teeming activity underneath. Not country houses, but ghettos where young kids carry guns and murder for crack and even younger kids are sodomised. Corrupt cops taking bribes from pimps and beating confessions out of luckless Irish boys. Rape victims infected with AIDS. Squats littered with used syringes and verminous mattresses and roaches feeding on stale vomit.'

'I don't have the slightest desire to read about stale

vomit,' said Miss Chilmark. 'You get enough of that on the television.'

'Precisely,' said Rupert. 'You switch channels and watch some sanitised story about a sweet old lady who makes nanas of the police through amateur detective work. The same formula week in, week out.'

'As a matter of fact, I hardly ever watch television these days,' Miss Chilmark told him loftily. 'I don't know why I still keep the set in my drawing room.'

Rupert's eyes glittered at the mention of Miss Chilmark's drawing room.

Polly cleared her throat and said, 'Did anyone wish to say any more about the classic detective story?'

'Is that what we were discussing?' Milo said with a disdainful look at Rupert. 'You could have fooled me. Yes, one of us obviously has to speak up for the story that challenges the reader, and as usual, it's me. I put it to you that the Golden Age writers between the wars brought the art of mystification to perfection. Regardless of what some of you were saying just now, I could name a dozen novels of that time, and probably more, that for the brilliance of their plotting stand comparison with anything written in the last half-century. You may talk about the intricacy of a le Carré novel or the punching power of your hard-boiled Americans, but for me and for many others the test is whether the writer has the courage to lay out a mystery – a fair puzzle with clues – and say to the reader, "Solve this if you can" – and then pull off a series of surprises topped by a stunning revelation at the end.'

'But at the cost of many of the other merits one looks for in a decent novel,' said Jessica with more restraint than Rupert.

'Such as . . . ?'

'Character, pace, sharp dialogue and, above all, credibility. The books you're talking about were excellent in their time, Milo, but they were never more than pleasant diversions.'

25

'Pastimes,' suggested Shirley-Ann and got a nod from Jessica.

'That's a word you don't hear so much these days,' said Polly abstractedly. 'Pastimes. Nice word.'

Milo was not to be overridden. 'Of course, the most basic and fascinating form of detective puzzle is the locked room mystery.'

Rupert groaned and slid down in his chair with his long legs extended.

Milo ignored him. 'The master of the locked room mystery was John Dickson Carr. The "hermetically sealed chamber" – as he called it – was a feature of many of his finest novels. I don't know which of you has read *The Hollow Man*.'

Shirley-Ann gingerly raised a hand. The only other reaction came, surprisingly, from Sid, who gave a nod without removing his gaze from his flat cap.

Milo said, 'In that case, I shall definitely bring my copy with me next week. Quite apart from being one of the most entertaining detective stories ever written, *The Hollow Man* has a famous chapter devoted to locked room mysteries. Dr Fell, Dickson Carr's sleuth, holds up the action to deliver a lecture on the subject that is a delight from beginning to end. Am I right?' He looked towards Sid, who gave another nod.

'Yes, why not?' Milo went on. 'I shall read it to you next week, and I'll warrant that Dr Fell will make some converts among you, even if I can't.'

Rupert confided loudly to Shirley-Ann, 'He's hooked on this hogwash, poor fellow. We'll never get him off it. Belongs to the Clue Klux Christie and the Daughters of Dorothy L. and the Stately Holmes Society. Quite mad. They think of themselves as scholars, these people. Believe me, my dear, the only fan club worth joining is the Sherlock Holmes Society of Australia. They meet once a year, get totally plastered, fire guns in the air and sing, "Happy Birthday, Moriarty, you bastard, happy birthday to you!"'

Shirley-Ann felt some sympathy for Milo. He had been outnumbered even before Rupert's arrival.

Polly nudged the tiller again. The best way to focus the discussion, she said, might be to move on to the part of the evening when members spoke about particular books they had read recently. Miss Chilmark offered to begin, but the resourceful Polly remembered that Milo had somehow missed his turn at the previous meeting, so he went first. His announcement that his chosen text was *The Hound of the Baskervilles* was received with an enormous, deeply embarrassing yawn. For a moment no one escaped suspicion. Then the dog Marlowe, lying on his side, yawned again and there were suppressed giggles.

Undaunted, Milo made a spirited claim that *The Hound of the Baskervilles* refuted the arguments levelled against the classic detective story. The power of Conan Doyle's setting and the drama of the plot far outweighed the whodunit puzzle, which was revealed long before the final chapters.

Rupert went next, after first admitting that he, too, admired much of Conan Doyle's work, but found *The Hound* one of the least satisfying examples. He spoke about an Andrew Vachss novel, *Blossom*, based on a real case about the tracking of a sniper who murdered teenagers for sexual kicks. Vachss, he told the Bloodhounds, was a New York child-abuse lawyer who drew on genuine case histories and whose books unashamedly crusaded on behalf of young victims. They were written in anger, with a missionary zeal.

The evening was drawing on, Marlowe had given up yawning and was whimpering intermittently, and Miss Chilmark could be constrained no longer. Milo objected that they had often before been lectured on *The Name of the Rose*, but Rupert, his face radiant with mischief, pointed out that it was a multi-layered book. He gave Marlowe a push and the dog rolled on its back and went quiet. Miss Chilmark was allowed to continue on the understanding that she would talk about aspects she had not touched on before. To her credit, she had some insights to offer on Eco's use of the monastery library, symbolically and as a device to enhance the mystery. All this did take longer than anyone else's contribution and as a consequence Shirley-Ann wasn't called upon.

'Care for a drink?' Jessica asked her when the meeting closed. 'The Moon and Sixpence is just across the street.'

She wasn't used to pubs, and said so. The only thing she knew about the Moon and Sixpence was that there was a plaque on the wall outside stating that it was the address from which the world's first postage stamp had been posted. This piece of philatelic history was open to dispute; there was *another* notice making a similar claim for the postal museum higher up the street. They were currently exhibiting the famous stamp, on special loan from its owner. Shirley-Ann knew next to nothing about stamp-collecting, but she'd been highly amused one Sunday morning at discovering the conflicting statements. Trivia of that kind fascinated her.

Jessica pointed out that it was still raining, so they might as well take shelter in the pub and see if it stopped. 'That is, if your partner isn't expecting you, or something.'

Shirley-Ann was flattered to be asked. She'd placed Jessica in a more sophisticated league than her own. Obviously this chic creature had never once seen the inside of a charity shop, the source of most of Shirley-Ann's clothes. Jessica, she felt sure, was one of that select breed of women who dressed out of the classiest boutiques – where the sales staff started by showing you to a chair and serving you with coffee in bone china cups. It had emerged during the meeting that Jessica was assertive and resourceful and confident at dealing with men. Shirley-Ann told her that Bert wouldn't be back from the sports centre for at least another hour.

So they skirted the front of the church and nipped

across Broad Street and through the cobbled passage to the Moon and Sixpence. 'Some of the people here are far too hearty for my taste,' Jessica confided as they went in. 'I prefer the crowd across the street in the Saracen's Head, but there's one drawback.'

'What's that?'

'The Saracen's is Rupert's favourite watering-hole. He dives straight in there after Bloodhounds. Rupert can be fun, but in small doses, as I imagine his wives discovered.'

'Wives?'

Jessica held up the four fingers and thumb of her right hand.

Trade was brisk in the bar of the Moon and Sixpence. It took them some time to get served. 'You don't know who to blame most,' said Jessica in a carrying voice. 'The blokes piling in like a loose scrum or the barmaids who refuse to catch your eye.' Promptly they were served with their halves of lager. Jessica spotted a corner table just vacated by a middle-aged couple.

'I brought Sid here a couple of times,' she told Shirley-Ann.

'The quiet man?'

'Yes, silent Sid. He's slightly better at communicating one-to-one. The poor guy's impossibly shy.'

Shirley-Ann said, 'I noticed Polly is very gentle with him.'

'She mothers us all. What a bunch!'

'Why did Sid join if it's such an ordeal?'

'Someone told him he should get out and meet people or he might easily flip his lid. He reads crime, so he found his way to us. It must have taken incredible guts to come down those stairs the first time.'

'What sort of crime?'

'The lot, like you, everything from Wilkie Collins to Kinky Friedman. And he knows what he likes. He's quite an authority on John Dickson Carr, the writer Milo was on about.'

29

'Does he ever say anything about himself?'

Jessica laughed. She had the whitest teeth possible. 'Does he ever say anything? I think he might loosen up in thirty years if I worked at it. He does security work, I gather. Not MI6. Just a glorified night-watchman. That's when he gets his reading done, I expect.'

'He isn't married?'

'Doubt it. I haven't asked.' Jessica took a sip of lager and gave a penetrating look. 'You said you aren't?'

'Married?' Shirley-Ann shook her head. 'Bert and I live together and that's enough for the time being.'

'How did you meet?'

'I joined a self-defence class he was running.'

'And he got through your defence?'

She smiled. 'No trouble. How about you?'

A sigh from Jessica. 'I'm cash and carried, as they say. Nine years. Barnaby works in ceramics. Well, that's the way he tells it, and it sounds impressive. Actually he makes those miniature houses. You know? About this high. They sell quite well. People will collect anything. They finish up with a whole village on top of the telly.' She spoke of her husband without warmth, Shirley-Ann noted. She'd had no difficulty sounding warm over almost everything else she'd mentioned.

'And do you have a job yourself?'

Without conceit Jessica told her, 'I manage an art gallery in Northumberland Place. It's called the Walsingham, but really it's mine.'

'Gracious. I've passed it hundreds of times.'

'Come in next time. I won't sell you anything, honest to God. I might even offer you a sherry.'

'You must know a lot about art.'

'Just certain things I specialise in.'

'Modern?'

'Contemporary. You have to be careful over terms. I don't deal in abstracts, which is most people's idea of modern. I'm a shop window for some talented young artists who can actually manage to produce landscapes

30

without zip-fasteners across the middle, or bits of news-paper pasted onto them.'

'Local artists?'

'From all over.'

'Do you paint?'

'God, no.'

'But you obviously know what's good.'

'It's ninety per cent bluff, darling.' Jessica bent her right hand and inspected her long fingernails. 'What did you make of the Bloodhounds, then? A rum lot, aren't we?'

'I enjoyed the discussion,' Shirley-Ann answered with tact.

'You'll get weary of it. We have that argument about escapism versus realism every week in some form or other. The puzzle versus the police procedural. Country houses versus mean streets. It's never resolved. Never will be. Milo and Rupert are at opposite poles. I'm somewhere between, I suppose, but I refuse to give support to either of them.'

'I expect it's amicable.'

Jessica dissented by letting out a breath and vibrating her lips at the same time. 'I wouldn't count on it. They're capable of murder, both of them.'

Shirley-Ann laughed.

'I'm serious.'

'You can't be.'

She put her hand lightly over Shirley-Ann's. 'Darling, if ever I've met a group of potential murderers anywhere, it's the Bloodhounds. It wouldn't take much. They've read about killing, come to terms with it in their minds. I mean, aren't we all participating mentally when we read a crime novel?'

'I'm not sure,' said Shirley-Ann. 'I've never thought of it like that myself.'

'We're the experts, we people who read them steadily. We know all the plots. We've read the gory bits. We know what the police look out for. If anyone could do the job and get away with it, one of us could.'

From across the room came a peal of laughter. Someone had reached the punch-line of a joke. It seemed well timed. Shirley-Ann looked to see if Jessica was smiling, but her face was serious.

FIVE

On Thursday, another meeting was hastily arranged. Putting on his glasses and picking up a file, the new Assistant Chief Constable said, 'Gentlemen, I'm sorry about the short notice, but this is a matter of some urgency. You'll recall that we had an encouraging report from Mr Wigfull only last Monday evening on crime prevention here in Avon and Somerset.' He nodded towards Wigfull.

'Sir?' said Wigfull brightly.

Peter Diamond, seated opposite, surprised himself by recalling another verse from long ago: 'How doth the little busy bee improve each shining hour.' Wisely he didn't speak it aloud.

The ACC was thinking along the same lines. 'This has Bumblebee written all over it. Yesterday we received a tip-off that a major crime is being planned in Bath. A theft. Just out of interest, I wonder if any one of you could name the most valuable piece of property owned by the city.'

'A building?' said Tom Ray, the Chief Constable's staff officer.

'Portable property.'

'Something in the Roman Baths, sir?' suggested Wigfull, his whiskers positively twitching with the challenge. 'A gold torque?'

'Not so ancient as that.'

'Precious metal in some form?'

'No.'

'An antique object?'

33

'You could describe it as such, but antiquity is not what makes it so valuable.'

'A work of art, then?'

The ACC bestowed a smile on Wigfull. 'You're almost there. Anyone else with a suggestion?'

It was apparent from the faces around the table that there would be no takers except Wigfull.

'I don't know a lot about art, sir. Where is it housed? In the Pump Room?'

'The Victoria Gallery.' Sensing astutely that he had reached the limit of his officers' knowledge of fine art, the ACC unveiled the truth. 'It is Turner's painting of the Abbey. A watercolour. Anyone been to see it?'

Total silence.

He added, 'It's worth over a million.'

'One picture?' said Tom Ray, rolling his eyes.

'J.M.W. Turner was probably the greatest painter our nation has ever produced. This was one of his earliest works, completed before he was twenty-one.'

'Hope it's insured,' said Diamond.

The ACC gave him a shocked look. 'We're not giving anyone the chance to steal it.'

'Isn't the gallery guarded by Impregnable?'

Impregnable was the private security firm entrusted with the safety and security of the mayor, the officers and all the public buildings of Bath. Among the police, there was an unending series of jokes about Impregnable.

'Yes, but that doesn't mean we abdicate our responsibility.'

'Good Lord, no,' said Wigfull. 'If the Turner was taken, we'd get stuffed by the press, not Impregnable.'

'Who's Deep Throat?' asked Diamond.

'Deep who?'

'Your source, sir.'

'That's uncertain,' the ACC admitted. 'The tip-off reached us by an indirect route. A CID officer in Bristol – Sergeant Plant – seeking information on another matter, picked it up from one of his snouts.'

34

'I like it,' said Diamond, his belly quivering with amusement.

'What?'

'Sergeant Plant, our plain-clothes man. Who was the snout – Mr Grass?'

The ACC reddened ominously. 'You'd do well to take this seriously, Superintendent. Plant is a promising young officer.'

Diamond made an effort to contain his amusement by thinking about the list of jobs waiting to be done in his new home in Weston. This meeting shouldn't drag on much longer if the Turner was the only topic.

'The point is,' the ACC resumed, 'we have the opportunity to prevent a major theft. I'm ordering a review of security at the gallery. Mr Wigfull, the Bumblebee team will be responsible. You can liaise with Impregnable. We're not trying to score points here. The painting is kept upstairs in the permanent collection. Check the windows, the roof, all points of access. See that the alarms are functioning and the guards are aware of the threat. Art thieves are among the most professional of all the criminal fraternity.'

'Right, sir,' said Wigfull. 'If you don't mind my asking, is the prime objective to scare them off?'

The ACC hesitated. 'Well, I see this as an exercise in crime prevention, don't you?'

'Absolutely, but . . .' His voice trailed away.

'What's your point, then, John?'

Wigfull picked his words judiciously. 'I may be out of order, sir, but it seems to me that we have the opportunity of, er, staking out the gallery and pulling in these villains.'

'Ah.' The ACC's response was flat, still uncommitted.

'If so, it might be wise not to make a show of strengthening the security.'

'You think so?'

'We don't want them getting suspicious.'

'You're thinking of setting a trap?'

35

'With the Bumblebee team and a few others, I could catch them in the act, sir.'

'Good thinking.' Wigfull's plan had got the nod.

'I'll need officers I can rely on, sir, preferably people I know. As we were told that the murder squad isn't overburdened at this time—'

At the mention of his murder squad, Diamond jerked forward in his chair. 'Hold on. How long will this panto-mime go on for? I can't spare men to sit in an art gallery for weeks on end.'

'It might improve their minds,' said Tom Ray.

'You're not busy,' said Wigfull. 'You may not have a murder in the next month.'

'I may commit one,' muttered Diamond.

He had little chance of defending his empire. It was decreed by the ACC that four of the murder squad should be seconded at once to Operation Bumblebee. Wigfull picked them himself. He had the gall to pick Inspector Julie Hargreaves, Diamond's best detective.

'I can't release Julie.'

'I need a woman,' insisted Wigfull.

Tom Ray said, 'Tell us something new.'

Wigfull gave him a fish-eyed stare and said, 'She'll be just right for this. She can sit behind the desk and sell postcards.'

'Terrific,' said Diamond. 'Would you like her to dust the picture frames as well?'

SIX

On Friday, the paper had a News in Brief item at the foot of page two about the murder of the Saltford bank manager and the magistrates' court appearance of the chief clerk. Stephanie Diamond spotted it by chance when she was looking for the weather forecast. The *Guardian*'s layout always defeated her. Peter wasn't mentioned by name, but now she understood why he was working so late these evenings. He'd muttered something about a meeting as he'd climbed in beside her the wrong side of midnight. Most of his time at work seemed to be spent in meetings or filling in forms.

She timed his breakfast to perfection, lifting the two lightly coated eggs from the pan and placing them on the slice of fried bread beside the bacon and tomatoes just as he came downstairs. The pampering he got at breakfast helped him through the day. She reckoned it was a fair trade for the cup of tea he brought her in bed these chilly October mornings. She couldn't move a muscle without her fix of tea. And he often cooked dinner when he was home.

He reached for the paper and glanced at the football results. Missed the item on page two. Then he yawned.

'Any chance of an easier day today?' she asked him.

'Every chance,' he said bleakly.

She felt a stirring of concern. 'You haven't done anything rash?'

'Like what?'

'Like resigning again?'

He smiled faintly. 'No. It's just gone flat.'

'What do you expect in Avon and Somerset? The Himalayas?'

He cut into a fried egg. 'I'm not ambitious. I'd settle for the Mendips, but all I see is the Somerset Levels. Take that murder that happened on Monday. The genius who did it walked up to me, shook my hand and confessed.'

'That must have helped your clear-up rate.'

He didn't answer. Statistics had never appealed to him.

'You can't have it all ways,' Stephanie remarked. 'We live in a gorgeous old city. It's going to be quiet. If you want serious action, you'd better start applying for jobs in Glasgow or Manchester, but don't ask me to come.'

'Thanks.' He put some more food in his mouth. 'But you're wrong, Steph. Avon and Somerset isn't short of villains.'

'You mean they're all in the police.'

He grinned.

Stephanie said, 'Which villains, then? Local farmers protesting about the bypass?'

'Professionals, I'm talking about. The smartest piece of shoplifting I ever heard of happened in my patch.'

'In Bath?'

'Bristol. Didn't I ever tell you? They did one of those ultra-expensive dress shops.'

'A boutique?'

'Yes, in Southmead. It was a night job. I don't know how many thousand quids' worth of designer gowns. They didn't break in, didn't smash anything, didn't leave any prints, didn't even set foot on the premises. We never caught them. Took us a long time to work out how it was done.'

'If they didn't break in, they must have had a key,' Stephanie guessed.

'No.'

'Then it was some kind of inside job.'

'It wasn't.'

'Didn't set foot in the shop, you said?'

'Didn't need to.'

'I give up. How was it done?'

'They worked through the letterbox with a twelve-foot boat hook. Dragged the display racks across the floor and tugged out the dresses one by one. Even the owner said she had to admire their cheek.'

The kettle boiled and he made instant coffee for them both, his thoughts on the day ahead. There was still three or four hours of form-filling for the Crown Prosecution Service. The chore couldn't be delegated. All his best people were on Operation Bumblebee now.

Stephanie turned up the volume on the radio. Diamond finished his breakfast in silence.

On BBC Radio Bristol some harbinger of gloom was wittering on about the traffic. If Steph was first downstairs she generally switched on the local station. When Diamond was forced to listen to anything at all in the morning he found it easier to tolerate the more po-faced Radio Four.

The short interval after he'd eaten and before he got up from the table was when Steph found it easiest to broach things she was planning. This morning, it was more of a confession she had in mind. 'I don't think I told you,' she began, not entirely honestly, because she knew for sure that she hadn't raised the subject until now. 'A few weeks ago, soon after we moved in properly, when you were at work and I was trying to get some more of those damned tea-chests unpacked, I heard a noise behind me. Gave me a fright. It was this little cat, no more than a kitten really, playing about with the newspaper we'd wrapped the plates in. You'd think he belonged here.' Steph saw an ominous look in her husband's eye and talked on rapidly. 'I'd no idea where he came from. Naturally I asked around. Pete, he was a dear little thing with enormous ears and feet for his size and just a few stripes in the middle. I tried the people who were here before us, but they didn't know.

In the end I did the right thing and took him up to Claverton.'

'The home for strays?' Diamond said. 'Yes, you did the right thing, Steph.'

She nodded. 'They get a lot of animals brought in. I didn't like leaving him really, being so young.'

'Too young to care, probably.'

'Oh, I don't know about that. Anyway, the young girl there said she'd let me know if he was claimed.'

'And was he?' Diamond asked hopefully.

'Er, no.'

'And where is he now? Still there?'

'I went to see him yesterday.'

'To Claverton? What did that dingbat say?'

She swung around defiantly. He'd gone too far this time.

But Diamond wasn't insulting the people who took in strays. He got up from the table and reached for the radio. The speaker was well into some item: '. . . so if any of you geniuses listening out there can make better sense of it than we can, call me now. I'll give you the number presently. Is there something we ought to know? Is it like a Valentine message? Is it in code? Is it a cryptic crossword clue? I tell you one thing, for sure. It had better not be some wiseguy trying to slip a commercial into BBC local radio or we're all in shtuck. No, my money is on a good, old-fashioned riddle. I understand we're not the only radio station to have received it. And the same message was sent to the local press. The whole region is going to be racking its brains over this. Let's prove that Radio Bristol has the most intelligent audience. We can crack this together.'

'Give it to us again, then,' said Diamond, and you would think he had been heard, the response was so quick.

'I'm going to give it to you one more time before we move on to the sports news. Make sure you have something to write it down. Ready?

> *J.M.W.T.*
> *Surrounded by security.*
> *Victoria, you challenge me.*
> *I shall shortly come to thee.*

Got it? Chew on that for a bit. Must move on now. Sports news coming up next. But I kid you not, listeners, the message was received this morning, early, but early, and we have no idea what it means, or who sent it. What or who is J.M.W.T.? Who is Victoria when she's at home? Over to you.'

Diamond reached across the table for the pen and the *Guardian*, placed ready for Stephanie's daily assault on the quick crossword. He made a note in the margin.

Stephanie remarked, 'You're always telling me puzzles are a waste of time.'

'Crossword puzzles, yes,' he said, tearing off the scrap of paper and pocketing it.

She said, 'About this kitten. I know if you saw it, you'd be captivated.'

He said abstractedly, 'Yes.'

'Then you don't mind if . . .'

He said, 'Anything you say, my love. Got to get off to work now.'

At Manvers Street Police Station he found a worried John Wigfull in the communications room. The big, black moustache was drooping ominously.

'I suppose you've heard,' Wigfull said.

'Depends what you mean.'

'This message about the Turner. It's all over the city. The radio. The papers. People are phoning in.'

'I did catch something on the radio while I was having breakfast. There's no doubt in your mind, then?'

'J.M.W.T.,' said Wigfull. 'Turner's initials. And the mention of the Victoria Gallery. "*I shall shortly come to thee.*" I'd say that's pretty conclusive. I'm up against a nutter.'

'Sounds like a poet to me.'

'Same thing.'

'A public relations expert, anyway,' said Diamond. 'He's used the local media to some effect.'

'Is it just a stunt?' Wigfull asked, as though Diamond in his infinite wisdom might be able to confirm the fact. 'If you're aiming to steal a picture, you don't broadcast it to all and sundry.'

'Is the picture still in place?'

'Yes, thank God. I spoke to Julie Hargreaves a few minutes ago. She's at the gallery. I keep checking with her. Up to now, everything is in order.'

'What's the problem, then?'

'No problem. Just that I'm bloody annoyed. First I get the tip that someone is about to stage a robbery and then, when I put a team in place, this message goes out, all over the city. Someone is doing his best to run rings around me.'

Diamond suppressed the smile that wanted to come. 'No chance you can spare Julie for a couple of hours, I suppose?' I'm a bit pushed collecting statements of this Saltford incident. I've got all those bank clerks to interview. Julie does it so well.'

'Sorry,' said Wigfull. 'She was assigned to me.'

'If I went down to the gallery I could look at the security for you. I'm sure you've got it under control, but sometimes another pair of eyes will spot something.'

'Do you think so?' Wigfull's eyes betrayed a flicker of uncertainty.

He parked illegally in Bridge Street under the statue of Queen Victoria that stands in a niche high up in the gallery's façade. For a Georgian city, Bath commemorates Victoria's name quite generously, with a park, a bridge, several streets, a pub and a burger bar, as well as the art gallery. Considering that Britain's longest-reigning monarch shunned the city for the whole of her reign, she scarcely deserved so much. She was brought there for

42

a brief visit as a young girl, before she was Queen, and the story goes that while she was standing on the hotel balcony she was deeply offended to overhear someone remarking how thick her ankles were. Bath was struck off her visiting list for ever.

Glancing up at the old killjoy as he got out of the car, Diamond weighed those words he had heard over breakfast: *Victoria, you challenge me. I shall shortly come to thee.* Did the message mean what Wigfull had assumed, a threat to plunder the gallery of its Turner, regardless of the extra security? Or might it be interpreted another way?

It was not impossible that the cryptic message didn't refer to the owner of the thick ankles at all, but to some living Vicky who had a connection with the Turner. A curator? A gallery attendant? For God's sake, Diamond, he chided himself, it's Wigfull's problem, not yours.

A local journalist he recognised as from the *Bath Chronicle* was at the corner of Bridge Street, by the entrance, waiting to hear the latest. So much for the puzzle the whole region was supposedly racking its brains to solve.

'Are you on this case, Super?'

'What case?' Diamond rapped on the door, annoyed by that 'Super'. The gallery wasn't open to the public yet, but the security team would be inside.

'The Turner. Has it been knocked off?'

'I've no idea what you're talking about.'

'Come on, Mr Diamond. I've got my job to do, same as you.'

'Nothing to my knowledge has been knocked off,' said Diamond.

'It's still there?'

'Far as I know.'

'You must be taking it seriously. You must be worried that they mean to have a go.'

'Do I look worried?'

He heard the sound of bolts being withdrawn. One of the great wooden doors opened a fraction and part

43

of a face was briefly visible, followed by the sound of static from a personal radio. The door opened widely enough to admit him. The reporter said something about co-operation and then Diamond stepped inside and the door slammed in the face of the press, if rather more heavily than the constabulary intended.

The last time Diamond had seen the black and white marble tiled vestibule was when the lower floor had been in use as the public library. Now both floors were used as galleries and the permanent collection was upstairs. He was escorted up the stone staircase past some paintings of rustic scenes, most of them featuring sheep, or what were intended by the artists to pass for sheep, but could have been giant, cream-coloured rats, or armadillos. Landscape painters, he decided, weren't on the whole successful with sheep.

Not the sort who spent his leisure hours looking at art, he'd never ventured up here before, and it was grander than he expected. At the top of the stairs was a tiled area surrounded by columns supporting the dome of the building, the underside of which was decorated in gilt with the signs of the zodiac. He stepped into the gallery, and was surprised by its size. It is a fine example of Victorian pomp, big enough for a ballroom, some fifty feet high, with a copy of the Parthenon frieze extending right around the walls below the glazed, arched roof that extends the length of the room. There are no windows. The pictures in their ornate gilt frames were attached to maroon-coloured walls, and some were displayed on purpose-built units along the centre of the room.

'Safe as the Bank of England, I would have thought,' he remarked to Julie Hargreaves, who had got up from behind the attendant's desk to greet him. 'I suppose he could try a Rififi-style entry from the roof.'

A look of incomprehension crossed Julie's face and he realised that the film *Rififi* must have been made before she was born. Not for the first time, he had to remind himself that his best support in the murder squad was

44

female and not much over thirty. Julie was a colleague he could rely on absolutely. She was as bright as a brand-new coin, and it was a measure of her professionalism that he disregarded her good looks. He hoped it wasn't a measure of his advancing years.

'It was a film,' he informed her. 'Maybe you saw one called *Topkapi*? Same method of entry ... No? Never mind.'

'Two men spent the night on the roof,' she told him.

'Two of ours?'

She laughed. 'I hope so. There are two more up there now.'

'I take it that the picture is still in place?'

'I expect you'd like to see it.' She led him across the gallery to one of the display units in the centre. 'It's not so big as I imagined.'

He looked at the fixings before he examined the painting. The Turner was secured to the wooden unit with nails driven through small metal plates projecting from the back of the frame. A thief equipped with a crowbar wouldn't take long to achieve his purpose, but no system has been devised that will withstand that kind of assault. Galleries are better employed installing alarm systems and strong locks.

As for the painting, he was less than impressed. It was a muted watercolour, a view of the Abbey from across the churchyard at an angle that to Diamond's eye was distorted, making the West Front outrageously taller than it is. He'd often sat on one of the wooden seats in the yard and looked at the building from that direction. Bath Abbey projected a sort of charm, but it had never pretended to be lofty. It wasn't as if the painting had other merits to compensate. He could see nothing remarkable in the pale blue and yellow ochre colouring or the brushwork. The total effect reminded him of a dull Sunday. Towards the bottom of the picture was an empty sedan chair with two attendants beside it and elsewhere the artist had tried to add some interest by including several figures of women in long skirts.

'Would you hang it in your front room?' he asked Julie.

She smiled slightly. 'I think it ought to be here, where everyone can enjoy it.'

'Be honest. Turner may have painted some wonderful pictures, but this one is crap.'

She said, 'There's a lot worse. There's one on the wall over there called *The Bride of Death* that gives me the creeps. It's really depressing.'

He told her that he was reclaiming her from John Wigfull and the relief on her face was obvious. She preferred real people, even if it meant statement-taking, to looking at Victorian deathbed scenes. She called up one of the sergeants on duty downstairs and instructed him to take over in the gallery until her replacement arrived.

SEVEN

Polly Wycherley said over a cup of *café au lait*, 'You didn't mind meeting here, I hope? It's one of my favourite places. I always think of dear Inspector Maigret here.'

The call had come unexpectedly, before 8.30, when Shirley-Ann was in the shower and Bert was about to leave for work. He'd handed her the mobile phone and a towel and followed up with an intimate fumble that had made her squeak in protest. What it must have sounded like on the other end of the line she dreaded to think. Anyway, it hadn't stopped Polly from suggesting coffee at Le Parisien in Shires Yard.

Not knowing what the weather would do on a mid-October morning, Shirley-Ann had put on a pink trouser suit overprinted with what looked like large blackberry stains. She had bought it for a song last May in the Save the Children shop in Devizes, along with the white lamb's-wool sweater that she was wearing under the jacket. Polly was less colourful, in a dark mauve padded coat. As it turned out, there was some fitful sunshine, so they sat under a red and white umbrella at one of the marble-topped tables outside. Faintly, from the interior of the café, came a song just recognisable as '*J'Attendrai*'.

Polly was right. This little sun-trap tucked away between Milsom Street and Broad Street could have been lifted from the Latin Quarter. Le Parisien and the Café René existed side by side and the waiters really were French. 'To be truthful, I think of Rupert Davies lighting his pipe.

47

You wouldn't remember him, dear. You're too young. It was in black and white, on Monday evenings.'

'Television.'

'And that elegant Ewen Solon, who played Lucas, his sidekick. A dreamboat in a porkpie hat. *Soigné.*' Polly gazed wistfully across the yard. 'I could have forgotten I was married for Lucas.' She pulled herself together. 'I wanted to talk to you about Monday night.'

'The Bloodhounds?'

'Did you find it off-putting? We weren't at our best and I didn't want you to go away thinking you wouldn't bother another time.'

'I enjoyed myself immensely,' said Shirley-Ann, and meant it.

Polly didn't seem to have heard. 'Rupert really is the limit, with that dog. He's a much nicer man than he appears, but he makes no concessions to what I think of as decent behaviour. He thinks we're all terribly bourgeois and deserve to be shocked, but that's no reason to let the dog misbehave.' Her hand shook as she lifted the coffee cup.

'It didn't bother me at all. Really.'

It seemed that Polly identified so closely with the Bloodhounds that the incident upset her personally. But as the conversation went on, recapitulating the meeting, it became clear that she was agitated about something more than Rupert's dog. She skirted the matter for some time, re-telling the story of the club's beginning over that dinner at the Pump Room in October, 1989, even using the same phrase about the deceased founder member, Tom Parry-Morgan: '. . . now dead, poor fellow.' Then she started recalling the names of people who had joined, stating the reasons why some had left, as if it was important to stress that they hadn't all been put off by Rupert. 'There was Annie Allen, a very old lady who gave up because of the cold evenings; a young chap who was more interested in films than books. Now what was his name? Alan Jellicoe. Another man, Gilbert

48

Jones, was out of his depth, I think, and lasted only three weeks. The Pearce sisters found that the evening clashed with lace-making when the evening classes started up.' The list continued: Colonel Twigg, who wandered in by mistake, thinking it was about crime prevention; Marilyn Slade-Baker, the delinquent girl, whose probation officer stopped her from coming; the Bentin family, just visiting from Oklahoma. More names followed.

Shirley-Ann wasn't counting, but upwards of fifteen had dropped out, and that seemed a high figure. Of the surviving six, Polly and Milo had been the founders; the formidable Miss Chilmark had joined soon after and bored everyone with *The Name of the Rose* ever since; then Rupert had arrived one evening looking like a convict after two weeks on the run; shy Sid had been introduced by his doctor; and Jessica had joined only last year. 'You could write a thesis about our reasons for sticking with it,' she summed up. 'All sorts of motives.'

'What's yours?' Shirley-Ann asked.

Polly seemed derailed by the suddenness of the question. 'I haven't really asked that of myself. I have my own thoughts why the others continue to come. I suppose I like being at the centre of something. The others seem to regard me as the mainstay. And I do enjoy crime novels.'

'And Milo? Why does he come?'

'For the companionship, I suspect, though he is the sort of man who joins everything he can. He's a long-standing member of the Sherlock Holmes Society, and Lord knows how many other clubs. The Agatha Christie, the Dorothy Sayers, the Edgar Wallace, the Saint. He belongs to them all, and others, I'm certain.'

'Has he given up work?'

'He's a retired civil servant.'

'I thought he must be.'

'Milo is single. Not over attracted to women, I get the impression, though he's perfectly sweet to us ladies, as men like that usually are. He lives alone, on one of those narrowboats on the canal. He calls it the *Mrs Hudson*, after Holmes's housekeeper. A beautiful gleaming boat almost entirely covered in pot-plants. We've had a couple of Bloodhound meetings on board. In fact, we had the last Christmas party there.'

'He's there through the winter as well?' said Shirley-Ann in surprise.

'Oh, I think a narrowboat can be quite snug in the cold weather. It certainly was when I was aboard.'

'I wouldn't care to live on a boat. You never know who's walking along the towpath, do you?'

'It takes all sorts, as they say. Did you find any like spirits among the others?' Polly probed, all too obviously.

'Jessica went to some trouble to welcome me.'

Polly said stiffly, 'I noticed that you went for a drink with her after the meeting.'

'Just while the rain stopped, yes.'

'She is quite an asset to the club,' Polly admitted, but grudgingly. Her habitual warmth of spirit seemed suddenly to have cooled, and Shirley-Ann realised that this was what she must have been so agitated over. For some unknown reason it had been a mistake to be seen leaving with Jessica.

'She's up with all the latest books,' Shirley-Ann remarked, trying to be neutral.

'Yes.' Polly took a sip of her coffee and the blue eyes watched over the rim. 'And she can be helpful at taking the steam out of discussions when they get overheated. She has a sharp sense of humour, which I like. She's very bright, I'm sure of that.'

Out with it, then, thought Shirley-Ann. How did she get up your nose?

Polly was saying, 'She runs that art gallery in Northumberland Place.'

'She told me. The Walsingham.'

'I think she part-owns it.'

'I got that impression.'

'We all have a standing invitation to drop in for a cup and a chat.' Polly was still testing the water.

'She did mention it.'

'It's not for me to interfere,' Polly went on. 'It's no business of mine, but I think you should be careful. Jessica is deeper than she first appears.'

'*Deeper* – what does that mean?'

'I'd rather not say any more than that.' Her gaze shifted away, over Shirley-Ann's shoulder. 'What's going on over there, do you suppose?'

Shirley-Ann turned. A policeman in uniform, rather senior from the look of his uniform, was standing with two other men in the passageway that leads to Broad Street. They were taking a lot of interest in the roof, or possibly an upper window of the building on the right.

'That's the Postal Museum,' said Polly.

'Yes. When you say Jessica is "deep", do you mean she has secrets, or something?'

Polly's mind was no longer on Jessica. 'I wonder if there's been a break-in. Some of those stamps are valuable. Have you ever been in?'

'Ages ago.'

'What a shame, if someone has broken in. It's a lovely little museum, entirely staffed by volunteers, I believe.'

'It might be nothing. They could be checking the security.'

'Let's hope that's all it is.' Polly looked at her watch. 'I have enjoyed our chat. And you *will* come next week, won't you? It's so encouraging to have a new member, especially such a well-read new member.'

'I'll be there if I possibly can.'

'Wonderful. I'll pay for this. I insist, my dear. And I can't help it – I'm going over to ask the policeman what's happened.'

'A case for Inspector Maigret, perhaps,' said Shirley-Ann, but the remark wasn't heard. Polly had dropped a

51

five-pound note in the dish that came with the bill and was striding across the yard.

After their coffee together, Shirley-Ann liked Polly a little less than she had on first acquaintance.

EIGHT

An air of urgency was gusting through Manvers Street Police Station when Peter Diamond and Julie Hargreaves returned from Saltford. Constables and civilians carrying faxes, files and clipboards hotfooted it along the corridors. Phones were cheeping like cicadas. Diamond stopped a chief inspector and asked, 'What's up? Everyone's behaving as if King Kong dropped in.'

'It's the ruddy media,' he was told. 'They won't leave us alone.'

'What media? The *Bath Chronicle*?'

'The nationals. Mainly the tabloids. Not to mention radio and TV. They're driving John Wigfull spare.'

'Why? What do they want?'

'A statement on the break-in. He's due to give one shortly, but they won't wait.'

'What break-in?'

'Where have you been all day? Someone did the Postal Museum last night and pinched the world's oldest stamp.'

'In Bath? I didn't know we had the world's oldest stamp.'

The chief inspector managed a weary grin. 'We don't any more.'

It emerged that the world's oldest stamp was not normally kept in the Postal Museum, but had been loaned by the owner (whose identity was a secret) for a special exhibition. It was in the city of Bath on May 2nd, 1840, that the Postmistress mistakenly date-stamped an unknown number of letters bearing the new Penny

53

Blacks four days before the service was due to start. An envelope bearing the famous stamp and date had survived for over a century and a half.

'What's the value?'

'Only two are known to exist. "Covers", they call them when they mean the entire face of the envelope. One like it was sold in auction in 1991 to a Japanese collector for one million, three hundred and fifty thousand pounds. It's in the *Guinness Book of Records*. The biggest price ever paid for a postage stamp.'

'Insured?'

'Their people are here already.'

'What was the security?'

'They have video-surveillance and strong locks on the doors. The stamp was on the upper floor in a special cabinet screwed to the wall. The thief got in through a window upstairs.'

'Where was this?'

'You know that passage leading up the side of the building, from Broad Street to Shires Yard? He had cutting gear to break into the cabinet. The SOCOs are saying that he left by way of the window he forced. It was a sash window. He must have used a ladder.'

'And nobody noticed?' Diamond said in disbelief.

'The theory is that he posed as a window-cleaner and did it in broad daylight between seven and nine in the morning. As everyone knows who is out early, a small army of window-cleaners is at work every day before the shops open, washing the windows. He could stroll up Broad Street with a ladder and a bucket and no one would give him a second look. He'd have his tools in the bucket covered with a leather.'

'Cool.'

'John Wigfull doesn't think so. We're taking a lot of flak from the broadcast media and the papers are going to have a field day tomorrow. The point is that we had a team guarding some painting in the Victoria Gallery and no one seemed to know about the stamp.'

As soon as they were alone, Diamond warned Julie that if asked, she should say she was working flat out on the Saltford bank murder. 'You can't be spared, even for half a day, right? You've got all those statements from the staff to check and it's opened up several new lines of inquiry.'

'Has it?'

'Well, if you want to spend the day mopping John Wigfull's fevered brow . . .'

He felt in his pocket for the scrap of newspaper he had tucked away that morning. After reminding himself precisely what he had written, he went in search of Wigfull. The man of the hour wasn't difficult to find in one of the offices on the first floor. All the activity was focused there. Faxes and files were going in at a dizzying rate. The chief inspector was entrenched behind a large desk heaped with paper. His body language – the hunched look as he talked into a phone – said everything Diamond expected. One hand was curled around the back of his head. The big moustache was lopsided, as if it had partially collapsed, the brown eyes glazed and bloodshot. You had to feel sympathy.

A sergeant Diamond scarcely knew said unnecessarily, 'He's terribly busy, sir. We're giving a press conference shortly.'

'That's what this is about.'

Wigfull put down the phone and immediately it started beeping again. Diamond's hand was on it first, keeping it in place.

'Half a mo, John.'

'I'm about to meet the press,' said Wigfull.

'I know. Have you thought it through?'

'Thought what through?'

'The statement you're about to make.'

'Certainly. I'm not wet behind the ears.'

'May I read it?'

'It's being photocopied right now. You'll get one if you want it.'

55

'What do you intend to say about Bumblebee?'

Wigfull looked into the distance like a camel unwilling to move. 'I won't be mentioning Bumblebee. The Turner's got nothing to do with this. I've no doubt that we prevented a possible crime in the Victoria Gallery, but there's no connection with the loss of this stamp.'

'I think you'll find there is, John, and I think the press boys will be on to it. They're not slow. You're going to face questions, so you might as well have something ready to say.'

'About the Turner?' Wigfull was still uninterested.

'The message we had on the radio this morning.' He fished it from his pocket again and read it to Wigfull.

> 'J.M.W.T.
> Surrounded by security.
> Victoria, you challenge me.
> I shall shortly come to thee.'

Wigfull stared at him without a glimmer of comprehension. 'Well?'

'Isn't it clear to you?' said Diamond through the din made by the phone. 'We were set up, John. The Turner was a distraction. The Victoria he was talking about wasn't the name of the gallery. It was the stamp. The Penny Black with Queen Victoria's head on it.'

'Do you think so?' Wigfull said. His weary eyes held Diamond a moment, slipped away and came back to him twice as large. '*Victoria, you challenge me.* My God. Why didn't I think of it?'

'There's nothing to be ashamed of,' Diamond generously said. 'It could have happened to any of us. So easy to get bogged down in one line of inquiry.'

'When did you put two and two together?'

'A few minutes ago, when I heard about the break-in.'

'The bastard's made a laughing-stock of me. He told us what he was planning and I didn't see it.'

'Which is why you should be boxing clever when you meet the press. They will have cottoned on to this, John.'

Wigfull raked his fingers across his scalp. 'How would you handle it?'

'Tell them it's no ordinary break-in. It was well planned and boldly carried out. You're dealing with a smart alec who takes pleasure in announcing his plans, but in cryptic form. Take them through the rhyme showing how devious it was. That "Victoria" could have referred to half a dozen locations in Bath. Tell them this alec is not so smart as all that because he won't be able to sell the stamp. It would be like trying to unload the *Mona Lisa*.'

'Good point,' said Wigfull. 'What does he hope to do with it – demand a ransom?'

'Probably. But I wouldn't open that can of worms with the press, even when they suggest it. If you'll take advice from someone who has dealt with those guys, don't be tempted to speculate on what might happen next. Deal with the facts as known. Tell them a full-scale investigation has been launched and leave it at that.'

'Peter, I appreciate this,' said Wigfull.

'Forget it.'

'No, I mean it.'

'All right. Don't forget it until you've bought me a drink.'

NINE

In the window of the Walsingham Gallery were two large
oils of clowns painted in such a way that the make-up
didn't entirely mask the features. The artist had sacrificed
some realism to reveal the character of the men and
women in performance, and it was skilfully done. It
took you a moment to see through the greasepaint,
but once your eye adjusted to the effect, you could tell
that one clown was grinning under the painted smile and
another was scowling; one appeared to be giving another,
a woman, a predatory look; she was staring out, aware of
his interest, yet disdainful. The idea was not remarkable,
but the artistry was. Shirley-Ann spent some time studying
the canvases before going in.

Instead of Jessica, a man popped up from behind an
arrangement of blue and yellow irises on a desk at the
rear of the gallery. 'Hi. Just looking round, or is there
anything in particular you wanted to see?' He was dressed
casually for the job, in a check shirt and black jeans. His
teeth were so regular that they must have been fixed. An
actor? Shirley-Ann didn't recognise him from television,
but the dark curls and brown eyes would have suited him
for a role as a heart-breaker in a soap.

'Actually, I just called in to see Jessica.'

'Shopping,' he told her. 'She won't be long if you don't
mind waiting.'

Something in his manner suggested he had a more
lofty status than a mere minder of the gallery. Shirley-Ann
wondered if this could be Barnaby, the husband. She

told him she hadn't come about anything important. She would call back another time.

He assessed her with a long look. 'You wouldn't be Shirley-Ann Miller by any chance?'

She felt the blood rise and redden her cheeks. 'How did you know?'

'Jess was talking about you. You just joined that coven she belongs to. The crime fiction people. What is it – the Baskervilles?'

'The Bloodhounds. I wouldn't call it a *coven*, but how did you recognise me?'

'She said you might call in some time.'

'Yes, but of all the people in Bath . . .' An uncomfortable thought had come to her. Had Jessica told him about the kinds of clothes she wore? Was it so obvious that she dressed out of charity shops?

'We don't get all the people in Bath dropping in and asking for her by name. I know most of the regular clients here.' He stepped from behind the desk and towards her with right hand extended. 'I'm known as A.J., and don't ask what it stands for because I don't much care for the name I was given.' His hand was cool, the grip firm. 'I'll put the kettle on, unless you want to sample the cheap sherry she keeps.'

'No, really,' said Shirley-Ann, telling herself that he couldn't be Barnaby the husband unless Jessica used the name he didn't care for – which wouldn't be very loyal.

'Really what?' said A.J. 'Really tea or really sherry or really you're in a frightful hurry? – because that patently isn't true if you dropped in for a chat with Jess. Sweet discourse makes short days and nights, so the saying goes, and I know of no one it fits better than Jess. My God, wouldn't she be flattered to hear that from me, always accusing her of being a motormouth?'

He was leaving her in no doubt that he knew Jessica extremely well. Personally, if Shirley-Ann had owned a gallery she wouldn't have left an overbearing man like this in charge.

'All right,' she said. 'Tea will be nice if you really think she won't be long.'

'Take a look round,' he said as he stepped towards the alcove where the kettle must have been kept. 'See what strikes you as worth the asking price. Between you and me, we have a new exhibition coming up later this week. You should come to the preview if you want to buy.'

She didn't care at all for that male assumption that women would do as they were told, so she went straight to a tall-backed Rennie Mackintosh chair and tested it for comfort, still wondering what A.J.'s role was in the business, and in Jessica's life.

When he appeared again and saw her in the chair he said, 'Careful, that's where you're supposed to sit to write the cheque.' He handed her the tea. It came in a white porcelain cup and saucer and there were two tea leaves floating, as if to let her know that he hadn't used a teabag. 'She'll be back any second. She can smell tea brewing a mile away.'

He was talking like a husband, but Jessica had definitely said she was married to someone called Barnaby. How could you get A.J. from that? Shirley-Ann tried some guesswork of her own. 'You look like a painter.'

'How come?' he said. 'Spots on my jeans – or did I leave a brush behind my ear? Yes, I paint figures.'

'The clowns in the window?'

'Christ, no. That isn't my style at all. I do nudes, but very Bath Spa, very tasteful, heavily shadowed over the naughty bits. She has three upstairs if you're interested. They retail at between eight hundred and a thousand. Two years back I couldn't keep up with the demand, but everything went flat in the recession, including my nudes.' He flashed the immaculate teeth. 'Joke.'

'So you combine painting with working in the gallery?'

'No. I don't work here. Just hold the fort for Jess on occasions. She's stuck with it all day, poor duck, so if I'm passing I look in and let her get some air. You're as hooked on crime as she is, I hear.'

'Crime fiction,' Shirley-Ann made clear.

'Jess buys books by the yard. You've got to find something if you're in here every day sitting on your butt. She doesn't get all that many callers. And about one in ten is seriously into art. Correction. One in twenty. Some people come in to ask the way to the nearest loo, for pity's sake. Or in the hope of making a killing with some faded print of *The Stag at Bay* that they picked up for a couple of quid in a car boot sale. Soul-destroying. But even that's better than no visitors at all. She can spend hours in here alone. Which is why she reads the Sara Paretskys and the Sue Graftons. The thick-eared action whiles away the time.'

Shirley-Ann found herself galloping to the defence of two of her favourite writers. 'Thick-eared? That's just what they aren't. They're intelligent. They take on issues.'

'Like feminism.' He barely concealed a sneer. 'Or should I say post-feminism?'

'You can't have read them. They say more about modern society – and more convincingly – than most of the so-called serious novels.'

He laughed. 'I was winding you up. And I haven't read them. Being an artist, I'm into graphic novels, told in pictures – what you would call comics for adults.'

'Thick-eared.'

'With a vengeance. But the artwork can be brilliant.'

'And do you enjoy winding people up, as you put it?'

'Enormously.'

'Women in particular?'

His lips twitched out of the smile that was forming. 'You're about to accuse me of sexism, or something worse. Women are just as good as men at piss-taking, you know. No, I treat 'em all alike. A sucker is a sucker is a sucker.'

'Is that what you took me for?'

He grinned. 'Just testing.'

In spite of bridling at almost everything he said, she was beginning to enjoy the exchanges. She wouldn't confide in a man like that except under extreme torture, but she found the argument stimulating. Men of his sort should be put to work like bowling machines in women's assertiveness classes.

The sparring went no further because Jessica burst in carrying a Waitrose bag full of groceries. On seeing Shirley-Ann, she put her hand to her blonde hair and pushed it back from her forehead, but there was no need. Even after the hassle of shopping she looked ready to step onto the catwalk in the pale blue suit she was wearing. 'Well, this is *so* terrific!' she exclaimed.

'I just dropped in as you suggested,' said Shirley-Ann. She had got up too quickly from the chair, teacup in hand, and slopped some in the saucer. She would never be poised like Jessica.

'I'm so pleased you did.'

A.J. added without the hint of a smile, 'And we just agreed that Mickey Spillane is the greatest crime writer in the world.'

'We did not!' protested Shirley-Ann.

'Or was it Peter Cheyney? *Dames Don't Care.*'

Jessica said, 'Give it a rest, A.J.' Then, to Shirley-Ann, 'He's full of crap. Do sit down.'

'He's one of the New Men,' said A.J. about himself. 'He made the lady a superb cup of tea. Pot's still warm. Want one?'

'Warm is no good to me. Make a fresh pot.' When they were alone, Jessica said to Shirley-Ann, 'Sorry you had to find him in charge. He can be fun in small doses. I'll get rid of him and then I can show you round in peace. He's extremely rude about all the work except his own.'

'He kept me entertained. Does he really know anything about crime fiction?'

'A smattering. Just enough to irritate. You don't want to tell him too much about yourself. He's a dreadful tease and he'll use anything he can discover.'

'That doesn't surprise me at all.'

When A.J. returned with the tea, Jessica thanked him

for standing in for her and said she'd just seen a traffic warden starting to check the cars in Walcot Street.

'Did you make it up?' asked Shirley-Ann, after A.J. had dashed out.

She smiled. 'He lives dangerously. Never buys a parking ticket. He'd do the same to me, only worse, much more bizarre. Probably tell me he saw a circus procession passing through and an elephant leaned against my car. And I'd fall for it, because the one time I disbelieve him you can be damned sure there *will* be a damned great jumbo sitting on my bonnet.'

'He's an artist, he told me,' Shirley-Ann said, keen to know more without probing too directly.

'Yes, that's how we got to know each other. His work sells quite well. Life studies, rather different from the usual thing. I'll show you presently.'

'Of women?'

Jessica shrugged. 'What would you expect? Male nudes don't sell unless they're by Michelangelo.'

'Is that so?'

'Think about it. Would you like one in your sitting room, however well hung?'

In a more relaxed situation Shirley-Ann would have giggled. She wasn't sure if the image she received was intended, so a smile did for an answer. She let her eyes travel to the far end of the gallery. 'It's bigger in here than I imagined.'

Jessica showed her round. Her policy, she explained, was to specialise in the work of a select group of artists. By refusing to crowd the walls with everything that was offered, she was putting her judgement to the test. Early on, she had made a decision not to show abstracts, not because she disliked them, but because she found that the sorts of people who called at her gallery wanted something that gave them a way in to the artist's vision. None of the work was slavishly representational. Each image from real life was enhanced by exciting and original use of colour and design. All this was said with conviction. The people

63

of Bath might be unadventurous in their taste, but Jessica wasn't knocking them.

They were large canvases, many priced in four figures, and Shirley-Ann thought with amusement of the shock it would give Bert to see her being escorted around this gallery. Her devoted partner had it firmly in his mind that she only ever bought pictures from charity shops, and it was true. The pictures of elephants and dancers in the flat they shared in Russell Street had cost under a pound, every one. She'd had to brighten up the walls with something, and quickly. All they had when they moved in was a collection of framed James Bond book jackets dating from Bert's days as a student at Loughborough College. He was quite fixated on Bond.

Up a white spiral staircase were more paintings, including A.J.'s nudes, which weren't the crude or flashy things she had expected. The figures were painted with subtlety and draughtsmanship, posed against strong light sources that cast much of the form into heavy shadow, letting the spectator's eye make sense of the areas exposed to the light.

'He's good,' said Jessica. 'I have to admit he's bloody good.'

'Who are the models?' Shirley-Ann asked, and heard herself saying, too late to hold back, 'Have you ever posed for him?' It was a tactless thing to have said, and she felt like slapping herself.

Jessica's large, shrewd eyes widened, but there was no obvious embarrassment. She answered coolly, 'No. Why should I? They're professional models, I imagine.'

They moved on to a view of a village church that Shirley-Ann was profoundly glad to recognise as one she knew. 'Oh, Limpley Stoke! It is, isn't it?'

It was, and the moment passed.

Downstairs, they made fresh tea. The evening paper had been pushed through the door and the headline was about a million-pound stamp theft in the city. It had pushed the story of the murdered bank manager off the front page.

'I don't approve of theft, but you've got to admire anyone bold enough to put a ladder against a window in broad daylight and climb up and nick the thing,' said Jessica after briefly studying the report. 'That's what happened, apparently. They're appealing for witnesses, of course, but they think people must have taken him for a window-cleaner. The guys with the squeegees are out in force before the shops are open. Scores of them. I have mine done every morning. It's essential. You wouldn't believe the state they're in sometimes.'

'The window-cleaners?'

Jessica smiled. 'The windows, lovie.'

'I saw the police looking up at the Postal Museum window this morning,' Shirley-Ann said. 'I happened to be having coffee outside the French café, with Polly Wycherley, as a matter of fact.' For the second time in a few minutes she wished she had guarded her tongue. The way Polly had spoken of Jessica should have made her more careful.

Jessica picked up on the remark at once. 'You were with Polly?'

'Just for a coffee, yes.'

'You knew her already, then, before the other evening?'

'No.' She thought of saying that she met Polly in Shires Yard by chance, but she had never been a convincing liar. 'She phoned me this morning when I was in the shower. She must be an early riser. I think she felt as Chair of the Bloodhounds that she ought to follow up on the meeting and find out if I was coming again.'

'Probably,' said Jessica.

'We couldn't have known that a real mystery was unfolding in front of us.'

The real mystery had ceased to interest Jessica. 'Did she have any advice for the new member?'

'Oh, I think it was just a friendly gesture,' said Shirley-Ann, resolved to stonewall.

'Polly is good at giving advice,' remarked Jessica, and it didn't sound like a compliment.

'Well, I'm grateful for all the friendship. I feel as if I belong already. I'm certainly going to come again.'

'Good – we can do with you,' said Jessica more warmly. 'It was getting polarised between the whodunit readers and the blood-and-guts lot. There's so much else we could talk about, but we hardly ever do.'

'Apart from Umberto Eco.'

Jessica smiled. 'Apart from him. They're charming people, but they will insist on taking up positions, and it's only because they don't read widely enough. If Rupert were to try a Peter Dickinson for a change, with that fertile imagination thinking up the most amazing plots and settings—'

'Oh, yes!'

'—and still worked out as puzzles, with clues and a proper investigation, he'd be jolted out of the rut he's in. And I'd *love* to get Milo reading American thrillers. I know the way in for him. It's through the Fletch books.'

'Gregory McDonald.'

'Yes. He'd adore the humour, and he'd appreciate the logic of the plots and he'd soon be into Westlake and McBain and Block and ultimately Ellroy.'

'There is a way in through women writers,' Shirley-Ann pointed out.

'True.' Jessica laughed. 'True in theory. But you don't know Milo.'

Shirley-Ann raised her eyebrows and Jessica nodded.

Much more gossip about the Bloodhounds would certainly have emerged, but Shirley-Ann didn't want to appear over-curious. She turned the conversation back to the art and was rewarded with an invitation to a private view on Wednesday of the following week.

'I won't pretend it's anything amazing,' Jessica explained. 'Rearranging the deckchairs on the *Titanic*, A.J. calls it. The same people tend to come each time, but it does pull in a few dealers and I sell enough to cover the cost of the buck's fizz and Twiglets. You'll see a couple of faces there you know. And don't, for God's sake, feel under any obligation to buy.'

THE SECOND RIDDLE

The Locked Room

TEN

When John Wigfull emerged from his press conference Diamond was in the main office reading the poem – if that isn't too grandiose a description of the four lines of verse that had misled everyone, including himself.

'Was it gruelling, John?' he asked with a matey grin.

'I didn't expect an easy ride.'

'You took my advice, I hope?'

'What was that?' said Wigfull in a hollow, preoccupied tone. 'Look, no offence, Peter, but I don't have time to talk. There are urgent things to attend to.'

'Like a strong coffee? The throat does get dry, answering those damnfool questions.'

Whatever the state of Wigfull's throat, his vocal cords had no difficulty in projecting his growing impatience. 'I'm heading a major inquiry. This is the world's most valuable stamp. It's far more serious than your shooting in Saltford.'

'Not in the eyes of the law, it isn't, and not to the bloke who was killed. So you're calling for reinforcements, no doubt?'

'I'll use every man and woman on the regional crime squad if necessary.' There was no doubting Wigfull's commitment. His jaw jutted like Churchill's uttering the 'blood, toil, tears and sweat' speech.

'And what are your lines of inquiry?'

'For a start, I'm going to have that bloody poem analysed by forensic.'

'What for – to see if it scans?' Before Wigfull reacted

to that, Diamond added, 'Because if you hope to learn something from the copies that were sent to the media, you'd better think again. I've got one here.' He held out the sheet of paper he had been studying, but Wigfull displayed no interest. 'There was a time when it was possible to look at a piece of typing and say which typewriter was used, thanks to some tiny flaw in one of the characters. "Pray examine this small irregularity in the letter 'W'. It proves conclusively that the note was typed on Professor Moriarty's Smith-Corona." Not these days, laddie. Moriarty puts it through a word-processor and runs it off on a laser printer that gives a perfect finish, indistinguishable from a million others. Then he photocopies it. Your forensic friends aren't going to help you, John.' A favourite theme of Diamond's, and worth repeating each time he got the chance.

Wigfull was not to be downed. 'Wrong. With fluorescence under laser illumination they can get good fingerprints off paper these days.'

'All the prints except the thief's.'

'You can't say that.'

'This guy is smart, John. He won't have left any prints. Have you checked the spelling?'

'The spelling?'

'Of the words in the note.'

'Let me have another look.' Wigfull snatched the scrap of paper from Diamond and stared at the words. 'I can't see anything wrong with this.'

'Nor I,' said Diamond, after a pause. 'Like I said, he's smart. We know the bugger can spell.'

That 'we' rang an alarm bell for Wigfull. He thrust his head forward combatively. 'You and I had better get one thing straight, Peter. This one is mine. Just because I listened to you about the press conference it doesn't mean you can muscle in.'

'Muscle in?' Diamond blandly echoed. 'You know me better than that. I'm far too busy talking to bank clerks.'

*　　*　　*

The grin faded as the week progressed. The bank clerks failed to revive it. Every one of them had a tale to tell of meanness, injustices and slights inflicted by the former manager. If only the chief clerk Routledge hadn't confessed, the liturgy of complaints might have been worth listening to, because the bank was chock-full of potential suspects, and a number of customers with grudges would have come into the reckoning as well. Dispiriting for a keen detective, there was no question that Routledge had fired the fatal shot. Forensic confirmed his statement. By Friday, Diamond was so bored with the business that he told Julie Hargreaves to finish up at Saltford without him. He spent the day in the office attacking the stack of paper that was spilling off his in-tray and across the desk.

Late in the morning he took a phone call from Dorchester. John Croxley was formerly one of the murder squad at Bath, a pushy young inspector with an ego like a hot-air balloon. His naked ambition had grated on the nerves of everyone. He had transferred to Dorset CID in the period Diamond was away, a sideways move that had been greeted with relief in Avon and Somerset.

'Thought I'd give you a call, Mr Diamond,' the voice made a show of sounding casual. 'I heard you were back. This isn't a busy moment, I hope?'

'Rushed off my feet – but carry on.'

'Are you handling the Penny Black case, then?'

'Not at this minute. I'm on the phone to you, aren't I? Must keep it short, I'm afraid. How are things down there in Dorset? Statistics perking up no end since you arrived, I bet.'

'To be perfectly honest, it's not entirely what I expected,' Croxley confided. 'I hadn't appreciated how much more rural this country is than Avon and Somerset.'

'More what?'

'Rural. You know, countrified.'

'You mean sheep-shagging?'

73

There was a pause. 'I don't know about that. I'm not getting much work in the field of murder.'

Diamond chuckled and said insensitively, 'Plenty in the field of turnips, however.'

'Not so much turnips as cattle, Mr Diamond,' Croxley said with total seriousness. His sense of humour had never blossomed. 'My main job just now is noseprints.'

'Is what?'

'Noseprints. It isn't widely known that every bovine noseprint is unique to the individual, like a fingerprint. You coat the animal's nose with printing ink and then press a sheet of paper against it.'

'You wouldn't be having me on, John?'

'I wouldn't do that, Mr Diamond. It's a scheme we've set up with the Dorset County Landowners' Association to combat the rustling of cattle. We've processed seven hundred cows already.'

Diamond was containing himself with difficulty. 'You get noseprints from cows? Go on, John.'

'Well, that's all there is to it. They've recently put me in charge. I don't know why. It isn't as if I was brought up in the country. And I don't see much prospect in it.'

'I don't know,' said Diamond, tears of amusement sliding down his cheeks. 'Things could be worse.'

'Do you think so?'

'If it's their noses you deal with, you're out in front, aren't you?'

'I suppose so.'

'Good thing you're not taking prints from the other end.'

'I hadn't thought of that, Mr Diamond.'

'Think of it when you're feeling low, John. This is new technology and you're the man who does it. Get your noseprints on the computer. You can set up – what is it they call it? – a data-base on all the cows in Dorset. You asked about prospects. You've got unlimited prospects, I would think. You could go on doing this for years.'

'That's what I'm afraid of,' said Croxley bleakly. 'I

was wondering if – with so much interest in the Penny Black business – you might be mounting a major inquiry, recruiting extra detectives.'

'You'd be willing to give up your exciting new job?'

'If there was half a chance.'

'No chance at all, I'm afraid. You know how it is with budgets as they are. I'd stick with the cows, if I were you. You could be the world's foremost authority on bovine noseprints.'

When he put down the phone he sat back and rocked with laughter for the first time in a week. He could hardly wait to tell Steph at the end of the day. But something else later that afternoon put it clean out of his mind.

On BBC Radio Bristol after the four o'clock news headlines, the presenter said, 'Something different here. I've just been handed a note that my producer believes could link up with that cryptic verse we gave you last Monday morning. Remember? The one the police later said was almost certainly linked to the million-pound stamp theft from the Bath Postal Museum. The Penny Black, right? Well, this looks like another poetic effort from the cryptic cat-burglar. It's printed on a sheet of A4 paper with no covering note. Came with the afternoon post, I gather. See what you make of this. Is it a hoax, or could it be a genuine clue? We'll be handing it pronto to the Old Bill, listeners, but you'll be able to say you heard it first on Radio Bristol. Are you ready with pen and paper?

> *Whither Victoria and with whom –*
> *The Grand Old Queen?*
> *Look for the lady in the locked room*
> *At seventeen.*

That's all. We know who or what Victoria is this time, I think, but do we know of any locked rooms? And how does the number seventeen come into it? I'm sure we'll get some calls about this. If you have any brilliant suggestions before the end of the programme, we'll be pleased to pass them on. I'll repeat the verse one more time.'

The producer had diplomatically phoned the Bath police before the item was broadcast, so a radio was tuned in and the entire control room heard it, including Diamond, whose sixth sense had told him something was afoot and got him from behind his desk at the critical time. The only notable absentee was John Wigfull, listening privately on a separate radio upstairs.

'This gets more and more like party games,' a detective sergeant commented morosely.

'Is it genuine?' someone else asked.

'Who can say? It's got to be taken seriously after the first one.'

'Yes, but why would they do this? Mr Wigfull was expecting a ransom demand, not another riddle.'

'Maybe they don't want a ransom. This could be some kind of publicity stunt, couldn't it? When is the university rag week?'

'Too early in the year for that. The students have only just gone back. If it is a stunt, then my money is on some smart-arse member of the glitterati.'

'The what?'

'The rich and beautiful. The in-crowd. Hooray Henrys. Leading the Old Bill up the garden path is their idea of fun.'

The debate was taken a stage further at a special meeting of senior staff convened by the Assistant Chief Constable. 'Since we are bound to treat this development seriously,' he said in preamble, 'I decided to pool our wits and experience. If the riddle is anything like the first one, it may involve knowledge of Bath and any one of you may have the piece of information that clarifies everything.'

From the expressions around the oval table no one was confident of clarifying anything.

'John, this is your inquiry,' the ACC said to Wigfull

with a motioning of the upturned palm, 'so why don't you give us your immediate thoughts?'

Wigfull cleared his throat. 'Well, sir, we can reasonably assume that the Victoria referred to is the cover.'

'The what?'

'The missing stamp, sir.'

'Why not call a stamp a stamp?'

'Because it's attached to an envelope. There's a date-mark. The whole thing is known as a cover. Like the first-day covers they sell in the Post Office each time a new set of stamps is issued.'

'That sort of cover,' said the ACC as if he'd known all along. 'Carry on.'

Wigfull referred to his notes. 'The first two lines:

> *Whither Victoria and with whom –*
> *The Grand Old Queen?*

must surely be a coded way of telling us that he is referring to the cover. I think we should focus our interest on the third and fourth lines:

> *Look for the lady in the locked room*
> *At seventeen.*

I venture to ask three questions: Which lady? Which locked room? And which seventeen? The lady may, of course, be another reference to Victoria, the cover, but we should not exclude other possibilities. Does it link up with the last line, giving us a lady of seventeen? Do we know of any seventeen-year-old ladies in the present or the past who may be connected with the case in some way?'

Nobody spoke.

'The locked room may help to fix it,' Wigfull went on. 'If there was a local memory or story of some young woman kept locked up, for example. A prisoner. A mental patient. A nun, even. These are my immediate thoughts.'

'Any response?' asked the ACC of the blank faces around the table.

Tom Ray said, 'I was thinking along different lines, sir. The seventeen could be part of an address.'

'That's rather good,' the ACC commented, seeming to imply that not one of Wigfull's theories was even half-good.

'Isaac Pitman, the inventor of shorthand, lived at number seventeen, the Royal Crescent. There's a plaque outside.'

'What's he got to do with this?' Peter Diamond asked. 'Did he have a seventeen-year-old sex slave?'

'I rather doubt it,' said the ACC frigidly. 'I happen to know a little about Pitman. He was a man of the highest principles. Like me he was a teetotaller, a vegetarian and a non-smoker.'

There was an uneasy pause. Not even Diamond was going to press the matter of Isaac Pitman's sex life, or the ACC's.

'It was a long shot,' admitted Ray.

Another theory was advanced by Keith Halliwell. 'Is it possible that the seventeen refers to a time, like five p.m., or seventeen-hundred hours?'

'If it does, we've missed it by ten minutes,' said Diamond, glancing at the clock on the wall. 'Personally I don't think this joker has given us enough to catch him. He wouldn't, would he? It's like that book *The Thirty-Nine Steps*. It's no good looking for the blessed steps. You know you're there when you find them. I mean, we could rabbit on all evening about seventeen this and that. Seventeen horse-power cars; seventeen trees in a row; the seventeenth day of the month; or fifteen rugby players and two reserves. It gets you nowhere without more information.'

'So your advice would be . . .'

'Ignore it. Continue with the other lines of inquiry.'

'What lines?' murmured Ray.

Wigfull said, 'We've been extremely thorough.'

'With what result?'

'Investigations can't be rushed.'

'I don't know,' said Ray. 'Peter Diamond nicks a bloke for murder two minutes after getting to the scene.'

The ACC drew a deep breath and said, 'Gentlemen, let's confine this to discussion of the stamp theft. To ignore this new development would, I think, be negligent. Peter may be right in saying that the thief won't give much away, but if we can make any sense of the riddle, it may link up with other evidence.'

'Was this character seen at all on Monday morning?' Diamond asked. 'Did anybody spot the ladder against the window?'

'Unfortunately, no,' Wigfull answered. 'But we have six or seven descriptions of window-cleaners near the scene reported as suspicious.'

'Have you ever seen a window-cleaner who *doesn't* look suspicious? What about forensic? Are they any help?'

'The thief seems to have used gloves. We've got an impressive list of fibres and hairs found in the room, but with so many people going through the museum by day, they could come from many sources. The display cabinet was forced with a rusty claw-hammer. That's about it.'

'And about the museum staff?'

'They're volunteers. Local stamp enthusiasts. They take turns to man the museum, at least two at a time. We've interviewed them all except two, who are away. Nobody seems to remember anyone casing the place in advance of the crime – but as several of them reasonably pointed out, how could you tell?'

Diamond let the meeting run its course without any more input from him. It was Bumblebee territory and he didn't intend to get involved. They broke up shortly after six. 'Have a good weekend, gentlemen,' he said as he went out.

'Aren't you coming in?' Ray asked.

'No need. My murder is put to bed.'

'So how will you spend the time?'

'House-training a new cat, if my wife can be believed.'

ELEVEN

Shirley-Ann was better prepared when she turned up at St Michael's for the next meeting of the Bloodhounds on Monday evening. Rummaging one afternoon through a carton of books in the Dorothy House shop she had pulled out *The Blessington Method*, a dog-eared and rare Penguin of some of Stanley Ellin's short stories. Having missed her turn the week before, she was sure to be asked to speak about a book she could recommend and Ellin seemed an ideal, uncontroversial choice. He was one of the American writers she admired most, particularly for his short fiction. She could hardly wait to discover how many of the group were familiar with his work. If any of them objected to short stories she would pluck up courage to remind them that Poe, Conan Doyle and Chesterton had laid the foundations of modern crime fiction with their short stories.

It must have been a lucky day, because she had also found a thick-knit purple jumper as good as new in Dorothy House for only a pound and she was wearing that tonight with a black corduroy skirt from War on Want.

The evening was distinctly colder than the previous Monday, but dry. Down in the crypt the warmth from the central heating wafted pleasantly over her face the moment she entered. Miss Chilmark, who seemed to make a point of getting there early, said the place was like a furnace and she was going to speak to the caretaker. She marched past Shirley-Ann with a determined look, but it turned out that she was only on her way to the cloakroom. If there was a complaint about the heating, it wouldn't get Shirley-Ann's support. Being so skinny – Bert called her slinky, which she rather liked – she could never get enough heat.

Jessica too was there already, snappily dressed in a charcoal-grey woollen dress. A wine-red scarf was draped with casual elegance across her shoulders and clipped with a huge silver buckle like a kilt fastening. 'Glad you've come,' she said, and seemed to mean it. 'You're going to make such a difference.'

Polly Wycherley waved a small, plump hand from across the room. She had already taken her place inside the circle and was removing things from her briefcase, determined to make amends for her lateness the previous week. 'Who are we missing?'

'Only Milo,' said Jessica.

'Rupert,' someone else spoke up. Chameleon-like, Sid in his fawn raincoat was standing against a stone wall. He had an uncanny ability to merge with the surroundings. 'Rupert is always late.'

An entire, unsolicited sentence from Sid. Perhaps he felt more comfortable with no other males present.

The door of the ladies' room opened and Miss Chilmark came out reeking of some musky perfume. She was no longer complaining about the central heating. 'I intend to make a stand on that dog tonight,' she announced.

'Bareback riding?' murmured Jessica.

Miss Chilmark hadn't heard. 'If it misbehaves, I shall tell Rupert I want it removed, and I expect the rest of you to support me.'

A click from Jessica's tongue showed that she, for one, would not be included. 'It only shook itself. Poor thing, it was wet. It's not as if it crapped on the carpet.'

'You don't have to be vulgar. I was drenched. We had to interrupt the meeting. Don't you remember?'

'Well, it isn't raining tonight, Miss Chilmark.'

'That's no guarantee of anything.'

As if she hadn't heard a word about Rupert's dog, Polly remarked, 'Milo isn't usually late.'

'Hardly ever,' said Miss Chilmark, scarcely aware that she had been diverted. She took her place opposite Polly. 'Milo and I attach a lot of importance to good timekeeping. We are always the first to arrive.'

'Perhaps he's ill,' said Polly, fumbling in her case. 'Once before when he was ill and couldn't come, he phoned me the evening before. I've got his number in my diary. I can phone him.'

'Good idea,' said Miss Chilmark. 'I'll take over in the chair until you get back. Let's get under way before the dog arrives and ruins it.'

'For heaven's sake,' said Jessica. 'It's ridiculous to phone the poor man. It's only five past seven.'

After everyone was seated, there was a short debate about whether Polly would be justified in making the phone call. The consensus was that Milo was a grown-up and didn't have to be accounted for. Jessica gave Shirley-Ann a grateful look that said sanity had won the day, and shortly after, Milo came in, full of apologies. A lorry had broken down on Brassknocker Hill and the traffic had been held up.

'Have we started, then?' said Miss Chilmark in a tone implying that she would have run the meeting more efficiently.

'I suppose we have,' said Polly.

'Because I have a suggestion,' Miss Chilmark went on. 'I don't know who else has been following the reports of this stolen stamp.'

'The Penny Black?' said Shirley-Ann. 'Just across the street from here. Isn't it exciting?'

'That isn't the word I would choose,' said Miss Chilmark, 'particularly as it shows our city in such a bad light, but, yes, that is what I had in mind. I thought for a change it would be an interesting exercise to address ourselves to a real crime.'

'We're readers, not detectives,' Polly pointed out, quick

to suspect that this might be a takeover. 'We discuss fiction, not real crime.'

'We talk about real crime most of the time, if you ask me,' asserted Miss Chilmark. 'Rupert is forever haranguing us about what happens on the streets. Well, now that something has happened on the streets that tests the intellect a little, let's see if our experience as readers is any help in solving it.'

Jessica said cynically, 'You mean set William of Baskerville onto the case?'

'Who's he?' Polly asked vaguely.

'The detective figure in *The Name of the Rose*.'

'Oh, yes.' Polly looked annoyed with herself for having to be reminded.

Miss Chilmark said stiffly, 'Mock me if you wish, but his methods stand the test of time.'

Shirley-Ann wondered if this was the moment to mention – after the put-down she had got the previous week from Miss Chilmark – that she had checked the date of publication of *Il Nome della Rosa*, and it was 1981, a full four years after the first of the Brother Cadfael series. But it didn't seem the right time for settling scores. She saved it up.

'Personally, I think you've made a marvellous suggestion,' said Milo, galloping to the support of Miss Chilmark. Theirs was a strange alliance, the elderly gay and the starchy spinster. Apparently, all that they had in common was that they usually arrived before anyone else. 'I'm fascinated to know if we can throw any light on the stamp theft. How about the rest of you?'

No one objected, not even Polly any more, so Shirley-Ann, who was quite fired up, said, 'It was extremely clever, if what the papers say is right, dressing up as a window-cleaner and climbing through an upstairs window.'

Jessica remarked, 'Extremely obvious, I'd have said. What intrigues me is why he did it.'

'Or she,' put in Shirley-Ann, scoring on the rebound.

'Or she. It's the world's most valuable stamp. They're not going to sell it.'

'People steal famous paintings all the time,' Miss Chilmark pointed out. 'They must have a reason.'

'Well, there's the theory that a fanatical collector wants to own them. He doesn't do it to make a profit, just to gloat over what he possesses.'

'Do such people exist?' asked Shirley-Ann. 'Outside books, I mean.'

'I'm sure they do. There are too many works of art that have just vanished over the years. And stamp-collecting is a lonely occupation anyway. I don't have any difficulty picturing some middle-aged man with a personality defect poring over his collection.'

'Or woman,' Sid managed to say, and when everyone had got over the surprise there were smiles.

'Actually, very few women go in for collecting,' said Jessica. 'This acquisitive impulse is a masculine thing.'

'Shoes?' Shirley-Ann reminded everyone.

'Hats, too,' said Polly. 'I have a cupboard simply stuffed with hats.'

'I meant useless things like stamps and beermats.'

'I don't think the person who stole it is a collector. I think they're going to demand a ransom,' speculated Shirley-Ann. 'That's what I'd do. Anyone who owns a stamp like that has oodles of money to spare. I'd ask for fifty thousand.'

'How would you collect it?' Milo asked, stroking his beard as if the prospect really beckoned. 'That's always the problem.'

'Oh, I wouldn't handle the money at all. I'd let the owner know that it had to be transferred through his bank to a secret Swiss account.'

'Do you have a secret Swiss account?' Polly asked Shirley-Ann in all seriousness.

'No, but with fifty grand as a deposit, I bet any bank would be only too happy to open one for me. I could afford to fly to Zurich and fill in the forms, or whatever.'

'It can't be so simple,' said Jessica.

'Can you think of anything better?'

Miss Chilmark interrupted the exchange. 'Madam Chairman, this is getting us nowhere. When I suggested this as a topic, I had in mind the much more fascinating problem of the riddles – if that is the word – that were on the radio and in the papers, apparently composed by the person who stole the stamp. Couldn't we address ourselves to those?'

'By all means,' said Polly, chastened. 'Do you remember how they went?'

'I have them here.' Miss Chilmark opened her crocodile-skin handbag and took out two press-cuttings.

'There's not much point in discussing the first one,' said Jessica. 'That's been solved by events. What was it ... *J.M.W.T.* ...'

> *Surrounded by security.*
> *Victoria, you challenge me.*
> *I shall shortly come to thee,*

Miss Chilmark read aloud.

'It's all been explained by the police,' said Jessica. 'They were tipped off that someone was planning to steal a Turner from the Victoria Gallery, so they doubled the security. But it was a bluff and the real target was the stamp. Let's look at the latest riddle. That's much more of a challenge. Have you got it there?'

Miss Chilmark obliged:

> *Whither Victoria and with whom –*
> *The Grand Old Queen?*
> *Look for the lady in the locked room*
> *At seventeen.*

'Is it by the person who wrote the first riddle?' said Milo. 'That's the first thing to ask.'

'It sounds similar to me,' said Shirley-Ann.

'The styles do have a certain textual affinity,' Miss Chilmark said with a donnish air. 'There's a touch of the archaic in the word "thee" in the first riddle that has an echo in the "whither" in the second.'

'Oh, come on. It's only some birdbrained idea of what poetry should sound like,' said Jessica. 'Straight out of *The Golden Treasury.*'

'Nevertheless,' insisted Miss Chilmark.

'You're probably right,' Jessica was compelled to admit.

Miss Chilmark was keen to show that she had done her homework. 'And of course there are allusions to other phrases. "The Grand Old Queen" is reminiscent of the epithet by which the Prime Minister W.E. Gladstone was known, the Grand Old Man, often abbreviated to the G.O.M.'

'Or the Grand Old Duke of York,' said Polly seriously. She wasn't given to humorous remarks.

Miss Chilmark chose to ignore that. 'Then "Look for the Lady" carries the idea of that card trick "Find the Lady", just as "in the locked room" suggests another piece of trickery, the locked room mystery – that Milo happened to mention only last week. The undertone of hocus-pocus is inescapable.'

'So what do you think it means?' asked Shirley-Ann.

If there was an answer, it wasn't communicated, because this was the moment when the door opened and the dog Marlowe padded in, headed straight for the circle of chairs, leapt on to the one beside Miss Chilmark and demonstrated affection for that horrified lady by lifting a large paw to her chest. In backing away, she tipped the chair backwards. Rupert, who had come in behind his boisterous pet, was quick to react. He darted forward and caught the back of the chair before it hit the floor. An unseemly accident was averted. Nothing worse had resulted than a display of rather more of Miss Chilmark's legs than she or her companions desired. She was wearing pop-socks. As if to apologise for startling

86

her, Marlowe jumped down and licked her lily-white left knee.

This was unfortunate. The dog had been much on Miss Chilmark's mind all week, there was no doubt of that. 'Get it away from me!' she cried out hysterically. 'It's going to bite me.'

Clearly Rupert hadn't trained Marlowe to respond to voice commands, so he grabbed him by the scruff and hauled him to the other side of the circle. Marlowe gave a growl of protest. 'He's frustrated now. He was only showing you affection,' Rupert told Miss Chilmark.

Jessica suddenly said, 'Does anyone have a paper bag?'

'What for?' said Polly.

'She's hyperventilating.'

'Oh, what next?'

Miss Chilmark was taking deep, rapid breaths and going ominously pink. Her eyes had a glazed look.

Sid reached under his chair for a plastic carrier bag. He rummaged inside and took out a brown paper bag containing something that proved to be a secondhand novel by John Dickson Carr. After removing the book he handed the empty bag to Jessica, who placed the open end over Miss Chilmark's mouth and nose.

'She'll suffocate,' said Polly.

'No,' said Jessica calmly. 'It forces her to rebreathe her own air. It should bring the acid-alkali balance of the blood back to normal and relieve the symptoms. Take the dog out of her sight, Rupert. You know it upsets her.'

The usually ungovernable Rupert responded to the unmistakable note of authority and led Marlowe to the door without a murmur on his part or a whimper on Marlowe's.

The others watched in fascination as the bag expanded and contracted against Miss Chilmark's face, making her appear uncannily like a tropical frog. After a short time the remedy produced an improvement in the breathing. Jessica spoke some calming words, mainly to reassure Miss Chilmark that the dog was no longer in the room. The bag was removed from her face. Polly offered to drive her home.

Miss Chilmark said in a small voice, 'I'd like to stay if you're quite sure the dog isn't coming back. I'm not entirely clear what happened.'

It was decided that Miss Chilmark would benefit from a cup of coffee, so the break was taken early.

Shirley-Ann told Jessica she was awfully clever knowing how to deal with the hyperventilation.

'Not at all. I had an aunt who was prone to it. She always had a spare paper bag with her.'

'Do you think Miss Chilmark is well enough to stay?'

Jessica smiled. 'She wouldn't dream of leaving. She's won her point, hasn't she? The dog has been outlawed. Now she wants to enjoy her triumph.'

This interpretation struck Shirley-Ann first of all as callous, later as discerning.

Presently Rupert returned, looking forlorn. 'I left Marlowe with some old chums in the Saracen's Head,' he informed everyone and added pointedly, 'He'll fit in anywhere if he's allowed to.'

They resumed the meeting, and when Shirley-Ann offered to speak about Stanley Ellin's short stories she was warmly received. The group were better informed about Ellin than Shirley-Ann expected. Rupert and Jessica had each read the famous and gruesome story *The Specialty of the House* and Polly, never to be underestimated, said she had copies of *The Eighth Circle* and *Stronghold* on her shelves at home. Fortunately no one had read *The Blessington Method*.

'What is the Blessington Method?' Jessica asked.

'That's what someone in the story asks. I'd better not say.'

'Is it a long story? Why don't you read it to us? There's time, I'm sure. We've often had things read out, but never a whole story.'

Fortunately Shirley-Ann rather enjoyed reading aloud. At school she'd won the Miss Cranwell Prize for Bible

Reading two years in a row. So the Bloodhounds learned the sinister secret of the Blessington Method as practised by the Society for Gerontology.

'You read it beautifully, but it's not to my taste at all,' said Polly when Shirley-Ann had finished. 'I found it chilling.'

Jessica said, 'His stories are chilling. That's the whole point.'

'I know, dear. I *have* read some of his novels. This one struck home rather more forcibly. 'I'm not so far from being an elderly relative myself.'

'It's not only about elderly people,' said Jessica. 'The principle behind it could be applied to any other potential misfits – the mentally ill, the unemployed, sexual deviants, racial minorities.'

Rupert fairly sizzled with approval. 'Have I discovered an ally at last? You're absolutely right of course. Crime writers have a duty to bring the complacent middle classes face to face with the festering sores in our society.'

'I didn't say that.'

He gave one of his gummy laughs. 'I said it for you, ducky.'

Jessica was incensed. She pointed a finger at him. 'Ducky, I am not – you patronising old fart. And I don't need you as a mouthpiece. I'll say what I want myself.'

Rupert turned to Milo and said, 'Hark at her.'

Someone needed quickly to defuse the tension. Milo glanced across at Polly. 'Is it time, I wonder, for my contribution on the locked room mystery? I brought my copy of *The Hollow Man*.'

'What a splendid suggestion,' said Polly.

'And then we'll all sing "Jesus wants me for a sunbeam",' said Rupert.

'What on earth makes you say that?' asked Polly.

'Darling, you've missed the point. If you're going to run this like a Sunday school, we might as well sing hymns.'

'Don't you patronise me either,' said Polly, taking her cue from Jessica.

'I wouldn't dare, ma'am, after what you did to my dog. I couldn't bear to be banished to the Saracen's Head for the rest of the evening.'

Polly conceded a smile. 'Milo, why don't you begin? We've heard more than enough from Rupert.'

Milo took a deep breath that threatened a lengthy dissertation. Some of the smiles around the circle froze. He began, 'A crime is committed in a sealed, locked room. Nobody except the victim is found there when the door is unlocked. A mystery *par excellence.* None applied more energy and brain-power to it than John Dickson Carr.'

Shirley-Ann noticed that Sid nodded in support, and she recalled that he was one of the three people present who had claimed to have read *The Hollow Man.* Remarkably, his eyes were fixed on Milo and his hands were rotating the flat cap on his knees. She had not seen him so animated before.

Milo was saying, 'Some of you have criticised the classic detective novel for being unrealistic. At our last meeting I heard the word "preposterous".'

'From me. I'll repeat it this week if you like,' said Jessica.

'No need. Improbability, John Dickson Carr boldly tells us in *The Hollow Man*, is not to be despised. It isn't a fatal flaw. On the contrary, it is the chief glory of the detective story – and that is as true of the books you people espouse as of those I prefer to read. We are drawn irresistibly to the improbable. Does anyone deny it? Rupert's mean streets and Jessica's lady sleuths are never more engaging than when some crime is committed in bizarre, unaccountable circumstances. And the supreme situation, the purest challenge to probability any writer has devised is the locked room puzzle.'

Rupert couldn't resist saying, 'Absolute piffle.'

Milo glared at him. 'You're going to tell us that no locked room murder ever really happened, no doubt. You'd be wrong. Before *The Hollow Man* was published, a Chinese laundryman was found murdered in New York in a locked room and there have been other cases since. But I won't be sidetracked. My words may not impress you, but I fancy that Dickson Carr's might.'

He brandished his copy of *The Hollow Man* like an evangelist preacher and Shirley-Ann secretly thought back to Rupert's remark about the Sunday school.

'Chapter Seventeen is entitled *The Locked-Room Lecture*. Ideally, fellow Bloodhounds, I should have liked to read it in the kind of setting Dickson Carr describes, after dinner, round the glow of a table-lamp, with the wine bottles empty and coffee on the table and snowflakes drifting past the windows. But I suppose a church crypt is not a bad alternative.'

With his audience well primed for the treat in store, Milo opened the book and glanced first at the Contents page. He turned to the right chapter. Then he blinked, frowned and said, 'How odd. I don't remember using this as a bookmark.' He picked an envelope from between the pages and glanced at it.

He went silent. The envelope was yellow with age, the address in fine copperplate so faded that it was barely legible. In the top right corner was a single postage stamp with the head of Queen Victoria on a black background and the words ONE PENNY along the lower border. The stamp was overprinted with a cancellation mark saying PAID. Just below and to the right was the postmark, remarkably even and clear:

BATH
MY 2
1840

TWELVE

'It's impossible,' said Milo, blushing deeply. He stared at the flimsy envelope lying across the open book. 'Impossible.'

Miss Chilmark, seated on his left, had her hand pressed to her mouth. She swayed away from Milo as if he were contagious. A second bout of hyperventilation could not be ruled out.

On Milo's other side, Jessica took a long look and then raised her eyebrows across the circle at the others seated opposite.

'What is it?' Polly asked. 'What have you got there, Milo?'

Rupert, having leaned across Jessica to see for himself, said, 'Hey ho. What a turn-up!'

'Somebody tell me,' said Polly, becoming petulant.

'It would appear to be the missing Penny Black,' said Rupert. 'Milo, my old fruit, I salute you. I wouldn't have dreamed that you of all people would turn out to be the most wanted man in Bath.'

'But I didn't steal it,' Milo blurted out. 'I'm no thief.'

'You're among friends,' Rupert went on as if he hadn't heard. 'If we're honest, most of us have a sneaking admiration for you. This was brilliantly worked out. You don't need to say any more. Just shut the book and we'll all behave as if nothing happened.'

Milo's hands were shaking. He fumbled with the book and practically knocked the envelope to the floor.

'Careful!' said Jessica. 'It's worth a fortune.'

'I didn't take it,' Milo insisted. 'I don't know anything about this.'

'You can be frank with us,' said Jessica. 'Rupert's right. We'll stand by you if you promise to give it back and say no more about it. We can keep a secret. That's a fair offer, isn't it?' she appealed to the rest of the circle.

'But I've done nothing wrong,' Milo shrilled. 'This is the first time I've ever laid eyes on the thing. Really.'

'How did it get into your book?' asked Shirley-Ann.

'I haven't the faintest idea.'

'None of *us* could have slipped it between the pages,' said Polly, and then undermined the statement by adding, 'Could we?'

'It's been here on my lap all the time,' said Milo. 'I'm not accusing any of you, but someone planted it on me and I'd like to know how.'

'What about when Marlowe came in and upset Miss Chilmark?' Shirley-Ann suggested. 'In the confusion—'

'No,' Milo interrupted her. 'I kept hold of the book. I didn't leave my chair. It must have been done before I got here, but I can't fathom how. Someone must have broken into my boat. Oh dear, this is so distressing.'

Shirley-Ann recalled being told that Milo lived on a narrowboat on the canal. 'Have you had any visitors lately? Anyone you left alone for a few minutes?'

'Not for weeks.'

'Do you lock the boat when you're not there?'

'Of course. I have a damned great padlock. I carry the key on my key-ring.' He produced it from his pocket. 'This one. You see? I bought it from Foxton's. You get a guarantee that no other lock with a similar key has been sold from the same shop – and they're the only people who sell them in the west of England.' He sighed heavily. 'What am I going to do?'

'Go to the police,' said Polly.

'They're going to give me a bad time, aren't they? They're not going to believe this.'

Nobody said so, but Milo's reading of events was

probably right. His camp manner wasn't likely to help him at the police station.

Shirley-Ann said, 'Couldn't you just send it back to the Postal Museum in an envelope?'

'That's what Rupert and I said in effect,' said Jessica. 'The trouble is, there are six of us who know about this. He's going to have to rely on us all keeping the secret. Who's to say that any one of us won't let the cat out of the bag in some unguarded moment? Then he'd be in far worse trouble.'

Polly said, 'I don't really agree that we should stay silent. I think Milo ought to go to the police directly.'

'So do I,' chimed in Miss Chilmark. 'Let the truth come out, whatever it is. What do the rest of you think? What about you?' she said to Shirley-Ann.

'I think the decision is up to Milo. I don't mind staying quiet if he doesn't want to get involved.'

'And you?' demanded Miss Chilmark, swinging round to face Sid.

Sid's shoulders were hunched as usual. He said without looking up from the floor, 'I can stay quiet.'

'No one will argue with that,' said Rupert. 'Milo, my old cobber, the house is divided. Four of us are willing to turn a blind eye and two want to hand you over to the rozzers.'

'That isn't right,' Polly protested. 'Milo tells us he knows nothing about this, and I'm willing to believe him. He has nothing to fear from the police. The sooner he reports this and gives them the chance to catch the real thief, the better.'

'My sentiments exactly,' said Miss Chilmark.

Milo gave a nod. 'You're right, of course. I'd better hand this in as soon as possible.'

'Do you want anyone to go with you?' Polly asked. 'We can all back up your story. We're solidly behind you, Milo.'

Milo thanked her and said he thought he would rather go alone. He placed the precious envelope tightly between the pages prior to closing the book. 'The amazing thing is that it was here, like a bookmark, at the very chapter I was going to read out.'

'The one about the locked room lecture?' said Jessica.

'Yes.'

'Did you have a bookmark here?'

'No need. I knew it was Chapter Seventeen.'

'But you'd opened the book to look at it?'

'Some time during the week, yes. I suppose when the thief opened it, the pages fell open at the chapter I'd been studying. But why me? Why do a thing like this to me, of all people?'

There was no response from anyone. If any of the Bloodhounds knew the answer, or had a private theory, this wasn't the moment to air it. Polly suggested closing the meeting early – it was still only 8.45 and there was no dissent. Milo put on his overcoat and fur hat and was the first to leave.

THIRTEEN

Shirley-Ann could hardly wait to tell Bert, her partner, about the dramatic moment when the Penny Black was found. She gave him the update as soon as she got back to their flat in Russell Street. Bert was a difficult man to impress, a modern embodiment of the stony indifference displayed by the English archers at the Battle of Agincourt. Admirable, but frustrating when you were the French army at the charge, so to speak, with lances raised and banners unfurled. He listened in silence, hardly raising an eyebrow until Shirley-Ann had finished. Then came the comment: 'I suppose we'll have the police round here asking questions next.'

Bert had this unerring ability to raise alarming images in Shirley-Ann's brain. She pictured two burly officers in uniform sitting in the living room. She, straight from the kitchen, caught wearing that vulgar PVC apron with its lifesize image of an over-developed female torso in basque and suspenders. No good saying her regular apron was in the wash and this one belonged to Bert, a silly prize won in the rugby club raffle. She visualised the policemen eyeing suspiciously her shelves of books stacked with crime fiction and perhaps even finding on the bottom shelf among the atlases and art books the Stanley Gibbons Junior Stamp Album she had kept since childhood. 'Interested in philately, are we?'

Shirley-Ann's brain was in such turmoil that she wouldn't be ready to sleep until much later. She didn't expect to hear much more from Bert until he'd finished his supper.

He always ate a big meal with a glass of red wine at the end of the day, and tonight it was a full-size Marks and Spencer steak and kidney pie, heated in the microwave. He survived all day at the Sports and Leisure Centre on dried fruit, pulses and apple juice. It seemed to suit his metabolism. He had the physique of an athlete, so hunky, Shirley-Ann sometimes told him, that he could have doubled for Arnie Schwarzenegger, which was a slight exaggeration. He jogged in the mornings and of course his work kept him in shape and burned up plenty of calories.

She wanted Bert's advice. He had a very clear-sighted view of things. She waited until he had cleared his plate and was finishing with a banana.

'Bert.'

'Mm?'

'Do you really think the police will want to talk to me?'

'It's obvious. You're a witness. You could be a suspect as well.'

'Oh, be serious. I didn't have anything to do with it.'

'They don't know that. If – what's his name, the gay bloke?'

'Milo.'

'If Milo can't explain how he got hold of the stamp, questions are going to be asked, aren't they?'

She nervously fingered a strand of her hair. 'I suppose you're right.'

'Don't know why you got mixed up with this lot.'

'That's down to you.'

He frowned. 'Me?'

'Because you're always at the Sports Centre in the evenings. You can't expect me to stay here on my own. It was in that "What's On In Bath" pamphlet you brought home. I found it under clubs and societies, remember?'

'So how are you going to handle it?' Bert asked, positive and forward-looking. Attractive qualities in a man, but not always easy to match.

'You mean if they come asking questions?'

'There's no "if" about it.'

'I'll tell the truth, I suppose. Mind you, I don't want to get Milo into more trouble than he's in already.'

'You can't turn your back. You might as well go to the police and tell them what happened – before they come to you.' Bert's urge to get things done was why a career in sport was so ideal for him. He called it 'sports management', but Shirley-Ann suspected it had more to do with demonstrating step-ups than sitting behind a desk.

'I don't want to do that,' said Shirley-Ann. 'I don't want to shop Milo. I don't even know for sure if he went to the police after the meeting ended. He said he was going, but you never know.'

'Shop him?' Bert repeated. 'You're talking like a criminal yourself.'

'Give over, Bert. I'm not going to the police, and that's final.'

Bert softened a little. He relented to the extent of offering her a segment of orange. He put on his worldly-wise look, the sort of expression he wore when showing some novice how to hold a table-tennis bat. 'You've got to admit that they sound an odd bunch. This Rupert – he's the character with the dog, right?'

She nodded. 'Character is the word for Rupert. He dresses like a stage Frenchman. Well, a rather gone-to-seed stage Frenchman. Black beret, striped jersey and jeans. And he has this terribly, terribly well-bred English accent. Have I told you this already?'

'Some of it,' Bert said.

'Listening to him, you'd think you were safe as houses, but he seems to cause havoc wherever he goes. He got the Bloodhounds banned from the Francis Hotel.'

'Why?'

'I don't know the details. He can be pretty outspoken, and it's a very carrying voice. I'm not sure if he knows the effect it has.'

'Better keep your distance, then. What about the women in the group? Are they more reliable?'

'There's Polly Wycherley. She's our chairman. A little white-haired lady with a fixed smile like you get across the jam and marmalade stall at the Women's Institute sale. She set up the group and she holds it together. I think it's very important to her self-esteem to keep it going.'

'Reliable?'

'I'd say "yes" like a shot except that Jessica – she's the one who runs the art gallery – seems not to trust her entirely.'

'Any idea why?'

'There's some friction between those two. Polly was quite miffed because I stayed for a drink with Jessica in the Moon and Sixpence last week. And Jessica wasn't too pleased when I mentioned having coffee at Le Parisien with Polly. So there's a slight question mark. But I like them both in their different ways. Jessica is bright and liberated. Fun to be with.'

'There's another woman in the group, isn't there?'

Shirley-Ann smiled. 'Miss Chilmark wouldn't care to be described as a woman. A lady, if you please. "There have been Chilmarks in the West Country for over seven hundred years." She can't abide Rupert. Or Polly. Or any of us, except possibly Milo. She'd like to be chairman.'

'So what's your opinion?' Bert asked. 'Do you think Milo pinched the stamp?'

'I'd be amazed if he did. He's an intelligent man, or so I thought.'

'But this wasn't a stupid crime,' Bert pointed out. 'The whole thing was set up as a kind of challenge, remember. There was that rhyme about Victoria that was on the radio and in the papers.'

She nodded. 'It was a jolly clever bluff. Everyone was fooled by it, including the police.'

'So you reckon there's a good brain behind this?'

She nodded. 'The way it was set up was really artful.

Brilliant, in fact. That rhyme fooled everyone. The stupid bit was tonight – if Milo is the thief – revealing it to everybody.'

'Unless he's still several moves ahead of the rest of you.'

Her eyes widened. Bert was second to none at spotting devious goings-on. There was a lot of jockeying for position in sports management.

'So what's he up to, do you suppose?' She leaned across the table with the point of her chin resting on her upturned thumb. Her lips were slightly open. She half hoped Bert would say, 'Who cares about Milo?' and lean closer.

Instead he asked, 'Does he know anything about stamps?'

Her chin came to rest less seductively in her cupped hand. 'I've no idea. No one has mentioned it. He seems more hooked on Sherlock Holmes than anything else.'

Bert rotated his finger thoughtfully around the rim of the empty wine glass. 'Do you think he fancies himself as Holmes?'

Shirley-Ann giggled a little. 'I suppose he might. He does wear a deerstalker. But I don't see why it should make him want to steal the Penny Black. Holmes didn't commit crimes, he solved them.'

He expanded on his theory. 'If he wanted to show off a bit, demonstrate his skill at solving a crime, he could pretend to find the stamp by Holmes's methods.'

'But he didn't, did he? It turned up in the pages of a book.'

'A stupid mistake. It proves he isn't in the same league as Holmes,' said Bert. 'He must have tucked it in there for safety and forgotten that he was using the same book to read from.'

She pondered for a moment. 'That sounds quite possible. What was he aiming to do with the stamp?'

'He'd have pretended to find it somewhere nobody else would think of, and he'd have got his fifteen minutes of fame as the modern Sherlock who outwitted the police.

The whole episode wouldn't have done anybody any harm provided that the stamp turned up again in perfect condition.'

'That's rather neat. I do hope you're right,' she said. 'I don't like to think of Milo as a thief.'

'I didn't say he wasn't one,' said Bert in a change of tone. 'They don't all wear flat caps and carry bags with "Swag" written on them.'

'Haha.'

'He could have demanded a ransom for it. Fifty grand, or he burns it.'

'He's a retired civil servant, for heaven's sake.'

'Maybe he's been waiting all his life to do something really exciting.'

'Silly!'

Bert said huffily, 'If you don't think much of my opinions, why ask me?'

Now she'd offended him. He was so touchy about anything remotely suggesting he was stupid, which he patently was not. She supposed he had to endure a lot of thoughtless remarks at work from users of the Leisure Centre who thought he was just a musclebound bloke in a tracksuit.

They cleared the table and watched television for an hour, but Shirley-Ann couldn't have told you what the programme was.

FOURTEEN

Peter Diamond was still up after midnight watching television, picking holes in the plot of an old film, *To Catch a Thief.* Stephanie had quit after the first commercial break. 'Far be it from me to drag you away from Grace Kelly,' she told him. 'See it to the end. I'm tired.'

She was amused to see that the new kitten stayed on the arm of his chair, ready to pounce on his hand if he moved. It still had no name. Peter had this weird theory that the kitten would let them know what it wanted to be called. She was content to let the little tabby do its own job of winning approval. On the first evening, after the predictable flare-up when he'd spotted the cat-tray, her bruiser of a husband, the tyrant of Manvers Street, had stayed up most of the night with the kitten in case it cried. Big softie.

Then the phone rang.

She was still sitting up in bed reading when he came into the bedroom to hand over the kitten. 'I'm going to have to go out, love. That was Wigfull.'

Her eyes widened. 'He isn't your boss, is he? What does he want at this time of night?'

'He's found a body.'

'Personally?'

'So he says. Murder is my pigeon, not his.'

'Where is it?'

'On a canal boat.'

'In Bath?'

'Limpley Stoke. That boatyard near the Aqueduct. I've got to go.'

102

'It's wickedly cold tonight. There's a frost.'

'I'll take it carefully down Brassknocker,' he promised.

'I wasn't thinking of your driving. I meant I'm going to freeze in this bed without you.'

He smiled. 'You'll have warmed up nicely by the time I get in.'

'Thanks – I'll really look forward to that. You'll be as cold as Finnegan's feet on the day they buried him.'

By daylight Brassknocker Hill offers a series of glorious, gasp-inducing views of the Limpley Stoke Valley. By night the descent from Claverton Down is even more dramatic, for you plunge into a vast, black void with just a scattering of lights. He would have driven cautiously anyway, without the frost warning. At the bottom he turned right at the Viaduct pub, joined the A36 and immediately left it by the traffic lights.

The entrance to the Dundas boatyard is an unprepossessing pull-in over uneven ground a few yards along the Bradford Road. The gate was open and a few frost-coated cars were parked inside. He bumped over a couple of potholes and stopped beside an empty police car. Nobody was about. There was some kind of notice at the far end of the parking area. He groped in his glove compartment for a torch. The notice informed him: *Your car is at risk from thieves.*

There was only one way to go: up a slope towards some temporary-looking buildings that turned out to be the boatyard offices. They stood beside a stretch of the old Somerset Coal Canal that was used for mooring. His torch picked out a small iron bridge and beyond it a row of narrowboats and other small craft.

Along the towpath he discovered that the moorings extended much further than he had first appreciated, using both sides of the canal. Fifty or sixty boats must have been tied up there. He flicked the torch over some names painted in the florid lettering that is the canal-boat style: *Henrietta, Occam's Razor, Charleen.* They were moored for the winter, he guessed, locked up, curtains drawn, with everything portable removed from the decks. If cars were at risk from thieves, then so were boats.

Presently voices carried to him. A torchbeam speared the darkness and dazzled him. He stepped out towards John Wigfull, two uniformed officers and a bearded man in a deerstalker hat. They were beside a red narrowboat called the *Mrs Hudson*. As if to proclaim that it was also a houseboat, some twenty conifers in pots stood along the roof and there was a television aerial. The interior was lit, but nothing could be seen; the venetian blinds were closed at all the windows.

'This is Mr Motion,' Wigfull said with a nod at the bearded man. 'He owns the boat.'

'Nice boat,' said Diamond to Motion. 'And you say there's a corpse inside?'

Wigfull said, 'We found it together.'

'*You* found it?' Diamond could have added that Wigfull was supposed to be fully stretched investigating a stamp theft, but there was no need. The point was made in the way he stressed the word *You*.

'Peter, can we take this from the beginning? We've got to wait for the SOCOs, so you might as well hear what happened. Mr Motion walked into Manvers Street this evening and informed us that the missing Penny Black had come into his possession.'

'So you've found it.' Diamond took a longer look at Motion in his deerstalker, but without shining a torch into his face it was difficult to assess the man in these conditions. 'A body *and* the stamp?'

Wigfull continued, 'It turned up in a book. He doesn't know how it got there. He happened to be reading from this book at a meeting. There's a club called the Bloodhounds that meets on Mondays—'

'Hold on a minute. The what?'

'Bloodhounds.'

'We're a group of local people with a mutual interest in crime fiction,' Motion explained in a tone that expressed some irritation with Wigfull. Clearly they'd been over this a number of times already.

Wigfull said, 'They bring their books to the meeting and read bits. When Mr Motion opened his, the cover was inside – and when I say cover, I'm using the stamp-collectors' term. I mean the envelope with the Penny Black. It was between the pages at precisely the section Mr Motion had chosen to read from. Have I summarised the facts correctly, Mr Motion?'

'Yes,' said Motion wearily.

'He opened the book and made the discovery in the presence of six other witnesses. When he realised what it was, he came directly to the station and reported it. That was at five to nine this evening. I was called in and interviewed him from nine-thirty onwards.'

'For almost three hours,' said Motion.

'This wasn't a missing budgerigar you brought in, sir,' said Wigfull, displaying some impatience of his own. 'It's the world's most valuable stamp.' He switched back to Diamond. 'Mr Motion insists that the book never left his hands from the time he started out for his meeting.'

'Literally?' said Diamond.

Motion gave a nod.

'I see that you're wearing an overcoat, sir. Did you wear it for the meeting?'

'Obviously not,' said Motion.

'You removed it, then, and still held on to the book? Not impossible, but not easy.'

'You're splitting hairs, aren't you? I put it on a chair for a moment, but it didn't leave my possession.'

'So we shouldn't take everything you say as the literal truth. Carry on, John.'

Wigfull said, 'We've been over this several times.'

'You mean you covered the question of the overcoat.'

'I established that nobody at the club had an opportunity to place the cover inside the book,' Wigfull said, sidestepping the overcoat question. 'It was likely that it was in the book before he started out – in which case, the perpetrator must have boarded this boat, got inside and found the book and planted the cover between the pages. Mr Motion insists that the boat is always locked. He uses a padlock with a key that is unique.'

'Unique? Most padlocks are sold with two keys,' said Diamond. Wigfull's complacent manner was bringing out the pedant in him.

'There were two originally,' Motion explained. 'One fell into the canal at least a year ago. I only have the one.'

'Couldn't someone buy a padlock with a similar key?'

'No. Not in England. It's German-made. A strong lock, and expensive. From that locksmith in George Street. Well, you can see for yourself.'

Diamond shone his torch on the steel padlock, now unlocked and hooked over an iron staple fixed to the top of the door. When the door was closed, the staple would slot into a hinged metal strap attached to the sliding hatch at the back end of the roof. It looked a secure arrangement. He wouldn't touch anything until the Scene of Crime Officers arrived. Certainly the padlock was heavy-duty. 'Do you attach this at all times?' he asked Motion.

'Except when I'm aboard. Then I can close everything and bolt it from inside.'

'And do you?'

'Do I what?'

'Always take the trouble to bolt yourself in?'

'Of course I do. I want my home to feel as secure as you no doubt wish yours to be.' Motion didn't jib at crossing swords with Diamond. He had the confidence of someone well practised with words.

Wigfull took up the narrative again. 'Naturally after questioning Mr Motion about the stamp I decided to accompany him here and see if his story held up. When we got here the boat was padlocked, just as he claimed. But when he opened it, we found the body inside, lying on the floor of the lounge.'

'Before your very eyes.'

'What?'

106

'Just like magic.'

Wigfull said huffily, 'I didn't find it particularly enchanting.'

'But you can't think how it was done.'

'Can you? Mr Motion swears that nobody was aboard when he left for his meeting.'

'What about the door at the front end?' asked Diamond.

'Prow,' said Wigfull.

'Bolted from the inside,' said Motion.

'The windows?' Diamond shone his torch along the side of the boat. There were five in view. 'Fair enough,' he said, for it was obvious that no one could have climbed through the narrow vents at the top. 'No other means of access? Hatches?'

'There's a hatch to the engine, but that wouldn't let you into the cabin.'

'You've got some explaining to do, sir.'

'*I* have?' said Motion. 'I'm more mystified than you are.'

'The funny thing is,' said Wigfull, 'the place in the book where the missing stamp was found is the start of a chapter with the title *The Locked-Room Lecture.*'

'Is that funny?' said Diamond.

'You can't deny it's a strange coincidence. What we've got here is a locked room puzzle. How did the body get into the boat when it was locked?'

'Right now, I'm more interested in the body. Do we know who it is?'

'He's face down.'

'So it's male?'

'I examined him briefly to see if he was still alive. There was blood beside his head. He'd gone. No pulse. I don't know if you can see anything between the blinds.' Wigfull crouched at the nearest window, but the slats on the venetian blinds were tightly closed.

'Do you have any idea who this man might be, sir?' Diamond asked Motion.

'None. I wasn't allowed to go in. I unlocked and reached for the light switch and saw the figure lying on the floor ahead of me and said "Oh my God!" or something similar and then this gentleman took over. That's all I can tell you.'

The drone of car engines entering the boatyard stopped the conversation. Two bobbing sets of headlights came down from the road and advanced along the towpath: the Scenes of Crime team in the Land Rovers. In no time they were climbing into white overalls and stretching barrier tapes across the towpath, regardless that no one was likely to come along at this hour.

'If you'd open the blinds, we can take a look at the scene without disturbing you,' Diamond suggested, but it was getting on for twenty minutes before this request was acted upon. The SOCOs had their procedures and stuck to them.

Eventually the senior man informed Diamond, 'Victim is a male, white, aged about forty-five. Light brown raincoat over a blue sports jacket, black trousers, white shirt and black tie. There's a cap beside him, brown. The only injury I can see is the head wound.'

'And the weapon?'

'Couldn't tell you. Nothing obvious in there.'

Diamond turned to Milo Motion. 'Know anyone of that description?'

'No.'

'You live alone here?'

'Haven't I made that clear?'

'Not to me.' He hesitated. 'I'm bound to ask this, sir. Do you have a companion?'

'Absolutely not.' Spoken with umbrage.

'They've lifted the blinds now. Would you look at this man and tell me if you recognise him?'

'He's face down.'

'From his clothes and general appearance. We can't move him until the doctor has looked at him.'

Motion bent closer to one of the windows. 'He looks

a little like ... But that's impossible.'

'Like who, sir?'

'Like a man called Sid. But he's one of the Blood-hounds. He does have a raincoat like that. No, it couldn't possibly be Sid. He was at the meeting with me until it ended. Besides, what would Sid be doing on my boat?'

FIFTEEN

Next morning in the briefing room at Manvers Street, Diamond assembled the Murder Squad. It didn't matter that half of them were officially seconded to Operation Bumblebee; Wigfull's people were ordered to attend. Murder took precedence over everything. Even so, the stamp's recovery had given the Bumblebees some encouragement.

Diamond soon put a stopper on that. 'You lot may be feeling chipper this morning, but I got sod-all sleep last night. If there's anything to be pleased about, I'd like to know what.'

A young inspector recently transferred from Radstock rashly told him what.

'That's the good news, is it?' said Diamond.

'Well, it sounds like good news to me, sir.'

'Good news, my arse. You don't know who nicked it yet. Can't take any credit. It was handed in. Jack the lad made us look like the plods we are. What kind of good news is that?'

'It's bad news, sir,' the inspector said in a sharp about-turn.

'Wrong again, squire. That isn't the bad news. The bad news is that somebody was killed last night. And there seems to be a link between the murder and the theft.' He addressed the entire room. 'The victim was a man of forty-six called Sid Towers, a night-watchman. Towers was last seen alive in the centre of Bath at eight-forty-five last night. The body was discovered by Mr Wigfull here and the man who handed in the stamp, name of Milo Motion. Got that? Milo Motion. Time: about one a.m. this morning. Location: on a narrowboat moored at the Dundas boatyard, across the road from the Viaduct pub. Victim was cracked over the head with some heavy object like a spanner. It hasn't been found yet. The divers are already at the scene in case it was thrown into the water, but I doubt it. This killer is smart – and that is an understatement. Milo Motion, who lives aboard the boat, locked up at a quarter to seven to attend a meeting in Bath and when he got back with John Wigfull at his side the padlock was still in place.'

'With the victim inside the cabin,' Wigfull himself put in.

'I'd better tell you about the Bloodhounds. Wipe the smile off your face, Keith. These are crucial facts I'm giving you. Milo Motion belongs to a club – a literary society, he calls it – known as the Bloodhounds. They meet in the crypt of St Michael's – that big church by the Podium – every Monday to discuss detective stories.'

He broke off the narrative to point at someone making a sly aside to his neighbour. 'Will you shut up and listen to this? Sid Towers, the murdered man, was a member of this Bloodhound club and was present at the meeting. And a strange thing happened. Milo Motion, the owner of the boat, had agreed to read a chapter from a book he'd brought with him. A book of his own, right? This chapter was on the subject of locked room mysteries, which I gather have a devoted following among people who read whodunits. He opened the book at the place he wanted and – what do you know? – there was the missing Penny Black lying between the pages like a bookmark. Everyone was shocked, not least Mr Motion. The meeting ended early and Motion came straight to us and spent the rest of the evening being put through the grinder.

'All told, it wasn't Milo Motion's day, getting lumbered with a stolen stamp and a murdered corpse. He insists that his boat was locked all evening and he was the only person in possession of a key. Yet when he unlocked, the body was found there. So do we charge Motion with murder? Do we, heck! He has a better alibi than the Pope. I told you Towers was alive at eight-forty-five. At five to nine, Motion was meeting the desk sergeant downstairs. He couldn't have travelled to the boatyard and back in ten minutes. And the rest of the time he was with John Wigfull. What we have, my friends, is a locked boat mystery.'

One of Wigfull's team said, 'He could have hired someone.'

'Motion could?'

'Couldn't he?'

'To do a killing on his own boat?' said Diamond on a shrill note of disbelief.

'You said we're dealing with someone smart, or better than smart. Maybe this is the ultimate in bluffing.'

'I don't see it, but I'm willing to listen if there's more to this theory.'

There was not. Julie Hargreaves filled the silence that followed by saying, 'Shall we discuss the stamp theft first?' She had worked with Diamond often enough not to be cowed by his black moods.

John Wigfull said, 'Actually, I was about to propose the same thing.'

'Do you want to take over?' Diamond offered. He spoke mildly, and it might have been sincerely meant. It was impossible to tell.

Wigfull didn't answer.

'This is your baby,' Diamond pointed out.

Wigfull was practically squirming in his chair. The stamp theft *was* his baby, only there was no way he could dandle it on his knee with any pride.

Julie cut the tension by saying, 'Sir, can we establish first that Milo Motion is a fall guy and not a thief? Whoever did the Postal Museum job – which was cleverly carried out, remember – he took some risks courting publicity with those verses – whoever did it was unlikely to hand the

112

stamp in meekly, as this man Motion did. It would be a surrender, and a pathetic one at that.'

'Go on.'

'Is that a fair point?' said Julie, unwilling to be hustled. 'I'd like to know if anyone disagrees.'

Diamond looked to his left. 'John?'

'It sounds reasonable to me,' Wigfull was forced to commit himself. 'After several hours with Motion, I can't see him as a master thief. He's bright, certainly. A loner. Eccentric, shall we say?'

'If you mean homosexual,' murmured Diamond, 'why don't you say so?'

'Because I don't know,' Wigfull snapped back. 'I didn't ask. His sexual preferences don't come into it. If you're asking me to make a guess, I'd say he probably is gay, but that's a superficial impression.'

'Say it, John,' said Halliwell. 'The man's a jam duff.'

'What does that make you?' said Diamond. 'A paper-weight?'

Wigfull was striving to make a serious point. 'I don't think Motion has the bottle to carry out a theft, let alone bluff his way out of it.'

'Are you sure there isn't a partner?' Diamond pressed him.

'He doesn't live with anyone, if that's what you mean. I just said he's a loner. To come back to your question, Julie, yes, he's been set up, in my opinion. We're looking for someone else.'

Julie said, 'Then we ought to look at motives. Why steal the stamp if you intend to give it back? The other day we were expecting a ransom demand. It didn't come.'

Keith Halliwell said, 'The stamp was just a pawn in a far more serious game.'

'You're linking it to the murder?' said Julie.

'Of course. You sacrifice a pawn to achieve a better position.'

'What better position?' asked Diamond.

'It ensured that Motion would go to the police and

113

be questioned for some hours. His boat was unoccupied. Time enough for the killer to murder Towers and get away.'

'Except that we don't know how he got into a locked boat or what brought Towers there.'

'The locked room mystery,' said one of Wigfull's team. 'Isn't it remarkable that the Bloodhounds meet to discuss locked room mysteries and now we have one of our own?'

'Two,' said Diamond, and now he began to function more constructively. 'There's the mystery of the stamp and the mystery of the murder. It may be that Keith is right, and the stamp theft was a tactical move in a more serious game. We'd better keep an open mind. Since the stamp came up first, let's confine ourselves to that for a moment. Milo Motion can't explain how the Penny Black got between the pages of his book, which incidentally was *The Hollow Man*, by John Dickson Carr – if that means anything at all to a crowd of bozos who never read anything except the *Sun*. He kept it on a shelf on his boat with his other books. He had no visitors during the past week. On the evening of the meeting, he removed the book from the shelf and took it to the Bloodhounds. It didn't leave his possession at all. He's very clear about that. So what are we left with? The stamp was already between the pages when he took *The Hollow Man* from the bookshelf. John and I have seen the boat. It isn't very long. About sixty-five feet. Motion says he bolts it from the inside whenever he's aboard and padlocks it from the outside when he isn't. If the thief planted the stamp, he found a way to beat the locks and bolts. The cabin area of that boat is a perfect locked room. No hatches. No way in by the windows, which just have a narrow vent at the top. There's a door at either end. One end is bolted from the inside. Chubb security bolts at top and bottom. We've seen them. The other is locked from outside with this strong, close shackle padlock and there's only one key – on a ring in Motion's pocket.'

Keith Halliwell suggested, 'Could the thief have un-screwed the fittings on the door?'

'The padbar and staple, you mean?' said Diamond. 'Nice try. We looked at it ourselves. The screws are rusty, so any recent interference would show. There isn't a scratch.'

'The hinges?' someone else put in.

'They aren't accessible from outside – and they haven't been tampered with.'

Halliwell said, 'Someone must have a duplicate key, whatever Mr Motion says.'

'We've checked with the locksmith. It isn't possible. It's a feature of these locks, which are German-made, that each one is unique. There *were* two keys, but he dropped his spare one in the canal over a year ago. I simply don't believe that some passing bandit could have fished it out and knew which padlock it fitted.'

Halliwell was a stubborn cuss. 'If he put his keys down somewhere, someone could have done the old Plasticine trick and got an impression.'

'*If*,' said Diamond. 'But he insists that they are always in the pocket of the trousers he is wearing.'

'There's the flaw. Can we believe him?'

'I'd say yes.'

'There's got to be some explanation.'

'You might be interested in what Dickson Carr had to say on the subject.' Diamond felt into his jacket pocket and with a flourish produced a paperback of *The Hollow Man*. 'Chapter Seventeen is *The Locked-Room Lecture*, the one Milo Motion planned to read to the Bloodhounds. The author states among other things that the explanation of a locked room problem is invariably disappointing.'

'"So simple when it is explained,"' murmured Wigfull.

'What?'

'A quote from a Sherlock Holmes story.'

'This is John Dickson Carr,' Diamond said brusquely. 'I was going on to say that in this lecture he classifies most of the methods used in locked room mysteries. I won't bore you with them all. He dismisses secret panels, secret passages and so on as trick stuff, beneath contempt. He's pretty scathing about murders that are committed without the murderer actually entering the room, by gases, mechanical devices and so on. And about suicide, when the gun disappears up the chimney on the end of a piece of elastic.'

The gun on elastic earned some chuckles.

'As a variation it can be whisked out of a window. Then there are bullets made of ice that melts without a trace. There are poisonous snakes, impersonations, disguises, tricks with time. But the section of most interest to us is the one on ways of tampering with door locks. As Dickson Carr sums it up, there are three categories. First, the murderer can use bits of string and metal to turn a key which is still in a lock, but on the wrong side of the door. This doesn't apply to our problem. Secondly, he can remove the door hinges, as someone suggested, but in our case it didn't happen. Thirdly, he tampers with the bolt, using string or metal. One of our sets of doors, you'll recollect, was bolted from inside. However, the bolts aren't the primitive things Dickson Carr was describing in 1935. They're finger-bolts, set into the wood, invisible from the outside, and I defy anyone to open them with string, plastic, or anything else. If the killer isn't Milo Motion – and it can't be, for reasons I've stated – then he or she must have found a way of unfastening the padlock.'

'Which is impossible,' said Wigfull. 'This is a sophisticated padlock with only one key, which remained in Mr Motion's possession throughout the time I was questioning him.'

'Are you certain it was locked when you arrived at the boat with Mr Motion?' Julie Hargreaves asked.

Wigfull nodded. 'I watched him closely. I had my torch-beam pointed at the lock. I saw him take the key from his pocket and use it. There was a click as he turned the key and the shackle of the padlock sprang open. I haven't the slightest doubt that I saw the padlock being unlocked.'

'Do we have a time for the murder?' Fred Baker, one of Diamond's more senior detectives, asked.

'You know what pathologists are like about times of death,' said Diamond. 'All he would say – if I can call the phrase to mind – was that the external symptoms were not inconsistent with a time of death up to four hours prior to when he examined the body. We know the poor sod was alive four hours before.'

'And what was the cause?'

'Give me a break, Fred. We haven't had the post-mortem yet. It was pretty obvious that he'd received a heavy blow on the head, but if I tell you he died of brain damage you can be damned sure the post-mortem will show he choked on a fishbone.'

After a short pause, Keith Halliwell asked, 'What do we know about the victim? Was there any bad blood between him and Motion?'

'Apparently not. Motion claims they were on cordial terms. He says Towers was an introvert, excessively shy. Hardly ever joined in the discussions at the Bloodhounds. Wouldn't even look you in the eye unless he was forced to. He worked as a night-watchman in a furniture warehouse. Monday was his night off.'

'Any family?'

'No. He lived alone in a top-floor flat in Oak Street, off the Lower Bristol Road, under the railway viaduct.'

'Did he drive?'

'Good point. How did he get to the boatyard? He owned an old Skoda. And before anyone asks, yes, it was one of the cars parked near the entrance. We can safely assume that Sid Towers drove there after the Bloodhounds' meeting broke up. On the passenger seat we found a plastic bag containing a secondhand copy of – you guessed – a John Dickson Carr novel.'

'*The Hollow Man*?'

'No. *The Three Coffins*. I haven't read it yet.'

'You'll be lucky to get the time, sir,' Baker was bold enough to comment.

'I will if you lot get your fingers out. The first thing is to find out about what happened last night at the Bloodhounds. Apart from Motion and the victim, there were five others in attendance: four women and one man. I'll give you the names presently. I want them interviewed this morning before the news of the murder breaks. If you're assigned to one of them, play it cautiously. You're on the case of the Penny Black as far as they're concerned. They know they witnessed something bloody unusual. They'll be expecting you, so get them to talk about the moment when Motion opened his book and found the stamp. Try and get a picture of what else happened at the meeting – whether anything was said by the victim or anyone else that could have provoked violence later. See if Sid Towers confided in anyone before he drove to the boatyard. I'm damned sure this murder has its origin in the Bloodhounds, so I want to know what drives these people, their hang-ups, their ambitions, the tensions between them, what they eat for breakfast and what keeps them awake at night.' He turned to Wigfull. 'John, have I left anything out?'

Wigfull cleared his throat. 'I don't want anyone forgetting that we're also investigating the stamp theft,' he said huffily. 'This is more than just a pretext for getting the facts about the murder. It's a serious crime that may or may not be connected with what happened to Towers. Be alert. Insist that you get a full account of the events leading up to the discovery of the Penny Black cover, and what happened after.'

'Got that? The Penny Black is Mr Wigfull's baby and the murder is mine. And if one of you messes up, you answer to me,' said Diamond. 'Now Inspector Hargreaves will read out the teams.'

He was content to let others carry out the interviews. An act of mercy to the witnesses, given the mood he was in. Instead, he decided to walk the short distance across Churchill Bridge and up the Lower Bristol Road as far as Oak Street to look at Sid Towers' flat. He asked Julie to come with him. On the way he thanked her for her contribution to the briefing. 'I was too heavy, even by my standards,' he admitted. 'You got the thing back to what it should be. I don't know what came over me. Lack of sleep, I suppose.'

'You're not at your best conducting meetings,' she was bold enough to tell him.

'Was I an ogre, Julie?'

'Can I be frank?'

'You generally are.'

'You were appalling.'

'That bad?'

'The way you jumped on that new man. He was only trying to answer one of your questions. He didn't know that the form is to stay quiet until you've had your say.'

'He will in future, won't he?'

'And I know there's a history between you and John Wigfull, but you didn't have to hammer him in front of his team. They know what he's like without you pointing it out.'

'I'm not running the Women's Institute.'

'A pity. They'd sort you out in no time.'

He laughed. 'You're probably right, Julie. My wife was a Brown Owl and she keeps me in order.'

She said, 'Since I've gone out on a limb already, I might as well say it. You'd get more input from the team if you weren't so domineering. They don't like to speak out.'

'Are they scared of me?' he asked, genuinely surprised.

'I don't think you have any idea how stroppy you sound.'

He stared over the bridge along the grey ribbon of water. 'If you want the truth, Julie, none of them is as scared as I am. Remember I've been off for a couple of years. I don't know everybody any more. I call a meeting and it's a minefield. I can give instructions. I can interview a suspect. Put me in front of a crowd of faces wanting to

119

see how I function as top dog and I won't say I panic, but my insides don't like it.'

'Well, it didn't show this morning.'

The traffic halted conversation as they stepped towards the mills and warehouses, long since converted into the engineering and construction businesses that line this stretch of the Lower Bristol Road. Diamond knew the area from the days when he lived on Wellsway. On a fine day, or when his car was giving trouble, he would come this way into the city, down the steps from Wells Road and under the railway viaduct, passing the arches where the winos and derelicts spent the night. It amused him to think that some of these same arches once housed a police station. There was also once a mortuary for the storage of corpses dragged from the Avon.

Most of the Lower Bristol Road was an eyesore that some city planner would want to flatten before long, but there was still a dignity to the mills with their wooden hoist-covers projecting above the street, just clear of the container lorries that rumbled past. This was Bath's oldest surviving industrial landscape, and it was pleasing that the buildings were in use, even if the quays behind them no longer functioned.

To their right was the Bayer Building, a tall red-brick structure more ornate than the others, with arched windows and Bath stone trimmings. Seeing an opportunity to strike a lighter mood, Diamond said, 'Bet you can't tell me what this was built for.'

Julie gave it a look. 'Something to do with engineering?'

'In a sense, yes.'

'Plumbing?'

'Stays.'

'I beg your pardon.'

'Corsets. Charles Bayer was the corset king. Our great-grandmothers had a lot to thank him for.'

'Questionable,' said Julie. 'Some of them suffered agonies.'

'Ah, but he also invented a little item that no woman should be without.'

'What's that?'

'The safety pin.'

Directly opposite the Bayer Building was the street where Sid Towers had lived until so recently. Presumably it had once housed the corset-workers. Directly below the viaduct – it actually ran under one of the arches – and so close to the main artery to Bristol, Oak Street was not a place many would have chosen to reside in, except from necessity.

The houses were on one side only; a scrap merchant had the other side, with his business concentrated in the arches. The sound of metal-cutting shrilled above the noise of juggernauts from the end of the street. Several houses appeared to be empty. One or two presented a trim front, but the majority had surrendered. They were two-storey terraced dwellings in local stone stained black at the top by coal-dust. Remarkably, considering how small they were, several had been converted into flats.

They had to go under the arch to find Sid's flat, past some children throwing sticks for a dog that looked as if it should have been muzzled.

'This is the number I was given,' Diamond said. There was nothing so helpful as a set of marked bell-pushes.

'You did bring the key?' Julie queried.

He produced it from his pocket and opened the front door. 'He lived upstairs, I gather.'

The house they had let themselves into smelt of cat and the probable offender bolted out of sight behind some rolls of lino at the far end of the hall. The stairs were bare and speckled with pink paint. But when they opened the door at the top, Towers' home turned out to be a barrack-room ready for inspection. A narrow passage carpeted in red had four doors leading off. The first, the bedroom, was in immaculate order, the clothes put away, the duvet squared at each corner. The furniture may have been cheap and functional, but everything was dusted.

121

'The sort of place that depresses me the minute I enter it,' grumbled Diamond. 'No photographs, no pictures on the wall. Where's the evidence of the man who lived here? It could be a bloody hotel.' He opened a wardrobe door and looked at the jackets hanging there and the shirts folded and stacked as if in a shop.

Julie said, 'Almost as if he knew he was about to die.'

'Not even a copy of yesterday's paper by the bed.'

'If he buys one, you can bet it was tidied away before he left the house,' said Julie.

'I get a sense of a stunted life when I see a place like this.'

'An organised life doesn't have to be stunted,' Julie commented. 'He put things away, that's all.'

'No use to us.'

They looked into the kitchen across the passage and still found nothing out of place. The contents of the fridge were meagre, but neatly positioned. There was a microwave oven and an electric hob, each spotless.

'Is this obsessive, would you say?' Diamond asked.

The living room was slightly more promising. It had one wall lined to the ceiling with white bookshelves, the books mostly without wrappers, though some had transparent covers and evidently came from libraries. There was a small televison set and an armchair facing it. A Victorian writing-desk interested Diamond. He opened the front and was gratified to find various things stacked in the pigeon-holes: a cheque book, some payslips, electricity invoices, an address book, a writing pad and envelopes and some second-class postage stamps.

'He liked his John Dickson Carr,' said Julie, standing in front of the books. 'He's got at least forty here. The other writer he collected has a similar name in a way – Carter Dickson. I wonder if there's a connection.'

'Does it matter?' said Diamond, leafing through the address book. It was full of blank pages. The man seemed to have no friends or family worth listing.

Julie removed a Carter Dickson from the shelf. '*The*

Reader is Warned. Good title.' She opened it. 'Written in 1939 – before the war. So were the Dickson Carrs, weren't they? When was *The Hollow Man* published?'

'Years ago. In the thirties.'

'Are these books valuable, do you think? Was he a collector?'

'What are you thinking – that some valuable first edition provided the motive? Hey, that's an idea.'

Julie picked a couple more books at random and opened them. 'One of these says "Withdrawn from stock. Warminster Public Library." The other was bought for 75p. I don't think a serious collector would give them shelf-room. He bought these to read.'

'At least we know something about the man,' said Diamond.

'I was right,' said Julie, having opened another book. 'Listen to this from the introduction. "Carr was so prolific that he kept a second publisher provided with a steady supply of crime novels under the pseudonym of Carter Dickson."'

Diamond's thoughts had moved on. 'It could be army training that makes a man so tidy. Or his schooling. Or prison. I wonder if he had any form. We'll run a check.'

'He wouldn't have been taken on as a night-watchman if he had a prison record.'

'He wouldn't tell them, would he?'

'Don't they make inquiries?'

'Yes, but it wasn't MI5 he was joining. He was only guarding office furniture.'

'Who did he work for?' Julie asked.

Diamond picked up the sheaf of payslips. 'Our old friends Impregnable.'

SIXTEEN

Left to finish her breakfast alone, Shirley-Ann took a slice from the toaster and covered it thickly in peanut butter – a secret indulgence. She didn't start work until ten and finished at four. Civilised hours in theory, but the conditions weren't always so comfortable as the hours, for she was employed handing leaflets to tourists in front of the Abbey. On a warm day in summer, it was pleasant enough. Part of the job was to reinforce the message in the leaflets by pointing out the benefits of a bus tour. She didn't mind talking to strangers. Most of them were easy to approach, regardless of whether they wanted the tour. But on wet days the work was cancelled – and that meant no pay, because she was on hourly rates. The most frustrating days were the indifferent, showery ones that are all too common in the English climate. She never knew when Mrs Battle, the supervisor, would materialise and tell her to go home. Soon it would be over for another season anyway. At the end of the month she would go back to stacking the shelves in Sainsbury's – if there were still vacancies.

Bert often told her that she ought to look for a full-time job. Her stock answer was that she was waiting for him to open the private health club he was forever promising to start in Bath. Then she would wear a white suit and be the receptionist. Bert really did have this dream of going into partnership with one of the top hotels and equipping it with the latest gym facilities, a swimming pool, steam rooms, saunas and sunbeds. The only problem was finance. Up to now, the bank hadn't been willing to float a loan.

This morning she left the flat slightly earlier than usual, and she was glad she did, because as she turned out of Russell Street a police car drove up. That they were coming to call on her was confirmed later, when she met Polly Wycherley. The astute Polly, who must have known where to find her, came up to her in the Abbey Churchyard and asked if she could take a few minutes off work. From the tense way Polly spoke, it was a request that couldn't be turned down. They cut through Church Street to the Bath Bun, the tea-shop in Lilliput Court, near Abbey Green.

The shop had a cosy, tucked-away feel, situated as it was in a sunken court off one of the less busy streets. Shirley-Ann often escaped there. The framed mirrors on the pink walls and the brown and fawn zigzag design on the carpet weren't to her taste, but not much natural light penetrated there, so something had to be done to brighten the interior.

No other customers were inside at this time, which meant that the corner table was available, the only one with padded chairs. On the wall to Shirley-Ann's left was a greenish print of the Rokeby Venus; the one showing the rear view of the naked goddess admiring herself in a mirror. Bert had once joked that they were the best buns in the shop. It wasn't the kind of humour likely to appeal to Polly. This morning her little mouth was pinched into something like a stitched wound.

'Have you heard about Sid?'

Shirley-Ann had not. She was deeply shocked when she was told. The news had been on local radio at eleven.

'It's worse,' said Polly. 'He was found on Milo's narrow-boat.'

'*Milo's?*'

'Last night, after our meeting.'

'Oh, no, Polly!'

'But Milo couldn't possibly have anything to do with

125

it,' Polly pointed out. 'He was at the police station telling them about the missing stamp.' She felt in her handbag for a tissue and blew her nose. Her hands were trembling.

'Sid murdered?' whispered Shirley-Ann. 'I can't take it in. He was such an . . . inoffensive bloke. Who would want to harm him?'

'I'm as puzzled as you are,' said Polly. 'And the police aren't giving anything away. Have you had them call on you?'

'No.' Shirley-Ann didn't like to say at this stage that she'd seen them stop outside her flat.

Polly said, 'They came to me soon after nine. They must have known, but they didn't let on. He was killed last night, you see. I thought it was just about the Penny Black, but obviously it wasn't.' Her face, usually pink, was blotchy this morning.

'You don't mind if I ask?' said Shirley-Ann. 'What did they want to know?'

'The police? Everything I could tell them about the meeting and the Bloodhounds. Even when I spoke of Sid they didn't give me a hint that he was dead.' Polly fumbled with a button of her coat. 'It was underhanded not to tell me. I said things I wouldn't have mentioned if I'd known he was dead, poor lamb.'

'What things?'

'Oh – that he's so quiet you forget he's there a lot of the time. And worse. I think I said he was dead wood. It makes me feel mean-minded.'

'I'm sure no one could accuse you of that,' Shirley-Ann tried to console her.

'Why me? Why didn't they go to someone else?'

'I suppose because you're the chair.' Shirley-Ann drew back and the conversation ceased while their order was taken. Once the girl had returned to the kitchen, she said, 'What was he doing on Milo's boat? Are they friends?'

Polly frowned slightly. 'Not so far as I know.'

'He must have had some reason for going there. How did he know which boat it is?'

'That's no mystery. We had our Christmas party on the boat. Sid was there. It's called the *Mrs Hudson*. I remember telling you.' Polly's pale eyes studied Shirley-Ann.

'So you did.' She held Polly's steady gaze.

Polly eventually said, 'Sid knew Milo wouldn't be aboard the boat. We all knew he was going directly to the police station and they were sure to keep him there for ages asking questions.'

Shirley-Ann asked, 'Do you think Sid was up to something?'

'It certainly looks like it, going out to the boatyard at that time of the evening. And the whole point is that he wasn't alone. The person who attacked him was aboard the boat as well.'

Shirley-Ann felt goose-pimples rising on her skin. 'The only people who knew Milo was going to the police were ourselves. That means one of the Bloodhounds must have murdered Sid.'

Polly folded her arms. Her lips twitched as if she couldn't bring herself to say any more.

SEVENTEEN

By midday the incident room for the narrowboat murder – as it was already known at Manvers Street – was receiving information faster than the two civilian computer operators could process it. Reports had been coming in since eleven from the detectives sent to interview members of the Bloodhounds; the Scenes of Crime team had sent in their preliminary findings; and a time had been fixed for the autopsy. 'Pity,' said Diamond when the message was handed to him. 'Any time but tomorrow morning would have been fine for me. I may not be able to attend. How would you like to stand in for me, Julie? One of us ought to be there.'

This may have sounded like a request, but it was an order, and Julie Hargreaves knew her boss's Byzantine reasoning well enough not to question it. The head of the murder squad didn't care to admit that he fainted at the sight of a dissecting knife, even though almost everyone guessed this was so. Over the years, he had resorted to all kinds of strategems to miss post-mortems.

Moving inexorably on, he asked her, 'Did you run that check on Sid Towers? Any previous?'

'A clean sheet, if that really is his name.'

'Pity. What was he doing in someone else's boat, then? What was he up to?'

Julie had no theory to offer. Instead, she said, 'I had a word with his employers. The big white chief at Impregnable says Sid was one of their most reliable men.'

'Night-watchman, wasn't he?'

'They don't call it that these days.'

He rolled his eyes upwards. 'Tell me then. What's the jargon? What should I have said? "Small hours surveillance specialist"?'

She laughed. 'Anyway, he was guarding office furniture.'

'And as we know, desperate men will stop at nothing to nick a filing cabinet.'

Julie went on staunchly supplying the facts. 'He's been with Impregnable for four years. He liked working alone, which suited them, because most security guards prefer to work in teams, particularly at night.'

'A loner.'

'Chronically so, according to the personnel director, only it didn't interfere with his work. He was conscientious, a good timekeeper, very observant.'

'We could have used him here.' He digested the information for a moment. 'Impregnable are a big organisation, aren't they? All kinds of security work. I've seen their vans around the city.'

'They do a certain amount with the banks and building societies,' said Julie. 'Sid had worked on the vans. They also install security systems.'

Seeing John Wigfull approaching, Diamond cut the conversation. 'Something new, John? Am I mistaken, or are the whiskers twitching?'

'I was thinking—' Wigfull began.

'Wish I had the time. What about?'

'That riddle. The second one. I believe I've worked out what part of it means.'

'Which part is that? Wait a minute, John.' He flapped his hand in the direction of some of his officers in noisy conversation. 'Zip it up for a mo, will you? Chief Inspector Wigfull is trying to make himself heard.'

'Well, it's the last two lines,' said Wigfull. '*Look for the lady in the locked room, At seventeen.*'

'Yes?'

'It struck me that seventeen must refer to the chapter

in the book, the John Dickson Carr book that Motion was about to read from. Chapter Seventeen. The Locked-Room Lecture. If the lady is Queen Victoria, then the riddle tells us to look for her in the locked room at seventeen, and that's precisely where the Penny Black cover was found.'

'You think so?' Diamond didn't sound bowled over by the deduction.

'It makes sense,' Wigfull insisted.

'Perfect sense,' Diamond said. 'But it's too late, isn't it? Too late for us to do anything about it. This clever dick who pinched the stamp wasn't really giving anything away in advance. How could we have known that the stamp was going to turn up in Chapter Seventeen of some obscure book written sixty years ago? We didn't stand a snowball's chance. Like the first rhyme we were given, it's easy enough to work out after the event. Did you get the first two lines? How did they go, exactly?'

Julie remembered them. '*Whither Victoria and with whom – The Grand Old Queen?*'

Wigfull said with understandable pique, 'It's obvious, isn't it? The last two lines were the puzzle.'

'So you worked out who the Grand Old Queen is?' said Diamond.

'Victoria, obviously.'

'Can't say I'm with you there, old boy,' said Diamond. 'For my money, it was a reference to Mr Milo Motion.'

Wigfull blinked and said, 'The man's gay! You could be right.'

'You have to be an insensitive brute like me to get the point,' said Diamond.

Wigfull said, 'You are right.'

'But where does it get us?' Diamond developed his theme. 'All we can say is that the stamp theft was done according to plan. The way your Penny Black turned up last night was no mistake. It happened exactly as predicted. Milo Motion was earmarked as the fall guy.'

Julie said, 'But it does tell us that the thief knew Milo

would take the book to the Bloodhounds meeting and open it at Chapter Seventeen.'

'Right!' said Wigfull. 'We can count the suspects on one hand.'

'Two,' said Diamond. 'And you may need your feet as well.'

'I'm speaking of the Bloodhounds.'

'There are six of them.'

'Ah, but we can eliminate Motion,' Wigfull pointed out. 'That leaves five: Mrs Wycherley, Miss Chilmark, Mrs Shaw, Miss Miller and the man, Rupert Darby.'

'What about Sid Towers?'

'He's dead.'

'He wasn't dead when the stamp was stolen,' Diamond reminded him. 'If it were me investigating the stamp theft, I'd keep Sid Towers in the frame, dead or not.'

'Was the man capable of such a theft?'

'Certainly. He was easily overlooked, but not dim. He knew all about security. He'd have known how to suss out a building for a break-in.'

'I can see that. But he doesn't strike me as the sort to compose riddles drawing attention to the crime.'

'Why not? He was a reader of whodunits. Plenty of time to himself to think it through. Setting a puzzle for the police might have appealed to him.'

Wigfull weighed the suggestion. 'I suppose it's possible. But why was he killed?' He raised a finger like an umpire as he answered his own question. 'Maybe the killer took offence at the way he chose to return the stamp. The obvious suspect would be Motion, but he's the one with the alibi.'

'Now, John,' Diamond said sharply. 'The murder is my business. I don't want interference.'

'You offered *me* some advice.'

'Here's some more, then. You said you could count the suspects on one hand. You've just added Towers. You must also add anyone Motion spoke to – anyone

131

who learned that he was taking the Dickson Carr book to that meeting.'

'That's scraping the barrel, isn't it? From all I hear, he's another loner.'

Diamond gave a shrug.

Wigfull was forced to concede. 'Technically, I suppose you're right. Has anything helpful come up in the interviews?'

'Nothing startling. They're still being fed into the system, but I've heard from all the officers who carried them out. We caught up with everyone in the end, all the Bloodhounds, anyway. A couple of them weren't at home and we nobbled them later.'

'My number one suspect is the man.'

'Why do you say that?'

A rare smile lit Wigfull's face. 'I'm speaking of *my* case, the theft of the stamp. I can't see any of those women walking through the streets of Bath with a window cleaner's ladder and bucket.'

'Sexist.'

'Two of them are middle-aged.'

'What matters to me is whether they could murder a man,' said Diamond, 'and a woman can crack a bloke over the head with a blunt instrument whether she's middle-aged or twenty. We had a case in Twerton before you joined the squad. Two old people, well over seventy, married fifty years, regularly coming to blows and ending up in casualty. In the end she clobbered him with a hammer because he threw away the *TV Times*. Killed him. I often think of that when I'm putting the papers in the bin.'

After a sandwich lunch, Diamond interviewed Milo Motion for the third time.

'Caught up on your sleep yet?'

Milo was temporarily installed in a bed and breakfast house opposite the police station in Manvers Street. He had come in to ask when he could expect to return to his floating home. The black beard accentuated the challenging tilt of his chin. Bushy was the word for it, Diamond decided. A family of small mammals could have found a habitat in that abundant growth.

'You can go back before the afternoon is out, I give you my word,' Diamond promised. 'It may not be restored to its former glory yet, because they took the carpet and one or two other items for forensic tests.'

'I simply want a change of clothes,' said Milo. 'I'm not proposing to sleep there after what happened.'

'Are you comfortable in the B and B?'

'Tolerably.'

'You don't have a friend who would put you up?'

He gave a prim click of the tongue. 'No.'

'Why don't you sit down?'

'Is it going to take as long as that?'

'A few things need clearing up,' said Diamond equably.

'If it's about the bloody padlock again . . .' Milo started to say.

'No, it's the Bloodhounds, sir. You were one of the founders, you told me. You should know everyone quite well.'

Guardedly, came the answer: 'That doesn't necessarily follow. I see most of them once a week, on Mondays. That hardly entitles me to speak of them with any authority.'

'But you've known Mrs Wycherley since the beginning.'

'True.'

'And the other lady, Miss, em . . .'

'Chilmark?'

'Miss Chilmark. You've known her almost as long. You told us last night that there was some sort of incident involving Miss Chilmark. Something about a dog.'

Milo sighed. 'It seems a century ago. The dog belongs to Rupert Darby. He's bloody inconsiderate, is Rupert. Miss Chilmark doesn't care for the dog at all, and of course it always makes a beeline for her. If he left it at home, or kept it on the leash, we wouldn't have any trouble. Last

133

night at the meeting Rupert came in late as usual and Marlowe – that's the dog—'

'Did you say Marlowe?'

'Marlowe, yes. That's its name.'

'Funny name for a dog.'

'It's the name of Raymond Chandler's private eye. You remember *The Big Sleep*?'

'It's still a funny name for a dog.'

'Rupert told us why. You must have heard that Chandler quote: ". . . down these mean streets a man must go who is not himself mean . . ." Well, that dog adores a mean street.'

Diamond nodded. 'Go on. Tell us what this dog did that was so obnoxious.'

'It jumped up beside Miss Chilmark and threw her into a panic. She had some sort of attack of breathlessness that was only brought under control thanks to swift action by Jessica – Mrs Shaw.'

'What kind of action?'

'She called for a paper bag. Sid produced one. His book was wrapped in it. Jessica held it against Miss Chilmark's face and the attack subsided. That's all it was.'

'Sid had a book with him?'

'I just said so.'

'Why would he have a book with him? He didn't read things out, did he?'

'No, he was far too shy. I imagine it was for private reading.'

'Did you happen to notice the title?'

'Of course. I'm not uninterested in books myself. It was *The Three Coffins*, by John Dickson Carr. Sid was an admirer of Dickson Carr's work.'

'Are you familiar with this book?'

'Extremely familiar, yes, but under the English title.'

'Isn't *The Three Coffins* English?'

'I should have said British. *The Three Coffins* was the title the book was known by in America. Publishers sometimes decide in their wisdom that a book will sell better over there with a different title. It's a blasted nuisance to collectors.'

'So what was the British title?'

'*The Hollow Man.*'

'Really? But that was the book you took to the meeting.'

'Yes, indeed. The first English edition, published by Hamish Hamilton in 1935. Unfortunately, my copy is without a wrapper, or it might be worth a few pounds.'

'Let's get this clear,' said Diamond. 'You and Sid Towers each took a copy of the same book to the meeting on Monday?'

'You make it sound suspicious,' said Milo, 'but it isn't at all. Far more suspicious things happened than that. The explanation is simple. At the previous meeting I announced to everyone that the next time we met, I would read the locked room chapter from *The Hollow Man.*'

Diamond mentally ticked one of the points he had wanted to check. Wigfull would be cockahoop. All the Bloodhounds who were present the previous week knew that Milo would bring his book to the meeting and open it at Chapter Seventeen. Any of them could have placed the stamp between the pages – any clever enough to find a way of doing it.

Milo was saying, 'I presume Sid brought along his copy to follow the text. In his quiet way he was quite an authority on Dickson Carr.'

'And so are you, apparently.'

Milo preened the beard, pleased by the compliment. 'I prefer to be thought of as a Sherlockian, but, yes, I have a sneaking admiration for much of Carr's work. He made the impossible crime his own speciality. Wrote seventy crime novels, which isn't at all bad considering he was notoriously fond of the bottle and also led a complicated love life. And of course he found time to write a fine biography of Conan Doyle. He was quite an Anglophile until the Labour Government was elected after the war. He couldn't abide socialism, so he went back to the States and only returned after Churchill was returned to power.'

'How does politics come into crime writing?'

'My dear superintendent, it's all about conservatism and affirming the social order, or was for almost a century.'

'The class system.'

Milo gave Diamond a sharp glance. 'However vile the crime, the reader can rest assured that order is restored by the end. Only in comparatively recent times have left-wing crime writers discovered ways of subverting the status quo. You're not a socialist, are you?'

'I'm a policeman,' said Diamond. 'We're neutral.'

Milo gave a hollow laugh. He was becoming confident.

Diamond said, 'Getting back to the incident with the dog—'

'You're going to ask me once again if I let go of the book in all the confusion. The answer is the same. I had it on my knees or in my hand throughout. No one could have tampered with it. No one.' Milo shook his head. 'Nothing like this has happened to me in years. Once in my youth I met a close-up magician and he did remarkable things that I still can't explain, like removing my watch without my being aware of it and having it turn up inside a box of chocolates. This business with the stamp is just as miraculous. I can only account for it as a brilliant conjuring trick. I can't guess the solution.'

'And the murder of Sid Towers – is that magic?'

'The circumstances are.'

'Trickery.'

'Magic or trickery, it's beyond my understanding.'

'That's a conclusion I'm not permitted to make,' said Diamond. 'I've got to catch the conjurer. Do you have any suspicions?'

'Of whom?'

'The other Bloodhounds.'

'How can I?' said Milo. 'They're charming people, all of them. Oh, Miss Chilmark has the reputation of being a sourpuss, but she's all right when you take a little trouble with her, butter her up, you know. And Jessica Shaw went out of her way to help poor old Sid fit in. She took him for a drink on more than one occasion. No, I'm afraid if you're looking for suspects, they're a very unlikely bunch. Not like a detective story at all. In this case, I can't think of anyone with a grudge against poor old Sid.'

EIGHTEEN

Later the same afternoon, Diamond drove Milo Motion to the Dundas boatyard to collect his change of clothes from the *Mrs Hudson*. A thick-knit sweater was likely to be among them, because now that the sun was disappearing behind the willows on the far bank, there was an unmistakable threat of frost in that cloudless sky. The Scenes of Crime team had finished work and left. The only police activity – apart from one luckless constable rubbing his hands to keep his circulation going – was a pair of divers searching the canal bottom for the murder weapon, and they didn't seem too happy either. What they were doing in the shallow water couldn't be described as diving; more a matter of wading about and bending double. On a blue tarpaulin on the towpath they had assembled their finds – a horseshoe, two plastic milk crates, a bicycle pump, a birdcage, about twenty beer-cans and several pieces of stone – the result of three hours' scavenging for fifty yards either side of the narrowboat. Diamond told them to give up for the day. The chance was slim that a killer so artful as this would have disposed of the weapon in so obvious a place, but procedure had required the search to be made. He asked Milo to check for any object missing from the boat that might have been used to crack Sid Towers over the head.

Milo said he was unable to think of anything, but he would certainly look.

The constable had to open up for them because the door at the stern had been fitted with a fresh lock.

Milo's German-made padlock had been stripped down and examined at the forensic lab. Pressed by Diamond for their findings, the scientists had reported no flaw in the mechanism. No sign, even, of tampering. It was described as a high-security close-shackle padlock. The locking mechanism provided over six million key variations, bearing out the manufacturers' claim that each padlock they sold in Britain had a unique key-pattern.

Diamond had been over the narrowboat and its security arrangements many times in his mind without deducing how the body had been placed there, so this extra inspection wasn't embarked upon with much confidence. The murder of Sid Towers was becoming his own locked room mystery, his Gordian Knot. If Milo Motion had spoken the truth, the facts were indisputable:

1. Milo locked the boat when he left it.

2. The key never left his person.

3. The key fitted that padlock and no other. There was no second key.

4. The only other point of entry to the cabin was the door at the fore end and this was bolted from the inside.

5. The padlock was still in position when Milo returned to the boat with Wigfull. He had opened it with the key and discovered the corpse of Sid Towers in the cabin.

Each time he looked for a flaw in the logic, Diamond was forced back to that qualifier: *if Motion had spoken the truth.* The hardware, surely, was foolproof; the human assurances had to be tested further.

The two men dipped their heads to enter the cabin, now stripped of its carpet.

'I want you to think hard and long,' Diamond told Milo. 'Do you keep anything in here that might have been used as a weapon? Some ornament, perhaps, like a heavy beer-mug or a paperweight?'

Milo thought for a moment and shook his head. 'Books are about the heaviest things in here. You couldn't kill someone with a book, could you?'

'It would take something heavier than those,' Diamond admitted, eyeing the shelves of detective stories. 'A really big dictionary might do the job.'

'Can't help. I manage without one.'

'Lucky for you. Good speller, are you?' he asked companionably. Putting the man at his ease might encourage him to talk more freely about the evening of the murder.

'Correct spelling was part of the education when I grew up.'

'Mine, too.' Diamond switched to a confiding mode. 'I was at grammar school, but I never fully mastered the spelling. Bit of a handicap, because they deducted marks in every subject and it all went on a weekly report card. There was a ritual on Saturday mornings called "slackers' parade" – a painful encounter with the deputy head – and I was a regular on it. Then one of the English masters taught me the trick of avoiding words like "necessary". You can always write "needful" instead. Good advice. So the next time, that's what I did – and still finished up on the slackers' parade. Pity he didn't warn me "needful" has only one "l" at the end. Tell me, what's the attraction of detective stories?'

Milo blinked and frowned, derailed by the unexpected admission of frailty by the man he'd come to regard as the embodiment of authority.

'I've never understood what people see in them,' Diamond went on. 'True crime, yes, I can read with pleasure. Fiction I can't.'

'I suppose it's the not knowing.'

'The what?'

'The not knowing . . . until the end,' Milo explained.

'Not knowing who did it?'

Milo relaxed slightly. 'That's true of some books, certainly, but not all. There are other things the reader is keen to discover these days. I mean, some books tell you right off who the villain is. There's the fascination of not knowing whether he gets away with the crime,

140

or whether the good chap survives. There's much more emphasis on character these days, but there's always an element of surprise in the best mysteries. You should attend one of our Bloodhound meetings.'

'I may end up doing that. Would you mind stepping into the kitchen, or the galley, or whatever you call it?'

'You'd like a coffee?' said Milo.

'No, Mr Motion.' Abruptly he was the investigator again. 'We're checking for a possible murder weapon. Remember?'

'Ah.'

Nothing was missing from the galley that Milo could recall.

'You appreciate the importance,' Diamond said to take the edge off his sharp remark. 'The choice of weapon can tell us if the murder was planned or was just a response to something unexpected. Did the killer bring a weapon here with murder in mind, or was it just a matter of snatching up the first thing that came to hand?'

'I follow you,' said Milo.

'But you can't help me?'

'On this matter, no.'

'While we're here, let's go over the business of the pad-lock,' Diamond continued. 'I know you've been through it so many times you could say it in your sleep, but something else needs to be explained, doesn't it? The boat was totally secure according to you and yet a murder took place in here.'

'Don't you think I'd have told you by now if I knew the answer?' Milo said with injured virtue. 'It's utterly beyond my understanding. What is more, they got in twice. Someone must have broken in earlier to put the stamp inside my copy of John Dickson Carr.'

'There's no evidence that anyone broke in,' Diamond was swift to correct him. 'If they had, we might have an explanation. Not one of the doors or windows was interfered with. Nothing was broken.'

'What happened then? They couldn't have had a key. Mine is the only one in existence.'

'That isn't true, is it? There's the spare one you dropped in the canal.'

'If you want to nit-pick to that degree, yes.'

'How long ago did you lose it?'

'Last year. I told you.'

'Exactly when, Mr Motion?'

Milo sighed. 'Towards the end of the summer. It must have been September.'

'Can you recall the circumstances? I dare say it caused you some annoyance.'

'Well, it did. I lost my car keys at the same time.'

'So we're talking about a bunch – on a ring?'

'Yes.'

'Did you try to recover them?'

'It happened after dark,' Milo explained, tugging at his beard as if the whole episode was painful to recall. 'If you must know, I was the worse for drink. Pretty unusual for me. A night out at the Cross Guns.'

'The pub at Avoncliff?'

'Yes. Do you know it? Gorgeous on a summer evening. I had the boat tied up at one of the moorings just above the pub, that stretch of the canal before the aqueduct. Treated myself to a meal and a few beers and when I got back—'

'Alone?'

'Yes. I opened up and stumbled a bit pulling open the door. The damned keys slipped out of my hand and over the side. Bloody annoying, but I knew I had spares for all of them, so it could have been worse.'

'Next morning, did you try and get them out?'

He shook his head. 'Hopeless. They would have sunk into the mud.'

'Did you mention this to anyone else?'

'I may have done to the people in the next boat. Can't remember, frankly.'

'What about the Bloodhounds? Would you have mentioned it to them?'

'Certainly not. Why should I? It wasn't an incident I'm proud of.'

'We've got to think of all the angles.'

'All I can say is what I know to be the truth,' Milo stressed in a more defensive tone. 'You can see for yourself that when I'm aboard the boat, it's just about impossible for anyone else to come in here without my knowing. You can hear every step and there's nowhere to hide. It's all open-plan. Anyway, the cupboards are far too small to hide anyone.'

'What exactly are you driving at?'

'If the murderer found some way of stowing away while I was still here, and remained hidden when I locked up, it would be possible to unbolt the door at the far end – unbolt it from the inside – and admit the victim.'

Diamond almost snapped his fingers in triumph. Then, as the flaw in the revelation occurred to him, he converted the gesture into scratching his right ear-lobe. 'But when you and Wigfull entered the boat, it was bolted from the inside at that end and padlocked outside at the other. Unless the killer was still aboard, it couldn't have happened.'

'There you go,' said Milo with an air of resignation. 'I can assure you, there wasn't anyone here except poor old Sid. I'm as confused as anyone by all this.'

'And as you remarked just now, there's nowhere to hide. Everything folds against the walls. The only lockers are outside the cabin, back at the stern end.' Diamond paused, watching Milo. 'The crucial question is whether your memory is reliable when you say you locked the boat.'

'Of course it is!' Milo said petulantly. 'I remember rattling the damned padlock, testing it with my hand to be sure it was secure. And it was. Later, when I returned with your colleague, Mr Wigfull, I unlocked with my own key and had the shock of my life when I saw what was inside. It's impossible, but it happened. I am at a total loss to account for it. You need Dr Fell for this.'

'Who's he?'

'Dickson Carr's detective.'

'A detective in a book? Great.'

'Someone of his calibre, at any rate.'

'Thanks for the vote of confidence,' said Diamond. 'Well, I think we need someone smarter than Dr Fell. I've been through that chapter on the locked room lecture and it's no help. I ask you. You've studied it yourself. This is a puzzle that defies all Dr Fell's explanations.'

Milo nodded. 'I have to agree with you.'

'And the locked room is only part of the mystery. What was Sid's reason for coming here?'

'I haven't the foggiest,' Milo answered with a shrug. 'He wasn't in the habit of visiting me. Besides, he knew I wouldn't be here. I told everyone I was going straight to the police station to hand in the Penny Black. Do you think the murderer lured him to his death?'

Diamond didn't want to trade theories any longer. 'Look, why don't you pick out the clothes you need? I'll take a stroll along the towpath and see you in ten minutes.'

He needed more time for reflection. Milo, surely, was a reliable witness. This, after all, was the one member of the Bloodhounds who couldn't have murdered Towers. Yet there was still a doubt. Any lawyer will tell you that witnesses tend to present themselves and their actions in the most favourable light, sometimes obscuring serious flaws in their evidence. Suppose Milo hadn't after all locked the narrowboat before leaving for the meeting. Suppose through carelessness or overconfidence he had left the padlock hanging from the staple still unfastened. At first he may have decided not to mention it; no one wants to admit to negligence, particularly to the police. Later, as the investigation proceeded, he would find it increasingly embarrassing. An act of carelessness would grow into a deception. He might even have lied to cover it up.

Human frailty seemed a stronger bet than mechanical wizardry. Ingenious locked room puzzles were the province of detective story writers.

He went across to the divers. They had unpeeled their wetsuits and were stacking their van. He had another job for them tomorrow, he told them, further along, by the Avoncliff Aqueduct. A bunch of keys. They didn't sound overjoyed. With a wink at the constable on duty he stepped briskly along the towpath. This stretch of waterway now used for mooring was historically the route taken by the barges transporting coal from the Somerset mines. Much more narrow than the main canal, almost two centuries old and edged with ancient flagstones, it had its own character, though the aluminium lift-bridge where it joined the Kennet and Avon was clearly a modern replacement. He stood for a moment staring at this bridge, deciding how the lifting mechanism worked. Clearly it had to be raised for anything the size of a narrowboat to pass under. There were counterweights projecting from the fulcrum, but the walkway was bolted down on the opposite side. He hauled on it to make sure. At this late hour nothing was about to pass into the boatyard, so his curiosity had to be set aside. He turned and started back towards the solitary policeman.

The question of most interest to him now was the one Milo had raised only a few minutes ago. What could have induced Sid Towers to visit the *Mrs Hudson*? It was strange behaviour considering that Milo himself was not going to be present. Why visit a locked boat after dark? One possible explanation was that the murderer had suggested meeting him there. If it was a trap, what was the bait? Or was it a threat? Maybe Sid had been under some pressure to obey the summons.

Blackmail?

He stepped aboard the narrowboat and found Milo in the cabin filling carrier bags with clothes. 'I'm about ready.'

'Good. It's cold in here. I don't know how you put up with it.'

'Well, I've got no heating on. Normally it can be really snug.'

'I walked to the end of the canal,' said Diamond. 'As far as that lift-bridge. It *is* a lift-bridge?'

'Oh, yes. It has to be raised each time a boat goes out.'

'How do you lift it, then? So far as I can tell, the thing is bolted down.'

'It is. We unfasten it with a windlass. Everyone using the moorings has one. You get one from the office.'

'Like a spanner, you mean?'

'Yes.'

'That explains it, then. Let me help you with those.' He picked up one of the bags. 'Ready to leave?'

'Will the constable lock up?'

'We'll do it.'

They emerged from the cabin. Diamond pressed the strap over the staple and closed the padlock over it. 'Where do you keep the windlass? I wouldn't mind seeing what it looks like.'

'It's in the locker on the right. I keep the tiller in there with it.'

Diamond pulled up the lid of the locker and peered at the collection of tools. 'I can see the tiller. Can't see anything like a windlass.'

Milo bent over and shifted the contents about. 'Well, that's a damned liberty. It's gone. Someone must have pinched it.'

'Are you sure?'

'It's always here.'

'What size and weight is this windlass?' Diamond asked.

Milo extended his hands about eight inches. 'It's iron. Not a thing you'd put in your pocket and forget about.'

'Heavy enough to crack a man over the head and kill him?'

'Good Lord. Is that possible?'

'Problems?' said Julie, seated at a desk near the door.

Diamond made a sound deep in his throat like a growl, pushed a computer keyboard aside and perched his rear on one of the desks in the incident room. The civilian staff had finished work for the day.

He sighed. 'No worse than yesterday. I'm boxed in, Julie. I don't care for it.'

'Because of the way the body was found?'

'The whole shooting match. The bloody riddles. The missing Penny Black. This ridiculous Bloodhounds club. It's straight out of a whodunit. I'm a career detective, not a poncy Frenchman with spats and a walking stick.'

'Belgian.'

'What?'

'Hercule Poirot is a Belgian.'

'I don't care if he's from Outer Mongolia. He's a figment of some writer's imagination – that's the point. Everything up to now is detective story stuff from sixty years ago. It shouldn't be happening in the real world. I'm being asked to deal with a locked room murder, for Christ's sake. If I crack it – I mean *when* I crack it – what am I going to be faced with next? Invisible ink?'

Julie allowed a suitable pause. She'd worked with Diamond long enough to know that these occasional outpourings weren't entirely negative in effect. Then she remarked, 'Do you really need to crack the locked room mystery?'

He folded his arms. 'You'd better explain yourself.'

'Well, the great temptation is to go at this head on, as they did in those detective stories, puzzling over the locked room until we hit on the solution. That's what we're meant to do. Why don't we approach it another way?'

'Tell me how.'

'There's only a handful of people who could have committed the stamp theft. Agreed?'

'Certainly – but that's for John Wigfull to unravel.'

Julie refused to be deflected. 'I mean the Bloodhounds. They knew from the previous meeting that Milo would be bringing in his copy of *The Hollow Man* – an opportunity that the thief found irresistible. If Milo himself is not the thief, then it has to be the person who planted the stamp in his book.'

Diamond nodded. This was pretty obvious stuff.

She continued, 'Someone who must have been at the meeting the previous week when Milo promised to read from the chapter on locked room mysteries.'

'Or who was tipped off about what was said.'

'All right,' Julie conceded. 'But it's still a small group, right?'

'Right.'

'And so is the list of murder suspects.'

Diamond held up a finger. 'Careful, now.'

Julie got up and crossed the room to argue her case. 'Because the killer got inside the *Mrs Hudson*, just as the stamp thief did. Be fair, Mr Diamond. It's got to be the same person. I refuse to believe that two people independently worked out a way of getting inside that cabin without disturbing the lock. Two different people, each smarter than you? No way.'

'So?'

'So instead of all this brain-fag over the locked room, I suggest we get talking to the suspects. You and I, I mean. I know we have a batch of statements, but there's no substitute for getting face to face with people.'

'Doorstepping.' He smiled.

'No, I don't mean house-to-house enquiries. I'm talking about the suspects, and there aren't many of them.'

'That's your advice?'

She hesitated, detecting the note of irony. 'I'm trying to be helpful.'

'And you are.' This was sincerely meant. Listening to Julie had helped him take hold of a doubt that had been hovering just out of reach for some time. 'Only I'm not yet convinced that you're right about the thief and the killer being one and the same. Think for a moment about Sid Towers. What if he were the man who stole the stamp?'

'Sid?'

He gave a nod.

'The murder victim?'

Diamond gave his snap assessment of Towers. 'Unassuming, easily disregarded, yet not unintelligent. A reader of John Dickson Carr. Imagine the quiet satisfaction Sid would have derived from surprising the rest of the Bloodhounds – that opinionated lot who thought they knew all there is to know about detective stories. This is pure hypothesis, but let's suppose he stole the Penny Black simply to make a point, not with his power of speech which was so underdeveloped, but through the written word, with riddles and rhymes. "I'm smarter than all of you put together," he was saying in effect, "whatever you think of me." And what a marvellous notion to have the stamp turn up between the pages of Milo's book – thus demonstrating a locked room mystery unknown to Dr Fell or anyone else. Do you see what I'm getting at, Julie?'

'Sid was the thief? But Sid was murdered.'

Diamond sketched the scenario as he spoke, and it made a lot of sense, even to himself. 'Murdered aboard the narrowboat. Sid went back there, knowing Milo would be occupied at the nick for some time to come. Maybe he intended to leave a note, another riddle, even. He let himself in by the same brilliant method he used on the previous occasion – whatever that may be – only this time he was followed in by someone else, who picked up a windlass and cracked him over the head.'

'Who?'

'That's the question. Could be one of the Bloodhounds who followed him there. Could be someone else with a grudge against Sid. Could simply be some evil person who was on the towpath last night and decided to mug the occupant. In other words, anyone from your half-dozen suspects to the entire population of Avon and Somerset, plus any visitors passing through. That's why I'm cautious, Julie. But it's only a hypothesis. I may be totally mistaken.'

NINETEEN

Open-top tour buses are a feature of Bath that most residents accept with good grace in a city that welcomes tourists. The two companies in competition are distinguished by their colours: Ryan's Citytour in red and white and Badgerline's Bath Tour in green and cream. Citytours operate from Terrace Walk, near the Abbey. The Badgerline tours leave every thirty minutes from the bus station and are named after city worthies like Prince Bladud, King Edgar, Ralph Allen, John Wood and Dr William Oliver. All the buses stop at convenient points to allow ticket holders to get off and explore, continuing the tour on another bus if desired.

Miss Chilmark was one of the minority who disapproved of the open-tops of whatever colour. For one thing she had a house on the route and was convinced that people on the upper deck looked into bedrooms. And for another, as a person of refined literary taste, she found it deplorable that Jane Austen's name was on the back of a bus. You may imagine the shock she received when crossing Pierrepont Street at ten-thirty in the morning to hear her own name spoken, amplified, from one of these despised vehicles.

'Miss Chilmark!'

It must have been audible right across Parade Gardens.

She froze and tried to take an interest in a shop window, telling herself she couldn't have heard correctly.

'Miss Chilmark!' Louder still and unmistakable, like a summons to the Last Judgement.

Deeply alarmed, she turned her head enough to see a female figure speaking into a microphone on the upper deck of a Badgerline called Beau Nash. Twenty or more interested faces were staring down.

'Miss Chilmark, this is Shirley-Ann Miller, from the Bloodhounds. Could I talk to you?'

Miss Chilmark was in no position to stop her from talking, but she had enough spirit to answer, 'What gives you the right . . . ?'

She wasn't heard. Shirley-Ann's amplified voice drowned hers. 'Shall we say eleven, by the Abbey Door? Please be there if you possibly can.'

The bus started to move off. The commentary continued, 'Sorry about that, ladies and gentlemen. Personal. I happened to spot someone I know and it is rather an emergency. If you look to your left now you will see the archway leading to Pierrepont Place. At Number One from 1764 to 1771 lived the Linley family, and Mrs Linley once had a maidservant called Emma Lyon, later to become famous as Emma Hamilton. To your right across the street at Number Two is the house occupied for many years as a winter home by the Nelson family – yes, *that* Nelson. Unfortunately for romantics like me, the dates are wrong. It is most unlikely that Emma and Horatio met in Bath, but there is a romantic story about the dazzlingly lovely daughter of the Linleys, Elizabeth, who eloped . . .'

Miss Chilmark, her mind closed to the commentary, turned unsteadily along North Parade Passage, pink with the indignity. Not once in her life had she been hailed from the top of a bus. Generations of Chilmarks had lived with dignity and decorum in this city. She was mortified to have been singled out for such public humiliation. She needed a strong coffee and a Sally Lunn to take away the shock.

'Yes, I'm awfully sorry about that,' Shirley-Ann told her when they met. 'I didn't mean to alarm you. I'm not

151

very used to the public address system. Usually my job is handing out the leaflets, but today they were short-staffed, so I stood in for someone. It's a chance you don't turn down. A marvellous opportunity for me and only the second time I've done it. When I spotted you, I forgot I was holding the mike and it was live. And I desperately wanted to speak to you. Look, shall we sit down? You look dreadfully pale.' She was wondering what to do if Miss Chilmark had another attack of hyperventilation. She didn't have a paper bag with her.

They went over to sit on one of the benches in the Abbey Churchyard. A busker facing them was playing the recorder to an orchestral backing from a portable cassette-player, but it wasn't any bar to conversation. 'I like giving the commentary and I think I'm rather good at it,' Shirley-Ann said, giving a commentary to Miss Chilmark. 'I get a real buzz when I'm up there with the mike switched on and all those faces turned my way. They hear more from me than any other guide gives them. I must admit I depart from the script a bit. And today I was fairly bombarding them with information, more than I intended to say. I'm in a bit of a state myself, to be honest. We're all in a state and no wonder.'

'What do you want?' Miss Chilmark asked.

'Just a few words.'

'A few!'

What Shirley-Ann wanted was the chance to talk over the developments since Monday evening. It was right against her nature to suffer in silence. She had a chronic need to share her anxieties with some other woman. She couldn't trouble Polly again so soon after meeting her in the Bath Bun and she didn't like to call at Jessica's art gallery in case the man A.J. was there. Miss Chilmark wasn't an obvious choice for a tête-à-tête, but she was the only choice left. Spotting her from the bus had seemed like destiny intervening.

'You must have heard about poor Sid?'

Miss Chilmark gave a nod. She was wearing a small

version of Robin Hood's hat with a feather, and the feather was vibrating, whether with rage or the breeze it was impossible to judge.

Shirley-Ann did what she could to make this seem like a shared concern. 'I heard the news from Polly. She had the police round yesterday morning. Well, so did I later. I dare say you did. But Polly is terribly upset. She cares so much about the Bloodhounds. We're like her own family to her.'

Miss Chilmark said acidly, 'If that's her idea of a family, she must have had a deprived upbringing.'

'Well, you must know what I'm trying to say. The police are bound to think of us as suspects. This was a locked room murder – the very topic we were about to discuss on Monday evening.'

'Not at my suggestion,' Miss Chilmark was quick to point out.

Shirley-Ann sighed. 'It doesn't really matter who suggested it. We all knew that Milo was going to read from the book and we're all under suspicion. Did the police visit you?'

Grudgingly, Miss Chilmark said, 'They did call briefly.'

'You drive, don't you?'

'I beg your pardon.'

'You have a car of your own?'

'I do.'

'Then it's perfectly possible for you to have driven to the boatyard after the meeting finished. You're a suspect.' Shirley-Ann added with more tact, 'We all have cars, so far as I know.'

Outrage had spread ominously across the suspect Miss Chilmark's features and the feather was positively flapping.

Shirley-Ann said, 'The detective who came to interview me made the point that it was the crime of someone of high intelligence.'

Miss Chilmark looked a mite less outraged. 'Low cunning, more like. I know whom I suspect.'

'Rupert?'

'Who else?'

'But why? Why would he want to kill Sid? They weren't enemies.'

'How can you tell?' said Miss Chilmark, her eyes on the Abbey front. 'Sid – Mr Towers as I prefer to think of him – was a quiet man. Who can say what his private opinions were? He wasn't the sort to articulate them at one of our meetings.'

'But Rupert isn't a man to bottle up his feelings – and I can't recall him saying an unkind word about Sid, ever.'

'He's a degenerate.'

'Rupert?'

'You only have to look at him. That face.'

'Now that really is unfair.'

'Evil.'

'I don't think of him as evil. Rather hollow-cheeked, I grant you, and he could do with some more teeth. He's no oil painting, but I find it a very watchable face. Anyway, it would be terrible if people were judged on their looks.'

'His are clearly the result of many years of bad living.'

And yours, Shirley-Ann thought, of mean-mindedness. 'Or neglect.'

'Depravity. He's constantly in public houses, so far as I can make out. His choice of reading is indicative – all that violence he wallows in.'

'Really, Miss Chilmark, I've read a lot of those books myself and I'm not depraved, I hope. Millions of people read them. You admire *The Name of the Rose*, but it doesn't mean you want to go into a monastery, I mean a nunnery – oh, I don't know what I do mean, except that the books people read are no guide to their behaviour.'

Miss Chilmark turned to Shirley-Ann, her broad face pitted with disfavour. 'Let me remind you that Mr Towers worked for a security firm. They're ex-policemen, a lot of them. They know the ne'er-do-wells in this city. If something came to his notice in the course of his duties, something particularly unpleasant regarding one

154

of the Bloodhounds, and that person felt at risk of being exposed, you wouldn't have to look hard for a motive for murder.'

Shirley-Ann had forgotten that Sid was a security guard. It was the first reasonable comment Miss Chilmark had made. 'But that could apply to any of us. Any of us could have a skeleton in the cupboard.'

'Speak for yourself,' said Miss Chilmark.

'Even if I had, I wouldn't see murder as the solution,' Shirley-Ann said thoughtfully. Mentally she was reviewing the other Bloodhounds, wondering what skeletons they might prefer to keep hidden. Jessica? Polly? She had been going to suggest a meeting, if only to compare notes on what the police had said. Now, she was less enthusiastic.

'Poor Mr Towers didn't batter himself to death,' said Miss Chilmark. 'Someone wanted him dead.'

'At the meeting last night,' said Shirley-Ann, 'do you remember anything that Sid said or did that might have caused someone else to kill him?'

'I was too distressed to notice.'

'Before that. Before Rupert arrived.'

'The only thing I can recall him saying was at the beginning, before we started. There were four of us present – Mr Towers and the three lady members. Polly asked who was missing – as if she couldn't work it out for herself – and Mr Towers spoke Rupert's name, adding that Rupert is always late. It was so unusual for Mr Towers to say anything that I noticed it particularly.'

'He said something later,' said Shirley-Ann. 'Now what was it? A quip of some sort. Just a couple of words. I know! Jessica was giving us her theory about the stealing of the Penny Black. She said it could easily be a collector. She could picture some middle-aged man with a personality defect gloating over his stamps, or something like that, and Sid said, "Or woman," and we all smiled about it. You do remember, don't you? After all, you were the one who suggested we discussed the stealing of the stamp.'

155

'I can bring it to mind now, yes. But I don't see that it makes any difference. None of us took offence, the ladies, I mean.'

'Do you think it was Sid who took offence? Do you think he took the remark personally, about the personality defect? He could have thought it was aimed at him.'

'Conceivably. Who can say?'

Shirley-Ann trawled through her memory of the evening. 'After that, you gave us your theories about the riddle and Sid made no comment at all, did he?'

'I can't remember any.'

'The next thing was that Rupert's dog appeared.'

'Spare me that.' Miss Chilmark looked away at the recorder-player.

'I don't remember Sid saying anything while you were distressed, but when Jessica asked for a paper bag, he supplied one. He took it from his carrier bag. A book was wrapped in it. So it was thanks to Sid that she had the means to cope with your attack.'

Miss Chilmark appeared to wish to dismiss the episode from her mind. At any rate, she said nothing.

Shirley-Ann picked up the thread again. 'Soon after, I read the Stanley Ellin story, and then Milo opened his copy of *The Hollow Man*.'

'Before that, he insulted Mrs Wycherley.'

'Who did?'

Miss Chilmark looked as if she had bitten into a sour apple. 'Who do you think?'

'Rupert?'

'You remember, don't you? "Jesus wants me for a sunbeam"?'

'Oh.' Shirley-Ann tried to stop herself smiling.

'It was meant to wound, and it did.'

'Yes, but it didn't have anything to do with Sid.'

'It demonstrated the depths the man will sink to.'

'Rupert. But we were talking about Sid and the things he did and said that evening,' said Shirley-Ann. 'And now I've remembered something else. At the end of the evening,

156

after Milo opened his book and found the Penny Black, we were talking about what Milo should do next. Some of us said there was no need for him to get involved. He could send the stamp back to the Postal Museum and no one need say anything about it. Someone – I think it was Rupert – asked Sid for his opinion and he said, "I can stay quiet." You must remember because you were one of the people who said he had a duty to go to the police. You and Polly insisted. Everyone else was inclined to turn a blind eye.'

'Don't talk to me in that accusing tone of voice,' said Miss Chilmark. 'It was the proper thing to do.'

'If he hadn't done it, he would have gone straight back to the narrowboat. Very likely, Sid wouldn't have been murdered.'

'That, if I may say so, is about the most stupid thing I have heard you say,' commented Miss Chilmark. 'It's pure speculation and quite pointless. No one can say with certainty what would have happened. Anyway, my recollection is that Milo made up his own mind. It didn't require advice from me or anyone else. He would have gone to the police regardless, and quite right.' She stood up. 'And now, if we have quite finished this futile exercise, I have some business to attend to. Good morning.'

She headed off in the direction of Waitrose.

TWENTY

Julie Hargreaves routinely cleared the surface of her desk at the end of each day's work. She wasn't compulsive about tidiness, but the desk was quite modest in size and she would transfer everything she could to the filing cabinet and the wire trays. For the pens, pencils and clips, she had an arrangement of cylinders called a desk tidy. All she expected to find in front of her when she arrived for work next day was the mail, if any. So this Wednesday morning Peter Diamond, whose desk was a disgrace, was making mischief. He had heaped her space with objects in transparent plastic bags – Sid Towers' possessions, ready to be collected for forensic examination. An outraged howl was the least he expected.

She deflated him by saying mildly, 'It's a little early for Christmas, isn't it?'

He said, 'You're an optimist.' He still hoped for an eruption.

But she moved the dialogue smoothly on to professional matters. 'Surely he didn't carry all this in his pockets.'

'It's all the loose stuff from his car as well.'

'Anything of interest?' She picked up one of the bags and rattled the contents. 'Keys.'

'For the car, the doors to his flat and the warehouse where he worked.'

'Nothing so helpful as the key to a certain pad-lock?'

'You're a super-optimist.'

She handled a bulkier package. 'This will be the book

158

he had with him at the Bloodhounds' meeting. *The Three Coffins.*'

Diamond frowned as a fresh thought popped into his brain. 'Where's the brown paper bag we heard it was wrapped in?'

Julie shifted some of the objects.

'Should be here somewhere,' said Diamond, joining in. 'Every bloody item has its own plastic bag and label.'

'I don't see it, do you? Here's a carrier bag.' Julie picked up the packet and read the label. '"Waitrose carrier used to contain book, *The Three Coffins.*" No mention of a brown bag.'

'Come to think of it, he wouldn't fancy using it for his precious book after Miss Chilmark had been hyperventilating into it. Probably binned it.'

'I expect so,' said Julie, continuing to examine the collection. Packaged and labelled like this, anyone's possessions would have looked pathetic. There was about thirty pence in small coins. A five-pound note. A handkerchief. A comb. Two ballpoints. Half a tube of Polo mints. 'Does it matter?'

'The bag? Only if it's missing,' said Diamond, beginning to question his own assumption. '*Would* he have thrown it away, seeing that it came in so useful? Suppose the old dear had another attack. They could have needed it a second time.'

'Unless it got torn.'

'Nothing was said about that. Who held the bag to Miss Chilmark's face?'

'The art gallery owner. Jessica Shaw. She knew what to do.'

'Then I wouldn't mind betting she kept hold of the bag, at least until the meeting ended.'

Julie gave him a long look. He had this way of pursuing to tedium points that seemed trivial. Once in a while this paid a dividend. Still, it was difficult to understand why the fate of a brown paper bag had any importance.

'And the meeting broke up in some disorder after the

Penny Black was discovered,' he continued, talking more to himself than Julie. 'She may not have returned the bag to Sid. Well, she couldn't have, or it would be among these things.'

'Unless Sid got rid of it later.'

Diamond didn't think much of that suggestion. 'She could have left it in the crypt, in which case some cleaner will have tidied it up.'

'Or she may have taken it with her.'

'Jessica? Stuffed it into her handbag, you mean?'

'Or a pocket.'

He liked that better. 'Right. We'll ask her now. We'll take a walk to that art gallery she manages.'

'What do I do with all this?' she asked with her hand on the heap of plastic packets.

'Leave it there.'

'Cluttering up my desk? No thanks.'

'You're not a slave to tidiness, are you?'

'But there's money here.'

'This is a police station, Julie. If you can't trust the police . . .' He spread his hands like the Pope and tried to look as benign.

She gave him a long look and said, 'It's not your money.'

'Yours neither. Get your coat. We've more important things to do.'

She looked at her watch. 'Can't do it. Sorry.'

'Why not.'

'Actually, I've got an appointment.'

His blood pressure rose several points. She had no business making appointments in police time. 'What's that?'

'The post-mortem on Sid Towers. You asked me to go – remember?'

'Ah.' He'd dismissed it from his mind. 'What time?'

'Noon, at the RUH.'

'We can fit this other thing in first. I'll get you there on time, I guarantee.'

'If you say so.' Not for the first time in her dealings

160

with Diamond, Julie showed restraint. She could easily have remarked that if he could drive her to the RUH, it was odd that he was prevented from attending the autopsy himself.

The Walsingham Gallery window was being dressed and Jessica Shaw was directing, gesturing to a man on the other side of the glass exactly where a painting on an easel should stand. She was engrossed and so was a small crowd of bystanders, making it difficult for anyone to reach the other end of the narrow, flagstoned passage of Northumberland Place. Jessica seemed to be well aware that this was street entertainment. In a cherry-red woollen dress and with a thick white cardigan draped around her shoulders, she was conspicuous among her audience in their drab padded jackets and windcheaters.

'Mrs Jessica Shaw?'

She didn't even turn to answer Diamond's enquiry, but carried on giving instructions. 'More to the right. The right, the right, the right.'

'Police,' said Diamond. 'CID. This may be inconvenient, but are you Mrs Shaw?'

'It is inconvenient, yes.'

'And you are Mrs Shaw?'

'I am. That's it, A.J.! Perfect!'

In a tone of formality amounting almost to a warning, he gave his rank and name and Julie's, too. 'Could we talk to you inside, ma'am?'

'But I have talked,' she said, still staring at her window arrangement. 'I had a sergeant here yesterday and he wrote down everything I said.'

'This is the follow-up.'

She sighed and turned her face to him for the first time. 'And I'm trying to get this ready for a private view this evening. I've got over a hundred people coming. What do you think of it so far?'

'The window? I like it. Not so keen on the picture. Meant to be Avebury, is it?'

161

'God help us,' said Jessica Shaw. 'What a brutal expression that is. *Meant* to be. We just have to be grateful the artist isn't here.'

They went inside. A.J. was sent to fetch more pictures and unwrap them. 'I hope this won't take long,' Jessica said to Diamond. 'It's interfering with my livelihood, all this third degree.' She found them chairs at the rear of the shop. 'You want coffee?'

'That's going to delay the questions even more,' Diamond pointed out.

'Not if A.J. makes it. White with how many sugars? Two?'

She'd guessed correctly. 'Thanks. You should be doing my job,' Diamond remarked.

Eyeing his bulk, she commented, 'It's not much of a deduction. And no sugar for you, right?' she said to Julie. She gave the order to A.J. as he shuffled past with a large wrapped painting, then she confided to Diamond, 'A.J. is a brick. It's all voluntary. I don't pay him a cent. I only wish I could sell more of his work.'

'His work?'

'He's an artist.'

'Is that his stuff in the window?'

'Lord, no. I keep him upstairs.'

'Lucky fellow,' said Diamond, then wished he had guarded his tongue. The look he got was all he deserved. She didn't blush, or betray any embarrassment. She simply gave him a cold stare. 'First question,' he said quickly. 'When did you join the Bloodhounds?'

'Last winter. I was one of the last to join, except for the new woman, Shirley-Ann. She's only been a couple of times.'

'So was Sid Towers already a member when you joined?'

'Sid? Yes.'

'Had you met him before?'

'No.'

'Did you know any of them previously?'

'Only Polly Wycherley. I joined at her invitation. She

came into the gallery a couple of times towards the end of last year and noticed what I was reading. We discovered we shared an interest in crime fiction, so she told me about the meetings in the crypt. I went along reluctantly. She's a great persuader, is Polly. Have you met her?'

'Not yet.'

'She's cooled towards me for some reason. Probably something I said. People like you and me ought to think before we speak. But I don't go to please Polly any more. I go to be entertained. The members are well informed, but I can tell you there are some pretty eccentric ones among them.'

'Lost their Marples, you mean?'

She raised her eyebrows. 'Did I hear right? Was that meant to be a pun?'

'"*Meant* to be." What a brutal expression.'

Now she laughed and it was clear from the look she gave him that she was beginning to alter her assessment of this paunchy policeman. 'Anyway, "eccentric" was the word I used. The Bloodhounds aren't so dim. They're well read. I like scoring points off them when I can.'

'The meetings can be lively, then?'

'Lively? Deadly, as it turns out.'

Now Diamond smiled.

'Yes,' Jessica went on. 'There are personality clashes. Rupert gets people excited.'

'Mr Darby, you mean?'

'Do I? I only think of him as Rupert. He's harmless, in my opinion, though others will tell you different. A classic case of arrested development. He's locked into the nineteen-fifties, when it was chic to hang around Soho smoking Gauloises and going to jazz clubs. You'll get on famously with him, by the look of you.'

Diamond's hand curled protectively over the trilby on his knees. 'There were incidents with Miss Chilmark, I'm told.'

'Silly old duck, yes. She's a frightful snob. The Chilmarks once owned half the city, if she can be believed. She can't

163

understand why we don't prostrate ourselves each time she appears. What really gets to her is that Rupert is manifestly several points above her in the social scale and doesn't give a toss about decorum.'

'How is it manifest?'

'His accent. To borrow a phrase from Dylan Thomas, he talks as if he has the Elgin Marbles in his mouth.'

'There was an incident on Monday, I heard.'

'There's an incident on most Mondays. He insists on bringing his dog and she gets herself into a state about it. She started to panic and we calmed her down.'

This account was all too perfunctory. Julie intervened to say, 'You're understating it, aren't you?'

'In what way?'

'Wasn't she hyperventilating? And didn't you act quickly to stop it?'

'Just the old remedy of holding a paper bag to her mouth,' said Jessica dismissively. 'She soon responded.'

Diamond wasn't going to let this crucial matter get by. 'What happened to the bag?'

'What do you mean – what happened to it?'

'Afterwards.'

'I don't remember, unless . . .'

'Unless what?'

'. . . I kept it.'

'Did you?'

'I may have done. In fact, I believe I did, just in case she started up again. She insisted on staying for the rest of the meeting. Rupert removed the dog, but I didn't want to take any chances, so I kept the bag by me. Now what happened to it at the end?' She hesitated. 'Is this important?'

'Possibly not, but I'd like to know.'

'Sid produced it in the first place.'

'I know,' said Diamond.

'I don't have any memory of returning it to him.'

'Would you have thrown it away?'

'Doubtful. Not after it came in so useful. I'm wondering

now if I kept the thing. I didn't want it in view, right in front of Miss Chilmark. I may have stuffed it in my handbag.'

'You would have found it later, then.'

'Not me. I carry things for years before I turf them out. It's probably still in there. Want me to fetch my bag?'

'Presently,' said Diamond. The questioning had settled to a tempo that he didn't want interrupted. Give her half a chance and she would go back to her window-dressing. 'Tell me about Sid.'

'That won't take long,' she said. 'He was a member before I joined. Polly told me once that he came on the advice of his doctor. He was painfully shy, poor bloke. The doctor's idea was that he was a crime fiction buff, so he would be encouraged to chip in. He hardly ever did.' She smiled. 'It was so rare if he did that we all turned our heads and scared him rigid.'

'Did anyone try making friends with him?'

'Polly fussed over him sometimes like the old hen she is. If anyone else had spoken more than a couple of words I'm sure he would have run a mile.'

'And I understand you spent some time with him in the Moon and Sixpence on more than one occasion.'

She coloured slightly. 'Are you trying to trip me up, or something? You make it sound like infidelity. I felt sorry for the guy, that's all. I thought someone should try and draw him out a bit, for his own sake. The others simply ignored him.'

'No one was hostile?'

She shook her head. 'There was nothing you could dislike about Sid.'

'Someone must have objected to him.'

'I know,' said Jessica.

The coffee arrived in bone-china cups, A.J. bearing it in on a lacquered tray. Potential buyers of the art had to be cosseted. From the efficient way he handed the cups around, A.J. had performed the duty more than once. 'If it doesn't seem frightfully rude,' he said, 'I'll take mine to the front of the shop and carry on with what I was doing.'

Alert to the possibility that A.J. was something more in this set-up than a volunteer window-dresser, Diamond watched him with interest. The man had an air of confidence that belied the menial tasks he was performing here. There was poise in the way he moved, and a suggestion of anarchy, as if any second he might execute some Chaplinesque trick with the tray, and his dark curls and mobile brown eyes reinforced the idea, though he was actually quite tall. However, Jessica was content to treat him as a domestic in spite of the approving things she had said earlier. They both appeared at ease with each other.

Intriguing.

But there were things still to be asked. 'On Monday after the meeting ended, what did you do?'

'Went home,' Jessica answered.

'Immediately?'

'Yes.'

'Where's home, Mrs Shaw?'

'Widcombe Hill.'

'You've got a good view from there, I dare say.'

'A view of a chapel roof with the words "Prepare to Meet Thy God" painted in big white letters across it, if that's what you call a good view.' She laughed. 'A nice message to see each morning when we pull back the bedroom curtains.'

'If that's the Ebenezer, it must have been there when you moved in.'

'Of course. Actually, it doesn't bother us. I was just amused when you mentioned the view.'

'When you got home that evening, was Mr Shaw there?'

She put down her cup of coffee. 'This is becoming rather intrusive.'

'I'm sorry. That's my job,' said Diamond. 'I need to know if anyone can vouch for the time you got in.'

'So I'm a suspect?'

'We're doing our best to eliminate you.'

'That's precisely the message I see from my bedroom window.'

He laughed. This had become an interview to savour. It was all too rare to meet a witness so adept at verbal sparring. Jessica Shaw had a quick intelligence. He told her, 'You haven't answered the question yet.'

'Which one? Oh, was Barnaby at home? No, he was not. He didn't get back till late. Lions.' She folded her arms, enjoying Diamond's puzzled reaction to the last word, making it plain that she wasn't intending to add anything.

'Live lions?' he asked after taking a sip of coffee.

'Very lively, so Barnaby tells me.'

Diamond's thoughts were on the safari park at Longleat. Julie was quicker on the uptake.

'You mean the Lions who collect money for charities, like the Rotary?'

'Didn't I make it clear?' said Jessica, eyes twinkling.

'You said he got home late,' said Diamond. 'What's late?'

'Oh, God. I don't keep a stopwatch for him. After I was in bed. Towards midnight. You don't regard *him* as a suspect?'

'We're trying to fix some parameters, that's all,' Diamond hedged.

She rolled her eyes. 'Could you fix my wonky exhaust while you're at it?'

'So you have a car?' He wasn't so slow himself when an opening came.

'Of course I have a car. I'm running a business here. And in case you were about to ask, I didn't use it on Monday evening. I didn't need to. It's just a short walk to St Michael's and back.'

'Would you give me the make and number?'

She told him it was a new Peugeot 306. White. It seemed there was money in art, even in these straitened times. Or perhaps Barnaby Shaw was the provider.

'Your husband. Is he in business?'

'Houses.' She paused, playing her game of letting the wrong assumption take root, only this time Diamond was more alert. He wasn't thrown when she held her thumb and forefinger about three inches apart. 'This high. He makes miniature houses.'

He smiled.

She said, 'Gullible people buy them for exorbitant amounts. He does a police station with a blue lamp at fifty pounds if you're interested.'

Diamond was more interested in the way the pupils of Jessica Shaw's eyes reduced in size and the edge of her mouth turned down when her husband was mentioned. He said, 'Maybe we should check your handbag now.'

'What do you mean – *we*?' She got up and crossed the room to where a leather shoulder-bag was hanging over a tall-backed chair. 'I'm not having my personal objects pored over by policemen, thank you.' She released the catch, felt inside and straight away withdrew a folded brown paper bag. 'This I have no further use for.'

TWENTY-ONE

A message was waiting for Diamond when he returned to Manvers Street after delivering Julie to the Royal United Hospital for the post-mortem. Would he contact DCI Wigfull as a matter of urgency?

Generally he avoided the man. From experience, he was willing to bet that this was a gripe over areas of responsibility, but in a police station matters of urgency can't be sidestepped. He picked up the phone.

'Well, have you found your stamp thief?' he asked while Wigfull was still self-importantly giving his name.

'Is that DS Diamond?'

'Who else?'

'As a matter of fact, I have found him.'

'And is he a dead man?'

Was it an intake of breath he heard, or the wind abandoning Wigfull's sails?

'You still there, John?' Diamond asked. 'Was it Sid Towers?'

'What makes you think it might be?' Wigfull parried, the annoyance coming through clearly.

'Doesn't everything point to him?'

'I wouldn't have said so.'

'So you nicked someone else, then?'

'I didn't say that.'

'Aren't you going to say anything, John?'

'Has someone been talking to you?'

'No, I worked it out.'

'Have you also worked out how he got into the locked

room?' Wigfull asked more warily.

'No. Have you?'

A distinct note of self-congratulation crept in. 'I believe so.'

'You've cracked it? Nice work,' Diamond, profoundly surprised, was gracious enough to say.

'That's why I asked you to get in touch,' Wigfull said with more élan. 'I'm here in my office with the Assistant Chief Constable, wrapping up my part of the case, so to speak. Why don't you join us?'

Mr Musgrave was by common consent the most approachable of Avon and Somerset's three Assistant Chief Constables. His florid countenance and portly shape attested to thousands of pints taken convivially with colleagues. A good listener, fair in his dealings and appreciative of jobs well done, Arnold Musgrave was the ideal man to have drop into the office at an auspicious moment.

When Diamond arrived, Wigfull was saying with the air of a man confident of a commendation at the very least, 'I dare say you're familiar with the detective stories of John Dickson Carr, sir.'

'I dare say I am,' the ACC chanced his arm. 'My failing is I read these things and don't recall who wrote them or what they were about.' Spotting Diamond at the door, he gave a broad smile. 'Peter! You're looking chipper.'

'It's all show,' said Diamond. 'I'm up to my ears in problems. Unlike John Wigfull here.'

'He's about to tell us how he solved the case of the stolen Penny Black.'

'So I heard.'

'Could ease a few of your problems, Peter.'

'My fingers are crossed, sir.'

Both looked expectantly towards Wigfull, who smirked, producing a confident upward twitch of the large moustache. 'We were speaking of Dickson Carr,' he said with a donnish air. 'These detective writers of fifty years ago were expected to set puzzles for their readers, the sort of

170

brain-teaser you could do to while away a train journey as a change from the crossword, and Dickson Carr was one of the best of them. He still has a devoted following, I gather. His forte was the locked room puzzle.'

'Then I must have read one of them at least,' the ACC decided. 'Mind, I couldn't give you a title for love nor money.'

This didn't matter to Wigfull, into his flow now. 'A strange experience for me, dealing with a case like this one, with the hallmarks of an old detective story – the cryptic rhymes, the ingenious theft, the locked room puzzle and the closed circle of suspects. But I relished the challenge. Something out of the ordinary. Once I knew of the connection with this group of detective story readers, the Bloodhounds, who meet in the crypt of St Michael's, I was able to concentrate my inquiries.'

Mr Musgrave nodded. 'Piece of good fortune, John, having one of them come to you with the missing stamp.'

Wigfull wasn't having that. 'The thief didn't do me any favours. It was deliberate, sir. Part of the plot. The way I see it, he was poking fun at the police, trying to show us up as, er—'

'Bumbling idiots?'

'Er, less than efficient, anyway. He stole the stamp and then handed it back, as if to prove he'd been toying with us. It was sheer bloody arrogance, coming on top of the rhymes he broadcast to all and sundry.'

'So you rose to the challenge?' said Mr Musgrave. 'Good man.'

Diamond observed all this in a tactful silence. Mr Musgrave's genial manner masked a sharp wit. He was leagues ahead of Wigfull.

'I realised it was no ordinary theft,' said Wigfull.

'Well, you would,' Mr Musgrave amiably agreed.

'Exactly, sir. It *was* a theft, but it was also a stunt. And it could only have been planned by someone with inside

171

information. The perpetrator had to know in advance that one of the Bloodhounds, Mr Milo Motion, was going to bring his copy of *The Hollow Man* to the next meeting and read from it. They were due to discuss locked room mysteries, and Dickson Carr's book contains the famous chapter on the subject. That is to say, famous to people who still have an interest in such things.' Wigfull gave a superior smile. He liked to project the image of a modern man, more excited by information superhighways than detective stories.

'The missing Penny Black cover was dramatically discovered at precisely that chapter in the book – just as Mr Motion was about to read it aloud.' Now Wigfull leaned forward, eyes gleaming. 'In the classic tradition of the detective story, we had a closed circle of suspects and, even more intriguingly, a locked room puzzle of our own, because the book had been on the boat all week and the boat was kept locked. Naturally I interviewed Mr Motion at length – to his credit, he came to us at once – and I satisfied myself that he was not the man we were looking for. What would have been the point – giving himself away? He was genuinely shocked, I'm certain, and at a loss to explain what had happened. He insisted that the boat was remarkably secure. Bolted inside at the prow and padlocked outside with this.' Dramatically Wigfull produced a sturdy-looking padlock from his drawer and held it out for inspection like Houdini preparing to perform.

'Is that it?' asked the ACC. 'The very one?'

'The very one, sir.'

'May I see?'

Mr Musgrave first felt the weight of the padlock in the palm of his hand and then turned it over. 'Looks pretty solid. German-made?'

'Yes, sir. It's a heavy-duty padlock, all right. Bought from Foxton's, the best locksmith in the West Country. This is top-of-the-range equipment.'

Mr Musgrave turned to Diamond. 'Care to examine it?'

'Thank you, sir, but I already have.'

Wigfull took hold of the padlock again and gave a fair impression of a sales rep, pointing out its special features, stressing that each padlock sold was unlike any other. 'They are supplied with two keys. Mr Motion informed us that he accidentally dropped one of his in the canal some time ago. I have no reason to disbelieve him. So for all practical purposes, the remaining key is unique. Mr Motion is adamant that it never left his possession. It was on the key-ring that he carried in his pocket with his car keys. I have it here now. You see?' Wigfull produced a key about two centimetres long, inserted it into the slot and turned it clockwise. The steel shackle sprang open. 'You push the top down again and it closes. Would you care to try it, sir?'

This whole presentation was so spirited that it would have been churlish to refuse. Obligingly Mr Musgrave took the padlock and tried the mechanism.

'One key,' reiterated Wigfull. 'I myself watched Mr Motion unlock the padlock on Monday night prior to discovering the body aboard the boat. I am perfectly satisfied that it was properly locked and that he opened it with this key from his pocket. Yet there was Sid Towers in the cabin, dead. The impossible crime.'

At this point Diamond thought Wigfull was over-egging the cake.

Mr Musgrave said, 'You must have considered the possibility that Motion left the boat earlier without securing the padlock?'

'Indeed, I did, sir. I questioned him closely. He insists that it was locked.'

'What other explanation is there?'

'If you'll bear with me, I'm coming to that. He says he has a clear memory of pressing the shackle home and rattling the padlock to make sure it was secure. After all, that boat is his home.'

'You believe him?'

'I do, sir.'

173

Diamond gave a nod. 'He satisfied me, for what it's worth.'

'All right,' said Mr Musgrave. 'How was it done?'

Wigfull placed the padlock and key on his desk and pushed them aside as if they no longer mattered. 'Most of my inquiries – and I dare say yours, Peter – have centred on the events of last Monday evening. Who had the opportunity and a reason to visit the narrowboat? But the point about the crime, the theft of the Penny Black, I mean, is that it happened the previous week. On the Thursday we had that erroneous tip-off from Bristol and on the Friday the first of those rhyming riddles, and on the same morning the theft occurred.' He raised a finger to give significance to his next statement. 'The whole thing was planned ahead.'

'Most crimes are, in my experience.' Even Mr Musgrave seemed to have decided that Wigfull's theatrical manner was starting to reek of ham.

'How right you are, sir, but I'm suggesting that this was intricately plotted. Dovetails, every part: the tip-off to Sergeant Plant; the riddles; the theft at the Postal Museum; and the planting of the stamp in Motion's book. It was a high-risk undertaking, and the planning was worthy of the SAS. And it worked like a dream. The thief always intended to return the stamp after making monkeys out of everybody – ourselves and the Bloodhounds.'

'With some success.'

'True. But let's concentrate on the locked room.'

'Good idea.'

'Chummy knew a week in advance—'

There were limits to Diamond's tolerance. 'For Christ's sake, John,' he appealed to Wigfull. 'Let's not call him "Chummy". We both agree Sid Towers is the man.'

'Is he?' said Mr Musgrave, showing more interest than he had for some minutes.

'He fits the frame, sir,' said Diamond. 'The silent man with a lot to prove to some of those motormouths in the

174

Bloodhounds. Trained in security, so breaking into the Postal Museum wouldn't be such a problem. He'd know plenty about locks and bolts. An expert on Dickson Carr. And of course he was found in the boat. Either Towers or the killer must have found a way into that cabin, and the logic is that it was Towers and he was followed in there and killed. Agreed, John?'

Wigfull muttered his assent, peeved that Diamond had hijacked the narrative.

Mr Musgrave said, 'This is fine as far as it goes, but it's all circumstantial, isn't it?'

Keen as he was to lead the discussion again, Wigfull had no answer. He turned to Diamond.

'Everything I just mentioned is,' Diamond admitted, and added, straight-faced, 'unless Mr Wigfull here has some evidence I'm not aware of.'

Wigfull's eyes narrowed. The opportunity was there and he still had nothing to say.

For Peter Diamond, the silence was as good as a fanfare. 'In that case, I'd better show you mine,' he announced. Resisting the flourish he might have made – there was no need – he took from his inside pocket the brown paper bag he had recovered from Jessica Shaw. He unfolded it. 'This, gentlemen, was the bag Towers produced on Monday evening when Miss Chilmark was hyperventilating. I'm sure you heard about the incident. He handed the bag to Jessica Shaw, who knew what to do. She held it against Miss Chilmark's face and stopped the attack. Afterwards, Mrs Shaw kept the bag, in case of a recurrence. Miss Chilmark felt well enough to remain at the meeting, you see. In the confusion at the end, Mrs Shaw popped it into her handbag and forgot about it. I recovered it from her this afternoon.'

'Is it important?' asked the ACC.

'The bag on its own is not, sir. But if you look at it . . .' Diamond smoothed the bag against the surface of Wigfull's desk and handed it to Mr Musgrave.

'There's writing.'

Wigfull got up and came around the desk to look. 'May I see?'

'Doesn't make a lot of sense,' said Mr Musgrave.

There were three lists of words in rows, written in an untidy hand in black ballpoint:

JACK	LOTION	TOMB
FLAK	OCEAN	DOOM
KNACK	POTION	WHOM
MAC	NOTION	GLOOM
LACK	DEMOTION	BLOOM
SMACK	DEVOTION	
BACK		
CRACK		
SLACK		

'They rhyme,' said Wigfull. 'They're rhyming words.'

'Take a little time over it,' Diamond suggested, as if he were coaching a five-year-old in reading.

Mr Musgrave said, 'Looks to me as if he was working on a piece of verse.'

'The very thing I was about to say, sir,' said Wigfull.

'Do you think he was composing another riddle?' said Mr Musgrave.

'Look at the middle row,' Diamond gently nudged them on. 'What else rhymes with "lotion"?'

'These other words?' said Wigfull.

'Apart from those other words.'

'Ha – you're ahead of us,' said Mr Musgrave. 'Motion. He wanted something to rhyme with Milo Motion. Good spotting, Peter. This does look like the notes for another cryptic riddle. So how about "Jack"?'

'"Attack"?' suggested Wigfull, still thinking about hyper-ventilation, and in some danger of succumbing to it himself.

'"Black",' said Mr Musgrave. 'Penny Black.'

Diamond gave a nod. 'That's my best guess, sir.'

'And "tomb"?'

'Locked room,' Diamond guessed again.

'I'll buy that. Ha. Neat. So Towers was jotting down words to make his next press release. This isn't absolute proof, of course, but I'm satisfied, Peter. You've linked him to the crime.'

Wigfull straightened in his chair. 'Why didn't you show it to me before?' he demanded in a high, aggrieved tone. 'It's evidence.'

He was answered first with a long look, and then: 'I got it from Mrs Shaw less than an hour ago.'

'Then she was withholding evidence.'

'A paper bag?'

'If it's written on . . .'

'She hadn't noticed. Anyway, she'd forgotten about it. It was still in her handbag.'

'Are you sure she hadn't noticed the writing?'

'Even if she had, why should she have thought it important?'

'Crafty old sod,' said Mr Musgrave. But it was Sid Towers he was talking about, not Jessica Shaw. 'What's the old saying? "Who knows most, speaks least."'

Some of the steam dispersed as they all thought about silent Sid, dismissed by most of the Bloodhounds as a nonentity. This, surely, was the proof that he had stolen the world's most valuable stamp and devised a locked room puzzle capable of baffling the best minds.

John Wigfull's mind excepted.

'You were going to tell us how it was done,' Mr Musgrave prompted him.

Wigfull had a mountain to climb after that revelation. You could almost sense the effort of lacing his boots again and pulling on the rucksack. 'Yes, sir.'

'You're not going to keep us in suspense, I hope.'

'No, sir.' Manfully, Wigfull started again. 'The crime, as I was saying, was meticulously planned. Sid Towers must have been working on it for weeks, if not months. He needed to find a way of getting inside the narrowboat when Milo Motion wasn't present. He had an opportunity to see the *Mrs Hudson* for himself the previous Christmas, when the Bloodhounds held their party there.'

'Aboard the boat?' said Mr Musgrave. 'Good place for a party.'

'I checked and he was certainly there, in spite of being so shy. I picture him at the party unwilling to mix, moving about the boat, looking at things. It's probable, isn't it, that a professional security officer like Towers would take an interest in the locks and bolts? I reckon he noted the type of padlock at that early stage. No doubt he'd come across such locks before. Probably knew they were supplied by Foxton's. If not, it was easy to note the name of the manufacturer and find out who stocked them.'

'What was the point?' Mr Musgrave asked.

'An amazingly obvious one. No disrespect, sir. Most of these locked room puzzles are obvious when they're explained. I think he went to Foxton's and bought one of those German padlocks himself. He waited for his chance to make a substitution.'

'Good. I'm with you.'

'Exactly when he made the switch I can't be sure. May have been months ago, or as late as the meeting before last.'

'Are you saying he changed over the padlocks at the Bloodhounds?'

'Not exactly, sir.' With a startling sense of drama for such a prosaic man, Wigfull pictured the scene. 'Motion takes off his coat and hangs it on one of the coathooks near the door. Towers chooses a suitable moment to go to the gents. On the way he dips into Motion's overcoat pocket and finds the bunch of keys. He removes Milo's padlock key from the ring and replaces it with one of his own that fits the new padlock. Returns the keys to the pocket.'

'Now he can unlock the boat.'

'Right, sir. He leaves before Motion and drives fast to the boatyard to make sure he gets down there first. With the old key he unlocks the original padlock and replaces it with the one he bought.'

'And when Motion gets back to his boat he uses the key on his ring to let himself in.'

'In the usual way,' said Wigfull, 'unaware that the switch has been made.'

'Neat,' said Mr Musgrave. 'I like it.'

John Wigfull beamed. 'And of course Sid Towers is now in possession of a spare key. He can visit the boat any time he likes.' He brought his hands together in a gesture of finality. Then in case it appeared he was applauding himself, he rubbed them vigorously as if using a drying machine in a public toilet.

'The locked room mystery solved,' said Mr Musgrave. 'What do you say, Peter?'

Diamond digested what had been said and then gave a nod. 'Full marks, John.' He meant it sincerely. He was genuinely impressed. The explanation had no obvious flaw. 'And the reason we didn't find the key on Towers' body is that the murderer must have taken it with him.'

'Or her,' Wigfull was quick to point out.

Mr Musgrave said to Wigfull, 'You'd already thought of that, I'm sure.'

Wigfull smiled. He'd scaled his mountain and was on the summit posing for pictures.

Mr Musgrave reached for the padlock again. 'It doesn't look as if it was bought recently,' he said, turning it over in his hand.

Wigfull had an answer to that. 'He'll have done what any forger of coins does – roughed it up a bit to take off the sheen. They stick them in a bag with other metal objects and shake them about. Sometimes they bury them. They soon look worn.'

Diamond had never judged Wigfull as short in intelligence; it was the sense of humour that was lacking. This wasn't an occasion for sour grapes. The man had just made a crucial contribution to the case, to *his* case, as well as Wigfull's own. 'Wish I'd thought of it,' he admitted. 'I didn't come near to working it out.'

TWENTY-TWO

For Julie's benefit, as he put it, Diamond had been over Wigfull's explanation of the locked boat mystery point by point and they could find no flaw. The substituted padlock and key answered every problem.

Finally he said, 'I'm thinking of handing the whole thing over to Wigfull.'

Julie blinked and frowned. She had sacrificed her lunch hour attending the post-mortem, an unsavoury duty she shouldn't have been lumbered with, and now he hit her with this. 'What do you mean? Let him take over the murder inquiry?'

'Locked rooms and cryptic rhymes. It isn't my scene, Julie. He's motoring through it. Firing on all cylinders while I'm . . . I'm stuck in the pits.'

She stared across the office at the big man as he stood by the window watching the traffic in Manvers Street. 'What does that make me – a worn tyre?'

Diamond was not easy to work with, but his saving grace was a sense of humour. Such a remark would usually produce a smile, whatever the pressures he was under. This time he sighed. He had taken heavy punishment. Actually he wasn't indulging in self-pity; this was about confidence. At this minute he genuinely believed John Wigfull would make a better fist of the case than he could. The strongest comment Julie could find to add was, 'If you do anything so dumb, I'll ask for a transfer.'

He turned to look at her, eyes widening.

'We've put all that Dickson Carr stuff behind us,'

180

Julie insisted. 'We're down to brute murder. Nothing unexpected came out of the post-mortem. No unexplained injuries. He was bashed over the head a couple of times with some solid implement. That isn't exactly a master-criminal at work.'

This earned a glint of amusement.

She added, 'And you said yourself that the locked room mystery isn't a mystery any more.'

'Thanks to Wigfull.'

'All right, thanks to him. Is that important? What we're left with is a straightforward case of murder.'

'About as straightforward as a plate of spaghetti.'

Julie grinned and held out her hands in appeal. 'Come on, you've got the tricky stuff out of the way. We know Sid Towers stole the Penny Black and wrote those rhymes. And incidentally that was your persistence that gave us the proof, not John Wigfull's.'

This tribute didn't register anything with Diamond.

Staunchly, Julie continued to put the case in its most promising perspective. 'Sid thought up this brilliant plot and carried it out and then he was killed. We've got to find the killer. Is it too much to believe that it was a casual murder?'

He said a flat, 'Yes.'

'Then surely it must have been triggered by Sid's actions.' She looked towards Diamond, inviting him to pick up the thread.

But he would not.

So she pressed on. 'I'm suggesting that one of the Bloodhounds felt deeply angered or threatened by what happened at the meeting.'

There was, at least, a response from Diamond, even if it was not helpful. 'The stamp turning up in Milo's book?' he said in a hollow tone. 'Where's the threat in that?'

Julie turned a shade more pink, not in reaction to Diamond's ill-humour, but because a theory – a persuasive theory – was forming in her brain. 'Let's not forget that the stamp is worth millions. Suppose Sid wasn't working alone. What if he had an accomplice?'

He gave her a look that was only a fraction less bleak. She added, 'And what if their plan was to demand a ransom for the stamp?'

'Then they fell out, you mean?'

'Exactly. It wasn't in the plan to return the stamp unless and until they got a thumping great pay-off. But Sid wasn't the hard man he made himself out to be. He got nervous and decided to return the stamp. The accomplice would have been shocked and deeply angered when it turned up in the book as it did, without a penny changing hands. It's enough, isn't it, to provide a motive for murder?'

Diamond was less excited about the theory. 'It would be, if you can believe Sid capable of teaming up with anyone. My judgement is that he was a loner. That flat of his, upstairs at the end of a cul-de-sac; the job, the night work, the shyness everyone mentions. I can't see a man like that confiding what he thinks of the bloody weather, so how does he get around to teaming up with a fellow-criminal? Sorry, Julie. I don't buy it.'

'Why was he killed, then? Can you think of a reason?'

If nothing else, her persistence finally nudged him out of that negative mood. His brown eyes held her for a moment, looked away and then came back to her. 'Could have been something he found out. I suppose if one of them – one of the Bloodhounds – had a dodgy past, a criminal record, say, a man in Sid's line of work might have got to hear about it. Have you checked their form?'

That evening, Bath's glitterati descended on the Walsingham Gallery in numbers. Jessica Shaw's private views were not usually so well patronised, but since the papers were full of the Narrowboat Murder and it was known that the victim had attended a Bloodhounds' meeting the same evening and Jessica was a member, the chance of some inside information was too good to miss. With luck, some of her fellow-members would also be invited. There was even the thrilling possibility of rubbing shoulders with a murderer – for it was stated in the papers that everyone at Monday night's meeting in the crypt of St Michael's had been interviewed by the police. So the buck's fizz flowed and the eyes darted eagerly about, looking not so much at the art as the other guests. As some wit pointed out, it would have assisted everyone if instead of using those little red stickers to mark paintings that were sold, Jessica had attached them to her Bloodhound friends.

The minute she arrived, Shirley-Ann heard an unmistakable voice declaring in syllables brought to perfection by generations of privilege that most of the art on display was absolute balls.

On tiptoe to see over the mass of expensively coiffed heads, she glimpsed a black beret and moved determinedly in that direction. Gratifyingly, Rupert recognised her at once. It didn't matter that he greeted her as 'Sally-Ann'; the warmth was genuine. He introduced the people beside him in his own florid fashion.

'My dear, in my endless quest for culture I once located this unlikely duo in a watering-hole in Bradford on Avon, of all places. Tonight I met them in the Saracen's, sinking one or two before the party. Stephen and Pat Volk. Stephen's a screenwriter and a crafty old fox, he won't mind me telling you. Remember that extraordinary hoax about psychic phenomena that went out on television one Hallowe'en and petrified the nation? With Parkinson playing it straight as the presenter. What the devil was it called, Steve?'

'*Ghostwatch.*' The playwright, reassuringly substantial, broad of shoulder, scant of hair and dressed entirely in black, with owlish glasses, seemed subdued by Rupert's eloquence, but who was not?

Almost by definition, the most brilliant hoaxers were going to be self-effacing, Shirley-Ann mused.

'"Heads must roll at the BBC"! Loved it,' Rupert was crowing. 'And speaking of heads, this is Pat, who sculpts them. Marvellous, strong, archetypal heads in amazing colours. If you can force a way through this drunken mob, as you must, you'll see her work upstairs. I was on the point of telling her she's the only one of this lot I'd consider buying.'

Pat Volk smiled wryly. Rupert might talk like a patron of the arts, but his scuffed leather jacket, patched jeans and the black beret speckled with dandruff didn't inspire confidence. Shirley-Ann smiled back. It was about all anyone could do when Rupert was in full flow.

'Sally-Ann joined the Bloodhounds just as we all became suspects in a murder case,' he continued, projecting loudly enough for all the room to hear. 'She's incredibly well informed about detective stories. You could ask her anything at all and she'd know. Try her. Here's one at random. Name the poison Agatha Christie used most commonly in her books.'

Shirley-Ann felt as if half the room had suspended conversation to hear the answer. 'Cyanide?'

'I wouldn't know, my dear,' said Rupert, displaying his gaps in a fiendish grin, 'but I'm sure it's a splendidly efficient poison, quite impossible to trace in buck's fizz.'

From somewhere to Shirley-Ann's left, a familiar voice spoke up. 'Of course she's right. It occurs in fourteen of the books, twice as many as morphine, which comes second.' Milo, back in circulation and seeming no worse for his skirmish with the police.

'Ah, perpetual Motion,' said Rupert. 'The man's unstoppable. Why don't you join us, Milo? Hit Sally-Ann with some really searching questions.'

Shirley-Ann saw an opportunity and seized it. 'If it doesn't seem frightfully rude, I forgot to pick up a catalogue.' She turned her back and was away. Talking to strangers was preferable to that sort of embarrassment. How could she have been so misguided as to think Rupert was a safe haven?

She had not travelled far across the room when further progress was barred by a plate of canapés. Predictably, Jessica stood out from her guests in a gorgeous outfit, a shimmering black sequin jacket over a peacock-blue dress. 'I was on my way to rescue you,' she said. 'That Rupert! Cyanide in the buck's fizz! Believe me, I won't be wasting good poison on him. I'll strangle him.'

'At least he doesn't have the dog with him.'

'I wouldn't count on it. Have one of these, and come and meet my husband.'

The husband.

This was one encounter Shirley-Ann hadn't anticipated. She followed eagerly as Jessica crossed the room, greeting almost everyone by name, and finally turning to remark, 'I won't inflict him on you for long. Anyway, he's supposed to be handling the sales. I don't know how much trade he's doing.'

Jessica's way of introducing Barnaby, as he was called, was to wave the plate of canapés and speak their two names. Then she moved away. Barnaby was seated behind a table with an account book in front of him, a tired-looking man of about forty-five with tinted brown hair and one of those dark blue suits with a broad white pinstripe that are worn by MPs on the far right of the Tory Party. At his side, in charge of the cashbox, was A.J., of all people, and the two appeared relaxed with each other. She'd taken it as likely that A.J. was Jessica's secret lover. Maybe he was; if so, he was putting on a fine show of innocence, or Barnaby was astonishingly tolerant.

'Shirley-Ann and I met last week,' A.J. informed Barnaby. 'She set me straight on my leisure reading. No more graphic novels. I'm under orders to read the American female private eye from now on.'

'I didn't say anything of the sort,' Shirley-Ann protested.

Barnaby's eyes slipped away to another part of the room, absenting him from the conversation.

She drew him back in. 'How's it going? Have you sold any?'

He nodded. 'Three so far.'

'Nothing of mine,' said A.J., so egocentric that he was unaware whether anyone else really cared. 'The only things that sell these days are insipid pen and ink drawings of the Royal Crescent.'

'Three. Is that good?' Shirley-Ann asked Barnaby.

He gave a shrug.

A.J. answered for him, 'The commission from three won't cover the cost of the party, but Barnaby doesn't mind. He isn't in this for the profit.'

Barnaby became slightly more animated. 'I'm not in it at all. It's Jessica's show, not mine.'

'Your money, pal,' said A.J.

The husband flapped his hand dismissively.

A.J. was determined to make his point. 'I'm an old friend of these two, so I can say this. Without Barnaby there would have been no party tonight. The wretched artists of Bath would be deprived of all this. The whole point is that he isn't all that interested in art. He does it because he likes Jess to be happy. Isn't that terrific?'

Shirley-Ann said that it was. She hadn't detected a trace of sarcasm or irony in A.J.'s tribute. She was confused now. They truly were like old friends and she was going to have to revise her theory about them. Her admiration for Jessica soared. It isn't unusual for a brilliant and beautiful woman to win the devotion of two men, but it takes exceptional talent to keep them on friendly terms with each other.

Someone from the press butted in, wanting to be introduced to one of the artists, allowing Shirley-Ann the opportunity to smile politely and move away. She took a glass of buck's fizz from a waitress and headed for the side of the room that wasn't being dominated by Rupert. Possibly she would find someone else she knew, though she doubted if it would be another of the Bloodhounds. Who was missing? Only Polly and Miss Chilmark. The frost between Jessica and Polly, though unexplained, was apparent. And Miss C., poor old duck, with her potential for apoplexy at the sight of Rupert, would be more of a liability than an asset.

She got into an amusing conversation with two sparky women who had gatecrashed. Neither knew anything about art. They were looking for two hunky men to invite them to a pub, or, better still, a restaurant, when the party was over. They weren't sure about Rupert. He was probably good for the invitation, they estimated, but not good for much else except brilliant conversation. And he didn't seem to have a friend. The girl-talk might have continued for some time longer if Jessica hadn't appeared suddenly at Shirley-Ann's side. Her vivacious expression of minutes before was supplanted by a look of stark anger.

'Did you see it when you arrived?' she demanded of Shirley-Ann.

'Did I see what?'

'Outside, on the window. Come and look.'

Jessica practically scythed a way through her guests to the door, with Shirley-Ann following apprehensively. Outside in Northumberland Place, Barnaby and A.J. stood together examining the Walsingham Gallery window.

'What do you think?' demanded Jessica. 'What scumbag could have done this to me?'

Shirley-Ann looked.

Someone had been busy with a spray-can, writing a message in large, crude, white letters across the main window:

SHE DID FOR SID

There was a moment while Shirley-Ann absorbed the meaning of what was written. Then she said, 'That's horrible.' She was truly appalled and outraged on Jessica's behalf. 'What kind of person does a thing like this?'

'A rat, not a person,' said Jessica. 'A stinking rat. To think that all my guests must have seen it when they arrived. And I, in all innocence, was greeting them inside. Barnaby, I'm nauseated.'

'We'll clean it off,' said A.J.

'I didn't notice it as I came in,' said Shirley-Ann. 'And nobody was talking about it. I think this must have been done after the party started.'

'With the lighting as it is, you don't notice it from inside,' said Barnaby, quick to chime in with the reassurance. 'I couldn't tell you when it was done.'

A.J. rubbed at one of the letters with his fingertip.

'Don't do that,' said Jessica.

He said, 'I'm just seeing if it's still wet.'

'We don't want your fingerprints on it if we call the police.'

'Is that what you want to do – call the police?' asked Barnaby. 'Is that wise?'

'What do you mean – is it wise?'

'Jess, my dear, it's a rotten thing somebody has done, but it's hardly a serious matter in the eyes of the law.'

'It's vile,' said Jessica.

'Yes, it is, but you're not going to get much redress. In fact, it wouldn't surprise me if they took more interest in what's written here than in catching the bastard. It will bring you more grief than satisfaction. My advice is to rub the window clean and forget about this.'

'Look,' said A.J., 'why don't you go back to your guests and leave this to me? I can clean it up before anyone else sees it.'

She said through gritted teeth, 'I want to know who did this. Someone must have seen.'

'Not necessarily,' said Barnaby. 'It wouldn't take more than a few seconds with one of those cans. The writing is rough. It's obviously been done in haste.'

Jessica turned to Shirley-Ann. 'What's your opinion?'

A difficult one. 'If it were me,' she said after a moment's consideration, 'I think I'd rather it was cleaned off now. It's going to ruin the party if you call the police. And it's bound to get in the papers.'

Jessica sighed. 'I can't win. All right. Rub it off.'

TWENTY-THREE

Julie was keen for some human contact after her long session with the Police National Computer. 'Ready to demonstrate your sleuthing skills, Mr Diamond? Let's match you against the PNC. Which one of the Bloodhounds has a police record?'

'Only one?'

'That's all.'

'The fellow with the mean-streets dog. Rupert Darby.'

She shrugged and smiled. 'You could have saved me nearly two hours of eye-strain. Two prison terms, of six months and eighteen months, for obtaining money by deception. Seven fines for drunkenness and one for indecency.'

'When was this?' Diamond asked.

'The indecency?'

'No, the bird.'

'1977 and 1983.'

'Long time ago. What was the scam?'

'I don't know. The PNC doesn't go into the details.'

'But you will, won't you, Julie? That's where the human brain scores over the computer.'

'It isn't the brain,' she said. 'It's hard slog.'

'Put a hard slogger on the job, then. Delegate, Julie. I do. And get the facts on the indecency, will you? That could mean anything from streaking at a test match to pissing in a shop doorway.'

She didn't complain. She wouldn't have told Diamond, but she was encouraged that the murder inquiry was back on track.

Diamond was off on another tack. 'Funny idea,' he said, 'calling a dog after a character in a book. We've got a cat – well, a kitten, really. Steph brought it home. Haven't thought of a name for it yet. I wouldn't call it Marlowe.'

'That wouldn't do,' Julie agreed. 'Is it a tom?'

'Yes.'

'You could call it Sherlock, or Wimsey, or Father Brown.'

He pulled a face. 'It'll let us know.'

Sitting in bed, clutching a mug of cocoa, Shirley-Ann told Bert about the writing on the Walsingham Gallery window. And why shouldn't she? It wasn't as if she had been asked to keep the incident to herself, though she appreciated that the words had been cleaned off in the hope that no one else would find out. She always told Bert everything. It would have made her feel furtive not to have spoken to him.

'Who did it, then?' he asked, yawning. He was already horizontal, physically tired. So much of his day was spent doing sport that if the truth were told he wasn't much of a sport at night.

'Wrote the words on the window? I've no idea,' said Shirley-Ann, with energy still to burn. Even the weekends were filled with football-refereeing that tired Bert. 'It could be anybody. Milo was at the party and so was Rupert, but I wouldn't read anything into that. It may have been done by someone who didn't come.'

'Someone bitter about not being invited?'

'Well, yes.'

'Who, for instance?'

'I didn't see Polly or Miss Chilmark there. I suppose either of them could have sneaked up and got busy with a spray-can.'

'Just out of spite?'

'I don't know them all that well, but I wouldn't put it past one of them. They're formidable ladies, those two.

190

The only thing I doubt is whether they'd use that way to register a protest.'

'It doesn't have to be one of the Bloodhounds,' Bert pointed out.

'Do you think so?' Shirley-Ann said dubiously.

'It could be some artist with a grudge. Someone whose work wasn't included in the exhibition.'

'I suppose that's possible,' she admitted, disinclined as she was to look outside the Bloodhounds.

'Someone who knows about the Narrowboat Murder,' said Bert. 'The thing that was written *does* refer to the murder, doesn't it?'

'I'm sure it does.'

'Plenty of people in Bath must have read the papers or seen something on TV. All the reports mentioned that the victim was at the Bloodhounds meeting earlier in the evening. Almost anyone could have linked Jessica to the murder.'

'So?'

He said wearily, 'So is there any point in trying to work it out?'

She was silent for a while. However, she remained sitting up, taking sips of the cocoa. Eventually she said, 'Bert, do you think there's anything in it?'

Bert twitched. He had almost dozed off. 'What?'

'I said do you think there's anything in it? Is it possible that she did for Sid?'

'Who – Jessica?'

'Mm.'

He said, 'I'm pretty tired, you know.'

'It isn't fair asking you,' said Shirley-Ann with more consideration. 'You haven't met her, so how can you have an opinion?'

There was an ironic laugh from under the quilt. 'You've told me enough about her. You never stop talking about that lot. If you want my opinion, yes, I think she's well capable of murder.'

'You *do? Jessica?*'

'All she had to do was follow the bloke – what's his name?'

'Sid.'

'Follow Sid after the meeting that night, catch him off guard and crack him over the head with some heavy object. A woman could do that as well as a man if she crept up behind him.'

'Why? Why would she do it?'

'Why would anyone do it? Nobody knows. All I'm saying is that she's as capable of clocking the bloke as anyone else. What age is she?'

'Around thirty, I'd guess.'

'Well, I tell you this. Most of the women in my over-forties group tonight could lay a man out cold with a blow on the skull, no problem. I wouldn't like to tangle with some of them.'

'But she liked Sid. She took him into the Moon and Sixpence a few times, she told me. She knew quite a bit about him, his job and everything. She said he had guts to come to the Bloodhounds. She admired him.'

'That doesn't mean she's innocent. She had a high opinion of him, you're saying. She believed he was all right. That's exactly the sort of person who gets angry and homicidal when it turns out they were mistaken.'

'I don't see Jessica like that at all, Bert. She isn't hot-headed.'

'Ice-cool, is she?'

'She's well in control, anyway.'

'Calculating?'

'Now you're twisting my words.'

For a time, no more was said. Bert began to breathe more evenly while Shirley-Ann weighed Jessica's capacity to kill. She finished her cocoa and put her Snow White mug on the bedside table. The clock showed it was past midnight. Bloody nuisance. Bert had really set her brain into overdrive, yet she needed her sleep in case she was offered another chance as tour guide in the morning. She spoke her thoughts aloud. 'I suppose if she found out there was another side to him . . . if he wasn't the placid, unassuming bloke she took him for, and she caught him in the act of letting himself into Milo's boat – which meant that he, Sid, of all people, was the stamp thief – then she might have got mad with him, but I still don't see it. Not Jessica. She's too intelligent. She operates in far more subtle ways. No, the only way I see Jessica getting violent is if . . .' She caught her breath at the idea, at the same time bending her legs to her chest and clasping her hands around her knees. 'That's it! They were in cahoots. They worked together. Are you listening, Bert? Jessica and Sid worked out this brilliant scheme to amaze the Bloodhounds. Sid was a security man, right? He knew how to beat the video cameras and special locks at the Postal Museum. And he had some way of getting into Milo's boat as well. I don't think he'd have done it by himself. It was Jessica who put him up to it. At those meetings at the Moon and Sixpence, they planned the Penny Black job. Sid's expertise and Jessica's intelligence – quite a combination. I reckon she made up those riddles. And together they devised a way of getting into Milo's narrowboat and placing the stamp in his copy of *The Hollow Man* so that it turned up at the meeting. Okay, what they did was dangerous and illegal, but they returned the stamp and they didn't expect anyone to work out how it was done. Only something went wrong. For some reason Sid decided to go back to the boat. Maybe he thought it was an opportunity to do some real burglary while Milo was talking to the police. Or he could have left some trace that he thought they were sure to find. Jessica was suspicious and followed him. She was furious. The perfect crime she'd planned was about to be undermined by Sid. She hit him over the head, locked him in and left. That's it, Bert! . . . Bert, are you listening?'

She grabbed Bert's shoulder and gave him a shake. He had drifted into a shallow sleep and heard nothing. He said from a long way off, 'Yes?'

'I said she did it, Bert. Jessica did for Sid.'

'All right,' muttered Bert apathetically.

'Only somebody worked it out and tried to make it public tonight. I wonder who.'

'Who what?'

'Who sprayed the words over Jessica's gallery window.'

'Someone with one of those aerosols, I expect,' said Bert in an interval of clarity.

'Well, you don't have to tell me that,' she said.

'Must have got some on their clothes,' added Bert. 'You can't use one of those things outdoors without some of the spray getting on your clothes.' It was his last contribution that night.

She pondered that for a time. Then something stirred in her memory that would keep her awake another two hours. She pressed her hands to her face and said, 'I thought it was dandruff. Well, would you ever?'

TWENTY-FOUR

So comprehensively has Bath been facelifted in the last twenty years that it is quite a treat to discover streets that have escaped the restorers and stonewashers. One charmingly down-at-heel example is Hay Hill, north of the centre, which is actually just a convenient short cut from Lansdown Road to the Vineyards and the Paragon. A short cut for pedestrians, that is to say, for no cars run through it. You know that Hay Hill will give some relief from Georgian formality as soon as you reach the betting office on the corner of Lansdown Road. A strip of worn paving descends between undistinguished eighteenth-century artisan houses. The dozen or so dwellings are irregular in style, height and colouring, and the railings fronting most of them supply only a semblance of order. The rest of the ironwork on view – basement grilles, inspection covers, lamp-posts and drainpipes – is a hotchpotch. Few of the windows match in style; in fact, some have been bricked up. Here and there graffiti scar the walls, but it might be argued that the people who painted one of the buildings in layers of pink, yellow and brown, like a monstrous cake, were guilty of vandalism before the marker-pen writers got to work.

To Hay Hill, then, came Diamond and Julie Hargreaves the next morning to call on Rupert Darby. Rupert's house was the one with more flake and crumble than any other, and with weeds growing up the walls.

The bell-push on the door may have been working; it was difficult to hear for the noise of traffic cruising down

Lansdown Road. Anyway, there was no response. Diamond tried rattling the letter-flap and instantly wished he hadn't. It was a plastic thing that fell off. A low, vibrating noise like a power-drill driving into wood came from inside. As he bent to look through the gap there was an almighty thump against the door, and he found himself inches from the bared teeth of a large dog.

He stepped back and turned his attention to the window, which was coated in dust. A faded gingham curtain blocked any view of the interior. After some unproductive tapping on the glass – the main panel had a crack the width of the frame – he went back to the door, tried the handle and discovered that it opened.

Julie warned, 'I wouldn't if I were you.'

But he had a confident way with dogs. Opening the door a fraction, he presented the back of his right hand for inspection. There was some sniffing, some contact with a moist nose and then a reassuring warm lick. He increased the gap just enough for Marlowe's brown head to look out. With German shepherd in its genes, this beast wasn't going to roll over and have its chest scratched, but it had quit growling.

'Show him your hand, Julie.'

This sounded like an order. He thought of adding, 'Trust me,' but he wasn't certain she would take encouragement from that.

She had two dogs of her own, and she knew enough to be cautious in a situation like this. After some hesitation she did as Diamond had done. There was no rending of flesh. By degrees Diamond opened the door fully and Marlowe padded out to the pavement. The big dog didn't growl any more, but neither did it make any concessions to friendship. It sniffed at their shoes, circled them, trotted to the house opposite and sprayed the neighbours' wall. Diamond took this as approval. He stepped through the open door.

A first impression of the interior was that this place was more of a crash-pad than a home. It smelt of stale beer

196

and old socks and dog. The board floor was littered with clothes, books, papers, crockery, beer-cans and cardboard boxes. In the far corner was a mattress and on it a body was lying covered by an army greatcoat.

Julie went to the window to admit more light. Dust peppered her hands when she tugged at the curtain. It hadn't been disturbed in months.

The body under the greatcoat spoke. A voice as mellifluous as Gielgud's, totally out of keeping with the surroundings, told them, 'Please go away, whoever you are, and try again at some civilised hour.'

Diamond said, 'It's gone ten, Mr Darby, and we're the police.'

Marlowe heard his master's voice and lolloped in from the street. Picking up a tin plate between his teeth, the big dog carried it across the room, leapt on the mattress and put in a claim for breakfast. There was a clang as the plate struck Rupert's head.

Rupert misinterpreted the knock. 'I can report you for this,' he said without stirring. 'It's police brutality and it's outrageous.'

'It's your dog,' Diamond told him. 'It's asking for food.'

'The hell with it. What's a dog for, if it doesn't keep the fuzz from marching into one's home?'

'Do you want us to feed it while you wash?'

'If you can find one of his cans. There might be some under the window.' Rupert gave a moan and stretched. One of his feet, wearing a striped sock, appeared from under the greatcoat. He propped himself up on one elbow, rubbed his eyes, and said, 'Is it the state of my head, or is one of you wearing a skirt?'

Diamond formally spoke their ranks and names. Expecting the usual snide remarks about female cops, Julie busied herself locating some tins of Pal under a beret and opening one for Marlowe.

Rupert was too sleepy for snide remarks. He needed all his concentration to stand up. His night attire (and no doubt the basis of his day attire also) was a T-shirt and boxer shorts. He tottered to an open doorway that must have led to whatever passed for a bathroom in this unedifying set-up.

Diamond warned him, 'We haven't got all day.'

Rupert riposted over the sound of running water, 'My day doesn't start till noon.'

He emerged after a few minutes wrapped in a grey blanket and cradling a mug of coffee. 'I'd offer you some, but I can't find a spare cup. You're welcome to look if you wish.'

Diamond spoke for them both. 'I don't think we want any. What we'd appreciate is a place to sit down.'

Two chairs had to be cleared of the items heaped on them. Rupert found his beret and jammed it on his head. Apparently it was a vital accessory, though like everything else in this place it looked shabby, speckled with white particles that he didn't bother to brush off. He squatted on his mattress wrapped in the blanket, looking like an exotic species of toadstool.

'Convenient place you have here,' Diamond said politely, since there was nothing polite he could say about the way it looked.

'You mean with the Lansdown Arms at one end and the Paragon Bar and Bistro at the other?' said Rupert, with a grin. 'Yes, that was a consideration, I admit. Tell me what this is about.'

'We're inquiring into the death of Sidney Towers.'

His face lit up. 'Thank God for that. I thought it was something I'd done.'

'Isn't it?' said Diamond.

'Certainly not.' The shrill note in his voice made it sound as if he were the last person you ought to suspect of anything.

'You're one of this group who call themselves Bloodhounds, right?'

'That's no crime, is it?' said Rupert, now ready to defend his reputation. 'Well, the name may be a crime, I grant you. A gift for the gutter press. It wasn't my suggestion, officer. If I had my way, we'd call it the Crime Noir Club and attract a different class of member.'

'When did you join?'

'At least three years ago. I think only Polly Wycherley and Milo were ahead of me. No, I tell a lie. The Grand Duchess was already in.'

'You must mean Miss Chilmark.'

He smiled. 'She who must be indulged.'

'And Sid?'

'Joined six months after me, though you would hardly have noticed. He made being inconspicuous into an art form.'

'You don't sound all that enamoured of the other members, Mr Darby, yet you stuck with the club. Why?'

'Oh, it gets me out of my local for a couple of hours.' Rupert gave his smile that resembled a country churchyard. 'And I have a mission. I want to persuade those poor, blinkered bastards to read some books that deal with the real crimes of our time and the misery and despair that they engender. You can't make converts overnight. They're fixated by ancient puzzle stories with maps in the front and snobbish characters suffering from xenophobia.'

'What's that?'

Julie murmured, 'Hatred of foreigners.'

Rupert went on, 'And they also talk endlessly about timetables.' Without more preamble, he launched into an extraordinary monologue. ' "By your leave, my lord," declared the inspector, with a deferential cough. "There is only one possible killer. He left here at 7.10 and got to the station by 7.14 to catch the 7.15, but the 7.15 was delayed because of the fog, and the first train in was the 7.07, running twelve minutes late. On the 7.15, which actually arrived at 7.32, he would have missed his connection at 7.27, but the 7.07 got him to Crewe by 7.25 and he caught the 7.27 and was in Little Fartington precisely at 8." ' Rupert paused and grinned wickedly. ' "Or so he believed. Actually it was still only seven o'clock. He knew how to use a timetable, but *he didn't know about British Summer Time*, so the murderer has to be the German, Herr Von Krapp."'

This earned some genuine laughter. 'Did you make that up, or was it done from memory?' Diamond asked.

'I'm still pissed from last night,' Rupert said, without answering the question. 'My point is that these people know nothing of real crime.'

'And you're well qualified to tutor them.'

Diamond got a sharp look for that. 'If you mean that I read books that give it to you straight,' said Rupert, 'with the smell of blood and the pain and the suffering, yes.'

Tempting as it was to go into Rupert's criminal record, Diamond held off. At this stage he needed the man in good humour. 'Tell me about the meeting last Monday,' he said. 'You were late, I believe.'

'Very likely,' said Rupert airily. 'I'm not much of a timekeeper. When I got there, Marlowe – that's my dog –' Marlowe lifted his head from the plate of Pal and looked round. 'Marlowe happened to go in ahead of me. He likes the meetings. As far as I can gather, the poor animal – who's just an overgrown puppy – well, look at him – unwittingly caused a panic by showing affection to that old bat, Miss Chilmark. I don't know why. She's never done a blessed thing to deserve a friendly lick from Marlowe or anyone else, for that matter. A more disagreeable old crone would be hard to find. When I got in, she was acting up, making a big production number out of it and having hysterics. It took a bag over her face to calm her down. Thank God for Jessica. Jessica Shaw.'

'We know Mrs Shaw,' said Diamond.

'Capable woman. I didn't see the end of this performance. I had to take Marlowe next door to the Saracen's Head and settle him there with some drinking chums of mine. Of course he was no trouble at all. When I got back to the crypt, order was restored. Well, of course it was. Milady manufactured the whole melodrama so that she should have her way. You should have seen the triumphant look she gave me.'

'And then?'

'Oh, the new woman read us a short story.'

'The new woman?'

'Shirley-Ann Miller,' said Julie.

'Is that her name?' said Rupert. 'I never discovered. She joined a couple of weeks ago.' He chuckled. 'And regrets it now, no doubt. As I was saying, she read us something by Stanley Ellin, an American with a nice gift for the macabre. After that, I made some innocent remark that Polly took personally, silly old coot. They're such wimps, these people. What's wrong with some lively confrontation? Milo attempted to calm us down with his piece on the locked room puzzle. We all resigned ourselves to being bored out of our skulls for the rest of the evening – well *I* did – and then, of course, he gobsmacked us all by opening his book and finding the bloody stamp.'

'Good. I'd like to hear more about that,' said Diamond. 'Can you remember what was said?'

'Give me a break, I'm barely awake yet!' He took a sip of coffee. 'As far as I recollect, Milo went crimson and kept saying what happened was impossible. I found it excruciatingly funny and said so. I remember trying to rib Milo about it, but he was far too shaken to take a joke. His first comment was that one of us must have planted the stamp on him somehow. Then he backtracked a bit. After all, whoever pinched it in the first place had committed a serious crime. Milo had to admit that he hadn't let the book leave his hands, not even when Miss Chilmark was throwing her tantrum. So without a clue as to how the thing was done, we got around to talking about what to do next. Polly – our top banana – said firmly that Milo should go straight to the police.'

'Polly made this suggestion?'

'Yes.'

'You're sure?'

'Yes, Polly. Does that remove her from your list of suspects? Have you met her?'

'Not yet,' said Diamond.

'Watch her eyes when she smiles. They don't change at all. But Milo was reluctant to throw himself on the mercy of the Old Bill. He expected a workover from you people. Well, he's more fruit than vegetable, isn't he? I'm sure you treated him with the utmost consideration, but there was solidarity from some of us. I was willing to keep quiet, and said so. So was Jessica. As for the new woman, Sally . . . ?'

'Shirley-Ann.'

'Thank you. I may be muddled about the name, but I've got her number all right: the sort of bright-eyed little body who wears a knitted hat and knows about homeopathy. She suggested he sent the stamp back by post. Good thinking. He might have got away with that. The trouble was, as Jessica pointed out, we all had to agree to button our lips and two of the company weren't willing to do that.'

'Polly and who else?'

'Who do you think?'

'Miss Chilmark?' said Diamond.

'Right. The Grand Duchess.'

'How about Sid? Did anyone ask him?'

'Yes. He said he could stay quiet.' Rupert threw back his head and guffawed. 'Sid offering to stay quiet! It was the funniest thing all evening. He should have taken a bow for that. None of them saw the joke except me. So there it was. Two in favour of blowing the whistle and four against. But of course to work, the vote had to be unanimous. Milo isn't slow on the uptake. He could see that. He marched off to do his duty as a responsible member of the public.'

'Leaving the rest of you to talk it over?'

Rupert shook his head. 'There was no more talk, squire. The meeting broke up. I've no idea what time it was.'

'Eight-forty-five, I was told,' said Diamond. 'What did you do?'

'Went into the Saracen's to collect my dog.'

'Who with?'

'No one. We all went our different ways. I may have had one drink. I wasn't there long. I rescued Marlowe and took him for a walk. The poor old tyke was bursting. Some people's idea of fun is tanking up my dog with Guinness.'

'So where did he lift his leg?'

'This is rather personal, isn't it? Along the river bank.'

'And then did you come back here?'

'Yes. I needed to eat by then.'

'Can anyone vouch for your movements?'

'I can.'

'I mean an independent witness, Mr Darby.'

'No one I can think of. Look, you don't seriously suspect—'

'Have you got wheels?'

'What?'

'Wheels. A car.'

'Now, come on,' said Rupert, drawing the blanket closer around him.

'Have you?'

He sighed. 'An ancient Lada that I keep in Beehive Yard by special arrangement with a drinking chum who has a business down there. I suppose you'd like to know if it's taxed and insured.'

'No,' said Diamond. 'I'd like to know if you used it last Monday evening.'

'Absolutely not, seeing that the tax ran out in August.'

'Would that stop you?'

Rupert wasn't meant to respond, and didn't. Most of the questions he couldn't have answered more directly, thanks to the conditioning of his education. He was a pushover, the type of suspect Diamond generally found easy to entrap – when there was anything inconsistent. There was the police record with this one, too. Yet he

203

was a fellow who made you smile, even when he was on the defensive. His comments on the other Bloodhounds had brought them vividly to life. It would be almost a pity to put the boot in.

'Fair enough,' said Diamond. 'Let's talk about Sid Towers.'

'There isn't much to say, is there?'

'Did you ever meet him in any other place than the crypt of St Michael's?'

'You mean the pub afterwards?'

'I mean anywhere at all.'

Rupert closed his eyes in thought. 'Aboard Milo's boat last Christmas. The Bloodhounds' party. Sid was there, trying to merge with the woodwork.'

'Nowhere else?'

'Can't remember an occasion.'

'Perhaps he was in touch some other way,' suggested Diamond. 'A letter?'

'The phone?' Julie contributed.

'What on earth about?' asked Rupert, his gaze moving suspiciously from Diamond to Julie. 'He and I had practically nothing in common.'

Diamond couldn't hold off any longer. He'd kept the goodwill flowing past the point when it was still productive. His voice took on a harder tone. 'I have to think of every possibility, Mr Darby. Let's face facts. Sid worked with a security firm. They keep files on people. I want to know if he got nasty with you. Demanded money in return for his silence over your prison record.'

A muscle twitched in Rupert's cheek.

'You wouldn't want your literary friends to know you've done bird, would you?' Diamond pressed him. 'Obtaining money by deception. Twice. And the other convictions aren't too edifying. How many fines is it for drunkenness? Indecency? What are you – a flasher? What would Miss Chilmark say about that if she found out?'

'She wouldn't say a word. She'd be hyperventilating again,' said Rupert, buying time with an easy jibe. There was a pause while he adjusted mentally. Then: 'If you want to know, it was a joke that misfired. I was up for the fifth time before Bath Magistrates on a drunk and disorderly charge and it was December 23rd. After the beak fined me fifty quid I lowered my trousers and treated him to a view of my backside with the words Merry Christmas stuck to it. It was a paper decoration off a Christmas cake. I was done for contempt of court and indecency. "Pull up your trousers and face the bench, Mr Darby. You may have thought that seasonal goodwill justifies some leniency over this disgusting exhibition, but the law is not to be mocked. You are fined one hundred pounds for the contempt and a conviction for indecency will be entered on your record. Merry Christmas to you, too, and, let us hope, a sober New Year."'

Diamond wasn't smiling. His disappointment was crushing; after Julie's work on the PNC he'd really thought he had a handle on Rupert Darby. The blackmail theory had just sunk like a punctured balloon. The man wasn't a sexual deviant. He was a clown. A couple of prison terms for fraudulent deals weren't going to worry an extrovert like this.

He turned to Julie and told her they were leaving.

They passed St Michael's as they returned down Broad Street. Diamond decided to look into the crypt. 'It's where the bloody thing started, Julie. And the way things are going, we'd better send up a prayer while we're there.'

Inside, a playgroup had taken over for the morning. While three-year-olds were squabbling over wooden trains it was difficult to picture the Bloodhounds in session discussing locked room murders. The woman in charge was monopolised by a tearful girl who wouldn't budge from her lap, so Diamond sorted the problem of the boys and the trains. It was a wonder to Julie that his bulk and his gruff manner didn't frighten children. She'd seen plenty of adults in awe of him. The reason seemed to be that he didn't patronise kids; he listened to them solemnly and talked back to them with sincerity. He'd told her once that his wife Stephanie had miscarried several times. He'd said nothing else.

Now that harmony was restored, they looked at the layout of the crypt. There was a row of hooks near the door. The playgroup supervisor had her coat hanging there and the children's were beside it, tiny garments with gloves attached to elastic and dangling from the sleeves.

'This, presumably, is where Sid Towers switched Milo Motion's keys,' said Diamond. 'Fished the bunch out of his coat pocket, slipped the original off the key-ring and replaced it with a key he'd bought from Foxton's. He could turn his back to the circle of chairs and make the switch without being seen. Simple.'

'The quiet man. Everyone under-estimated him,' said Julie.

'Except wily John Wigfull.'

She smiled, 'That really irks, doesn't it?'

He nodded. 'But I blame myself.'

Back at Manvers Street, there was a message asking Diamond to contact PC Hogarth.

'Who's he?'

'I thought you knew, sir,' said the woman who had taken the call. 'He seemed to know you.'

'Where was he calling from?'

'I'm afraid he didn't say.'

'What was it about?'

'He wanted to speak to you personally.'

'Well, that's a fat lot of use. He isn't one of my detectives, I can tell you that.'

Julie hadn't heard of the man either.

It was another hour before PC Hogarth called in again.

'He said he's down at Avoncliff, sir,' said the woman from the wireless room.

'Avoncliff? Avoncliff?' A light bulb switched on in his head. 'Jesus Christ. The divers.'

TWENTY-FIVE

Without looking up, Julie was aware of someone in a brown suit, carrying a tray. She was sure from the way he was moving steadily between the tables in the police canteen that he would come to hers. Her first impulse was to leave, but she still had most of her lunch in front of her. Although she rarely ate much at this time – today's meal was just a tuna salad and some yoghurt – she knew some food was essential to get her through the afternoon.

'You don't mind?' John Wigfull said, as he pulled out a chair.

She minded, but she knew he wouldn't go away whatever she replied. A grin like broken glass was spread under that great broom of a moustache. He wasted no time over pleasantries. 'I hear your boss goofed over the divers, poor blighters. What was that old catchphrase: "Don't forget the diver"?'

'There was never any question of forgetting them,' Julie found herself distorting the truth in defence of Diamond. 'It was always going to be a long job.'

'A soul-destroying job, I should think. Not even a proper diving assignment. It's only a few feet deep at the most. More like wading than diving. They weren't too thrilled, I was told.'

'Really?'

'It's a bit much, being left that long.'

'They were just getting on with the job, I expect,' she said casually. 'They didn't want one of us standing over them.'

208

'You're very loyal, Julie. Always have been.'

She forked some food into her mouth.

He didn't hand out compliments without wanting some return on them. The pumping started. 'How's it going? Is he getting anywhere with the murder?'

She answered with as much conviction as she could muster, 'We're following several leads.'

Wigfull allowed that claim to wither and die in silence. 'Personally,' he said finally, 'I'd have handled it differently.'

'Oh, yes?'

'I'd have given you more freedom to act. He doesn't delegate, does he?'

'If you don't mind, it's no business of mine to discuss Mr Diamond's handling of the case,' she was quick to tell him.

'Yes, but what's your part in the investigation? Sitting in front of the PNC. Don't deny it. I saw you yesterday. You should be out conducting interviews, not stuck in front of a ruddy screen by the hour. That's a sure way to get a headache.'

She couldn't resist saying, 'I thought you were all in favour of information technology, Mr Wigfull.'

He swayed to one side, as if riding a blow. He was still cockahoop over Diamond's lapse. 'You can say that again, Julie, but I wouldn't put my best DI on the job. We employ civilians to operate the hardware. Whose form were you checking? One of the Bloodhounds?'

'It was just routine,' she said, fencing as well as she could.

'Leaving no stone unturned, eh?'

'Well . . .'

He followed up quickly. 'The divers will vouch for that, poor buggers. They must have run out of stones to turn over.' This amused him vastly. The whole table shook and he spilled some of his coffee.

Julie remained impassive.

He went on to say, 'He isn't a team man, is he? If you worked for me—'

'But I don't,' Julie cut in, wanting to put a quick end to this.

'Any time you'd care to . . .'

'Thanks,' she said in a tone that made clear how unwelcome the prospect was.

Now the offer turned into a threat. 'It could happen sooner than you think. I sorted the stamp theft, didn't I? Proved that Towers was the man and showed how he did it. That didn't go unnoticed. Someone's going to give me a crack at the murder soon. They want a result.'

End of commercial. The talk turned to performance-related pay. Wigfull was one of the few at Manvers Street in favour of it. He had nothing to fear from appraisals, he said.

When she finished and was carrying her tray back to the collection point, Wigfull called after her.

She turned. 'Yes?'

'Tell your boss.'

'Tell him what?'

'What I said: "Don't forget the diver."'

That afternoon there was some rare autumn sunshine and Shirley-Ann Miller took a slow stroll through Sydney Gardens and along the canal towpath. In the winter months this is a part of the city where you may walk for stretches without seeing anyone, yet once it was the fashionable place to be and be seen, a park you paid an entrance fee to visit, with a bandstand, grottoes, a labyrinth and regular firework displays. It was all so cherished by the Georgians and Victorians that when the canal-builders and railway engineers wanted to cut through, elaborate measures were insisted upon to disguise the construction. So there are tunnels, balustrades and wrought-iron bridges that are a credit to the planners, though rarely seen by modern visitors. Shirley-Ann was not the sort who looked for solitude, but after a morning doing her damnedest to hand out leaflets about the bus tour and getting not much response and a couple of vulgar suggestions, she wanted a break from people.

She had decided to walk as far as Top Lock, along the last, spectacular section of the canal before it joins the Avon. Here, after a wooded stretch, you suddenly look right and become aware that you are on an escarpment above most of the city except the church spires. That view always lifted Shirley-Ann's spirits. This lunchtime she would walk as far as the lock-keeper's cottage, a small gothic building of great charm restored by the Canal Trust – in no way as notable or noble as the sights she pointed out when she was giving her commentary on the bus, but pleasing to Shirley-Ann because she thought of it as a personal discovery. Today, however, she was distracted along the way by a discovery of a different kind. At Sydney Wharf Bridge, where George Street crosses the canal, the towpath switches sides. She climbed the cobbled slope on one side and passed over the bridge to rejoin the path by way of the descending steps by the Mercedes-Benz showroom. Her view of the towpath was hidden until she stepped on to it – which was why she was surprised by the man and woman coming towards her. She felt herself blush scarlet. The woman was Jessica Shaw.

Jessica, the murderer.

She did for Sid.

After the long, sleepless night when her mind had fizzed with the facts that pointed to Jessica's guilt, this was the last person on earth Shirley-Ann wished to meet.

Worse still, the man was A.J. Meeting Jessica at all was rotten luck; catching her out with her fancy man was a double blow from the fates. Of course she'd been sure in her mind that Jessica had something going with A.J., but up to now the liaison hadn't been paraded in front of her.

On the narrow towpath she couldn't avoid them without making it obvious.

They weren't actually arm in arm or holding hands,

but so close to each other that they were practically in contact. Recognising her, they broke off the earnest conversation they were having. Jessica said, probably in case A.J. hadn't spotted who it was, 'Shirley-Ann, what a nice surprise.'

A.J. half-lifted his hand in greeting and said, 'Small world.'

Shirley-Ann couldn't have felt more embarrassed if she had caught them in bed. She managed to say, 'Isn't this a treat? The weather, I mean.'

'Glorious.' Jessica seemed unfazed. In a short, wine-red padded coat trimmed with black fur and with black leggings and ankle-boots, she looked more suitably kitted for the catwalk than the towpath.

Since the weather hadn't yielded much in the way of conversation, Shirley-Ann remarked, 'I passed some swans back there. A pair, with their family. At least five cygnets. Fairly grown up, but really sweet.'

'I expect we'll see them, then,' said Jessica.

'They're worth looking out for, and the place is easy to spot. There's some pampas grass and a little wild area where they nest. They mate for life, don't they?' *Dear God*, she thought, *what am I saying?*

'I've no idea,' said Jessica evenly.

'Nor me,' said A.J.

Words, words in profusion, were Shirley-Ann's instinctive means of dealing with embarrassment. She had a horror of silences. She had to communicate something to get her over the mating swans gaffe. 'By the way, I did enjoy the preview last night. A party like that must have cost you an arm and a leg – all the buck's fizz and the refreshments. It seemed as if the whole of Bath had crowded in there. I hope you sold lots of pictures.'

'We just about covered our costs,' said Jessica. 'An evening like that isn't only about the money you take. It's a way of spreading the word.'

'PR,' said A.J.

Jessica added, 'Most of them there last night have never

212

bought a piece of work from the gallery and never will, but that isn't the point.'

'I understand.'

'It was a near-disaster, actually,' she went on. 'I'm still hopping mad about that vile thing that was written on the gallery window.'

'We've dismissed that,' said A.J. quickly. 'We agreed to erase it from our minds, didn't we?' He was addressing Shirley-Ann now.

'Absolutely,' she confirmed with all the conviction she could summon up considering she had thought about little else since the party.

Jessica said, 'I'd like to know who it was. I've got my suspicions.'

'Let go, Jess,' A.J. urged her, talking like a husband.

'If that's their game, they could try again.'

'It was a prank,' said A.J. 'Someone with a warped sense of humour. You don't think anyone could seriously suspect you of murder? I mean, you had a lot of time for the bloke who was killed. He was a bit of a loner, you told me, lacking in confidence. You took him under your wing.'

Took him under your wing and used him to pinch the Penny Black, thought Shirley-Ann cynically. Then clobbered the poor beggar because he stepped out of line and put the plot at risk. She was finding it a great test to keep her conclusions to herself.

'That isn't the point,' said Jessica. 'We all know I wouldn't have harmed Sid in a million years, but if this evil-minded bastard points the finger at me again, I'm going to the police.'

'He won't,' said A.J.

'How do you know it wasn't a woman?' Jessica demanded, and Shirley-Ann, with her weakness for speaking first and thinking afterwards, almost told her why.

A.J. grinned and said, 'Fair point, but I'm sure it's a closed book now. Hadn't we better get back and open the gallery?'

They moved on.

Shirley-Ann's thoughts were in ferment again as she continued towards Top Lock. She didn't give a thought to the marvellous view or the cottage. She was puzzled over the relationship between those two. Was it the modern morality that had stopped them from showing any embarrassment at being seen in each other's company? True, she had seen them together before, in the gallery, but this was something else, surely, being met along a secluded towpath. It was evident to anyone that they knew each other extremely well, almost like brother and sister. Yes, that was *exactly* the feeling she got from them, an intimacy that didn't give rise to shame.

Up to now Shirley-Ann had always believed she could tell if a woman was concealing a relationship. She'd spotted the signs quite early in several of her married friends. This was baffling because there was no suggestion of concealment. In A.J.'s company, Jessica behaved as if she had every right to spend major time alone with him.

And there was still a huge question in Shirley-Ann's mind. Where did Sid Towers fit into this ménage? To plot the theft of the Penny Black, there must have been meetings with Sid, long meetings to work on the details of an intricate plot. They must have cased the Postal Museum and talked over ways of gaining entry. They must have worked out their diversionary tactics, the riddles, and how to publicise them. There was the challenge – still a mystery to Shirley-Ann – of getting into Milo's locked boat. All of this must have been talked through by Sid and Jessica. Long sessions, debating ways of carrying out such an elaborate plot. How had Jessica achieved this without alerting A.J. or her husband? Or was either of them involved as well?

She walked on, unenlightened.

'He said what?'

Julie repeated the phrase for Diamond's benefit. '"Don't forget the diver."'

214

'Ah.'

'His idea of a joke.'

'It's one of those radio catch-phrases, if I'm not mistaken. When I was a kid we listened to the radio a lot.' He eased back in his chair, ready to reminisce, surprisingly untroubled by Wigfull's barbed message. 'I enjoyed them. *Ray's a Laugh*, *Take it from Here*, *Educating Archie* and, of course, *The Goons*. The characters had their set phrases. All they had to do was repeat them each week and the audience would be rolling in the aisles. And applauding.' He smiled. 'Mind, "Don't forget the diver" was before my time or Wigfull's.'

'I should hope so,' said Julie. 'I looked it up. It goes back to the nineteen-twenties.'

'The *twenties*?'

'It seems there was a one-legged man who used to dive off the pier for pennies at New Brighton. It was his catch-phrase in the first place. Then it was taken up by Tommy Handley during the war.'

'That would be *ITMA*.'

'Yes.'

'I don't remember *ITMA* either,' said Diamond. 'Did John have any other gags to share with you?'

'That was the only one,' said Julie. Truth to tell, she'd thought twice about passing that one on, but it was obvious that something had put her boss into a sunny mood. When she'd walked into his office he'd been humming 'Yellow Submarine'. 'No, there was another joke,' she said, 'but it was unintended. He expects to take over the case.'

He chuckled. 'I've heard that one before, too.'

'Once he did take over,' she reminded him.

'Only after I resigned. It's not going to happen again.' He opened the drawer in front of him and took out a rusty object and let it fall on the desk with a metallic clunk. 'Keys, Julie. A bunch of keys. The reason those divers got in touch was that they'd finished the job.'

'Those are . . . ?'

'The keys Milo Motion dropped into the canal.'

'Brilliant.' She understood his singing now. 'So now we know Milo was telling the truth about where he lost them.'

'Yes. Only there's more to it than that.' He took a padlock from the same desk drawer. 'This is the one that was on the door of the *Mrs Hudson* on the evening Sid Towers was found dead. Watch.'

He picked up the bunch of keys and selected one, and a powdering of rust dropped on to the desk. He inserted the key into the lock and turned it. The shackle sprang open. Still holding the padlock, he watched for Julie to react.

She put her hand to her mouth.

'Say it,' he said.

She was frowning. 'You say that's the padlock that was on the boat?'

He nodded.

'And those are Milo's original keys?'

'Yes.'

'Then it wasn't a substitution. According to John Wigfull's theory, Sid Towers fitted a new padlock to the boat, but that can't be so. This must be the original padlock. We've been working on a false assumption.'

For a man who had been working on a false assumption, Diamond didn't look at all downhearted.

Julie said, 'John Wigfull's theory about the locked room doesn't work after all.'

'Right, Julie. He's up shit creek without a paddle.'

A fresh thought struck her. 'Aren't we also?'

'Yes,' he said blithely. 'And isn't it refreshing?'

TWENTY-SIX

'Aren't you going to tell John Wigfull he was wrong?'
Julie asked.

'Not yet,' Diamond told her. 'What time is it?'

'Twenty to four, near enough.'

'Jiminy Cricket!'

'Something you forgot?'

'Get your coat. We have an appointment at four with
Miss Chilmark.'

'An appointment? Sounds like the dentist.'

'Miss C. is the sort of woman you don't visit without
prior notice. I fixed it this morning.'

'And you want me there?'

'In case she has an attack of the vapours.'

'Oh, thanks,' she said, flushing at the man's insensitivity
to her rank and experience. 'What do I bring – smelling
salts and a paper bag?'

'Just a pair of handcuffs.'

Julie's eyes opened wide. Her resentment was put on
hold. 'You don't seriously think she's the murderer?'

'I'm seriously asking you to have a set of cuffs with
you.'

The address, appropriately for someone of Miss Chilmark's
reputation, was the Paragon, a terrace dating from the
eighteenth century. Jane Austen stayed there when she
first came to Bath. It was in the area they had visited that
morning, actually quite close to Rupert's seedy abode in
Hay Hill. Rather to Julie's surprise, Diamond proposed
to walk there.

'Why not?' he said. 'We won't be late if we step out.'

'But if you're planning to bring her in . . .'

'You think the lady might object to walking half a mile in handcuffs?' He grinned at the picture it conveyed. 'If necessary we'll radio in for transport. All right?'

Diamond was not a quick walker, so the timing was about right. They stepped up to a white painted door at two minutes past the hour. The gracious curve of the Palladian terrace stretched away in pleasing perspective. Traffic zoomed past unendingly, but the broad pavement with its triple-stepped kerb kept the vehicles from encroaching too obviously on the Georgian formality.

After some delay the door was opened by a frail white-haired old lady in a lavender-coloured suit.

Diamond was slightly thrown. This wasn't the kind of person he'd been led to expect. 'Miss Chilmark?'

'I'm afraid you've come to the wrong door. She lives in the basement. Don't worry. It happens all the time.' She extended a shaky hand towards the railings to their right.

Miss Chilmark in the basement? They leaned over the railings and peered down. True, it was in better order than basements generally are, whitewashed, clear of litter and with a dwarf conifer in a pot by the door. They went down the stairs.

The bell was answered quickly by a sturdier woman, probably twenty years younger, who ushered them inside. The light was poor down there. Diamond's strongest impression of Miss Chilmark was of the heavy floral scent that wafted from her. In the cramped entrance he couldn't avoid passing so close that his eyes watered. She was in a black jacket over a garish multi-coloured dress that rustled when she moved. She glittered at the ears, throat and fingers.

'We came to the wrong door,' Diamond explained, just to get the conversation started, but it was an unfortunate start.

'Oh,' said Miss Chilmark in a long, low note of despair. 'Did you tell her who you were?'

'No, ma'am. Simply asked for you and got directed down here.'

This wasn't reassurance enough. 'Where's the police car? I suppose she saw that.'

He told her that they had come on foot, and got such an improved reaction that he wished he had started with it. They were led through a narrow hallway at some risk to the china plates clipped to the walls. Shown into what Miss Chilmark announced as her drawing room, they had a first impression of a dry atmosphere smelling like the inside of a biscuit tin. It was a place noticeably less colourful than its owner. Faded Indian carpets on a wood-block floor. Pale blue emulsioned walls with a number of gilt-framed portraits of po-faced Victorians and smug, tweed-suited figures from between the wars, judging by their clothes. Two ancient armchairs and a settee with blue and beige covers. A gas fire from the nineteen-sixties with a mantelpiece over it, on which were six or seven books and some rock specimens acting as paperweights for letters. Above that a large print of a cathedral with a spire.

'You see, it isn't a basement at all from this side,' Miss Chilmark was quick to point out, striding to the window to draw the chintz curtain further aside. 'I have the ground floor and the garden.'

'This is because it's built on a slope?'

'Yes. That's Walcot Street at the bottom. The whole house belongs to me, only it's too much for a single lady, so I let out the other floors.'

This might have been more credible if she had retained the floor above as well, with the front door access. She was not the kind of woman who willingly moved into a basement in her own house, even with the view of Walcot Street from the rear. The furnishings told a different, more convincing tale; that this was the last retreat of someone who had known more affluent times.

'Salisbury, isn't it?' Julie remarked, having stepped to the fireplace to admire the print.

219

'The tallest spire in England,' Miss Chilmark said with some pride. 'And built seven hundred years ago of Chilmark stone.'

'You own a quarry?' said Diamond.

'The stone came from the village of Chilmark.'

'You own a village?'

'Of course not.' Lesson One: she had little sense of humour. 'I thought everybody had heard of Chilmark stone. It's known as the architects' stone, because it's unmatched as a building material. Salisbury Cathedral, Chichester, Wilton House. I'm afraid my best sherry ran out when I had some visitors at the weekend and my wine merchant hasn't delivered yet. Would you care for Earl Grey tea instead?'

He told her not to bother. 'We're here to investigate a crime. You heard about the death of Sid Towers, no doubt.'

'Dreadful,' said Miss Chilmark. 'Such an inoffensive man. Why do these things always happen to the nicest people?'

'Is that a fact?' Diamond said, tempted to challenge such a sweeping statement, but needing to move on. 'You and he belonged to the same club, of course. The Bloodhounds.'

'Yes.'

'You're one of the senior members, right?'

'I joined a long time ago, so I suppose I'm entitled to be so described.'

'Before Sid?'

'Yes. Why don't you sit down?'

Acting on the suggestion, he felt the shape of a spring press into his rump, confirming that the settee, like its owner, had seen better days. 'We're finding it difficult to get a sense of what Sid Towers was like. Maybe you can help us, ma'am. Outside the Bloodhounds, did you know him at all?'

She reddened. 'What on earth are you implying, Super-intendent?'

'Is the answer "no"?'

'Of course it is.'

'I meant nothing defamatory. He worked in a security firm. What's the name? Impregnable. Have you had any dealings with Impregnable, Miss Chilmark?'

'I can't think why you imagine I should.'

'Have you got an alarm system, for example?'

'On the house? Certainly not. One of those bells would be unthinkable on a listed building like this.'

'Security inside? Sensors, fingerbolts, window locks?'

'I have excellent locks. I've no need for anything else.'

'That's clear, then,' said Diamond. 'On the evening he died, last Monday, you went to a meeting of the Bloodhounds. I'd be grateful if you would tell me what you remember of that evening, and of Sid in particular.'

She clicked her tongue. 'It was all extremely distressing for me personally, I can tell you that.'

'Before you tell me that, what happened at the very start? Were you the first to arrive that evening?'

'No, Polly – Mrs Wycherley – was there before me, and so was poor Mr Towers.'

'Those two arrived first? I want you to think hard about this. When you got there, were they in conversation?'

'Mr Towers never had anything amounting to a conversation with anyone.'

'Where were they standing?'

'How do you mean?'

'It's clear, isn't it? Where was Mrs Wycherley?'

'She wasn't standing at all. She was already seated inside the circle. We arrange the chairs in a circle.'

'You do this yourselves?'

'Yes, whoever gets there first. I helped Mr Motion the previous Monday, when we happened to be the first there. On this occasion he was a little late, held up by the traffic. He drives, you know, from Limpley Stoke, where the boat is.'

221

'So Sid and Polly Wycherley must have got the room ready this week?'

'I presume so. I wasn't there early enough to see.'

'Polly's the chairman, isn't she?'

'She does her best,' said Miss Chilmark, examining the back of her hand.

'You sound as if you don't have complete confidence.'

'Oh, I'm old-fashioned enough to expect a chairman to lead the discussion. On this occasion I took some initiative myself and it was generally welcomed, I may say.'

'How did that come about?'

'Well, at the start of the meeting – this was before the whole thing descended into chaos – I suggested that we applied our experience of detective stories to a discussion of the real crime that happened in our own city – the theft of that stamp from the Postal Museum.'

Diamond glanced towards Julie and then back to Miss Chilmark. 'Did you now? What made you think of that?'

'As soon as I read the report in the *Chronicle* I knew it was right up our street. For once we had the chance to test our wits on a real unsolved crime.'

'Can you remember what was said?'

'I have a very clear recollection, yes. First, we addressed the question of why it was done, stealing such a well-known stamp. Mrs Shaw, the lady from the Walsingham Gallery, who isn't backward in putting across her opinions, gave us the theory that it was stolen at the behest of some fanatical collector. Miss Miller, who joined only the previous week, thought it was more likely that a ransom would be demanded. She even had a theory as to how the money could be collected through a secret bank account in Switzerland. Then they turned to me, and I moved the debate on to the far more intriguing question of the riddles that were sent by the thief.'

'Ah, the riddles.'

'I had copies with me. We quickly decided that it would be sensible to apply our minds to the latest one.'

'"*Whither Victoria and with whom,*"' chanted Julie.

'Yes.'

'And did anyone throw any light on it?' asked Diamond.

A look of self-satisfaction passed fleetingly over Miss Chilmark's face. 'I flatter myself that I did. As a graduate in English Literature I was able to demonstrate that the two riddles had textual similarities that suggested they were composed by the same person – the archaisms such as the use of "thee" in the one case and "whither" in the other, for example.'

'Very astute,' said Diamond. 'And what was your answer to the riddle?'

'Oh, we didn't get that far,' said Miss Chilmark. 'This was the point when that degenerate chose to appear and chaos ensued.'

'You're speaking of Rupert Darby now. This incident.'

'Only the latest in a series of incidents,' said Miss Chilmark, going pink at the memory. 'He behaves deplorably. He has from the beginning. One looks to the Chair for discipline, or at least some effort to maintain order. She doesn't check him. One week without so much as a word of warning he arrived with the dog – a savage brute – and expected us to ignore it. A large, untrained, malodorous, terrifying dog. Mrs Wycherley did nothing about it, in spite of my protests. Last week it came into the circle and shook its coat, drenching us all and ruining my clothes. This week it attacked me.'

'Bit you?'

'I'm sure it meant to bite. They had to drag it off me. No wonder I had difficulty breathing.'

Julie, who kept two large dogs of her own, couldn't stop herself saying, 'If it meant to bite you, I'm sure it would have. They don't mess about.'

Diamond said quickly, 'So you think Mr Darby brings the dog to cause you distress?'

'I'm certain of it.'

223

'Some personal grudge?'

'I've given him no cause for one.'

'He lives quite close, doesn't he, across the street in Hay Hill?'

Miss Chilmark drew herself up in the armchair. 'What are you suggesting now?'

'I'm not suggesting anything, ma'am. I'm stating a fact. You're almost neighbours.'

'The man lives in squalor,' she said with distaste.

'You've visited him?'

'God forbid! I wouldn't need to. The state of the windows. The curtains. I try not to look when I am compelled to walk past.'

'Considering the way you feel about this man, I'm surprised you haven't given up the Bloodhounds. It can't be any pleasure.'

Her lips contracted into a tight, orange-coloured knot. 'Why should I allow him to hound me – literally hound me – out of an activity I've enjoyed for two years or more? Tell me that.'

The defiance was admirable, the English gentlewoman at her finest. She was at one with the steely-featured ancestors whose portraits lined the walls.

'Forgive me, I'm still trying to understand the appeal of this club,' said Diamond. 'From all I've heard, you have very little in common except that you all read detective stories.'

'Isn't that enough? People don't have to be like peas in a pod to function as a club. We speak of books we can recommend. Tastes differ, of course, and one doesn't have to agree with everything that is said, but discussion can be stimulating. Some of them will never break out of Agatha Christie and Dorothy Sayers. You can see that. Personally, I favour a more demanding writer. I don't suppose you are familiar with Eco.'

Diamond had heard of the so-called eco-warriors, who occupied the trees at Swainswick when the bypass was under construction, and he doubted if they would have

224

Miss Chilmark's seal of approval, so he said, 'No, ma'am, I can't say it's familiar.'

'He. Eco is the name of an author.'

Julie looked equally unwilling to commit herself.

'Umberto Eco,' Miss Chilmark said, rolling the 'r' and chanting her syllables like a native Italian, 'the greatest of modern writers. To describe him as a crime writer would be to belittle the man, regardless that *The Name of the Rose* is, beyond question, the finest detective story ever written.'

'I saw it,' said Julie. 'With Sean Connery.'

Witheringly Miss Chilmark said, 'I wasn't speaking of a film.'

'It was good,' said Julie.

'I doubt it. How could any film live up to the achievement of such an intricate and intelligent book?'

Julie retorted evenly, 'So what is your opinion of *Foucault's Pendulum?*'

It was a delicious moment, the more enjoyable for being so unexpected. It didn't matter that Diamond had no idea who Foucault was or why his pendulum was of interest. The question hit Miss Chilmark like a cannonball.

She became inarticulate. 'I, em, I can't say that I, em, that is to say, got on with it too well.'

Before she could repair her defences, Diamond said, 'Do you drive?'

'You mean a car?'

'Well, I don't see you on a motorbike.'

'I own a small car, yes. A Montego.'

'Where do you keep it?'

'I rent a garage in Lansdown Mews.'

'The colour?'

'Blue. Dark blue. Why do you ask?'

'Registration?'

She gave the number. An 'F' registration: quite a seasoned car.

'Did you use it on the Monday evening after the meeting?'

'Of course not. It's only a short walk from here to St Michael's. Besides, I was far too shaken by my experience with the dog to take the wheel of a car.'

'So what happened? Did you walk home?'

'Yes.'

'Didn't anyone offer to drive you?'

'I can't remember. If they had, I wouldn't have accepted. You see, I was well enough by then to make my own way back here.'

Miss Chilmark's fitness interested Diamond. During the interview he had been assessing her physique. Though probably around sixty, she was a sturdy woman, not incapable, he judged, of cracking a man over the head with a heavy implement.

'And after you got home, did you go out again?'

'No. Why should I?'

'Was anyone here that evening? A visitor?'

The look she gave him removed any doubt that if roused she was capable of violence. 'How dare you?'

Diamond smiled faintly. 'Miss Chilmark, I wasn't suggesting anything risqué, I was trying to find whether you had an alibi for the time when the murder took place.'

'Surely you don't believe . . .' Shocked, her voice trailed off.

'But it turns out you don't have one,' said Diamond. 'Shame.' He heaved himself up from the settee and crossed the room to examine one of the portraits, of a moustachioed man in a grey suit with a cravat, one thumb tucked into a waistcoat pocket to give a good view of a gold watch-chain. His young wife stood at his side in a long blue dress. She was holding an ostrich-feather fan. Three small boys were grouped in front, one of them in a sailor suit looking up adoringly at his father. 'Family?'

Miss Chilmark's mind was on other things. There was a pause before she responded. 'Er, yes. My grandparents, with Papa and my Uncles Esmond and Herbert.'

'Handsome family.'

'Grandpapa was mayor of Bath before the First World War.'

'Really? Did they live in this house at the time?'

'Yes.'

'It passes down through the family?' He swung around from the painting and looked at her. 'You did say it belongs to you still?'

She made a murmur of assent and nodded.

'Of course, if we had any doubt we could check who pays the Council Tax,' Diamond dropped in casually to the dialogue.

There was an uncomfortable silence.

He then added, 'Or we could ask the old lady upstairs.'

'You can't do that!' said Miss Chilmark in a panic. 'Well.' She cleared her throat. 'Technically, the house isn't in my possession any longer. Living here, as I have all my life, I still tend to think of myself as the owner.' She had just been caught out, but she was doing her damnedest to gloss it over.

'Technically?' repeated Diamond. 'You sold the place?'

'On the firm understanding that I may remain here for life.'

'And how long ago was this transaction?'

Miss Chilmark rested her hands on her thighs and pushed out her chest in an attempt to reassert herself. 'I don't see that this is a matter for the police.'

'It is if you mislead us,' said Diamond. 'We expect truthful statements, Miss Chilmark. If we don't get them, we ask why.'

'A misunderstanding.'

'I don't think so, ma'am. When did you sell?'

'In January, 1993.'

'A painful decision, I'm sure.'

'One's circumstances alter,' said Miss Chilmark philosophically.

'You had some hefty expenses to meet?'

'Do I have to go into this? It isn't easy for a single lady to exist on a private income in these expensive times.

My savings were depleted through inflation and some bad investment advice, so I took stock of my position, my future, and decided it was wise to realise the asset of the house. I have no family to pass it on to. I can now face my declining years with reasonable confidence.'

They left soon after. Outside in the street, Julie said, 'You pressed her hard about her circumstances.'

'And I haven't finished,' said Diamond. 'She's gone through a mint of money. I'm not convinced about the bad investments – unless it's something like a gambling habit. We need to do some digging, Julie. You see, if she sold the house – what? – a couple of years ago, she must have made a bomb. You wouldn't buy an entire house in the Paragon for much under four hundred grand – even with a sitting tenant in the basement. What's happened to the money?'

'Banked, I expect,' said Julie.

'There wasn't much sign of spending, was there? That basement could do with some redecoration. Furniture ought to be replaced – that settee, anyway. She runs a five-year-old car. Is this a woman who came into several hundred grand?'

'People do live meanly sometimes.'

'The jewellery – all that sparkly stuff – wasn't genuine, was it?'

'It looked like imitation to me,' Julie admitted.

'I want you to make some discreet inquiries,' he told her. 'Go through the local papers for 1993. Find out which estate agent handled the sale. Go and sweet-talk them. Get the price if you can, the bank she used and the name of the new owner, presumably the old lady we first met. Once we know the bank . . . Can you handle this?'

'Without breaking the Data Protection Laws?'

'I didn't mention them, did I?'

'But you'd like to see a bank statement if I can rustle one up?'

'I would.'

'If you say it's necessary, I'll do my best.'

He turned to look her in the face. 'What's this "*if you say it's necessary*"? Do I sense a whiff of insurrection?'

She shook her head. 'It's just that I still have a pair of handcuffs in my coat pocket. You asked me to bring them, but they weren't needed.'

'Only thanks to you, Julie.'

'Oh?'

'The cuffs were there to shock the old bat. Break down her defences. You did that in a much more subtle way, with your knowledge of Chinese literature.'

'*Chinese?*'

'Foo So.'

She laughed. '*Foucault's Pendulum*. That isn't Chinese. It's a book by Umberto Eco, the writer she was talking about.'

'I don't care. It was brilliant, Julie. It shook her rigid. Shook me, too. How on earth did you know about that?'

She said, 'I don't think I'll tell you.'

'Come on.'

'You'll be disappointed. It was pretty obvious really.'

'No!' he said, thinking back, picturing the room. 'It wasn't one of those books on the mantelpiece?'

'There you go. Am I still brilliant, or have you changed your opinion?'

He didn't answer. They were interrupted by the beeping of Julie's personal radio. She took it out. 'DI Hargreaves.'

'Do you have Superintendent Diamond with you, ma'am? Over,' the voice from Manvers Street asked.

'Yes, I do.'

'Would you tell him he's wanted urgently here? A message has just been received. We think it could be another of those riddles.'

THE THIRD RIDDLE

Suspense

TWENTY-SEVEN

The Assistant Chief Constable, Arnold Musgrave, sat behind his desk with his hands covering his eyes as if they were sore. Across the room, from armchairs in opposite corners, John Wigfull and Peter Diamond watched in the uncomfortable knowledge that everything they had patiently and plausibly stitched together had just been unravelled.

Mr Musgrave took a deep, troubled breath and dragged his fingers slowly down his fat features. Finally he propped his chin on his clenched fists. 'To sum up, then,' he said, his voice edged with reproach, 'we're back with the locked room mystery we started with. Your neat theory about the narrowboat has been blown to smithereens, John.'

'So we're led to believe, sir,' Wigfull said with a sideward glare at Diamond.

'Sometimes I wonder if you two are singing from the same hymn-sheet,' Mr Musgrave dressed him down sharply. 'You can't argue with the facts. Nobody changed the padlock. It was the same one Milo Motion bought originally. The key picked up by the divers at Avoncliff fitted it perfectly. Right?'

'Right, sir,' admitted Wigfull.

'Worse than that, the thief is still at large,' Mr Musgrave turned the spit relentlessly. 'This new riddle turns up this afternoon, proving you were wrong about Sid Towers. He can't have been the evil genius who thinks up these damned rhymes and stole the Penny Black.'

'I thought we all had a stake in that theory, sir,' the

maligned Wigfull couldn't stop himself from stating. 'If you remember, last time we met, DS Diamond produced the paper bag with those lists of rhyming words scrawled on it. That seemed to clinch the case against Towers.'

Mr Musgrave took a breath, as if to exercise self-control under extraordinary provocation. 'I don't say you're alone in your delusions, John. If this latest riddle is genuine – and I believe it is – we've all cocked up.'

'Would you mind repeating the verse, sir?' Diamond asked before his own shortcomings were opened to scrutiny.

The ACC picked a slip of paper off the desk and read the words in a monotone that underlined his distaste:

> *To end the suspense, as yours truly did,*
> *Discover the way to Sydney from Sid.*

There was a pause before Diamond said, 'To *Sydney*?'

'It's the way this blighter works,' said Wigfull. 'It's gibberish. He doesn't want us making sense of the thing until after the event.'

'That isn't my understanding of gibberish,' Diamond said. 'The other riddles did make sense.'

'Yes, but only when we had all the information. There's no way we could have worked out from that first riddle that the Postal Museum was about to be done over.'

'We do have a better chance now,' said Diamond. 'We know how two of the riddles worked out. We have some insight into the man's thinking.'

'Or woman's,' said Mr Musgrave. 'Let's not make any sexist assumptions. But you're right about that, Peter. Just because we didn't crack the other riddles, it doesn't mean we give up on this one. I'm as baffled as you are about this reference to Sydney. Does anyone in this case have an Australian connection?'

Diamond glanced towards Wigfull. 'It hasn't come up.'

'What about the first line: *To end the suspense, as yours truly did?*'

Wigfull, touchingly eager for some credit, now took a more positive line: 'That "yours truly" is worth noting – the sort of old-fashioned expression that was used before, with words like "thee" and "whither". Not quite so dated as those, I have to say, but it fits the style of the earlier pieces.'

Mr Musgrave said, 'I don't think there's any question that this comes from the same source. The typeface is the same and I'm pretty sure the paper is as well.'

'How was it delivered, sir?' Diamond asked.

'The same as before – all the local media got it first.'

'Another thing, sir,' said Wigfull, trying to be more positive. 'This time the whole tone of the message is more direct, as if the writer *wants* us to get the solution. *To end the suspense* . . . It's almost as if he or she has a need to be unmasked. Look at it from their point of view. They commit a masterly crime and put out these clever rhymes and get no recognition. In the end, the desire for glory gets the better of them.'

'That's an optimistic view.' Mr Musgrave turned to Diamond. 'What do you think of that?'

'I hope John is right. God knows, we need a break-through.'

'All right. What about this second line: *Discover the way to Sydney from Sid*. We know who Sid was. Who the devil is Sydney if it's not Sydney, New South Wales?'

'We have some Sydneys in Bath,' suggested Diamond. 'Sydney Place, Sydney Road, Sydney Gardens, Sydney Buildings, Sydney Wharf.'

'Sydney Mews,' put in Wigfull.

'This is better,' said Mr Musgrave. 'Any connections with the Bloodhounds?'

'None that I know,' said Diamond.

'Not one of them lives in any of those streets?'

'No, sir.'

'Nothing there of interest, then. What about Sydney Gardens?'

'Well, you have the museum there,' said Wigfull, and

as soon as the words were out he gripped the arms of his chair. 'Oh Lord, do you think they're planning another theft?'

Diamond, not often to be found imbibing culture in his spare time, needed to be reminded which museum this was. The Holburne of Menstrie, a converted hotel in the park at the end of Great Pulteney Street, possesses collections of silver and ceramics that rank among the best in Europe, as well as paintings by Guardi, Zoffany, Turner and Gainsborough.

'Better tip off the security people in case,' said Mr Musgrave. 'Do it now.' He picked up his phone and held it out to Wigfull. When the call had been made, he said, 'Let's shelve the riddle for a moment. Where exactly are we with the murder inquiry, Peter?'

'Still interviewing, sir.' This sounded lame, and Diamond knew it.

'The Bloodhounds?'

'Yes. They've all given statements to the murder squad. I'm doing the follow-up with DI Hargreaves. Talked to Mr Motion, of course, Mrs Shaw, Mr Darby and Miss Chilmark. There are two to go – Miss Miller and Mrs Wycherley.'

'Any angles?'

'No one can be eliminated yet, sir, except Milo Motion, who was here being interviewed when the murder took place. It was physically impossible for him to have got back to the boatyard and murdered Towers before he clocked in downstairs. Otherwise, not one of the Bloodhounds has an alibi worth mentioning. So far as I can make out, every one of them had the use of a vehicle, so they could have got out to the boatyard.'

'Do you seriously think a woman could have done this?'

'Cracked Sid over the head? No problem.'

'Miss Chilmark?'

'She may be getting on a bit, sir, but she's still a sturdy woman.'

236

'What about the motive?'

'For Miss Chilmark? Something emerged that made me wonder. Julie Hargreaves is working on it now.'

'What's that?'

'She seems to have got through a mint of money in recent years. She sold the house in 'ninety-three. Ought to be in the lap of luxury now, but she isn't. I want to find out why.'

'Blackmail?'

Diamond spread his hands. 'Her reputation is very important to her.'

'Did anything useful emerge from the other interviews? Miss Shaw?'

'Very little. It's more a matter of what she didn't tell than what she did. I knew from another source, from Milo, in fact, that she made definite attempts to be friendly with Sid. Out of sympathy, possibly. I'd be very surprised if any of it was meant as a come-on. She took him to the pub on more than one occasion after the Bloodhounds finished. When we talked, she told me about Polly Wycherley fussing over him, but she volunteered nothing about the drinks she had with him herself. I brought that up, and then she was forced to admit to it.'

'You think she was holding back?'

'Before I mentioned it, she was saying that if anyone else had spoken more than a couple of words to Sid, he would have run a mile.'

'But she did?'

'Yes.'

'And did *he*?'

'Run a mile? I've no idea.'

'Does Mrs Shaw have anything to hide?'

'Not that I've noticed. She's on pretty close terms with the fellow called A.J. who helps in the gallery. There could be something in that, but I don't get a sense that they're having an affair. I couldn't raise a blush from her, anyway.'

'Is that the way you work?' said the ACC. 'You seem to be staking a lot on Sid as a blackmailer.'

'What other motive is there, sir? He wasn't shafting anyone's wife.'

'Let's have the rundown on Rupert Darby, then.'

'Talk about blackmail. On the face of it, Rupert was a plum ripe for picking. A prison record that Towers could easily have checked on.'

'Through his links with Impregnable, you mean?'

'Yes, sir. Only Rupert doesn't turn a hair when you talk about his form. He could hardly wait to tell me the story of his conviction for indecency – for mooning at a magistrate. He gave his impression of the beak pronouncing sentence, quoting every word. Spot on, and amusing, too. The man glories in his image as an old lag. He likes to shock.'

'Not a victim, then?'

'I don't see it.'

Mr Musgrave vibrated his lips as if he suddenly felt a draught. 'If you discount Darby as a suspect, you're left with the women.'

'I don't make sexist assumptions, sir.'

This wasn't well received. The ACC drew back in his chair and pointed his finger. 'Don't make assumptions of any sort, Peter, least of all about me. Better get through those interviews PDQ. We've got the media on our backs. You're going to nail this joker fast.'

TWENTY-EIGHT

Annoyed with himself for having provoked such an outburst from the ACC, who was normally the most agreeable of the high-ups, Diamond returned to the second floor resolved to channel his discontent into the pursuit of the killer. This case was a brute, but there was no point in taking it out on the people upstairs.

He found Julie in the incident room holding a phone to her ear. She rolled her eyes upwards.

'Who is it?' he asked.

She mouthed the words, 'The bank.'

Miss Chilmark's bank. Julie must have made progress to get this far. While he'd been baiting the top brass, she had been beavering away on the things that mattered. Thank God for Julie. She had made this sort of exercise, ferreting for information, her speciality. She kept tabs on the networking between local government, business and trade. She always knew someone to approach.

'Any joy?'

She shook her head and continued to listen to the phone while fiddling with a pencil, standing it on one end and then sliding finger and thumb down its length and reversing it. At last she thanked her informant and put down the receiver. She gave Diamond a smile, not of satisfaction, but resignation. 'Confidentiality. They won't tell me anything without authority. I did get a few things clear from an estate agent – and not the one Miss Chilmark dealt with. In this town the agents all know each other's business. The house was sold to a Mrs

239

Nugent-Thomas in January, 1993, just as Miss Chilmark stated.'

'For how much?'

'Three hundred and thirty thousand, with a clause inserted to allow her to remain a tenant for life.'

'And what did she do with the proceeds?'

'That's what I was trying to discover.'

'Who from?'

'A bank cashier. I thought she was sure to be good for some inside info. I used to babysit for her. It was worth trying. Doesn't matter. Plan B should get us there, even if it's a more roundabout route.'

He shook his head. He hadn't the patience for Plan B, whatever that was. He'd been a front-row forward in his time. 'Get the number again and ask for the manager.'

Julie gave him a do-you-think-this-is-wise look and pressed the redial button.

'Ringing?'

She nodded.

'Tell the switchboard you have a personal call for the manager from, er, Douglas, Isle of Man. Give my name but not the rank.' Front-row forwards weren't picked for their subtlety, but occasionally they used the dummy pass.

Julie's eyes widened. She knew her boss well enough not to hesitate. After getting through and repeating his instruction precisely, she handed the phone across.

Diamond's face underwent a change. Suddenly he was a picture of affability, pink and smiling as if his day so far had been spent feeding the pigeons in Abbey Green. 'Who am I speaking to? . . . Right. This is Peter Diamond, Douglas, Isle of Man branch. How are you, old boy? Must be all of ten years since we last spoke. At staff college, wasn't it? Look, this is probably nothing, but one can't be too careful. We've got a young fellow here wanting to open an account with a single cheque drawn on a personal account at your branch. There's more than a slight question mark about the cheque. Do you happen to have a Miss Hilda Chilmark as a customer? . . . Good.

That's the name of the account-holder. I dare say you have a terminal in front of you. It might be worth pressing a couple of keys ... Already? You're quicker than I am with the damned thing. First it's a question of whether the balance covers the amount. Even if it does, I have my doubts whether your customer filled this in as it now appears ... Actually three thousand two hundred pounds, but it looks to my cashier as if the words "Three thousand" might be an addition, squeezed in front, you know, and so, to my beady eye, is the number three where the digits go ... The name of the drawer? John Brown, if you can believe that ... Ah! I'm glad you agree ... Well, I'd be grateful if you would ...' He smiled at Julie.

She murmured, 'I didn't think you were capable of this.'

He put his hand over the mouthpiece. 'You didn't hear any of this, Julie.' In a moment, the manager was back in contact. Diamond now put on a caring expression, listened and then said, 'Well, this does sound like a try-on. Most of her current balance, you say? ... It looks as if we may be on to something rather unpleasant. You won't mind me asking. Have there been any other four-figure debits on the account recently? ... Indeed! ... But by the lady herself at your branch? One can't argue with that. Between you and me, I wish I lived in such style. This does look like a one-off. Look, I'd better get back to this chappie right away. Rest assured that we'll stop it at this end and get a proper investigation under way directly. Doubtless you'll be hearing from Head Office shortly ... Not at all. It's our job to keep a look-out. Thanks.' He put down the phone and told Julie, 'She's been drawing a thousand a week in cash for at least a year. What are the odds on blackmail?'

Julie's thinking hadn't got past the thousand a week. 'That's a stack of money to get through.'

'Every week. You couldn't do it.'

'Couldn't I?' she said. 'Give me the chance.'

'Let's keep our minds on the job, shall we?'

She smiled. 'What next, then? Back to Miss Chilmark?'

'Not tonight. I want to interview Shirley-Ann Miller.'

She didn't often query a decision, but this one seemed hard to justify. 'Do we need to bother? I mean, if Miss Chilmark was being blackmailed . . .'

'We don't know if she was.'

'You brought it up, Mr Diamond,' she reminded him. 'It may not be true, but it's worth putting to her, surely?'

'This morning you were prodding me into visiting all the suspects.'

'Yes, but nothing was happening then. Now we're inundated. You must have heard about this new riddle sent to the press this afternoon.'

'I was informed by the Assistant Chief Constable,' he said with an air of martyrdom. 'When did you hear about this?'

'Only a short while ago. It's all over the front page of the *Chronicle*. The desk sergeant had a copy.'

'Into print already? And what do you make of it?' he asked.

Julie shook her head. 'Sounds very like the other riddles to me, except that they were about the Penny Black. Could be some publicity-seeker, I suppose. I mean, I thought we'd agreed that Sid wrote the others. We have the writing on the paper bag as evidence. True, it was just a list of rhyming words and not lines of verse, but I thought that was pretty conclusive.'

'So did I until an hour ago,' said Diamond. 'All we've got is conflicting evidence, Julie. An impossible murder in a locked room, a dead man who continues to taunt us with riddles and a woman who lives in a basement and gets through a grand a week. You were right about the other suspects. We want the whole picture. Get your coat.'

They'd done enough walking for one day, Diamond decided; this time, they inched towards Russell Street in the evening line of traffic. He used the time constructively, justifying the decision to visit Shirley-Ann Miller. At this stage of the investigation she was the least likely suspect, he cheerfully conceded, but she was potentially the most valuable witness. As a newcomer to the Bloodhounds, she must have observed each of the members acutely, getting those first impressions, alert to the dynamics of the group, the antagonisms and suspicions, link-ups and alliances that undoubtedly existed. In the two meetings she had attended, she may well have seen the crucial events that led to the murder. By all accounts she was not reticent. Her recollections ought to be worth having.

It was after five when they rang the bell at the Russell Street flat. An appetising smell wafted from the interior the moment Shirley-Ann Miller opened the door. Her PVC apron was quite a knockout, the lifesize image of a torso and thighs clad in a black basque and suspenders and worn in the appropriate position. Unfortunately Shirley-Ann's large round spectacles and pale features under the helmet of dark hair didn't square too well with the rest of the effect.

'Obviously not a convenient time to call,' Diamond mentioned apologetically after introducing himself and Julie.

'Oh my God!' Shirley-Ann looked down at the apron and tried to cover it with her hands. 'I forgot I had this on. What on earth must you be thinking? It isn't mine, actually.' She reached for the bow at the back, tugged off the apron and bundled it on to a chair before escorting her guests to the back of the house.

'I meant your cooking,' Diamond explained. 'Don't let it burn.'

'It's all right. It's only a beef casserole I took from the freezer. I can give it as long as I like.' She showed them into an open-plan area where the aroma was well-nigh irresistible. This was a once-gracious, high-ceilinged Georgian reception room now ruined by a divider, a central shelf unit that failed to mask a kitchen sink, refrigerator and dishwasher. On the near side of the unit was a carpeted living area with armchairs, television and low tables cluttered with newspapers, books, junk mail and crockery.

'Do sit down. Just park everything on the floor. You'll have to take me as you find me. With both of us working, Bert and me, it's difficult to keep up with the housework.'

'Bert being . . .'

'My partner. That's the whole point, really, that we're partners. When two of you share a place, it's two homes squeezed into one. Neither of you wants to throw anything away in case the relationship comes to an end, so you end up with two of everything. It's only been six months. Tea?'

Julie had tuned in to the quick tempo of Shirley-Ann's speech and she spoke for them both. 'Please.'

The rate of words actually increased, at no cost to the beautiful articulation. 'Bert does his best to keep the place in order. He's much more orderly than I am, but he isn't here as much, so my untidy habits win the day. You don't need to tell me what this is about,' she said, crossing to the kitchen area to fill the kettle. 'I expected you before this. Well, I've talked to one of your sergeants already and he told me to expect another interview. Not that I can help very much. I don't believe I spoke a single word to the poor man who was killed, and that's pretty unusual for me.'

'You joined this group, the Bloodhounds, quite recently?'

'I've only been twice. Quite an experience, both times. Had no idea what I was letting myself in for.'

'What prompted you to go along?'

'Force of circumstance, really. Bert is out most evenings at the Sports and Leisure Centre, where he works. That's when it's used most, so he has to be there. It's all very well having a gorgeous hunk for a lover, but you pay a price. I do a lot of reading in the evenings, only there are limits. When I heard about the Bloodhounds, it sounded right up my street.'

'How did you hear?'

'From one of those little booklets listing what's on in Bath. Bert brought one home from the Centre, knowing how I wallow in detective stories and thrillers. He's never moved on from James Bond, which he knows like some people know their Bible, I may say. They're not for women, those books. Bert doesn't like anything else, so our conversations about reading are rather limited. Anyway, I went along to the meeting and they were glad I joined, I think. They could do with some new members. I was told quite a number have left since it was set up. You have to be a real enthusiast.' She picked some mugs off the floor and took them to the kitchen sink to wash.

'Did you know any of the others before you joined?' Diamond asked. He had found a rocking chair and cleared it of golfing magazines. Julie, too, had made herself a space and was seated in a deep armchair.

'No. They were all new faces to me. But they went out of their way to be friendly. Some of them did, anyway. Jessica – that's Jessica Shaw, who owns that art gallery in Northumberland Place – took me for a drink at the end of the first meeting and I also had an invitation to the preview at her gallery this week. Then Polly Wycherley – she's the chair, and one of the founder-members – invited me for a coffee at Le Parisien a day or two later. I've had coffee twice with Polly. I think she takes her duties seriously.'

'What do you mean?'

'The second time was the morning after poor Sid Towers was killed. Polly came up to me when I was at work. I was only handing out leaflets about the bus tour, so it was easy to take a few minutes off. It was the first I'd heard about what happened. Polly had been interviewed by some of your people that very morning and she was worried because she'd made some ghastly, insensitive remark about Sid before they told her the bad news.'

'What remark was that?'

'I don't remember. No, wait, I do. She told them he was dead wood, meaning he didn't contribute very much to the Bloodhounds.'

'Unfortunate.'

'Yes. She was mortified.'

'Did she have anything else to say?'

'Let me think. She was very shaken. Well, it was obvious to both of us that one of the Bloodhounds must have murdered Sid.'

'How did you come to that conclusion?'

Shirley-Ann switched off the kettle and warmed a fancy teapot shaped like the face of Sherlock Holmes, with a deerstalker lid. 'We knew Sid drove to Limpley Stoke after our meeting and into that boatyard where Milo had his houseboat. The policeman who gave Polly the news told her Sid's car was found down there. Didn't know what he was up to. Whatever it was, he must have thought there wasn't much chance of being disturbed, with Milo having gone to the police station and sure to be there some time, to explain about the stamp. Obviously he was wrong. Someone else went to the boat as well. And it had to be one of the Bloodhounds because we were the only people who knew Milo wouldn't be home.'

'Polly had worked this out?'

'She didn't actually put it into words. I did.'

'You're a bit of a sleuth yourself, then,' said Diamond, watching her pop two teabags into Holmes's head.

'I'm sure Polly was of the same opinion,' said Shirley-Ann. 'She's very astute and she was in a fine old state about the murder.'

'Why do you think she confided in you?'

She blushed. 'I don't know. Perhaps she thought I was so new in the club that I was the only one who couldn't possibly have a motive for murdering Sid – which is true when you think about it. Everyone else had known him some time.'

'Fair enough. They'd been coming for years, some of them. Mr Motion, Mrs Wycherley.' Casually, Diamond tossed in Miss Chilmark's name, as one of the long-standing members. 'Quite a formidable lady, from all I've heard.'

'I thought so at first,' said Shirley-Ann. 'She presents

a strong front – seven hundred years of Chilmarks, and that sort of patronising nonsense that people of her sort sometimes use to justify their pretensions. I think she's brittle, though. She panics easily.'

'The episode with the dog?'

'Rupert's dog, yes.'

'You're sure that was genuine?'

She frowned. 'Do you mean: was she acting? I didn't think so. She worked herself up in anticipation, but that's different. We had a bit of a scene the previous week, when Marlowe – that's the dog – shook himself dry and made some of us wet in the process. She'd obviously fretted all week over that. At the beginning of the next meeting, before Rupert arrived, she was asking the rest of us to support her in excluding the dog. When the crisis came, it was real, I'm sure.'

'The hyperventilation?'

'Yes.'

'Rupert was the thorn in her flesh?'

'Absolutely.'

'Did you happen to notice how she behaved towards the other men?'

Shirley-Ann's eyebrows lifted a fraction at the question.

Diamond couched it another way. 'A maiden lady, rather brittle, to use your expression. Is she nervous of men?'

'If she is, it doesn't show. She gets on well with Milo, helps him to put out the chairs when they arrive early.'

'And Sid Towers? She wasn't in awe of him?'

'I don't think so. Like the rest of them, she behaved as if he wasn't there most of the time – which is probably the kindest way to treat a painfully shy man.'

Diamond moved the questioning on. 'I'd value your opinion, Miss Miller. You know that Sid was murdered later that evening and you observed everything that happened at the meeting. Did you form any theories?'

'About who did it? No.'

'No suspicions, even?'

'Well . . .' She poured the boiling water into the teapot, busying herself with the task. 'Not at the time.'

'You've got your suspicions now?' Diamond pressed her.

She was trying to hold back, which clearly went against nature for Shirley-Ann. 'Oh, nothing I'd call a suspicion.'

'What would you call it, then – an inspired guess? Woman's intuition?'

This dart hit its target, but failed to achieve the desired result. It brought out the militant in Shirley-Ann. 'Would you like the tea in a mug, or all over your head?'

At this point Julie had an intuition of her own: to wade in, but on Shirley-Ann's side. 'I wouldn't even ask,' she told her. 'He's like this all the time. You wouldn't believe the things I've heard him say to women. God knows, you wouldn't hint at something you know unless it was properly thought through and based on common sense. Intuition, be blowed!'

From the expression on Diamond's face, he might as well have had the teapot up-ended over his bald patch. Luckily he was lost for words and it was the effusive Shirley-Ann who supplied them.

'You're spot on. I *do* know something. I wasn't going to mention it.'

'But you will, to make a stand for women,' said Julie, dangerously close to overdoing this.

Shirley-Ann, fired up, proceeded to tell them about the words she'd seen sprayed on the window of the Walsingham Gallery and cleaned off by Jessica's husband, Barnaby. 'And those are facts,' she said finally. 'To hell with intuition.'

Julie's onslaught had wrongfooted Diamond, but he was grateful for the result. '*She did for Sid* – those were the words?'

'Yes.'

'You saw them yourself?'

Now that she had an ally, Shirley-Ann was becoming assertive. 'Didn't I just say so? Jessica practically dragged me into the street to look.'

'Who else was there?'

'Her husband Barnaby and A.J., the artist.'

'We've met A.J.,' said Julie. 'He seems to be around a lot of the time.'

'You can say that again,' said Shirley-Ann, all discretion abandoned. Her sisterly bond with Julie was bringing spectacular results. 'I'm surprised the husband puts up with it.'

'With what?' said Diamond.

'Oh, I've met them out, walking along the towpath at Bathwick like a married couple.'

'Arm in arm?'

'I didn't say a courting couple.'

'Side by side, then?'

She nodded. 'That suggests a much more permanent relationship, to my jaundiced eye.'

'I see. But you say the husband was present when the writing on the gallery window was discovered?'

'That's what's so amazing. He and A.J. were together all evening, looking after the picture sales. They don't act like rivals. In fact, they seemed to be getting on rather well.'

'And whose decision was it to rub out the writing?'

'Barnaby's. Jessica was all for calling the police, but he advised her that if she did, it was quite likely the words would be taken seriously.'

'It was entirely Barnaby's decision?'

'Well, not entirely. Jessica turned to me and asked what I thought, and I had to say it would ruin the party if they called the police. Sugar?' She handed a mug of tea to Diamond.

'So it didn't get reported.'

'Not until now. They're going to be furious with me for speaking out.'

Withholding information was apparently of trifling importance. Diamond let that pass for the present.

She continued, 'I've been agonising over this ever since it happened. At the time I thought it didn't matter if it wasn't reported. It seemed so obviously dotty, the suggestion that Jessica would have harmed Sid. She really liked the poor man, felt sorry for him, anyway. She's told me that herself.'

'And have you changed your opinion?'

'Actually I have.' She gave them the theory she'd worked out in bed the previous night, the conspiracy between Jessica and Sid that had gone wrong and resulted in Jessica murdering Sid. 'What do you think? Is it feasible?'

Diamond was too wily to say. 'What interests me right now is who shares your suspicion, who put the message on the window.'

'I can tell you,' Shirley-Ann said, and then clapped her hand over her mouth.

'You saw it happen?'

'No.' The flow of words stopped abruptly.

'But you know who was responsible, do you?'

She didn't answer.

Instead of a rebuke, she received the unexpected warmth of Diamond at his most charming. 'You've been very candid with us, Miss Miller, and I appreciate that. We'd never make progress at all without the help of honest people like you. If you know the identity of this person—' He stopped at the sound of someone entering the flat.

Shirley-Ann said, 'This has got to be Bert. He nips home before the evening session.'

Diamond got up from the rocking-chair as the door opened.

Shirley-Ann said, 'Hi, darling, you're early. Don't be alarmed. This lady and gentleman are from the police.'

Diamond supplied their names.

For one worrying moment it appeared as if Bert was stripping for a fight. Without a word he unzipped the

250

top half of his black tracksuit. He wasn't particularly tall, yet the muscle formation around his neck and shoulders – he was wearing a pale blue singlet – spoke for many sessions with weights. In fact he didn't become aggressive. Shedding the tracksuit top was his way of asserting that this was his territory, his home. He tossed it over a chair-back and asked mildly if the kettle was still hot.

Julie happened to be nearest the teapot and offered to pour him some, only to be told by Shirley-Ann, 'Thanks, but Bert has his own herb tea.'

'From an 007 pot, I dare say,' Diamond commented.

Bert shot him a surprised look.

Shirley-Ann said, 'I was telling them what a wiz you are on James Bond.'

'Don't exaggerate,' said Bert. He had a high-pitched voice for such a hunk of manhood.

Shirley-Ann went close to him and gripped his solid upper arm. 'Oh, come on. If I had to have someone answering questions on *Mastermind* to save my life, I'd pick you.' Turning to Julie, she remarked, 'There's a wise head on these chunky shoulders.'

Bert basked briefly in the compliment. Then he reminded her, 'That isn't what they came to talk about.'

She said to him, 'We've had our talk.' Turning back to Diamond, she explained, 'Bert's very law-abiding. He told me I should have reported what happened, and I've told you everything.'

Diamond wasn't interested in Bert's probity or Shirley-Ann's lack of it. Bert's arrival had put a stop to a promising conversation. 'Not everything, ma'am. You didn't finish. You were on the point of telling us who wrote those words on the Walsingham Gallery window.'

Hearing it put so bluntly caused Shirley-Ann to bite her lip and say, 'Was I?'

Julie gave a confirming nod.

Shirley-Ann deferred to Bert, spreading her hands as if uncertain whether she should go on.

251

He said, 'You can only describe what you saw. They can put two and two together, the same as we did.'

She nodded, cleared her throat and said to Diamond, 'I hate to get anyone into trouble, but I did happen to notice someone that evening with tiny spots of white on him, like snow or something.'

'Who?'

'Rupert. Rupert Darby. It was on that beret he wears all the time. The spots showed up against the dark material. At the time I thought it must be dandruff. It was lightly speckled, mainly towards the front. I remembered much later.'

'We were in bed,' Bert confirmed.

She added, 'That was when it dawned on me that it could be something other than dandruff.'

'Paint from a spray, you mean?'

'Well, yes.' She nervously fingered some strands of her dark hair. 'I could be mistaken. Probably there's some innocent explanation.'

'Did it look like paint from an aerosol?'

'I think so.'

'You must be reasonably sure. Were the spots even in size?'

'Yes, and very small. Look, even if Rupert did write the words, it must have been meant in fun. He'd had a few drinks already with some people he met in the Saracen's Head. He was probably tipsy.'

'Was he sprayed on his clothes, or hands at all?'

'I didn't notice.' She thought a moment. 'There may have been some on his shoulders, I think, which put the idea of dandruff into my mind.'

'Who else have you told about this?'

'Only Bert.'

'You haven't spoken to Rupert?'

The idea horrified her. 'He's the last person I'd speak to. I scarcely know him, anyway. He gets my name wrong. Look, if you speak to him about it, you won't bring me into it, will you?'

252

'Was Rupert at the party in the gallery?'

'Yes, he was already there when I arrived, with the people I mentioned.'

'Did you catch their name, by any chance?'

'Yes, it was unusual. Faulk, or Volk, or something like that. She was a sculptor and had some work in the exhibition. He was a television writer.'

'He'd met them in the Saracen's?'

'So he said.'

'And when do you think the words were sprayed onto the window?'

'I've no idea. I didn't notice them as I came in, but I didn't look specially. I just went to the door, as you do. With all the spotlights on inside, and the people, you tended to look straight *through* the window, not at it.'

'Since the party, have you spoken to anyone at all, any of the Bloodhounds, that is?'

'Only Jessica and A.J. this morning on the towpath. I told you about that.' She was becoming twitchy, making little nervous movements, probably regretting what she had told.

'You met them this morning?' Bert said. 'Was that wise?'

'They just happened to be there, love. It wasn't planned. I couldn't avoid saying something.'

Diamond took over again. 'You didn't tell us what was said. Was the incident discussed?'

'I'm not sure.' Swiftly, Shirley-Ann corrected herself. 'I mean, yes, it was. Oh, I do feel dreadful about this now. A.J. said we were going to erase it from our minds, and I sort of agreed. He said it must have been done by someone with a warped sense of humour. Jessica was still furious about it and said she wouldn't have harmed Sid in a million years. She said if the bastard – I'm using her words now – if the bastard pointed the finger at her again, she was going straight to the police.'

'You've done her a good turn, then,' Diamond summed up. 'Saved her the trouble.' He smiled.

Shirley-Ann didn't smile back.

'You didn't tell her about the spots on Rupert's beret?'

'Good Lord, no!'

'And you won't be mentioning what you saw to anyone else? Not Polly, not Milo, not Rupert, not anyone?' Having secured a nod from Shirley-Ann, he turned to Bert. 'Nor you, sir. I'd like us all to be clear about that.'

TWENTY-NINE

Outside the Assembly Rooms, where they had parked, Diamond asked Julie, 'What did you make of that?'

'The story about the beret?'

'Yes.'

'It's got to be true, hasn't it? And we can check. Even if Rupert has noticed by now, and been busy with the white spirit, some microscopic paint spots are going to remain. Forensic will find them. Simple.'

'Simple?'

'Well?'

'First, catch your beret.' He stood by the car, jingling the keys, coming to a decision. 'Look, Hay Hill can't be more than three minutes away. We can cut through by the toyshop and it's just at the end of Alfred Street. We'll leave the car here.'

Halfway down the passage called Saville Row, he paused to study the menu in the window of La Lanterna, in the amber glow of the streetlamp that gives the place its name. His gastric juices were threatening mutiny since being exposed to the aroma of Shirley-Ann's casserole. For a man of his appetite, it had been too long since lunch. 'I don't want to spend the rest of the evening over this damned beret. It may be just a distraction.'

'Would you rather leave it to me?' Julie offered.

'No, I want to see the man, as well as his beret.' He suppressed the thought of food and started walking again. 'To tell you the truth, Julie, I'm mightily intrigued. This kind of schoolboy stuff, writing slogans on windows, doesn't fit my impression of Rupert at all.'

'Too sneaky, you mean?'

'You've got it. He gives it straight from the shoulder, whatever his other failings may be. If he had his suspicions about Jessica, he'd tell her, wouldn't he?'

Julie agreed with a murmur. 'Unless he's the killer himself.'

He didn't respond to that. He walked on in silence past antique shops that had iron shutters over their windows.

'Deflecting suspicion,' Julie explained.

'I get the point.'

'If he felt we were closing in, he might do something like this in desperation.'

After another long and awkward pause, he said, 'You know, it's a curious thing: although Rupert is the one disreputable character in the Bloodhounds, the jailbird, the barfly, the cause of all the upsets, I haven't seriously cast him as the killer up to now. Maybe it's time I did.'

In the evening gloom, Hay Hill looked and felt even less enchanting than it had on their previous visit. A strong breeze was gusting between the houses, disturbing dead leaves, paper scraps and a discarded beer-can that rattled against the railings before dropping into someone's basement. No lights were at Rupert's windows. The only response was from Marlowe the dog, barking at them through the space where the letter-flap had been.

They decided to ask at the local. The landlord at the Lansdown Arms thought they might find Rupert in the Paragon Bar at this stage of the day. The waitress in the Paragon said he'd had a skinful at lunchtime and he was probably out to the world until later. He usually came in some time after seven. Sabotaged by appetising whiffs of seafood cooking, Diamond was willing to wait there for Rupert. He persuaded Julie into discovering if the Paragon's 'Meal in Itself' – of French fish soup with croûtons, cheese and grain bread – was a fair description. In Julie's case, it was.

Julie asked him how the kitten was settling in.

'Too well,' said Diamond. 'He really likes the football on TV. I'm trying to watch and he's up against the screen patting it with his paw. He can't understand why the little men won't let him have the ball.'

She smiled. 'Has he got a name yet?'

'Most of the names I've called him aren't complimentary. He nicks things and stashes them away: keys, combs, pens, watches, a toothbrush. I found a stack of little objects in one of my shoes. You go to put them on in the morning and your toes hit an obstruction.'

'A genuine cat burglar?' said Julie. 'You ought to call him Raffles.'

'Raffles!' His eyes lit up. 'He might approve of that.'

Customers crowded in. Most of Bath seemed to know the tiny bar. Rupert had not appeared yet. To justify keeping the table (there were only three in this tiny room), Diamond ordered himself an extra dish of crêpes with trout, broccoli and cheese filling. But eventually, about seven-forty-five, they paid their bill and left.

More knocking at the house in Hay Hill succeeded only in goading Marlowe into hurling himself against the door.

They returned to the car and drove up Bathwick Hill to Claverton, a mile east of the city, to interview the only suspect they had not met.

Polly Wycherley lived alone in a semi named Styles in a quiet road behind the university. A few pink rose blooms were enduring October staunchly in the small front garden.

A halogen floodlight came on as they walked up the path. 'Better defended than I am,' commented Julie.

'She may not have two large dogs.'

Diamond glanced up and noted the burglar alarm high on the front of the house.

But no dogs. They heard slippered footsteps respond to the doorbell, then bolts being drawn. The door opened as far as the safety-chain permitted and a suspicious-sounding voice asked who it was. Diamond gave their names and presented his ID at the narrow opening.

From inside came the sound of the chain being unfastened. 'Before you open up,' Diamond said, 'are you Mrs Wycherley, ma'am?'

She confirmed that she was.

'That's all right, then,' he said, and added with a wink at Julie, 'we can't be too careful.'

Polly Wycherley didn't take it as the waggish remark it was meant to be. Opening the door fully, she said, 'That's a fact. You hear of such horrific things these days. You can't even feel safe in your own home.'

And no wonder, Diamond thought when he stepped into the hall. The walls were hung with objects that suggested anything but safety: a Zulu shield and crossed assegais; a leopard-skin; a war drum; and what looked like a witch-doctor's mask. It was quite a relief to pass into the living room, filled mainly with bookshelves, each volume protected by a transparent wrapper that Polly must have fitted herself. The relief was short-lived when he caught sight of some of the titles: *Kiss Me Deadly*, *The Beast Must Die*, *Blood Money* and *The Body in the Billiard Room*. On one of the shelves was a box opened to display a set of duelling pistols. Here was your sweet silver-haired lady, bolting her door against the horrific world outside before settling down with a grisly murder, surrounded by her collection of weapons. Mind, a sense of order prevailed. But on the whole he preferred the clutter at Shirley-Ann's.

'I know practically nothing about books,' he said, to get things started, speaking from an uncomfortable Hepplewhite-style sofa with wooden arms and back, 'but this looks to be a fine collection, Mrs Wycherley. You obviously take care of it, too.'

'You mean my plastic covers? They protect the dust jackets,' she explained as if that were self-evident.

'But isn't that unfair to dust jackets?'

'Why?'

'They don't want protecting. They want to get on with their proper job.'

She saw the logic in that and laughed. 'They lose their value if the jackets are damaged.'

'So this is an investment?'

'It's more than that,' she said. 'I couldn't put into words the excitement to be had from finding a good first edition.'

'In its jacket?'

'The jackets are indispensable.'

'But the book you read is the same whether it's a clean copy like these or some dog-eared old paperback from a charity shop.'

'I have hundreds of those,' she said. 'I keep my reading copies in a spare room upstairs.'

'You don't read these?'

'No.'

'What have you got upstairs? Just crime?'

She smiled. 'My dear Superintendent, there's nothing unusual in that. People have always enjoyed a good mystery, from Prime Ministers to ordinary folk like me. I didn't have so much time for reading when my husband was alive. We travelled a lot. But in the last twelve years I've become quite addicted.'

Diamond had no need to steer the conversation. Polly moved smoothly on to the prescribed route.

'That was how I came to found the Bloodhounds. You go to a function and meet other enthusiasts and find you have a lot in common. We've had six very enjoyable years. This dreadful tragedy is going to put an end to it, I fear. I've already cancelled the next meeting. Just imagine! We'd all be staring at each other wondering who was capable of a real murder. You couldn't possibly talk about books. Let me get you a nice cup of tea.'

'No, thanks—'

'Then perhaps Inspector Hargreaves . . . ?'

'Nor me,' said Julie. 'We just had something.'

'But a cup of tea always goes down well. Or coffee? I'm due for one about now.'

Diamond said firmly, 'You don't mind if we talk about the evening Mr Towers was killed?'

'I do have decaffeinated, if you prefer,' Polly offered, unwilling to be denied. It was almost a point of principle to provide hospitality. Perhaps she wanted time in the kitchen to marshal her thoughts.

'You were one of the first at the meeting, I understand.'

She gave a nod. 'To make up for the previous week, when I was late. Stupidly, I dropped my car keys down a drain in New Bond Street. I got them back, but I hate being late for anything, so I made a special effort this time. I do wish I could get you something. A drink?'

'No, thanks. You drove down to the meeting?'

'I always do. I could take the minibus, I suppose, but it does involve some walking, quite late in the evening, and you can't . . .'

'. . . be too careful.'

She smiled. 'I was the first to arrive. Sid came soon after.'

'Did you notice his behaviour? Did he seem nervous?'

'No more than usual. In fact, rather less. He actually said things a couple of times during the meeting.'

'Do you remember what?'

She fingered a button of her cardigan. 'I can try.' After a pause, she said, 'Yes, at the beginning, someone wondered who was missing and Sid mentioned Rupert, and added that Rupert was always late – which is true.'

'Anything else?'

Polly dredged her memory. 'We were talking about the missing stamp. Miss Chilmark had suggested we might be able to throw some light on the mystery. Someone – Jessica, I'm sure – came up with the theory that some fanatical collector may have taken it. She suggested he might be a middle-aged man with a personality defect,

260

and Sid interrupted to say that it might equally have been a woman.

'Sid said as much as that?'

'No, he just interrupted with the words, "Or woman," but that was essentially the point, and quite fair. I don't think he spoke again until nearly the end of the meeting. However, he did produce a paper bag at an opportune moment. I expect you've heard about Miss Chilmark's attack?'

Diamond nodded. 'But let's stay with Sid. You said he spoke at the end?'

'I mean after the discovery of the stamp. There was a difference of opinion as to whether Milo should go directly to the police. He was in two minds, you see. He felt he might come under suspicion and – please don't take offence at this – several of them clearly believed he might be treated roughly. In fact, only two of us, Miss Chilmark and I, were for Milo going to the police. Sid was asked and what he said was that he could stay quiet – which nobody doubted.'

This was the first Diamond had heard of a split of opinion at the end. 'If the majority favoured staying quiet, how was it that Milo came in to report the matter?'

She smiled, and Rupert's comment came back to Diamond. *Look at her eyes when she smiles.* She said in a self-congratulatory way, 'Good sense prevailed. Milo listened to us and saw that he had a public duty. The others may have been willing to turn a blind eye—'

'But you weren't?'

'It didn't come to that. Nobody made any threats. Milo reached his own decision.'

Diamond understood now. Democracy wouldn't have worked. Polly and Mrs Chilmark had felt they had a public duty. Milo had been left with no option.

'Getting back to Sid,' he said, 'the more I hear about him, the more I think he wasn't the doormat that his quiet behaviour suggested.'

'That's a fact,' Polly said firmly. 'Sid may have been

reticent, but he was no fool. He knew as much as any of us about detective stories, with the possible exception of Milo. John Dickson Carr was his special interest.'

'I've seen the books in his flat.'

This drew an interested 'Oh?' from Polly. 'I always imagined he must have a collection.'

'They wouldn't be of use to you,' he told her. 'Most of them had no jackets, and those that did were withdrawn from libraries. Do you collect Dickson Carr, ma'am?'

She waved vaguely across the room. 'I have a few of the collectable ones. He was very prolific.'

'A writer of crafty plots, I gather. I can see why the locked room stories appealed to Sid, considering his line of work.'

'As a security officer? Actually I doubt if he came across that sort of thing working for Impregnable. It doesn't often happen in real life, does it?'

Diamond let that pass. He had a sense that Polly was doing her best to manipulate the interview now that she was over the surprise of their visit. The image she presented, of the homely woman in twin-set, tweed skirt and slippers, with her soft curls, teapot and sweet smile, had slipped once or twice already. He remembered the reservations about her that he'd got from Jessica Shaw and Miss Chilmark. 'I understand Sid joined the Bloodhounds on the advice of his doctor.'

'Dr Newburn, yes. My doctor, too. A lovely person. Dead now, unhappily.' The saccharine smile appeared again. 'Of natural causes. Dr Newburn got in touch with me and asked if I thought it would work. He knew of my involvement. Sid was recovering from a breakdown. I said I couldn't promise anything, but he was welcome to come along and I'd make sure he wasn't put under more stress. My conscience is clear in that regard, anyway.'

Spoken serenely, ignoring the logic that Sid's introduction to the Bloodhounds had led to his death.

'This breakdown. What was the cause?'

'I couldn't tell you. He did let drop the fact that

his house had once been burgled. A horrible thing to happen to anybody. Would that lead to a breakdown, do you suppose?'

'Your guess is as good as mine, ma'am.' After a suitable pause he said in the tone of someone testing a theory, 'I'd appreciate your reaction to a thought I had. We know that Sid enjoyed a locked room puzzle. I'm wondering whether the reason he drove to the boatyard was simple curiosity, to work out for himself what must have happened. What you had was a Dickson Carr set-up. Milo did make this clear?'

'Indeed, yes. He showed us the key to the padlock and said where he'd bought it and how impossible it was for anyone to have a spare key.'

'Quite a challenge for a man like Sid, a student of the locked room puzzle. Trained in security, too. The question is: did he go down to Limpley Stoke to have a quiet look round the narrowboat and see for himself?'

'You could well be right,' said Polly.

'Then either he surprised the murderer or the murderer followed him there and surprised him. That's the logic of it, isn't it? Either way, Sid got the worst of it.'

'Poor Sid,' said Polly. She got up and went to a sideboard and took out a box of chocolates. Her need to be seen as hospitable was almost pathological. 'All soft centres,' she said as she offered them.

Diamond shook his head and Julie took her cue from him. 'But don't let us stop *you*, ma'am,' Diamond said. He was still weighing up this woman, trying to picture her wielding a windlass at the unsuspecting Sid. Was it plausible? She was sixty, at least, short and overweight, with a tendency to wheeze when she breathed, yet if she had caught him from behind, say, or bending forward, one blow could have done the job. A couple of blows were what the pathologist had reported.

The motive was harder to pin down. What about opportunity, then?

'Just for the record, Mrs Wycherley, would you mind

telling me where you were between the hours of nine and midnight on that evening, the evening Sid Towers was killed? I have to ask everybody.'

She took the question placidly enough. 'Here, for most of the time. I drove back here directly after the meeting. It's in the statement I made to the sergeant who called.'

'Directly?'

'Well, I spoke to one of the others for a short time. Who was it? Miss Chilmark, I think. I thanked her for supporting me. We agreed it was the proper course of conduct. She's a difficult person, I have to say, but on this occasion I was glad to have her on my side against the Young Turks in our club.'

'Were you the last to leave the crypt?'

'I generally am. I like to close the door myself. Miss Chilmark was just ahead of me. Don't misunderstand me. We probably didn't talk for more than a couple of minutes after the others had gone.'

Julie came in with a useful question. 'Did you notice who left first?'

'After Milo, do you mean? He was the first out.'

'Yes.'

'Sid. But he always is quick to make his getaway. I mean *was*, God bless him. He was in dread of anyone getting into a conversation with him. I think some time ago Jessica Shaw practically dragged him by the coat-tails to one of the local pubs. She caught him once more, but he was wary after that.'

'Who left after Sid?' Diamond asked.

'You *are* asking some questions. It must have been our new member, Shirley-Ann, followed by Jessica or Rupert, I'm not sure who. Then Miss Chilmark and I. We were all out within five minutes and going our different ways.'

'And you drove straight here?'

'I thought that was clear, Superintendent.'

They established next that no one could vouch for Polly's presence in the house on the night of the crime.

She had watched *News at Ten* and an old Stewart Granger film, but that was no alibi.

At Diamond's request, Polly then dictated a list of all the Bloodhounds since the club had begun in 1989. Her memory appeared to be functioning brilliantly. 'Tom Parry-Morgan, Milo, myself, Annie Allen, Gilbert Jones, Marilyn Slade-Baker, Alan Jellicoe, the Pearce sisters, Colonel Twigg, the Bentins from Oklahoma ...' She completed it without pause until she got to Rupert's name and Diamond asked how this charming, but wayward, man had come to join.

'Quite by chance,' Polly recalled. 'We used to meet in the Francis Hotel. A corner of the Roman Bar. We were more informal then. Rupert happened to come in for a drink and overheard our discussion and joined in. He's like that, loves an argument. He gets very animated after a few drinks. We were asked to take our meetings to another venue after one evening when he was particularly noisy. That's how we moved to the crypt.'

'What did Rupert think of that?'

'Well, he couldn't say much, could he? He was the cause of our ban. The crypt isn't licensed, but it's next door to the Saracen's Head, which suits him well, I fancy. He's a mischief-maker at times, but brilliant in his way, and I thought it was in all our interests to keep him as a member.'

They got up to leave. Diamond thanked Polly for seeing them at such a late hour.

She said, 'I hope I've been of some help, but I doubt it. I can't think how this ghastly thing happened.'

'It's becoming clearer to me, ma'am,' he told her. 'And, yes, you have been helpful. The Bloodhounds have been meeting for six years. That's mainly down to you. I mean you put a lot into it. I've heard this from several sources. For you, it's more than just a way to pass a Monday evening.'

She said modestly, 'It isn't any hardship.'

'Ah, but you do make a point of encouraging them.

A phone call here and there. The odd cup of coffee.'

'I enjoy it.'

'Keeping up with the other members, I mean. Did you
get to know Sid away from the meetings?'

She returned his gaze with cold eyes. 'Not at all.'

'Never met him outside the crypt?'

'He was unapproachable.'

'Of course.' At the front door, he paused. 'I noticed
you have a burglar alarm fitted on the front of your
house.'

'Yes, I do.'

'Very sensible. You have it serviced on a regular basis,
I'm sure.'

'Of course. They send a man every six months.'

'That's all right, then.' He put on his trilby, stepped
away from the house and turned to look up at the
box fitted under the eaves. 'It's too dark to see. Out
of interest, Mrs Wycherley, does it happen to be one
of the Impregnable alarms?'

'No,' she said with just a hint of mockery, 'it's a
Chubb.'

Down at the central police station, John Wigfull was
lingering in the incident room. The civilian clerks had
long since finished. One sergeant was trying to look busy
in front of a screen.

'Working late, John?' Diamond commented.

Gratified to be found still on duty, Wigfull actually
smiled. 'Needs must. I'm just back from the Holburne
Museum, making sure the night squad are on their toes.'

'Expecting some action tonight?'

'That's the pattern. There isn't much delay after the
riddle is sent. The Penny Black was taken the night
after, and it turned up on the day the second riddle
was received.'

'Good thinking. So it's a strong presence down at the
museum?'

'Six men.'

'Strategically posted?'

'It's not an easy building, but I think six should be enough.'

'To end the suspense?'

Wigfull frowned uncertainly.

'I'm quoting the riddle, John. *To end the suspense, as yours truly did . . .*'

'Ah.'

'. . . *Discover the way to Sydney from Sid.* And that's what you've done. Six good men posted in Sydney Gardens should end the suspense sooner than Johnny expects.'

'I'd like to think so,' said Wigfull.

'So are you off home?'

He shook his head. 'I'll stick around, I think. Stay in touch with the lads down there.'

'A chance for some quiet reflection, eh?' Diamond said. 'You're still pondering over the locked room mystery, I dare say. Any fresh theories?'

Wigfull's moustache moved strangely, and Diamond thought he might be grinding his teeth. He had no theories he wanted to share.

When invited for a coffee in the canteen, he declined.

'So whodunit, Julie?'

They had the canteen entirely to themselves apart from the woman who had served them, and she was reading a Barbara Cartland in the kitchen. This was to be the last coffee of the day. Diamond had an apricot pie to go with his. By the time he got home, Steph would have eaten.

Julie couldn't give an answer, and was wise enough not to guess.

'We've seen them all now,' Diamond reminded her chirpily. 'Heard all their stories.'

'And got more questions than answers,' she said.

'Clues, then. Let's examine the clues.'

'Rupert's beret?'

This wasn't high on his own list, and he explained

why. 'I'm keeping an open mind on that one. If we *ever* get hold of the damned thing – and I mean to have one more try tonight – and if we find it spotted with paint, what does it tell us – only that Rupert may have written an unkind message on a gallery window.'

Julie was unwilling to dismiss the beret. 'It means we ought to question him again for sure, in case he really found out something about Jessica.'

He made no response, preferring a bite of the pie. 'Another clue?'

'The paper bag, if you prefer,' she said.

'It isn't what I prefer,' he said, 'it's what we have to deal with.' Both of them were tired, and it was showing.

Julie said, 'Since we're talking whodunits, I think the bag is a red herring. I mean the writing on the bag. We thought it proved that Sid composed the riddles. We were obviously mistaken.'

'You mean if this third riddle is authentic?'

'Yes.'

'Very likely is, Julie. Similar type, similar paper, similar distribution.'

'So what are we to make of the writing on it? They *are* lists of rhyming words.'

'True.'

'And they seem to refer to what was going on. You pointed out yourself that one of the lists rhymes with the word "Motion", and another with "Black", presumably for Penny Black.'

'And "Room" – for locked room.'

'What was Sid up to, then, if he wasn't working on a new riddle?'

'You're making an assumption there, Julie, that I can't automatically accept.'

'What's that?' She screwed up her face, trying to work it out. Not easy, after more than thirteen hours on duty. 'You're questioning whether Sid made those lists?'

He finished the pie and wiped the edges of his mouth. 'Think of that paper bag as evidence we pass on to the

CPS. What do they want from us? Continuity of evidence. Remember your promotion exams. First, they want to know where it originated.'

'A secondhand bookshop.'

'By no means certain.'

'They nearly always use brown paper bags.'

'So do plenty of other shops.'

'It did contain a book.'

'All right. Who owned the book?'

'Sid.'

'Yes, but where was it from? We can't say. Maybe not from a shop at all. Maybe from another collector, someone else in the Bloodhounds, someone who jotted lists on a paper bag.'

'And gave it to Sid by accident?'

'Or design.'

'That's really devious.'

'This murder is, Julie. I'm not saying this is what happened. As well as examining the start of this chain, you have to look at the end. What happened to the bag after it left Sid's possession?'

'It was jammed against Miss Chilmark's face.'

'But who by?'

'Jessica Shaw.'

'And then?'

'It ended up in Jessica's handbag. Oh!' She put her hand to her mouth. 'She could have written the lists.'

He said nothing, letting this take root.

Julie moved to the next stage in the logic. 'But she handed us the bag. If she'd used it herself to make lists, she'd never have done that. She isn't daft. She would have destroyed it.'

'Unless she wanted us to see the lists.'

Julie frowned. 'And assume they must have been written by Sid. Why?'

'To shift suspicion.'

Her eyes widened amazingly for one so tired. 'I hadn't seen it like that at all.'

'It's only one end of the chain, remember.'

'Can we get a handwriting expert on to this?'

'I sent the bag away with a sample of Sid's writing,' he said, 'but I'm not optimistic. Graphologists like joined-up writing. This wasn't. And – before you ask – none of the words was misspelled. No point in running a little test for our suspects.

She said, 'It does bring us to another clue.'

'What's that?'

'The writing on the gallery window. *She did for Sid.* Someone – probably Rupert – believes Jessica is the killer.'

'Or wants us to believe she is.' He was finding this session helpful. He moved on to the most elusive of all the elements in this case: the motive. Succinctly, he laid out the options for Julie to consider. The best bet was that Sid had been a blackmailer. At Impregnable he had unusual opportunities to pick up titbits of information about people's private affairs. He had access to confidential files and he worked with ex-policemen with inside knowledge of the indiscretions of some of the most outwardly respectable residents of Bath. Certainly there were questions about Miss Chilmark's regular withdrawals of large sums from the bank. Jessica, too, might be vulnerable to blackmail if she was having an affair with A.J. Rupert had a past, but he was quite open about it. Of the others, Polly seemed well defended in every sense and Shirley-Ann was surely too new on the scene to have fallen a victim.

There were two big problems with the blackmail theory, he admitted to Julie. Firstly, there was no evidence that Sid had received money in any appreciable amounts. He lived in that depressing flat in the shadow of the viaduct in Oak Street and worked unsocial hours as a night-watchman. Surely a blackmailer's lifestyle would have shown some improvement? And the second problem was the manner of Sid's death. Why would a blackmail victim choose to put an end to the extortion in such an elaborate fashion, in a locked cabin on a boat?

So he outlined his alternative theory, the one he had

touched on while interviewing Polly. This postulated that the killing had not been planned. It was sparked by the Penny Black turning up in the astonishing way it did. Sid – the Dickson Carr fanatic – was so excited, so intrigued, by a real-life locked room puzzle that he went to the boat to examine it for himself. There he met the person responsible. Sid was killed because of what he discovered, not who he was.

'What was the murderer doing there?' Julie asked.

Diamond gripped the edge of the table as a thought struck him. His eyes shone. 'Julie, that's the whole point. Brilliant! You haven't told me whodunit, but you've given me the solution to the locked room mystery.'

It was after ten that evening when he returned to Hay Hill, this time alone, Julie having been released from duty as a reward for her brilliance.

Rupert's house still had no light inside. The dog barked furiously.

The waitress in the Paragon Bar and Bistro told him Rupert must have gone somewhere else for a change. She hadn't seen him all evening. Neither had the landlord at his other local, the Lansdown Arms.

He looked at the clock and decided there was time to try the Saracen's Head, a mere five minutes away, down the hill in Broad Street. The Saracen was still doing good business towards closing time, but there wasn't a beret to be seen. Diamond was given some abuse by a well-tanked customer for giving a shout out of turn. A glare put a stop to that, and got the barman's attention as well. After a quick consultation among the bar staff, one of them pointed to a table in one of the partitioned sections. Here, it seemed, Rupert occasionally held court, telling tall stories about his encounters with the great and the not-so-good, surrounded by a delighted crowd of regulars. These were the people who looked after Marlowe the night that unruly animal was banished from the Bloodhounds' meeting.

It emerged that Rupert had indeed called in for a beer much earlier, about seven. One glass of bitter. He had been dressed as usual in beret, black leather and blue cords. Less usually, he hadn't brought Marlowe because, he had explained, he had been invited for drinks at another pub and dogs weren't welcome in some houses. He had left after five minutes. Nobody knew any more about this arrangement.

There are one hundred and forty public houses in and around Bath.

Diamond treated himself to a brandy before going home.

THIRTY

For John Wigfull there was no sleep that night. About midnight he parked his car opposite the entrance to the Bath Spa Hotel and walked briskly through Sydney Gardens to the Holburne Museum. A less conscientious officer might have parked closer to the building, in Sydney Road, say, just around the corner. Wigfull was determined to give nobody a clue as to his presence, and that included his own men. When the side door of the museum opened and the sergeant looked out, Wigfull put his finger to his lips and went silently in.

The Holburne is not an easy building to make secure. It looks like a cross between an English country house and a Greek temple. Built towards the end of the eighteenth century as a hotel with a classical façade of a pediment and four columns mounted above three arches, the original structure has undergone several alterations in its two-hundred-year existence, notably the addition of an extra storey and balustraded walls at each side. The front is open to the road. Where once there were railings, there remains only a low wall facing Great Pulteney Street. Two watchman's boxes have a purely decorative function now. At the rear, a combination of drainpipes and footholds between the stone blocks would be as good as a ladder to an intruder. Fortunately, the alarm system is modern and efficient and there are floodlights at the front and security lights right around the building.

The six policemen posted strategically inside and on the roof were in radio contact and Wigfull made sure that they were alert. As well as calling them a number of times on their personal radios, he took the extra precaution of visiting them half-hourly. He made no friends that night, but nobody slept on duty.

By 6.30 next morning, nothing suspicious had occurred. Disappointed at having failed to trap the villain, but relieved that the museum was intact, Wigfull stood on the roof eating chocolate and watching the first glimmer of dawn over Bathampton Down. It was safe, he decided, to return home for a few hours' rest. Leaving instructions to the senior man to keep up the vigil until the relief team arrived at 8 a.m., he took the short cut through Sydney Gardens towards his car. A light frost had blanched the lawns.

Cold as it felt outdoors, this was a charming place to be at this early hour. In years past, Sydney Gardens had been a mecca for Bathonians. It had brass bands, a bowling green, a maze, grottoes and firework displays. Two emperors, Napoleon III and Haile Selassie, had walked these paths. So had Jane Austen, Emma Hamilton and Lord Macaulay. This morning John Wigfull, Chief Inspector, justifiably content after a night's policing, had the entire place to himself.

Except for one dog.

He spotted it in the distance coming over the narrower of the two railway bridges, a large black poodle, trotting with that air of purpose special to dogs. Instead of staying on the path, the poodle started across the broad sweep of lawn towards the laurel bushes on the far side. Wigfull, almost as purposeful, continued his brisk walk, thinking of other things. Ahead, he knew, was the railway cutting. All that could be seen of it was a massive stone retaining wall and he wondered why a number of park benches were positioned opposite, as if users of the park might wish to turn their backs on the lawns and trees and stare at blocks of grimy stone. In 1841 Brunel had been permitted to navigate his Great Western Railway through the gardens provided that the trains would not spoil the vista, so the track was laid in a deep gully impossible to see from the benches. Brunel had fulfilled the contract handsomely. The bridges for pedestrians were a pleasure to use, elegant and unobtrusive. Wigfull would need to cross the railway and the canal a short way on to reach his car. He didn't get that far because his attention was caught again by the dog.

That it was a poodle had been clear from the moment he had seen it, for it was clipped. Large standard poodles are not often seen these days. This was a fine specimen and probably should not have been off the leash. The owner had not appeared. In his days as a beat officer, Wigfull might have gone to investigate, but this morning he had more important things on his mind than a stray poodle.

The poodle had other ideas. Halfway across the lawn, it switched direction and came lolloping towards Wigfull. Only then did he notice something odd. He was no expert on poodle-clipping, but he had always thought they were supposed to have pointed muzzles, whatever outcrops of hair were permitted around the top of the head and the mane.

This one had a beard. Or sidewhiskers growing below the jawline like some Prussian aristocrat of a century ago. A strange extravagance, and not symmetrical. There was definitely more of it on the right of the jaw than the left.

Wigfull stopped to look.

He had been mistaken. He wasn't looking at a beard, but something the dog was carrying between its teeth. Something as dark as the rest of the coat.

'Here, boy!'

He stopped and held out his hand.

The dog approached to within a few yards before changing its mind and racing away.

But in that short time, Wigfull saw clearly what the dog had in its mouth: a black beret.

'Oy! Come back!'

The beret could have belonged to anyone, been discarded by anyone. But there are not many owners of berets in Bath. He knew of one of them. He decided he had better go in pursuit.

There is no chance of outrunning a dog, but they don't usually dash at top speed for long. This one stopped after thirty yards or so and looked back, wagging its pom-pom tail.

Wigfull called some encouraging words. The dog dropped the beret and barked. It was ready for a game.

'Come on, then!'

It didn't come. It ran off again – not without picking up the beret.

Wigfull wondered if this was worth the trouble. His shoes were going to be ruined. He looked about him to see if the poodle's owner was anywhere in sight. No such luck.

Away to his left, on the far side of the lawn, was a Roman temple, or, rather, a twentieth-century reconstruction, an upmarket rain-shelter. The poodle was heading towards it fast. If he could only trap it in there . . .

He covered the distance quickly. The dog had gone inside and was crouching under the stone seat that extended around the three enclosed sides. The beret was still in its mouth.

Wigfull was wary of going too close. If the poodle felt cornered, it might get aggressive. Up to now, it had seemed playful, but this was a new situation.

He ventured just inside the temple and tried clicking his tongue in a friendly way. The dog gave a low growl.

'It's all right, old fellow,' Wigfull said reassuringly. 'I'm just a friend. Are you going to give me a present? I'd like that.'

The dog growled again. In the gloom of the temple its eyes had a reddish glint that Wigfull didn't care for.

Then he remembered the bar of chocolate he had in his pocket to sustain him through the night. There were still several pieces left. Did poodles eat chocolate?

'How about this, then?' He held a piece out. 'Just the job, eh?'

The dog was definitely interested. It raised its head and sniffed. Only it didn't move from under the seat.

'Come and get it, then.'

No chance, the poodle seemed to say.

In case he was more of a threat standing up, Wigfull crossed to the side opposite the dog and sat down, still holding out the chocolate in his open palm and speaking encouragingly.

There was a break in the deadlock. The dog let the beret slip from its jaws and took a couple of deep sniffs. Then it got up, leaving the beret, and crossed to where Wigfull was sitting, put its nose to the chocolate, decided it was edible and took it.

He noticed it was wearing a collar with a name tag, but he didn't dare put his hand under its neck. He found two more pieces of chocolate. The first he fed to the dog, and the second he planned to throw through the temple pillars on to the path outside. The dog would run after it and Wigfull would retrieve the beret.

But it didn't happen like that. A voice from nowhere, echoing around the stone walls, impressive as an oracle, spoke the words, 'What are you feeding that dog?'

Wigfull jerked his hand away and looked guiltily to his right.

A man carrying a spade like a weapon stepped from behind a pillar. He was dressed in a scuffed leather jacket, black jeans and gumboots. He looked dangerous.

'Only chocolate,' said Wigfull.

'You've no business feeding him anything,' said the man with the spade. 'What's your game?'

Wigfull explained that he was a detective, a chief inspector, and he was trying to remove the beret from the dog, because it might be evidence in a case he was involved in. It sounded unconvincing, even to him, and on this, of all mornings, he wasn't carrying his identity card. He'd changed into a padded jacket for the night and left the ID in his suit at home.

The poodle growled at Wigfull.

The man said, 'Bloody liar.'

Wigfull pointed across the temple at the beret, still lying on the floor.

The man said, 'Chief inspector, my arse. You were feeding him something. You weren't after the beret. You hadn't even bothered to pick it up. You were after my dog. He's a thoroughbred poodle, is Inky, and you well know it.'

'He's yours?' said Wigfull.

'Why else would he be running loose in the park? I'm the deputy head gardener here.'

The dispute continued for some time before Wigfull convinced the gardener that he was, indeed, one of the top men at Manvers Street and not a dog-snatcher. Finally, they went their different ways, Wigfull with the beret in his pocket, and the gardener leading Inky to a council van.

Annoyed with himself, Wigfull walked on towards the far end of the gardens and crossed the railway and the canal, thinking of things he should have said. He was so preoccupied that he failed to notice something far more sinister than a poodle with a beret.

THIRTY-ONE

About twenty to seven the same morning, a jogger on his regular route along the towpath, approaching the point where the canal passes under Cleveland House and Sydney Road before entering Sydney Gardens, caught sight through the tunnel of the first of the two wrought-iron bridges. He always looked forward to this point of the run. Aside from the boost of knowing that he was two-thirds of the way home, there was the sheer pleasure in the spectacle of the white-painted bridge framed by the arch of the tunnel.

Except that this morning something was different.

When you are jogging for exercise, you don't stop to get a better view of things along the way. As he approached the tunnel, the jogger thought he could make out an object suspended beneath the arch of the bridge, but he couldn't tell what it was. It isn't possible to run through the tunnel, so he climbed up to Sydney Road to enter the Gardens, cross by the iron bridge and take the little gate down to rejoin the towpath. When he got closer he saw that he was not mistaken. Something was hanging from the bridge, and it was a body.

This section of canal is one of Bath's secrets, as charming as anything in the city, almost two centuries old, yet constructed with visual appeal, with sweetly curved passing-places, and glimpses under the arches of several bridges, their reflections patterning the water.

By eight, the reflections included an inflatable dinghy, police, park officials, a doctor and two ambulancemen.

The entire area was cordoned off. The body was photographed in situ and seen by the police surgeon before police performed the tricky operation of cutting it down and lowering it into the dinghy. The dead man was dressed in a black leather jacket, striped shirt, navy blue corduroy trousers and black shoes. He was thin, about six feet tall and looked about forty-five. His neck was obviously broken, confirming a considerable 'drop'. This, the surgeon pointed out, must have been an efficient hanging. Most suicide victims use a chair or a ladder and rarely break their necks and in consequence die slowly.

The pockets of the leather jacket were found to contain a five-pound note, some loose change, a set of keys on a ring and a padlock. An alert constable pointed out that the padlock was of the same make as the German one featured in the locked room case currently being investigated by the murder squad. The incident room was informed at once.

Peter Diamond had no breakfast that morning. He drove the short distance from his home in Weston to the Royal United Hospital in time to see the body brought into the mortuary. He was allowed to unzip the body-bag and confirm that the dead man was Rupert Darby. And the noose was still around his neck. The rope had been cut higher up.

A real sense of loss affected the big detective on seeing Rupert's gaunt face, the bluish lips parted, revealing the gaps between a few nicotine-stained teeth. In that one short meeting the previous morning he had enjoyed talking to Rupert, quickly getting attuned to his irreverent wit and warming to his vitality. What remained of the man was wholly pathetic.

He would have liked to examine the arms and torso for possible bruising, but that was the pathologist's prerogative. To remove the clothes prematurely would be a major breach of procedure.

After viewing the corpse, Diamond went home briefly.

Steph offered to cook his usual bacon and eggs but he didn't fancy anything except a black coffee. He told her he expected another long day.

John Wigfull arrived an hour later than usual, with heavy shadows around his eyes, and was startled to find so much activity in the incident room. For a few nerve-racking minutes, he wondered if in the short time he had been away, the thief had got into the museum.

Diamond told him about Rupert Darby.

In turn, Wigfull told Diamond about the beret he had found. He didn't go into the problems Inky the poodle had given him, merely stating that he had picked up the beret soon after six-thirty. 'I'm bound to say I wondered about it when I saw it,' he added.

'Where was it?' Diamond asked.

'Em, I picked it up in that temple thing near the railway bridge. Do you know where I mean?' He produced the beret from his pocket. 'By the look of this, some animal has chewed it about a bit. A dog, I'd say. Do you think it was Rupert's?'

'Sure of it.' Diamond flattened the beret on a table. 'You can see where the paint spray got to it.'

Wigfull hadn't heard about the paint, or the graffiti on the Walsingham Gallery window. He had to be told. He studied the tiny paint spots that covered about a third of the beret and said humbly that if he'd realised how crucial a piece of evidence this was, he'd have treated it more carefully.

Diamond had not deliberately withheld information, he made clear; he'd only heard about it late the previous afternoon. There had not been an opportunity.

Wigfull, floundering in his own deceit, made no objection. Instead, he said, 'He must have taken off the beret to fit the noose over his head. Probably left it on the bridge and a dog picked it up.'

'His own dog, I expect,' said Diamond, reasonably enough.

'I shouldn't count on it,' said Wigfull, going red. 'I did happen to see a large poodle running loose in the gardens – quite near the temple, actually.'

'Could have been the poodle, then.'

'Doesn't really matter, does it?' said Wigfull, trying to emphasise the larger considerations. 'The crucial thing is that we found it and confirmed what you heard about the paint marks. Pretty damning. This writing on the gallery window was a desperate attempt by Rupert to throw suspicion on someone else, wouldn't you say?'

'Looks that way,' Diamond said.

'And when it didn't succeed, when you followed up yesterday, asking for him in all his usual haunts, he heard we were on to him and topped himself.'

Diamond wasn't having that. He hadn't hounded Rupert to his death. 'You're wrong there, John. This hanging wasn't something he thought of yesterday evening. It couldn't have been.'

This drew a frown from Wigfull.

Patiently and without condescension, Diamond explained, 'It was in the third riddle:

> To end the suspense, as yours truly did,
> Discover the way to Sydney from Sid.'

Wigfull's long, silent look showed that he dearly wanted to know what Diamond was getting at.

'The riddle predicted this hanging,' Diamond went on. '*To end the suspense*: that's what happened this morning. Rupert was suspended from the bridge. When he was cut down, we ended the suspense. It was a play on words, John, a gruesome double meaning. So it was all planned. *Discover the way to Sydney* is what we did, except that we guessed wrong and picked the bloody museum instead of the bridge. If we'd thought more about every sodding word in the riddle, we might have anticipated this.'

'Might not.'

Really Diamond had to agree. The lines had tantalised,

as the previous riddles had. To have penetrated their true meaning would have required the brilliance of one of those fictional sleuths the Bloodhounds revered. He knew his limitations.

Wigfull took a more positive line. 'At least you have your murderer and I have my locked room thief,' he pointed out. 'All we have to do now is work out how it was done.'

'You're assuming Rupert Darby is your man?'

'Aren't you?' said Wigfull, blushing scarlet.

Diamond said, 'If you really want to know, John, I think you couldn't be more wrong. I know how it was done, but I'm damned if I know who did it.'

'You're talking about the locked room mystery? You think you've cracked it?' said Wigfull on a shrill note of disbelief.

Diamond had cracked it all right. He was certain now, after thinking it through, going over it many times in his mind since getting the flash of inspiration the evening before. As he'd told Julie at the time, the breakthrough had come with her question: *What was the murderer doing there?*

Between them, on a table, labelled and bagged, were the contents of the dead man's pockets. Diamond pointed to the polythene bag containing the padlock. 'Take a look. Is it, or is it not, indistinguishable from the padlock on the narrowboat?'

Wigfull turned it over several times. 'It's the same make, certainly. But we've been through this before, my theory about a substitute padlock. You know we have. I thought I had the answer until you showed it was impossible. This padlock can't have been used. Milo's was on the door when we opened it that night, and he had only the one key. You proved that yourself when your divers found his old bunch of keys in the canal and the damned thing fitted. This doesn't prove anything unless the keys happen to be identical, and we were told by the locksmith that such a thing couldn't happen.'

'Just in case, let's put that to the test,' said Diamond. He went to a drawer and took out Milo's padlock and the key that fitted it. 'Pass me the other bag, would you – the one containing Rupert's keys?'

'Do you think you ought to be handling them?' said Wigfull.

'The keys, please.'

Wigfull shook the bag and dropped the key-ring on the table-top. He wasn't going to risk leaving *his* prints on them.

All work was suspended in the incident room. Everyone in there – detectives, filing clerks, computer operators – gathered around the two senior men. Julie Hargreaves was there, and Keith Halliwell, on tenterhooks to hear the explanation.

There were four keys on the ring: one of the Yale type that looked like a front-door key; a plastic-topped one that was probably for a car; and two small narrow ones, identical in shape. Diamond slotted one of the latter into Milo's padlock and tried unsuccessfully to turn it. To leave no one in any doubt, he tried the other, still with no result.

Wigfull said smugly, 'You see. It doesn't match. Let's compare it with Milo's key. I'm willing to bet the whole shape is different.'

He was right. When placed together, the two keys were clearly cut for different locks.

Diamond was not discouraged. Far from it. 'Right. This is the way it was done. It's going to make you groan, it's so simple. This is Milo's padlock, right? And this is the key that fits it, the one key available at the time. Milo had possession of the key, so Milo was the only person who could open the padlock at any time. Everyone agreed?'

There were some cautious murmurs. Nobody really wanted to be shown up as gullible.

'Now imagine Milo going to his locked boat any time you like. He uses his key to open the padlock. Now what does he do?'

Halliwell said, 'Removes the key and replaces it in his pocket.'

Diamond wagged a stubby finger in confirmation.

'Right. The keys go back into his pocket. What about the padlock?'

'He doesn't put that in his pocket,' said one of the computer operators. 'It's too bulky.'

'So what does he do?'

'Leaves it hanging on the staple.'

'Correct. Locked or unlocked?'

A moment's hesitation. Then, from Wigfull: 'Unlocked, presumably. No point in locking it while he's at home. If he wants privacy, he can use the fingerbolts on the inside of the door.'

Diamond gave a nod and referred the matter to everyone else by spreading his hands. 'Reasonable? Now, let's take this on a bit. Milo is aboard his boat, sitting in the cabin watching TV or cooking. The door is bolted from the inside. The padlock is hanging from the staple outside the door with the shackle – this arched bit at the top – unfastened. Anyone could lift the padlock off. Are you with me still?'

There were nods and murmurs all round.

'Now along comes our villain with a similar padlock – different key, of course – unhooks Milo's padlock and substitutes his own. Done in a moment without Milo being aware of it. He goes away and waits for his opportunity.'

There were definite sounds of understanding.

'You're on to it, aren't you?' said Diamond. 'Milo decides to go out. And what does he do to lock his door? Simply closes it, lifts off the padlock – the new padlock, believing it to be his own – and slots the hasp over the staple. Puts the padlock in position and presses it home. He doesn't need to use his key. They lock automatically, as anyone who has used a padlock knows.'

They were not only up with his explanation now; they were ahead. The murmurs were of appreciation.

'But of course,' Diamond said, 'the padlock he's just attached to his boat belongs to the villain, who can now unlock it at will. So the villain lets himself in, does his dirty work, and leaves. And when he leaves, he fixes

Milo's padlock on the door and presses it closed. Milo comes back later, unlocks as usual, and can't fathom how someone could have got inside his cabin.'

Julie said, 'Nor could anyone else until this moment.'

Halliwell said, 'You've cracked it.'

Even Wigfull was nodding.

A couple of people applauded and almost everyone joined in.

Diamond flushed with embarrassment and reminded them that there was work to be done. His stock had never been higher at the Bath nick.

Later, at the bridge in Sydney Gardens, he examined the scene of the hanging. The approaches were still cordoned off. The scenes of crime officers had come and gone. Part of the rope was still attached to the iron parapet.

'If you wanted to end it all,' Diamond said to Julie, who was with him, 'there are worse ways than this. You sit on the railing here with one end round your neck and the other attached to the bridge and jump down. Mercifully quick.'

'Is that what happened?' Julie said. Something in his tone had suggested otherwise.

'He certainly broke his neck.'

She nodded. 'Only I notice you haven't used the word "suicide" once.'

'Because I'm not sure,' he said.

'Murder by hanging would be pretty unusual, wouldn't it?'

'Very.'

'Have you ever come across one?'

'Never. The victim is going to struggle, isn't he? I reckon you'd need a couple of people to carry it out. It's not as if his arms and legs were pinioned, as they are in a judicial hanging. Unless he were very feeble for some reason, or so pissed out of his mind that he didn't know what was happening—'

'That might be true in this case,' she said.

'He was out early last evening,' Diamond confirmed. 'I did establish that he had a quick pint in the Saracen's

Head about seven and went off to meet someone else.'

'Did he say who?'

'No. But it was at some other pub, which was why he didn't have the dog with him. He told them in the Saracen's that you couldn't count on every pub accepting animals.'

'So it *was* a boozy evening,' said Julie. 'Do we know what time he died?'

He shrugged. 'They can never tell you with any precision. Between midnight – when Wigfull came through here – and six-thirty in the morning.'

Julie tried to picture the scene. 'If he was drunk by then – I mean so helpless that someone could hang him – this would be a long way to bring him. Can you get a car along these paths?'

Diamond's immediate response showed that he'd given the problem some thought already. 'Yes, you can drive straight in from Sydney Place. There's no gate.'

'Difficult to prove,' Julie remarked.

'Impossible.'

'I meant the possibility of murder.'

'You never know what the post-mortem may show up,' he said. 'I've asked Jack Merlin to do it.'

Merlin was the top forensic pathologist in the west of England. He would have to drive seventy miles, from Reading. He and Diamond knew each other of old, but he would have needed some convincing that a routine suicide by hanging was worth the journey.

'You do believe there's something suspicious,' Julie probed.

He made some indeterminate sound and pulled a face. 'Nothing very solid.'

To draw him out, she said, 'There wasn't any suicide note. If he did this from a sense of guilt, you'd think he would want to confess.'

Again, he gave a shrug. 'It's early days to worry about a note. Could be at his house, or in the post. The thing that makes me pause for thought is the padlock being found in his pocket. If you were going on a bender with a friend, would you carry a damned great padlock with you? What would be the point? It's not as if he was going to try the locked room trick on Milo's boat again. No point in that, surely? The only reason I can think of is to link him with the killing of Sid Towers. That *may* have been Rupert's way of telling us he was guilty. But as you just pointed out, he could have done that better in a written confession.'

'And if we're talking murder,' said Julie, 'the padlock in his pocket is a lot easier to plant than a fake confession. It still frames him.'

Diamond turned and looked along the strip of blue-green water towards the second iron bridge. 'Another murder on the canal? I wonder, Julie. I wonder.'

The first task after entering the house in Hay Hill that afternoon was to open a tin of dog food and pour some water into a bowl. Marlowe was ravenous.

Julie saw to it. 'Poor thing – he's been alone here since seven last night. I'm going to take him for a walk. You don't mind?'

'If it doesn't take long.'

He opened some windows.

The second task was to find the suicide note, if one existed. He looked in the obvious places, over the fireplace and by the bed. On the kitchen table. Beside the ancient typewriter in the back room.

No joy.

He found some cash, about thirty pounds, in an old box file, along with an out-of-date passport, letters from the local Job Centre and the Social Security office, unfilled tax declaration forms, doctors' certificates and beer-mats with some names and addresses scribbled on them that meant nothing to Diamond. Nothing so helpful as a diary. A testament to a chaotic existence. He was learning nothing new about Rupert.

While his thoughts were still full of the dead man, he felt a sudden pressure against his leg. 'Jesus!'

Marlowe was back from his walk and wanting more food.

Julie followed the dog in. 'He's a super old thing really,' she said. 'Just wants some training. I'm sure he'd pick it up.'

'You'd better open another tin before he has my leg,' said Diamond, less enchanted.

'Found anything useful?' she asked.

He shook his head.

'So we wait for the post-mortem?'

'Well, I did ask the police surgeon to take a blood sample. There may be some news on the alcohol content. We'd better be getting back to the nick, anyway.'

'What about the dog?'

Diamond's mind was on other things.

Julie said, 'We can't leave him here and forget about him. What's going to happen to him?'

He yawned and said as if such details were beneath him, 'The Dogs' and Cats' Home at Claverton, I reckon.'

Julie's blue eyes moistened at the thought. 'We can't just stick him in a home.'

'My cat Raffles came from there.'

'He's not a young dog, you can see that. No one would want to take him on.'

'There's no alternative.'

'There is. He can come home with me. I'll have him.'

His eyes widened. 'You've got two dogs already, haven't you?'

'So I'm used to it.'

He felt compelled to ask, 'What's your husband going to say?'

'Charlie? I'll talk him into it.'

'But if you've got the dog with you already . . .'

She smiled. 'Exactly. When he sees Marlowe, he won't turn him away.'

He didn't pursue it. Julie's domestic arrangements were her own business. They drove back to Manvers Street with Marlowe seated contentedly on the back seat spreading gusts of his doggy breath around the car.

THIRTY-TWO

Back at Manvers Street, there was a message waiting from the police surgeon: Rupert's blood alcohol level had been high, at 100mg/100ml, but not excessively high. Diamond screwed it up and tossed it into the bin. 'I'd have expected double that figure if he was legless.'

Julie pointed out that 100mg was above the legal limit for a driver and Diamond said offhandedly that this wasn't about pinching a dead man for drunk driving.

She was treading on eggs, but she wasn't going to let him get away with a cheap jibe. 'It's worth remembering when the blood sample was taken, about eight this morning. We don't know when he had his last drink, but the alcohol must have been metabolising for some time. It would have been a higher reading if we'd got the blood earlier.'

He rolled his eyes at her use of the word 'metabolising' and said, 'Too bad we didn't, then. You must be right, I suppose. I'm a dead loss at science. You've got to make allowances, Julie.'

She surprised him by saying, 'You, too, Mr Diamond.'

'What?'

'You've got to make allowances.'

'What for?'

'For the metabolic factor.'

'Ah.' He grinned faintly.

Still unhappy with the result, however, he arranged for a driver to collect the sample and take it at once to the Home Office forensic laboratory at Chepstow. They would check for other substances; it was not inconceivable that one of

290

Rupert's drinks had been spiked. But of course a test for drugs would take time. He hated delays.

His mood didn't improve when he looked into the incident room. The impetus seemed to have gone out of the inquiry, as if everyone there was just cruising now. The general idea was that Rupert's hanging had confirmed him as the murderer, even though no confession had yet come to light. Diamond, they felt, was just being bloody-minded now, and he added more fuel by ordering an immediate search for witnesses and yet another check of all the suspects and the people they lived with, this time to establish their movements since seven the previous evening – an exercise guaranteed to create more resentment and hostility.

He said he would take his share of the flak by checking on Jessica Shaw and the men in her life. Halliwell and a detective constable were sent to the Paragon to interview Miss Chilmark. Julie went off to the Badgerline offices to find where Shirley-Ann Miller was this morning, and after that to the Sports and Leisure Centre to check on Bert, the husband. DS Hughes and DC Twigg were despatched to Claverton to call on Polly Wycherley. And, just for the record, as Diamond put it, DS Mitchell went out to the boatyard to talk to Milo Motion.

Instead of going directly to the Walsingham Gallery, Diamond started at the Locksbrook Trading Estate, west of the city, where Jessica's husband rented a unit for his ceramics business. It was high time to meet that patron of the arts, Mr Barnaby Shaw.

Asked to wait in the showroom, he felt like Gulliver in Lilliput, surrounded by what must have been the entire range of miniature buildings in Barnaby's stock: houses by the hundred, stately homes, churches, pubs and castles. Finely made as they were, to a man as incorrigibly clumsy as Diamond, such exquisite little pieces represented a thousand potential hazards. He stood uneasily in the only space of any size that he could find, trying to stay clear of the slowly revolving display stands. It was a mercy when Barnaby's assistant called him into the managerial suite.

Having negotiated the showroom without mishap, the big man tripped on an Afghan rug and lurched forward, grabbing Barnaby's welcoming hand and practically dragging him to the floor. Bits of china around the room rattled, but nothing was broken.

'Never look where I'm going,' he admitted. 'When I was a kid, my knees were permanently covered in scabs.'

The p.a. escorted him to an armchair.

Barnaby looked more shaken than his guest. Trim in a grey suit, with a maroon shirt and toning tie and pocket handkerchief, he wasn't dressed for wrestling. Diamond watched the way he scooted back around his desk; he looked used to staying out of trouble.

They discussed the miniatures politely. Barnaby had started making matchstick models thirty years ago and progressed by stages to ceramics. He sometimes did commissions, for people who wanted their homes immortalised, but it came rather expensive. Diamond said honestly that he considered it a waste of money, adding tactfully that he was always breaking things.

Barnaby submitted easily to the questioning.

'Yes, I was here until late yesterday evening catching up on the orders. It gets very busy in the run-up to Christmas.'

'Christmas already?' Diamond said in mock horror. 'Anyone with you?'

'Last night, you mean?'

'Yes.'

'Not after six, when the staff left.'

'So what time did you get home, Mr Shaw?'

'Must have been well after midnight. About one-thirty, I'd say.' He was fluent in his replies, unaware (presumably) of Rupert's death, giving the impression of a small businessman pressed to the limit, but cheerful. But he obviously found time to dress well, even if the three-piece suit seemed a little wasted on the trading estate.

'Did you speak to anyone at all in that time?'

'Certainly – on the phone.'

'But you weren't seen by anyone?'

'No.'

'When you got in, was your wife in bed?'

'I presume she was.'

'You don't know?'

'We sleep in separate rooms.'

That fitted, Diamond thought. He was hard pressed to think what Jessica Shaw found attractive in this dull, overworked man, unless it was the money he made from his titchy houses. No, to be fair, he was dapper. And he took the trouble to tint his hair.

'Do you happen to know how Mrs Shaw spent the evening?'

'You'll have to ask her. I haven't seen her since early yesterday. She was still asleep when I left this morning.' He put his hand to his mouth as a thought struck him. 'Look, nothing's happened to Jess, has it?'

'Not to my knowledge.'

'Someone else? A.J.?'

'I was going to ask you about him, Mr Shaw. A close friend of the family, obviously.'

'Well . . . yes,' said Barnaby, as if he needed to ponder the matter before confirming it. 'He's extremely helpful.'

'In what way, sir?'

'With the gallery.'

'You mean setting up the exhibitions, and so forth?'

'Financially, also. He has a large stake in the business.'

This was new information – though Diamond tried to make it seem familiar. 'Well, he would want to see it succeed – as one of the exhibitors, I mean.'

'I doubt if Jess could keep it going without his help,' Barnaby placidly agreed. 'I certainly couldn't fund it out of my profits. I chip in when I can, but the overheads are terrific. You wouldn't believe the business rate in the city. The heating bills, the publicity. A.J. takes care of all that.'

So Barnaby was the patron of the arts. 'Out of his sales?'

'Lord, no. He doesn't sell much at all. He's a proficient artist, but not commercial. He has a private income.'

'And did he help with the party the other evening – the, em, preview?'

'He was a great help, yes.'

'I meant financially. Did he pay for the booze?'

'No. Actually, that was my gift to Jessica. I chip in when I can. It's easier to fund a one-off event like that than meet the regular bills, as A.J. so generously does.'

Barnaby's own generosity of spirit was increasingly puzzling to Diamond, trained to look for the jealousies and rivalries in relationships. This wanted probing further. 'He does this out of friendship, does he?'

'Essentially, yes,' Barnaby confirmed. 'He has a stake, in a sense, because he hopes to sell his paintings, and probably he could insist on a one-man show if he wanted. However, he's content to be treated as any other artist wishing to exhibit.'

'That is altruistic.' Diamond took a deep breath and dived in. 'I don't wish to be offensive, Mr Shaw, but haven't you ever wondered about his motives?'

'I don't understand you.'

'Your wife's an attractive woman.'

'Oh, I see,' said Barnaby coolly. 'You're suggesting a liaison of some kind?'

'In your shoes, I would have given it more than a passing thought.'

'But you're not – and you don't know Jess.'

'I've met her.'

'What I mean, Superintendent, is that she can be trusted absolutely. I understand why you mention the matter. She's a modern, intelligent woman, but she has an old-fashioned notion of fidelity. I won't pretend that she and I are locked into a passionate marriage. I just know that Jessica would never be unfaithful.'

'That must be a great consolation.'

'When she spends so much time in the company of another man, you mean?' said Barnaby. 'I know exactly what you're getting at. I've no doubt that she and A.J. are close. Intellectually, they may be flirting outrageously. Physically, no.'

'Would you mind enlarging on that?' asked Diamond.

'On what?'

'Flirting intellectually.'

Barnaby Shaw smiled. 'If you haven't indulged, it's hard to explain. Let's put it this way. The attraction two people feel for each other is channelled in certain ways. If there is sexual energy, it may find an outlet through other means. Music, perhaps. Or food.'

'Lunchtime walks?'

Barnaby gave him a sharper look. 'I'm not explaining myself very well, am I? Intelligent people – and the two we're discussing are very bright indeed – may indulge in a kind of ritual, finding some means of amusement, some game, that diverts their energy and is fulfilling.'

'That's enough?'

'It would be enough for Jessica.'

Such sophisticated goings-on were outside Diamond's experience. He wasn't sure that he was convinced by the rationale. It was not impossible that Barnaby was trying to convince himself.

'I'd like to ask you about the graffiti that appeared on the gallery window on the evening of the party,' he said.

For the first time, Barnaby was rattled. 'Who told you about that?'

'It came to my attention.'

'The young woman with the glasses and the fringe? Miss Miller?'

'I think it's fairly common knowledge, Mr Shaw. There were plenty of people at the party.'

'Yes, but they didn't all see the writing. In fact, nobody remarked on it until we noticed it ourselves. It wasn't very obvious with all the lights on in the gallery. One tended to look through the windows, not at them.'

'I see. And did your wife have any idea who was responsible?'

'No idea whatsoever, but she was pretty upset about it.'

'Which was why you decided to wipe it off without reporting it?'

'Left to herself, Jess would have called the police.'

'Why didn't she?'

'Because we persuaded her that it wasn't a serious matter. It was better to ignore it.'

'You say "we". Who was involved in this decision?'

'A.J. and I and Miss Miller.'

'So Shirley-Ann joined in, did she?'

'Jessica brought her out of the party to look at the writing. I think she was the first one of the Bloodhounds she could grab. There were others there, but—'

'Which others?'

'Milo Motion and that character with the beret. Rupert.'

'Anyone else from the Bloodhounds?'

'No, the two women, Miss Chilmark and Mrs Wycherley, aren't on the gallery mailing-list.'

'Why is that?'

'You'd have to ask Jessica.'

Diamond resolved to do that. Before leaving Barnaby, he had one more question of significance. 'You saw the message on the gallery window. Has it crossed your mind, just fleetingly, that it might be true?'

'That Jessica did for Sid?' Barnaby was candid. 'I gave it some thought later, yes. But I honestly couldn't think of any reason why she would do such an immature thing. My wife is an unusually clever woman.'

In the car he took a call from Keith Halliwell reporting that Miss Chilmark wasn't at home. The old lady upstairs in the Paragon house had said that she might have gone away. She'd seen her the previous evening getting into a taxi – a black cab – and carrying a small suitcase.

'*Miss Chilmark did a runner?*' Diamond piped in amazement.

'It seems so.'

He told Halliwell to start checking with taxi firms and heard the faint sigh of despair.

He drove to Orange Grove, left the car in front of the Empire Hotel, and walked the short distance up the High Street to Northumberland Place. A.J., unflustered, welcomed him to the gallery and offered him a coffee. Jessica, he told Diamond, should not be long. She was with a dealer upstairs. 'If your business can wait a few minutes, Superintendent, I'm sure she'll be immensely grateful. It isn't often she gets a chance to do business with the big boys from London.'

'I'll start with you, then.'

'With me? I shouldn't think I can help much.'

'You can save Mrs Shaw from some tedious questions about things that happened last week.'

'Is that all?' A.J. was reassured. The smile was reinstated. 'Fire away, then. I thought this must be about the frightful business this morning in Sydney Gardens.'

'You heard about it?'

'From Shirley-Ann Miller a short time ago. Of course, we know nothing first-hand.'

'She was quickly on to it,' said Diamond, slightly deflated.

'The jungle telegraph works well in Bath. I think she works in public relations, doesn't she?'

'Tourism.'

'Well, she's pretty hot at public relations as well. Did you say you'd like a coffee?'

'No, thanks.'

He was shown to the tall-backed Rennie Mackintosh chair. After making up his mind that it really was a chair, though unsuited to his physique, he tried his weight on it, perched awkwardly, and then got up saying, 'I'm happy to stand. You knew Rupert Darby, sir?'

'A slight acquaintance only,' said A.J. 'Jessica invited him to the preview we had here. Rather a carrying voice, which can be an asset at a party, because everyone else then raises the volume and it all sounds wildly successful.'

'You hadn't met him before that?'

'No. I'd seen him around in Bath. Easy to recognise from Jessica's description. The beret, the voice, the dog.'

'Was the dog at the party?'

'No, I'm speaking of seeing him in the street. You want to know about the party. He and I didn't exchange more than a few passing words as he came in. He isn't the sort who waits to be introduced to people. He was in there straight away. I wouldn't have thought he was the suicidal type.'

Diamond gave a shrug. His thoughts were no longer on Rupert's personality. At this minute A.J. interested him more. He might have stepped out of a holiday brochure with his welcome-to-paradise smile and designer shirt and jeans. Barnaby had spoken of a private income and some of it must have gone on the teeth, which were as even as computer keys. Was this young buck likely to be content with 'intellectual flirting'?

'I understand you have a large stake in the gallery, Mr, er . . . ?'

'A.J. will do.'

Diamond was shaking his head. 'Not any longer, sir. I'm gathering evidence, you see. I have to insist on full names.'

A.J. frowned. 'Does it really matter? The "A" is for Ambrose. I cringe each time I have to own up to it.'

'And the "J"?'

'Jason. Hardly much better.'

'That isn't your surname, is it?'

'No. That's' – he cast his eyes upwards – 'Smith. Ambrose Jason Smith. Now can we talk about something more important, for pity's sake?'

This business over the name had quite upset A.J. All the more incentive for Diamond.

'Are you a local man . . . Mr Smith?'

A glare. 'No. Born in Devon, but the next twenty years I spent in and around Winchester. I went to school there.'

'The public school?'

'Yes. If you want the whole sordid truth I was not a credit

to them. Got expelled eventually. Went to art college and then had a few poverty-stricken years in Paris.'

'And now you're stricken no longer?'

'That is correct.'

Diamond waited.

A.J. explained, 'The family forgave me.'

'To come back to my question, you have a large stake in the gallery. Is that so?'

'I help out with the overheads. I'm also a regular exhibitor. I wish you would tell me what this has to do with the police.'

'You're a close friend of Mrs Shaw's.'

'That's a sinister-sounding phrase. She's a married woman, Superintendent. If you're inferring what I think you are, you'd better have a care what you say.'

'Some words were sprayed on the gallery window on the night of the preview party.'

A.J.'s reaction was less dramatic than Barnaby's. He was still well in control. His brown eyes looked into Diamond's and then towards the window. 'How did you hear about that?'

'The words, I was informed, were *She did for Sid.*'

'So?'

'You were one of the people who decided to remove them without reporting the matter.'

'To put it in context,' said A.J., adopting a lofty tone, 'it was obviously a piece of misplaced fun. We were having a party. People have a few drinks and do daft things. We thought it was in bad taste and wiped the window clean. If that's a crime, you'd better arrest us all.'

From above came the sound of footsteps. Jessica was about to descend with her dealer.

'Another question,' said Diamond. 'Where were you last night from seven onwards?'

'God, you really are taking this seriously. In the bar at the Royal Crescent Hotel and afterwards at the Clos du Roy Restaurant, where I dined alone. But if you wish to make enquiries, a dozen bar staff and waiters can vouch for me.'

'And after you'd eaten?'

'I went home and watched television. Would you like me to tell you what the programme was?'

Jessica's black-stockinged legs and blue strappy shoes appeared at the top of the spiral stairs. She led down a small silver-haired man in a black overcoat and a bow tie. Quick to sense that the deal she'd been doing upstairs might be undermined if she introduced a policeman, she said smoothly, 'My dear Mr Diamond, how good of you to call again. This is quite a morning. If you'll forgive me for a moment, Mr Peake has come specially from London and he has another gallery to see. I'll just point him in the right direction, and then we'll do business, I promise.'

Diamond nodded, allowing the subterfuge to pass, before starting up with A.J. again. 'You live in Bath?'

'Queen Square.'

'Nice and central.'

'Yes.'

'Is there anyone . . . ?'

'I am a bachelor.'

'Did you go out at all last night?'

'I went home to sleep, Superintendent, and sleep is what I did.'

Back came Jessica. 'Wonderful. He wants seven, including that big one of yours, A.J. We've got to celebrate. Is there any bubbly left over from the party?'

'Before you do—' Diamond began.

'You're to join us,' said Jessica. 'It isn't every day we do three grands' worth of business.'

'Sorry, but you're joining me,' said Diamond, 'and there's no bubbly on offer. We might run to coffee in a plastic cup, but that's the best I can promise.'

'I don't think I understand.'

'I'm taking you in, Mrs Shaw. For questioning.'

THIRTY-THREE

Out of consideration for his passenger, he drove to the back of the central police station and they entered through a side door. Even so, several heads swivelled when he escorted Jessica, teetering high-heeled along the corridor in the pale blue Armani suit she'd put on for the London art dealer.

In Diamond's office the phone was flashing like a burglar alarm. He pulled out a chair for Jessica and asked if she wanted that coffee tasting of plastic. She requested water.

He read the written messages left on his desk. Julie Hargreaves had spoken to Shirley-Ann Miller and confirmed that she had a good alibi for the previous night. Halliwell had traced Miss Chilmark to Lucknam Park, the country house turned hotel at Colerne, and was on his way there; lucky bastard, he wouldn't be drinking out of plastic cups. And Jack Merlin, the pathologist, couldn't, after all, get to Bath next day; the post-mortem on Rupert Darby would have to be postponed unless someone else took over.

After collecting tea for himself, Diamond sat opposite Jessica, observing her, deciding on his strategy. She was drumming her fingers on the desk. There didn't seem much advantage in gentle sparring.

'Mrs Shaw, why did you write those lists of words on the paper bag?'

The finely shadowed eyes narrowed, but there was nothing else to register the body blow this was meant

301

to be. This lady wasn't simply going to roll over and tell all.

'The bag you used to treat Miss Chilmark's hyperventilation. I have it here.' He opened his desk and took it out, enclosed in a transparent cover. 'They happen to rhyme, these words. *Jack, flak, knack, mac* . . . It looks like working notes for a poet – or at least a writer of verse. In this case, they rhyme with Black. There's a second column rhyming with Motion and a third with Room. I could be wrong, but those are words that feature in the case under investigation: Penny Black, Milo Motion and Locked Room. Working notes?'

Jessica's only response was the merest movement of the padded shoulders.

'You did write them yourself, didn't you?' he pressed her. 'Sid Towers had nothing to do with it.'

Not even a flicker this time.

'It can't have been Sid because of the fresh riddle in verse that was published yesterday. Sid is dead. He couldn't have been our poet.' He watched her minutely. This wasn't achieving anything. 'I'll be frank,' he said. 'Until this morning I still wasn't certain. You know what happened this morning?'

No answer.

'Mrs Shaw?'

A sigh. 'Yes, I heard what happened.'

'Another death,' he said. 'Rupert Darby's death.'

She said calmly, 'You're not telling me anything I don't know.'

Encouraged that there was two-way traffic now, he said, 'Let's go back to the riddle for a moment.

> To end the suspense, as yours truly did,
> Discover the way to Sydney from Sid.

In style, it was not dissimilar from the other two. It was on similar paper, in an identical typeface and distributed in the same way to the local media. That wasn't some

302

publicity-seeker messing about, Mrs Shaw. *To end the suspense* . . . It was written in the knowledge that a man would shortly be found hanging from a bridge in Sydney Gardens. Isn't that plain?'

'If you say so.'

'You must have read the riddle in the paper.'

'Yes.'

'Did you write it? – that's the question.'

'I did not.'

'Did you write the others?'

'No.'

He paused, letting the gravity of her situation take root. He studied the paper bag as if he hadn't seen it before. Then he looked up and started again, but less abrasively. 'Until yesterday afternoon, I was taken in by these lists. Thought they were written by Sid. Had to be.'

She held his gaze with her dark brown eyes.

He said, 'If Sid wrote them, it was natural to assume that he was our poet, the composer of the riddles, the joker who stole the Penny Black and magicked his way into a locked boat. They looked like working notes, the first notes for a riddle that never appeared, because Sid was killed before he completed it.' He spread his hands. 'I boobed. We all make mistakes. But what am I left with?'

He took his time. Passed his hand around the back of his neck and massaged it. 'What I'm left with, Mrs Shaw, is the alternative. You wrote the lists.' Another pause. 'Do you follow my thinking? The bag was Sid's. He handed it to you. You handed it to me. True?'

She sighed – a reluctant admission. Yet the logic of what he had said was inescapable.

'We call that continuity of evidence, Mrs Shaw. That's why it's clear that if Sid didn't write the lists, you did.' He leaned forward, hunched over his desk, watching her. 'Makes you my prime suspect.' An exaggeration, but he had to find some way of getting through. 'I'm trying to give you every chance. This isn't a formal interview. If there's an explanation, now's your opportunity.'

She looked down at her fingernails, not persuaded, it seemed.

He said, 'The post-mortem hasn't been done on Rupert yet, so this may be premature, but I expect it to confirm that he met his death by foul play.'

She caught her breath – the first unguarded response. 'He hanged himself.'

'He was found hanging.'

'I don't follow you.'

'I think you do. We took a blood sample. The man was well tanked up, some way over the limit, probably incapable of rigging up a noose.'

She said, 'This is in the realm of speculation.' Fair comment, too.

He found himself analysing his performance so far. This isn't the approved interviewing technique, he told himself. It isn't an interview at all yet. I'm laying out all my cards while she sits there denying everything.

He picked up his cup and did damage to the inside of his mouth. Tea from the machine was always too hot or tepid. 'Could I have a sip of that water? I'll get you some fresh.'

She pushed the beaker across the desk.

He said, 'It may be speculation now, but we'll know soon enough. The post-mortem will show if there was a struggle. You can't string a man from a bridge without handling him roughly.'

Jessica drew herself up in the chair and said scornfully, 'You're not seriously suggesting that I did this to Rupert?'

'You probably couldn't have done it alone,' he conceded.

'Why should I do it at all?'

'That's no mystery,' he said. 'We recovered his beret and it has traces of sprayed paint.'

Another sharp intake of breath. The wall of indifference was crumbling.

He told her, 'I know all about the graffiti sprayed on the gallery window. Mean.'

She started to say, 'How—'

'I've discussed it with your husband and your friend A.J.'

'*They told you?*'

He moved relentlessly on. 'Rupert was at the party with paint on his beret.'

She said, 'Are you sure of this?'

'I can show you the beret if you like. The real point is that it gave you, and possibly someone else, a clear motive for silencing Rupert. He would have exposed you.'

'I didn't know it was Rupert.'

He got up, walked to the window and looked out.

She repeated, with more fervour, 'I didn't know it was Rupert.'

He let a few seconds pass. Then, without turning from the window: 'Do you still deny writing the riddles?'

'Of course I deny it,' she said passionately. 'I didn't write them. I didn't kill anyone.'

'But you wrote those lists of words on the paper bag.'

'It doesn't mean I'm a killer.'

He said, 'But you wrote the lists. You will admit that much?' By now, he reckoned, she ought to be ready to admit to the lesser crime.

She showed she had spirit. 'Is this going to take much longer, because I have things to do? I assume I can walk out whenever I wish. I'm not under arrest, or anything?'

He said in sincerity, 'Mrs Shaw, I brought you here so that we could talk in private, away from the gallery. I'm giving you the opportunity to explain your actions.'

Coolly, she asked, 'What actions? I've done nothing illegal.'

'At the very least, fabricating evidence.'

'How can you say that?'

'Look, if you didn't write the lists as notes for a riddle, you wrote them for another purpose. You were taking a considerable risk, of course, but it was – what's that term bridge-players use? – a finesse. The winning of a trick by subtle means, playing a low card. And you played it with a skill anyone would admire. You didn't volunteer the bag. You waited for me to ask if it was still in your possession. And when you handed it across, you didn't draw my attention to the lists. You let me find them myself and conclude that Sid wrote them. You conned me and my team. Why? Why mislead the police? You must have had something to hide.'

She shook her head.

'Someone to shield, then?'

The colour rose to her face.

He said mildly, 'A.J.?'

A jerk went through her like an electric shock.

THIRTY-FOUR

Lucknam Park, an eighteenth-century mansion at Colerne, north-east of Bath, and latterly converted into a four-star conference hotel, might not have been the obvious choice for a bolthole, but it was Miss Chilmark's. No backstreet hideout for milady, thought Diamond with amusement, as it became obvious that the drive through the grounds would add another half-mile to the six he had just completed.

On arrival, he was welcomed like a paying guest and given a phone message. It was from Julie. Would he call her urgently? He didn't recognise the number.

He found himself talking to a switchboard operator at the Sports and Leisure Centre who told him Inspector Hargreaves was waiting for his call.

'Mr Diamond?' The note of relief in Julie's voice was gratifying and disturbing at the same time. 'I'm so glad I've caught you.'

'Trouble?'

'It's about Marlowe.'

'Who?'

'Marlowe. The dog. Rupert Darby's dog. I took him on. Remember?'

He said in amazement, 'You're calling me about the dog? What's it been up to now?'

'Nothing. He's done nothing wrong.'

'Well?'

'I'm here at the Sports Centre to interview Bert Jones, Shirley-Ann Miller's partner.'

'I know that, Julie.'

'Yes, but before going in, I thought I'd better give the dog a chance of a walk, if you know what I mean. I walked him round the edge of the car park at Manvers Street, but he didn't seem to get the idea, so I thought I'd give him another opportunity here.'

'Of lifting his leg, you mean? Do we have to go into all this, Julie?'

'Yes, Mr Diamond, we do,' she said earnestly, 'because as we were walking about, I happened to look closely at his coat. Marlowe has this dark brown hair, as you know, but I noticed that one area of it seems to be going white.'

'He's an old dog, you mean? You'd rather not take him on at his time of life?'

'Please listen, Mr Diamond. The white bit is only on his left side. It isn't natural. When I looked at it closely, I saw it was lots of little points of white. It's paint from an aerosol spray.'

He was stunned into a brief silence. He'd been reluctant to give his full attention to Julie's fussing over the dog, and now this was hard to take in. 'Are you sure?'

'Certain. I scraped some of the specks off with my fingernail.'

'Julie, Rupert didn't have the dog with him at the gallery party.'

'That's the whole point. Do you see what it means? If the dog was sprayed with the aerosol, it must have been done at some other time.'

He was ahead of her now. 'Right. It means we can't be certain when the paint got on the beret.'

'Exactly. We've been assuming it was done when the gallery window was sprayed. We can't any more.'

He was silent for a moment, pondering the significance. The evidence of the beret, linking Rupert to the graffiti, was undermined. The spray had been used elsewhere and Rupert's dog had got a burst of paint. Rupert could have been trying out the aerosol, practising.

Diamond was humble enough to say, 'You've had time to think about this, Julie. What do you make of it?'

She started to say, 'I'm as confused as . . .' Stopping in mid-sentence, she began again. 'There may be a way of finding out whether there was spray on the beret before Rupert got to the gallery that evening. If you remember, he was supposed to have arrived with some people he met at the Saracen's Head.'

'Right, and if they happened to have noticed . . . What the devil was their name? Shirley-Ann gave it to us.'

'Volk. They're from Bradford on Avon.'

'I'll get someone on to it. Have you finished with Bert Jones yet?'

'I haven't even started. I wanted to catch you first.'

'You did the right thing, Julie.' Before putting down the phone, he added, 'Sorry I was short with you. Thought you wanted advice about the bloody dog. How is Marlowe, by the way?'

'He's not a bloody dog, Mr Diamond. He's great. I'm just keeping my fingers crossed that Roger accepts him.'

'Your husband?'

'No, Roger is one of my other dogs. He's rather unpredictable.'

'So is Marlowe, by all accounts.'

He made a call to Manvers Street and despatched a car to Bradford on Avon. After replacing the phone, he stared blankly around the elegant entrance hall with its enormous fireplace and portraits; after the brain-stretching session on the paint-spray, a conscious effort was required to remind himself why he was here.

Keith Halliwell was with Miss Chilmark in a spacious guest room overlooking the croquet lawn. Clearly in a state of some embarrassment, if not distress, the lady didn't even look up from the chintz armchair where she was seated. Her appearance had undergone a change that Diamond couldn't immediately define, until he realised he was meeting her without make-up. The green eye-shadow and orange lipstick and foundation had created a different woman from the one he was presently seeing. Of the two images, he thought he preferred this paler, more vulnerable version.

He took note of a plate of canapés and a half-empty glass of what looked like whisky on the occasional table in front of her. He also noted the glint of a second whisky glass on the floor and partially obscured by a fringe around the base of the armchair Halliwell must have been using, and was informed, 'I sent for something to calm her down, sir. A drop of Scotch is supposed to be good for the nerves.'

'And was it good for yours?'

Halliwell gave a twitchy grin.

Diamond turned to the matter in hand. 'You gave us a fright, Miss Chilmark, disappearing like that.'

She said nothing.

'How long have you been here?'

Halliwell said, 'Since yesterday, sir.'

'Control yourself, Keith. I'd rather hear it from Miss Chilmark. You remember who I am, Miss Chilmark? I visited you in the Paragon. Nice place. Nice address. I'm surprised you left it.' He lowered himself into another armchair opposite her. The furniture here was built for people of his size. He usually had to back into chairs like a carthorse easing between the shafts. 'I was getting worried about you. Two of the Bloodhounds are dead. Did you hear about Rupert Darby?'

She nodded, still without looking up.

'Caught it on TV West, did you?' Diamond pressed on, with a jerk of the head towards the appropriate section in the wall unit. 'They filmed me standing on the bridge over the canal where it happened. Sydney Gardens. Do you know the place? You must do.'

Another nod.

'Can't expect you to waste much sympathy on Rupert Darby,' he said. 'He was no friend of yours, was he?'

She looked up, which was some encouragement, even if her broad, colourless face was registering nothing.

'I said he was no friend of yours. You don't have to stand on ceremony with me, ma'am. It's good riddance

310

as far as you're concerned, isn't it? He made your life a misery.'

She found her voice. 'You've no right to put words into my mouth, Superintendent.'

'In the absence of any words from you, ma'am, I was having to speak for both of us. I said Darby made your life a misery. Isn't that so?'

She gave him a distrustful look. 'What are you suggesting?'

He said on a quieter note, 'Simply helping you to get started, ma'am. There are things to be explained, aren't there?'

She shifted in the chair, nervously rubbing her hands. She sighed.

Generally Diamond preserved a formal neutrality when interviewing. It seemed unlikely that this old dowager with her tendency to hysteria would evoke any sympathy at all from him, yet curiously she did. Her life was narrow, her values based on little else but status and snobbery. Everything she espoused had been undermined. Here she was, ashamed, discredited, being questioned by the police. To restore any self-respect was probably beyond her.

She closed her eyes at first, as if it made speaking less painful. 'I'm not at my best. I don't know what to say about him – Rupert Darby. Since I heard about his death, I've been trying to understand him, if not forgive him. At the time of the various incidents at the meetings, I was incensed by his behaviour. I felt sure he really set out to persecute me. Now that, em—'

'Now that he's dead?'

'Yes. I'm less certain. I can't be sure. Possibly what happened with the dog was due mainly to negligence on his part.'

'Failing to control the dog, you mean.'

'Yes. He couldn't really have known that it would run straight to me and leap on me. So I'm trying, I'm beginning, I'm *wanting* . . . to take a more charitable view of what happened. Do you understand?'

By Miss Chilmark's lights, this was a turnaround on a par with Count Dracula turning out to be the tooth fairy. Was it Rupert's passing that had prompted it? Diamond wondered. Or had a much larger crisis put the incidents into a new perspective?

She said, 'I had no idea he was suicidal.'

Diamond told her, 'I wouldn't worry about Rupert if I were you.' He changed his posture. Instead of leaning forward, demonstrating concern, he rested his back against the chair. 'It wasn't anything to do with Rupert that brought you here, was it, ma'am?'

A little shudder went through her. 'No, it was another matter.' Then, silence.

'You may not feel you want to speak about it,' Diamond spoke the obvious, 'but if you do, I think it may become easier to live with. Locking it in is not the best way.'

She said with a penetrating stare, 'You know, don't you?'

'A certain amount, ma'am, enough to understand how difficult this is for you. but it can't go on, can it? The cost—'

'How did you find out?'

Swiftly he changed tack. He didn't want her knowing he'd tricked her bank. 'I was going to say the cost in stress is more than you can bear.'

The evasion was transparent. Miss Chilmark closed up again. 'Anyway, I don't see that my private affairs have anything to do with the police.'

The story had to be coaxed from her. He wished he had Julie with him instead of Halliwell standing there like the recording angel. 'Keith, I may be getting a call downstairs. Do you mind?'

Halliwell had the sense to leave.

Diamond smiled faintly, wanting to convey encouragement. 'See it from my point of view, Miss Chilmark. Darby died last night. You went missing. I'm bound to be concerned. I accept that the two events weren't connected, but I have to ask your reasons. I believe someone has been taking advantage of you. Threatening you, perhaps. Am I right?'

She gave a convulsive movement, a sob like a hiccup. From her sleeve she produced a paper tissue and put it to her face and sobbed several times more.

Diamond waited uneasily.

Finally Miss Chilmark looked at him intently through a film of tears. 'If I tell you, will you promise not to pursue it?'

Without knowing what she was about to say, how could he give such an undertaking? He answered, 'If it doesn't bear on the matters I'm investigating, I wouldn't wish to get involved.' A 'promise' worthy of Machiavelli, but she scarcely seemed to be listening, she was so distressed.

In a voice threatening any second to dissolve into weeping, she began to tell her story. 'It goes back to when my parents were killed in an accident, a car crash in France, in 1961. A head-on smash with a lorry near Rouen. It was dreadful. They were in their early fifties, both of them. I was twenty-six, their only child, very naive. I'd been given an extremely sheltered upbringing. You may imagine the shock, and the problems, the responsibilities, I had thrust upon me. I was at a loss, quite unable to cope.'

'Anyone in your shoes . . .' Diamond murmured.

She went on, 'There was all the complexity of the inquest and of getting them home. I knew Mummy and Daddy would have wished to be brought home and buried here. As often happens in a crisis, someone came to my rescue, a solicitor who worked with Daddy. Did I say Daddy was the senior partner in Chilmark, Portland and Smales? This young man – I'd rather not give his name – shouldered the whole thing. I was nominally the executrix, but he arranged everything for me. Went to France and brought them back. Saw to the funerals, the wills, the shares. Advised me on how to invest my legacy, which was considerable. I couldn't have got through without him. And he was only a name to me before. I don't believe Daddy had ever mentioned him – but then he

313

never spoke much about his work. And I have to say that his behaviour to me in all this time – vulnerable as I was – was impeccable. He was the perfect gentleman.'

She reached for the whisky. 'Do you mind? I must. My voice.'

'Take your time.' He suspected it was not so much the voice as the gentleman under discussion who made the long sip of whisky a necessity.

Miss Chilmark continued in a low, confidential tone, 'The next thing that happened was a mystery to me at the time, and not at all unpleasant. I received a Valentine, the only proper one I've ever received. Oh, people sent silly, jokey things at school, but this was beautiful, like a Victorian card, with lace edging and a silk ribbon. There was a lovely verse inside, but no clue to the sender. Nothing. I was deeply curious, of course. I would lie awake wondering who sent it, hardly daring to hope it might have been the young man who had done so much to solve my legal problems. Then about six weeks after, he phoned me with the good news that the probate had come through. At last I could invest the money, write cheques, and so on. Not that I had any great plans, but it was a kind of landmark. I suppose I looked on it as the end of my parents' tragedy. I could look forward now, and think of my own life.'

'Were you working at this time?' Diamond asked.

'In employment? No. Daddy didn't want me working. He belonged to that generation that thought women of good class should not go into employment. I worked hard in the house and garden, but not for a wage.

'I was telling you about the probate. My kind solicitor said we ought to celebrate with a meal out the same evening. I didn't know what to say. I knew enough about the profession to be sure that my father would never have suggested such a thing to a client, but he was another generation. Part of me wanted to accept. He'd been so kind throughout, and now that the legal part was over ... Well, to cut the story short, I went out to dinner with

314

him the same evening at the Hole in the Wall, which at that time had a reputation unrivalled in Bath. He was a charming companion. He wasn't terribly good-looking, or anything, but he had an unusually attractive voice, like an actor's. He bought champagne and towards the end of the meal he told me the Valentine had come from him. Of course I was overwhelmed by the whole thing. I had no experience of men. I think the champagne affected me, too.

'After the meal, he walked me back to the Paragon. It was raining, and he had an umbrella and he asked me to take his arm while he held it over both our heads. I was extremely happy. As we approached the house, he said he hated mixing business with pleasure, but he had a couple more papers for me to sign. I half knew it was just an excuse for him to come inside, but I wanted the excuse. I don't condone my behaviour.'

'It's all in the past,' said Diamond.

She lowered her eyes. 'You won't need telling what happened. I was a willing participant and I have to say that he was considerate. Gentle and understanding. People's attitudes to such things have undergone a revolution since then, but by the standards of that time, we were wicked. That evening I didn't care. He didn't stay for more than an hour, I suppose. If I'm honest, I was relieved he didn't spend the night with me. I don't think I was ready to sleep with a man, literally sleep with him, I mean. He left before midnight, and I sank into my bed and slept until quite late next morning, when I woke and felt like a scarlet woman. These days the only thing that makes a young woman feel guilty seems to be eating a bar of chocolate.'

He gave an encouraging smile. To make a remark even faintly resembling a joke, she must have been feeling calmer.

'That evening wasn't the only occasion,' Miss Chilmark went on. 'He came to the house at other times in the weeks that followed. He was usually there on some pretext. A letter about my bank arrangements, or something. I have to say that I invited him as often as he suggested coming. We would go to my bedroom and . . . he never stayed long. We didn't really go out together, and I suppose that made me suspicious that there was a reason why he didn't want to be seen with me in public. I didn't really want to admit it to myself, I wanted so much to keep him. Then the inevitable happened. I discovered that I was pregnant.'

So honest was the recollection that Diamond's image of the solid middle-aged woman opposite had been supplanted by a mental picture of the desperately vulnerable twenty-six-year-old she had been. He remembered those times and the moral climate and the pains and blunders of young love.

'Of course it was a shock, a tremendous shock, but in a way I'd been hoping something like this would happen. He'd always been vague about our future together. This was going to force us to a decision. I saw it as my chance to bring him to the registry office, if not the altar.'

She shook her head, sighing deeply. 'When I told him, his whole manner towards me changed. He told me to get rid of it. Those were his actual words. "It" – as if the child inside me was an object. I was horrified. I said something about getting married, and he told me quite brutally – as if I should have realised already – that he was already happily married with two children of his own. As I say, I'd guessed it really, but refused to admit it to myself. I was his mistress. He regarded my pregnancy as my mistake, a hazard that you have to face. We'd taken no precautions. I don't know if you can understand this, but I would have felt that birth control in any form would have made me into a loose woman.'

'So you had the child?'

She nodded. 'Alone. He refused to have anything more to do with me. His attitude was that if I wasn't willing to go to an abortionist, it was my bad fortune. So I made my own arrangements. I confided in a cousin, a woman who lived in Exmouth and worked in a private nursing home. We'd spent holidays there sometimes, and I'd got to know her quite well. She was the only person I could think of asking. I said I wanted to have the baby, but I wouldn't be able to keep it. I couldn't face the shame of bringing up a fatherless child. So my cousin Emma told me she knew of women who were desperate to adopt and had been turned down for some obscure reason by the adoption agencies. If I was really willing to give up the child within a short time of the birth, she could arrange it. So that's what happened. When I got towards the end of the pregnancy – when it was getting obvious, I mean – I went away to Exmouth. The child was born. I suckled him for a week or two, and then Emma took him away. He was registered as someone else's child, you see. It was highly illegal, but he was legitimised. Part of the understanding was that I should not be told the identity of the couple who were given him. I came back to Bath and resumed my life. I've never had another serious relationship.'

'Did you name him?'

'No. It was thought to be better if the adoptive mother gave him a name.'

'And you were not to have any more to do with them?'

'That was the understanding.'

'Hard, I'm sure.'

'Very – but I understood the thinking behind it. Over the years I've had times when I've wept a little, and times when I've wondered just what my son was like, but I kept my side of the bargain. I made no attempt to trace him. Fortunately I couldn't, not even knowing his name.'

She paused. She had shredded the paper tissue in her lap. She picked up one piece and dabbed the corner of her eye.

Diamond prompted her. 'You said you kept your side of the bargain as if someone else did not. Did the father – your lover, I mean – did he know of these arrangements?'

'No. He had nothing more to do with me.'

'So it was someone else.'

She nodded. 'About two years ago, I received a letter from someone who clearly knew a great deal about what had happened. He mentioned the date of birth, the place and the name of my cousin Emma, who died in 1990. He asked to meet me at a stated time by the west door of the Abbey. It wasn't exactly a threatening letter, yet there was so much in it that only I could have known. So I decided to go along.'

'A blackmailer?'

'No.'

'But you paid money. You've been making regular payments.' She had been frank, and so would he.

'He's not a blackmailer. He's my son.'

'Your *son*?'

'I couldn't refuse him, could I?'

'Are you certain?'

'Absolutely.'

'How do you know?'

'A mother's instinct. Whatever one thinks of him – and I know he has taken advantage – that first meeting outside the Abbey was a revelation. He wanted to know what his own mother was like as much as I longed to see him. It was genuine, I swear to you. We went for a coffee together and for a long time simply looked at each other. An opportunity I never expected to have. A miracle. We weren't breaking faith with anyone, because he'd long since left his adoptive family.'

'What's his name?'

She shook her head. Her expression tightened. 'I'm not going to say and you can't make me. What has happened between us is strictly private. It isn't illegal. I'm allowed to support my own child, for heaven's sake.'

Diamond sighed. 'When did he tell you he needed money? Right at the start?'

'It was obvious. He's thirty-two. He should be making his way in the world, but these are dreadful times for his generation. He was sent to a good school. It ought to help, but he's been unable to get regular work. I had more than enough money, so I gave him some. He was living in Radstock, with no prospect of employment, so I persuaded him to come here – to Bath, I mean. There are more opportunities here.'

'What does he do, then?'

Miss Chilmark clicked her tongue. 'You won't get it out of me that way. Can't you be satisfied with what I've told you already?'

Diamond tried some gentle persuasion. 'Look at your situation. In a couple of years you've gone through most of your fortune for this man. You sold your family home to stay in credit with the bank. You must have realised you were running through the money – or, rather, he was. You came here because you can't bring yourself to tell him it's the end of the line for this particular gravy-train. You ran away. Are you going to be able to pay the hotel bill?'

She covered her eyes.

He asked, 'Do you have any idea where all the money has gone?'

No answer.

He said, 'If what he's been doing is legal, we can't touch him.' More tenderly, he said, 'I'm going to arrange for Inspector Halliwell to drive you back to your home. You can't run away from your son. You haven't the funds. You've got to tell him you're almost skint. Or I have. I'm willing to talk to him. I think I know who he is, you see.' He paused. 'Would his name be Ambrose Jason Smith?'

Miss Chilmark gave a cry as if of pain and thrust her face more deeply into her hands. She wept uncontrollably now, for her son, and her mistakes and the cruelty of fate.

THIRTY-FIVE

Keith Halliwell was in his car having a nap when a heavy tread across the gravel alerted him. He woke instantly, like a dog expecting a walk.

'Any joy, Mr Diamond?'

'"Joy" isn't the word I'd use,' said Diamond. 'Anyway, she's packing her case up there. Going home. I've offered you as chauffeur.'

'Right, sir. And a message came through from Sergeant Filkins. That Bradford on Avon enquiry. He spoke to the people. The em . . . ?'

'The Volks.'

'Yes. And it's quite definite that Rupert Darby's beret was marked with paint before the art gallery party. They say he actually complained about it when they met him at the Saracen's Head.'

Diamond's interest quickened. 'Rupert mentioned it himself, did he?'

'Apparently there was an incident at the Lansdown Arms, his local. He went in with his dog early in the evening, his usual time, for a quick drink. On the way out, some merchant banker was playing about with what Rupert took to be a tin of hairspray.'

'Merchant banker?'

'Rhyming slang, sir. Rupert's expression.'

After a moment's thought, Diamond responded with a distinct note of affection, 'I can hear him saying it in his plummy accent, too.'

'Some of it got on his beret. Later he found it was paint.'

A low rumbling like a growl came from deep in Diamond's throat. 'I wish we'd known this earlier. What about this character with the spray? Is there a description?'

Halliwell shook his head. 'Rupert had nothing else to say about him.'

'Well, it tells us one interesting thing: Rupert didn't recognise the bugger.'

'Is that useful?'

'It is if we're dealing in murder here. It eliminates just about all our suspects.'

'You think Rupert was murdered, sir?'

'I can't rule it out.'

'Shoved over the bridge and hanged?' Halliwell sounded sceptical. 'That wouldn't be easy, would it? It would take some strength to get the noose around his neck and heave him over the railing.'

'Two people could do it.'

'No question . . . but where are we going to find *two*?'

Diamond turned and looked up at the window of the room he'd just left. 'Be patient with the old girl, Keith. She's had some shocks.'

'I'll treat her like my own mother, sir.'

'I wouldn't go that far.'

'What's next for you, Mr Diamond?'

'A little culture.' He ambled across to his own car and started up.

For once he didn't curse when he saw the usual queue for the roadworks beginning to form on the London Road approaching Bath. He was in a more positive frame of mind. A pretty demanding investigation was coming to its climax. Mysteries that had seemed impenetrable had been solved by – what? – steady detective work, or brilliance? Either way, he had now disentangled the problems of the locked room puzzle, the riddles, the paper bag and Miss Chilmark's secret payments. There remained only the unmasking of the killer.

Or killers.

This was when the likes of John Wigfull would run to their computers and start keying in information in the expectation that a mighty buzz from the megabytes would produce a perfect offender profile. *Your murderer is a writer of verse in possession of a ladder and window-cleaning materials and a car or other means of transport, with access to a computer and printer, possessing also a twisted sense of humour, a better than average knowledge of philately, detective stories, padlocks and the topography of Bath. Now arrest the bastard, you dim plods.*

The solution to this one, Diamond had long ago decided, wasn't going to come out of a computer. It required deductions on a more sophisticated level, an understanding of the strange workings of the human mind, fathoming why such a bizarre series of crimes and murders had been necessary or desirable. The sequence of events had almost certainly started with some weirdo wanting to score points, whether from frustration, a grudge or just a wish to impress someone else. The Bloodhounds had been picked as the patsies. Then the thing had erupted into violence, into murder. Was the first murder always part of the plan, or an unwished-for consequence? And was the second, the killing of Rupert – if murder it was – made necessary by something Rupert knew, or was it cynically carried out to derail the investigation? The latter, surely. It seemed inescapable that the staging of the 'suicide' was an attempt to frame Rupert as the conscience-stricken killer of Sid Towers. In other words, to draw a line under the case.

And it hadn't worked.

Ten minutes later, he walked into the Walsingham Gallery, only to be told by a young woman with cropped, blonde hair that it was Jessica's day off. He was also informed with just a hint of a smile that A.J. wasn't expected in today either.

'Any idea where I can find them? It's important.' He showed his ID card.

'You could try the house. You can phone from here if you like.'

With maddening inevitability, an answerphone message came down the line from Jessica's.

He turned to the blonde woman. 'Do you have a number for A.J.?'

She shook her head. 'They could be out for a walk. They walk by the canal sometimes.'

'It's a bloody long canal.'

He tried Barnaby Shaw's business number with a little more success. Barnaby thought Jessica had spoken about going to the framer's. An artist had delivered a picture with a chipped frame and she wanted a new one for it.

'Which framer?'

'The Meltone Gallery, in Powlett Road.'

'Can you find me the number?'

There, the trail went cold. Mel, of Meltone, hadn't seen either of them all day.

It was Keith Halliwell, back at Bath Central, who got the inquiry back on course. Spotting Diamond as he stomped in, the frustration writ large, he reported that Miss Chilmark was now installed at the Paragon again. 'She blubbed a bit, but I did my best with her and she cheered up no end when she got back. There was a nice note from someone saying he'd call later. I went out and got her a box of Mr Kipling's.'

'Jesus Christ.'

Halliwell went white. 'Did I do wrong?'

'Did this note say what time?'

'I don't know. Teatime, I suppose. That's why she wanted the cakes. What is it now?'

It was ten to four. Diamond actually ran out of the building to his car. He drove white-knuckled, at the limit of his nerve, bucking two sets of traffic lights on the way to the Paragon. Leaving the car to create the mother and father of all tailbacks in the homeward traffic, he dashed across the pavement and down the basement steps.

A.J. had not yet arrived. The disappointment showed when Miss Chilmark opened the door. She had changed into one of her high-necked oriental dresses and restored the make-up in lashings. She would be in thrall to that extortionist for as long as he cared to trouble her.

Diamond told her he would wait inside.

She protested, 'But I'm expecting a visitor.'

He said, 'That's who I want to see.' Then he banished her to the kitchen at the back.

Ten minutes went by, Diamond just to the left of the door, trying to be invisible through the frosted glass, whilst squeezed behind the foliage of a tall benjamina.

About four-twenty, someone descended the steps in a businesslike way to the basement. The doorbell rang. Diamond stepped out and flung open the door. The uniformed police constable standing there started to say, 'Is that your car parked out . . . ?' Then he practically choked as he recognized Diamond.

Miss Chilmark came eagerly from the kitchen, saw the policeman and said hysterically, 'Oh, my God, what's happened?'

'This officer has come to tea – that's what's happened,' Diamond told her through gritted teeth, tugging the man inside and slamming the door. 'Give him his Mr Kipling and I'll see to him later.'

A short time after, came the visitor Miss Chilmark was expecting. Upon seeing Diamond, A.J. did a double-take, turned about and bolted up the stairs, but Diamond's large right arm groped through the iron railing, grabbed a leg and pulled the man off balance. He fell heavily and gashed his hand on the edge of the bottom step.

'Looks like you're nicked.'

The emergency was not over. Before relieving the traffic chaos outside, Diamond called Bath Central and had a message radioed to all units. He wanted Jessica Shaw brought in. She might be heading away from Bath in a new white Peugeot 306. He gave the registration.

Back at Manvers Street, A.J. was waiting in an interview room, stroking the fresh Band-Aid on his hand. He had recovered his composure enough to tell Diamond, 'I don't know what the fuck this is about. You're going to pay for this.'

'Save it.' Diamond ignored him, and fiddled with something on the desk. His cackhandedness defeated him. 'Someone's got to get this bloody contraption working for me.' He walked out again.

A further twenty minutes passed before he came back with a sergeant, who attended to the tape recorder. 'You'll have to wait, squire,' Diamond now informed A.J. 'They're bringing in Mrs Shaw. Like I thought, she was heading out of town in the car.' He grinned. 'Luckily, there's still one hell of a snarl-up on the London Road.'

He went down to the canteen for sausages, eggs and chips. It was half a lifetime since he'd eaten. Casting around for a vacant table, he glimpsed a large moustache topped by a pair of tired, red-lidded eyes. Eyes that made contact. John Wigfull gestured to him to come over. Difficult to ignore. Promising himself that he would soon escape, he carried his tray across.

Wigfull actually came to life and pulled out a chair. 'You've cracked it, I hear. Pulled in Mrs Shaw and her boyfriend.'

'I really need this,' said Diamond. 'Haven't eaten since breakfast, and that was cold toast and marmalade.'

'Letting them stew, are you? Want some brown sauce?' Wigfull glanced around for some, but Diamond didn't seem to care. He had already started eating. 'It did cross my mind more than once that two people had to be involved.' Wigfull was clearly expecting a rundown on the case. 'And when Darby was strung from the bridge, it really had to be them working together.'

Diamond spoke between mouthfuls. 'Wise after the event, John?'

'No. I don't mind admitting I was confused up to that point. But the hanging clinched it, to my mind. Just about impossible for one person to hang a man. You'd have to be exceptionally strong – or the victim feeble. And this plot

325

was always too complex to have been masterminded by one individual. They're an odd pair, those two. Too clever by half. Milking the old lady's bank account, weren't they?'

A nod from Diamond. 'That's how the art gallery kept going.'

'And the smart new Peugeot she was driving?'

'I expect so.'

'Surprising, really, that the husband didn't object.'

'To the gallery being funded like that? He didn't mind.' Against his inclination, Diamond found himself being drawn into a dissection of the case. 'To Barnaby, A.J. was just a third-rate artist with a private income. If he wanted to throw money at Jessica, fair enough.'

'I meant the relationship,' Wigfull explained. 'Why didn't he object to A.J. screwing his wife?'

'Because it wasn't happening. This is the whole point. They aren't lovers. Barnaby convinced me of that. Intellectual flirting, he calls it.'

'Get away,' said Wigfull.

'Straight up. Their relationship is non-sexual. They get their kicks in other ways. The courtship display stops short of the act itself. These two are games players. That's their turn-on. It's like a grown-up version of truth, kiss or dare, ultimately leading to destruction. The crimes arose out of A.J.'s need to impress her. He's given her most of the money he creamed off from Miss Chilmark, but that wasn't enough. He planned a spectacular stunt.'

'Stealing the Penny Black and having it turn up at the Bloodhounds' meeting? That was spectacular, no question. It proved he was smarter than any of them. The riddles. The business with the padlocks. Bloody clever.'

'Yes, but it went wrong,' said Diamond. 'He didn't reckon with Sid. Here was a bloke who was a Dickson Carr buff with an interest in locked room puzzles, so naturally he was fascinated by what had happened. He drove out to look at the narrowboat and came along the towpath while A.J. was in the act of replacing the padlock. I think A.J. heard him coming and hid inside the cabin, grabbing a windlass for a weapon. Everything had worked brilliantly up to then. He'd almost got away with a perfect crime. He was angry and scared at the same time, and he panicked. He cracked Sid over the head, probably meaning to knock him out, no more, but it killed him. You can never tell with skulls until you give them a bash.' He forked up some more chips. 'And everything after that was done to cover up.'

Wigfull had been over that scene a thousand times in his mind and never pictured it so vividly before. He tried to sound casual. 'So when did Jessica come into it?'

'After Sid was killed. She suspected A.J. was responsible, and she didn't want us to find out. With luck, he'd get away with it. There was a chance that everyone would assume Sid had stolen the stamp and staged the locked room trick.'

'And we did,' said Wigfull.

'Well, it fitted the facts. After all, he was the Dickson Carr expert, and he had plenty to prove to that lot who thought him thick because he didn't ever have much to say for himself. This theory was an ideal cover for A.J. It meant anyone at all – not just someone in the know – could have been on the towpath that night and attacked Sid. Tidy. It let A.J. off the hook. And then the writing on the paper bag seemed to confirm that Sid had written the riddles.'

'Jessica did that.'

'Yes. She admitted it to me. She was covering up for A.J. To be fair, I don't think he'd told her anything. She's not slow, that woman. She worked out that he'd done it. Later it all began to unravel, of course. So Plan B was devised to frame Rupert and fake his suicide.'

'They were both in on that?'

'By this time, yes. This killing was not accidental. It was planned in cold blood. They staged the graffiti incident, making sure Rupert was well sprayed first. It was simple to surprise him coming out of his local. A.J. must have done that. Rupert hadn't met him.'

'Fair enough,' said Wigfull, 'but what about the message

– *She did for Sid*? Why on earth would they draw attention to their own guilt?'

'First, it wasn't true. She didn't do for Sid. A.J. did. Second, if anything went wrong, who would suspect that they wrote up the message themselves?'

'And they got Rupert tanked up the next night and hanged him?'

'After writing another riddle supposedly by Rupert, predicting his suicide. Case closed. End of story.'

'So they hoped,' Wigfull said, and sighed. 'You're good, Peter. I've got to admit you're better than I am.'

'Yes,' said Diamond abstractedly, glancing at the clock. He'd practically finished the snack. A portion or two of treacle pudding would go down a treat. Very soon he would start the first interview. He was hoping Wigfull would take the hint and leave. A couple of minutes alone would be nice. With any luck, Julie would be back from the Sports and Leisure Centre by now. She ought to be in on the interviews.

But Wigfull still had something on his mind. 'What about this character, A.J.? Is he really Miss Chilmark's long-lost son?'

'She seems to think so,' Diamond said, making it clear that his mind was on other things.

'If he isn't, and it's all a con, he ought to be done for that as well as murder.'

'Maybe.'

'Well?'

Diamond said irritably, 'Well what?'

'Is he the son, or isn't he?'

'Most probably not. It's a side issue.'

'Could he have conned Miss Chilmark?'

'Easily. It was part of the arrangement when the child was given away that she wasn't told the name of the parents or the child. Anyone of approximately the right age could have knocked on her door and claimed to be the son if – and it's a big "if" – they knew the story.'

'Why does he call himself A.J.?'

'Doesn't like the name he was given. Ambrose Jason Smith. It is quite a mouthful. At one time . . .' His voice trailed away. He really didn't want to prolong this.

'Yes?' said Wigfull. 'At one time, what?'

'Oh, I had another theory about A.J.'

'You've got to tell me now you've started,' said Wigfull. 'It won't take a minute, will it?'

Diamond sighed and felt into the inside pocket of his jacket. He had several pieces of paper there. He started sorting through them as he talked. 'I asked Polly Wycherley to write down the names of everyone who had ever been a Bloodhound, thinking, you see, that there might be some former member with a grudge against Sid. Here it is.'

'No one called Ambrose Jason Smith, I'll bet,' said Wigfull.

'No, but there was a name – this one – Alan Jellicoe, that made me pause.'

'The initials?'

'Yes,' said Diamond. 'Coincidence, I expect.'

Wigfull was more suspicious. 'I wouldn't count on it. Don't you think this is worth following up? After all, he could have made up the A.J. Smith identity just to con Miss Chilmark.'

Diamond didn't want to push this. Wigfull had a point. It ought to be checked, but if there was anything in it, the truth would come out. There were hours of interviews stretching ahead. Call him Smith or Jellicoe, he was still sitting in an interview room waiting to be charged.

'If I were you,' Wigfull went on, 'I'd ask Mrs Wycherley to come down here and have a look at him. Has she seen him lately?'

'No, she wasn't invited to the gallery party. She and Jessica don't get on too well.'

'All the more reason to check.'

Diamond yawned. 'You're a persistent bugger, John. All right, I'll arrange it. Alan Jellicoe. It is a little out of the ordinary.' His eye scanned the list again. Something else was stirring in his brain. Tom Parry-Jones, Milo

Motion, Polly Wycherley, Annie Allen, Gilbert Jones, Marilyn Slade-Baker . . .

'There's another coincidence for you.'

'Someone you know?'

'Put it this way,' said Diamond. 'I know someone called Bert Jones.' He handed the list to Wigfull to read.

'This says Gilbert. You don't shorten Gilbert to Bert, do you?'

'Some people might. It's the name of Shirley-Ann Miller's partner.' He looked up at the canteen clock. 'Julie was going in to interview that bastard over two hours ago. I've heard sweet Fanny Adams since.'

He was on his feet and out of the canteen before Wigfull had time to draw breath.

THIRTY-SIX

The Sports and Leisure Centre, built in concrete and reconstituted stone in 1972, is a structure more functional than decorative, a prime example of what has been called the packing-case style. By day, it manages to be unobtrusive, sited on the Recreation Ground away from Bath's grander architecture. At six-thirty this October evening it was a garish yellow monolith, caught in the artificial light.

They found Julie's car at 5.25 p.m. at the far end of the car park. Rupert's dog Marlowe, on the back seat, had set up a fit of barking and yelping that considerably helped the search.

Instantly this was upgraded to an emergency. Every available officer was called in. By 5.45, over forty mustered in the floodlit area in front of the main entrance off North Parade.

Diamond addressed them through a loudhailer. There were two missing persons, he impassively announced. DI Hargreaves, a female officer, was known to many of the search party. She was five foot eight, with short blonde hair and was dressed in a light brown leather jacket over a black sweater and black leggings. She was possibly being detained by Gilbert – better known as Bert – Jones, aged about thirty, five foot nine, with a body-builder's physique, dark hair and brown eyes. He was an employee of the Sports and Leisure Centre, probably dressed in a dark blue tracksuit. Jones was not known to be armed, but was under suspicion of violent crimes and should be treated with extreme caution.

Diamond explained that in a few minutes the fire alarm would be sounded to evacuate the building. Users of the Centre were to be directed by uniformed officers towards the main doors, where a watch would be kept for the suspect. If he was not found, a full search of the building would then take place, starting with the ground floor and moving up. Senior staff from the Centre would give assistance. Particular attention was to be paid to enclosed spaces, changing-rooms, saunas, store rooms and cupboards.

Assistant Chief Constable Musgrave materialised at Diamond's side and said, 'I hope you've got this right, Peter. We're going to take some stick if not.'

Diamond had the foresight to turn off the loudhailer before saying tersely, 'She hasn't radioed in. The car is still here in the car park. What else do you expect me to do, sir?'

'But can this really be our man?'

The blare of the alarm put a timely stop to the exchange. Diamond stepped towards the main doors to keep a watch on people as they streamed out of the building. The task was fraught with difficulty: he was the only police officer capable of recognising Bert Jones, and he was having to rely on the help of three of the Centre staff who worked with the man.

The response to the alarm was quick, almost too quick. Early evening was a peak time at the Centre. The foyer filled quickly and a bottleneck formed at the one exit Diamond allowed to be used. Reasonably enough, he wanted a sight of everyone leaving the building. Inside, uniformed police were doing their best to control the exodus and calm nerves, but there were still people complaining. It could easily tip over into panic.

And if there wasn't trouble within, there were problems developing outside. The public assembling on the fore-court were dressed in a variety of skimpy sports kits. On

332

a cool October evening, middle-aged women in leotards were not going to stand in the open for long. There were shivering kids from the swimming pool without even a towel to dry themselves; someone on the staff was sent for a stack of towels to hand round.

Upwards of two hundred people had passed the check-point before the real flow stopped and only a few more stragglers were seen emerging. The alarm was silenced and the search party went in. A few officers remained to deal with the public. Keith Halliwell suggested letting the people back inside the foyer, but Diamond was totally absorbed in the search, increasingly sure that serious harm had come to Julie.

Halliwell tried again, 'I think we should let them back in, Mr Diamond, I really do.'

Diamond thrust the loudhailer into his hands. 'Do it, then.'

He kept track of the operation with a personal radio. A few who had believed the alarm to be false were being winkled out and so were others who had insisted on returning to the changing-rooms before leaving. There were protests from some of the women caught half-dressed by young policemen; they were unconvinced by the logic that the rooms were supposed to be unoccupied.

The search of the ground floor did not take long. Much of the space is taken up by the main sports hall, a vast place like an aircraft hanger, divided only by netting, where badminton, aerobics and netball can take place simultaneously. The swimming pool and the indoor bowls hall were equally simple to check.

The searchers moved upstairs, into a warren of corridors and offices, viewing galleries and smaller rooms for table tennis, weight training and aerobics. This took longer. A party of rebels was located in the bar and restaurant, called the Winning Post, and some angry exchanges were brought to a stop only by an angrier instruction from Diamond over the radio link. He had other priorities than getting involved with a crowd of bolshie drinkers.

Soon after 6.30 p.m., the word came through that every part of the building had been searched.

'She's got to be here somewhere,' Diamond insisted to Mr Musgrave. 'Her car is still outside. She knew the dog was in there. She wouldn't have left it that long. Either she's hurt, or she's being kept against her will.'

'Was the car park checked?' Mr Musgrave asked. 'It goes right under the building, you know.'

'Of course.'

'Yes, but is Jones's car still here? Do we know what he drives?'

It was a useful suggestion and Diamond acted on it at once. One of the Sports Centre people said Jones drove an old white Cortina. A check with the Police National Computer confirmed this and supplied a registration number. A search was started.

With some reluctance, Diamond acceded to Mr Musgrave's suggestion that the public be allowed to return to their activities. 'If the car is missing,' said the ACC, 'we can safely assume he's abducted Julie and driven her away. Then we're into a full-scale emergency.'

'Aren't we, already?' muttered Diamond, striding off to look at cars.

Within a few minutes, Jones's white Cortina was found in the section reserved for staff. Diamond walked around it, looking through the windows. Then he had the boot forced open – a stomach-churning moment, but it turned out to be empty except for some sports clothes. He had the engine immobilised.

'In that case,' he said, 'there's only one place the bastard can be. I want torches and ladders. And I want twenty men and at least three authorised shots for this. Keith, get the floodlighting turned on at the rugby ground.'

The Centre had a vast flat roof with several levels. It was decided to start from the side nearest the road. Ladders were not after all required because there was access by way of the restaurant balcony on the top floor. About twenty of the searchers lined up on the roof and began a slow sweep

334

of that level under Diamond's personal supervision, with the marksmen positioned to target any figure making a break. It wasn't so open an area as Diamond expected; a number of ventilation shafts were capable of providing cover for a fugitive.

On any investigation he experienced moments of numbing despair; he couldn't change his nature. But this was infinitely worse. It wasn't mere depression; it was hell. He despised himself. It wouldn't take much more to persuade him to jump off this bloody roof. He'd made a whopping misjudgement, totally failing to see the danger in sending Julie to interview Jones. The neatness of the case against A.J. and Jessica had blinded him to other suspects. Up here, on this God-forsaken roof, Peter Diamond was getting his pay-off. He had a reputation for decisiveness. When the decision led to a disaster ... if, as he had to expect, Julie was found dead ... then only one decision would be left to him.

His thoughts went back to his last conversation with Julie, over the phone, when she'd been trying to alert him to her discovery of the paint-spots on the dog, and he'd made the idiot assumption that she was reconsidering keeping the dog. Trivial, but it shamed him now. He'd never valued Julie sufficiently. She was ace, a clear thinker. He knew it, so why hadn't he listened first time?

The line moved steadily across the roof, towards the edge that overlooked the Recreation Ground. There was a brisk wind up here, making it difficult to be heard. He was directing the operation with a torch, waving it in a circular motion to bring the line forward and holding it still above his head when he needed to stop them. They seemed to have got the idea.

Quite suddenly, the whole area ahead was illuminated. Keith Halliwell had acted on his order and the flood-lighting on the rugby ground, where Bath RFC played its matches, was switched on. The Sports Centre was sited next to the ground, and the lighting, on masts, was close enough to make a real difference.

At the same time, Diamond thought he heard a shout from a woman. There were women in the police line and he couldn't be sure if one of them had reacted to the lights. He held the torch high and asked for silence by a sweeping motion with his free hand.

The wind increased in strength.

He could hear nothing more. He waved the line forward again.

Almost immediately there was another cry. It *was* a woman's voice, no question, and it seemed to be saying, 'Here!'

No one was in sight ahead, where the sound seemed to have come from. They had passed the last of the ventilation shafts.

He signalled another halt and asked the man nearest to him if he'd heard the voice. He said he thought he had, but he couldn't understand where from. Diamond considered ordering everyone to do an about-turn; clearly there was no one ahead of them, so maybe it was some acoustic effect.

Then he heard it again and this time it was a cry for help.

He took some quick steps forward and understood. The roof of the Sports Centre came to an end, but beyond it, at a lower level, was the new stand of the rugby club, the Teacher's Stand, built only a season or two ago. Its superstructure of seventeen white cones, like the tops of so many medieval jousting-tents, was silhouetted against the floodlighting.

'She's down there,' he said. 'That's where she's got to be.'

The gunmen had moved forward and taken positions on the edge of the roof. He hissed an order to them to get out of sight.

There was a way down to the back edge of the stand roof. The buildings were virtually linked. Making the descent was awkward for a man his size, but he was first there. Three of the party followed him.

He gestured to the others to stand still.

He called her name.

Nothing.

'Julie, this is me – Diamond.'

A clear voice, shrill and urgent, answered, 'Here!'

She was alive! He still couldn't see her, but the voice was unmistakable. It seemed to have come from in front of the cones. There was a chunk of equipment projecting above the level of the roof.

He took a few steps to his right, then ducked down fast.

Two figures were lying flat, almost obscured by a satellite dish. If Jones, powerful man that he was, had Julie by the throat, he could snap her neck. This couldn't be rushed. And it was no use relying on the guns.

Diamond crept forward, commando-style, flat to his stomach. He beckoned the others on.

Then Julie spoke again. 'For God's sake hurry up, Mr Diamond. I've made the arrest. All I want is someone to take him away.'

Sheepishly, he stood up. Once more he'd underestimated her. Julie had Bert Jones in an arm-lock, her leg braced and keeping him immobile in a very effective hold.

A couple of constables handcuffed Jones and got him upright.

Diamond put out a hand to help Julie up, and she hesitated. He asked if she was all right and she said she'd injured an ankle, and hadn't wanted to take any risks, so she hadn't attempted to bring Jones down herself. They'd been lying there for over an hour.

'I don't know how you managed it,' Diamond said without thinking that his surprised tone might give offence. 'He's a fitness expert.'

'I've done my training, same as you or anyone else,' Julie said. 'I know how to restrain a man.'

'A body-builder?'

'My instructor said you grab his arm before he grabs yours.'

'Did he, indeed!'

'Did *she*.'

'Right,' he said in a dazed way. 'Right, Julie.'

They used Diamond's car to drive back to Manvers Street. Marlowe travelled with them, giving an occasional whimper; he'd spent too long cooped up in the other car.

Julie explained what had happened when she had gone to interview Bert Jones in his office on the first floor. 'He didn't seem troubled that I was there – not at first, anyway. I asked him about his movements the previous evening and he said he'd been working late at the Centre on some paperwork, ordering equipment. It sounded reasonable. I asked if anyone else could confirm what time he left and he said it was after midnight and he'd been alone in the building. He often worked late. He had an arrangement with the security staff to let himself out. Then I asked if he used the computer to order this equipment, and immediately I could tell he didn't like the question. It wasn't unreasonable: the screen was sitting on his desk between us. He came over all aggressive, asking what the hell it mattered whether he'd been using the computer or sitting with his feet on the desk. I tried to explain what I was getting at with my question.'

'You'd better explain to me,' said Diamond.

'Some computers log the time and date when they're in use. We could have looked it up and seen on the screen that he clocked off at midnight and that would have provided proof of his statement. Just as good as a witness. He said this computer didn't have a function like that. It was obvious there was something he wanted to hide, so I probed a little more. I asked to see duplicates of the order-forms he'd been preparing. He tried to stall me. I insisted it was important. I had him worried, even if I wasn't sure why.'

'You were on to him,' said Diamond. 'I reckon the riddles were printed on the Sports Centre equipment. We could have compared the typefaces.'

'Well, he certainly took it seriously,' said Julie. 'He got up and went to the door, saying he had to go somewhere to look for these forms. I was getting suspicious and said I'd go with him. In the corridor outside, he suddenly started running. He bolted up a fire escape to the roof and I followed. There was one hell of a chase up there, and it ended on the rugby club stand.'

'With one of the best tackles all season.'

'Maybe,' she said with a smile, 'but I twisted my ankle doing it and . . .'

'The trainer was a long time coming on.'

'You said it, Mr Diamond.'

After the ordeal on the roof, Julie was more than entitled to go off duty, but she insisted on being present when Bert Jones was interviewed. There was much that she still wanted to know.

Jones sat with arms folded in the interview room, his facial expression saying I'll see you in hell first. Diamond impassively went through the preliminaries of a recorded interview. He had seen this kind of posturing so often before from suspects.

'Let's start with your name. Most people know you as Bert, but it's Gilbert Jones, isn't it?'

A nod.

'You signed up for the Bloodhounds – four years ago, was it? – as Gilbert.'

Another nod.

'Why?'

Jones frowned and said sullenly, 'Why what?'

'Why Gilbert? Why not Bert?'

No response.

'It's not such a dumb question,' Diamond told him. 'I want to understand your motive in all this. You're smart. You know enough about people's perceptions to see that the likes of Mrs Wycherley and Mr Motion would be more impressed with a Gilbert than a mere Bert. Right?'

'If you say so.'

'No. I'm asking you.'

Jones hesitated. 'All right, some places I'm known as Bert, some as Gilbert. That isn't a crime, is it?'

'Right. You work in – what do you call it? – sports administration. Some people think a man who goes round in a tracksuit and trainers all day can't have a serious thought in his head. Just a jock. Just a Bert, anyway. Put on a jacket and tie and call yourself Gilbert and they'd see you in a different light. The truth is that you're quite an intellectual. You read a lot. James Bond, isn't it?'

Reddening suddenly, Jones thrust a finger across the table at Diamond. 'Don't talk down to me.'

'That's what I'm saying,' Diamond cheerfully pointed out. 'You're entitled to respect. You had to get a qualification for the job you do, right?'

'Three years' training and a diploma,' said Jones.

'Where did you do it?'

'Loughborough.'

'The best – and bloody hard work.'

Jones eyed the big detective, uncertain now whether his achievements were being mocked.

Diamond stared back. He was convinced that the source of this man's behaviour was a grudge, a deep conviction that the world undervalued him. 'Head work,' he stressed. 'I don't say there isn't a physical element – of course there is – but there's a damn sight more bookwork and study than any outsider appreciates, right?'

No response except a twitch of the mouth that seemed to signal assent.

'You're an expert on Ian Fleming's work. An authority,' Diamond said without a flicker of condescension. 'You went along to the Bloodhounds as Gilbert Jones, ready to talk about Fleming, and something went seriously wrong because you only lasted a couple of weeks. I have a suspicion why. I've met these people, full of self-importance. Something was said about you, or your background, or the books you read, that turned you right off the Bloodhounds and left you feeling bitter. It doesn't matter what.'

Jones was spurred into saying, 'It matters to me.'

'What was it, then? What did they say?'

His face creased at the mention of it. This was an open wound. And it was still hurting. 'They called them blood and thunder thrillers. Ignorant bastards. They as good as told me I was wasting my time and theirs by talking about them. What do they know about it? Far better people than them appreciate Fleming – President Kennedy, Kingsley Amis. I still shake when I think about it. Those books changed the face of the spy story. The research was terrific. The attention to detail. Just because something is a worldwide success, it doesn't mean it's pulp. Agatha Christie sells in millions, but the Bloodhounds were willing to talk about her.'

'Was that really what this was about – Fleming's reputation?' Diamond asked. 'Or was it yours that was being rubbished?'

A muscle twitched in Jones's neck. 'They knew nothing about me. I didn't tell them what my job is.'

'It was even more of a slapdown, then. They judged you personally, by your voice, your manner . . .'

'It wasn't a slapdown. They chose to ignore me once they knew I admired Fleming and no one else.'

'So you quit after three weeks?'

'Should have quit after one.'

'And then forgot the whole thing until an opportunity came to get revenge?'

Jones wouldn't accept that. 'No. I didn't forget.'

Of course he hadn't forgotten. The wound had festered for years. 'Then you met Shirley-Ann Miller, who moved in with you. Like you, she's a reader of crime stories.'

'She reads everything.'

'So you had James Bond in common. She decided to join the Bloodhounds.'

'Off her own bat,' Jones was keen to make clear. 'I didn't put her up to it.'

'You didn't?' Diamond glanced at Julie; the lie hadn't escaped her. Shirley-Ann had told them herself that Bert brought home a brochure from the Leisure Centre and pointed out the existence of the Bloodhounds, knowing how much she enjoyed detective stories. It was a side issue, and Diamond chose not to pursue it. Even if Shirley-Ann had been used, she wasn't an accessory in these crimes.

'She doesn't know a thing. She has no idea I once went to some of their meetings.'

Probably true. 'You sat back and waited to hear what she said about these know-it-alls who snubbed you. It was the opportunity you wanted. You decided to have some fun with them.'

'Fun?' said Jones, as if it were a foreign word.

'Show them up.'

'Right.' He preferred that. His actions weren't motivated by humour. He'd been deadly serious.

Diamond underlined the point. 'You wanted to show up their tiny minds.' This was emphatically the right way to handle Jones. The man craved admiration.

'I saw my chance and I took it. Specially when she told me the same old gang were still running it. The gay bloke with the ridiculous beard and that old witch Polly. Shirley-Ann likes telling me things. She sometimes says she could talk for Great Britain. I don't mind. I was riveted. I was given a very accurate account of that first meeting she attended.'

'When they agreed to discuss the locked room puzzle?'

'Yes.'

'And you decided to act – hit them with a real locked room puzzle, to prove that a James Bond reader was smart enough to frame the lot of them with one of their favourite plots.'

'Something like that,' agreed Jones, though the irony of what he had done seemed to escape him. This had never at any time been a mere intellectual exercise. It was the revenge of a deeply embittered man.

'You thought up a way of stealing the Penny Black early one morning when the window cleaners were out in force. Your partner wouldn't suspect anything, because you go jogging in the mornings anyway. This time, you took a ladder and a bucket. You must have visited the museum before then and found the weak link in the security. So you put your ladder to the window, let yourself in and came out with the stamp. Is that a fair summary?'

Jones said, 'I didn't take it for personal gain.'

'We're agreed on that,' said Diamond amiably. 'This was all about proving a point, not making a profit. By this time, you were ready to garnish the plot with the first riddle. You composed it on your computer at work and ran it off on the printer in the evening when no one was about. Correct?'

Jones gave a nod. He was willing, even eager, to claim responsibility for the clever stuff with the stamp and the riddle. Would he be as ready to admit to murder?

'What made you choose Milo as the fall guy, I wonder? Why was he singled out as the one who would be offloaded with the stolen stamp? Was it something he said at those meetings you attended that caused such offence?'

'He said they were written for people with sick minds.'

'That *is* over the top,' agreed Diamond, regardless that Jones himself had a mind that was sick *and* over the top. 'Practically everyone has read Bond. I have. What did he mean?'

Julie murmured, 'The violence.'

Diamond said, 'It's all very tame by today's standards, isn't it?'

'I doubt if Milo Motion has read anything written in the last thirty years,' said Jones.

'So you took your revenge on Milo?'

'Yes, and you don't know how it was done.'

'Don't I?' said Diamond, his own ego challenged. 'Don't I?'

'Let's hear it, then,' Jones sneered.

He heard it from Diamond, point for point. The extra padlock from Foxton's. The switch while Milo was aboard the boat, enabling Jones to unlock it later.

The deflating of Gilbert Jones was satisfying to behold.

343

'All right, you worked it out,' he eventually conceded, 'but not one of them could.'

'I'm sure you're right. Your planning can't be faulted. It would have been a perfect crime if Sid Towers hadn't got curious and driven out to the boatyard just as you were replacing the original padlock.'

Jones didn't deny it. He said, 'I didn't mean to kill him. I mean I hit him from behind, but I only wanted to make my getaway. He hadn't seen me. If he'd survived, you would have been none the wiser.'

'And Rupert?' said Diamond, leaping ahead. 'Why was he killed? He hadn't insulted your brain-power. He wasn't even a member when you joined the Bloodhounds.'

This was the crux of it. Sid's death may not have been planned, but Rupert's was. Stringing a man from a bridge isn't accidental.

Jones was silent for some time. Then he shook his head. 'You've got to see it my way. You were closing in. I was worried. It was only a matter of time before you got round to me unless I did something dramatic to put you off. I'd be up for manslaughter at the very least. Maybe murder. I needed someone to take the heat off me. First I thought of Jessica Shaw. She's clever. Clever enough to have written the riddles. And she was holding a party at the art gallery. I decided a message on the window would get some attention. If nothing else, it would create a distraction.'

'And buy time?'

'Well, yes. But I needed someone else to be blamed for writing up the graffiti. Rupert Darby.'

'Why Rupert? He hadn't even crossed your path.'

'That's exactly the point,' said Jones with the pitiless logic that had sentenced Rupert to death. 'He was a stranger to me.'

'You marked him with the paint-spray,' said Diamond. 'You'd never met him, but he was easy to recognise with the beret.'

'And it struck me then that Darby was a better choice

344

than Jessica. And if he committed suicide, or appeared to—'

'You mean if you were to murder him.'

Jones didn't balk at the mention of murder. It was secondary to his plan. His locked-room crime was the proof of his brilliance in the face of the Bloodhounds, the police, his workmates, all the people who had ever slighted him. It had to remain undetected, regardless of the consequences. The killing of two hapless men had been incidental. What mattered was that he succeeded. Murderers of his kind are rare, but they exist; they lose all sense of proportion and nothing is allowed to thwart them.

'It would look like he'd killed Sid Towers and decided to do away with himself. Especially if I wrote another riddle.'

'Which you did. You've got some talent there,' said Diamond. 'Pity you didn't leave it at poetry.'

Jones shrugged.

Diamond said, 'Killing a man you hardly knew at all.'

'But the riddle had to work out,' Jones said, his blue eyes widening in a way that revealed his unbalance. 'It had to work out.'

Adding a confession of his own, Diamond said, 'When I first saw the body hanging from the bridge, I was sure it was the work of two people. I overlooked your strength-training. Even so, it couldn't have been easy.'

'He was in no state to struggle.'

'Drugged?'

'I did add something to his seventh vodka.'

'In which pub?'

'Don't ask. It was some night,' said Jones. 'He told me himself it was one of the best benders of his life.'

'And then what? You drove him to Sydney Gardens . . .'

'He couldn't stand straight by this time. I stuffed the padlock in his pocket.'

'The one you used to get into the narrowboat?'

'Yes. And I found his key-ring in his pocket with his house-key and attached the padlock keys to it. He had no

345

idea what I was doing. Then I dragged him out of the car to the bridge, fixed the rope to the railings, slipped the noose over his head and heaved him over.' There was a chilling sense of satisfaction in the way it had been done.

'In the end it was down to muscle power, your perfect crime,' said Diamond.

'It's the way you use it,' said Jones.

'We know all about that,' Diamond told him. 'How's your arm feeling now? Capable of signing a statement?'

Nothing would be gained from protesting at the callous way two likeable men had lost their lives. Gilbert Jones was irredeemable.

At home in Weston, in his armchair in front of the TV, with Raffles chewing his shoelaces, Diamond asked Stephanie what she was reading.

'It's that book you brought home the other day,' she said. '*The Hollow Man*.'

'I meant to read it,' he said. 'I only looked at one chapter in the end.'

'Will you get round to it?'

'I shouldn't think so. Detective stories aren't my thing at all. I've got no patience with them. Nothing like the real thing.'

'The bank murder, you mean?'

He gave her a sharp look. 'That was another story.'

Diamond Dust

1

The prisoner stared at the jury as they filed in. Every one of them avoided eye contact.

The foreman was asked for the verdict and gave it.

A few stifled cries were heard.

Peter Diamond of Bath CID, watching from the back of the court, displayed no emotion, though he felt plenty. Unseen by anyone, his fists tightened, his pulses quickened and his throat warmed as if he'd taken a sip of brandy. This was a moment to savour.

'And is that the verdict of you all?'

'It is.'

'But I'm innocent!' the man guilty of murder shouted, his hands outstretched in appeal. 'I didn't do it. I was stitched up.'

Yes, stitched up well and truly, Diamond thought, in a Pink Brothers shirt and a fine Italian suit that didn't fool the jury, thank God. Any minute now the lowlife inside those clothes will say something nakedly uncouth.

'Stitch-up!' a woman supporter screamed from the public gallery, and more voices took up the cry. The people up there began chanting and stamping their feet as if this was a wrestling match.

The judge slammed down his gavel and ordered the court to be cleared.

Almost an hour after, the prisoner was back for

sentencing, a short, swarthy man with eyes like burn holes in a bed-sheet.

'Jacob Barry Carpenter, you have been found guilty of murder, a murder as callous as any it has been my misfortune to come across. If there was the slightest uncertainty in the minds of the jury, it will have been removed upon hearing your criminal record. You are a man of habitual violence, and you have acted in character once again, and this time you will not escape with a light sentence.'

'You got the wrong man, for Jesus' sake.'

'Be quiet. As you well know, the mandatory sentence for murder is life imprisonment, and that is the sentence of this court. As you are also aware, a life sentence has a discretionary element. It need not mean life in the literal sense. In your case – are you listening? – I recommend that it should. You are such a danger to the public that I cannot foresee a time when it will be safe to release you.'

The man reverted to basics. 'Arsehole! I was fitted up!'

'Take him down.'

Shouting more abuse, Carpenter was bundled from view by the prison guards.

The judge thanked the jury and discharged them. The court rose.

Peter Diamond turned to leave. His pudgy face revealed no joy in the verdict, nor concern at the prisoner's outburst. A mature detective learns to conceal his feelings when a verdict is announced. But when his deputy, DI Keith Halliwell, said, 'Are we going for a bevvy?' the suspicion of a smile appeared at the edge of his mouth.

'You bet.'

The pub was just across the street from the Bristol Crown Court and some of the team would already be there, celebrating.

Daniel Houldsworth, the QC who had led for the Crown, put a hand on Diamond's shoulder. 'Pleased with the outcome, Superintendent?'

'It's the right one.'

The lawyer made it clear he wanted to say more, so Diamond told Halliwell to go ahead. He would join the team shortly.

'I expected the abuse at the end and so did the judge,' Houldsworth commented, as if he felt some of the gloss had been taken off the triumph. 'They're a cancer, the Carpenters. They've run Bristol for too long.' He went on in this vein for some time, until it became obvious he was fishing for larger compliments.

'Top result, anyway,' Diamond said, and that seemed to do the trick. He shook hands with Houldsworth and a couple of junior lawyers and left the court. Funny how everyone wanted credit: barristers, solicitor, jury, and, no doubt, judge – when it was obvious the murder squad had done the job. With a shake of the head unseen by anyone else he made for the exit across the flagstoned corridor where the principals in another case waited nervously. He'd missed one round of drinks, and maybe another.

Thinking only how much he would savour that first cool gulp of bitter, he came down the Court steps into Small Street on a beeline for the Bar Oz. Stared up at the sallow February sun, the promise of brighter times ahead. Didn't glance at the small group in conversation on the pavement. Didn't even react when a woman's voice shrilled, 'There he is, the shitbag.' Simply reached the bottom step and started forward.

His sleeve was tugged from behind. He swung around and got a gob of spit full between the eyes. There was a blur of blond hair, a shout of 'Sodding pig!' and the woman clawed her fingernails down the right side of his face from eye to neck. The nails ripped the skin, a searing, sudden pain. She was screaming, 'Stinking filth. He done nothing. My Jake done nothing, and you know it.'

The next strike would have got his eye if he hadn't grabbed the woman's wrist and swung her out of range. In this frenzied state she was a match for any middle-aged man and she lunged at him again, aiming a kick at his crotch. He jackknifed to save himself, caught his heel against the steps and tripped, falling heavily. He lay there trying to protect his groin, and instead got a vicious kicking in the kidneys.

No one stopped it. People outside the Guildhall stared across Small Street with glazed expressions and pretended they hadn't noticed. What do you do when a woman is assaulting a man twice her size?

What do you do if you're that man? Diamond struggled upright and tried to hobble away. Where were the police? Someone should have seen this coming after the rumpus inside the court.

Still she vented her hate on him, pummelling his back and screaming abuse. If he turned and swung a punch at her it was sod's law someone would get a photo and sell it to the papers. So he moved on stoically. Then, thank God, spotted a taxi and waved to the driver.

The cabbie stared at this man with a bleeding face and a screaming woman raining punches on his back and, not unreasonably, didn't want them in his vehicle. He shook his head and drove off.

Further up the street, a second taxi had been hailed by one of the junior barristers on the case.

Diamond charged towards it and shoved the lawyer aside. 'Emergency,' he said with as much authority as he had left.

His attacker had come after him and still had a hold on his coat. He elbowed her off and slammed the door. 'Police. Foot down,' he told the driver.

'Where to?'

'Out of here.'

The woman and her friends were running beside the cab beating the windows.

The cabbie drove off fast towards Colston Avenue. 'Friends of yours?'

'Leave it.' He ran a finger over his smarting face and looked at the blood.

'Top cop, are you?'

'Not really.'

'Got to be Jake Carpenter's bird, hasn't she, the blonde? Wasn't he on trial?'

He confirmed it with a murmur.

'Guilty, then?'

'As hell.'

'She's marked you. You could do her for assault.'

'No chance.' He'd been onto a loser the moment she attacked. Really, he had only himself to blame, leaving the court unaccompanied like that. If he nicked her, she'd use it as a publicity stunt, a chance to go over the trial again. And her counsel would plead extenuating circumstances and she'd get off with a caution.

'So where shall I put you down?'

They were heading south, towards the river. He was in no shape now to join the celebration in the pub.

'Bath. I'm going home.'

2

'You'll tell me if it hurts, won't you?' Stephanie Diamond was dabbing her husband's scratched face with TCP. 'Is that painful?'

Without thinking, he started to shake his head, and felt the full pressure of the swab. 'Jee-eez!'

She drew it away. 'Sorry, love.'

'My fault.' Mortified for being such a wimp, he said, 'Iodine's the stuff that hurts. They always used that when I was a kid. Wicked. Why, I couldn't tell you.'

Steph waited, swab in hand. She was still in her work clothes, a white jumper with a magnolia design on the front and a close-fitting black skirt. She moved closer again and rested her free hand on his shoulder. 'These are deep. She must be a vicious woman.'

'Just angry.'

'She's marked you with all four fingernails. Do you think I should take a photo?'

'Whatever for?'

'Evidence.'

He grinned. 'Like when someone runs into the car, you mean?' Patiently, he explained that he wouldn't be charging the woman, and why.

Steph, with her strong sense of right and wrong, didn't appreciate the explanation. 'She shouldn't get away with it.'

He was basking in her concern, even though it had to

be cooled. 'She believed he was innocent. I expect he told her he was fitted up and she believed him.'

'That doesn't excuse it.'

'It means she acted out of genuine outrage, not just spite.'

Steph sighed. 'Well, the scratches are genuine enough. They're going to be on your face for some time. What are you going to tell people – that I did it?'

He smiled at the idea, and felt his cheek sting when the muscles stretched. 'Would you rather I said it was one of my many mistresses?'

'Do you want a scar on the other cheek? I could match them up, no problem.'

'Okay. I'll think of something better.'

'I could mask it with a concealer-stick if you like.'

'A what?'

'Make-up.'

'I don't think make-up would play too well at the nick.'

Later the same evening, after supper, the rich aroma of beef casserole lingered. Diamond, in his favourite armchair, warmed by the cat at full stretch across his lap, was thinking life was improving. Then Steph asked, 'What exactly did he do?'

'Who?'

'Jake Carpenter. All you've told me is that he's a well-known criminal.'

'And he is.'

'But you haven't said anything about the case.'

'True.' He made it obvious he didn't intend saying much.

'Is it as bad as that? You don't usually shield me from the facts.'

'I'm not shielding you, Steph. I wouldn't do that.'

'The well-bred English gent sparing his delicate wife the gory details?'

'Cobblers. I just didn't think you wanted to know.'

'I do now.' Her eyes were on the scratches again.

He yawned, and stroked Raffles under the chin while considering where to begin. 'They're Bristol's Mafia – the Carpenters, Jake and his brothers Des and Danny. They live in luxury and make their money out of protection and pimping. They've all got form – done time inside. They're feared. Anyone standing up to them is dealt with, usually by one of their gorillas. But when we succeed in pinning things on any of the brothers they mysteriously get light sentences.'

'You mean the law is bought off?'

'So it appears. It may not be cash passing hands, but it happens. This time was different. A mandatory life sentence if he was convicted.'

'He'd murdered someone?'

'A call girl by the name of Maeve Smith. Irish. Seventeen years old. Pretty, dark-haired, and a big earner. Unwisely, young Maeve tried to transfer to another pimp, so Jake made an example of her. Two of his thugs took her to a tattooist and had her breasts and buttocks personalised with his initials.'

'Beast.'

'That's tame for the Carpenters. Girls who step out of line sometimes have acid thrown in their faces. This one was still a top earner, so they left her face alone. After the tattooing he slept with her several times. I suppose he found it a turn-on seeing his initials on her.'

'How could she, after what he'd done?'

'I didn't say she agreed to it.'

Steph took in a sharp breath.

'In court, he claimed she was his girlfriend to support his case that he wouldn't want to hurt her. He failed to see that it gave him a stronger motive when she slipped the leash again.'

'Was that why she was killed?'

'Yes, he considered her his property. Her naked body was found in the Avon below the Suspension Bridge, but she was dead before she was thrown in the water. She'd been beaten about the face and head. Really beaten, I mean. The face was pulp, unrecognisable. The tattooed initials helped us link her to Carpenter, so the rat did himself no service when he ordered that punishment. And this time the forensic stuff led us straight to him. Traces of her blood and DNA material in his car boot and on one of his shoes.'

'No doubt about it, then?'

'Not a jot.'

Steph looked away, her face creased in sympathy for the young victim, and then her eyes turned back to Diamond. 'This other woman – the one who scratched you – must be deluding herself. If she was at the trial and heard the evidence, she knows he slept with the girl. And she knows he's a sadist. How can she defend a brute like that?'

'You tell me.'

'I'm saying, Peter – she's deluded. She's trying to convince herself you faked the evidence. She turned her anger on you.'

He spread his hands, and the cat jumped off his lap, surprised by the movement. 'Steph, I've no interest what her motives are.'

'Do you know who she is?'

'A minor player.' He stretched and stood up, wanting to talk of other things. 'Hasn't been around long.'

'I still think she shouldn't get away with this.'

He went over to her and touched her hair, letting a strand rest between finger and thumb. 'Leave it, eh?'

'Now you've told me about it—'

Gently but with decision he interrupted. 'There are more important things.'

'Like?'

'Like let's have an early night.'

She hesitated, needing first to shut out the horrors of his work, then laughed and flicked her hair free. 'Fancy your chances, Scarface?'

The taunt brought back the bittersweet agonies of nearly twenty years ago, being in love without being sure of her. They'd met in Hammersmith, when he was in uniform, doing a stint as community involvement officer, which meant lecturing groups on road safety and crime prevention. Much of it was with the very old or the very young. At that time Steph was not long out of her divorce and trying to forget it by being Brown Owl to a troop, or pack, or whatever it was called, of Brownies. Diamond turned up to do his talk and made a total balls of it because he couldn't take his eyes off Brown Owl. At the end he asked her out and she declined. Wouldn't even give him a phone number. So he put in an appearance next week with some leaflets he said he'd forgotten to hand out to the girls. Then made himself useful changing a fuse when the lights failed. Week after week, using flimsy excuses for being there, he let her know how committed he was. These days it might well be called harassment. By degrees, she softened. It was a curious, chaste courtship, with each move witnessed by small giggling girls in brown uniforms. The turning point was the summer camp, when he breezed in unexpectedly with Bradford and Bingley, two donkeys he'd borrowed from the Hammersmith desk sergeant, who'd set up a donkey sanctuary as a retirement venture. Bradford and Bingley gave rides for the next two days. From that moment the girls called Diamond the Donkey Man and convinced Steph he deserved to be an honorary member of the Brownies.

Brown Owl married the Donkey Man the following

spring, and it was a strong, loving relationship still, thanks in no small part to Steph's calmness under stress. There had been desperately bad moments, like her miscarriage (she'd suffered three already with her first husband) and the hysterectomy that had followed. There were the plunges in Diamond's rollercoaster career: the board of inquiry, the resignation, the move to the poky basement flat in London, being sacked from Harrods, and the spell of unemployment. Steph had kept them going by being positive and finding a funny side to every experience.

But rollercoasters have their upsides, and the police had needed him back. He returned to his old job as murder man in Bath CID. Since then, life had been kinder – their own house in Weston, a playful cat called Raffles, good neighbours and a Chinese takeaway at the end of the street.

Upstairs, he poured two glasses of Rioja before getting into bed. Steph had been to Spain twenty-five years ago as a student and always remembered the wine. She would cheerfully have migrated to Spain or France. No chance hitched to a man like Diamond, with GB plates welded to his soul.

'When did you get this?' she asked. The Diamonds didn't have wine in store. When they bought a bottle, it was for immediate consumption.

'On the way back from Bristol.'

'Nice surprise.'

'Mm.'

'There's the difference between you and me,' she said. 'I don't mind surprises.'

'You're saying I do?'

'You hate them. That's why you're such a good detective. You take out the surprise element by thinking ahead, every angle.'

'I wish it were true.'

'Of course it's true.'

'Yeah? How many times have I needed your help to second-guess a suspect? More than I can count.' He held up his glass.

'Is this to anything special? Another villain off the streets?'

'No, this is to my pretty, wise and understanding wife. Cheers, Steph.'

Accepting a compliment is one of the hardest things to handle. She could have made some flippant response, but she didn't. Coming from her Peter, the awkward little speech was as near as he got to a love poem. She felt for his hand and held it, and they sipped their wine.

'Speaking of surprises,' she said presently, 'certain of your old colleagues know you're reaching a landmark this year.'

'My fiftieth?' He stared at her in alarm. 'How the hell did they find out?'

'You had your picture in the papers last summer when there was all the hoo-ha about the body in the vault.'

'Oh, and the bloody press always give your age. "*Peter Diamond, forty-nine.*" It doesn't take a genius to work out I'll be half a hundred this year.' His eyes read her face. 'They're not planning anything?'

'It was being whispered about. They asked me, and I did my best to cool it. I said you wouldn't appreciate a surprise party one bit.'

'Dead right. Who was this?'

'I'm not at liberty to say.'

'They've dropped the idea, I hope.'

'I think so, but we may need to think of something ourselves.'

'Like being away for the week?'

'Good thinking. I like it.' Steph smiled. 'You're way ahead of me. What do you have in mind – a cruise?'

He vibrated his lips. 'I can't think of anything worse.'

'A surprise party is worse.'

'Christ, yes.'

'Oh, come on. They only thought of it because they're fond of you, in spite of the hard times you gave them. They want to show you some affection.'

'Who *are* these misguided people?'

'I promised not to say.'

'They should know I get all the affection I want from you.'

'Hint, hint?' She put aside her wineglass and turned to kiss him.

Still troubled by the thought of opening a door on a roomful of smiling faces, he curled his arm around her and returned the kiss in a perfunctory way. She wriggled closer and the second kiss was warmer and they got horizontal in the same movement.

'Well, now,' Steph said as he pressed against her. 'You're quite a surprise party yourself.'

3

By morning the scratches on his face had darkened and were more obvious. He checked them in the car mirror on the way to work, in a line of traffic on the Upper Bristol Road. No sense in kidding himself people wouldn't notice. Nobody at the nick would be bold enough to ask how they'd got there, but he was damned sure the place would hum with gossip. His team would have noticed he hadn't turned up at the pub, of course. 'I had to go to another scene,' he'd tell them without saying that the other scene was his home.

He had this bullish reputation that shielded him from comments on his appearance, but inwardly he was more self-conscious than anyone realised. So he entered the nick by the back door, went straight upstairs to his office and closed the door. No one came in.

Just after eleven he was summoned upstairs to Georgina's lair. Georgina Dallymore, the Assistant Chief Constable, gave the scratches a look and may even have winced a little, but made no reference to them when she gestured to him to sit down. 'So one of the Carpenters is off the streets now. Nice work, Peter.'

'Don't know how long for.'

'Yes, he's going to appeal. His solicitor said so on TV.'

'Did he? I didn't watch the box last night.'

'His friends outside the court made a lot of noise.'

'Rentamob, ma'am.'

Georgina picked up a pen and scrutinised it as if the writing on the side held some important message. 'They're a dangerous family, Peter. I wish we had something major on the other two.'

'Des and Danny? No chance,' Diamond said. 'They don't soil their hands.'

'It's all contracted out, you mean?'

He nodded. 'The only reason we got Jake was that he let this girl become a personal issue.'

'He's not the smartest of the brothers, then?'

'Smart enough to live in a swish pad in its own grounds in Clifton – until yesterday.'

She examined the pen again. 'What will they do now? Regroup?'

'I expect so. Vice, or Drugs, have better tabs on the empire than I do.' He sensed, as he spoke, that he was walking into something, and Georgina's eyes confirmed it.

'Right on,' she said. 'It's organised crime.' She leaned forward a little and her eyes had a missionary gleam. 'You'd be good at that – detecting it, I mean.'

He reminded her guardedly, 'I'm your murder man, ma'am.'

'And a very effective one. But there are times, like now, when all we have on the books are the tough cases from years back that nobody ever got near to solving.'

'Doesn't mean we give up on them.' He didn't like the drift of this one bit.

'I'm thinking your skills might be better employed elsewhere, particularly as you know a lot more about the Carpenter family now.'

Elsewhere? He looked away, out of the window, across the grey tiled roofs towards Lansdown. There was an awkward silence.

'You might need to work out of Bristol Central, but it's

not like moving house. What is it – under an hour's drive from where you live?'

He waited a long time before saying, 'Is this an order, ma'am?'

'It's about being flexible.'

'Well, you're talking to the wrong man. I'm not flexible. Never have been. I'm focused.'

Georgina's voice took on a harder note. 'Focus on the Carpenters, then. Yes, it is an order – while nothing new comes up on the murder front. Liaise with Mike Solly and George Eldon. Get an oversight of the entire operation – drugs, prostitution, protection. Put a surveillance team together if you want. This is the time to strike, Peter. They've lost Jake, so they have to put their heads above ground.'

'Have you finished?'

'Careful what you say,' Georgina warned him.

'That's someone else's empire. Not mine.'

'I've issued an order.'

'You want me out of Bath – is that it?' The old demons raged in his head, savaging any good intentions that might have lingered there. He hadn't felt so angry since the day he'd faced another Assistant Chief Constable in this room and resigned from the Force.

'It's not personal. It's about effective management.'

'Effective?' He threw the word back at her.

'I think you'd better get out.'

'Piss off.'

'How dare you!'

'I'm just summing up what you said to me. You've got no use for me here, so you want me to piss off to Bristol.' He turned and walked.

Down in his own office, he stood shaking his head, getting a grip on his emotions. Organised crime had nothing to do with this, he believed. Georgina wanted him out. While he'd been tied up with the court case she'd been plotting his removal. Wrongly, she thought he couldn't take orders from a woman. She didn't understand that he didn't let *anybody* push him around. No doubt she planned to put some pussycat in his place. John Wigfull was out of hospital and supposed to be returning to work any time. Bloody Wigfull would fit in beautifully: the Open University graduate who did everything by the book, never raised his voice and kept his desk as tidy as a church altar. Yes, she'd love to upgrade Wigfull to head of the murder squad.

He spent the next hour with his door closed, looking at the paper mountain on his desk, the filing cabinets that wouldn't close and the stacks of paper on the floor. Was it admitting defeat to tidy up? Wasn't it better to leave everything as it was, just to demonstrate that he'd be back?

He didn't go to the canteen for his usual coffee. And they had the sense not to disturb him.

At lunchtime he got out of the place for a walk, not towards the Abbey Churchyard, where he sometimes went when life had dealt him a wicked hand, but round the back of the railway station, across Widcombe Bridge and along the bank of the Avon as far as Pulteney Bridge – as dull a stretch of river as any he knew. Whenever he told people where he lived, they said how lucky he was, but in truth he wasn't attracted to the postcard scenes of Bath. The stately buildings, the rich history, the setting among green hills didn't excite him. He would have been just as content to work in Bristol if he'd been posted there six years ago. But he hadn't. Stuffy old Bath was his patch. He was in tune with it now. That was why he resented Georgina's attempt to move him.

He picked up a 'ploughman's' baguette – a contradiction, in his opinion – and a can of beer and sat on a

bench in Parade Gardens. By now his rebellious thoughts
were being toned down. He was starting to accept the
inevitability of obeying orders. Georgina hadn't proposed
a permanent move to Bristol Central. The best tactic was
to let everyone know this was a short-term investigation.
He'd make a point of calling in most days at Manvers
Street and keeping track of what was going on there.

Still far from satisfied, he ambled back to the nick
without any urgency. After all, nobody could expect him
to drop everything and beetle off to Bristol the same day.

There was a sense of important things going on when
he walked through the door.

'Mr Diamond, there you are,' the desk sergeant called
across the room.

'Something up?'

'A shooting in Victoria Park. A woman is dead.'

His spirits soared. Bad news for someone could be a
lifeline for him. 'Suicide?'

'Apparently not.'

'So who's dealing with it?'

'DI Halliwell.'

Keith Halliwell was his deputy, and well capable of
sussing out the scene. 'Even so, I think I'll take a look,'
he said as calmly as if a rainbow had appeared over the
city. 'Which part of the park?'

'Crescent Gardens. Down at the bottom, back of the
Charlotte Street Car Park.'

On his way through the building he thought about
leaving a message for Georgina – just to rub in the fact
that sudden deaths did occur in Bath – and then decided
against it. First, he'd find out for himself what this
shooting amounted to. It could be one of those incidents
that get cleared up the same day.

Please God, no.

*   *   *

The Royal Victoria Park, on sloping ground to the west of the city, is in effect two parks, one rather gracious, with lawns descending to a wooded area providing the Royal Crescent with its leafy view; and the other, larger and containing the Botanic Gardens, a fishpond and a children's playground overlooking the gasworks. They are bisected by Marlborough Buildings and its long gardens. The shooting had happened in the gracious part, near the bandstand on the south fringe of the park below the Crescent.

They had sealed off the scene with police tape. The inevitable gawpers had gathered at the margin, but helpfully the trees screened the place from the car park.

The scene-of-crime lads – with at least one lass – in their white zipper overalls were already at work. Halliwell was standing with the constable guarding the access path. Spotting Diamond, he came over to meet him, rubbing his hands.

'We're back in business, guv.'

'What do we know?'

'Middle-aged woman, shot twice in the head at close range. No sign of the weapon.'

'Apart from two holes in her head.'

Halliwell grinned. 'Well, I guess that counts as a sign.'

'Let's have a look, then.'

Halliwell led the way to where the SOCOs were combing the ground for traces of the crime. The corpse was covered with a white plastic sheet.

'Who found her?' Diamond asked.

'A Mr Warburton, walking his dog. About ten-twenty this morning he heard the shots and came over.'

'Did he see the killer?'

'No. Too far away. He was up the hill, not far from the Crescent. When he got here, there was just the woman lying dead.'

'Other people must have heard it. Well into the morning. People are about. The car park would have been filling up.'

'Yes, but he was the only one who bothered to check.'

Diamond didn't question this. The common reaction to the sound of shooting isn't to go and investigate. Most people dismiss it as a car backfiring. If they know it's a gun they head in the opposite direction. He stood over the covered corpse. 'What am I waiting for – someone to introduce us?'

Halliwell stooped and lifted the sheet from the head.

Diamond ran an experienced glance over the blanched face, one blood-red hole almost exactly in the centre of the forehead and another in front of the left ear. Then he stared. His skin prickled and his muscles went rigid as if volts were passing through them.

From deep in his throat came a sound more like a vomit than distress. He sank to his knees and snatched back the plastic sheet and looked at the woman's clothes. No question: she was wearing the black Burberry raincoat she'd bought from Jolly's last summer and the blue silk square he'd given her on her last birthday. He fingered a strand of her hair and it felt like straw. 'It's Steph,' he said, gagging on the words. 'The bastards have shot my wife.'

4

Halliwell was speaking into his mobile. 'We have a positive ID on the body in Crescent Gardens. Confirmed as Mrs Stephanie Diamond, wife of Detective Superintendent Diamond. I repeat . . .'

Diamond remained on his knees beside his dead wife, registering nothing of what was going on around him. This was not self-pity. The focus of his grief was entirely on Steph, and her life so abruptly ended. Dry-eyed and blank-faced, he was weeping inwardly for her, for her compassion, her wisdom, her sense of humour, her integrity, her serenity, her mental strength, her brilliant insights. It had been almost a psychic gift, that ability of hers to draw his attention to hidden truths. With uncanny timing, she had reminded him only the night before how he hated surprises. Here was the worst surprise ever. He hadn't remotely imagined it could happen. Had she? Without the faintest idea of why she had come to this place, he wasn't going to make sense of it now, or in the next hour, or the next day. He knew only that Steph had been the one love of his life and she had been shot through the head at point-blank range. Too dreadful.

Halliwell put a hand on his shoulder and suggested he sat in the car for a bit.

He said from the depths of his grief, 'Back off.'

Wisely, Halliwell did.

The SOCOs continued their fingertip search of the

area, less talkative now. Professionals working at murder scenes often insulate themselves from the horror with black humour that might offend anyone unused to what goes on. Diamond was quite a joker himself. *No sign of the weapon – apart from two holes in the head.* Trust him to make a crass remark like that. Since word had passed round that she was his own wife, the jesting had stopped.

The police photographers (a civilian couple) arrived and Halliwell explained the situation. 'Hang on a minute, and I think he'll move away.'

They waited five minutes.

'Can't you tell him we're here?' the woman said. 'He knows the routine as well as anyone.'

'He's not functioning as a cop at the moment.'

'Who's in charge, then? You?'

'Technically, Mr Diamond is, but . . .'

They looked across. Still the big man knelt, hunched beside his dead wife. 'How long has he been there?'

'Ten, fifteen minutes. It's one hell of a shock.'

'Was he the first officer on the scene, then?'

'No, I was.'

'Didn't you warn him?'

Halliwell reddened. 'I didn't recognise her. I should have, because I've met her a couple of times. I didn't look at her as you would a living person. Saw the injuries and shut myself off from the victim. Your mind is on what happened and what has to be done. Didn't dream it's someone I know.'

'He's got to move away if we're going to get our pictures.'

'All right, all right.'

Halliwell went back to his boss and explained about the photographers. Diamond didn't take in one word of it. He was holding his dead wife's hand, cradling it between both of his.

Halliwell tried again. 'They've got to get their pictures, guv.'

Nothing.

'The photos of the scene.'

He wasn't listening. The police and their procedures were part of another existence.

Halliwell turned away and went back to the photographers. 'I can't shift him.'

'Someone's going to have to.'

'You can wait, can't you?'

The woman made a performance of looking at her watch. 'We're self-employed, you know.'

'Bollocks.' Halliwell stepped away from them and took a call on his mobile.

It was Georgina, the ACC. 'Is this true – about Mr Diamond's wife?'

'I'm afraid so, ma'am. He's here at the scene.'

'Dear God. I'd better come and speak to him.'

'With respect, ma'am, I don't think he's fit to speak to anyone just now.'

'Where is he exactly?'

'Kneeling beside his wife.'

'Poor man . . . I don't think he has any other family, does he?'

'None that I've heard of.'

'Close friends?'

'Outside the police? I wouldn't know.'

'It's up to us to help him through, then.'

Difficult. Halliwell doubted very much if Diamond wanted the ACC to help him through, but he'd told her already to stay away and he couldn't keep repeating it. He looked towards Diamond and saw him reach for the plastic covering and replace it over his wife's face. 'I'm going over to him now, ma'am. He may be ready to leave.'

Diamond stood up, paused for a moment more beside the body and then walked across to Halliwell. His eyes had the unfocused stare of the freshly bereaved, but he was able to find words now, and he made it clear that he wasn't thinking of leaving. 'What have we found, then?' he asked in a flat voice.

'Not much so far, sir. It looks professional.'

'You're searching for the bullets?'

'Of course.'

'And the cases? If they used an automatic . . .' He lost track of the sentence for a moment, his voice breaking up. Then he managed to control it. 'The weapon could still be around. Get some back-up. All this area has to be combed. Every yard of it.'

'Right, sir. Can the photographers get their pictures now?'

'I'm not stopping them.'

The hiatus was over. He was making a huge effort to show he was capable of carrying out the familiar routines. He checked that the police surgeon had been by to certify death, and Halliwell confirmed it.

'And the pathologist?'

'On his way, sir.'

'Middleton, I suppose?'

'Sir.' Halliwell found himself slipping in that 'sir' far more than usual. Normally he was more relaxed with his old boss. 'I'd just like to say—'

'No need,' Diamond cut him short. 'We understand each other. Take it as said.'

The cover was removed entirely from the body for the photographs and video record. More sightseers had gathered behind the police tapes to watch. A violent death in broad daylight was a rare event in Bath. Stephanie Diamond was fully clothed, yet it still seemed offensive that she should be an object of ghoulish interest. Her husband knew if he told them to move on, more would take their places.

So the painstaking process continued. The body was on the grass to the rear of the old bandstand, obscured from Royal Avenue, the road that crossed the lawns below the Crescent. The Victorian shrubbery nearby fringed the car park and trapped the litter that blew across the open lawns. The search for traces of the killer would be a long job.

The forensic team arrived in their vans. While they were putting on their sterile overalls, Halliwell hurried across to warn them who the victim was. Diamond didn't want sympathy from anyone, but he could be spared the backchat that went with the job.

The next twenty minutes passed slowly and mostly in silence, with the white-suited figures clustered around the body.

Someone must have tipped off that old motormouth, Jim Middleton, the forensic pathologist, before he arrived – a merciful act. He said nothing. Just put out a hand and rested it briefly on Diamond's shoulder in a gesture of support. Then took the taped route to the corpse and studied the scene. Diamond followed.

'Has anyone touched her?' Middleton asked.

'The police surgeon,' Diamond said. 'And forensics. And me. She hasn't been moved.'

Middleton crouched for a closer inspection. 'Bullet wound to the frontal, almost dead centre. Very close range. You shouldn't be here, you know. You're too involved.'

'I can handle it.'

'I don't doubt you, old friend, but that isn't the point.'

'This is the work of a hitman,' Diamond said, ignoring the criticism.

'Do you know something?'

'I'm talking about the bullet wounds.'

'Two, to be sure, you mean? I wouldn't read too much into that. They look very deliberate, measured almost, but that's speculation. Could equally be some crazy with a gun who happened to point the muzzle towards her and pull the trigger twice.' Middleton crouched and peered closely at the powder burns around the neat hole the bullet had made in her forehead. 'Are you sure you want to be here?'

Diamond didn't answer, but remained where he was.

Middleton took a small tape recorder from his brief-case and started describing the wounds. He lifted each eyelid, the beginning of a slow, methodical examination. He inserted a thermometer into a nostril and noted the temperature. Felt the arms and tested for rigor by moving one. Looked at the hands and fingernails. Loosened the clothes around the neck and searched for other signs of injury. Turned the body and studied one of the blood-encrusted exit wounds at the back of the head.

'Have they picked up the bullets?'

'Not yet.'

'Buried in the ground, I dare say.'

'We can use a metal detector.'

The pathologist remained for over an hour before signalling to the waiting funeral director that he was ready to have the body removed to the hospital mortuary. Diamond stood back and watched his dead wife being lifted into a plastic zipper-case, and then into a plain fibre-glass coffin, which was carried up the slope, through the crowd, loaded into a van and driven away.

With self-disgust he thought back to his first reaction to this, how he had been elated at the news of a shooting. And later joked about waiting to be introduced to the victim.

'Big shock,' Middleton said to Diamond. 'You want to go home now, take a Valium.'

'There's work to do. You know as well as I do – the first twenty-four hours are crucial.'

'Yes, but it shouldn't be you.'

He didn't dignify the suggestion with a response. Instead, he walked over to Halliwell. 'The bloke who found her – where is he?'

'Went off home, guv. He had the dog with him.'

'That's no reason to leave.'

'We took a short statement.'

'A dog doesn't need to go home. Dog would stay in the park all day if it got the chance. Does he live nearby?'

'The Upper Bristol Road.'

'Which end?'

'This end, I think.'

'Get him here fast. I want to speak to him.'

He escorted Middleton to his car. 'Anything else you noticed?'

The pathologist said, 'What you don't find can be just as informative as what you do. Did you look at her hands?'

'I held them.'

'No damage. No sign that she put up a fight. When someone holds a gun to your head, you try and push it away. You fight for your life. This was quick, Peter. She didn't know much about it.' He opened the car door and got in. 'I wouldn't expect too much from the post mortem.'

Diamond watched him drive off.

Some time after, a constable approached him with a tall, thin man in tow. 'Sir, this is Mr Warburton, the gentleman who found the, em . . .' His voice trailed off.

Warburton, in his thirties, had a down-at-heel look, lank, dishevelled hair, his hands deep in the pockets of a black overcoat that was coming apart at the shoulder-seam. The shock of the morning's discovery may have left him looking troubled, or it may have been his stock expression. He swayed a little.

'You've been drinking?' Diamond said.

'A wee drop,' Warburton answered. 'It helps me sometimes. I got the shakes.'

'You found the body, I believe?'

'Heard the shots, didn't I?' He flapped his hand in the general direction of the Royal Crescent. 'I was right up there with my dog, causing no trouble, and I heard it go off and came down here.'

'What time?'

'Couldn't tell you.'

'We logged the call at ten-twenty, or thereabouts. See anything?'

'No.'

'Are you sure? How long after the shots did you get here?'

'Dunno.'

'Two minutes? Five? Ten?' As he said it, he knew he wouldn't get a precise estimate. The man was three-quarters slewed.

'Thought it was someone taking a pot at a rabbit.'

'Here?'

'I've seen them.'

'Why bother at all, then, if you thought it was someone after rabbits?'

'Followed my dog, didn't I?'

'Was nobody else about?'

'Not that I saw.'

'Had you been drinking?'

'Might have. Don't remember.' Pure bad luck that the only witness happened to be a wino.

'So what happened?'

'Like I said, I followed my dog. He found her first. He's a lurcher. Kind of stood over her waiting for me to get there. I thought it might be one of my mates, fallen asleep. Then I see the bullet holes.'

'What then?'

'Scared me, it did. I looked around for help and there wasn't none.'

'Did you hear anything? Movements in the bushes? The sound of anyone running off?'

Warburton shook his head. 'I belted down to the car park and there was a geezer just drove in. He had a mobile and I asked him to call the Old Bill.'

'Was anyone else in the car park? Anyone leaving?'

'Give us a break, mate. I was so shit-scared I wouldn't have noticed me own mother walk by.'

'And I suppose they told you to wait here and not touch anything.'

'If you know it all, why ask me?'

'And pretty soon the first police car drove up?'

'And found little old me holding the fort.'

'You didn't find anything near the body?'

'Like what?'

'Like money, for instance? A handbag?'

'Here, what do you take me for? That's a fucking insult considering I did my public duty.'

'If anyone did take anything from the scene, they're in trouble. It's a serious offence.'

'Don't look at me. I did nothing wrong.'

Diamond was inclined to believe him. 'Don't drink any more. That's an order. I may want to speak to you again.'

He found Keith Halliwell and told him to remain at the scene. 'I'm leaving you in charge. I want to check on certain pieces of lowlife and their movements earlier today.'

'Shall I do that?' Halliwell offered.

'You find the bloody bullets. And look for spent cartridges as well.'

* * *

He made the mistake of returning to Bath Police Station to begin his check on the Carpenters. Georgina walked into his office before he'd picked up a phone. She must have asked the desk to alert her the moment he returned.

'Peter, we're all devastated. I can't begin . . .'

He nodded. 'I'll cope . . . thanks.'

'We'll get them – whoever did this. I promise you that. I've put Curtis McGarvie in charge.'

His tone changed sharply. 'You what?'

'DCI McGarvie, from Headquarters. A good man.'

'It's my case.'

Georgina hesitated. 'Peter, there's no way—'

'My wife. My case.'

'That's the point. You're personally involved. If you took this on – as I'm sure you could – we'd lay ourselves open to prejudice, a personal vendetta. If it came to court, prosecuting counsel would cut us to ribbons.'

Diamond shook his head. 'I have the right—'

This time Georgina interrupted him. 'You don't. I'm sorry. This is hard for you to take, but you don't have the right. You know perfectly well that someone else has to handle this. Curtis is already on his way to Victoria Park.'

'He's too bloody late.'

'What?'

'She's been moved.' His brain churned out a compromise. 'Look, I don't mind working with McGarvie, if that's what you want. A joint investigation. As far as the CPS is concerned, it can be his case.'

'Absolutely not. You're staying right out of it. You're a witness.'

'To what? I saw nothing.'

'Be serious, Peter. This looks like a contract killing. The first line of enquiry has to be your enemies in the criminal world. He's going to want a list of everyone you put away, every villain you crossed since you came here.

Your evidence is going to lead us to the killer, and the people behind the killer if – as I suspect – they hired a hitman. You can't be the investigating officer and chief prosecution witness as well.'

The truth of that got through to him, but it still denied him what every sinew in his body was straining to begin: the pursuit of Steph's killers. 'What am I supposed to do? Take a holiday?'

'You'll be involved, providing information. Oh, of course you should take time off to get over the shock.'

'What – sit at home with my feet up, surrounded by memories of Steph? That isn't any use to you or me. I want a part of the action.'

'If you'd like counselling . . .'

'Don't push me, ma'am.'

'I mean it. You've got to rebuild your life. We have trained people we can call on. Why refuse?'

'Because I sort out my own sodding problems, thanks very much. I don't want time off and I don't want to see a counsellor.'

'When you have a chance to reflect, you may see the sense of it.'

'I think not.'

'Well, I'm going to insist you take a couple of days at least. You can forget our conversation this morning.'

He had forgotten it already.

'About organised crime,' she reminded him, 'and going to Bristol. You'll need to be here when Curtis wants you for interviews. And, anyway, you can't investigate the Carpenters.'

'Why not? Have they become a protected species?'

'It would prejudice the case – if they're behind this ghastly crime.'

'So I'm sidelined.'

'I wouldn't put it that way. Take it day by day. I've asked

you to take some time off. You'll need it, believe me. And in the meantime, let's hope for quick results from Curtis McGarvie.'

'That's it, then?'

Georgina nodded.

When he'd almost left the room, Georgina said, 'Peter.'

He swung around. 'Mm?'

'Don't defy me.'

5

People in shock are liable to come out with extreme statements. Steph's sister, when Diamond phoned her with the news, said, 'I knew something like this would happen. I told her she was making the biggest mistake of her life marrying a policeman. She wouldn't listen.'

'Are you saying it's my fault she was killed?'

'Well, it wouldn't have happened if you'd been a school-teacher.'

With an effort he restricted himself to, 'Maybe we should talk again when you're over the shock.'

'She was my sister and I'd say it again.' Then she softened enough to ask, 'How will you manage? Do you want us to come down?'

Like the plague. 'No need.'

'We'll have to come anyway for the funeral. When is it?'

'She only died this morning.'

'So you don't have it arranged?'

'No.'

'You'll tell us the minute it's fixed?'

'I'll be in touch.'

The prospect of a funeral hadn't fully entered his mind until now. Steph's *funeral*, for pity's sake.

Unreal.

He spent the next hour making more calls to family and friends, and there were repeated offers of help.

Genuine offers, too. Steph had been held in high regard – no, *loved* was the word. Her friends wanted to rally round for her sake. He was under no illusion that they had any strong affection for him. Politely he turned down all the offers, saying he would cope.

Then he called the nick and asked Halliwell what had been happening.

'We found two bullets, guv. Used a metal detector, like you said. They've been taken away by forensics. One of them is in fair shape. The other was a bit flattened, as if something drove over it.'

'Christ. How about cartridges?'

'No. I suppose a revolver was used.'

'We shouldn't suppose anything yet. You probably heard I'm off the case.'

A tactful pause. 'Yes, guv. DCI McGarvie has taken over.'

'He knows about the Carpenters, I hope?'

'Everything. I'm sure of that.'

'Not quite everything. After the case ended, I had some aggro from a woman outside the law courts. She was screaming about me sending down her Jake, so I guess she was the girlfriend.'

'You think she could have done this?'

'I don't know, but McGarvie ought to be told. She was hyper.'

'I'll tell him.'

'And make sure he checks the Carpenter brothers – where they were this morning.'

'That's in hand, guv.'

'Right. You'll keep me in the picture, Keith.' It was more of an order than a request.

He put down the phone, and this time left it down. The urge to keep talking to people, shutting out the silence in the house, was strong. But the pain had to be faced. A number of times in his career he'd knocked on someone's door to tell them a loved one had been killed – the duty every cop dreads. He thought he'd understood something of the way those people had felt. How wide of the mark he was. You lose your grip on reality.

He was an alien in a spacesuit exploring Planet Earth. All his senses were blunted. He looked out through a glass visor. He heard things only when he made huge efforts to listen.

Georgina had been right to take him off the case. He admitted it now. He was in no state to investigate anything. The incentive was there, but he wasn't capable of making himself a cup of tea, let alone running a murder inquiry.

He sat at the kitchen table with his hands propping up his chin, and stared at the chair where Steph sat in the mornings. The *Guardian* was still there, folded to the crossword page, most of the squares completed in her neat lettering. Beside it, the mail she'd received that morning, a couple of junk items she hadn't bothered to open and a postcard from one of her ex-Brownies, on holiday abroad. She'd kept in touch with many of those little girls of years ago, encouraging them, taking real pride in their successes at school and university. He'd been to more weddings and christenings with Steph than he could remember now.

Those ex-Brownies would see on the TV news that she'd been murdered. For Steph's sake, he thought suddenly, he ought to warn them all. They were family to her. Her kids – and his. Somewhere she kept her own address book. He got up and started opening drawers. She had always kept her things organised, and he soon found it with the stationery. What a task, though. The 'A's alone ran to three pages.

This was what she would have wanted, so he made a start. Even if he didn't get through, he'd give it his best shot.

It was hard, hearing the shock in their voices, and harder listening to the loving things they said about her. Some were former Brownies, some friends she'd made through her work in the charity shops, others she'd kept up with since long before he knew her. So many – and so much love. After some time, he poured himself a brandy, then started another page.

Almost hidden among the 'D's he found the number for Steph's first husband, Edward Dixon-Bligh. Was it worth calling that tosspot? he wondered. He doubted if Dixon-Bligh and Steph had spoken since the divorce. The man had been an officer in the RAF Catering Branch (Diamond had dubbed him the Frying Officer) who had let her down badly at the time when she'd most needed help, after three miscarriages. The last they'd heard, he had swapped his commission for a Michelin star and was managing a restaurant in Guildford, Surrey, with a partner almost half his age. Still, he had a right to be told.

Waiting with the phone pressed to his ear, he recalled something Steph had once told him about her ex-husband that seemed to sum the man up. They had once rented a beach hut on the south coast and after the rental expired he'd kept a key. He'd go down to the beach for years after and if no one was using the hut he'd open it and brew some tea and sit there all afternoon, an over-grown cuckoo in the nest.

It turned out that he was no longer at the private number they had in the book. He'd moved into central London. That seemed a good enough excuse to forget him, but out of loyalty to Steph he tried directory enquiries. He was glad of the chance to leave an answer-phone message.

He abandoned this phone marathon when the people he called started telling him they'd heard already on the evening news. Outside, it was dark and he was only up to the 'G's. He drew the curtains.

What would Steph have wanted next? It was weird, but he almost heard her say in her calm voice, 'Tidy my things, Pete.' She would hate to leave disorder. Against all logic he went upstairs and emptied the basket where she put her clothes for washing. Picked her nightdress off the pillow and for a moment held it against his face and got a faint smell of her and said, 'Oh, Steph.' Brought the clothes down and loaded the machine. Went back upstairs and stripped the bed. Tightened the lid on a pot of foundation cream she'd left on her dressing table.

He said in a whisper, 'Is that better?' and then shook his head at his own stupidity.

He heard a car draw up outside and someone coming to the door, so he went downstairs and opened it.

A camera flashed.

The press.

He said to the woman on his doorstep, 'Shove off, will you. Leave me alone. There's no comment. There won't be any comment.' And slammed the door.

The phone rang.

He snatched it up, ready to give them a blasting.

'Curtis McGarvie here.'

'Oh.'

'First, I want to tell you how sorry I am.'

'Thanks.'

'And any number of people asked me to pass on their sympathy and support. Everyone is gutted. You can be sure we won't rest until we've caught this jerk. Do you mind if I talk about it?'

'Feel free.'

'The bullets are with forensics. They'll check them against their database and tell us the class of weapon. I've asked them to give it top priority. Some kind of handgun was used, obviously, and I'm assuming it was a revolver.'

'Why?'

'There'd have been cartridges lying around if a self-loading pistol was used.'

'Not if the killer was careful.'

'Picked up the cartridges, you mean?' McGarvie was silent, absorbing the point. 'Well, there weren't any, I promise you.'

'The striker pin marks the cartridge differently with each gun,' Diamond said with the confidence of the weapons training he did in his time with the Met. 'Important to ballistics. A professional would know that. He might well decide not to leave them there to be found. I think we should keep an open mind about the weapon.'

'I intend to,' McGarvie said, stressing the first word. 'Otherwise not much came up in the search. Do you know if your wife normally carried a bag of some kind?'

A bag? He meant a handbag. Of course she carried a handbag. 'Black leather, quite large, with a shoulder strap and zip. Didn't you find it?'

'Nothing so far. Maybe you could look around the house and see if it's gone for certain.'

'I'll do it now.'

'No rush.'

'I said I'll do it now.'

'Okay. And I'd like to come to your place tomorrow and talk to you.'

'I'll come to the nick.'

'No, I'd prefer to visit your home, if you don't mind. That way, I'll get a better sense of your wife.'

He would have done the same. 'All right.'

'Is nine too early? If you can find a recent photo, we'll need to appeal for witnesses. Have you been bothered by the press at all?'

'Told them to bugger off.'

'If it happens again, tell them we're calling a press conference for midday tomorrow. Should get them off your back.'

'Thanks. Do you want me there?'

'No need at this stage. Is anyone with you? Friends or family?'

'I'm alone.'

'Would you like—?'

'It's my choice.'

He searched for that handbag without any confidence that it would turn up. Steph always took it with her if she went out. Just as he expected, it wasn't in the house – which raised a question. If the killer had picked it up, what was his reason?

Would a hitman walk off with his victim's handbag after firing the fatal shot? Unlikely.

It raised the possibility that the hitman theory was wrong, and that Steph had been shot by a thief.

He stood in the living room with head bowed, hands pressed to his face, pondering that one. Had she been killed for a few pounds and some credit cards? That would be even more cruel.

He called the nick and left a message for McGarvie that the bag was not in the house.

During the evening he answered the door twice more to reporters, and told them about McGarvie's press conference. And the phone rang intermittently. The word 'condolences' kept coming up. And 'tragic'. And 'bereavement'. Death has its own jargon.

But he was pleased to get a call from Julie Hargreaves, his former deputy in the Bath murder team – the best he'd ever had. Julie always knew exactly what was going through his mind.

When she'd expressed her sympathy Julie said, 'Let

Curtis McGarvie take this on, whatever your heart tells you. He's well up to the job.'

'Have you worked with him?'

'Yes, and he's good without making a big deal out of it.'

'Better than me?'

'For this case – yes. You want a result. If you handled it yourself, you'd get one, I'm sure – only for the CPS to throw it out because you're too involved.'

'I've been told that already.'

'But your heart won't accept what your head tells you. You can still play an active part by telling Curtis everything you know.'

'It isn't the same, Julie. I want to roll up my sleeves, make decisions.'

'Why don't you put your energy into giving Steph the kind of send-off she deserves? A lot of people will expect it, you know. She had so many friends.'

'That's for sure.' He paused, letting her comment sink in. 'What exactly are you suggesting?'

'Would she have wanted a church funeral?'

'She was a believer.'

'Then I really think you should arrange it at the Abbey.'

'The *Abbey*?'

'Do your public servant number on the Dean, or whoever decides these things. But insist on having the service the way Steph would have wished.'

'Which is . . .?'

She caught her breath, as if surprised she had to spell it out. 'The music she liked. Whoever takes the service should be someone who knew her personally. One or two of her family or closest friends should do readings. You, if you can face it.'

'I'd feel a hypocrite. I'm an agnostic if I'm anything, Julie.'

'It doesn't have to be out of the Bible. Well, to be honest, I wasn't thinking of you. But you could speak about her if you felt up to it.'

'I don't think so.'

'You're confident in front of people.'

'Barking out orders to a bunch of coppers, maybe, but not this.'

'Okay, if you want, you could write something about her life and include it with the Order of Service. Then when it's over, you invite people to lunch, or tea, or whatever, at some local hostelry.'

He took all this in before saying, 'You're right, Julie. This is what I should be doing. I'll see to it as soon as the coroner releases . . .' He didn't complete the sentence.

'One more thing, if I can be really personal,' Julie said.

'What's that?'

'I can only say this because we worked together so long. You're tougher with people than anyone I know, but not so tough as you are on yourself. It wouldn't be the end of civilisation as we know it if, when you're alone, you shed a few tears – for Steph, and for yourself.'

At the low point of the night, before dawn, he remembered, and wept for the first time in over forty years.

6

He nicked one of the scratches shaving and it bled on his shirt: too little concentration after too little sleep. He'd finally flopped onto the sofa and drifted off for about two hours – only to be roused by the *Guardian* being shoved through the door. Then he was forced to accept the unthinkable over again.

'You look rough,' McGarvie told him unnecessarily.

'So do you.'

Actually McGarvie was one of those people who always look rough – no bad thing in CID work. Still in his early forties, he was marked by too many late nights and too many whiskies. Under-nourished, pock-marked, with bags under his eyes, he had a voice like the third day of a God-awful cold.

He'd brought Mike James with him, a newish, far-from-comfortable DC who Diamond himself had plucked from the uniformed ranks.

Diamond offered coffee and admitted, when asked, that he hadn't eaten breakfast. He chose not to reveal that he hadn't been able to face food since yesterday.

'So where are we on this?' he asked while they stood in the kitchen watching the kettle. 'What have we got?'

McGarvie hesitated. That 'we' obviously troubled him. 'I've got a hundred and twenty officers on this. Fingertip search. Door-to-door in all the streets nearby. Incident room up and running.'

'What I meant is what have we learned?'

'Forensics take their time. You appreciate that.'

'But you do know certain things – what time she was shot. Ten-twenty.'

'If we're to believe the guy who found her.'

'She was at home in Lower Weston when I left at eight-fifteen.'

'That was one thing I was going to ask.'

'And the Carpenters?' Diamond pressed him.

'Des and Danny appear to be watertight for yesterday morning.'

He shook his head. 'Surprise me.'

'Des was motoring back from Essex and has a credit card voucher for fuel placing him on the M4 at Reading Services at ten-thirty.'

'I'd check the forecourt video if I were you.'

'It's in hand.'

After spooning instant coffee into two mugs Diamond moistened the granules with a dash of milk from a bottle that must have been on the table since yesterday. 'You like it white?'

McGarvie frowned at the lumpen mess. 'Sure.'

Mike James just nodded. He was so ill at ease in the home of his bereaved boss he would have drunk the cat's water if it were handed to him.

'And the other one? Danny?'

'At the gym in Bristol for an hour until ten, signed in, signed out, and vouched for by the staff there, and afterwards went to his solicitor in Clifton.'

'Who of course recorded precisely when he arrived and left? They really wrapped this up.'

'You think they used a hitman?'

'Don't you?'

McGarvie left the question hanging. Diamond poured hot water into the mugs and handed them over.

Curds and black granules rose to the surface. McGarvie
picked up the spoon and stirred his. They carried them
through to the living room. The curtains hadn't been
pulled.

'DI Halliwell was telling me about this woman who
attacked you after the trial,' McGarvie said. 'Had you seen
her before?'

'Just a faint memory of her sitting in the public gallery.
She must have been one of the crowd who screamed at
the judge.'

'But you didn't come across her when you worked on
the case?'

'No. It's possible some of the team did. I didn't do all
the legwork myself. Do we know who she is?'

'Not yet.'

'Blond, shoulder-length hair. Tallish. Five-seven, five-
eight. Probably under thirty. Long fingernails.'

'I can see.'

Diamond put his hand to his face. The scratches were
still there, though the incident seemed like a century ago.
'She was in some kind of trouser suit. Black or dark blue.'

'Did you see who she was with?'

He shook his head. 'Some of the Carpenter mob.
Heard them shouting. I was avoiding eye contact at the
time.'

'I wonder if anyone got it on video. There must have
been camera crews around.'

'Didn't notice any.'

'Let's get back to your wife.'

'Wish I could.'

McGarvie glanced at Diamond, who gave a sharp sigh,
more angry than self-pitying.

'Sorry. Go on.'

'This has to be asked. Can you think of anyone with a
grudge against her?'

He shook his head. 'Steph didn't make enemies. I never knew anyone who disliked her.'

'The opposite, then. Someone who fancied her?'

The idea caught him off-balance. 'A stalker?'

'It happens. Had she mentioned anyone giving her the eye in recent weeks?'

'No.' This line of enquiry was a waste of time in his opinion. 'I've got to face it – she was murdered for no better reason than being married to me.'

'I'm trying to keep an open mind. How did she spend her time?'

'She's always done charity work, serving in the Oxfam shop, and Save the Children at one time, organising the rota, running the stall at this or that event.'

'Was that where she was going yesterday?'

'What day was it? I have to think. I've lost track.'

'Tuesday.'

He shut his eyes to get his brain working. 'Tuesday was the morning she kept clear for shopping and so on.'

'She didn't tell you what she was planning?'

'She would if it was out of the ordinary. I guess it was going to be the same as any other Tuesday.'

'If she'd arranged to meet someone, she'd tell you?'

'Always.'

'Did she write it down anywhere? A calendar? An appointments book?'

'Diary.'

McGarvie's eyebrows arched hopefully.

'In her handbag,' Diamond added. 'Did you find it?'

'No.'

'It's not here. I can tell you that. She always had it with her if she went out. I was thinking last night it's strange the bag was taken – unless someone else came along after she was . . .'

'Possible,' McGarvie agreed.

They both reflected on that for a moment before
Diamond said, 'I don't think a hitman would take it.'

'Probably not.'

'And I can't believe she was mugged.'

'Why not?'

'Shot dead – for a handbag?'

'You don't want to believe it,' said McGarvie, 'and I
can understand why. But there are yobbos out there who
hold life as cheaply as that. We can't discount it. Why was
she in the park? Was it a place where she liked to walk?'

'No.'

'You mean not at all?'

'That's what I said.'

'Never went there?'

'Hardly ever. And she didn't go for walks on Tuesdays.
She was always too busy catching up with herself. It was
her day for jobs, shopping, some cooking sometimes,
housework.'

'Was there a phone call?'

'Before I left, you mean? No.'

'Could she have made one?'

'Not to my knowledge. You'd better check with BT.'

'It's in hand,' McGarvie said. He seemed to be doing
the right things. 'Did she carry a mobile?'

'Do we strike you as the sort of couple who carry
mobiles?'

'In other words, no.'

'Are you thinking she was lured to the park?' Diamond
said.

'Possibly. Or driven there. Met the killer somewhere
else.' He glanced around the room. 'He could have come
here.'

'I don't think so.'

'We can't be sure.'

'She's not going to invite a stranger in. She knew better

than that. And you're wrong about being driven there. Steph wouldn't get into a car.'

'Unless she was forced.'

'She'd have put up a fight.'

'There are no signs of it.'

This was true, he knew. He remembered holding her cold, limp hands. And the pathologists's remark about the state of them. 'Is Middleton doing the PM?'

'Eleven-thirty.'

He closed his eyes and was silent for a moment. 'Who's going to be there?'

McGarvie steered the conversation away. 'You said she had no enemies, so let's talk about yours.'

'Waste of time.'

'Why?'

'Come on. This has the Carpenters written all over it.'

'In my shoes, you wouldn't say that. You know the danger of going for the obvious. No disrespect, Peter, but you've roughed up more villains than just the Carpenters.'

'Ancient history.'

McGarvie drew a long breath to contain his patience. 'Don't you think you owe it to her to help me?'

The tactic worked. Diamond dropped his opposition. 'Villains with old scores to settle? Here, you mean? In Bath?'

'Let's start here, any road. I remember the case that made your name here, the body in Chew Valley Lake, but that wasn't your first.'

He nodded. 'There were five before that, three domestic, the others drugs-related. Far as I know, all of the killers are banged up.'

'The kid who murdered Mrs Jackman?'

'Bore me no grudge.'

'The con who escaped from Albany?'

'Back inside.'

McGarvie displayed a more than superficial knowledge

of Diamond's career as he went through the principal
investigations of recent years. He must have studied the
files overnight. You couldn't fault the man's thoroughness. But as Diamond had warned at the outset, nothing
useful came out of it. The killers he'd put away had been
mainly loners, not one of them connected with organised crime in the way the Carpenters were.

'What about your private life?'

'My what?'

'People you know outside the job.'

'You're thinking I pick fights with the neighbours? I
haven't got the energy. I pay my bills on time – well, Steph
does. Call at the pub for a quiet pint once in a while, and
I mean quiet. They don't know who I am. Come home,
feed the cat, mow the lawn – the daily grind.'

On cue, Raffles came around the door, sized up the
visitors, decided DC James was the softer touch and began
pressing his side against the young man's shins. James
tried to ignore it.

'Forgive me – I have to ask this,' McGarvie said. 'Your
marriage. Was it going well?'

Diamond said with a slight break in his voice, 'It was
all right.'

'No possibility that she—'

'None.'

For a while the only sound was the cat's purring as it
continued to lean against James's trousers.

Finally McGarvie said, 'I have this major problem with
the Carpenter theory. If it's a contract killing, as we
suppose, why did they target your wife? *You* should have
been the mark. You, or some witness, or the lawyers, or
the judge. Not your wife. You and I know what these scum
are like. If they take revenge it's not at one remove.'

Diamond shrugged. He couldn't understand it either,
and he had nothing to contribute.

'Can I feed him?' DC James asked.

'What?'

'The cat. He's hungry.'

Diamond hadn't even noticed. 'If you like. The tins are in the kitchen. Shelf over the cupboard.'

When the two older men were alone, McGarvie once again raised the possibility that Steph had a secret life Diamond had not been aware of. 'We work long hours, get home tired. It's not surprising if our women don't always tell us everything that happened.' Seeing Diamond's expression he spread his hand and held it up. 'Don't get me wrong. I'm not suggesting she had a relationship. Just the possibility that she got into something she didn't want you to know about, something slightly dodgy that got out of control.'

Diamond glared. 'Such as?'

'I don't know. I'm guessing. What do middle-aged women get up to? Gambling?'

'Not Steph.'

'She didn't owe money to anyone?'

'Forget it. She wouldn't borrow a penny.'

'I suppose she didn't do drugs?'

'This is bloody offensive.'

'Would you mind if we searched her bedroom?'

'Christ – what for?'

'Peter, I haven't the faintest idea what might turn up, but it needs to be done.'

'Now?'

'It's as good a time as any.'

He stared out of the window. 'I'd tell you if there was anything.'

'But have you been through her things?'

Of course he hadn't. That would be a breach of trust. They'd always respected each other's privacy. He was damned sure Steph had nothing to hide from him.

Being brutally honest with himself, if he were investigating some other woman's murder, he'd insist on a proper search, just as McGarvie was doing. You don't rely on the husband to tell you everything.

'Come on, then.'

He led McGarvie upstairs.

Their bedroom was ready for inspection, the bed made, clothes put away, though that hadn't been his purpose when he tidied up the day before.

McGarvie started with the dressing table, removing the two drawers entirely and placing them on the bed. Steph's make-up, combs and brushes were in one, her bits of jewellery in the other. Apart from her wedding ring, which was on her finger when she died, she hadn't the desire to deck herself in what she called spangles and fandangles. Much of the stuff never saw the daylight and had been inherited from aunts and grandmothers. McGarvie opened every one of the little boxes and looked into the velvet bag containing the single string of pearls Diamond had bought her on their wedding day.

He asked which of the two chests was Steph's, and Diamond pointed to it. With the same thoroughness he pulled the top drawer completely out and felt among her underclothes, watched sullenly by Diamond. At the back of the second drawer was a shoebox full of letters. 'Do you know what these are?'

Diamond went over to look. When he saw his own handwriting on one of the envelopes he grabbed the box with both hands. 'You won't want this.'

'How do you know?'

'They're from me, ages ago.'

McGarvie held out his hands. 'Sorry, but there may be other letters, more recent ones. I've got to go through the box.'

'It's too bloody personal.' He didn't hand it back.

Wisely McGarvie chose to let him mull over that, and continued with the search. That second drawer had evidently been Steph's storage place for photos, invoices, vouchers, visiting cards and newspaper cuttings. It would take a team of detectives to follow up every lead. 'I'll have to take all this away . . . as well,' McGarvie said.

Diamond didn't commit himself. He doubted if there was a clue to the killer in there, but he didn't want to impede the investigation. 'Why don't you look in the wardrobe?'

McGarvie was thorough. Every pocket of each coat, each pair of slacks, was searched, but he found no more than a few pence and some tissues. He looked on top of the wardrobe and beneath it and pulled the bed across the floor to see if anything was underneath.

'Bathroom?'

The search moved on. Mike James joined in and they went through each of the rooms.

On the landing, McGarvie glanced upwards. 'What do you keep in the loft?'

'She never goes up there. Can't stand spiders.'

They took his word for it, which was something. He had some police property up there, including a gun and ammunition. In his present state he didn't care a toss about being compromised. He just didn't want anything to deflect from the hunt for Steph's killer.

They took the search downstairs and still found nothing of interest. McGarvie looked at his watch. He didn't need to say he was thinking about getting to the post mortem. 'Did she keep an address book?'

'Yes, but you can't take that away. I'm phoning people all the time.'

'I'll have it photocopied. You'll get it back inside two hours, I guarantee.'

Her whole life laid out, as if for inspection. With a

sigh, he picked the book off the table by the phone.

McGarvie handed it to Mike James. 'That's your job. Get it copied and back to Mr Diamond directly.' To Diamond, he said, 'Is it okay if I take that drawer from the bedroom?'

With reluctance, he gave in.

'And the box of letters? Trust me. I'll examine everything myself. Nothing will be passed around.'

It was the best offer he would get. He knew the way things were done.

7

He descended into limbo – or grief – drifting through the days without any sense of what else was happening in the world. He kept strange hours, often sleeping in snatches through the day and sitting up most of the night. Nothing seemed to matter. When friends called he told them he was all right and didn't want help. He rarely answered the phone and didn't open letters or look at the newspaper or listen to music or the radio.

It was a call from the coroner's office that ended this hiatus. All the forensic tests had been completed and the coroner was ready to release Steph's body for disposal. They needed to know which undertaker was in charge of the funeral arrangements.

Shocked out of his zombie state, he remembered his conversation with Julie Hargreaves, about putting his energy into giving Steph the sort of send-off she would have wanted.

'What day is it?'

'Wednesday.'

'The date, I mean.'

'March the tenth.'

'*March?*' More than two weeks had drifted by and he'd done nothing about it.

'I'll get back to you shortly.'

He snatched up the Yellow Pages and looked under

Funeral Directors. The process took over. The same afternoon, clean-shaven and showered, wearing a suit, he went
into Bath, from the undertaker's to the Abbey to the
Francis Hotel, making decisions about black Daimlers and
brass handles and orders of service and bridge rolls and
chicken wings. He was functioning again.

8

Awkward and totally out of his element he followed the coffin into Bath Abbey and up the main aisle. An early plan to use one of the apsidal chapels had been abandoned when it became clear how many wished to attend the service. Three to four hundred were seated in the main Abbey Church. The story of the shooting had featured for days in the national press and on television and people who had known Steph from years back had made the journey. The police alone numbered over sixty, among them the Chief Constable and three of ACC rank, as well as most of Bath CID and about twenty old colleagues from his years in the Met. The biggest contingent was of friends Steph had made through her work in the charity shops, customers as well as staff. There was her 'family' of Brownies grown into adult women. Then there were former neighbours from the series of places he and Steph had occupied in London and Bath.

The small family group of Steph's sister Angela with her husband Mervyn and Peter Diamond's own sister Jean and her eccentric partner Reggie looked and felt humbled by the scale of the affection represented here. None of them had known of Steph's gift for making lasting friends of almost everyone she met. Diamond knew of it, but even he hadn't expected them to come in such numbers.

One of the few who hadn't bothered to respond was

Edward Dixon-Bligh, Steph's first husband. If he *was* in the congregation, Diamond wouldn't know. He'd seen photos, but never met the man. In view of the unhappiness of that first marriage, his absence would trouble nobody.

Julie's advice to make a fitting occasion of this had been spot on, though in his heart of hearts Diamond wanted it over. He'd taken leave of Steph already, in those wrenching minutes kneeling beside her damaged body in the park. The service in the Abbey was for her, because she had been a believer, and for everyone else who loved her and had faith that she was going to a better place.

At odds with his agnostic leanings, he joined in the hymns as well as he could and heard the address, the readings and the prayers and wished peace and rest for her. And then followed the coffin out again and was driven to the crematorium at Haycombe for what the undertakers had termed the committal.

There, not for the first time in recent days, he had the strange sensation that he was detached from what was going on, with the power to switch off as if it were a TV programme. Some roguish part of his brain was telling him it was all a nightmare and he would go home and find her there. He had to make an effort to concentrate.

All the illusions came to a stop when the curtains slid across.

Back to the Francis for the 'light refreshments'. The pitying looks and well-meant words of consolation from her friends – and his – rammed home the certainty that she had gone and his life had altered immeasurably.

A few went so far as to ask what was happening about catching the person responsible. He answered that he didn't know. The case was out of his hands.

In truth, he did know. Things were happening, for sure. There was an incident room. Appeals to the public. Over a hundred officers at work. They knew what time the murder had taken place and where, what calibre of gun had been used, what bullets. McGarvie's first reaction had been correct. The murder weapon was a revolver, a .38. But as for the killer, they were still at a loss.

'Are you back to work yet?'

'Tomorrow.'

'Best thing, old man.'

Next morning everyone at the nick went out of their way to be sympathetic. He had to run the gauntlet of good-will before he could close his office door. He didn't count the number of times he was told it was nice to have him back. On his desk were bundles of letters that could only be messages of condolence. He shoved them to one side and leafed through the internal memos instead.

About ten-thirty came a call from McGarvie, who had the sense to treat him like a fellow professional. 'If you can spare a few minutes, I need your help.'

'On the case?' He couldn't disguise his eagerness.

'Yes – but don't get me wrong. This doesn't put you on the team. I want your services as a witness, to take a look at a suspect.'

'A line-up?'

'No. We've brought in a woman we think may be the one who scratched your face outside the law courts. You can look at her on camera, tell us if we're right.'

'You think she could be the killer?'

'Did I say that?'

'You said she was a suspect.'

'For the assault on you.'

'That? I don't want anyone done for that,' Diamond said at once. 'I haven't laid a complaint.'

'Hold on, hold on. It gave me a reason to pull her in,' McGarvie explained. 'I've no plan to press a charge.'

'Ah.' His brain wasn't sharp at all.

'We'll see what else comes out. If she's so passionate about the Carpenter verdict, she might say something helpful.'

'I'm with you now.'

'Say twenty minutes?'

His confidence in McGarvie was growing, in spite of the lack of any obvious progress. He fetched a coffee from the machine at the cost of another 'nice to see you back' from one of the civilian staff, and took it to the observation room, where you could monitor interviews.

The woman was being questioned by McGarvie and a female detective in Interview Room C. Diamond had to watch the screen for a while before making up his mind. The last time he'd seen this woman she was practically foaming at the mouth. Now there was no discernible aggression. She was in control of herself, if not entirely at ease.

But definitely his attacker.

McGarvie was saying to her, 'You don't deny you were in court?'

'That's no crime.'

'What was your interest in the case?'

No response.

'You're a friend of Jake Carpenter's – is that right?'

'If you know it all, buster,' she said with a flat nasal twang more London than Bristol, 'I don't know why you bother to ask me.'

'I'm giving you the chance to explain what happened.'

'Oh, sure.'

'You were also seen outside the court demonstrating – if that's the word – about the verdict.'

'It's a free country.'

'So you don't deny you were one of the people shouting?'

She showed more interest. McGarvie was making headway, even if she insisted on ducking the last question. She flicked some blond hair from her face, and tilted her chin to a more challenging angle. Defiant, but sexy. Meticulously groomed and fashionably dressed in a black suit and wine-red polo-neck. It was easy to see why Jake Carpenter had been attracted.

'Did you follow all of the trial?' McGarvie asked. 'Did you hear all the evidence?'

'Evidence? I call it a stitch-up.'

'So I'm told. Were you there right through?'

'Not every day. I couldn't stomach it, watching a fine man brought down.'

In the observation room, Diamond said, 'I feel like throwing up.'

McGarvie pressed on. 'What's the truth of it, then, in your opinion? The poor woman was violently murdered. Her face was raw meat when they took her out of the river. You wouldn't argue with that?'

'Jake ain't a violent man. He may have his faults, but he don't treat women like that.'

'The blood in his car matched hers.'

'Piss-easy to arrange, innit?'

'Watch it, Janie.'

'Some nutter killed her,' she said. 'She was on the game. It's a risk they take.'

'Jake was her pimp,' McGarvie told her. 'She flew the coop and paid the price with her life.'

'Your lot were out to get him, and this gave you the excuse.'

'Her blood was on his shoe as well.'

'Of course it was. A few spots in his car wouldn't do the trick. It stands out a mile what you did. You wrap it up as science and the stupid jury swallows it.'

They could have gone on like this indefinitely.
McGarvie had the sense to change the script.

'How long have you known the Carpenters?'

'Seven months.'

'You're not local, are you, Janie? Where are you from?'

'Dagenham.'

'But you don't know Bristol very well, or you wouldn't
be holding a torch for the Carpenter brothers. Where
did you meet Jake?'

'Nightclub.'

'Local?'

'London.'

'And he brought you here and set you up in a nice
apartment in Clifton? Did you stop to think what the price
tag is?'

Her eyes blazed. 'Sod off, will you?'

'So it was pure romance,' McGarvie said with heavy
irony.

'I'm not on the game. Never have been.'

'Nor was Maeve Smith before she met Jake. Get real,
Janie. He's evil.'

'Take a running jump.'

McGarvie paused before shifting to another line of
questioning. 'Who were the people you were with outside
the court?'

'His mates.'

'Family?'

'Don't ask me. We just stood together to make ourselves
heard.'

'You didn't know them by name? They were mainly
women.'

'I told you.'

'One of the women attacked Superintendent Diamond,
the senior detective on the case.'

She said vaguely, 'Oh, yeah?'

'Scratched his face and kicked him when he fell. That's assault on a police officer.'

'Serve him right.'

'What?'

The temper ignited. 'He framed my boyfriend, got him sent down for life. What do you think I'm going to do? Cook him a fucking fruitcake?'

'Are you admitting to the assault?'

'Bollocks.'

'You know his wife has been murdered?'

She switched to defence. 'Oh, come on – you can't pin that on me just because . . .' In time, she managed to stop herself saying any more.

'You appreciate how serious this is?'

'I never . . . It's a load of crap. Is that why you pulled me in? I wouldn't do a thing like that to my worst enemy. I didn't even know the woman. I don't have a shooter. I never handled one in my life.'

'Don't get hysterical,' McGarvie said. 'Listen, Janie. No one is pinning anything on you. I may even take a lenient view of the assault on DS Diamond if you can put me on the trail of the killer. What have you heard?'

'Now he wants to do a deal,' she said as if to the unseen gallery. 'I keep telling you, I know sod all about the murder of this lady.'

'Was it a contract job? You could tell me that.'

'Go to hell.'

McGarvie tried different tacks, but either she was too afraid to speak, or she knew nothing. Presently he broke off the interview and came out, leaving Janie and the woman officer facing each other in silence.

He came to the observation room. 'Well?'

'She's the one with the sharp nails,' Diamond confirmed. 'What's her name?'

'Mary-Jane Forsyth, apparently. Likes to be known as Janie. Twenty-six. No previous. Calls herself a beautician.'

'And what's your take on her?'

'She's small change in the Carpenter set-up. Doesn't know much. But she's been around enough to know I won't press charges for the assault on you.'

'You're going to let her go?'

'When I'm ready.'

'If you like, I could try and get a reaction.'

'Peter, you're a glutton for punishment. Thanks, but no. I don't want you involved, and you know why.'

'Are you going back in?'

'Yes, but you don't have to stay and watch.'

'Try and stop me.'

When the tape was running again, McGarvie resumed with a fresh approach. 'Did you visit Jake while he was on remand?'

'Course I did,' Janie said.

'You're still number one in his life?'

'He's always been kind to me.'

'Have you been to see him in Horfield Prison, since the trial?'

She shook her head. 'They don't get many visitors.'

'But you're his girl. He'd like to see you more than anyone else.'

'I expect I'll get a turn. His brothers want to go first and talk about business things. Family stuff.'

'I bet they do. Did they warn you off, then?'

'Celia – that's his brother Danny's wife – said I have to be patient and they'll let me know.'

'So you know that side of the family?'

'I met them once. They came round to Jake's place for a barbecue on one of them hot days in the summer.'

'Got on all right?'

'All right.'

'Was Celia one of the crowd you were with outside the court?'

'No.'

'And Des – the other brother?'

'I don't know him.'

'What's happening about your flat?'

'It's on a lease until next month. Jake paid six months upfront.'

'Generous. What are your plans?'

'I'll have to go back to London, won't I?'

It ended on that downbeat note. McGarvie went through the motions of warning Janie to respect the law in future and told her she wasn't going to be charged this time. If he'd entertained thoughts of using her, they were dashed. It was starkly clear she wouldn't get her turn to visit Jake in prison. She was history so far as the Carpenters were concerned.

Yet she was better off than Maeve Smith.

And Stephanie Diamond.

Diamond was summoned to the ACC's office early in the afternoon. Clearly there had been discussions before he arrived. Georgina was holding court with McGarvie, Halliwell and two others of DCI level in attendance. An empty chair was positioned centrally.

He had a sense straight away that he had walked into a trap. Georgina looked uncomfortable. No one looked at ease. 'Peter,' she began, meeting his eyes in a way that could only promise conflict, 'I don't have to tell you that the investigation into your wife's murder has been running for almost a month. We've put all the resources we can into it. Curtis here has been working long hours, excessive hours, trying for the breakthrough.'

'I know,' Diamond said with caution. 'I've no complaints.'

'That's good. Unfortunately, the results are disappointing. The obvious suspects, the Carpenter brothers, have very good alibis.'

'Can't fault them,' McGarvie chimed in. 'Everything checks.'

Diamond said, 'They hired someone.'

Georgina didn't challenge the statement. 'The theory of the professional gunman? Obviously that's high on the list.'

'Top of it. Must be.'

She let that pass. 'The most likely way we'll get a line on a hitman is through informants. We're asking all the sources we know, and the Met are making soundings as well, because it's more than likely – if it happened – someone was brought in from London. But so far, nothing has come up. Meanwhile, we must explore every other possibility.'

He shrugged. Couldn't argue with that.

Georgina looked to McGarvie to pick up the baton.

'Can't ignore the stalker theory either,' McGarvie said.

'She wasn't a pop star.'

'Come on, Peter. Ordinary people get stalked. If you're unlucky enough to grab the attention of some crazy, you get stalked, whoever you are.'

'No one was stalking Steph.'

'She may not have mentioned it.'

'She'd have told me. I don't buy this at all.'

'But you'll agree as a detective it has to be given an airing?'

He leaned back in the chair. They seemed to want his endorsement. 'Air it, then.'

'All right. She worked in the charity shop. Any woman – anyone at all – who works in a shop is on display. A stalker knows where he can see her, and when. It's the kind of shop anyone can step into and browse around without being asked what he wants. Sometimes he can walk by and just look in the window. He fantasises that she'll take an interest in him. Maybe he asks a question, or buys something. She was an outgoing woman, good at her job, pleasant to the customers. He takes it as a come-on.'

'You don't have to labour it,' Diamond interrupted. 'Why does he turn nasty?'

'When this obsession is at its height, he finds out she's happily married to you. In his eyes, that's disloyalty. The love turns to hate. If he can't have her, neither will you.'

Diamond rolled his eyes upwards and let out a long sigh. McGarvie was right. It couldn't be discounted. 'Any other scenarios?'

McGarvie nodded and said, 'The mugging that goes wrong. Some drug-user desperate for cash points a gun at the first woman he sees in the park. She tells him to get lost and he pulls the trigger.'

'If someone pointed a gun at Steph and asked for money, she'd have the sense to hand it over.'

'Her bag was missing.'

'Anyone could have picked that up, including the wino who found her.'

'I know, I know.'

There was an awkward silence while McGarvie exchanged a look with Georgina. Neither seemed ready to go on. Finally Georgina cleared her throat.

'We have to explore every avenue. Do we agree on that?'

'Doesn't need saying.'

Still she hesitated over the real purpose of this meeting. 'Well, in a straightforward case of murder, there are procedures we use almost without thinking.' Another pause. 'You don't have to take this personally, Peter. The first person questioned is the spouse.'

He gripped the arms of the chair and looked at each of the embarrassed faces. Now he knew what this panto-mime had been about: easing him into the frame. 'Isn't that what's going on now?'

'I'm speaking of something more formal.'

'You're serious?'

'We can't make any assumptions,' Georgina went on. 'Of course it's an imposition. You're a trusted colleague. None of us seriously believes . . . In short, I've asked Curtis to conduct an interview with you.'

'What do you think I'm hiding, for Christ's sake?' he demanded. 'He's been to my house, been over every room, taken things away. I've told you all I can.'

'You're one of us,' McGarvie said without any convic-tion at all, fingering the knot of his tie, 'and that's the problem. I can't put certain questions to you without giving offence.'

'Such as?'

'I don't propose to start here. This should be done in a structured way, in an interview room, on the record.'

'An *interview room*? Give me strength.'

'It may seem over-formal, but . . .'

'You really do have your suspicions.'

'An open mind.'

To think he'd been impressed by McGarvie.

Georgina tried her best to give it an ethical spin. 'We owe this to Stephanie, you know, leaving absolutely nothing to chance. You wouldn't want us to skimp. Why don't I send for some coffee before we do anything else?'

'I'd rather get on with it,' Diamond muttered from deep in his gut.

9

In Interview Room C, in the same chair his attacker, Janie Forsyth, had occupied only an hour ago, Diamond listened in a dazed, disbelieving way to the familiar preamble to a taped interview with a suspect. Was told the identity of his interrogators, McGarvie and Georgina Dallymore, as though he had never met them. Was advised that he was attending voluntarily and was entitled to leave at will unless informed that he was under arrest.

The world had gone mad.

'For the record,' McGarvie was saying, 'I'd like to clarify your movements on the morning your wife was shot. You were at home first thing, I gather?'

'Mm?' He stared blankly.

'What time did you leave the house?'

'The day it happened? I told you already. Eight-fifteen.'

'Can anyone confirm the time? Did you see a neighbour? The postman?'

He shrugged. 'I got into my car and backed it out and drove off.'

'Leaving your wife at the house?'

'You don't have to make it sound like a crime.'

'Do you sometimes give her a lift into town?'

'Only if she wants one.' With each response he was stifling the urge to tell them it was no business of theirs. Until now he hadn't ever considered how closely he guarded his private life.

'She didn't want the lift on this occasion because it was her morning off. Right?'

'Correct.'

'How was she dressed at the time you left?'

'Is that important?'

'Night-things? Day clothes?'

'I see. The things she was found in, apart from the raincoat and scarf.'

'So you drove here, to work?'

'Yes.'

'Arriving at what time?'

'Must have been before nine. I didn't check exactly. Ten to?'

'It takes you that long?'

'The traffic is heavy that time of day.'

'Which way did you enter the building?'

'From the car park.'

'Using the back stairs?'

'Does it matter which stairs I used?'

'Anyone see you arrive?'

'I've no idea.'

'You didn't pass the time of day with anyone, in the car park, or coming upstairs?'

'Don't remember.'

'Okay. Where did you go?'

'My office.'

'Without speaking to anyone at all?'

'You asked that already.'

'And then?'

'Took off all my clothes, stood on my head and recited *The Charge of the Light Brigade*. For the love of God. What does anyone do when he comes into his office in the morning? Opens the window, looks at the stuff on the desk, kicks the wastepaper basket. One day is like another, and I can't tell you what I did.'

'Perhaps you used the phone?'

'First thing? I doubt it.' Eyes closed, he made an effort to think back. 'At some point I was called by Helen, the ACC's PA, and asked upstairs.'

'We know that.'

'Then you don't need to ask. And you know what time it was.'

'Shortly after eleven. Were there any callers prior to that?'

'Not that I remember.'

'In short, you can't name anyone who can place you at work in your office between nine and eleven o'clock.'

'Someone could have come in. I don't recall.' He was in difficulty with this line of questioning. Everything prior to Steph's murder was very hazy indeed. It was almost like the after-effect of concussion, with the trauma blocking out everything. He hadn't expected to be questioned about it, and until now hadn't given a thought to what he had been doing.

'Two hours, alone in your office?'

'Things were quiet in CID. I was keeping my head down. If you show you're at a loose end in this place you get dumped on.' Having said this, he knew it wouldn't win any sympathy from Georgina, but it was the truth and he was too far gone to care. Georgina was tight-lipped.

McGarvie drew his right hand slowly across the table as though testing for dust and pressed his palms together, rubbing them lightly. He was ill at ease, and his next question showed why. 'Forgive me. I have to ask this. Was your marriage in good shape?'

Diamond heard the words, played them over in his head, and had an impulse to grab the man by the shirt and head-butt him. He'd asked the same insulting question when he came to the house. This was bloody incitement.

Then Georgina chose to come in with her smooth talk,

learned in all those management courses for high-ranking officers. 'You appreciate that we need to know for sure. It is a legitimate question, Peter.'

Legitimate? It was a bastard question, and they knew it. 'I didn't have any reason to shoot my wife, if that's what you're asking.'

'No,' McGarvie said, 'that isn't what I asked.'

He pressed down on his legs to stop them shaking. The stress had to break out some way. 'Steph and I were happy together, happy as any couple can be. Is that what you want to hear?'

'Do you own a gun?'

Another crass question. He hesitated before answering, 'No.' It was the truth . . . just about. The Smith & Wesson revolver in his loft at home was police property, acquired years ago when he worked in London.

'In the Met, you were listed as an authorised shot.'

'I let it lapse some years back.'

'The .38 that was used to shoot your wife could well have been a police weapon.'

He took a sharp, deep breath. 'What are you on about? I don't believe this.'

Sensing that it was time to draw back a little, McGarvie said, 'In the days leading up to the incident, did your wife mention any concerns, anything that might have suggested she was under stress?'

He'd been over this in his own mind many times. 'No. Nothing at all.'

'Was she at all secretive?'

'If you'd known her, you wouldn't ask that question.'

'Had there been any change in her routine?'

'Not that I noticed.'

'Had she received any threatening phone calls or letters?'

His patience was draining fast.

'For the tape,' McGarvie said, 'the subject just shook his head.' Then he tossed in another grenade. 'Did she have links with the criminal world?'

'What? Steph? Are you completely out of your mind?'

It wasn't the kind of response McGarvie wanted for his precious tape, but the gist was clear. He sniffed and moved on. 'Did she have a car of her own?'

'No. We shared it.'

'She could drive, then?'

'Oh, yes. But I was using it.'

'We need to establish how she travelled to the park. Would she have walked?'

'Could have, quite easily. It's scarcely a mile from where we live, but not too nice when the traffic is heavy on the Upper Bristol Road. It's more likely she caught a minibus. They pass the end of the street every fifteen minutes, so she generally took one if she was going into town.'

'She'd be at the park in a very short time.'

'Depending on the traffic.'

'We reckon she'd have got off at the Marlborough Lane stop to make her way up to the park.'

'If she took the bus, yes.'

'We've questioned each of the drivers on that route. Not one remembers a passenger of your wife's description. Of course they don't necessarily take note of every middle-aged woman who boards their bus.'

'You could ask the passengers.'

'The regulars? It's being tried. Nothing so far.'

Diamond remarked, 'All this presupposes she went to the park of her own free will.'

'You think otherwise?'

'I don't know any reason she would go there.'

'By arrangement?'

'Then she would have told me.'

McGarvie commented tartly, 'If she told you everything.'

He leaned forward, showing more of his bloodshot eyes than Diamond cared to see. 'Before you take offence again, consider this. The whole thing is strange, you've got to admit. You tell us she was acting normally that morning, had no secrets from you, had no reason to visit the park, yet that's where she was shot within two hours of your leaving for work.'

'If I knew why, I'd have told you.'

'At what stage were you told she'd been shot?'

'Nobody told me. I found out for myself.'

There was a pause while the horror of that moment was relived, and when McGarvie resumed again, there was less overt hostility. 'Okay, to be accurate, you heard that a woman had been shot and you went to the park and recognised the victim as your wife?'

'You know this. Do we have to go over it?'

'DI Halliwell was competent to deal with the incident. What prompted you to go there?'

Amazing. Even his attendance at the scene was viewed as suspicious. This experience on the receiving end, having to account for everything he had done, would change for ever his attitude to interviewing a suspect.

'I said we hadn't seen much action.'

'Point taken. Spurred on by the prospect of something happening, you went to the scene. You saw who it was, and you ignored procedure at the scene of a crime and handled the victim—'

'She was my wife, for pity's sake.'

'We're going to find blood on your clothes.'

'How inconvenient.' He'd taken enough. 'You know what really pisses me off about this farce? It's not the personal smear, the assumption that I might have murdered her. It's knowing the real killer is out there, and every minute that goes by his chance improves of getting away with this.'

'This isn't our only line of enquiry,' McGarvie said. 'I've got over a hundred men on the case.'

'For how much longer? What happens when Headquarters ask for your budget report? They'll cut the overtime. The whole thing will be scaled down.'

Georgina said with determination, 'I'll deal with Headquarters.' She asked McGarvie if he had any more questions and he said he was through and they stopped the tapes.

'I've had it up to here with you lot,' Diamond said. 'I'm going home.'

But he didn't. Instead, he drove out to the crime scene, now abandoned by everyone, and restored to normal except for the wear on the turf of hundreds of police boots. The one place where the ground had not been trampled was a small oval of fresh grass where Steph's body had lain. Someone had placed a bunch of flowers there. No message. He could have brought some himself, but he knew Steph would have been troubled by the idea of cut flowers without water. She wouldn't willingly deprive anything of life.

If he'd written a message, it would have been the one hackneyed word people always attach to flowers they leave at murder scenes. 'Why?'

He looked around him, taking in the setting. Previously he'd been aware of nothing except Steph lying dead on the ground. Now he saw a curved path lined with benches about every thirty yards. In spring, he remembered, the daffodils sprouted here and made a glorious display. The shoots were already visible. Lower down, the remains of the Victorian shrubbery, a long line of trees and bushes, hid the Charlotte Street Car Park from view. You wouldn't believe all those cars were actually only a few paces away.

Higher up the slope was the unprepossessing rear of

the old bandstand with its domed roof. He walked up to
it and around to the front.

The façade was much more elegant than the back, being
visible from the Crescent. He could imagine an audience
seated here listening to one of the German bands that
were so popular around the turn of the century. The shell-
shaped design was more modern in concept than the
weathered stonework suggested.

At either side, separate from the bandstand, two large
stone vases with handles, chipped and stained, but
evidently marble, were raised on plinths. Each was
protected by a flat stone canopy mounted on pillars and
surrounded by a low railing. Along the top of the
stonework was an inscription stating that the vases were
the gift of Napoleon to the Empress Josephine in 1805,
something Diamond had never noticed until now. They
were spoils of the Peninsular War, presented to the city
by some Bath worthy. The overgrown bushes almost hid
them from view, but he could make out the letter 'J' in
an Imperial circlet of leaves. It was the kind of detail that
fascinated Steph, and forgetting everything for a second,
he looked forward to telling her what he had found and
bringing her here to see it.

Caught again. This wasn't the first time. He supposed
it was what psychologists referred to as denial.

He moved back to the spot where Steph had been found.
Why had the murderer chosen this location? For one thing,
the park was reasonably quiet, even now, in the afternoon,
and fairly well screened by trees. If it was right that she
had been lured here, her killer could have remained
hidden among the bushes, or behind the bandstand, until
the last minute, and then approached her, keeping the
gun concealed. Since there had been no evidence of a
struggle, it was reasonable to assume the weapon had been
held to her face and fired twice in a swift, professional

action. Most gunmen knew you couldn't be certain a single shot would kill, even at point-blank range. Apparently he (or she, though it was difficult to visualise a female assassin) had quit the scene by the short route to the car park – which was huge, with more than one exit. So that was the special appeal of this location: the certainty of getting away fast. All in all, a well-chosen place.

The biggest problem must have been persuading Steph to come here.

For the first time since the murder, he was functioning as a detective. Until now he had been too devastated to think straight. For that reason alone it was right that someone other than he should head the team. Moreover, the official line made sense: having the victim's husband in charge would undermine any prosecution. Fine – so long as McGarvie was a competent, energetic stand-in. But after that farcical interrogation, Diamond's confidence in the man was in tatters. The competence was flawed, the energy misdirected. There was a sense of desperation in what was going on.

A single crow stalked the lawn, foraging for worms. The bleak look of this scene reinforced the lost opportunities.

Steph deserved a good investigation.

No sense in offering advice. Georgina and McGarvie wouldn't listen to a man they were treating as a suspect. No, the only way to get results was to go solo. Throughout their marriage Steph had put up with his cack-handed attempts at all things practical: shelves that fell off the wall, doors that stuck in the winter and let in draughts in the summer, electrical wiring that blew the fuses. She had never directly benefited from the one skill he had: sleuthing. She was entitled to it now. He would find her killer, and to hell with the problems it raised.

*   *   *

His spirits improved. He was putting his career on the line and maybe his life. Bugger that, he thought. This is the right decision. I refuse to be sidelined. She's my wife and no one can make me walk away from her.

At home that evening he opened a can of lager and dug about in the freezer and cooked himself a satisfying meal of one of Steph's beef casseroles with fresh potatoes and carrots. He watched a repeat of *Fawlty Towers* on TV and smiled for the first time in weeks.

Towards midnight, he woke in the armchair and realised he'd dozed off. He'd been dreaming, an anxious, vivid dream of being shot in the leg by an invisible man with a gun. Of limping away and feeling more shots, and dripping blood. The shots fitted the film that was running on the box, some spaghetti western with Clint Eastwood. Clint looked in fine shape still. The film bullets had obviously missed.

Diamond fingered his own leg.

'Daft.'

But it had got to him, that dream. He decided to fetch his handgun from the loft. In the coming days he might need to defend himself. He had no plans to use it, except as a deterrent. So he went upstairs, opened the hatch and let down the folding ladder. Switched on the loft light and of course the sodding thing flickered and went out.

No matter. He knew where the shoebox was that contained the gun wrapped in a cloth with two rounds of ammunition. At the top of the steps he put his head and shoulders through the hatch, reached and found what he wanted at once.

But there was no weight to the box. Nothing was inside. He took off the lid. Not even the cloth was in there.

Impossible.

He groped around the plasterboard where the box had

been. Dust and cobwebs. Nothing else. No other box, no Smith & Wesson .38 wrapped in cloth.

Deeply worried, he collected a torch from downstairs and replaced the light bulb. Spent the next hour searching the whole of the loft, struggling with old suitcases, among unwanted rolls of wallpaper and discarded carpets. He tried to remember if anyone except himself had been up there. A plumber, to look at the cold storage tank? Electrician? TV aerial man?

Not to his knowledge.

What in Christ's name was going on?

10

The two men talking in a London taxi knew only as much as the media had told them about the shooting of Stephanie Diamond, but after the shock wave of a killing there are ripples washing up on some unlikely shores.

'It's beautiful, Harry.'

'It always is at the beginning,' the voice of experience spoke. 'I hate to disillusion you, old friend, but the beauty soon wears off. By the end it's revoltingly ugly.'

'Not this time, I promise you.'

'Would you care to take a bet on that?' Harry Tattersall gazed out of the window at the traffic in Piccadilly. At forty-two, he'd seen many a pretty plan turn to dross. 'Who else is in?'

'That's the beauty,' Rhadi said. 'We are a small, talented team. Five only.'

'Who?'

'Wait and see.'

'I don't work with failures.'

'These are pros. You're going to be impressed.'

'Where's the meeting?'

'This is a top job, Harry. Top job needs a top meeting place.'

The cab wound its way around Trafalgar Square, under Admiralty Arch and up the Mall towards the Victoria Memorial. Tourists stood snapping the sentry at the gates of Buckingham Palace.

'Not there?' Harry said, only half joking. This was such a weird set-up, he was ready to believe anything.

'No, not there.'

They were driven up Constitution Hill to Hyde Park Corner and came to a halt outside one of the more exclusive hotels. A white-gloved hand opened the door.

'Didn't I tell you?' Rhadi said.

'It takes more than one flunkey to impress me,' Harry said. He had been to a good public school and liked everyone to know it.

A doorman ushered them in and a black-suited young man wished them good afternoon in a way that asked to know their business.

'We're expected,' Rhadi said with a princely air. 'The Napoleon Suite.'

'Very good, sir.'

In the lift, Rhadi said, 'What do you think? An improvement on the Scrubs?'

'So long as it isn't a short cut back to the Scrubs,' Harry said. He'd done one six-month stretch in an otherwise unblemished fifteen-year career of confidence trickery, and he hadn't cared for it one bit. 'I'd better warn you, I'm not going to be bounced into anything.'

'Lighten up, old friend.'

Rhadi knocked and the door was opened by a Middle Eastern man.

'What's this – Ali Baba and the Forty Thieves?' Harry said.

He'd known Rhadi so many years that he never thought of him as an immigrant. Wasn't even sure where he came from originally. Confronted now by two more Arabs in expensive suits, he felt outnumbered. Rhadi hadn't said a word about the nationality of the personnel involved.

'Is there a problem, Mr Tattersall?' one of them asked,

a near-midget with a set of teeth that wouldn't have disgraced a camel.

'I didn't expect . . .' Harry started to say, and let his voice trail away when he saw the second Arab's hand slip inside his jacket.

'This is Ibrahim,' the teeth said, 'and I am Zahir. You were not expecting to be involved in an international enterprise, I dare say.'

'If it's terrorism, I'm leaving.'

Rhadi gave him a gentle push in the back. 'Go in, Harry. Forget about terrorism. This is big-time.'

'It had better be,' he muttered. 'Where are you all from, anyway?'

Zahir ignored the question. 'You want a drink? It's against our religion, but there's plenty here if you want something.'

'I think I will.' It wasn't a mini-bar, either. This was a drinks cabinet, courtesy of the hotel. He poured himself a large single malt while he pondered that remark about religion. He didn't think he'd been invited to a prayer meeting.

Ibrahim had closed the door. Harry took stock. Zahir, the spokesman with the teeth, had to be Mr Big, though not in stature. Ibrahim, silent, built like a water buffalo, was the muscle. The fifth man apparently hadn't turned up yet.

'You were at King's, Canterbury, I believe?' Zahir said out of nowhere.

'Is my old school important?'

'That's true, then? Straight up, as they say?'

'Anyone can check the register.'

'Did you row?'

'No. I was a cricketer. Opened the batting.' Harry refrained from revealing that he opened for the third eleven and ended the season with an average of nine.

'In that case,' Zahir said, 'we wouldn't have met. I coxed the first eight. Eton.'

With the pecking order established, Zahir invited Harry to take a seat. 'Rhadi tells us you're the smoothest con artist in London.'

'Rhadi isn't bad at it himself,' Harry commented.

'You once took one of the big merchant banks for a cool fifty thousand?'

'Three banks together,' Harry said. 'It was a matter of persuading them it was a notional adjustment.'

'And none of them understood what was going on?'

'They still don't.'

'Rhadi also tells us you might not be averse to another payday.'

'That depends.'

'Naturally. Have you ever dealt in diamonds?'

'Diamonds?' He twitched and frowned. 'I'm not a diamond man.'

'Don't look so alarmed,' Zahir said. 'No one is asking you to do anything outside your experience.'

'So what's the scam?'

Zahir hesitated. 'This is more than a scam. We're not talking thousands, Mr Tattersall, but hundreds of thousands. We can all retire on the proceeds. But you'll understand that I need your total commitment before I unfold the plan.'

'Before? That's asking a lot. I don't know you. Rhadi is an old friend, but the rest of you . . .'

'Well, it's a good thing some of us aren't familiar to you. You wouldn't want to be getting into bed with a bunch of well-known criminals, would you?' He flashed the enormous teeth.

'You've got a point there.'

'Let's see if we can resolve this. What if you were guaranteed a hundred thousand pounds?'

'A hundred grand? What are you snatching – the Crown Jewels?'

'Better. These are uncut stones. Some of the finest gem-crystals in the world.'

Harry was silent for a while, still cautious. 'It sounds wonderful, but why have you come to me? What am I supposed to do?'

'What you're best at doing, Mr Tattersall. Conning people.'

'Ah, but I know damn all about the diamond industry. I need to understand what I'm talking about.'

'No you don't.'

'Sorry, my friend,' Harry insisted. 'That isn't the way I work. I absolutely refuse to wing it.'

'You're not listening, Mr Tattersall. Your part in this project doesn't involve the diamonds. You don't need to talk about them. In fact, you are expressly forbidden to mention them. You will be a go-between. We require someone who is English, not Arabian, a true-blue English gentleman.'

'That I can do.'

'So you're on the team?'

'Hold on,' Harry said. 'First I want to know the job – and who else you've signed up for this.'

'You know Rhadi, and you've just met Ibrahim and me.'

'I was told there are five.'

'Who told you?' Zahir's eyes flicked to Rhadi. 'The fifth man must remain anonymous for the time being.'

'Why?'

'He's the key to everything.'

'The peterman?'

'The what?'

'Safe-breaker. The fellow who liberates the rocks.'

Zahir's face was a study in distaste. 'We're not proposing to break into a safe, Mr Tattersall.'

'How else are you going to lay hands on them?'

Rhadi broke into the dialogue in some excitement. 'This is the beauty, Harry.'

Zahir said, 'We're having the diamonds delivered to us.'

'*Delivered?* Who by?'

'The owners. The top dealer in Hatton Garden, the home of the London diamond trade.'

'How do you arrange that?'

Zahir exchanged more looks with Rhadi and Ibrahim. 'This is what will happen. Rhadi will go to Hatton Garden and inform the dealer that a prince of the Kuwaiti Royal Family has come to London to buy rough diamonds and is staying at the Dorchester Hotel. In Hatton Garden they know that the Kuwaitis are rich beyond dreams. They will arrange to take their best stones to his suite for inspection.'

'Before you go on,' Harry said, 'these Hatton Garden people aren't fools. They'll check with the hotel.'

'And when they check, they'll find that it's true. There will be a Kuwaiti prince on the hotel guest-list.'

'You, I suppose,' Harry said, not over-impressed.

'No. A true member of the blood royal. The Kuwaitis visit London frequently and stay at the Dorchester. They have a financial stake in the City. Anyone checking will find this is totally on the level.'

'Get away. The fifth man is a Kuwaiti prince?'

'No, no. You're still not listening. The prince isn't in the plot. We time our heist to coincide with the visit.'

Harry still needed convincing. 'How will you know when one of the princes is over here? Private visits by royalty are arranged in secret. They're very aware of security.'

'Rightly so,' Zahir said, unfazed. 'We'll know because we have a man inside the Dorchester.'

Harry digested this.

'Clever,' he said, after a pause. 'The fifth man?'

'Yes. He's on the staff, on the catering side. When royalty are coming, they have to order food supplies specially, so he's one of the few to be entrusted with advance information about VIP guests. He will advise us – through you – when one of the princes has a booking. We will then book one of the best suites for you under the name of Lord this or the Earl of that. Your job. You can impersonate one of the aristocracy, I hope?'

'With ease.'

'Good. I suggest you are disguised. Dyed hair, glasses, moustache. You will check in, and occupy the suite. Presently I will arrive with Ibrahim. Within a short time you will remove your disguise and leave by the back stairs. Your job will be over. It's as simple as that. Shortly after you depart, the Hatton Garden dealer will arrive, and be met in the foyer by Rhadi, posing as the emissary of the Kuwaitis.'

'He may have security with him,' Harry warned.

'We're prepared for that. Rhadi will escort him to the suite, where I will be waiting, with Ibrahim, both dressed in the *jubbah*. If they bring a security officer, he will be ordered by Rhadi to remain outside the door. You don't bring functionaries such as that into the presence of the blood royal. The dealer takes out his parcel of diamonds and we relieve him of them. As smoothly as possible. Minimum violence. He is tied up and gagged. We leave by another door.'

'Isn't that the neatest scam you ever heard?' Rhadi said.

'Sounds all right,' Harry grudgingly admitted. 'But why do you need me?'

'For your special talent, and our protection. You have two functions. First, you are the go-between, as I mentioned. Our man on the Dorchester staff will communicate with you, not with Arabs, which might arouse suspicion. There is sure to be a security enquiry after the heist. He will, of course, deny having given information to anybody.'

'And secondly?'

'You are the decoy – the peer who booked the suite. It will take some time for them to realise how it was done. For all they know, you may have been a genuine peer abducted by the gang.'

Harry was silent for several seconds as he reviewed the plan. Certainly it had attractions. No safe-breaking, fiddling with security systems, no guns, no excessive violence. The concept of the dealer being conned into bringing the rocks to the hotel was neat, as was the idea of timing the scam to coincide with a genuine royal visit. Yes, it appealed. His own part didn't sound too demanding. He'd taken bigger risks in the past.

'And if it all goes to plan,' he said, 'how will you fence the diamonds? If they're tiptop items, they'll be well known in the trade.'

'These are uncut stones, Mr Tattersall,' Zahir reminded him. 'The industry is worldwide now. Huge. There are factories in Bombay, Tel Aviv, Smolensk. Every damned place. There is no difficulty in unloading top quality roughs for a decent price, believe me. They will be out of Britain within hours and cut and polished within days. And once a stone has been cleaved, it changes personality, just as you do for a living, or so I'm told. Are you in?'

'For a hundred K guaranteed?'

'Guaranteed.'

'I'll incur some expenses.'

'We can take care of that.'

'Over and above my hundred grand?'

'Expenses – yes. What do you have in mind? The disguise?'

'A suit. I can't walk into the Dorchester in what I'm wearing.' It was worth the try, Harry thought, and he was mightily impressed when it got a result.

'I was thinking the same,' Zahir said, looking him up and down. 'Fifteen hundred in expenses, then.'

'Upfront?'

'Rhadi will see to it.'

They shook hands.

'What next?' Harry asked, trying not to show his awe at the deal.

'You buy some decent clothes, and then you wait. We all wait.'

'For the word from your fellow in the Dorchester?'

'Which he will give to you.'

'Is this hotel man reliable? One hundred per cent?'

'Be assured of that. He held the Queen's commission. He was an officer in the Royal Air Force Catering Branch.'

11

'How did you . . . ?'

'Your door was open.'

'Bloody liar. You put your boot against it.'

'So it was open,' Diamond said.

He didn't usually force an entry when calling on a witness, but the rules change for winos. Warburton clearly wasn't in any shape to get up and greet a visitor. He was on the floor, his back propped against a greasy leather armchair on which the lurcher was curled up asleep, oblivious of Diamond's arrival. Maybe it, too, was pie-eyed. Empty cider bottles were scattered about the floor.

'You're that copper,' Warburton said through his alcoholic haze, as if Diamond needed reminding.

There was another chair, an upright one, with a plate on it with the dried remains of a meal of baked beans. Diamond chose to remain standing. He was trying to decide if the man was capable of coherent answers. *In vino veritas* is a maxim reliable only up to a certain intake of the vino.

'What you want?' Warburton asked.

Diamond ignored him and walked through to the second room of this foul-smelling basement.

A mattress on the floor and an ex-army greatcoat slung across it, presumably for bedding. More empty bottles.

He stooped and looked under one side of the mattress. And then the other. Nothing except some dog-eared pages from a girlie magazine. He brushed his clothes in case of lice.

Back in the main room, watched by the still-supine tenant, he sifted through the few possessions. From a carton containing cans of dog food, baked beans and a stale loaf, he picked out a supermarket receipt.

'What's this? Thirty-eight pounds fifty-three? You had a good splurge on the twenty-third. In the money, were you?'

'Me social, wasn't it?'

'On a Tuesday? Come off it, Jimmy. This was the day you found the woman in the park. You nicked the cash from her bag, didn't you?'

'I never.'

'So what did you do with the bag?'

No answer.

'Where is it, Jimmy? No messing. This is a murder inquiry.'

Warburton blurted out in a panicky voice, 'I never killed her. I reported it, didn't I?'

'You did the right thing, there. And I've been asking myself why you bothered, Jimmy. So public-spirited that you felt compelled to raise the alarm? I don't see it.'

''S a fact.'

'Now that I have this . . .' Diamond held up the till receipt '. . . I'm starting to get the picture. You're not such a hero. I was asking myself how a down-and-out like you reacts when he comes across a body in a park. Does he get to a phone immediately and report it? Does he hell. He's on the lookout for goodies. You found the handbag.'

Warburton shook his head.

'It won't do, Jimmy,' Diamond told him. 'The date matches. You raised the alarm, yes, but there can only be one reason. Someone came along when you had your thieving hands in the bag. They saw you right beside the body, maybe even thought you'd fired the shots. You were forced to play the innocent, pretend you were just about to call the police. You stuffed the handbag under your coat and hightailed it to the car park and did the decent thing because they were breathing down your neck. Am I right?'

'Has she been onto you?'

Diamond pounced. 'She? It was a woman, then? Better unload, Jimmy.'

The man looked so sick that Diamond wasn't sure what he would unload.

'Tell me about her, this woman who spotted you.'

'Nothing to tell.'

'What was she like? Where did she come from? What did she say? Come on, man. Do I have to shake it out of you?'

'Dunno,' Warburton said. 'Came from nowhere. I looked up and she was there.'

'What age?'

He shrugged. 'Thirty. Thirty-five.'

'Wearing what?'

'Tracksuit. Blue. Dark blue.'

'A jogger?'

'Yeah. Could be.'

'So what colour was her hair?'

'Christ knows. She had one of them woolly hats.'

'Wearing trainers?'

'Didn't see.'

'How tall?'

'Average.'

'Brilliant. What happened?'

Warburton dragged his hand down the length of his face, pressing the pale flesh as if to squeeze out some memory. 'Asked what I was doing and I told her I found the stiff on the ground, which was true. She said we ought to tell someone, so I got up and legged it to the car park—'

'With the handbag under your clothes?'

'Don't want to talk about that.'

'Spill it out, Sonny Jim, or I'll have you for obstructing the police as well as withholding evidence and theft. Have you done any time?'

He didn't answer.

Diamond took a step closer. No one could look more threatening. 'What happened to that handbag? Is it here?'

'Chucked it, didn't I?' Warburton said.

At least he hadn't pinned the blame on the jogger.

'Where?'

'Dunno.'

Diamond took a handhold on Warburton's T-shirt just below the throat and screwed it into a knot.

'I could have stuffed it out of sight,' Warburton piped up.

'We know that. Where? The car park?' There were big collection bins at one end, for newspapers, bottles and cans. Maybe he'd got rid of it there.

'Can't say.'

'Get up.'

'What?'

Warburton found himself hauled off the floor. 'You're going to have your memory jogged.'

The lurcher woke up and wagged its tail, uninterested that its master was being forced outside against his will. The chance of a walk was not to be missed. Except that it wasn't going to be a walk, simply because Warburton wasn't capable of staying upright that long.

In the car, the dog stood with its front paws on the back of Diamond's seat, licking him behind the ear. Warburton immediately fell asleep.

They drove up Charlotte Street and took the car park turn. Diamond stopped beside the bins. 'Recognise them?'

No answer.

He rammed an elbow into Warburton's ribs. 'Is that where you got rid of the handbag?'

'No.'

'You're certain?'

Charlotte Street Car Park is vast, the largest in Bath, with tiers of parking space separated by hedges. A hedge wasn't a bad place to get rid of an unwanted bag, but these had already been combed by McGarvie's search squad. Whilst Warburton lolled against the headrest with his eyes closed, Diamond toured the car park trying to picture the scene. He drove to one of the higher tiers nearest to the old shrubbery. Every parking slot was taken, so he just stopped between the rows, got out and dragged Warburton from the car. The dog jumped out as well.

'Now. Where exactly did you find the guy with the mobile phone?'

Warburton looked vaguely about him. He flapped a limp hand that seemed to take in the whole of the car park.

'Do you know who I'm talking about? You asked him to dial nine-nine-nine.'

'Could have been right here . . . Or over there . . . Or there.'

'Did you have the handbag with you?'

'What?'

'Under your coat – did you have the woman's bag under your coat?'

No response.

'Listen. I'm trying to get this straight. The jogger came along while you were beside the body going through the bag. She told you to get to a phone, and you made a show of looking for help. You came here, to the car park, and I think you had the bag with you.'

'I did – 's a fact.'

'Good. And we know you found the guy with the mobile and he got the number and you spoke to the operator and she put you through to the police and they asked for your name and told you to wait at the scene. Right?'

'Mm.'

'This was seen by the man who owned the mobile. Must have been. So I don't think you dumped the handbag here, with him watching. I think you took it back to the park.'

'Yeah.'

'So what did you do with it there?'

'Dunno.'

Diamond clenched his fist. The urge was strong. Somehow he suppressed it. Warburton was barely capable of standing upright without support. The fresh air seemed to be sobering him up a little. A poke in the guts wouldn't help. 'Okay. We're going to reconstruct the scene, do the walk, just like you did.' He opened the car and took out the pack containing the vehicle service record and documents. 'This will do for the handbag. Where did you have it? In your shirt? Under your arm?'

Warburton took the pack in his hands, eyed it in a puzzled way, and then looked to Diamond for guidance.

'We're pretending this is the handbag.'

'Ah.'

With an effort at co-operation, Warburton lifted the flap of his jacket and shoved the documents out of sight in the front of his jeans.

'Good. What next? You've called nine-nine-nine. Do you go back directly to the scene?'

'Yeah.'

'The guy with the mobile – what did he do?'

'Got in his motor and pissed off quick.'

So much for the great British public. In all probability Warburton would have quit the scene as well if he hadn't stupidly given his name to the operator.

'So you went back to wait by the body?'

'Yeah.'

'Still carrying the handbag?'

'Yeah.'

'Let's walk it through, then.'

The lurcher led the way up the path. After stumbling a little and being steadied, Warburton began to move rather better. Diamond was trying to think himself into this man's befuddled brain on the day of the shooting. There was this short period before the patrol car responded to the call. The jogger had moved on and the man with the mobile hadn't wanted to get involved. This, surely, was the opportunity to see what was in the handbag, remove any money, and then get rid of the bag before the police arrived. But where?

In the open area beside the bandstand a man was helping a child fly a kite, obviously unaware that someone had been murdered in this place. Victoria Park was back to normal. Life had moved on. Diamond had seen it happen before when murder scenes were reclaimed for everyday use, watched the families of victims unable to understand how the rest of the world could be so unfeeling.

They reached the spot where Steph had fallen. That sad bunch of flowers was still in place, yellow tulips spread wide, roses dropping their petals.

'Right. You came back here. You had a few minutes in hand. Was this when you helped yourself to the money?'

Warburton didn't answer.

'I'm giving you a chance. Tell me what you did with the bag and I may not charge you with theft.'

The last word sank in. Warburton looked about him

as if coming out of a trance and then started walking to the left side of the bandstand where one of the Empress Josephine's vases stood. He reached under his shirt and tugged out the document wallet. 'Want me to chuck it in there?'

'In the vase?' The great stone amphora was large enough to take a dozen handbags. Surely the searchers had looked inside. Or was it possible they'd been so absorbed in their fingertip search of the shrubbery, lawns and car park that they'd omitted something so screamingly obvious?

'If you're wasting my time . . .'

'Not.'

Diamond stepped over the railing, pushed aside an overgrown rose bush and climbed on the plinth. Put an arm into the huge vase and groped around. Dead leaves, for sure. He felt for something more solid and brought out a rust-covered lager can and chucked it angrily aside. The lurcher chased it.

'There's no bag here, you berk.'

'Some bleeder took it, then.'

'Bullshit.' He climbed down, scratching his hand on the rose. 'Where is it, Warburton?'

'It was in there. I swear.'

'You don't even remember, you piss artist. Give me that.' He grabbed his car documents. 'Find your own way home. I've wasted enough time.' He turned and marched back to the car, angry and disappointed.

Driving home, he tried telling himself that it hadn't been totally fruitless. He was sure now that Warburton had taken the money. Probably the bag had been slung into the river, or a builder's skip. It might yet turn up.

The frustration was that he'd appeared to be succeeding where McGarvie had failed. The bag *could* have been lying inside that pesky vase.

He was halfway to Weston when he thought of the obvious. Talk about Warburton's bosky state: what kind of state was *he* in?

He did a fast, illegal U-turn, and drove back to the park.

The handbag was in the second vase.

12

Curious as to what this fascinating object might be, Raffles arrived on the table with an agile leap whilst Diamond was performing a delicate operation with salad-servers and a chopstick.

'Get out of it.' He didn't want paw prints on Steph's handbag.

Raffles jumped down and went to look at the feeding dish instead.

Neither did he want more of his own fingerprints. He must have left some when he picked the bag out of the stone vase. Since then he'd been careful to handle only the strap. Forensics would bellyache about contaminated evidence. So he eased the sides open with the chopstick and started removing the contents with the salad-servers.

Plastic rain-hat.

Kleenex tissues, soggy and disintegrating. The damp had penetrated the bag.

Compact.

Oxfam ballpoint.

Lipstick (a devil to grip with the servers).

Purse, unzipped and empty except for a few small coins. But the credit cards were still in place in the side pocket. Warburton must have known no one would believe he possessed a credit card. He'd gone for the cash.

Keys.

Aspirin bottle.

Her little book of photos, of her parents, a group of her Brownies and Diamond himself, in uniform, the year they'd met. The pictures had suffered in the damp.

But where was the one thing he wanted to find?

He probed with the servers. Held the entire bag upside down on the end of the chopstick. A Malteser fell out and rolled across the floor. He watched Raffles hunt it down and flick it with a paw before discovering it was coated in chocolate. One item forensics would have to manage without.

They would get everything else. Presently he'd go into work and take quiet satisfaction in presenting McGarvie with the handbag and saying he'd found it at the scene. What was the figure they kept quoting – over a hundred officers involved in a fingertip search?

In truth, he knew how easy it was to miss something as obvious as the stone vases. Could have happened to anyone.

He poked with the chopstick at the objects on the table, trying to work out where Steph's diary was. Not in the house. She *always* had it with her. That little book was essential to the way she ran her life. Dates, times, important phone numbers and addresses. She didn't use it as some people use a diary, to write up a daily record of their lives. Recording the past was alien to her outlook. She was forward-looking. She scribbled in appointments, names, birthdays.

That diary was of no conceivable interest to anyone else.

So where was it?

He said, 'Stupid arse.'

The answer was as obvious as the stone vase in the park. In the lining inside the bag was a zip. She kept the diary in an inner pocket. Impatient now, he dropped the chopstick and used his finger and thumb to open the zip and feel inside.

Result.

The diary was dry and in near perfect condition. He turned to the date of the murder, Tuesday, February the twenty-third, and found an entry. Steph had written in her blue ballpoint:

T. 10 a.m. Vict. Pk, opp. bandstand

He frowned at the page, baffled, disbelieving, shocked. He'd been telling everyone it was most unlikely Steph had arranged to visit the park – because she hadn't said a word to him. But why hadn't she mentioned it? She was so open about her life. Always told him everything.

Didn't she?

All at once his hands shook.

He hesitated to check the rest of the diary. It would be an invasion of her privacy. Already he felt shabby for opening it. Then an inner voice told him the murder squad would pore over every page after he handed it in, and he was more entitled than they to know what was in the damned thing.

He had this gut-wrenching fear that his trust in Steph was about to unravel. Up to now he'd never had a doubt about her loyalty. Theirs had been an honest, blissful marriage. That had been one of the few certainties in his case-hardened life. Was it possible he'd been mistaken, that she had secrets she'd never discussed with him?

This looked horribly like one, this appointment in the park. Did 'T' stand for a name, someone she'd met, or – please, please – something totally different and innocent that happened in parks, like ... like what, for Christ's sake?

Tennis?

Outdoors, in February? Ridiculous.

T'ai Chi, then?

Why not? Steph was forever trying therapies, holistic this and alternative that. Didn't always speak of them, because she knew he dismissed all of it as baloney. It was not impossible she'd joined a group who exercised in the park.

Somehow, he couldn't picture it.

Briefly he was tempted to destroy the diary without looking at any more of it. If he'd been living an illusion, wasn't it preferable to hold onto precious memories, even though they might turn out to have been unfounded?

He dismissed that. The diary was pivotal evidence, whatever else was in it. The killer had to be caught, and this proved Steph had made an appointment to go to her place of execution. The chance that some casual mugger had killed her was now so unlikely that it could be discounted. She'd obviously been lured to her death. The murder squad had to be told.

So he started leafing through. It was a small diary with seven days spread over two pages, and Steph's entries were short. They took some interpreting. 'Ox' meant her stints at the Oxfam shop. They varied a bit from one week to the next, so she had to keep a record of them. She'd also scribbled in appointments with the doctor and dentist, family birthdays, dinner invitations and theatre bookings. He was looking for other things.

Disturbingly, he found them.

Monday 15 February Ox 2–5 P out. Must call T.

With that, the T'ai Chi theory went down in flames.

Wednesday 17 February Ox 10–1. Hair (Jan) 1.30.
Friday 19 February P out. Call T tonight.

On the following Tuesday – Shrove Tuesday, the diary

reminded him – she'd had her fatal meeting in the park with the person she called 'T'. These were crucial entries and he copied them into a notebook of his own.

It was deeply worrying, not to say hurtful. The first mention of 'T', on Monday the fifteenth, seemed to be linked with the note that he, 'P', was out. He remembered. It had been one of his regular, mind-numbing PCCG meetings with local residents' groups. Evidently on the Wednesday she'd had her hair done, which was usually a sure sign of some important occasion ahead. Another call to 'T' on Friday. And she'd said not a word about all this.

Hold on, he told himself, this is your wife Steph. Don't read too much into it. But the suspicion of a secret affair was planted. How could he interpret it as anything else?

For crying out loud, be realistic! Steph wasn't two-timing me. I'd have picked up some signals. She was as loving as ever in those last few days of her life, on our last night together. There's another explanation. Has to be.

He went methodically through the eight weeks up to the date of her death and found no other mention of this 'T'. It was no use looking for last year's diary, because she always threw them away at the end of the year. His hands still shook as he replaced this one in its pocket of the handbag and closed the zip.

There was no sense of triumph in handing the bag to McGarvie. He simply walked into the incident room, passed it over and said where he'd found it.

'I thought those bloody great things were solid stone,' McGarvie said as if Diamond himself had conned him. 'I suppose you looked inside?'

He nodded. 'You'll find some of my prints on it. And Warburton's, no doubt. The purse is in there, minus the money. And her diary.'

'The diary.' The tired eyes widened.

'She had an appointment in the park the day she died.'

'Who with?'

'Someone she called "T".'

McGarvie looked around the incident room. 'Did you hear that, everyone? This is the breakthrough.' He looked animated for the first time in a month. 'Any thoughts?'

Diamond shook his head. 'Like I said, she hadn't mentioned a thing.'

'Boyfriend?'

'Some boyfriend, if he put a bullet through her head.'

'Sorry. I've got to cover every angle. And you think Warburton took the cash?'

'I'm sure of it.'

'And tossed the bag in the vase?'

'He told me he did. Took me to the place. There was only forty quid. If you're thinking of charging him, don't. He gave me his co-operation.'

'I'll handle this my way. I still want to speak to him. Look, I'm grateful you found this.'

'But . . .' Diamond said.

'You know what I'm going to say?'

'Save it. I'm not trying to take over. I'll keep my distance.'

'That's not good enough, Peter.'

'It's the best you'll get.'

Specially, he thought, when I'm ahead of you.

He turned right outside the police station and walked the length of Manvers Street and beyond, where it became Pierrepont Street. At the far end he turned left into North Parade Passage, and straight to Steph's hairdresser, called What a Snip.

He asked for Jan. She was with a client.

'If it's about an appointment,' the receptionist said with a dubious look at Diamond's bald patch, 'I can do it from the book.'

'You can show me the book. And you can tell Jan to break off and speak to the police.'

She went at once.

Steph's name was in the book for one-thirty on Wednesday, February the seventeenth.

'Does this tick beside her name mean she definitely came in?' he asked Jan when she appeared.

'She did. Mr Diamond, I can't tell you how shocked I was when I heard what happened,' Jan said. She was the senior stylist and manager, meaning she was all of twenty-one with the confidence of twice that, blond, elfin, with eyes that had seen everything and dealt with every kind of client. You wouldn't mess with Jan. Steph must have liked her.

'I want you to cast your mind back to that Wednesday. I'm sure she chatted as you were doing her hair.'

'A bit, yes.'

'Can you remember any of what was said?'

'That's asking. The weather, naturally. My holiday in Tenerife. The night before's television, I expect. And the kind of cut she wanted.'

'Did she say anything about the reason for the hairdo?'

'Not that I remember.'

'Try, please. She wasn't one for regular appointments, as you know. She only booked you when she had something coming up. Did she mention what it was?'

She shook her head. 'I would have remembered if she'd said anything. People often do, and I like to know about their lives. But I never ask if they don't want to say. I don't believe in being nosy.'

'Are you sure she didn't tell you something and ask you to keep it to yourself? – because if she did, it's got to come out now. You don't have to spare my feelings, Jan. I need to find her killer before someone else is murdered.'

'And I'd tell you if there was anything to tell, but there isn't.'

He believed her.

The phone was beeping and the cat mewing when he came through his front door. He ignored the phone, but Raffles got fed. Then he heated some baked beans, cut the stale end off a loaf and made toast, topped with tinned tomatoes and a fried egg that smelt fishy. Looked at the post without troubling to open anything. The solicitor, the bank, the funeral director. They could wait. In less than twenty minutes he was out again, driving to Bristol.

He called at two pubs in the old market area and asked for John Seville, an informer he'd known and used a few times. No snout is totally reliable, but Seville was better than most. The problem was that nobody had seen him since the Carpenter trial. Bernie Hescott, hunched over a Guinness in the Rummer, was definitely second best.

'Haven't clapped eyes on him in weeks. I wouldn't like to think what happened. He was too yappy for his own good, I reckon.'

'Maybe you can help.' Diamond showed the top edge of a twenty-pound note, and then let it slide back into his top pocket. 'You heard what happened to my wife?'

'It was in all the papers, wasn't it?' said Bernie, a twitchy, under-nourished ex-con in a Bristol Rovers shirt. 'Wouldn't wish that on anyone.'

'It was done by a pro.'

'You think so?'

'I was going to ask John Seville if he'd heard a whisper about a hitman.'

'Was you? Well, he's not around.'

Diamond fingered the note in his pocket. 'I could ask you, couldn't I?'

Bernie shrugged and took a sip.

'Who do the Carpenters use – their own men, or someone down from London?'

'What – for a contract?'

'Yes.'

'Job like that – I'm talking theory now – she was gunned down in broad daylight, I heard – job like that doesn't look like a local lad. There's no one I can think of in Bristol.'

Diamond took the folded banknote from his pocket and placed it on the table with his hand over it. 'I could show appreciation, Bernie, if you put out some feelers.'

'Bloody dangerous.'

'You can't help me, then?'

'It'll cost you.'

'This is personal. It's worth it.' He took his hand off the banknote and revealed a crisp new fifty. He lifted it and the twenty was underneath. He returned the fifty to his pocket and slid the twenty across the table. 'I'll be in again Friday or Saturday.'

He drove up College Road to Clifton, looking for the house where Danny Carpenter lived. Back in the early nineteenth century when the city had been infested with cholera, the affluent Clifton residents instructed their servants to leave blankets and clothes halfway down the hill for the poor wretches in Bristol, and the place still has a determination not to be contaminated by the noxious life below Whiteladies Road. Danny's residence was on the Down, in one of the best positions in the city, with views along the Gorge to the Suspension Bridge. Old stone pillars at the entrance with griffins aloft gave promise of a gracious house. In fact, the original building at the end of the curved drive had been demolished at the time when architects went starry-eyed over steel and concrete. To Diamond's eye the replacement was an ugly pile of lemon-coloured, flat-roofed blocks. Even so, its location and scale represented money.

Before he got out, the security lights came on. A dog barked. A large bark. No need, really, to touch the bell push, but he did, and was rewarded with the first bars of *Danny Boy*.

The door opened a fraction and a snarling muzzle was thrust through.

Diamond took a step back. Someone swore, and hauled the dog inside. A man's face appeared, without doubt the face of a minder. 'Yeah?'

'Danny at home?'

'Yeah.'

'I'd like to see him, then.'

'Yeah?'

'The name's Diamond. He's heard of it.'

'Yeah?'

This might have continued for some time if a woman's voice had not said from the inner depths, 'Who is it, Gary?'

Silence. Gary had forgotten already.

Diamond called out his own name and presently Gary's ravaged head was replaced by one easier on the eye, one Diamond knew, red-blond and green-eyed. She had been in court for much of the Jake Carpenter trial.

'Evening, Celia.'

She said, 'You've got a bloody nerve.'

'I'm here to see Danny.'

'Not by invitation, you're not.'

'About the murder of my wife.'

'We don't know nothing about that. He spoke to your people and he's in the clear.'

'Then he hasn't got a problem. He can see me.'

'Aren't you forgetting you banged up his brother for

a life term? Why don't you go forth and multiply, Mr Diamond? Danny's busy.' She turned her head and shouted, 'Gary, we may need that dog again. The visitor is leaving.'

'I've got some questions for you,' Diamond said.

'*Me?* What have I got to do with it?'

'Do you want to come down to Bath, or shall we talk inside?'

'Hang about,' Celia said. 'What's this about?'

'I don't conduct interviews on doorsteps, Celia.'

'I've done nothing wrong.'

'So it's a trip to the nick, is it?'

She opened the door wider. 'You'd better come in, you sly bastard.'

The entrance hall was virtually a foyer, circular, with doors off, a grand staircase and a marble fountain. A life-size statue of a nude woman held up a shallow bowl from which the water cascaded.

Celia showed him into a reception room that seemed to have been removed from a safari lodge, with zebra skin hangings, Zulu shields, crossed spears and huge wooden carvings of animals.

She told him, 'I'm not saying a word without Danny here.'

That suited Diamond. 'Good thinking. You'd better fetch him right away.'

She was so flustered at being fingered as a possible suspect that she didn't realise Diamond had got his way.

He stood at the window taking in the view and musing on these villains' overview of all the little mortgaged houses like his own.

He heard someone behind him say, 'You've been upsetting my wife.'

'Someone murdered mine.'

He turned. Danny Carpenter, the best-looking of the

brothers, still dark-haired at forty-five or so, stood in a red polo shirt and black jeans in front of a mural of a stalking lion. Celia wasn't even in the room. No matter, now Danny had been flushed out. His short, bare arms had the muscle tone of a regular weight-lifter.

Diamond added, 'I'm trying to find the reason.'

'What reason?'

'Why she was murdered.'

'Not here, you won't,' Danny said. 'We're clean. Your people spoke to me already.'

'You've got nothing to hide, then.'

'I was at the gym.'

'And afterwards with your solicitor. I heard. A five-star alibi.'

Danny displayed his gold fillings in a slow, wide grin.

This stung Diamond into commenting, 'It's almost as if you knew something was going to happen.'

'Watch it.'

'Your brother Des is watertight, too.'

'This is going nowhere, squire,' Danny said.

'Don't tell me the Carpenter family draw the line at killing women. You could have used one of your heavies. Or hired someone.'

'You've got to be joking,' Danny said. 'Who do you think we are – Fred Karno's Army? Listen, if we wanted to get at you, we wouldn't top your wife.'

Put like that, it chimed with Diamond's own assessment, the main objection to the Carpenters as the killers: their uncomplicated notion of revenge would have resulted in his own death, not Steph's.

'If you want us off your back,' he said as if he was speaking for the entire police operation, 'you could tell me what the latest whisper is. Have you heard anything?'

'About the shooting?' Danny shook his head. 'What sort of piece was used?'

'Point three-eight revolver.'

'Doesn't say much.'

'It will when we find the weapon.'

'He'll have got rid of it, won't he?'

'Not necessarily,' Diamond said. 'This was a professional job, and professionals get attached to their pieces – don't they, Danny?'

'Let's leave it there before you say something that really gets up my nose.'

Not yet, he thought. Up to now, he'd got no signal that Danny knew more about Steph's murder than he wanted to admit. The purpose of this call was to assess the man, tease out the guilt if possible.

He tried another approach. 'You think your brother Jake's conviction was down to me, don't you?'

'You were on the case, sunshine.'

'He wasn't fitted up, you know. The girl's blood was on his shoes, in his car. This was no contract job. He flipped when she tried to sling her hook. You didn't see what he did to her face. I did. Seventeen, she was.'

Danny stared out of the window, unmoved.

Diamond said, 'There was never any doubt. The jury took under an hour.'

Still the brother was silent.

'PC Plod could have handled the case,' Diamond pressed on recklessly. 'Okay, Celia and the other women stood outside the court giving me lip, and one of them clawed my face, but they know it wasn't down to me. Your brother Jake is a stupid, sadistic killer.'

'Still family,' Danny said in a low voice, without challenging the statement.

'What's happening to Janie, then?'

'Who?'

'His girlfriend. The woman who marked me.'

Danny shrugged. He appeared to have no interest in

Janie. Or what she had done to Diamond.

Diamond reminded him, 'She was wanting to visit Jake. She said you and Des monopolised all the visits.'

'She'd better piss off back to London,' Danny said. 'She's nothing to Jake.'

'You haven't spoken to her since the trial?'

Danny shook his head.

'Is it possible Janie felt so strongly about the case that she fired the shots?'

'Don't ask me.'

'I'm trying to get your opinion, Danny. You said if the family was out for revenge you wouldn't target my wife. You'd go for me. Well, Janie isn't family. Is this a woman's way of settling the score? Does she have a gun?'

Danny turned to face him. 'You're boring me. Why don't you leave?'

'Maybe I should.'

He'd got as much or as little from this member of the Carpenter family as he was likely to. The trick in making home visits to known criminals is judging when to leave.

13

Ten days went by.

Ten more days in the process of grieving, this grudging acceptance of the stark reality. One day he decided he would take all Steph's clothes to a charity shop because that was what she would have wished (so long as it was not the one where she worked). He carried the dresses downstairs and draped them across the back seat of the car so as not to crease them. If the helpers in the shop decided to throw them in a corner in the back room or stuff them into plastic sacks, so be it. He wouldn't do it himself. Then, in a fit of sentiment he picked out one of her favourites, the fuchsia-coloured silk one she'd worn to the theatre last time they'd gone, carried it upstairs again and returned it to the wardrobe. It should have gone with the rest. There was no logical reason to keep it. He simply couldn't part with it yet. And when he looked at the other clothes, he couldn't be separated from them either. He drove around with those dresses on the back seat for days, reaching back to touch them at moments when he felt really down. You're a pathetic old idiot, he told himself when he finally removed them from the car and put them back on their hangers.

Of course he tried immersing himself in work, but that was fraught with problems he hadn't experienced before. The danger of working in isolation, he learned the hard way, is that you are forced to rely on hunches and theories. In a CID team, you have information coming in all the time, ninety-five per cent of it useless, but at least your brain is occupied reading reports and statements and checking the records. In the Yorkshire Ripper inquiry they had so many statements on file that the floor of the incident room started to cave in. The storage problem is less in this computer age, more a matter of pressing the right keys. McGarvie could cross-reference all known cases of murder using .38 revolvers; shootings in public parks; suspicious deaths of police and their families. He could analyse statements, classify the long list of objects found in Victoria Park and Charlotte Street Car Park, go through years of Peter Diamond's case notes looking for people with grudges. Bloody McGarvie had plenty to occupy him.

This parallel investigation of Diamond's had to be run on a wing and a prayer. A certain amount leaked out of the incident room, of course, through old colleagues, and he barged in there repeatedly on the flimsiest of pretexts, but it was obvious the team were under instructions not to tell him things.

One afternoon, in a quiet corner of the canteen, Keith Halliwell confided to him, 'The lads are on your side, guv, even if it doesn't look like it. There's a lot of anger about the way you're being treated.'

'I'm not looking for sympathy, Keith. A result is all I want.'

'It isn't sympathy. Well, you know what I mean. We do feel for you. Of course we do. This is something else. Personality.'

'The Big Mac?'

'He doesn't speak for the rest of us. We want you to know that.'

'He's doing the same as I would. I'm a hard-nosed git when I'm on a case, as you well know.'

In truth, he wasn't impervious to sympathy, or support from his colleagues. However, he would trade it for hard facts on where the investigation was leading – if anywhere. Too many theories are a pain. They keep you awake at night. They're difficult to disprove without the back-up of the murder squad.

His only back-up was the snout, Bernie Hescott, and he hadn't anything to offer when Diamond drove to Bristol for the fourth time and looked him up in the Rummer. 'I'm working on it, Mr D. Got more feelers out than a family of bugs. I'm not sleeping at nights.'

'Join the club.'

'Give me another week and I might have something for you.'

'This isn't what I came to hear, Bernie.'

'It's all the people I have to see.'

'You wouldn't be stringing me along?'

'No way. Wednesday, then. And Mr D . . .'

'Yep?'

'I've run through my expenses.'

He got twenty more.

Next morning, appallingly early, Peter Diamond's lie-in after a night of little sleep was disturbed by a heavy vehicle drawing up outside the house, followed by a voice issuing orders. He would have sworn and turned over in bed if the voice had not been pitched so low that it was obvious something underhand was going on. He groaned, sat up, shuffled to the bedroom window, and was amazed to see men in police-issue Kevlar body armour scrambling out of the back of a van. Two of them carried an enforcer, the 'fifty-pound key' used by rapid entry teams as a battering ram. Curtis McGarvie got out of a separate car and marched up the short path to the front door.

Diamond belted downstairs in the T-shirt and shorts he slept in and flung open the door. 'What the fuck is going on?'

McGarvie raised his palms in a pacifying way. 'Stay cool, Peter. We need to make a further search.'

'Go to hell.'

'Can we speak inside?'

'You're out of your mind.'

'I'd rather not have this conversation on your door-step.'

'What are you looking for?'

'The firearm used in the murder of your wife.'

'For crying out loud.'

'So I'm formally requesting permission to search your house and garden.'

'You can piss off, McGarvie.'

'I thought that would be your response.' He handed over a sheet of paper. 'This is your copy of a warrant issued by a magistrate last night.'

'A *search warrant*? This isn't happening.'

But it was. And you don't argue with a warrant unless you want your door smashed in. Diamond stepped aside, and three of the ninjas moved in. 'Why wasn't I told? You can pick up a phone.'

'Do you want it straight? I had reason to think you might dispose of the evidence.'

He was speechless.

McGarvie admitted more men, and every one avoided eye contact with Diamond. They obviously had their orders. They must have been briefed before dawn. Some went straight upstairs, others through to the kitchen.

Diamond slumped into a chair in the front room.

McGarvie told him, 'You know you have the right to ask a friend or neighbour to witness the search?'

'I don't need lecturing on my rights.'

'Don't you want to see what's going on?'

'No. This whole charade is a waste of time.'

'In that case why don't you get dressed? I'm going to take you in, whether we find anything or not.'

'You'll find sod all. You're out of order. I'll hang you out to dry for this.'

'It's all according to the book.'

'I opened the place to you before. You've been through here already.'

'That wasn't a full search.'

'God help us.' Diamond trudged upstairs and saw what he meant. Three men in the bedroom were ripping the fitted carpet from its stays. His entire wardrobe had been emptied and the clothes were on the bed. All the drawers had been removed from the chests and sideboard.

He looked out of the window. Two officers with metal detectors were at work in the garden.

He grabbed a pair of trousers and got into them.

At the nick – his own nick – they offered to call his solicitor. He said he'd done nothing wrong, so he didn't need one.

They kept him waiting over three hours.

His anger hadn't subsided. In the interview room with the tapes running he stared McGarvie out like a boxer at the weigh-in. A sergeant he'd never seen before was in the other chair. He was damned sure Georgina and most of the senior detectives were watching on video monitors.

McGarvie said in that voice like a rusty lawn mower, 'At the previous interview, you stated that you didn't possess a gun. Is that still your position?'

His thoughts flew to the empty shoebox in the loft.

They couldn't have found anything. He'd gone through the place. 'Yes, it is.'

'When you served in the Met, you were an authorised shot – right?'

'We've been over this.'

'For the tape, would you confirm it?'

'I was trained to use firearms, yes.'

'Were there occasions when you were issued with a handgun?'

'Yes.'

'A Smith & Wesson revolver?'

He said with mounting unease, 'That was the standard sidearm before they switched to automatics.'

'Point three-eight?'

'You know as well as I do.'

'At Fulham, where you served, guns were issued and returned according to procedure, were they?'

'To my knowledge, yes.'

'You always returned the guns you carried?'

'Of course.' This could only be leading one way, he thought with disaster bearing down on him. How could McGarvie have learned that he acquired that gun back in the nineteen-eighties? It had been signed out and signed in again.

'Before we go on,' McGarvie said with obvious relish in prolonging this, 'I'd better give you some background. We've been in contact with the Met.'

'The Met – what for?'

'A certain Smith & Wesson revolver at Fulham – where you served – went missing in nineteen eighty-six, about the time the change to automatics took place. It hasn't been traced since.'

'Nothing to do with me.'

'You were the last to be issued with it.'

'And I bet I returned it. Always did.'

'Yes, the paperwork was in order. But after that, there's no record of the gun with that serial number.'

'Not my fault. You can't stick that on me.'

McGarvie smiled with the confidence of a player with trumps in hand. 'Procedures at Fulham in the eighties were somewhat relaxed – shall we say? It's not impossible the issuing officer made a mistake.'

'Not in my case, he didn't. You just agreed it was returned and signed in.'

'The officer in question later appeared before a disciplinary board charged with negligence. A number of weapons couldn't be accounted for. Clearly the rules were breached in some way.'

'Am I missing something here? What has this got to do with my wife's murder?'

'She was shot with a point three-eight revolver. When I questioned you before, you denied owning one. You just repeated that denial.' McGarvie's brown eyes glittered. Reaching under the desk he took out a sealed evidence bag and passed it across. 'For the purposes of the tape, I am now showing the witness exhibit DO3, a police-issue point three-eight Smith & Wesson revolver recovered this morning from the garden of his house in Lower Weston.'

Diamond's voice shrilled in disbelief. 'What are you saying? You found this in my garden?'

'With some ammunition. Wrapped in a cloth in a biscuit tin buried in the vegetable patch.'

Vegetable patch? This had to mean the little plot where Steph grew tomatoes last summer. He was silent while his brain raced, trying to make sense of it.

McGarvie added, 'The serial number confirms this gun as one missing from Fulham since nineteen eighty-six. You were issued with it and apparently returned it. Do you have any explanation?'

He was up to his eyeballs now. A horrible hissing started in his ears – the old blood pressure problem threatening. After a long pause he said, 'I wasn't strictly straight with you just now. This gun has been in my possession ever since I was in the Met.'

McGarvie gave a grunt of satisfaction. 'So you lied.'

'Well—'

'You lied.'

'They were dangerous times. We had some hard men on our patch.'

'Face it, Peter.'

'You asked if I *owned* a gun. I don't. It's still police property.'

'Now you're playing with words.'

'Okay. I should have come clean when you asked me.'

'What stopped you?'

'Didn't want to draw you up a blind alley. All this horse-shit about the gun has nothing to do with my wife's murder.'

'Ho.' McGarvie turned to exchange a look with the sergeant beside him. 'And if it turns out to be the murder weapon . . . ?'

'No chance. It was in the loft of my house, in a shoebox.'

'Until when?'

Another crushing uncertainty hit him.

'Don't know,' he was forced to admit. 'After you interviewed me last time, I went up to the loft to look for it, and the box was empty.'

'Is this another half-truth?'

'No.'

'Why did you need the gun?'

'For protection. If you want it straight, I was losing confidence in your investigation. I thought I might need to open up some fresh lines of inquiry.'

'With a gun in your hand? Going it alone, eh – contrary to the ACC's instructions?'

Diamond shrugged. There were more important issues now than defying Georgina.

'If the gun wasn't in the loft, who could have moved it except you or your wife?'

'I've tried to think ever since I noticed it was gone. I don't have an answer.'

'You don't have answers to much. Sure you didn't panic after we visited the house? Sure you didn't take the gun from the loft and bury it in the garden?'

'I didn't bury it.'

'You didn't?'

He sighed heavily.

'Then who did? Someone trying to fit you up, I suppose?' McGarvie said with sarcasm.

'I've no idea. This is a total shock to me. Listen, if I wanted to get rid of the thing, why would I bury it in my own garden?'

'No one suggested you wanted to get rid of it. Far from it. You thought you might need it again.'

'This is unreal.'

'It isn't looking good, Peter. There's a time period on the morning of the murder when you have no alibi. You say you came into work, but no one here saw you before eleven.'

'I was in my office.'

'Keeping your head down – to quote you. Then, ten days ago, you brought in your wife's handbag.'

Incensed at the way things were being twisted, he blurted out, 'That was a responsible act.'

'In the bag was her diary with certain entries suggesting she'd been in contact with someone referred to as "T", and who – apparently – she'd arranged to meet in Victoria Park on the morning of her death.'

'Well?'

'We can't say for sure if those entries were written by your wife.'

'Jesus! Of course they were.'

'We've checked the record of phone calls made from your number. There's nothing on the fifteenth or the nineteenth. Both days are blank. There were no calls to "T".'

'Doesn't mean they didn't happen.' He cast about for an explanation. 'Maybe she used the phone at work, or went out to the callbox up the street.'

'Why?'

'For privacy. Or maybe she intended to call, but "T" called her first. There won't be any record of incoming calls.'

'I think it's more likely the diary entries are forgeries. Manufactured evidence.'

'Oh, come on.'

'An attempt to deflect attention.'

'It's Steph's handwriting, for Christ's sake.'

'I wouldn't call it handwriting. Most of the entries are printed.'

'Her printing, then.'

'Easy to fake.'

Diamond gave an exasperated sigh.

McGarvie added, 'You had plenty of time to work on it.'

'The diary was in the bloody handbag in the stone vase in the park.'

'That's open to question. Our search team didn't find it.'

'Because they didn't look in the right place.'

'They tell me they did.'

'They're covering their arses. Ask Warburton. He slung the bag in there.'

'He's a dipso. His memory isn't reliable.'

'He remembered enough to tell me.'

'So you say. You didn't pass the information on to us. That bag was potentially crucial evidence and you recovered it yourself, if your account is true, with no witness. Hours later, you handed it in.'

'I told you at the time, I looked at what was inside.'

'Did you write anything in the diary?'

'Did I *what*?'

'You heard me.'

'Oh, get away! You're losing it, McGarvie.'

McGarvie reached for the package containing the gun and drew it back across the table like a gambler who has scooped the pool. 'The next step is to have this test-fired and see if the rifling matches the bullets found at the scene.'

'You really want to stick this on me, don't you?' Diamond said. 'Have you given any thought at all as to *why* I would murder my wife?'

McGarvie was unfazed. 'Why would anyone murder her? She appears to have been a popular, charming, inoffensive woman. If anyone has a reason, it's you, and it's well hidden. I don't know what happened in your marriage, but it'll come out – unless you want to open up now.'

'You disgust me.'

'In my shoes, you'd think the same, Peter. The husband has to be the number-one suspect, and when he brings suspicion on himself, you act.'

A telling comment.

Diamond said bleakly, without conceding anything, 'What happens now?'

'I'll get you to write a statement about the gun. When ballistics have checked it, we can talk again. I'm not going to hold you here.'

'Am I supposed to be grateful? In the meantime, the real killer is laughing up his sleeve.'

'We're pursuing every possible lead.'

'Oh, sure.'

'Interview terminated at four twenty-six.'

14

The phone was going when he finally got home after six. He'd had all the hassle he could take for one day, so he didn't pick it up. They'd give up presently. He and Steph had experimented with an answerphone for a time. It hadn't survived long. It was faulty (or, more likely, his attempt to install it was faulty) and kept running the messages into each other. You'd get a 'Hi, Diamonds' from Steph's sister and then a male voice would come in selling double glazing, followed by the tail end of a message about a parcel some unknown firm had been trying to deliver for days. He'd ripped out the contraption in a fury and plugged in the simple phone they'd used before.

He took a brief look around. A search team executing a warrant was supposed to do its work with 'minimum disruption'. The door of the living room wouldn't open over the rucked-up carpet, the pictures were still off the walls and the drawers in the wall unit wouldn't close and were in the wrong places. Steph would have spent the evening straightening up. He ignored the mess. Out in the garden, he stood looking balefully at the place where the tin box containing the gun was supposed to have been found. No use denying there was a hole in the ground. One more weird twist to this nightmare. He had no explanation. His world had gone so crazy that he actually asked himself whether he could have buried the gun himself and wiped the episode from his memory. So much had been squeezed into the five weeks since Steph's death that certain things already seemed remote, if not unreal. Why would he have wanted to hide the gun – unless his brain had flipped and he'd done the unimaginable thing he'd been denying?

'Christ, no,' he said aloud. 'You may be so dumb you couldn't find your arse with two hands at high noon, but you would never hurt Steph.'

He returned indoors and the phone started again, so he lifted the receiver and clicked it dead. Made himself tea and tried to decide if he could stomach beans on toast again.

The cat wanted to eat, for sure. It pressed against his leg, making piteous sounds. He opened a tin and put down some food.

Then the damned phone went again. 'You're bloody persistent, whoever you are,' he said before finally putting it to his ear. 'Yes?'

'Where have you been?' a familiar voice asked. 'I've been trying to reach you for days.'

'Julie. If I'd known it was you . . .'

'Great! You just let it ring, do you? What if it was a real emergency instead of an old oppo wanting to know how you're coping?'

'What do you mean – "a real emergency"? Don't you think I'm in a real emergency already?'

'Still getting to you, is it?' Julie's voice sounded more concerned. As his deputy until a couple of years ago, she knew all about his mood swings. They'd led in the end to her request for a transfer to Headquarters.

'I'm up shit creek, Julie. The prime suspect. They searched my house this morning, with a warrant – would you believe? – drove me to the station and put me through the grinder. McGarvie thinks I'm Dr Crippen.'

'How ridiculous. Whatever for?'

He told Julie about the gun.

'That *is* a facer,' she agreed. 'Whatever possessed you to keep a gun? Oh, don't bother. What are they doing? Testing it?'

'Yes, and when it turns out to be the murder weapon, I'm screwed.'

'How could it be?'

'You tell me. I didn't expect it to turn up in a tin box in my garden.'

'You think someone is trying to frame you?'

'Trying? It's done and dusted.'

'McGarvie wouldn't stoop to that. You may not like him, and I understand why, but he's honest.'

'And so wide of the mark, Julie. He should be out there catching the real killer instead of breathing down my neck.'

'Yes,' she admitted. 'I thought he was going to make a fist of this. I misjudged him.'

'You're not alone.'

'But I told you he was good. I'm sorry.' She tried sounding a brighter note. 'What about you? I bet you haven't been sitting on the sidelines these last weeks. What have you dug up?'

'Sweet f.a., apart from Steph's diary.' He told her how he'd tracked it down with the help of the wino, Warburton, and how McGarvie was alleging that the entries relating to 'T' were faked.

'That man has certainly got it in for you. How did you get up his nose?'

'You know me, Julie. A touch hot-headed.'

'Only a touch?'

He sensed that she was smiling.

She asked, 'What else have you been up to?'

'I'm still convinced this was a contract killing. I called

on one of the Carpenter brothers – Danny. I can hear you saying "That wasn't wise", and you're right. He'd think nothing of topping me. He's bitter about Jake, never mind that the toerag got what he deserved. But Danny Carpenter wouldn't see the point in having Steph killed. That's too devious for him.'

'You count him out?'

'Unless there was some motive I'm not aware of.'

'But who else would hire a gunman?'

'I've been over that many times, Julie. McGarvie took me through all the cases I've had anything to do with in Bath and Bristol. Most were domestic. No one fits the frame.'

'How about earlier – when you were in the Met?'

'Bloody long time to harbour a grudge. More than ten years. It's true I came up against professional criminals more often in those days. But, Julie, the hard men think like Danny Carpenter: if they wanted to hit me, I'm a big enough target.'

Julie asked suddenly, 'In your time with the Met, did you ever rub shoulders with a DCI Weather?'

'Say that again.'

'Weather.'

Anything outside the focus of his attention was an effort to take in. 'In the Met, you said? There was a copper of that name at Fulham. We called him Stormy, of course. He could be the same guy. Chief Inspector now, is he? Why – have you met him?'

'No. His wife is missing. She's ex-police. A sergeant at Shepherd's Bush until a year or so ago. Pat Weather. I read about her in one of those Scotland Yard bulletins that get sent out – the ones you never bother with.'

'How long has she been gone?'

'More than a week.'

'Problem in the marriage, I expect.'

'I just thought I'd mention it. If some evil-minded crook was looking for a way to settle old scores, he might be targeting detectives' wives.'

He weighed the suggestion. 'You think this missing woman is dead?'

'I just wonder.'

'It's a big assumption, Julie.'

'At this point, yes. But if anything *has* happened to her . . .'

'Let's hope not, for both their sakes. But thanks. I'll keep tabs on this one. Stormy Weather. Right now I don't remember anything about the guy except his nickname, but he could have been involved in cases I was on. Let's see how it plays. Can't call him with the news that my wife was murdered when he's hoping his is still alive.'

'So what are your theories about the diary?' she asked him.

'This "T"? I'm foxed. Can't link it to anyone. And not for want of trying. I've been through our address book as well as Steph's.'

'If it's the killer, you can bet you won't find the name in your address book.'

'Right. The odds are on a new contact.'

'Does McGarvie have any leads?'

'I told you. McGarvie has convinced himself I forged the diary entries as some kind of red herring. Working out who "T" might be is not high priority.'

'Are you certain it's Steph's writing?'

'No question. It's printing, actually, but she often wrote things like that.'

'You made a copy?'

'Yes.'

'Then I think you should put all your efforts into cracking this one.'

'Tell me about it!'

'Maybe the people in the charity shop heard her mention something.'

'I'll give it a go. I drew a blank at the hairdressers'.'

'You'll crack it, I'm confident of that. Could "T" stand for a surname?'

'If you ask me, Julie, it's invented. The killer isn't going to give his real name, is he?'

'Depends. If it was someone she knew already, they wouldn't use a false name.'

'Good point. Actually, I can't see it being a surname. Steph liked to be on first-name terms with everyone. I reckon if she met the Queen, she'd be calling her Liz in a matter of minutes. I tried going through all the Christian names from Tabitha to Tyrone, but I'm convinced this is someone I haven't heard of.'

'Nicknames? Taffy? Tich? Tubby?'

'Those, too. I won't give up. I just have to cast the net wider.'

She asked how he was coping with living alone and he told her everything was under control, at the same time eyeing the curtain the search team had tugged off the rail. Why burden Julie with his problems? She didn't want to know that he hadn't slept properly since it happened, that he still reached across the bed for Steph, expecting the warmth of her smooth skin, and still ached for her wise advice, her marvellous gift of defusing the troubles he faced.

'Raffles has taken it harder than I have.'

'Poor old Raffles.'

'Cats aren't so forgiving as humans. He didn't like his litter box being searched.'

'That's a liberty.'

'Hasn't used it all day.'

'Where does he go?'

'Outside when I open the door – at the double.'

She laughed. 'At least they dug a hole for him.'

'You haven't seen the size of the hole. For a cat it would be like squatting over Beachy Head.'

'And you still can't think how the gun got from the loft to the garden?'

'No idea. That's something else I need to find out.'

'You ought to get the locks changed.'

'I should. There's plenty to keep me busy.'

'You're going to need some domestic help. A cleaner.'

'I'll cope, thanks. Life is complicated enough.'

'A cleaner would simplify it.'

'I can manage without.'

'You were always too stubborn for your own good.'

'Thanks, Julie. I'll have that on my tombstone.'

'No, there's a better epitaph than that,' she said. '"*Stuff 'em all.*" Good luck to you, guv.'

He was starting to speak his thoughts aloud. A bad sign, so he'd always heard. Worse, he was speaking to Steph as if she were there in the room.

'You've got some explaining to do, my love. Either you buried that shooter yourself, or you know who did. I don't see a sign of anyone breaking in. It happened while you were here, didn't it? But why, Steph?'

He'd never told her he'd kept the revolver all those years. She didn't know the threats he was under when he left the Met. That was why he'd hidden it in the loft where she hardly ever went because of her fear of spiders.

'Well, now,' he continued, as if she were standing in the room. 'Just suppose you *did* go up there for some reason and found the damned thing. You must have been deeply shocked. You hated guns and weapons of all kinds. It would get to you, having a handgun in the house. So I guess you may have decided you couldn't live with it. I can understand that. I can even understand you thinking of burying it. What I just can't fathom, Steph, is why you didn't mention it to me. I was secretive, yes, and I'm sorry for that, more sorry than I can say. But you were always open about everything. You would have told me, wouldn't you?'

He filled the silence with a sigh.

There was something else she hadn't told him. She hadn't mentioned a word about 'T' – whoever that was. There were three references in the diary to this 'T'. Two phone calls, and the meeting in the park, all in the two weeks prior to her death. And she'd had her hair done specially. All this cloak-and-dagger stuff was so unlike Steph. Maybe she didn't think it was important enough to mention. Was that a reasonable assumption? If 'T' was a woman friend, for instance, someone Steph knew well, and not a man, as the demons in his head kept whispering, might she have made these diary entries without saying a word about it?

Unlikely. She *always* told him things.

At best, she had acted out of character. At worst, there was a secret liaison with someone who turned out to be a killer.

And now, instead of talking to Steph, he turned on himself. 'You're a flake, Diamond. You're starting to mistrust her. While she was alive, she never gave you a moment's uncertainty. She was loyal right to the end. How can you think this way?'

15

This was a sharp suit, a two-piece by Zegna, in a pale grey woollen cloth with a faint blue thread. Harry Tattersall bought it for nine hundred pounds, off the peg at Selfridges. With his slim build the only tailoring he ever needed was to the leg length. The silver-tongued West Indian salesman told him he looked as smooth as a dolphin, which was meant as a compliment. Harry would have preferred to look like a lord – the object of this exercise – but he guessed he would also need a good white shirt and an old boy's tie to get the aristocratic effect.

The Arab way of doing things appealed to Harry. Who else paid cash upfront to kit out their team? These fellows had style. And the good thing was that his part in the scam would be over before the punch-up began. He'd be out of the Dorchester and hightailing it to a safe distance. Even if the others were all nicked, he'd still be sitting pretty in his dolphin-smooth Zegna suit with six hundred in the back pocket.

Rhadi called him at the weekend and asked if he was ready.

'Is this the lift-off, old chum?'

'No, no,' Rhadi said. 'I'm just checking that you'll be prepared when the time comes.'

'At concert pitch. I've bought the suit.'

'You had enough dosh to cover it?'

'Enough for a shirt and shoes as well.'

'And the disguise?'

'All under control.'

'Don't go downmarket for the hair colouring, will you?' Rhadi cautioned. 'Nothing looks worse than badly dyed hair.'

'A cheap wig.'

'You're wearing a *wig* for this?'

'No. You said nothing looks worse. I'm telling you a cheap wig does. Don't fret. I'll look the part.'

'Have you picked a name yet?'

'How does Lord Muck strike you?'

'For the love of Allah take this seriously, Harry. I told Zahir you're totally dependable. If you mess up, if he even *thinks* you might mess up, we're both dead meat.'

'He's as dangerous as that?'

'He's all right if you do the job. Now what are you calling yourself?'

'Sir John Mason. There are several in *Who's Who*. A computer-hacking friend of mine has found me the credit card details of one of them, and I've had my own card made by someone in the business. Satisfied?'

'It will do, I guess.' Rhadi cleared his throat nervously. 'Now, these are your instructions. Listen carefully. When the time is right – and we don't know when that will be – you'll get a call from someone who won't give his name.'

'This ex-RAF type?'

'He'll simply tell you that the goods you ordered are coming in on . . . and he'll name a date.'

'The payday?'

'Yes. Thank him and put the phone down. Don't say any more. Then it *will* be all systems go. First, you pass on the info to me.'

'This will be the date the Prince has booked at the hotel?'

'Right. Then you go to a payphone at some suitable place – let's say the Festival Hall – and call the Dorchester as – who was it?'

'Sir John Mason.'

'. . . and reserve one of the roof garden suites. Say you want it for a week.'

'A week from when?'

'The day following the date you have just been given. The Prince will be well installed by then.'

'I give them the credit card details. If they check, they'll find it's all kosher.'

'All right. You still have some money left, I hope?'

'A little. Good suits don't come cheap.'

'You will also need some new luggage. A case, of superior quality. Fill it with bulky objects unconnected with yourself. Cushions, newspapers – something like that. Be careful not to leave fingerprints.'

'I wasn't born yesterday.'

Rhadi said primly, 'I'm telling you all this because we won't be in contact again – not until after it's over. On the day, you must arrive in disguise, by a taxi hired outside one of the main railway stations. You will be carrying the suitcase. You check in to the Dorchester at two in the afternoon. No earlier, no later.'

'How do I let you know which suite I've been given?'

'Do you have a mobile?'

'Of course.'

'Get a new one. New number. Use it only for this. Once you're alone in the suite, call Zahir and tell him where you are. This is his number. Got a pen?'

'Go ahead.' Harry noted it. 'Do I call you as well?'

'No need. Shortly after, Zahir will knock. You will admit him, and Ibrahim, and your job will be over, apart from leaving discreetly.'

'I think I can manage that.'

'Where will you go?'

'Straight to Ireland. I have a cottage there.'

'Good man.'

'But I'll be back for the payout. A hundred grand, we agreed. I have to say this, Rhadi. Perish the thought, but if your friends should be so unwise as to change their minds about my share, I know enough to put you all away, and I can arrange it at no risk to myself.'

'Harry, that won't happen. These are men of honour. When they give their word, they keep to it.'

'They'd better.'

Georgina looked into Diamond's office on the Thursday, two days after the search of his house. 'Don't get up.'

Unusually he was at the computer, checking the Scotland Yard site for the latest on the missing wife of DCI Weather, the old colleague Julie had mentioned. There was nothing new.

'You look busy,' she told him.

'Raking through the embers, that's all.' He looked at her over the screen, fearing the worst. 'Have you heard from forensics?'

'About the gun? No. You know what they're like. It could take another week.' She remained standing, with her hands on the back of the chair in front of his desk. 'Peter, I'm sorry the search had to be done the way it was, without even telling you in advance. I sanctioned the application for the warrant after Curtis McGarvie convinced me you probably had the gun in your possession. It wasn't just a hunch. He looked at your service record, found you were an authorised shot.'

'He told me.'

'The point is that the fatal bullets could have been fired from a police handgun. The calibre—'

'I know this, ma'am.'

'And when he learned there were problems over the firearms issued from Fulham in your time there, and asked to see the records and found you were the last to use that particular gun, it couldn't be shirked. You'd already denied owning a weapon. You weren't going to put your hand up unless we produced it.'

'Which you have.'

'We're not being po-faced about this. You wouldn't be the first officer, or the last, to acquire a gun for his own protection. Because you denied it, we don't automatically disbelieve everything else you said.'

He listened in silence, thinking this wasn't the heart-to-heart it was meant to appear. She was doing her best to soften him up. When this didn't work, McGarvie would put the boot in.

'There's tremendous sympathy for you in CID – as there is throughout the station,' Georgina went on. 'You're under huge stress even without the extra pressure of the investigation. I have to say that Curtis has risked a lot of unpopularity from the ranks.'

'My heart bleeds.'

'He knew what the job implied when he took it on. He'll get to the truth.'

'He's taking his time.'

'That isn't fair, Peter. He's working flat out, and so are the team. If you'd been frank about the gun, you'd have saved him many hours of work.'

That angered him. 'If you really want to know, I didn't own up to the gun because I knew it would distract them. Yes, I'm out of order to have kept the thing, but everyone's wasting their time on it. It's six weeks since the murder and the trail's gone cold.'

'We don't know that. Other lines of enquiry are being followed.'

'Give it another two weeks and you'll be standing people down. We both know the score.'

'We're giving this top priority.'

'Next you'll be telling me budgets don't exist, Headquarters aren't already breathing down your neck for a budget report.'

'Peter, people are working overtime for nothing because of their loyalty to you. They want this killer caught.'

He nodded. 'So why are you talking to me, ma'am? What's behind this?'

Sounding almost maternal in her concern to keep him sweet, she said, 'Is there anything else you haven't mentioned? Anything we should know?'

She was fishing for the motive. The confession that his marriage was in trouble.

The devil in him made him lead her on a bit. 'Off the record?'

'There are only the two of us here.'

He could almost feel the heat of her charm.

'I'll come clean, then.' Leaning forward, he said, 'I loved my wife. Still do. Long after McGarvie has folded his tent and crept away I'll be on the case. It may never come to court, but it'll be solved, I promise you.'

Georgina's voice altered. He'd touched a raw nerve. She told him, 'How do I get through to you, Peter? We can't allow you to get involved. It would sabotage everything. You know that.'

'But I *am* involved. I'm your number-one suspect.'

'Now, come on. That's a bit much.'

'So who's in the frame apart from me?'

She was unprepared for that one. She could only counter it with an impatient sigh.

He said, 'If I don't point you in the right direction, I'm hung, drawn and quartered.'

'Oh, be reasonable.'

'Be reasonable? My place was searched twice. You authorised a warrant. You've taken away my wife's private letters, interviewed me on tape, looked for dirt in my career record, accused me of forging the things in her diary. Is it any wonder I'm starting to sound paranoid?'

She said, 'I've told you I'm sorry about the way some of this has been handled. You and Curtis are totally opposite in most ways, but you share one thing. You don't believe in sugaring the pill. I should have seen there would be personality problems when I asked for him. He's still the best detective I could get. He has my confidence – I want to make that clear.'

'You have, ma'am.'

'And in case you're wondering whose idea this conversation was, it was mine. I haven't known you as long as most of the people in this place, but I share their respect for you, and their concern. I want to see you come through this.'

'I will,' he told her. 'I will.'

On Monday morning he attended the inquest. It was mercifully straightforward, since the salient facts of Steph's identity, and where, when and how she came to be dead were manifestly clear. As the coroner explained, apportioning blame was outside his jurisdiction. The jury might decide murder was done, but the process of identifying who was responsible would be up to the criminal court. Diamond listened to the two main witnesses, Warburton, passably sober this morning and wearing a suit, and Jim Middleton, the pathologist. The facts of the case were so firmly lodged in Diamond's own mind that he could listen impassively, even when the phrase 'an execution-style shooting' was used. His own testimony was limited to stating when he had last seen Steph alive and explaining that he couldn't account for her being found in the park.

The police were represented by McGarvie, who gave evidence about the recovery of the bullets and the finding of the handbag and the diary entry. He said nothing about the discovery of the handgun in Diamond's garden, merely informing the court that enquiries were continuing.

The coroner adjourned the inquest, pending further investigations.

Outside, Diamond declined to make any kind of comment when the press converged. They took their photos on the move, while he marched briskly to the car park.

And then stopped.

McGarvie was beside his car. 'I know you've been waiting on the ballistics tests, as we all have,' he said. 'I called them first thing this morning.'

'And . . . ?'

'The results are inconclusive.'

'You mean the bullets weren't fired from the gun?'

'No. They can't say either way, so they're test-firing again.'

'At your request, I suppose.'

'Yours, also, I expect,' McGarvie said with a faint smirk. 'It's in everyone's interest to have the truth, I would have thought.'

'Did they find any prints on the gun?'

'Wiped. It was wrapped in a cloth.'

Diamond got into his car and drove back to Bath.

'Inconclusive' meant that the rifling on the test round was not identical with the bullets they'd found, but close enough for suspicion. One bullet had been crushed by some emergency vehicle and was probably unsuitable for ballistic analysis. The other had passed through bone and possibly struck stone when hitting the ground, and the match was likely to be less than perfect. Like fingerprinting, ballistic proof depends on sufficient points of similarity.

So he still faced the sickening possibility that Steph had been murdered with the gun he had stupidly kept all those years. How the killer had found it, he could only guess. He had two hypotheses, equally painful to accept. Firstly, it was possible Steph had discovered the gun herself and instead of asking him what the hell he was doing with it she had confided in someone she mistakenly believed she could trust – this 'T'. Theory number two: she had trusted someone, some Trojan Horse, so well that he was given the run of the house and went up into the loft and found the gun. It seemed fantastic, but a fantastic crime required a fantastic explanation.

He bought a burger and a beer and sat in his usual seat below the west front of the Abbey where the mediaeval stone angels scarred and mutilated by five hundred years of weather clung resolutely to their ladders. Watching them at the edge of his vision he sometimes caught them on the move. He'd fix his gaze on the left side, and the angels on the right would climb up a rung or two, always upwards. He knew it was impossible and an optical illusion, but it lifted his own spirits when it happened.

The events of the last twenty-four hours were being manipulated by the police to make him break faith with Steph. Uncomfortable facts had to be faced. What other construction was there to put on the entries she'd made in the diary than that she was meeting somebody she'd never mentioned to him? None he could think of. Fair enough, she was his wife, not his ten-year-old daughter, and she had a perfect right to meet people without telling him every detail. She didn't demand to know how he spent every hour of each day. Yet it wasn't in Steph's nature to have secrets from him. She was open about everything. She would enjoy telling him how she'd spent each day and he'd looked forward every evening to hearing her lively slant on the things she'd done and the contacts she'd made. This had been one of the strengths of their marriage. Nothing had been off-limits.

Nothing except . . .

He sat forward and his hand went to his face. There *was* a part of her life they scarcely ever mentioned. Her first marriage, a time of such unhappiness that it never lost the power to hurt.

Her dipstick ex-husband, who hadn't bothered to turn up to the funeral, nor even leave a message that he regretted her cruel death, had been called Edward. That was the name she'd used on the rare occasions she spoke of him. Edward. The formality distanced him from her.

Edward Dixon-Bligh.

What a mouthful.

Surely when she lived with him she would have called him Ted.

His eyes travelled up the Abbey front. One of those angels had just moved.

16

That evening he repeatedly tried the London number he believed was Dixon-Bligh's and kept getting the same answerphone message: a plummy voice asking the caller to leave a name and number and 'I'll get back to you toot-sweet.' It grated after the third or fourth try, especially as the message didn't supply a name. Never having met the man, he couldn't tell for certain if the voice belonged to Steph's ex.

He left a message saying it was extremely important that they spoke, however late.

But in this case, 'toot-sweet' meant 'not tonight'.

Lying awake waiting for the call that didn't come, he tried to think of a reason why that pig of a husband might have resurfaced in Steph's life. The most plausible was that he'd run through his money and appealed to her for funds. She'd always been a soft touch, helping scatty friends who couldn't pay the phone bill and were threatened with disconnection. She sometimes bought the same *Big Issue* three times over to help homeless people. It wouldn't have required much of a sob story from Dixon-Bligh to have her reaching for her chequebook. She hadn't forgotten the misery of life with him, but she'd still fork out.

Even Steph, generous as she was, must have sensed that it wasn't a good idea to meet her ex-husband. She would have preferred dealing with him by phone and post. Most likely he concocted some reason for meeting her in the park. It had been written in her diary, so it was fixed ahead of time. Maybe he'd offered to hand over something that belonged to her.

Surely he wasn't blackmailing her?

Blackmail?

At night, a tired brain can dredge up dark thoughts, and Diamond's years in the police had given him plenty of practice. Was it possible Dixon-Bligh had evidence – letters, photos, press clippings – touching on some part of Steph's early life she had wanted to forget? Some youthful indiscretion? A drugs episode? Drunk-driving? A relationship with some notorious character? No, it wasn't about covering up old scars. It had to be more damaging. Could she have committed some criminal act that had gone undetected?

Come off it, he told himself. This isn't Steph you're thinking about. She was no more of a saint than any other spirited woman, but she wasn't into crime.

He turned over and looked at the clock. One-fifteen.

Then he sat up and switched on the light. This had to be thought through. If he was dealing with anyone else but Steph, he'd put blackmail top of the list. It was a classic set-up: the no-good ex-husband worming back into her life and threatening to tell all. He'd offer to hand over the evidence in return for cash. She'd agree to meet him on neutral ground. The diary appeared to confirm it.

Then what?

My God, he thought, as the scenario flashed up in his brain. She had armed herself. She must have gone up to the loft one ill-starred day and found that sodding gun. When Dixon-Bligh resurfaced in her life making threats and demanding money she'd taken it with her to meet him in the park. Most likely she had no thought of killing him. She'd meant to produce the gun and demand the return of whatever he was using as the basis of blackmail. That much was consistent with Steph's character. She had a streak of defiance and was as fearless as a tigress.

She had taken the gun with her, but she had no experience of handling it. Dixon-Bligh had grabbed it and shot her. If charged, he would offer that well-tried defence: there was a struggle and the gun went off.

But right now, he'd be thinking he'd got away with it. He'd have judged, correctly, that Steph wouldn't have mentioned the blackmail to anyone else. He wouldn't know about the diary entries.

Certain he wouldn't get to sleep for hours now, Diamond got up and pulled on the clothes he'd dropped in a heap in the corner a couple of hours before. He needed physical activity. Fresh air.

Fresh it was. A sharp east wind was blowing up Weston High Street, shifting the discarded packs and paper cups outside the takeaway. He pulled up the collar of his overcoat and jammed his old trilby more tightly over his bald patch. The occasional car passed him, but no one else was desperate enough to be walking the streets.

It was painful, this process of speculating on the bits of Steph's life she may have wanted to keep from him. It was alien to their relationship. She had known the worst about him and taken him on with all his faults, and he'd always told her everything. No, he thought, that isn't true. Who am I kidding? I kept things back. I didn't tell her I kept the gun all those years, mainly because I knew she'd hate to have such a thing in the house. And if I wasn't open with Steph, and she found out, she was entitled to feel let down. Was it any wonder she kept quiet about what happened after she found it?

Those diary entries hurt him, just as she must have been hurt when she found the gun. You work at your marriage, trusting, believing, and the more honest the relationship is, the more devastating is any deceit. The people we love the most are capable of inflicting the greatest pain.

Still, if there were ugly things in her past, he couldn't ignore them. He might feel guilty probing, but he'd sworn over her dead body he would find her killer. That outweighed everything.

His thoughts were interrupted. A car had crept up and was cruising beside him at walking pace. He'd got to the top of the High Street and was approaching the Crown. They came so close that he heard the nearside window slide down. Someone who'd lost his way, he thought, and turned to see.

It was a police car with two young officers inside.

'Do you mind telling us where you're going?'

'Home, eventually,' he answered.

'And where's that?'

'Just up there, off Trafalgar Road.'

'Out for a walk, are you?'

'That's the idea.'

'At this time of night?'

'There's no law against it.'

'Most lawful people are in bed and asleep. Don't I know you, chummy?'

'You should . . . constable.'

There was a murmured consultation inside the car, followed by, 'Christ!' Then a pause, and, 'Sorry to have troubled you, sir. There was a break-in higher up, on Lansdown Lane, and we—'

The voice of the driver said, 'Leave it, Jock.'

'Night, sir.' The car drew off at speed.

He shook his head and walked on.

In the morning he called the nick and told the switchboard he'd be late in. These days nobody objected. They were relieved when he was out of the place. He was an unwelcome presence, reminding everyone of the poor progress so far. He had the files of unsolved crimes to keep him occupied, supposedly, but he was forever finding reasons to look into the incident room.

He took an early train to London and was in Kensington by ten. The last address he had for Dixon-Bligh was in Blyth Road, behind the exhibition halls at Olympia, not far from his old patch. He wasn't in a nostalgic mood.

The tall Victorian terraced house was split into flats and the motley collection of name cards stuffed into slots beside the doorbells didn't include a Dixon-Bligh. He stepped back to check the house number again. Definitely the one he had.

He rang the ground-floor bell. This was not the kind of establishment that operated with internal phones. After several tries no one came, so he pressed the next bell up, and got a response. Above him, a sash window was pulled up and a spiky hairdo appeared. Male, he thought.

'Yeah?'

He said he was looking for Dixon-Bligh and didn't know which flat he was in.

'Dick who?' the punk said.

'No, Edward. Edward Dixon-Bligh. Man in his forties. Ex-Air Force. Used to own a restaurant in Guildford. May be sharing with a younger woman.'

'Never heard of him.' The head disappeared and the window slammed shut.

It wasn't unusual for people in London flats to know nothing of their neighbours. Diamond studied the names beside the remaining doorbells, and wasn't encouraged. Both looked foreign.

He pressed the first and got no response. The second was answered eventually by a woman in a sari who came down two flights of stairs with a baby in her arms.

He stated his question again.

She shook her head.

'You don't know, or you think he's moved?'

She took a step back and smiled and shrugged. She didn't understand a word he was saying.

But at least he got inside the building. Picked up weeks of junk mail heaped on the floor to his right and – eureka! – found a seed catalogue addressed to E. Dixon-Bligh. Without a date stamp, unfortunately. Showed it to the woman, pointing to the name, but she didn't understand.

He moved past her to the door of the ground-floor flat. There was a note pinned to it: *Sally and Mandy are at the shop all day.* Didn't sound like Dixon-Bligh. He went upstairs, past the punk's door, to the second floor. The woman in the sari followed. No one answered when he knocked at the door of the second-floor flat. According to the bells downstairs the occupier was a V. Kazantsev. He was probably at work, spying on the Foreign Office.

The woman joined him on the second-floor landing. The child was asleep.

He tried once more. 'Edward Dixon-Bligh?' Used his fingers to mime an RAF moustache, though he had no idea if Dixon-Bligh had one. This was desperation time.

She shook her head.

He returned downstairs, frustrated, and sorted through the junk mail and found a couple more addressed to Dixon-Bligh. No clue as to how long they'd been there. It was unhelpful that the Post Office didn't frank mass mailings.

What next?

He wouldn't leave this building without a result. Up he went to the punk's level. The door was vibrating to enormous decibels from inside. Pity the people upstairs and down. He hammered on it with both fists. At the third attempt he was heard. The punk looked out and said, 'Piss off, mate. You're wasting my time.'

Diamond's foot was against the door and he grabbed the man by his T-shirt. 'Who's the landlord?'

'Get off, will you?'

'The landlord.'.

'How would I know? I pay my rent to the agent.'

'Which one?'

'Pickett. North End Road.'

The woman in Pickett's was guarded. 'We never give information about clients.'

'This one seems to be an ex-client.'

Her eyes widened. 'Who's that?'

'A Mr Dixon-Bligh.'

Client confidentiality no longer applied. 'Certainly we know a Mr Dixon-Bligh. He was a tenant in one of our Blyth Road properties for three years, but he moved out at the end of February.'

'Where to? Do you know?'

She gave a bittersweet smile. 'I was hoping you would tell me. He left no forwarding address. We'd like to trace him ourselves. He owes two months' rent.'

'You didn't give him notice?'

'He did a flit. The first we knew of it was when Mr Kazantsev came in and said he'd heard there was an empty flat.'

'Kazantsev? So Dixon-Bligh had the second-floor flat?'

She checked the card index. 'Second floor. Yes.'

'Do you think Kazantsev knew him?'

'No. He heard from one of the other tenants. Blyth Road is a desirable address. Places there are snapped up fast.'

'Do you know what line of work Dixon-Bligh was in?'

'We never ask.'

'References?'

'Not these days. If they can put down the deposit – and he did – we take them on.'

In case the agency traced their runaway tenant, he left his phone number, but he rated the chance no better than a meeting with Lord Lucan.

He sat in a North End Road café eating a double egg and chips and pondering the significance of what he had learned. Dixon-Bligh had upped sticks at the end of February, just about the time of the shooting. He may well have returned from the murder scene in a panic, determined to vanish without trace. He was top of the list of suspects now.

But the trail stopped here.

He had no idea where to go looking for Dixon-Bligh. He doubted if it could be done without help.

Well, he'd served in the Met. That was the obvious place to start. He'd look up his old nick in Fulham. See if any of the team had survived into the new century.

The sight of the tarted-up new building was not encouraging and neither was the face across the desk. They were getting younger all the time. This one probably had to shave once a week.

'Afternoon, sir.'

'Is it already?' Diamond said. He introduced himself and asked if anyone was there who had served in the mid-eighties, and almost added, 'Before you were born.'

'I doubt it, sir. Do you know about tenure?'

He'd heard of it, and very unpopular it was in the Met, the system of moving officers between squads and stations. Nobody was allowed to dig in for ever. 'Maybe somebody I knew – somebody really ancient like me – has done the rounds and returned to base. Is there anyone fitting that description?'

He was invited to the canteen to find out, and there

he was recognised at once by the manageress, a big Trinidadian called Jessie. Her smile made his day. She wanted to feed him – even though he insisted he'd just eaten – so he settled for rhubarb crumble, Jessie's speciality.

'Have you seen Mr Voss yet?'

'Louis?' he said, his spirits rising. 'Louis Voss is still here?'

'He come back January. Civilian now. They make him computer king. On first floor with all the pretty chicks in tight skirts.'

That rhubarb crumble disappeared in a dangerously short time.

Louis (spoken the French way) had been a detective sergeant, a good ally through some hair-raising jobs at a stage when each of them had more hair to raise. They'd lost touch when Diamond had moved to Bath.

He'd altered little. The slow smile was still there, and the irreverent gleam in the eyes. He'd kept slim, too. 'Amazing,' he said, and Diamond guessed it was a comment on his own disintegration.

Louis must have read in the papers about Steph's murder, because he spoke of it at once, probably to save Diamond from bringing it up. He didn't ladle out the sympathy, but just said he was more stunned by the news than words could express. He remembered Steph from before they were married. 'Let's get out of this place and have a drink,' he suggested. 'If there's a problem, they can call me on the mobile.'

In the saloon at the Fox and Pheasant, a Victorian pub just off the Fulham Road, Diamond gave his version of the past five weeks, the full account, including the finding of the handgun.

Louis listened philosophically. He wasn't surprised that

the Met had passed on information to the Bath police about the lax firearms procedure back in the eighties. 'There's been such a stink over corruption in the past few years that this is small beer, the odd gun going astray. Old Robbo faced a disciplinary board and was retired early, as you know, but he still got his pension.'

'Is he still about?'

'Died some years ago. I'm surprised you kept the gun.'

'Forgot about it for years. It was up in my loft – or was until someone decided to bury it. You don't expect to have your own house searched.'

'Did Steph know you had it?'

He smiled and shook his head.

'She wouldn't have approved?'

'That's putting it mildly. I ought to have had more sense. But it's a side issue, this gun.'

'Unless they prove it was the murder weapon. You say they've done tests?'

'Inconclusive so far. The killer used a point three-eight revolver, same as mine, but there are thousands in circulation.'

'Looking on the black side, what if they prove it was your gun that was used?'

Louis had always been a dogged interviewer. Diamond took a long sip of beer and outlined his theory about Dixon-Bligh attempting blackmail, and Steph taking the gun to the park to demand the evidence.

'Wouldn't she have talked to you before doing something as drastic as that?'

'Normally, yes.'

'But blackmail isn't normal?'

'Right. And I guess she felt she could deal with Dixon-Bligh herself. I can't think what he had on her. I suppose we all have things in our lives we're not particularly proud of.'

'How long was he married to her?'

'Just a few years. Four or five.'

'And she didn't stay in touch with him?'

'No, it ended in bitterness.'

'Enough for murder?'

'I never thought so. He was the problem, not Steph.'

'If he did fire the shots, how would the gun have ended up buried in your garden?'

'Big question, Louis.'

'You must have thought about it. Wouldn't he have got rid of the thing some other way?'

'I can only guess he wanted to incriminate me.'

'But he wouldn't have known it was a police-issue weapon. It's a big risk, when he knows he's killed her, visiting your place.' Louis glanced at his watch. 'Would you like another?'

'Just a half, then.'

Louis had made a sound point. Reflecting on it, Diamond was less confident about his theory. But *someone* had taken the risk of burying the thing.

They were drinking Black Baron, a speciality here. When Louis returned, Diamond asked him, 'Did you hear about that woman going missing, the wife of Stormy Weather, one of the Fulham crowd from the old days, though I can't recall him too well?'

'Saw something about it on my screen. Marriage tiff, I reckon.'

'That's what I thought.'

'Changed your mind?'

'Obviously, I hope she's okay, but . . .'

'Hope you're wrong,' Louis said. 'I've known her for years. You'd remember her yourself, I reckon. She was around in your time here. Fresh face, bright blue eyes, dark hair. Bit of an organiser. We called her Mary, after Mary Poppins.'

'It rings a bell, but faintly.'

'Nice woman, anyway, and good at her job. She got to be a sergeant at Shepherd's Bush. Then she changed careers. Went into business on her own running some kind of temping agency.'

'Where do they live?'

'In the suburbs. Raynes Park, somewhere like that. Stormy is still in the Met, I think.'

'Just hope his wife is all right.' Diamond returned to the main purpose of his visit. 'So how am I going to find Steph's ex-husband?'

'He was local, you say?'

'Blyth Road – until the end of February.'

'Has he got form?'

Diamond shrugged. 'I wouldn't know. Owes a couple of months' rent.'

'Then it's going to be difficult, Peter. I can put out some feelers. Dixon-Bligh is an unusual name, and that may help. If you did this through official channels you might get a quicker result.'

'Can't do that,' Diamond said. 'It's only supposition up to now. A few entries in her diary that could – or could not – refer to him. Some things are starting to link up, but not enough for a general alert.'

They walked back together. The chance to air his thoughts to an old colleague had given him a lift. But the parting handshake they exchanged outside the entrance to Fulham nick was a reminder that he was going to have to battle on alone.

17

Two months had gone by since Harry Tattersall had bought the suit. He'd worn it a few times around the house so that it would feel comfortable and hang well on his trim physique. Two months. He was beginning to wonder if the diamond heist had been cancelled. Nobody had been in touch, even though his answerphone was always switched on. Arabs, of course, are well known for taking the long view, hardly ever giving way to impatience – something to do with riding camels vast distances across the desert. Or drilling for oil. He had to take the long view himself. A hundred grand would be worth the wait.

Finally the call came one Sunday evening about eight-thirty, and he was at home to take it in person, watching *The Sting* on TV.

'Yes?'

'Mr Tattersall?'

'Speaking.'

'The goods are coming in on the tenth of next month.' An accent redolent of blue-grey serge and brass buttons and high tea in the officers' mess, well up to Dorchester Hotel standards.

The phone clicked, and that was it. Harry thought: I wonder if he gets a hundred K just for that?

Slightly under two weeks, then. He poured himself a large Courvoisier.

He was relaxing with the drink, spending the money

in his imagination, with the movie still running on the box, when a troublesome thought popped into his head. Suppose this entire operation was a clever sting. There was a way of checking if the call came from the Dorchester. He got up and dialled 1471. The caller had withheld his number.

No sweat, he told himself. Any professional would do the same.

Next morning, positive again, he took the tube to Waterloo, came up the escalator to the mainline station and strolled in sunshine along the South Bank walkways to the Royal Festival Hall, where he used one of the public phones in the foyer.

He called the Dorchester and reserved one of the roof garden suites in the name of Sir John Mason for a week from the tenth.

Simple.

He called Rhadi and told him the booking was made for the tenth. They kept the conversation short.

Then it all went quiet again. He swanned around London enjoying the good weather, the parks and the pubs. Two days before the heist was due, he went into Boots in Oxford Street and picked some hair colouring to go nicely with the moustache he'd already bought. He spent a long time choosing. Sir John Mason, he decided finally, would favour Rich Chestnut. Personally he favoured rich anything.

18

McGarvie was suspicious when Diamond asked for the return of Steph's letters and papers. 'Why do you need them?'

'They were my wife's property and they belong to me. You've had them nearly two months.'

'You won't let go, will you? You won't leave this to us?'

'It's a simple request.'

'You can have them at the end of the week.' From McGarvie's tone it was clear he'd be going through every scrap of paper again in case there was something incriminating he had missed.

Diamond asked, 'What's the latest on the gun?'

'Still with forensics.'

'They're taking their time.'

'Does that bother you?' McGarvie said, his eyebrows arching. 'If you know you're in the clear, why do you keep asking?'

'Because all this concentration on me is bogging down the whole inquiry. You have a budget for overtime now, and it's being wasted. They'll scale you down soon.'

'You're not the only line of enquiry, Peter. The hitman theory is still a strong runner.'

'Well, obviously.'

'I'm glad we agree on something. The shooting looked professional. Two shots to the head.'

The image darted into Diamond's brain once more – and it hurt. He was getting better at hiding his grief. 'Who would have put out a contract?'

'Someone you sent down for a long stretch. It's not impossible to organise a murder from behind bars.'

'Like Jake Carpenter?'

'Or some other villain.'

'Apart from Carpenter, it's a long time since I tangled with a big-time crook.'

'We know that.'

'You'd have to go back to my service in the Met. The eighties.'

'Which we are doing.'

'Are you? I thought about this myself.'

McGarvie was quick to say, 'Would you care to share your thoughts?'

'Don't mind.' He knew they must have trawled through his career already. 'There was the Missendale case that got me into so much trouble.'

'The black boy?'

'Yes. Murder in the course of an armed robbery. A building society job. One of the customers tried to tackle the gunman and was shot in the head. Hedley Missendale was a known robber, and we pulled him in and he confessed. I wasn't the SIO – that was Jacob Blaize – but I did the main interview. Missendale was sent down for life, and then after two years someone else put up his hand and said he'd found Jesus and the murder was down to him.'

'Jesus?'

Diamond glared. 'No, this born-again Christian. He produced the gun to prove it. Missendale was pardoned and Blaize took early retirement and I was up before a board of inquiry. Well, you know. It's on my file.'

'You were cleared.'

'Officially, but there was stuff in the report about my methods. "*His physical presence and forceful demeanour were bound to intimidate.*" What was I supposed to do? Buy him a box of chocolates?'

McGarvie wisely passed up the chance to comment on Diamond's demeanour. 'So do you think it could be Missendale getting back at you?'

He shook his head. 'Hedley had a few dodgy friends, but I don't see him or his chums harbouring a grudge all those years. They lived for the moment.'

'He's in Maidstone Prison,' McGarvie said. 'Been there two years for RWV.'

'Is that so? He seems to be in the clear, then.'

McGarvie turned to another of Diamond's cases. 'You were on the Brook Green shooting.'

'Headed it. That night was just like the OK Corral, except they were using Kalashnikovs. Three men died. Basically it was a skirmish in a drugs war. Two barons claiming the same patch. We collared Kenny Calhoun and two of his heavies. They all got life. Calhoun was in Brixton, the last I heard.'

'He died last year,' McGarvie said.

'Did he? Can't honestly say I'm sorry.'

'The other two?'

'Logan and Crampton. Thickos. Guys who wouldn't remember their own names, let alone mine.'

'This isn't much help. Can you think of any other villain you crossed?'

'I'm doing my best. There was a mean character called Joe Florida we nailed for a protection racket. He was American, I think. Scared the shit out of Asian shop-keepers. He got a twelve-stretch, which means he could be out now and back to his bad old ways. Yes. Joe Florida.'

'Was it personal, between you and him?'

'It seemed so at the time. I haven't heard of him for years.'

'Was he the sort who'd gun down your wife?'

'Hard to say. He'd have gunned me down, that's for certain.'

'Was he organised?'

'You mean did he run a gang? Sure.'

'Joe Florida. I'll see what the Met knows. Are you sure there's nobody closer to home, apart from the Carpenter family?'

There was – but for the present, Diamond preferred to deal with Edward Dixon-Bligh himself. The case against Steph's no-good ex-husband was tenuous, and he didn't want McGarvie rooting around for the evidence of blackmail. So he shook his head. 'I've been over and over.'

And on Wednesday evening at home he had a call from Louis Voss. 'I think we've traced your man. One of the two women in the ground-floor flat did some detective work of her own. She has a business in Walham Green selling weavings – wall hangings, curtains, throws, that kind of thing – and she lent him a few items to brighten up his flat. She does that, apparently, and it helps to get her work known. When he did his flit, he took off with all the choice items she'd lent him, and she went berserk.'

'She found him?'

'She told everyone who came into the shop. That's the way to get the word around. One of her customers saw him walking out of Paddington Station last Sunday afternoon and followed him. He's living in some crummy street at the back of the station, right under the Westway flyover. Seventeen Westway Terrace. You'll be glad to hear Sally has recovered all her wall hangings.'

'I'll be overjoyed if she left him in one piece.'

'Will you come up again?'
'Tomorrow. And thanks, Louis.'

Seedy as Blyth Road had looked with its peeling stucco, it was state of the art compared to Westway Terrace. A hundred years of coal dust from the trains was sealed with the mud and oil sprayed from the flyover. A sane person would not have ventured there without a protective suit.

The first mystery: how did the place come to be named after a flyover when it obviously pre-dated it by half a century or more? He could only assume it had been called something else in Victorian times and was given a change of name during the twentieth century. One possible explanation for a change of street name was that the address had become notorious because a murder had been committed there. He was willing to believe it.

No doorbells here. He knocked at number seventeen and got no answer. These were labourers' dwellings of the two-up, two-down sort. He tried peering through the window and made out a square table with a newspaper on it. Some cardboard boxes stacked against a wall. He felt certain Dixon-Bligh was not at home. What mattered was whether he had left altogether after being tracked there by Sally – or was it Mandy? – the angry weaver.

He tried the houses on either side, and still failed to rouse anyone. He thought he heard a faint sound from within the second place, but they weren't answering for sure. It was the kind of temporary home illegal immigrants are dumped in after a long, expensive journey in a container. They'd hardly want to come to the door.

A forced entry was an option he preferred not to take. Better, surely, not to alert the suspect. Within walking distance was the Grand Union Canal and the upmarket area of Little Venice, with its trees, pubs and cafés. Maybe Dixon-Bligh had found work there. He'd been in the catering trade. For Diamond, it was a good enough incentive to leave this depressing street and go looking.

He had not gone far when a cyclist turned the corner and pedalled towards him: the first sign of life. A man of around his own age, dressed in a blue suit and flat cap, riding along in that focused way cyclists have. Diamond didn't hail him, as he might have done. Westway Terrace was a cul-de-sac, so it was certain that the cyclist would stop at one of the houses and there was just a chance . . .

His hunch was right. The man came to a halt outside number seventeen and felt in his pocket for keys.

A change of luck was overdue.

'Mr Dixon-Bligh?'

The cyclist turned and stared. There was panic, or guilt, or both, in the look. His hands gripped the bike as if he was considering escape. He didn't say a word.

Diamond stepped purposefully towards him. 'I'm Peter Diamond, Steph's second husband.'

He watched it register. *Diamond the policeman.* Saw the eyes widen, the jaw gape. Any jury would have convicted on that reaction.

'Mind if I come in?' Diamond asked, with a huge effort to sound friendly and disarming. 'I'm up from Bath to see you.'

'What on earth for?'

'It'll be easier inside.'

Dixon-Bligh unlocked and wheeled the bike in first, leaning it against the wall just inside. Diamond stepped in after him and closed the door. The place smelt damp and the wallpaper was coated with mould.

'I tried to reach you on the phone. The number I had was obviously out of date. Are you on a mobile these days?'

Dixon-Bligh was not saying.

'You did know she was killed?'

He nodded. It had been in all the papers and on radio and television, so he could hardly have failed to find out.

Diamond added, 'I tried to let you know about the funeral. She had a good one, in the Abbey. Lots of people came.'

The funeral didn't interest Dixon-Bligh. 'What do you want from me?' he succeeded in saying. He still hadn't taken off the hat.

'A cup of coffee wouldn't come amiss. Didn't get one on the train. Can't stand those paper cups.'

Glad, it seemed, of any opportunity to mark time while he marshalled his thoughts, Dixon-Bligh stepped through to the kitchen, and Diamond made sure he was close behind. There wasn't much in there, considering this was a professional caterer's kitchen. A packet of cornflakes and a cut loaf. One mug. Dixon-Bligh looked around for another and took one out of a box, still wrapped in newspaper from the house-move.

'You don't have many visitors, then?' Diamond remarked. 'I'm having to get used to being a loner myself. Can't say I'm much good at it.'

No matey response to that.

'Is this where you keep the milk?' He opened the small fridge to the right of the door and took out a packet of semi-skimmed and checked the sell-by date. It was just about drinkable. 'I expect you get a main meal at work, like me. You *do* work?'

Dixon-Bligh nodded and picked up the kettle and filled it. The old-fashioned gas ring had to be lit with a match. Then he took off his cap and hung it on the door, accepting the obligation to say something. Now that the words came, they were fluent and articulate. 'I'm sorry about the way she died, truly sorry. Thought about coming to the funeral, and decided against it. The point is, there was a residue of bitterness after we parted. The marriage had been a mistake. I'm sure Stephanie must have told you. Harsh things were said, deeply wounding on both sides. I'm ashamed, looking back. I gather she was happier with you.'

'It worked,' Diamond said, not trusting himself to say more.

The man was pouring on the oil now he was over the first shock. 'I decided turning up at the funeral would have been hypocritical. I should have let you know, written a note or sent a card at the very least. I have this tendency to turn my back on things I can't handle.' He took a packet of teabags from an otherwise empty cupboard. 'I expect her family came to the funeral. Her sister . . . the name has gone.'

'Angela. Yes, she was there.'

'Didn't approve of me.'

'Me, neither,' Diamond said to encourage confidences. 'She thinks my job contributed in some way to Steph's murder. She could be right.'

'Really? I hadn't thought of that.'

'Do you have any idea who would have wanted her killed?'

'None whatsoever. She didn't have enemies. She wasn't that kind of person, as you know.'

This comparing of notes by the two men Steph had married was taking out some of the tension. Dixon-Bligh may not have dropped his guard yet, but he was willing to respond to questions.

Diamond said, 'I was going to ask if you remember anyone who took against her, with or without cause.'

'From that far back, you mean? It's a long shot, isn't it?'

'You were in the Air Force when she met you, I believe.'

'True, and there were some weird characters around

then, but Steph didn't come across them. We weren't housed in married quarters. We had a flat in the city, and she didn't see much of the other officers. Even on mess nights, when some of the wives attended, Steph stayed at home because I was always on duty supervising the catering staff. Wouldn't have been much of a night out for her.'

'Where was this?'

'Hereford. Not a bad posting.'

'Hereford, right,' Diamond said placidly, making immense efforts to suppress his gut feeling that the man had murdered Steph. 'She spoke of it quite often, and I didn't link it up with the RAF. I thought she'd lived there at some earlier stage of her life. She liked it there. She more than once mentioned the view of the Black Mountains from the kitchen window.'

'Typical.'

'What's that?'

'Steph remembering the view. You could see it on a fine day, but most of the time it rained.'

'She was an optimist. And how about you? Did you like Hereford?'

'Unreservedly. Great pubs, good cider, terrific steaks.'

Diamond's eyes widened. 'Was Steph eating steak in those days?'

Dixon-Bligh grinned faintly. 'No, that was a personal memory.' The water had come to the boil, and he tossed a teabag into each cup and poured some in.

Judging that the preliminaries were at an end, Diamond sat at the table and asked, 'Do you mind talking about what went wrong in your marriage?'

'I don't mind,' he answered evenly. 'We went into it blindly, that was what was wrong. We were attracted to each other, very considerate when we were going out together, full of plans. After we married, after the nuptial bliss, I relaxed – or relapsed – and became the selfish bastard I am. To Stephanie, this came as a shock. Service life makes heavy demands anyway. A career officer is expected to spend time in the mess and she couldn't understand why I was out so often.' With a sigh, he said, 'If you want the absolute truth, I had affairs. My duties in the catering branch meant I had more women around me than men, and – well, you know how it is – there are always those who are game for some fun.'

'Did she find out?'

'Not for a while. She had her suspicions, I'm certain. Even so, our sex life was normal. I'm a twice-a-day man, or was, given the opportunity. I think if we'd had the child she wanted, we might still be married, regardless of my playing around. She was so keen to get pregnant.'

'I know.'

'The miscarriages did for us. She was weak and weepy and I couldn't handle that at all. I played away more blatantly than before. She found out and angry things were said and we split. Simple as that.'

'Had you spoken since the divorce?'

'Only when necessary. Some couples stay friendly, I know. In our case, it was impossible.'

'You say "when necessary". Did you get in touch in the weeks before her death?'

'No.' A flat denial without a glimmer of guilt. This was not what Diamond had come to hear.

'You're certain? Her diary mentions phone calls and meetings with someone.'

'Not me, old chum.'

The cockiness of that 'old chum' got to Diamond. He went for the kill.

'She called you Ted, I expect?'

'Hardly ever. I was Ed to her.'

'Easy to say now.'

'But true.' Dixon-Bligh widened his eyes. 'Why? Is this important?'

'The diary entries speak of somebody called "T".'

'And you thought . . .' He flushed deeply. 'Christ, I nearly walked into that, didn't I? No, she didn't call me Ted. Ever. You ought to know that. She must have spoken about me. Did she ever refer to me as anything but Ed?'

'She rarely mentioned you, and then it was always Edward. Never Ed.'

'Never Ted either, I'll bet.'

'I've been looking at witness statements. Various men were seen in the vicinity.'

'Matching me? I don't think so.'

The frontal attack hadn't succeeded. He made a tactical switch. 'Any idea who this "T" could be?'

'I'd have to think. It's not going to be someone from our Air Force days, surely. No, I'm at a loss.'

'When were you last in touch with her?'

'Must be at least two years ago, some photos of her parents I found among my things. I was running a restaurant, then, living in Guildford. I phoned Stephanie to ask if she wanted them sent on.'

'And that was the last time?'

'Absolutely.'

'Sure you didn't ask her for money?'

Dixon-Bligh shot him a hostile look. 'That's insulting.'

'True. Answer the question.'

'I didn't ask her for anything.'

'Maybe you demanded it.'

'Get lost.'

'You're skint. This place is a comedown from Blyth Road and you owe two months' rent there.'

'They'll get their money. That was a flat, and bloody noisy. This is a house.'

'It's a tip.'

'It's temporary – until I find something better.'

'Not the sort of place I'd expect to find an ex-RAF officer living in. What's the attraction? Are you working now? Something just a bike ride away?'

Dixon-Bligh said, 'What does this have to do with Stephanie's death?'

'Everything. If you're on the skids, and don't like to admit it, you could be lying about not asking her for cash. It's more than likely she was being blackmailed.'

'Blackmailed? What about?'

'Something in her past. Something you're well placed to know about.'

Dixon-Bligh sneered. 'You must have a lower opinion of her than I thought, you filthy-minded git.'

Weeks of bottled-up anger went into the punch Diamond swung at the man. The table tipped up and the chair crashed over. His fist struck the side of Dixon-Bligh's jaw and keeled him against his cardboard boxes with a crunch that must have shattered any breakable contents.

He was out cold, blood oozing from one side of his mouth.

Satisfying as it was, the blow had solved nothing. The encounter was over. Nothing useful had come of it.

Diamond walked out and slammed the door.

19

At the end of the week, he went to see McGarvie again.

'My wife's letters.'

'Ah.'

'You said you'd return them.'

'I did. And they're here.' McGarvie took some keys from his pocket.

What kind of man keeps his desk locked all day? Diamond thought. It doesn't demonstrate much trust in the rest of the team.

Steph's shoebox of old letters was pushed across the desk to him, together with a polythene bag filled with the invoices and assorted papers the search party had taken from her drawer.

'I expect you want me to sign for these.'

'If you please.' The sarcasm fell flat. McGarvie actually had a chitty ready. 'And there's something else.' He delved into the drawer again.

'What's that?'

Diamond was handed another polythene bag containing a single brown envelope. He was amazed to see his name on it, just the word *Peter* – amazed because it was written in Steph's hand.

'You can open it.'

'Seeing that it's addressed to me, I should think so.'

'I mean it's safe to handle.'

What did McGarvie think it was, then – a letter bomb? Steph taking revenge on her killer husband from beyond the grave?

'We've carried out the necessary tests.'

'Tests? What for?'

'Prints. Handwriting.'

'I mean why?'

'You haven't seen this letter before?'

Diamond frowned. 'Is that a trick question? No, I haven't. Was it with the others?'

'We found it in the biscuit tin.'

His heart pumped faster. 'What – the one the gun was buried in?'

'That's the only biscuit tin we've got.'

So Steph *had* written him a message. 'You didn't tell me,' he said, outraged. 'Why wasn't I told?'

'You'd better read it.'

Diamond unzipped the wrapper, took out the envelope and found a single sheet inside. In Steph's tidy handwriting was written:

My dear Peter,

Just in case you find this before I have the pluck to tell you, I had to brave it out with the spiders in the loft to look for my old violin, which I'd promised to give to the shop since I haven't played it for years – and I found the gun. It was a great shock, Pete. You know my feelings about guns. I left it there for a week, telling myself I would talk to you about it, and I kept putting it off, not wanting to cause an upset while you were so stretched on this dreadful Carpenter case.

I know you'll insist the gun was there for some good reason, but the knowledge that a weapon that could kill someone is in our home has been preying on my nerves. Please try to understand. Rather than creating

*a scene and making us both feel guilty I decided to
bury it and tell you when you're not under so much
strain.*

> *Your loving*
> *Steph*

He read it twice before asking McGarvie, 'Why wasn't I
told about this?'

'My decision.'

'I know that.'

'It could have been a forgery.'

'Who would have forged a letter like this?' His stomach
lurched as the realisation struck him. 'Me? You think I
might have written it?'

McGarvie gave a prim tug at his tie. 'Quite possibly,
as a diversionary tactic. I decided to have it tested for
prints. And have a graphologist look at it. You'll be
relieved to know it's genuine. And we found no trace of
your prints.'

'What do you mean: I'll be *"relieved to know"*? I've never
seen this before in my life.'

'Noted.'

'You could still have informed me when you found it.'

'Yes.'

'But you chose not to. Why?'

'If you *had* forged the note, you'd be puzzled as to why
we hadn't produced it.'

'Nice,' he said as the deviousness struck home. 'You
thought you could trap me into saying something about
it when I wasn't supposed to know it existed. Well, thanks
for the vote of confidence.'

'My priority is to get to the truth, Peter, not pander to
your feelings. You know as well as I do that in major
crimes it's standard practice to keep back certain information.'

He took a long, deep breath, trying to tell himself to stay cool this time. In McGarvie's shoes, would he have played it the same way? He couldn't be certain. The one sure thing was that the suspicion was real. It riled him that his so-called colleagues treated him as the major suspect. By now he should expect nothing else. He needed to put aside his anger and deal with the new evidence. And it was good news. It put him back on side, didn't it?

'If the note is genuine, then you know I didn't use the gun.'

'How do you work that out?'

He spread his hands to emphasise the obvious. 'Well, if Steph buried the gun herself, I couldn't have shot her with it.'

McGarvie shook his head. 'It's not so simple. She could have told you she'd buried it. She had every intention of telling you, just as she says in the note. It's possible she told you on the day the Carpenter trial ended.'

'Well, she didn't.'

'Then I ask myself how you reacted,' McGarvie ploughed on, ignoring Diamond's denial. 'You'd certainly have dug the gun up. You may have had a blazing row about it, just as she feared. It could have been the reason she was murdered. No, hear me out. If you shot her yourself, you had a neat get-out. Bury the gun again, with the note as your alibi.'

The blood pressure rocketed. 'You don't give up, do you?'

'Would you?'

He ignored that question and asked one of his own. 'If we had a blazing row and I shot her in the heat of the moment, how is it she was killed in Royal Victoria Park?'

'I didn't say anything about the heat of the moment. This was a planned murder.'

'What – to punish her for burying my gun?'

'The motive has never been established.'

Conversations with McGarvie were an incitement to violence. He bit back his resentment and tried all over again. 'Have you heard any more from ballistics? It's beginning to look as if mine wasn't the murder weapon.'

'They say they can't prove the bullets were fired from that gun.'

He held out his hands in appeal. 'So?'

'There's still a good chance they were.'

'What do you mean?'

'There are points of similarity, but insufficient for legal proof. As you know, the bullets weren't in the best condition. They may have been tampered with, prior to firing, to hamper the investigation.'

'How?'

'By scratching the jacket, or scoring it with a file to distort the rifling. It suggests a professional gunman – or someone with a knowledge of weapons.'

'Like an authorised shot?'

The drooping lids of McGarvie's eyes lifted a little, but he said nothing.

'Is that their last word on the subject?'

'Apparently.'

'Trust the men in white coats to foul up. So it's back to the drawing board, is it?'

McGarvie said with an air of self-congratulation, 'We're going on *Crimewatch*.'

'So you admit you've run into the sand?'

'Not at all. It's the right move at this stage. There must be more witnesses out there. After all, this happened in daylight, in the open, close to an enormous car park. We still haven't traced that jogger.'

Diamond had dismissed the jogger from his thoughts.

This was the woman Warburton had claimed he spoke to at the scene.

McGarvie added, as if Diamond had never seen *Crimewatch*, 'They'll do a reconstruction with actors. It's worked in the past.'

'And the best of British.'

'And what about you?' McGarvie said. 'What have you learned?'

'I'm not on the case.'

'Get real, Peter. We know you've been out and about talking to snouts – or is that just a blind?'

He wasn't being provoked into passing on information until he judged the moment right. He'd handle Dixon-Bligh himself.

'If I hear anything, you'll be told.' He almost said, *You'll be the first to know.* There were limits.

20

No question. Harry looked every inch the aristocrat when, precisely at two, he strode up to the desk at the Dorchester with a porter in tow wheeling in his smart suitcase filled with telephone directories.

'Sir John Mason. I made a reservation. You have my details.'

'Yes, Sir John. One moment.'

Harry glanced through his horn-rimmed frames at the staff behind the desk busy issuing keys and taking phone calls and printing out accounts. No chance of spotting the stoolie who had tipped him off. He'd be somewhere behind the scenes preparing medallions of venison with chestnuts.

'We've got you down for one of the roof garden suites, Sir John.'

'That's what I asked for.'

'Would you care to make a reservation for dinner?'

'Tonight I shall dine out, thank you.' True. Instead of sampling the *haute cuisine* of his fellow-conspirator he'd be grabbing a bacon sandwich at the airport cafe while he waited for his flight to Cork.

'Very good, sir. And would you care to order a newspaper for tomorrow morning?'

'*The Times.*' An uncollected paper outside the door was better than a 'do not disturb' sign at keeping the staff away.

'Jules will take you to your suite and show you how the key works. Enjoy your stay with us.'

'I intend to.'

He followed Jules to the lift and up to the roof garden level.

'Are you staying long, sir?' Jules asked.

Under an hour, if the Arabs are up to the job, he thought privately. 'Just the week.'

'London has so much to offer this time of year.'

'Let's hope so. Is the hotel busy?'

'Very.'

'Full of wealthy foreigners, I expect.'

'Quite a few visitors, yes.'

He hoped Jules might throw in a mention of the Kuwaiti Royal Family, but you don't get everything you wish for. And they didn't pass any white-robed gentlemen in the walk from the lift to the door of the suite.

He was shown how to use the plastic key and they entered a light, luxurious sitting room with original paintings on the walls. Jules hoisted the suitcase onto a stand and switched on the TV. A message flashed up saying 'Welcome to the Dorchester, Sir John Mason,' and giving a rundown of the facilities. Jules showed how the curtains worked and opened the doors to the bedroom and bathroom. Harry tipped him two pounds.

Alone in the suite, he took out his mobile and called Zahir.

'Yes?'

'Yes.' He gave the name of the suite.

So professional. Nothing more was said. He switched off and put on a pair of polythene gloves he'd thoughtfully brought with him, collected some tissues from the bathroom and busied himself wiping the suitcase to remove any prints of his own. His part in the scam was nearly over, thanks be to Allah. He looked at the time.

The doorbell buzzed. He opened it.

A woman in hotel uniform carrying a bunch of flowers. 'I'm Mary the housekeeper, just checking you have everything you require, Sir John.'

Everything except my dusky friends, he thought. 'I'm quite content, thank you.'

'May I change your flowers?'

He hadn't even noticed the lilies on the coffee table. 'If you're quick. I'm expecting visitors.'

She fussed with the vase and left with yesterday's blooms. Harry looked at his watch again.

Ten more minutes passed. '*Shortly after, Zahir will knock. You will admit him, and Ibrahim, and your job will be over.*'

Bloody long 'shortly after'.

He stood by the sliding windows and looked across the roof garden and noticed a movement behind one of the taller shrubs. First he thought it must be a bird or a cat. Then another movement showed it was larger.

Someone was out there.

The hairs straightened on the back of his neck. He backed away from the window, waited a few seconds and then took another look. The same figure ducked out of sight behind a bush, but not before Harry noticed he was cradling something that looked horribly like a sub-machine-gun. There was another movement at the edge of Harry's vision. Two of them at least. He had an impression of black uniforms.

Police marksmen.

Jesus.

He swung away from the window, back out of sight against the wall. It didn't take rocket science to work out that it was an ambush and he was cornered. They'd have men in the corridor as well, waiting to pick up the others if they hadn't nicked them already.

Hold on, he thought. They won't bust us until after the crime is committed. They'll let Rhadi bring the Hatton Garden man in here and they'll delay until the moment the diamonds are snatched.

They'll need to time it right.

The place must be bugged.

A listening device is so small you can hide it anywhere. There wasn't time for him to make a proper search.

His eyes darted left and right and lighted on the flowers the woman had brought in. Was she really a hotel employee? He stepped closer. Those enormous lilies could hide a microtransmitter with ease. The police couldn't have known in advance which suite would be used, so it was a cool move. He bent closer and examined the flower arrangement without touching anything.

The bug was there all right, lodged in the side of one of the spike-shaped buds.

He picked up the entire arrangement in its vase and carried it to the bedroom, placed it on the floor of the wardrobe and gently slid the door across. Then he returned to the main room, shutting the bedroom door after him.

He took out his mobile and called Zahir again.

An agonising pause followed. Then Zahir's terse voice asking: 'What is it?'

'Pull the plug.'

'What?'

'It's off. Cancelled. We've been shopped. Tell Rhadi, will you?'

'We can't do that.'

'Why?'

'He doesn't have a phone.'

'Christ.'

Harry switched off. Then he collected the flowers from the bedroom and replaced them on the table.

His old friend Rhadi was going to walk into the trap. Surely those bastards could stop him.

No, he thought. They'll save their own skins and to hell with everyone else. Thick as thieves, the saying went. Thick as thieves, my arse.

Think of a way out of this, Harry, he told himself. You're a con man, the very best. You can save Rhadi and yourself.

But it wouldn't be easy, up here on the top floor with armed men outside and every exit covered.

He made a rapid check of the rooms, looking for the ventilation shaft or the loft space he could use as an escape route. No such luck.

Determined not to be downed, he told himself he wasn't a goddamn escapologist anyway. He was a con artist. He'd do this his way. Sweet-talk his way to freedom.

He sat on the sofa, removed his gloves and gave the matter some thought.

Rhadi was going to arrive any minute with a Hatton Garden diamond merchant expecting to do business with a Kuwaiti prince. Or – far more likely – with a policeman posing as a Hatton Garden diamond merchant. The fuzz had obviously got advance information, so they would have planned this. They would send in one of their SO19 people, armed and ready for combat. At a signal from him, police gunmen would burst in from all sides.

Harry let out a long, nervous breath. He'd only agreed to do this because it didn't involve violence.

Every instinct urged him to get out now and plead ignorance and hope for leniency. Only his brain told him there was a better way.

The buzzer on the door sounded.

He got up and looked through the little spyhole and saw Rhadi in the corridor with two men, one carrying a briefcase.

He opened the door a fraction and peered out. Rhadi

saw him and looked horrified. It should have been Ibrahim or Zahir who opened the door. Harry should have been out of the hotel and on his way to the airport.

Harry said in the elegant accent he'd used when he was registering, 'A slight hitch in the arrangement, gentlemen. The Prince isn't here.'

'Not here?' Rhadi said in disbelief.

'We had an appointment for three o'clock,' the man with the briefcase said.

'Yes. His Royal Highness went for a massage and isn't back yet. You're welcome to come in and wait.'

'Who are you?' the man with the briefcase asked.

'Er – his secretary,' Harry said. 'Smith – Henry Smith. He's only at the fitness centre. He shouldn't be long.'

Rhadi stared at him. This wasn't in the script.

'Won't you all come in?'

The man with the briefcase exchanged a glance with his bodyguard companion, who gave the matter some thought and then nodded. The bodyguard stepped ahead and did a rapid check of the other rooms.

'Care for a drink?' Harry offered.

They shook their heads.

'Why don't we all sit down?'

Harry's mind was racing. He was certain these were policemen, and he was pretty sure the briefcase contained a video camera. There was an eyelet at one end that could easily be a hidden lens, and it was pointing at him. He said to Rhadi, 'We'd better remind the Prince about this. He's due at the Embassy at four. Why don't you go to the fitness centre and speak to him?'

'Can't you phone?' the bodyguard said.

'You don't phone a member of the royal family,' Harry said with scorn. 'Not when he's in the same building.'

'I'll go and speak to him,' Rhadi said, catching on at last.

The police were as undecided as anyone. Their game plan was in disarray and they had no way of getting fresh instructions without blowing their cover.

Rhadi was allowed to leave. If he had his wits about him, he'd bluff his way past the waiting policemen and go straight to the fitness centre and make his escape from there by a back exit. He was off Harry's conscience.

Alone with the heavy mob, Harry marked time for a bit. He noticed how twitchy they appeared. It made him feel more confident. He crossed the room to the drinks cabinet and was amused to see the briefcase being turned to follow his movement.

'Whisky, anyone? No? I think I will.'

He poured himself a generous measure. The next few minutes were to be a formidable test of the con man's art.

'How long have you worked for the Prince?' the cop with the briefcase asked.

Harry smiled, took a deep breath and answered in a West Coast American accent that amazed everyone. 'Matter of fact, my friends, I don't work for him at all. I'm on your side. I'm Roscoe Hammerstein, CIA.'

'Say that again.'

'CIA.' Harry put out his hand. 'Put it there, officer.'

The officer just gaped. His companion was frowning.

'Face it, guys,' Harry said, twisting the hand outwards and upwards in a gesture of candour. 'This is one gigantic cock-up. Don't know if my people are responsible, or yours. I spend fifteen months tracking these jerks, getting their confidence. Finally I make it. I'm on the team, and what happens? You guys pull the plug.'

'Are you saying you infiltrated the gang?'

'*Saying?* Why do you think I'm here? It sure isn't for my health.'

'You work for the CIA?'

'Didn't I say that?'

'What's the CIA's interest in these men?'

'Come on,' Harry said, almost convincing himself, it sounded so plausible. 'You know where they come from.'

'The Middle East.'

'Right on – and where do the world's most dangerous terrorists have their base?' He spread his hands. 'How do they finance their operations? From heists like this. A multi-million-dollar diamond job.'

'Can you prove any of this?'

'You mean do I have my ID with me? You think I'm crazy? There's no more certain way to guarantee a quick death.'

'You must have a control – someone we can call to verify this.'

'Sure,' he said smoothly. 'I can give you a number to call. But shall we decide what happens next? They could be back for a showdown any time now.'

'What was your plan, Mr Hammerstein?'

'To play along with them.'

'In robbery with violence?'

'I'm undercover. As an organisation we're not interested in how they raise their funds. We have a greater objective – the defeat of terrorism.'

'Are British security aware of your involvement?'

'I couldn't tell you. Listen, pal, I'm just an agent putting my life on the line. The top dogs decide who they tell.'

The other man asked exactly the question Harry had been waiting for. 'You say these are terrorists. What sort of terrorism are they involved in?'

'Bombings.'

He waited for it to sink in.

They weren't as impressed as he'd hoped. It seemed they still needed convincing that he was genuinely CIA. 'How did you know we were police?'

'It stands out a mile. There's the bug in the flowers.
The marksmen outside. The camera you're pointing at
me.' He stared into it and said, 'Hi, guys.'

'Do you think the other man sussed us?'

'Which other . . . ? You mean Abdul, the guy who
brought you up here? How would I know if he spotted
you?'

'He looked nervous when you opened the door.'

'Maybe he smelt a rat.'

'He could abort the job.'

'Sure.' Harry was content to let them find their own
rambling route to the point of panic.

'We'll know if they don't come back.'

'You bet.'

'They've been gone some time already. Which floor is
the fitness centre?'

'Couldn't tell you.'

The man with the briefcase said, 'We could be sitting
here like dummies while they make their escape.'

'Maybe.'

Another minute went by.

One of the cops looked at his watch. 'This isn't looking
good.' He got up and went to the window, returned and
sat with the others. 'What's in that?'

'In what?'

'The suitcase.'

Harry eyed the case he had personally filled with phone
directories and lugged here. He frowned. 'It's just for
show, I guess.'

'What's in it?'

'You've got me there.'

'You don't know?'

'I told you.'

The less talkative of the cops suddenly said, 'Jim.'

'What?'

'These people are bombers.'

'Jesus,' Jim said. The penny had finally dropped.

Harry stood up. 'You could be right. This damned case could be packed with explosives. They can detonate by remote control. We'd better get outta here.'

Jim was first through the door, followed closely by Harry. The corridor looked empty, but this was deceptive. Jim yelled, 'There could be a bomb in there. Clear the floor!' And immediately the doors of two other suites opened and men carrying sub-machine-guns came out. 'It's off,' Jim said. 'Everybody out.'

Harry had already picked his route. Instead of using the lift, which was open, he turned left and took the stairs. Before he was down the first flight he'd ripped off the moustache and pocketed the horn-rimmed glasses. On the third floor he emerged alone. The alarm system had just been switched on. Walking steadily, but without suspicious haste, he made his way along the corridors to the stairs on the opposite side of the building. He descended to ground level and strolled into the street and down the tube.

21

AND STILL THE KILLER WALKS FREE

Six months ago this week the wife of a Detective Superintendent was gunned down and murdered in Bath's elegant Royal Victoria Park, within view of the world-famous Royal Crescent. The most intensive investigation ever mounted in the city has so far failed to find the killer of Stephanie Diamond. In this special report, we examine the conduct of the inquiry and get the views of two of the principal men involved: Detective Chief Inspector Curtis McGarvie, who leads the investigation, and Detective Superintendent Peter Diamond, the victim's husband.

On Shrove Tuesday morning, last February 23rd, at 8.15, Peter Diamond kissed his wife Stephanie goodbye and drove to work as usual. It was the day in the week when Mrs Diamond caught up with household chores and shopping. On other days she worked as a volunteer in the Oxfam shop. That morning she was her usual cheerful self and showed no sign of stress. She didn't mention any arrangement to meet anyone, or visit the park, although a note was later found in her diary apparently fixing a meeting with someone she called 'T'. About 10.15, two shots were heard close to the Charlotte Street Car Park. An unemployed man walking his dog on the far side of the park heard the shots and presently found a woman's body in Crescent Gardens, beside the Victorian bandstand. Two bullets had been fired into her head at point-blank range.

Peter Diamond, the head of Bath's murder squad, arrived at the scene within a short time of the shooting, before anyone had identified the victim. One of several distressing features of this case is that he himself recognised the dead woman as his own wife. In spite of repeated appeals for witnesses, nobody appears to have seen the shooting. Police believe the gunman must have escaped through the car park, and video footage from the security cameras has been examined without any helpful result. A number of reports of drivers leaving around the time of the shooting have so far proved unhelpful. Eleven detectives and five civilians are working full-time on the case, which is believed to have cost three-quarters of a million pounds already.

The SIO (Senior Investigating Officer), DCI McGarvie, has appeared on *Crimewatch* and *Police Five* appealing to the public for assistance. A reconstruction was staged at the scene of the crime with a policewoman dressed in similar clothes to the victim. 'There was a huge response from the television audience,' the Chief Inspector told our reporter, 'and we fed every piece of information into our database, but we still lack the crucial evidence that will identify the killer.' McGarvie is convinced there are people who know someone who acted suspiciously at the time of the murder, and he urges them to get in touch as soon as possible.

THEORIES

Sitting in the incident room surrounded by photos of the victim, in life and in death, and a computer-generated map of the crime scene, DCI McGarvie outlined the main theories his team have so far produced:

1. The killer acted under instructions from someone in the underworld with a grudge against Det. Supt. Diamond. As a murder squad detective in the Metropolitan Police and Bath CID, Peter Diamond has been responsible for many convictions over a twenty-three-year career. The problem with this theory is that a criminal bent on revenge is more likely to attack the officer who put him away than his wife.

2. The killer was hired by the wife or girlfriend of a convicted man. It is felt that an embittered woman might have ordered the killing in revenge for the loss of her own partner.

3. The wife or girlfriend of a convicted man fired the fatal shots herself as an act of revenge. Such a woman with underworld connections might have access to a firearm, though shootings by women are rare.

4. Stephanie Diamond, an attractive woman looking some years younger than her age of 43, was shot by some obsessive person or stalker, a 'loner' who believed she stood in the way of their fantasies. Stalkers have been known to 'punish' the women they idolise for what they see as infidelity.

5. The 'T' mentioned in her diary was trying to blackmail Mrs Diamond about some secret, or supposed secret, in her past and killed her in frustration when she refused to pay up.

6. The killing was a mugging that went wrong. The killer drew a gun. Mrs Diamond resisted, or even fought back. The first shot was accidental and the second was fired in panic.

The difficulty with theories 4, 5 and 6 is that the shooting has the hallmarks of a contract killing. The murderer timed the shooting at an hour when Victoria Park was quiet. The scene of the crime was close to the Charlotte Street Car Park, enabling the killer to get away rapidly to a vehicle, if the police theories are correct. A .38 revolver was used. 'Two shots to the head are characteristic of a professional gunman,' says DCI McGarvie. 'People have been known to survive a single shot to the head. The second bullet makes certain.'

CONFIDENT

Curtis McGarvie remains confident of an arrest. 'This is by far the biggest test of my career in CID,' he admits, 'and it's taking longer than I expected. I thought there would be more witnesses, considering where the shooting took place. We've been unlucky there, unless someone else can be persuaded to come forward. We've done reconstructions, and we know the killer took at least ten seconds to leave the scene and return to the car park. We are pretty sure they used a car. Somebody, surely, heard the shots and saw the gunman return quickly to the car park and drive off.' He is conscious that the costs of this case are mounting and there is already pressure to scale down the investigation. 'Up to now, I've had unqualified support from the Police Authority. A long-running case is automatically reviewed by the top brass. We've had two such reviews, and my leadership hasn't been faulted. But I can't expect to carry on indefinitely at this pitch when we're up against manpower shortages and budgets.'

Detectives speak of unsolved cases as 'stickers' and hate to have them haunting their careers. The murder of a police colleague's wife is particularly hard to consign to a file of unsolved cases. 'Peter Diamond is a man highly respected by everyone who knows him,' says McGarvie. 'No one here is going to give up while there is the faintest chance of progress. He's in a difficult position, because even though he is a fine detective with substantial experience it wouldn't be right or proper for him to investigate the murder of his own wife. We owe it to him to slog away as hard as he would to find the killer.'

That killer, according to the profilers who these days assist the police on all challenging murder inquiries, is most likely to be male, efficient, unexcitable, with a link to guns, and some knowledge of Bath. He drives a car. His friends or relatives probably have suspicions about him.

FRUSTRATION

Detective Superintendent Peter Diamond, the victim's husband, is 50, and has an outstanding record in bringing murderers to justice. He admits to frustration at having to stay at arm's length from the investigation. 'I know the reasons and I respect them. If I got involved I would be open to charges of bias. But it's hard. My heart wants to do what my head tells me I can't. I'd like to be working round the clock on this for Steph's sake. I'm an experienced investigator, and I have my own ideas on what should be done.' But he refuses to be critical of the detectives working on the case. 'This is about as tough as they come. You need luck on any case, and they haven't had much up to now.' Echoing McGarvie, he adds, 'My main worry is that soon the cost of all this will panic the people who hold the purse-strings into scaling everything down.'

When asked which of the main theories he subscribes to, Peter Diamond is cautious. 'They should rule nothing out until evidence justifies it. There are compelling reasons to suppose it was some kind of contract killing for revenge, but it's still possible that the killer was a loner acting for himself – or herself. It's not out of the question that a woman did this. And there may be a motive the murder squad are unaware of.'

The shooting of Stephanie Diamond on that February morning put tremendous strains on her husband. 'You find out how much you depended on someone when they are taken from you. She was a calmer personality than I could ever be, very positive, with a way of seeing to the heart of a problem. She understood me perfectly. I don't know of anything you could dislike in Steph, which makes her murder so hard to account for. The killer has to be someone who didn't know her at all, or some deluded crazy person.'

After the shooting there was the added ordeal of being questioned about his own movements. Peter Diamond shrugs and says, 'It had to be faced. I'd have pulled in the guy myself, whoever was the husband. You always take a long look at the husband in a case like this.' But if he was at work in Bath Police Station, surely he had a perfect alibi? 'Actually, no. On that morning I went straight to my office and worked alone. There was no one who could vouch for me.' He adds wryly, 'I may look big and threatening, but off duty I'm a baa-lamb. I think I convinced them in the end that I wouldn't have dreamed of harming my wife.'

Peter Diamond's fiftieth birthday came four weeks ago. 'I didn't do anything to mark it – but then I wouldn't have done much in normal circumstances. Oddly enough I discussed the birthday with Steph the night before she was killed, and persuaded her I didn't want a so-called surprise party with old cronies from years back. That's not my style. We would have gone out for a meal together, Steph and I, and had a glass or two.' He is in regular contact with Curtis McGarvie and has co-operated fully with the murder squad, even to having his home searched and his wife's private letters and diary taken away for examination. He is as puzzled as the murder squad over the diary entries mentioning somebody called 'T'. 'This must be the killer,' he says, 'and the odds are strong that the letter "T" was meant to mislead, but the diary mentions phone calls and an appointment in Royal Victoria Park, which Steph hardly ever visited, so it has to be the best clue we have. What foxes me completely is that she didn't say a word about going to the park that morning. My wife wasn't secretive. She was the most open of people. I find it hard to accept there was something hidden in her life, but what other explanation is there?'

Peter Diamond continues his work at Bath Police Station, busying himself on other cases, trying to block out the knowledge that the incident room for his wife's murder is just along the corridor. Shortly before the shooting he gave evidence in the murder trial of Jake Carpenter, a notorious Bristol gang leader who was given a life sentence for the sadistic killing of a young prostitute. The possibility of some kind of revenge killing by Carpenter's associates was a strong theory early in the case. It has still not been ruled out entirely, but intensive enquiries in Bristol have so far proved negative. Diamond himself agrees that it was probably a mistake to link the killing to the Carpenter conviction. 'My own reaction was the same as the squad's,' he says, 'but with hindsight we may have leapt to a premature conclusion and missed other leads. The first forty-eight hours in any inquiry are crucial.'

TENSION

They work in separate offices on the same floor of Bath Police Station in Manvers Street, these two experienced detectives. Curtis McGarvie is the outsider, the man drafted in from headquarters. He is at his desk by 8 a.m. There is an air of tension in the incident room and it isn't just the pressures of the case. For this should be Peter Diamond's domain. He has led the murder squad for eight years. McGarvie refuses to let sentiment trouble him. He is a gritty Glaswegian, thin as a thistle, with deep-set, watchful eyes, a professional to the tips of his toes, focused and unshakeable. 'If I were this killer on the run, I'd be sweating. I wouldn't want Curtis on my trail,' says a colleague at Avon & Somerset Headquarters who knows McGarvie well. He has a long string of successful prosecutions to his credit. But his team in Bath are Diamond's men and women, loyal to their chief, wanting passionately to achieve the breakthrough, yet unfamiliar with their temporary boss.

Meanwhile Peter Diamond sits alone in his office

up the corridor sifting through other 'stickers', trying to give them his full concentration. He is a big, abrasive man who speaks his mind without fear or favour. Few in Bath's CID have escaped the rough edge of his tongue at some point in their careers. But right now there is a strong current of sympathy for this beleaguered man excluded from the action through no fault of his own. If commitment to the cause counts for anything, the killer of Stephanie Diamond will soon be found.

22

Reading the *Chronicle* piece, Diamond was surprised how much the journalist had coaxed from him. He couldn't fault the quotes. She'd done her job well. Deprived of Steph's company for all this time, he'd been a soft touch for a bright woman journalist. The interview, over coffee in Sally Lunn's, hadn't seemed at all intrusive. He'd found her interest agreeable, almost therapeutic, having his brain exercised with a series of unthreatening questions, the sort Steph put to him when he was more under pressure than usual. Thank God he hadn't said what he really thought of McGarvie.

For obvious reasons he'd kept quiet about the cringe-making incident of the revolver the search party had dug up, and he was glad McGarvie had not mentioned it either. His feelings about that gun were complex. There was a basinful of guilt. He deeply regretted being so stupid as to hang on to the damned thing all those years. It pained him that Steph had found it and been so troubled that she buried it. He was sick to the stomach that her last communication to him – a beyond-the-grave message – had to be a kind of rebuke, for all its sensitive phrasing. But he had to be grateful she'd written the note and buried it with the gun. One last rescue act. She had removed a great burden of suspicion from his shoulders. Imagine McGarvie's fury, just when he felt he'd got the sensational evidence he needed, at finding the note that put Peter Diamond in the clear. The counter-theory about Diamond finding the gun and murdering Steph with it and then reburying it had been the sophistry of a desperate, disappointed man.

Among those theories listed in the newspaper there was no hint of the suspicion about Steph's former husband, Dixon-Bligh. He'd given away nothing on that front because it was a line of enquiry he was pursuing alone. He didn't want Steph's past life dissected by the press or the police unless it proved absolutely unavoidable. If Dixon-Bligh or anyone else had tried to blackmail her, he would root out the dusty old secrets himself – and he didn't expect they amounted to much.

One question the gently probing reporter hadn't put to him: was it bloody-mindedness that set him against McGarvie at every turn? Bloody-mindedness? It's not so simple as that, ma'am. It's force of circumstance. I'm under an embargo, you see, orders from above to leave the detective work to the murder squad. But don't you feel bitter about all the horseshit thrown at you by McGarvie, the false charges, the invasion of your privacy? I've got broad shoulders. I can take it. Or the abysmal lack of progress in the investigation? It's a brute of a case, my dear. But if I'm totally honest, if you were to tease the truth from me, I'd be forced to admit that, yes, there could be a tiny chip on these broad shoulders of mine: I hate the man.

In the next week, doggedly pursuing his own line of enquiry, he took another trip to London and looked up Dixon-Bligh – or tried to. There was a twist in the plot, and not a welcome one. The house in Westway Terrace was empty. The boxes and the few bits of furniture had gone from the front room. A neighbour said she hadn't seen the gent for weeks. The Post Office had no forwarding address. Dixon-Bligh had done another flit.

*   *   *

The trains on the Portsmouth line to Waterloo had run better than usual lately. The winter problems of frozen points and leaves on the line had meant a few delays and cancellations earlier in the year, but compared to previous years the service was improving. Whether the credit went to Mother Nature or the railway companies was much debated by the regular commuters. But as long as the wheels continued to roll along the tracks it was all good-humoured stuff.

Then one September morning when it was still too early for frosts or leaves, an 'incident' (unspecified, except it was 'up the line') brought everything to a prolonged halt. People don't like sitting in stationary trains for any length of time. For one thing they have places to go to, appointments to keep; and for another they feel unsafe. There's that troublesome suspicion that the longer your train waits the more likely it is that another will come along behind and smash into it. There are signals to prevent such catastrophes, but signals have been known to fail.

In the 7.37 from Portsmouth, some people blocked out their nervous thoughts by turning to newspaper articles they would otherwise have skipped, about travel in the Greek Islands or training for the marathon. Others switched on their mobiles and rescheduled the morning. A few made eye contact with the passengers opposite and gave little tilts of the head that said you couldn't travel anywhere with confidence these days. This being Britain, not many words were exchanged at first, but after twenty minutes voices began to be heard.

'Where are we, exactly?'

'You talking to me?'

'I said where are we?'

'Almost at Woking, I reckon.'

'What do they mean – an "incident"?'

'Could be anything from a suicide to cows on the line.'

'I blame privatisation.'

'No, it goes back further than that. It all started going wrong about the time British Rail stopped calling us passengers. When I first heard myself being called a customer I knew they'd stopped trying to get us from A to B as their first aim. They were out to sell us things.'

'You mean the reason we're all sitting here is so they can empty the refreshment trolley?'

'Dead right.'

One man in a pinstripe let down the window and looked out. 'There's another train pulled up ahead of us. Must be the 7.07.'

'My sainted aunt,' a reader of the *Independent* said. 'They won't let us move until that one's well clear.'

The pinstriped man turned from the window and reached for his hat and umbrella.

'Where the blazes are you going?' the *Independent* reader asked.

'Up the line. I can't afford to sit here all day. I'm going to board the 7.07. It's a more comfortable ride, anyway. Better than this old rolling stock.'

'You want to be careful.'

'It's safe enough. I know what I'm doing.' He opened the door and stepped down onto the gravel at the side of the track and started walking.

'There's always one, isn't there?' a woman in a suit said, looking up from *Pride and Prejudice*. 'If he gets knocked down we'll have another hour to wait.'

But not two minutes later, pinstripe was back and asking his companions to open up and help him back inside. 'You're not going to believe this,' he said when the door was closed again. 'There's a leg down there.'

'What's he beefing about now?' the *Independent* reader asked.

'I said someone's leg is down there, or part of it, from the knee down.' Pinstripe put his hand to his spotted silk tie and tightened it. 'Horrible.'

'Where?'

'Just a short way along, by the side of the track at the bottom of the embankment. You wouldn't spot it unless you were down there.'

'It'll be a dummy from a dress shop.'

'No, it's real. I could see the raw flesh. It must have been chewed by a fox or something.'

'Leave it out, will you?' a *Sun* reader said. 'You're making me puke.'

'Has anyone got a mobile I can use? We ought to tell the police.'

'Do us all a favour, mate,' the *Sun* reader said. 'Leave it till we get to Waterloo. If you call the Old Bill now, we'll be here till lunchtime.'

Not everybody chimed in, but no one objected. Three minutes later, the 7.07 resumed its journey to London, and in another three minutes the 7.37 was in motion, leaving the leg behind.

The senior officers were sitting in armchairs and there was a table in front of them with filter coffee and chocolate digestives, but nobody was comfortable.

'As you know, I managed to get full backing from Headquarters,' Georgina was saying. 'We're in the seventh month of this inquiry, and they've given it one hundred per cent support.'

'So have my team,' McGarvie said. 'They've put in hundreds of hours of unpaid overtime.'

'I know. They've been terrific. We can be proud of them.'

Diamond said, 'But you're going to scale it down.'

'The office manager has shown me the costings, Peter. It's impossible to keep it running at this pitch.'

'You told me budgets didn't exist in this case. You'd
see it through, whatever.'

'That was in February.'

'And we're no further on. That's the truth.'

McGarvie took this as a personal attack. 'We're miles
further on. We've got statements, forensic reports, video
footage, we've recovered her bag, her diary and the
bullets, we've interviewed over six hundred people.'

'For what? Nobody's in the frame.'

'Are you saying I've mishandled it?'

'I'm saying this isn't the time to shut up shop.'

'Gentlemen,' Georgina called them to order. 'I don't
want this to get personal. We're all under stress, me
included. Headquarters are the paymasters, and I have
to listen to them. Curtis, you're going to have to manage
with six officers and two civilians.'

McGarvie swayed like a boxer riding a punch.

Georgina went on in the sock-it-to-them style she had to
use with these obstreperous characters, 'You'd better
decide who you want to keep. Peter, it's no use looking at
me like that. I know how you feel. This is no reflection of
how strongly we care about your loss and how keen we are
to bring this murderer to justice. The commitment is still
there. We have to face realities. Policing is about—'

'With respect, ma'am,' Diamond interrupted, 'I don't
need reminding about priorities and neither does he. We
both knew this was on the cards.'

'Right, then.'

'But why did you call me in?'

'You have a moral right to hear it.'

'Thanks.' He hesitated. 'I thought you might invite me
to take a fresh look at the evidence.'

Georgina's lips tightened. 'That is not my intention,
Peter, and you know why.'

'Off the record?'

'You're not to get involved. If you have any suggestions, you can pass them on now, and we'll be glad to look at them, but they won't get you on the team.'

He gave a slight nod, acknowledging the small, significant shift in Georgina's position. No longer was she treating him with suspicion, whatever the lingering doubts McGarvie harboured. 'So what's the focus now? Have we ruled out the Carpenters?'

Georgina looked towards McGarvie, who seemed reluctant to divulge the time of day while Diamond listened, but finally conceded, 'Our sources in Bristol haven't come up with anything. The word is that if some sort of revenge killing was authorised, Stephanie Diamond wouldn't have been the target.'

Georgina said, 'You mean they'd have targeted Peter?'

'Or the judge, or someone on the jury. Mrs Diamond would be well down the list.'

She said, 'That would hold true for any of the criminal fraternity seeking revenge for a conviction.'

'Yes,' McGarvie said, 'unless the killing of Mrs Diamond was seen as like for like.'

'Meaning?'

'Someone who was deprived of their partner – and blamed Peter for it – decided he should suffer the same way.'

'This is the theory that a woman is responsible?'

'Or a man whose wife was put away.'

Georgina swung towards Diamond. 'When did you last arrest a woman for murder?'

He cast his mind back. 'Before you took over, ma'am. Ninety-four. But there wasn't a man in her life.'

'So for all practical purposes we're looking at vengeful women,' Georgina said. 'What about the one who scratched Peter's face?'

'Janie Forsyth.'

'She was shouting about a stitch-up, wasn't she? And she was Jake Carpenter's girlfriend.'

'I've interviewed her twice,' McGarvie said. 'The big objection to Janie as a suspect is her behaviour after the trial. If you're planning a murder you don't draw attention to yourself by screaming in the street and assaulting a senior detective.'

'She was in an emotional state,' Georgina said as if that was the prerogative of her sex. 'She could have got a gun and shot Stephanie. Let's remember the shooting happened the very next morning.'

McGarvie said, 'Let's also remember where it happened. Mrs Diamond went to the park by arrangement. We're confident of that. The diary shows she was due to meet the person known as "T" at ten.'

'You're right, of course,' Georgina admitted at once. 'And she'd been in touch with "T" for some days.'

'Just over a week.'

'You now believe the diary is reliable evidence?'

McGarvie coloured a little and avoided looking at Diamond. 'We were cautious at first, but we now accept that the entries were written by Mrs Diamond. And if the first contact was at least ten days before the murder—'

'Remind us what it said.'

'"Must call T." That was on Monday the fifteenth of February. It suggests a prior contact.'

'All of which makes it unlikely that the Carpenter verdict was the motive for the shooting.'

'That's my interpretation, ma'am.'

'Mine, too,' Diamond said. 'Early on, before the diary was found, I was sure they were behind it. Shows how wrong you can be.'

'You have another theory.' Georgina spoke this as a statement. Whether she got it from intuition or the nuances of his tone, she spoke from confidence.

He wavered. He hadn't meant to bring Dixon-Bligh into this without more evidence, but the man was so elusive it was becoming clear back-up would be needed to stay on his trail. 'I don't know about a theory. Her first husband was called Edward Dixon-Bligh. I'm not certain of this, but she may have called him Ted.'

It was as if he'd just said the word 'walk' to a pair of dogs. They sat up, ears pricked, eyes agleam, and if they'd hung out their tongues and panted, they could not have looked more eager.

They continued to give him undivided attention while he told them everything – well, *almost* everything – he knew about Dixon-Bligh, and Steph's unhappy first marriage. The one thing he did not reveal was the thump he'd given the man the last time they'd met.

This new avenue of enquiry so intrigued them that nothing was said about Diamond defying the injunction to stay off the case. By now, Georgina and McGarvie knew they couldn't stop him doing his solo investigation.

'Did you ask him if he'd been in touch with her?' McGarvie said.

'He denies it, of course. Says the last time they spoke was two years ago when he found a photo of her parents and returned it.'

'And you think he's short of cash?'

'Either that, or he's on the run. He quit the Blyth Road flat at the end of February for a place no better than a tip.'

'The week of the murder?'

'Yes. And Westway Terrace looked a very temporary arrangement to me. He's moved on from there.'

'Where to?'

'Don't know. I haven't kept tabs.'

'We can ask the Met. Does Dixon-Bligh have form?'

'Not that I've heard of.'

'Does he strike you as capable of murder?'

He weighed the question, trying against all the odds to be impartial. 'He did the "I'm a reasonable man" bit. Said he'd put any bitterness behind him. Blamed himself and his affairs for the break-up. Called himself a selfish bastard. Said he was sorry about the way she died, but to turn up at the funeral would have been hypocrisy. I'm not the best person to ask, you understand, but listening to him, I had this feeling he was laying it on.'

Georgina said, 'He doth protest too much, methinks.'

Delving deep into the small cellar of quotes once laid down for his Eng. Lit. exam, Diamond said, 'Wasn't it the lady who protested too much?'

'Immaterial. I was making a general point.'

McGarvie, floundering, asked, 'Which lady?'

'Don't try me,' said Georgina sharply. 'Was he ever violent to her?'

'She never mentioned violence to me,' Diamond had to admit. 'She spoke very little about him.'

McGarvie, trying to recoup, thought fit to point out, 'As an ex-officer in the RAF, he'd have had weapons training.'

Georgina pulled a face. 'In the *catering* branch?'

'As part of his general training, ma'am. They all go through that. He may also have been issued with a handgun at some point in his career. A foreign posting in a war zone. Did he serve in the Gulf?'

'Couldn't tell you,' Diamond said.

'He's got to be interviewed as soon as possible,' Georgina decided. She asked McGarvie in an accusing tone, 'Why hasn't his name come up before this?'

There was some injured virtue in his answer. 'I was told he dropped out of her life a long time ago, and when he didn't attend the funeral . . .'

'It should have rung a warning bell, Curtis.'

*   *   *

Back in the office, still uncertain if it had been a wise move to put them onto Dixon-Bligh, Diamond listened to his voice-mail. The first voice up belonged to his old oppo, Louis Voss.

'Peter, I may have something for you. Could you call me back pronto?'

He closed the office door first. Then learned the hot news Louis had got from his computer, about a dismembered body found on the railway embankment near Woking. 'That's no big deal on its own,' Louis told him equably. 'Desperate people sometimes lie on railway tracks to kill themselves, but this doesn't sound like a suicide. This one has two bullet holes in the skull, and first indications are that it's a woman around forty.'

F or once Diamond did the approved thing: phoned the CID Headquarters at Surrey and asked if he might visit the scene. Making his pitch to a cautious-sounding inspector, he explained he was 'involved' in a case of fatal shooting that might conceivably be linked to the Woking incident.

Needless to say, his own CID wouldn't have regarded this as the approved thing. For the time being he preferred not to have them involved. McGarvie would be better employed trying to trace Dixon-Bligh.

'You're quick off the mark, sir,' the cautious Surrey inspector said.

'It's the computer age, isn't it?' Diamond remarked as if he spent all his time in front of a screen.

After a pause and some murmured consultations at the end of the phone, the decision was made. 'If you think it's worth your while, come down. Bowers is our man at the scene. DCI Bobby Bowers. He and his lads will be there the rest of today and most of tomorrow as well.'

'Is he extra thorough, then?'

'It's the location.'

'By the railway?'

'Horribly overgrown and on a wicked gradient and the body's in several pieces from all I hear. Are you still up for it?'

'Of course.'

'I'll tell Bobby to expect you.'

He looked at a map of Surrey. Woking is south-west of London, a short way south of the M25 and within five miles of another motorway, the M3. Convenient both for commuting and dumping a body.

It is also a main railway station on the Portsmouth line to Waterloo.

During the drive he prepared himself mentally for his first visit to a murder scene since that February morning that remained as vivid in his memory as anything in his experience. He wasn't sure how he'd react. The sight of the corpse should not trouble him, he thought. He'd seen plenty in his time, and they were all different. This one was in pieces anyway, and while that prospect might turn many people's stomachs, he would find it more acceptable than a recognisable body. The acid test would come when he met the professionals at the scene. He wasn't sure if he was ready yet for black humour. It was going to take an effort to stay calm, let alone join in.

In an effort to loosen up he tried to recall the wording of a press release – probably apocryphal – he'd laughed at many years ago during his training. It was along the lines of: 'Portions of the victim's dismembered body were buried in seven different locations. She had not been interfered with.' This time, it didn't amuse him.

Driving at his usual sedate pace, he eventually spotted the signs for Woking and by four-fifteen was there. It looked no different from any other dormitory town as the rush hour got under way. He crawled the last stretch in the queue along the A324 with the patience of a Buddhist. What's one murdered corpse when twenty thousand of the living have to get home for a meal and *The Bill* on television?

Surrey Police were well organised. Two caravans and several people-carriers were lined up in the street nearest to the scene. More promising than that, a mobile canteen was in place with some exhausted coppers in white overalls standing about drinking from cans. He parked as close as he could, introduced himself and accepted tea and a doughnut before moving on to a mobile caravan. He showed his ID to a uniformed sergeant and asked for DCI Bowers. The chief was down by the track.

The access was a short path through a public park where three little boys in the Manchester United strip were kicking a ball around. With just such little boys in mind, the railway embankment had been fenced off from the park, but the wire fence was rusty and holed in places. He could shake his head about young vandals, yet he remembered as a ten-year-old cutting holes in fences to trespass on his local stretch of track. The big dare was to leave pennies on the rails to see how the train wheels crushed them.

This July and August had been wetter than usual, producing a dense ground cover on the fenced-off side. The nettles and ferns were shoulder-high in places. From the top of the embankment Diamond parted some bracken and looked down on a sixty-metre stretch cordoned with crime-scene tape. Screens had been erected to shield the scene from passing trains. A team was at work stripping back the growth. Hot, backaching work. He'd done it in his time. You don't picture yourself scything a way through the jungle when you join the police. Sooner or later, it happens, and then you have to be grateful you're not excavating the council tip or up to your waist in stagnant water. That, too, can happen if you stay long enough in the lower ranks.

Someone pointed out the recommended way down to the trackside. It was a biggish detour, but the quick route would have been a steep slope straight through the search area. Surrey CID would not appreciate the big man from

Bath sledging in on the seat of his pants. He did the right thing.

Which of the search party was DCI Bobby Bowers was not immediately obvious. Three young men were directing operations from a chart of the search area pinned to a trestle table, and to Diamond's eye they looked like schoolkids. He gave his name and had his hand shaken firmly. Close up, Bowers, in a black polo shirt and faded jeans, looked marginally older than the others.

'You're from . . . ?'

'Bath.' He explained – with some telescoping of the facts – that he'd learned about the body from the police computer, and it might possibly have links with an unsolved case seven months back in Bath.

'Hope you're right,' Bowers said. 'We need all the help going.'

'What have you got so far?'

'Only what the animals left us. A well-chewed torso and one leg found here.' He tapped a finger on the chart. 'Skull, with two bullet holes and exit wounds, here, farther down the slope. The other leg – or part of it – on the gravel beside the track. And miscellaneous bits scattered over a wide area. Putrefaction well set in. The lads are calling her Charlie.'

'Ah,' Diamond said without fully catching on.

'Charlie – cocaine – she gets up your nose,' Bowers filled in for him. 'The pathologist estimates six months to a year on a first look, but he'll give a better estimate when he's had the maggots analysed.'

'Definitely female?'

'Unless it's a bloke in tights and a C-cup.'

'Age?'

'Too soon to make an estimate.'

'I was told she was about forty.'

'That's our impression from the clothes.'

'Any possessions? Handbag?'

'Not yet. We're still picking up bits.'

'Rings?'

Bowers shook his head.

'How about the bullets?'

'You're joking, I hope.'

'I suppose she was shot somewhere else and brought here.'

Bowers sniffed and looked away. 'Yeah, we worked that out.'

'Why wasn't the body noticed before today, with trains going by all day?'

'You didn't see the place before we started to clear it. You could hide the Red Army here and no one would know.'

'At this time of year, yes. What about six months ago?'

'The scrub would still have been dense enough to hide a stiff, no problem. There's years of growth. A railway embankment is a clever place to dispose of anything, when you think about it. Nobody much comes down here apart from railway workers.'

'So who discovered it?'

Bobby Bowers rolled his eyes. 'A prize nutter. All the trains are held up for some reason, stacked up waiting for a signal, so chummy decides to get out and board the one in front, the fast one he missed back at Guildford. He hasn't gone more than a few yards when he sees this half-chewed leg beside the track. Gets the screaming abdabs and climbs back on the train. But – mark this – he doesn't call nine-nine-nine till he gets to work. It's a crowded commuter train. You know what they're like these days with bloody mobiles going off every couple of minutes. Our wiseguy insists that the rest of the good citizens on the train told him not to call the fuzz right

away because it was sure to mean another delay. That's
your great British public. We finally got the shout at ten-
twenty.'

'You've made some inroads, then.' Encouragement is
always appreciated and Bobby Bowers sounded as if he
needed some.

And sometimes it has to be underlined. 'It's no picnic,'
Bowers said. 'My lads have a job to keep their footing.
The pathologist said he wanted danger money.'

'What did he say about the dismembering?'

'That's down to the foxes. They're rampant around
here. There's no sign she was hacked about by the killer.'
He glanced along the embankment. 'Ay-up – somebody's
found another bit.'

Conversation was suspended while they stepped along
the side of the track to where one of the search party was
waving. 'What have you got for me, Marty?'

'Two fingers, sir.'

'I know how you feel, but what have you got for me?'

Marty gave a tired grin. They clambered up the incline
to examine his find: the brown bones of the fingers with
enough skin still attached to link them at the base. They
were well camouflaged against the dark soil. The searchers
had to be eagle-eyed.

'You were asking about rings,' Bowers said. 'This will
be the little finger and the ring finger of the left hand.
We already found the right.'

'No joy, then.'

'None for us, anyway. The killer may have removed it,
of course.'

'Or she may not have had a ring.'

Some sinewy material remained attached to the bones,
and there were traces of varnish at the base of a fingernail, but there was no chance of finding the impression
of a wedding ring.

Bowers thanked his man and had the find marked and
called for a photographer.

Diamond asked about the skull. Was it still where they
had found it?

'No, the doc decided to lift it. It's in one of our boxes
waiting to be moved to the forensic lab. You can see it if
you want.'

They trudged back to the centre of operations. He had
the box opened and the skull grinned at him, or that was
the effect. The bared teeth and the curve of the jawbone,
picked clean by the joint efforts of foxes, magpies and
larvae, seemed to pass on the message 'Don't count on
me to give you any help'.

Trying to ignore that, he looked at the circular bullet
holes on the right side, just above the ear cavity. No exact
match with the pattern of Steph's shooting, but the firing
of two shots at such close range did suggest a professional
killing.

'Lift it out if you want,' Bowers offered. 'You might like
to look at the hair. Some is still attached at the back.'

'No need,' Diamond told him. 'I don't know what I'm
looking for. Dark, is it?'

'Tinted brown.'

He switched his interest to the teeth. 'One or two fillings, anyway. If you can find her dental records, you might
get a name.'

'A handbag would be quicker,' Bowers said. 'Did you
find one with yours?'

'Mine?'

'Your stiff.'

A pause.

Diamond made a huge effort to sound untroubled. 'Er
– it was hidden, but yes.'

'So you knew pretty soon who she was?'

'Right.' He put the lid on the smiling skull before it

unsettled him more. 'What about those clothes you mentioned?'

'We found a few. Want to see?' Bowers turned to a stack of cardboard storage boxes. 'These would tell you she's over thirty even if the bones hadn't. More Country Casuals than Top Shop.' He opened a box and took out two transparent zip-bags, each containing a shoe that didn't look the latest in snazzy dressing, even to Diamond's untutored eye. 'Size seven, squat, narrow heel. No bimbo wears things like this.'

Bowers opened another box and lifted out the tattered remains of a green padded coat in some man-made fabric. 'Ripped to shreds by the foxes. The fact that she was wearing a thing like this means she was probably shot last winter, or the spring.'

'It also makes it likely the shooting happened outdoors,' Diamond said more for his own benefit than anyone else's.

'Agreed.'

'What was she wearing underneath?'

'Woollen stuff for warmth, a thick pink jumper, though not much has survived. Black woollen skirt. Very little left of it. Imitation leather belt. Black tights. And Marks and Spencer underwear, same as yours and mine, I dare say.'

'Speak for yourself.'

There was a break in the dialogue while Bowers marked his chart with the latest find. The police work all seemed highly efficient except that each time a train went past one of the screens blew down and several of the search party had to shore it up again.

'What do you think?' Bowers asked, when the chart was updated. 'Any chance of a link between your stiff and mine?'

The force of that word struck home harder this time and it took some strength of will to let it pass. Bowers had no idea how close he was to being smeared all over his precious chart. 'It's a long way from Bath, of course,' Diamond succeeded in saying after a pause. 'The two shots to the head are the common factor, plus the sex and approximate age of the victims. Middle-aged women aren't killed this way. Mind, there are some differences in the m.o. Yours was hidden from view, mine left on the ground in a public park. She was found very soon after the shots were fired.'

'Who was she?'

'My wife, actually.'

Bobby Bowers gave a nod, then in a double take, a wide-eyed stare. 'Did you say . . . ?'

Diamond answered with formal precision, as if giving evidence, 'Her name was Stephanie. She went to the park to meet someone known as "T", according to her diary. She was gunned down in broad daylight.'

'Christ, I read about this.' Bowers raked a hand distractedly through his hair. 'Bloody hell. Didn't connect you.'

'Well, you wouldn't. You'd expect someone else to be on the case, and he is.'

This drew a frown from the young DCI. There is only so much you can take in at a time, even when you're a fast-track superintendent in a polo shirt and jeans.

With a candour that actually surprised himself, Diamond explained, 'I'm here unofficially, acting on my own. Way out of line, I know, but I mean to find out why my wife was murdered, and who did it.'

There was a forced interruption as a train went by.

Then, from Bowers: 'Have you found out anything of use?'

'Here? Not yet.'

'Are you working with the team on your wife's case?'

'Wish I was. Protocol doesn't allow it.'

'So you're doing a Charles Bronson?'

Diamond grinned faintly. 'Better not put it in those terms.'

'I'm glad you told me. I might have said something really tasteless. You don't mind me asking – were you and your wife—?'

'Happily married? Yes.'

'But you must have some theories why she was killed.'

'How much time have you got?' He was relieved the young DCI had taken it so calmly. That generation was less hung up on protocol, thank God. In the next five minutes he sketched out the main facts of the case, pausing only when another train thundered past. At the end of it, he said, 'If you hear all this again from a certain DCI McGarvie, do me a favour and try and sound interested.'

'McGarvie?'

'He's the SIO.'

'I may call him,' Bowers said.

'That's up to you.'

'Not much point till we know who the, em, victim is.'

'Right.' Diamond suddenly felt devious again, and he didn't enjoy it when Bowers had been so obliging. He had a strong theory who the dead woman was, but his maverick status made it necessary for him to keep it to himself. 'It shouldn't take long.'

Bowers looked less confident.

'So how do you think she was brought here?' Diamond asked.

'By road, almost certainly. As you saw, you can bring a vehicle really close.'

'You don't think she was pushed off a train?'

'Unlikely. Too many people travel on them. We're assuming she was driven here by night, already dead, and dumped on the embankment. Most of the torso was found high up the slope. You can park a van up there out of sight of any houses.'

'The killer knew the area, then. A local man?'

'I wouldn't bet on it,' Bowers said. 'The thing about Woking is it's so near the motorways. Driving the M25 is a joy at night. Any street map would show him how close he could get to the trains. He could have scouted out the route one evening and brought the body here the next.'

'He'd still need to have decided on that stretch of embankment.'

'Thousands of people use the trains. Some guy living as far away as Portsmouth could have planned it. Or equally someone in London.'

'Bath is way off the route,' Diamond said, as much to himself as Bowers. 'It's not too likely he came from Bath. The killer of my wife had local knowledge.'

'Doesn't matter where he comes from,' Bowers pointed out. 'A professional hitman does his homework first. They suss out the spot they want on a couple of visits.'

Fair point, Diamond had to admit. This young detective had a good grasp. He'd be an asset in any investigation.

When he drove out of Woking that evening, with the September sun shooting blood-red streaks above Bagshot Heath, he was mentally crossing theories off his list.

24

All the way back, chugging along in the slow lane of the M4 at a steady fifty (the fastest he drove under any circumstances), he argued with himself over his next move. He was home shortly after nine, and went straight to the phone and called Julie Hargreaves, the ex-colleague he could safely confide in. This link with Steph's murder – and he was ninety per cent sure it was a link – had huge possibilities, and no one else was aware of it yet. Ahead of the field now, he knew his dangerous tendency to rush fences, and even he could see that this one had a built-in hazard. Julie's advice was worth seeking.

They got the preliminaries out of the way. Yes, he was coping better than he expected, and yes, he was sorry he hadn't been in touch for months. The subtext, understood by them both, was the awkwardness he felt as a widower calling up a woman friend. You couldn't do it without suggesting you were feeling the strain of living alone. For her part, Julie said she was sorry they hadn't been in touch more. She'd tried phoning any number of times. She asked what had happened to the answerphone he'd once had.

'Binned it,' he told her, relieved to have something functional to speak about. 'More trouble than it was worth. And don't tell me I'm back in the Stone Age, or I'll come looking for you with my club. I want your advice, Julie, but not about phones.' He told her everything he

knew about the human remains beside the railway at
Woking. 'You'll understand what drew me there. Middle-
aged woman shot twice through the head, execution-style.
That's so rare in this country I can't recall any other case
except—'

'Neither can I,' she cut in. She was as keyed up as he
was.

'She's been dead six months to a year, they estimate.
It's mainly guesswork at this stage based on the clothes
she was wearing. The body's terribly chewed up.'

'And how long has it been since . . . ?'

'Seven months on Tuesday,' he said. 'February twenty-
third.'

'I suppose there could be a connection. On the other
hand,' she sounded a more cautious note, 'there are
obvious differences, aren't there?'

This was why he had phoned Julie, for her ability to
weigh the facts.

'Such as?'

'You said this woman was shot twice in the side of the
head.'

'I wouldn't make too much of that. Steph took one to
the forehead and one to the side. That could be down
to a head movement as the shots were fired.'

'All right. There's a bigger difference, isn't there? You
say this body at Woking was well hidden?'

'The weeds are shoulder-high.'

'Well then, the killer went to some trouble to take the
body there and hide it. She might not have been found
for years. Whereas Steph was shot and left in the open
where she was certain to be seen.'

'Okay, I'll give you that, Julie. It's not the same m.o.
at all.'

'And Woking is a long way from Bath.'

'That doesn't bother me,' he said.

Julie said, 'You're keeping something back, aren't you? Is she identified?'

'Not yet.'

'But you think you know?'

'An idea – that's all.'

She was there. It wasn't intuition or telepathy that made her say, 'The missing wife of that DCI? The ex-police sergeant. What was her name – Weather? Wasn't she found?'

Doubt flooded in. 'Was she?'

'I'm asking you,' Julie said.

He was mightily relieved. He'd built a mental case study of Mrs Weather's murder already. 'If she'd turned up, we'd have heard something, wouldn't we?'

'Maybe.'

'I'll check the Missing Persons Index.'

'What makes you think it's her?' she asked.

'Hang about, Julie. You put the idea in my head.'

She gave a quick, nervous laugh. 'Yes, I did.'

'And that was before this body turned up. Think about it. We know Mrs Weather went missing a week or so after Steph was shot. Early March. She'd have been wearing winter things.'

'Agreed.'

'You saw the computer item about her. Was there a description?'

'Nothing about clothes I can recall. There may have been something on her age and build. Hair colour. We can check again.' She paused before asking the key question. 'Why would anyone murder the wives of two policemen?'

'The wives of two detectives who worked out of Fulham nick in the early eighties,' he stressed.

She digested that for a moment. 'If it's true, it's going to transform the case.'

'Right – we can ditch all the cock-eyed theories and focus on this.'

'Where did Mrs Weather live?'

'Raynes Park, I was told by Louis Voss.'

'That's near Wimbledon, isn't it? How far from Woking?'

'Twenty miles, maximum,' Diamond said, sounding like Bobby Bowers. 'A hitman plots his route and goes where he needs to.' He hesitated. 'Julie, is this just one more theory, or have I struck gold?'

'I wouldn't go as far as that,' Julie said. 'But it deserves an airing. What's your next move?'

'That's my problem. Bowers is quick on the draw. It won't be long before he puts a name to his corpse. If she *is* Patricia Weather, they'll find out tomorrow, I reckon. All they have to do is check the MPI.'

'Against what?' said Julie. 'It's not so straightforward. They have some bones of a mature woman and some unremarkable clothes. No handbag, no rings.'

'Teeth.'

'That only helps if they can match them to a dental record.'

'They'll have a record for her.'

Still Julie doubted the efficiency of the system. 'They won't have her name – unless you suggest it. Remember there are different police services involved. I'll be surprised if anything is confirmed in the next twenty-four hours.' She paused. 'Is that what you wanted to hear?'

'If it buys me time, yes.'

'To outflank Curtis McGarvie?' Julie knew too well how he felt.

He said in his defence, 'It isn't personal. OK, I don't get on with the man, but I'm professional enough to put that aside. My confidence was shattered when he turned up on my doorstep with that search warrant. That was overkill, Julie. My worry is that when he gets this information, he'll cock up. The killer will get wise and head for the hills.'

'McGarvie is smarter than that.'

'I can't take the risk.'

She sounded sceptical when she asked, 'What can you do on your own?'

'If my gut feeling is right, and this body is Weather's wife, I'll know this goes back fifteen years, to my time in the Met. Some psycho out there has a major grudge against Stormy Weather and me. We need to compare notes.'

'You'd tell him?' Now there was definite disapproval in her voice.

'That's the size of it, Julie. Poor sod, he's going to be poleaxed when he finds out his wife has been lying dead for six months, half eaten by foxes.'

'You can't tell him that. You don't know for sure.'

'He'll read about the body in the paper tomorrow. It's going to cross his mind, isn't it?'

'That may be so, Peter, but I think you're making a mistake here. You should let things take their course.'

'What? Wait for everyone to find out?'

'Mm.'

'For Christ's sake, why?'

Julie said in the firm tone she'd learned to use when this ex-boss of hers was at his most overbearing, 'You're asking for my advice, and this is it. Talking to Weather at this stage isn't going to help you. He'll be in no state to think straight.'

He was silent, locked into his own thoughts, forced to accept the simple truth of her conclusion. 'That's a point. I wasn't.'

She waited a moment, making sure it had sunk in. 'So you'll stay clear?'

He sighed heavily. 'Of Stormy? I guess I'll have to. But I can do some ferreting of my own – with a little help from my old chum Louis Voss – getting up to speed with stuff I thought I'd never need to bother with again.'

'Case files from the nineteen-eighties?'

'Yes.'

'Property of the Met? Dodgy.'

'You're not going to give me another no, no?'

'I wouldn't dream of it, guv.'

After putting down the phone he fed the cat from one tin and himself from another. The basics of existence. Coping better than I expected, he'd claimed to Julie. True, in a way. He didn't have space in his life for self-pity. The drive to find Steph's killer occupied him totally.

But he would let Stormy Weather have one more night in ignorance.

He put in an early appearance at the nick next morning. Early by his standards. Curtis McGarvie, the focused, committed, hot-shit detective was always in by eight and expected the incident room to be humming when he arrived. An impressive regime – and what results had it achieved?

So Diamond looked in about eight-thirty, trying to fix his eyes on people rather than the photos of Steph's body displayed along one wall. There was a school of thought that said a murder squad worked better with visual reminders of the crime all around them. He'd never subscribed to it.

Keith Halliwell came over. 'All right, guv?'

'Fair to middling. Is robocop about?'

'Upstairs with the ACC. Something he saw in the papers.'

No prize for guessing. He'd catch up with the papers

shortly. 'Maybe you can tell me, Keith. What's the latest take on Dixon-Bligh, Steph's ex?'

'None that I heard. We asked the Met to trace him if they can. Thought it would be straightforward, but nothing has come through. He's covered his tracks apparently.'

'I put the frighteners on him. Between you and me, Keith, he gave me some lip and I stuck one on him. Better not tell your boss.'

'I won't. Is he a toerag, then?'

Diamond couldn't let it pass. 'Who do you mean?'

Straight-faced, Halliwell said, 'Dixon-Bligh.' He'd missed the point entirely, which was a good thing.

'Don't ask me,' Diamond said. 'I'm going to be biased, aren't I? Actually, I shouldn't have hit him. I was needling the bastard, trying to get a response, so it's no wonder he slagged me off. I hardly know the guy. What I heard from Steph didn't impress me much. No doubt you've checked his service record and everything else?'

'School reports, library tickets, vaccinations, birth weight and date of conception,' Halliwell said with a slight smile. 'We don't do things by half. He was running a restaurant after he left the Air Force.'

'Yes, he—' Diamond stopped before the rest came out. 'It was in Guildford, Surrey, that restaurant.'

'That's right, guv. Is it important?'

Diamond was asking himself the same question. Guildford was only five miles south of Woking, the next stop on the railway. Anyone travelling from Guildford to London would pass the stretch of embankment where yesterday's body had been found. 'May be nothing,' he told Halliwell. 'Just a passing thought. He had a partner in the restaurant. Did you find out her name?'

'Fiona Appleby. They parted, we understand. Then he sold the business and moved to London.'

'Blyth Road, Hammersmith, for a bit. Then Westway Terrace, Paddington.'

'Right. Then he goes off the screen. Do you really think he hoofed it because you showed up in his life, guv?'

'Could be. But I have to say Westway Terrace is not a place anyone would want to stay in for long. Does he have a job?'

'He isn't on the unemployed register.'

'Got on his bike and looked for work, I expect,' Diamond murmured. He heard someone enter the room behind him and noticed a change in the posture of the civilian computer operator, a definite bracing of the neck and shoulders.

Without turning, he said, 'Morning, Mr McGarvie.'

'Peter. Is this a courtesy call, or have you remembered something?' asked the Senior Investigating Officer with a touch of sarcasm. There was a distinct gleam in the bloodshot eyes this morning.

'Just comparing notes with Keith on Dixon-Bligh,' Diamond said. 'He's proving elusive.'

'Rather.' But McGarvie had something more urgent on his mind. 'Seen the papers?'

'Not yet.'

He had the *Daily Telegraph* folded open at an inner page. 'What do you make of that?'

Diamond skimmed through the report of the grisly find by the railway at Woking. 'Nasty.'

'Is that all you've got to say?'

'Shocking, then.'

'This woman was killed by two shots to the head.'

'I spotted that.'

'And you can't find anything more to say than "shocking"? Doesn't it strike you as a remarkable coincidence? A middle-aged woman?'

'Actually, no,' Diamond said in the bored voice of a

man who has heard nothing new. 'I don't think it's a coincidence at all. This is another shooting by the same gunman. I'd put money on it.'

McGarvie glared. 'My point exactly. I've just been with the ACC, and she agrees. We've contacted Surrey Headquarters and I'm going up to the crime scene this afternoon. It could be the breakthrough I've . . .' His voice faltered.

'Been waiting for?'

He'd laid himself wide open, and he knew it. 'I'll remind you that this case has twice been reviewed, and each time I've been confirmed as the SIO.'

'They must think highly of you. Enjoy your trip to Woking.' He managed to resist adding, 'Been there, done that.' He'd asked that bright young detective Billy Bowers to play dumb with McGarvie, and he probably would.

About the time McGarvie was motoring along the M4 to Woking, Diamond boarded the train to London. Whoever wrote the slogan about letting the train take the strain could have had the big detective in mind. Travel by motorway was on a par with ordeal by fire. In the comfort of the InterCity Express, he could review a case and decide on the next move. That was the theory, anyway. He read the report in the *Express* of WOMAN ON LINE SHOT 'EXECUTION STYLE' and woke up at Paddington unsure when he'd nodded off.

He was fully alert when he entered the Fox and Pheasant in Fulham. Louis Voss came in soon after with a briefcase under his arm.

'I feel like a character in a le Carré novel.'

'In your dreams, Louis. Inspector Clouseau, more like. Is it a lager for you?'

'Scotch.'

When Diamond returned with the drinks, he came

straight to the point. 'You've got something in the brief-case?'

'I thought it would be simple accessing the old files through the computer system, but of course you were pre-computer. I had to go downstairs to Records and talk my way in there. Then it was a matter of sorting through any number of dusty old packets tied with string.'

'And . . . ?'

'My clothes are filthy. I've a good mind to send you the dry-cleaning bill, but I think I found your main cases – except for Missendale.'

'That went to a board of inquiry. It wouldn't be down there. Doesn't matter. It wouldn't have any bearing. You found the protection case, I hope? Joe Florida?'

'That's there. And the Brook Green shooting. Two or three others.'

'Great work, Louis.'

'What you've got here are photocopies of the main documents. I couldn't copy everything.'

'Understood.'

Louis eyed him speculatively. 'Does a le Carré char-acter ever ask George Smiley what the hell he's up to?'

Diamond shook his head. 'They skirt around it. That's why the books are so long.'

'Would it have anything to do with the body found at Woking yesterday?'

'You read the papers, too.'

'Couldn't miss it. You want to be careful, Peter. There's a professional gunman out there. You may think you're on his tail, but he's on yours.'

'Thanks, Louis. I'll sleep better for knowing that.'

He left soon after with the files.

25

Julie was right. It took two whole days for anyone else to make the connection with DCI Weather's missing wife. Two days of inertia for Peter Diamond. True, he studied the case files Louis had photocopied. He combed them minutely, regardless that he'd extracted everything of substance inside an hour on his train ride back to Bath.

Top of the heap was the protection racketeer, Joe Florida, released from Wandsworth in 1995 after serving seven years of a twelve-stretch. Joe Florida's wish-list of slow tortures, emasculations and other cruel fates for police officers who had crossed him was well documented. He told Diamond in one of his interviews prior to being charged that he would 'blow you away, you pig' (though Diamond remembered some adjectives the transcription left out) and repeated the threat more graphically in court after sentencing. As he was being taken down he had shouted – and Diamond remembered this clearly – 'I've put a notice on you, copper. I'll do the business on you when I come out. You'll wish you'd never heard of me.' Such taunts from the dock were not uncommon, and the police and judiciary treated them philosophically in the knowledge that several years behind bars dulled the memory and weakened the intent. But in view of what had happened, Joe Florida had to be taken seriously. The probation service had kept tabs on him for three more years after release. He'd returned to West London, to a flat in an upmarket street in Chelsea, so he was obviously not without funds. Under 'Current Employment' on his file someone had written *Nothing known*, a succinct summing up. He was a career crook, well capable of slipping back into crime without drawing attention to himself.

Tucked away in a section about the surveillance operation on Joe Florida was a name Diamond noted with interest. He circled it with a pen. One of the team assigned to watch the suspect's flat had been DC Weather. A minor role apparently, but it was not impossible Stormy had helped make the arrest and got himself on Florida's wish-list.

The Assistant Chief Constable herself, Georgina Dallymore, brought the news late Monday afternoon when things had gone quiet, stepping unannounced into Diamond's cluttered office and exclaiming breathlessly, 'Peter, I think we have the breakthrough. Curtis has been talking to the Surrey Police at Woking, where the remains of that woman were found at the end of last week. They have an ID now, and she's confirmed as an ex-police officer, the wife of a CID officer *you may well have worked with in the Met.*'

'DCI Weather,' he said as if they were discussing nothing more enthralling than last night's television. 'Yes, I know the bloke.'

'You've heard already?' He'd just shot Georgina's fox, and she was not pleased.

He said in the same flat tone, 'Mrs Patricia Weather, aged thirty-eight, dark-haired, five-six, stocky, dressed in a dark green padded coat, black woollen skirt with an artificial leather belt, pink jumper, Marks and Spencer underwear, tights and low unfashionable black shoes, size seven with a narrow heel.'

'How do you know all this?'

This was not the time to mention his trip to Woking. 'Most of it is in the papers, apart from her name, ma'am. That's on the PNC under missing persons.'

Georgina eyed him warily, suspicious she was being gulled. Nobody associated computer science with Peter Diamond.

As an extra touch, he explained, 'And the Yard puts out these bulletins.'

'And you put two and two together?'

'It wasn't quite so obvious as that. I couldn't say for sure.'

'But you worked it out. Independently of our inquiry, you worked it out.'

'I do have an interest in the case, ma'am.'

Still huffy, she told him, 'I came to put you in the picture, and there's no need, apparently.'

'Ah, but it's nice to have it confirmed.'

She nodded and said with as much acid as she could convey, 'In the unlikely possibility that it *hasn't* reached your ears, I've called a case conference for tomorrow afternoon, and Surrey Police and the Met will be represented. I'd like you to be there as well. Any theories you have about this development will be of interest to us all.'

He thanked her, a necessary gesture. Even he recognised the need to kowtow on occasions.

Georgina unfroze a couple of degrees. 'Let's hope this brings a result. You're entitled to expect it. A fresh perspective ought to make a difference.' It was as near as she would come to saying McGarvie was all at sea.

Still she lingered, and Diamond waited. Eventually she said, 'I was never in the Met, so I can't speak from first hand about things that happened in the eighties. Everyone knows corruption was endemic then and the official inquiries didn't deal with the problem. Countryman should have made a difference and was wound up far too soon. What was that other inquiry run by Number Five Regional Crime Squad?'

'Operation Carter.'

'Yes, they collected some damning evidence and didn't deliver in the end, or were shut down. You were at Fulham in those days. You must have seen abuses.'

'They weren't the norm, ma'am.'

'Don't take this personally, Peter.'

Whenever he heard those words he knew something personal was about to be slung at him.

'You had to face a board of inquiry over that Missendale case. I know you took it to heart at the time.'

'I was angry.'

'You were exonerated.'

'With a rider about my overbearing manner.'

'Which everyone except you has forgotten. Will you hear me out? This changes everything, this identification. Both murders could well have roots in things that happened at the time I'm speaking of, things you'd rather forget. We need to know what they are, Peter. We've all had episodes in our past we gloss over. Speak frankly, and you have my word there will be no witch-hunt.'

'What about, ma'am?'

'Anything at all. The point is this. We have to stop this killer from murdering anyone else. That's paramount. Your iffy conduct fifteen years ago doesn't matter a jot compared to that.'

He was stung into a sharp riposte. 'No, ma'am,' he told her, feeling the blood rush to his face, '*this* is the point. My wife had two bullets put through her brain. If you think I'd hold back on anything to shore up my dodgy career, you must have a low opinion of me.'

'That isn't so,' she said through tight lips. She turned and left the room.

He felt a twinge of guilt. Georgina had come in spon-

taneously, genuinely wanting to share her news with him.
So often of late when she'd spoken to him, there had
been a hidden agenda. This time she'd dredged up his
past – or tried to – and said a couple of tactless things
and he'd reacted more tetchily than ever. He needn't
have put her down.

Too late to mention it.

Another of the case files he'd acquired from Louis
featured a white teenager, a crop-headed loner called
Wayne Beach who had a liking for guns. As a juvenile,
Beach had twice been caught in possession of firearms
acquired by his criminal family. For a short time in the
early eighties he had made a living robbing and shooting
taxi drivers. His method was simple and effective. He'd
hail a cab late at night when the driver had stacked up
an evening's fares in the West End and ask to be driven
to some street where he'd already parked a stolen car.
He'd get out and instead of paying the fare he'd pull out
a handgun and shoot the driver, usually in the leg, and
demand his takings. The drivers always paid up. He would
smash the two-way radio and put another bullet into one
of the taxi tyres before walking calmly to the stolen car
and escaping. One night in Edith Road an eagle-eyed
constable spotted a parked car reported as stolen three
hours before. On the off-chance that this was the taxi-
bandit a team headed by Diamond was issued with arms
and sent to lie in wait. Beach was ambushed and shot in
the hip. It was not stated in the file whether Stormy
Weather had been one of the DCs in support.

Beach had been given five years on that occasion and
had served several terms since for malicious wounding.
The significant feature in his case was the way he felt
about guns. He was a trigger-happy hard man with no
scruples about inflicting pain on innocent victims. It

wasn't enough to use the gun as a threat. He always fired.
The case notes said he had an image of himself as a hold-
up man in the old American West. He put bullets into
people without any compunction whatever. Killing hadn't
featured among his crimes, it was true, though one of
the drivers had almost bled to death. But he had to be
taken seriously as a possible killer now.

He'd been released from Wormwood Scrubs last
Christmas, in plenty of time to have shot Steph and
Patricia Weather.

Georgina said to the room in general, 'This is Detective
Superintendent Peter Diamond,' and added on a softer,
apologetic note, as if suddenly realising she was in the
holy of holies, the Chief Constable's suite, 'the husband.'

'Widower,' Diamond corrected her.

'We already met,' DCI Bobby Bowers said without elab-
orating, and nobody picked up on it.

The case conference was around the oval table where
officers' careers were blessed or blown away. Coffee was
served in porcelain cups and saucers instead of mugs and
there were Jaffa Cakes instead of chocolate digestives.
There was little else to report. It was a fact-finding exercise for all concerned, and no facts were found that were
new to Diamond.

At one stage someone made the ill-considered remark,
'Patsy Weather was a copper, one of our own. This time
we'll get this guy, whatever it takes.'

Diamond demolished him with a look.

Afterwards he offered to show Bowers the way down
to the car park.

'Nothing else at the scene, then?' he asked the young
DCI.

'Only bits of bone.'

'No bag? No rings?'

'I'd have mentioned it just now, wouldn't I?'

'When's the post mortem?'

'Tomorrow.' Bowers glanced at his watch. 'Would you have time to show me your crime scene?'

They drove out to Royal Victoria Park in Bowers' white Volvo. This late in the afternoon they found a space easily on Royal Avenue below the Crescent and walked across the turf to the place near the stone bandstand where Steph had fallen. The sympathetic tributes of flowers and wreaths had long since disappeared. No one would have known this was a murder scene. A couple of schoolkids locked in a passionate embrace behind the bandstand had not been put off. The proximity of strangers didn't put them off either.

Bowers stared across the lawns, velvety in low-angled sunlight, to the glittering row of parked cars along the avenue and above them the curve of the most-photographed terraced building in Europe. He took in the great trees to the left and the conifers away to the right. Turning, he noted how close were the tall bushes screening them from Charlotte Street Car Park.

'Hard to equate with my railway embankment.'

'You've got a park nearby.'

'Yeah, but this is so open.' He took out a pack of cigarettes and offered one to Diamond, who shook his head. 'And she was just gunned down and left here?'

He nodded, not trusting himself to speak without emotion.

'There was no attempt to move her?'

'Too risky.'

'You mean he would have been seen dragging her to his car?' Bowers cupped his hand over his lighter to get a cigarette going and exhaled a long sigh of smoke that seemed to express the difficulty he was having with this crime scene. 'Why wasn't he seen shooting her?'

'*He?*'

A pause. Bowers raised an eyebrow. 'You don't really suspect this killer is female?'

'I'm keeping an open mind – or trying to. But you asked about the risk of being seen. I've given thought to that,' Diamond said, more comfortable talking practicalities. 'You'd think a public park in broad daylight would be a stupid place to murder someone, but this was a cold morning in February at a time of day when most people were already at work – and I've checked more than once. It *is* deserted here around that time.'

'Do you think he – or she – worked that out?'

'Probably.'

'So he *could* have moved the body if he'd wanted to.'

'To a car, you mean?'

'The car park is right here behind us.'

Diamond was dismissive. 'No chance. Its use is totally different. By that time of the morning it's busy, three-quarters full and with cars coming in all the time. The people aren't coming this way. They're going down into town for shopping and looking at the tourist sites. You couldn't carry a body to a car without being seen. Besides, there are cameras, and, yes, every tape has been checked.'

Bobby Bowers raked a hand through his crop of dark curls. 'I seriously wonder if we're right to link these two shootings.'

'Tell me why.'

'Your wife was certain to be found in a short time. It was a bold, professional hit, as if they didn't care who heard the shots. But my shooting has all the signs of being covert. The killer took pains to move her to a clever hiding place. The body might never have been discovered. If he's so brazen about murder A, why go to all the trouble of concealing murder B?'

Diamond had no explanation. 'Have you spoken to DCI Weather?'

'Only to confirm identification. That was enough for starters. He was in shreds, as you must have been.'

'God only knows how I would have coped with chewed-up bones. I suppose he identified her from the clothes?'

'Yes. The bones were no help. Her dental records were sent for. They match.'

'When will you interview him?'

'It's being done as we speak, by the two DIs you met at the scene. I'll know more after I've heard the tape.'

'Will you see him yourself?' Diamond asked.

'Sure to.' A feral glint invaded Bowers' eyes for an instant.

Diamond's sympathy went out to Weather. 'He'll get the third degree like I did, the husband being the first suspect.'

Bowers declined to confirm this. He said, 'I don't know about the treatment you were given.'

Diamond enlightened him, and at the end of it said, 'I was saying Stormy Weather can expect the same.'

'Depends.'

'But you don't rule it out.'

'Would you, in my position?'

The chill of evening was in the air and the first lights were visible in the Crescent. Without either man suggesting enough had been said, they returned silently across the turf to the car, leaving the scene to darkness and the snogging schoolkids.

At home with a mug of tomato soup in his fist and a chunk of bread on his lap he watched the nine o'clock news on TV. Nothing. Maybe they had run the Woking story the previous night. He didn't watch much these

days. The news seemed as remote from real life as the
soaps.

He'd delayed for as long as he could manage. He
reached for the phone and pressed out the number he'd
obtained that morning from the incident room.

'DCI Weather?'

'Who is this?' The voice was defensive.

All too vividly he remembered being under siege by
the press. 'Peter Diamond. I don't know if you remember
me. We have a couple of things in common. I'm deeply
sorry to hear about your wife.'

There was no response at all. But what do you say in
the circumstances? '*So am I*'? '*No problem*'? '*Thanks*'?

Diamond waited, then said, 'We served together, you
and I, at Fulham, back in the eighties.'

'That's right,' the voice became a touch less combative,
yet still drained of animation. 'And your wife has been
shot like mine. They told me.'

'So I know how you feel. It's hell.'

'Worse.'

'Look,' Diamond said, 'may I call you by your first
name? It's so long ago I only remember—'

'The nickname.' The way Stormy Weather closed him
down made the tired old joke seem one more infliction.

'And your real name is . . . ?'

'Dave.'

'Dave. Right. A lot of guys came and went,' Diamond
said to excuse his defective memory.

'And I was just a DC in those days,' Dave Weather said.

'I'm Peter.'

'You said.'

'I'd like to meet up if possible. You're going to be
under all sorts of pressure. It may help to talk to someone
who knows what it's like.'

'I don't feel like talking.'

'I know. I didn't. But you want to find the dickhead who killed your wife, right? And the high-ups are telling you to keep away. They don't want the likes of you and me getting involved.'

'They've got their reasons.'

'Like leave it to us, it's in good hands?'

'Something like that. And as the husband I'm personally involved.'

'I heard it all seven months ago. I'm still waiting for some progress, let alone an arrest.' Diamond was trying his damnedest, and at the same time sensing he should have waited a couple of days. The man was shell-shocked, just as he had been.

He still refused to give up. 'You know they're treating the two killings as connected? There was a case conference here in Bath today. I was called in to give the dope on operations you and I were both involved in. Hard task, all these years later. When you feel up to it we really should compare notes.'

'Is that what they suggested?'

'No. This is my idea.'

The response remained lukewarm. 'If you think it will make a difference.'

'I'm certain,' Diamond said, elated at the small concession he'd winkled out. 'I'll come to you. You're in Raynes Park, aren't you?'

Dave Weather backtracked. 'My place is a tip. I've done sod all to keep it straight in the last six months and now I've had the CID all over it.'

Which Diamond treated as an R.S.V.P.

'Likewise. I'm still in chaos here. Dave, I don't give a toss what your place looks like. What's the address?'

26

The moment Stormy Weather opened the door of his mock-Tudor semi in Raynes Park, Diamond remembered him. How could he have forgotten a skin like that, the colour of freshly sliced corned beef? A man could spend his life shovelling coal into a furnace and not end up with so many ruptured blood vessels. You never knew when he was blushing because it was his natural appearance. Happily for Stormy, it wasn't off-putting for long. If anything, it endeared him to people. With a few exceptions, none of us likes our own face much, and it's a relief to be with someone who has more to put up with than we do.

Today the poor bloke was understandably careworn as well as florid. A faded black Adidas T-shirt and dark blue corduroy trousers hung loosely from his tall frame. He took a moment to register who his visitor was (Diamond put this down to his own hair-loss) and then invited him inside, through a hallway littered with newspapers still folded as they'd been pushed through the door. 'You'll have to make allowances,' he said, kicking some aside. 'Patsy would go spare if she saw the place in this state. She kept a tidy house.'

The sitting room was misnamed now, because there wasn't a seat available. The chairs and sofa were all piled high with drawers, books and CDs. It looked like the aftermath of a burglary. 'They went through the place a couple of days ago,' Stormy explained. 'I can't pretend it was tidy before, but they didn't help matters.'

'They' must have been a police search squad.

'It happened to me.' Diamond stooped and picked a framed photo off the floor, a black and white shot of a young woman at the wheel of a police Panda car. 'Is this your wife?'

Stormy reached for the photo and practically snatched it from him. 'I've been looking all over for that. I thought they must have taken it away.' He held it in both hands. 'Yes, this is Patsy about the time we met. Well, you must remember her. She was on the relief at Fulham when you were CID.'

'So I was told. Can I have another look?' Diamond stood beside Stormy, then drew back to get a clearer view. Soon he'd want glasses. More than once Steph had told him to see an optician. 'Of course I knew her. Didn't we call her Mary Poppins?' Instantly regretting he'd come out with anything so crass, he added, 'But her real surname – what was that?'

'Jessel.'

'Yes. Pat Jessel.' Clumsily, he tried to make up for his boorishness. 'I can't for the life of me remember how she got that nickname.'

Stormy sighed and told the story, and the canteen humour of twenty years ago jarred on the ear like an old LP. 'She was the fresh-faced rookie with very good manners who tried too hard to please. She had a perpetual smile and this amazing posh accent like Julie Andrews. One day Jacob Blaize sent down for a coffee and Patsy wanted to know if he liked it black or white and someone said "White, with just a spoonful of sugar" and the whole room started whistling the tune. She was stuck with it then. No one called her anything but Mary after that.'

'Right.' Diamond gave an apologetic smile. He now

remembered Mary vividly. 'We were a cruel bunch.'

'It was a bit OTT. She got tired of the whistling and singing. And of course every time an umbrella was handed in it was hung on her peg. Though I have to say she fitted the role in some ways. She was a born organiser.'

'So when did you marry her?'

'November, eighty-six,' Stormy said, and for a moment his face creased, but he controlled the emotion and stood the photo on the empty wall unit.

Diamond, too, was thoughtful, marvelling that a young woman as pretty as 'Mary' Jessel had fallen for the Bardolph of Fulham nick.

'She was younger than you?'

'Fifteen years.'

'And she got to be sergeant.'

'At Shepherd's Bush. Served all her time at two stations just down the road from each other. She would have made inspector if she'd stuck with it. She was a fine copper.'

'She jacked it in?'

'Only about a year ago. She set up her own secretarial agency from home. It was just starting to build when . . .'

'Was she ever with CID?'

He shook his head. 'Uniform for the whole of her career, and pleased to do it. Very good with the public, anyone from juveniles to junkies.'

'And no one looked better in a white shirt,' Diamond reminisced. 'So she wouldn't have been on any of the cases you and I got roped into?'

'Not as CID. Do you want tea? Or there's a pub only five minutes away.'

'Sounds good to me.'

From the way they were greeted by the landlord of the Forester, Diamond guessed Stormy – or Dave, as he was trying hard to think of him – had spent plenty of time here lately. The urge to get out of the house where every picture, every chair, every cup has the potential to strike at the heart is hard to resist, as he well knew.

Over a glass of bitter at a corner table in the saloon bar, his old colleague was more at ease. They had never been close companions, or even said much, but the shared experience drew them together. Diamond found himself speaking more frankly about the impact of Steph's murder than at any time up to now. 'There are days . . . The worst part is when you've been relaxing without knowing it – let's face it, forgetting what happened – and then something touches you like a finger, forces you back to reality, and . . . and . . . there's no other way to put it – she dies all over again.'

This drew a nod of recognition from Stormy.

Diamond added, 'What keeps me going is the promise I made to find the scumbag who did it. And I will. They keep telling me to stand aside and leave it to the murder squad. How can I? You feel the same, don't you?'

So much intensity from someone he'd known as a senior officer must have been daunting, but Stormy nodded at once.

Diamond was well launched. 'The murder inquiry is going nowhere. I've found out more through bloody-minded obstinacy than McGarvie and his television appeals and scores of men on overtime. It's incentive, Dave. You can't sit back. Even if they were right on the heels of the killer – which they're not – I'd still be going it alone. I owe it to Steph.'

'I know how you feel.'

Diamond took a long sip of beer, willing Stormy to open up a little, and he did.

'They kept saying she'd come back, hinting all the time that we'd had a run-in – as if it was something unusual.

We were always having dust-ups. We were one of those couples who scrap all the time and feel better for it. Doesn't mean we didn't love each other.' He looked down into his drink. 'When a grown woman goes missing, nobody takes it seriously, not for weeks. She's just another name on a list.'

'How did it happen?'

'Her leaving? Nothing happened. Everyone was hinting there must have been some great punch-up. There wasn't. I came home from work one evening and she wasn't there.'

'When was this?'

'A Monday in March. The twelfth.'

'Two weeks and a bit after Steph was killed.'

'Right. I actually read about your wife being shot, and I remembered you from the old days, and was really sorry. I didn't send a card or anything because I didn't think you'd remember me, and it's difficult to know what to write.'

Diamond gave a nod. 'What about when your wife went missing? Did it cross your mind what had happened to Steph?'

'No, I didn't connect them. I didn't think Patsy was dead. You don't. I hoped she'd walk through the door any minute. And I guess I didn't want to face up to the worst possible explanation. You think of everything else, loss of memory, an accident, a coma. Anything that lets you hope.'

There are different degrees of torture, Diamond thought. Steph's sudden violent death had seemed like the ultimate. Stormy's months of not knowing was another refinement, and he wasn't sure how he would have coped with it. 'It's very isolating. No one knows what to say to you. They shun you if they can.'

'Tell me about it.'

'And of course they don't want us to investigate. I don't

know if you've been told this, but the argument goes that a smart defence lawyer would cry foul if you or I helped to arrest our wives' murderers.'

'So get lost. Yes,' Stormy said, 'I was told that.'

Encouraged, Diamond moved a stage on. 'Yet if you and I put our heads together we'd be more likely to get to the truth than anyone else. We know who we crossed swords with. They don't.'

Stormy's brown eyes met Diamond's, slipped away and then came back. 'You're right,' he said with sudden fervour. 'Together we could nail this jerk.'

Warming to the man, Diamond took him into his confidence, telling him about the case files Louis Voss had copied.

Stormy heard all this with awe. He'd only just grasped that unofficial action was possible. Diamond's bull-necked attitude must have come as a shock. But as soon as the Joe Florida inquiry was mentioned Stormy recalled being on the surveillance team. 'He was given a long term.'

'Twelve. He was out after seven.'

'Out?' Stormy was appalled. 'That beats everything. That toerag. Most professional crooks have something to be said for them. Florida was evil.'

'You met him personally?'

'Twice. I sat in on interviews.'

'Questioned him?'

'No, I was only a DC at the time. Blaizy was in charge. You do remember Jacob Blaize?'

Too well, Diamond thought bitterly. 'Retired to Spain, the last I heard.'

'For some reason, he wanted me as the back-up in those sessions. I didn't mind. Saw myself as the up-and-coming detective, hand-picked by the guvnor. I didn't know Blaizy couldn't stay in an interview room for more than ten minutes at a time.'

Diamond frowned, then grinned as the explanation surfaced. 'His prostate problem? I'd forgotten about that.'

'It meant I spent more time alone with Joe Florida than anyone would wish to.'

'Did he talk?'

'Did he hell. He was after cigarettes. He could see I was a smoker. I may have been wet behind the ears, but I knew you don't dish out fags for nothing. So I took a fair amount of flak from Joe Florida.'

'Did he threaten you?'

'Let's say I wouldn't have needed a vasectomy if he'd got to me first.'

'He made his living out of threats,' Diamond recalled. 'I took a few. And in the protection racket you're not a serious player unless you mean what you say.'

'Joe did. Two shops torched, was it?'

'And a child almost died. She was in the cot upstairs. They got her out in the nick of time.'

'I remember.'

'So you spent time alone with him?' Diamond said eagerly. 'I didn't know that. Was there anything more serious from him than bumming a fag?'

'Such as?'

'He didn't try and make a deal? What I'm driving at, Dave, is something big enough for him to hold a grudge all the time he was in jail.'

'And then murder my wife, just to get back at me? No, there was nothing *that* extreme. I can't think of anyone who would behave like that. Even a shitbag like Florida.'

Diamond nodded. 'I keep saying the same. It's not just evil. It's twisted. Insane.' He paused. 'Do you think prison blew his mind?'

'He wouldn't be the first.'

'I mean to find out. I'm going to find him. If he murdered Steph, I'll have him.'

'I'm with you all the way.'

The hackneyed phrase had never meant so much to Diamond.

'Another beer?'

When he returned to the table, he said to Stormy, 'I was telling you about those files.'

'Files?'

'From Louis Voss at Fulham.'

'Right. I'm with you.'

'One was the Brook Green shooting.'

'I remember that.'

'You do?'

'Only I wasn't on the team.'

Diamond blew gently at the froth on his beer. 'Okay. There are others. Let's shuffle the pack again. How about a teenager by the name of Wayne Beach?'

The name brought a glimmer to Stormy's eye. 'Remind me, will you?'

'A loner. Armed robbery. Taxi drivers.'

'Ah – that little prick. We ambushed him one night in Edith Road.'

This was better than Diamond had hoped. '*We?* You were there? Tell me you were there.'

'I was. It was all very sudden. You were in charge, weren't you? You needed licensed shots and I was roped in, along with anyone else who happened to be there. I was behind a hedge in the garden opposite.'

'You didn't fire the shot?'

'No. That was another guy across the street. A sergeant. The name's gone now. But after Beach threw down his weapon I was one of the first to pin him. And I escorted him to the nick.'

'So he knows you?'

'I wouldn't think he remembers now.'

Privately, Diamond thought the opposite. Stormy's

geranium-coloured skin had instantly triggered his own memory when he called at the house.

'He'd remember you better,' Stormy added.

'Maybe. I did the interviews and gave evidence. The thing about Wayne Beach is that he's a gun freak. He's done several stretches.'

'He'd be in his thirties now.'

'Thirty-four. Released from the Scrubs last December.'

'December? Shortly before . . . ?'

'Right.'

'So we have an address?'

'Thanks to the Probation Service, yes. Some high-rise in Clapham. Are you game?'

Stormy raised both thumbs.

'He'll be armed,' Diamond cautioned. 'Do you have a shooter?'

'Sorry. Do you?'

'Not any more.' Diamond leaned back and rested his hands on his paunch as if that concealed a secret weapon. 'Just have to outsmart him.'

'We can do that,' Stormy said with confidence, raising his glass. 'Here's to us. Whatever it takes.'

'Whatever.' Diamond clinked his glass and drank deeply. He had an ally now.

The outsmarting of Wayne Beach needed neutral ground and the surprise element, they decided. It would court disaster to visit his flat. They sat in a CID Vauxhall opposite the graffiti-scarred building in Latchmere Road, Clapham, watching the residents come and go. Their man would emerge at some point to buy cigarettes or food, or place a bet, or pick up his social security. It went without saying that he hadn't gone into honest employment.

After a couple of hours with no result they were thinking about food themselves. They'd seen a number of dodgy-looking people enter or leave the building, but that was not remarkable. It was a run-down, fifties-built tower block, a place of last resort that probably housed more lowlife than Wayne Beach.

Towards four, when the butcher up the street started clearing his window, Diamond left Stormy in the car and went over to see if there was a pork pie left. He was lucky.

'You know, I'm thinking of Plan B,' he told Stormy while they ate.

'What's that?'

'Ask the neighbours.'

'Risky. He could hear.'

'He could be somewhere else.'

It was decided Diamond would go alone. After ten flights of stairs breathing heavily and not enjoying what he breathed, he emerged on Beach's landing. He'd passed no one.

According to their information, Wayne Beach occupied the sixth flat along, number fifty-six. There was a reggae beat coming from fifty-five.

'Hain't seen him, man,' the tenant said when Diamond asked after his neighbour.

'It's okay, I'm a friend.'

'Still hain't seen him in ages. Nobody in there. If you asking me, him Scapa Flow.'

Diamond risked a look through the window of fifty-six. The place certainly looked unlived-in. A free paper had been crammed in the letter box. He pulled it out, held the flap open and peered through. A heap of junk mail was inside.

'Man, he won't be back,' was the opinion of Diamond's informant, and in the circumstances he was probably right.

'Was he ever here?'

'Place is empty since Christmas. One time I hear

someone unlocking, walk in, walk out. Picking up his letters, I guess.'

Stormy insisted on driving Diamond across London to Paddington Station. 'We won't let it get to us, Peter,' he said. 'We're still ahead of the game.'

'Not for long,' Diamond said. 'McGarvie's no fool, and neither is Bowers. You can bet they spent today going through those old files, reaching the same conclusions we have. My worry is that they'll go in like the tank corps and the killer will see them coming a mile off.'

'Looks as if Wayne Beach already has.'

'He's using the place as a cover. As far as the social services are concerned, he's trapped in that slum, living from hand to mouth. No doubt he's got a nice pad somewhere else.'

'And a nice income as a hitman.'

'Could be.'

'So we wasted our bloody time.'

Briefly it seemed Stormy might be going cool on co-operation, but this proved false.

'There was something you said earlier, about us putting our heads together and finding the truth before anyone else. I was impressed.'

'You want to keep trying?'

'Definitely.'

If Diamond had believed in fate, he might have been awed by what happened to him that evening. Exhausted after so much waiting with no result, he fell asleep on the seven-thirty from Paddington and was out to the world when it stopped at Bath Spa. He ended up at Bristol Temple Meads Station some time after nine-thirty. Not for the first time. Only now there was no one at home to phone any more. Rather than cross the bridge and wait for a train, he made the best of his situation and took a taxi to the Rummer.

Bernie Hescott, his well-paid, worse than useless snout, was not in the public bar. 'Haven't seen him all week, squire,' the barman told Diamond.

'Doesn't surprise me. I'll have a pint, just the same.'

'Bitter?'

A fair expression of his state of mind. He settled down with the drink and let ten minutes go by. The place was warm and the music just about bearable.

Then fate gave an emphatic pull on the strings, for in walked the informer he should have used in preference to Bernie. John Seville caught Diamond's startled eye, turned and left the bar at once. He went after him.

'Can't help you,' Seville said while Diamond tried to keep pace with him, striding through one of the paved alleyways behind the Exchange.

'You don't even know what I want.'

'Jesus Christ, the whole world heard what happened, and I know sweet fuck all about it.'

Diamond grabbed his arm and shoved him against a shuttered shop front. 'John, if this is your way of raising the stakes, save your breath. I'll pay top dollar.'

'I'm not haggling, Mr Diamond. I got nothing for you. Nothing.'

'What are you scared of? The Carpenters? Forget them. They're in the clear for once. This wasn't local. This has a London connection. You do know what I'm talking about?'

'Your wife. What can I say? I wouldn't wish that on anyone. But I know nothing.'

'Someone, some hitman, gunned her down in a public park in broad daylight. He'd done his homework, John. Picked his spot. Got away fast. Did you hear of anyone –

a Londoner, maybe, a professional, who was holed up here six, seven months ago?'

'In Bristol?'

'Bristol or Bath, but he's more likely to have used here as his base. Bristol is bigger, easier to get lost in. What have you got for me, John?'

'I keep telling you—'

Diamond jammed a thumb under Seville's chin, forcing his jaws together with a crunch. 'I'm not messing. I want a result. I can pay fifty, or I can beat it out of you, or I can tell my chums at Bristol Central to make your life impossible. Which is it to be?'

'You just cut my tongue.'

'Too bad.' He relaxed his hold.

Seville wiped blood from the edge of his mouth and stared at his fingers. He darted looks to either side. No one was about. 'You said fifty?'

'This had better be kosher.'

'Take it or leave it, this is all I have. There's an ex-con living in clover in a smart house on Sion Hill, near the Suspension Bridge. Been around most of this year. Makes trips to London sometimes. The word is that if you want to buy a shooter, that's where you go. But don't bring me into it, for Christ's sake.'

'A local?'

'No, not from round here.'

'I'll need his name.'

'Beach. The name is Beach.'

John Seville got his fifty pounds.

Ever since the diamond heist went wrong, Harry Tattersall had dreaded hearing from his old friend Rhadi. He expected a witch-hunt. The deviser of the plot, that sinister little man Zahir, wasn't going to let the whole thing rest. Much as Harry hoped that the Arab philosophy might be to offer a thousand blessings to Allah for a lucky escape, he knew in his gut that it was not to be. Zahir would want to know who had shafted them.

Never mind that Harry was blameless, having acted like a hero and saved everyone from arrest. His Houdini stunt at the Dorchester wasn't going to work in his favour. With their devious minds the Arabs would think he'd been *allowed* to walk away. It wasn't true, of course. He'd been as horrified as anyone when things came to grief. He hadn't grassed, and he didn't know who had.

The first days after, he'd stayed out of sight, fearing Special Branch or one of the security services would come in pursuit. He hadn't gone to Ireland, as planned, in case that part of the operation had been blabbed. He'd stayed with a friend in Tunbridge Wells. As the weeks passed, he'd returned to London, deciding he was safe from the authorities. The real threat was from his fellow-conspirators. He'd heard disturbing stories of Arab retribution: thieves having their hands severed and adulterers being stoned. He didn't care to discover what happened to informers.

The call eventually came one Monday evening.

'I'm so glad you're in,' his friend Rhadi said, as if he was selling insurance. 'We need to talk.'

'Only you and me?' Harry said, more in hope than expectation.

'No. All of us. The team.' And it was obvious from Rhadi's voice that he wasn't alone. 'We wish to compare notes on our, em, disappointment. A de-brief, as they say.'

'A de-brief,' Harry repeated, thinking it sounded like the prelude to castration.

'We'll come to you. Be with you inside an hour. Don't go to any trouble.'

It was under the half-hour when the knock came. Little Zahir strode in first without even a nod of recognition, followed by Ibrahim and Rhadi. They were in black suits, like a funeral party.

Rhadi said, 'Sorry about this, but we need to frisk you.'

So much for team spirit. He submitted to Ibrahim's large hands.

'Isn't the other fellow coming?' Harry asked while this was going on. He'd given thought to the way he would handle the workover.

Zahir didn't answer for some time, and the others seemed to feel any response should come from him. He was sitting in Harry's favourite armchair, well forward so that the tips of his shoes kept contact with the carpet. 'Which other fellow?'

'The man from the Dorchester.'

'No, he can't make it.'

'We could be wasting our time, then, trying to work out what went wrong.'

'Why? Do you have a theory?' Zahir said, baring the big teeth.

Harry backtracked. 'Not as such. I simply thought we should all be in on the discussion.'

Zahir gave a shrug. 'Our colleague at the Dorchester can't be here tonight. Now, Mr Tattersall, sit down and let's discuss the fiasco. The first we heard from you, on your mobile from the hotel, was a positive message. You called me with the name of the suite.'

'Exactly as arranged,' Harry stressed, taking a seat as far from his interrogator as possible.

'You didn't say anything was amiss.'

'Nothing was at that stage.'

'A few minutes after, you called again and told me to pull the plug, or some such phrase.'

'Correct.'

'So something must have happened between the two calls.'

In an effort to react positively, Harry slapped a hand down on the arm of the chair. 'Indeed it had. First, a woman who said she was the housekeeper knocked on the door wanting to change the flowers. That made me suspicious.'

'So how did you react?'

'I let her in.'

'Why?'

'I was trying to act like a normal guest. You don't send the housekeeper away without good reason. It would have drawn attention to us.'

'So she came into the room. What then?'

'She put fresh lilies in a vase. As I mentioned, my suspicion was aroused. After she'd left the room, I went to the window and looked out at the roof garden and spotted a movement. I was horrified. There was this fellow hiding behind a bush and holding a sub-machine-gun. And there was another marksman as well. It was obvious we'd been rumbled.'

'*Rumbled?*'

Rhadi gave an interpretation in Arabic.

'I immediately checked the flowers, and found they contained a bugging device,' Harry continued, underlining his efficiency. 'I put them – flowers, vase, the lot – in a wardrobe to mask the sound and then called you on the mobile.'

'Yes.' It was a 'yes' pregnant with reservations.

'That's it.' Harry waited.

Zahir brought his hands together and cracked the knuckles. 'The operation was called off at your suggestion, yet you remained in the room. Why didn't you get out while you had the chance?'

His worst scenario. They suspected he was in collusion with the police. 'If you remember,' he said, feeling the blood drain from his face, 'I asked you to let Rhadi know the problem, and you said you couldn't because he didn't have a phone. It was clear to me he was going to get arrested if I didn't help. He'd walk straight into the trap. He's an old friend.' He glanced towards Rhadi, who was clearly uncomfortable and avoiding eye contact. 'There's such a thing as loyalty. So I waited until he came to let him know the whole thing had gone pear-shaped.'

'Pear-shaped?'

Rhadi interpreted, and there followed an earnest dialogue in Arabic between Zahir and Rhadi.

Finally Zahir said, 'Your old friend confirms that you sent him away. He believes you.'

Harry gave his old friend a look of gratitude. 'He would have done the same for me.'

Then the sting. 'Yet you remained in the room with the men we now know to have been detectives.'

'For a time, yes.'

Zahir's tiny feet curled upwards. 'Why, Mr Tattersall? Why?'

He tried to make it sound the most obvious thing in the world. 'That was my best chance – to bluff my way

out, and that's what I did by letting them think there was
a bomb in the suitcase. I told them I was CIA.'

'Are you?'

'Good God, no.'

'But they believed you?'

Rhadi said in support, 'He does a very good American
accent.'

'It got me out and away. The alarm system went off,
there was a hotel evacuation and I stepped out to the
street along with everyone else.'

'That's all?' The dissatisfaction was all too evident in
Zahir's voice.

'What else can I say except I'd like to know who stitched
us up, and why? It certainly wasn't me. I was going to get
a hundred K.'

'We were all looking forward to a share,' Zahir pointed
out. 'None of us had any obvious reason to play traitor,
yet someone did.'

The right moment, Harry decided, to point the finger
elsewhere. 'We were sold down the river before the scam
got under way. Those gunmen were in place when I was
shown into the room. The police knew where to lie in
wait. They must have been tipped off well ahead.'

'Wrong,' Zahir said.

'Why?'

'If they'd known in advance they'd have bugged the
room already. They wouldn't have needed to send a
woman in with flowers.'

Clever. This was a point Harry hadn't considered. He
frowned in the silence, grasping desperately for an explanation. Finally one came to him. 'Well, maybe the police
suspected some of the hotel staff were in on the scam.
They couldn't risk taking them into their confidence.
They played along with the plot and waited to see which
suite we were sent to. They knew it must be on the same

floor as the Prince's suite, so they posted their firearms team on the roof garden.'

Zahir's large, shrewd eyes studied Harry. After an interval he conceded, 'You could be speaking sense now. So if you are not the informer, who is?'

'How would I know?' Harry said. 'I didn't even meet everyone.'

'You met us all except one.'

'Yes, the inside man, the ex-RAF type on the staff of the hotel.' The injustice fired Harry to say more than he'd intended. 'I can't think why he gets special treatment. If he's on the team he should be here, ready to face the music like the rest of us.'

'Music?'

The phrase had to be explained. Then, as if such details were beneath him, Zahir gestured to Rhadi to enlighten his friend.

'The man at the Dorchester went missing the day after we were there. No one knows where he is. He's lost his job, moved out of his old address and gone.'

'Who is he?'

'His name is Dixon-Bligh.'

Harry had never heard of him. 'The police must be onto him if he quit the next day.'

'They're trying to find him, yes, but it's complicated. He's also wanted for questioning in connection with the killing of his former wife.'

'He's a killer?' Harry piped up. 'How did we get into bed with this monster?'

'I only said they want to interview him.'

'We all know what that means.'

'It isn't certain.'

Harry digested the information. He still felt he hadn't been given all the facts. 'He's done a runner, you said? Isn't it obvious he's the one who grassed us up? I don't know why you give me the third degree as if I'm the snitch when you could be looking for this bastard.'

No one answered.

'Wait a minute,' Harry said, as an ugly thought surfaced. 'You haven't already topped him, have you?'

28

The photocopier at Fulham nick must have been red-hot over the weekend. McGarvie was now in possession of a thick stack of paper: Diamond's entire record of cases with the Met. Three of the most experienced officers in the incident room had combed each page for the crucial mentions of DC Weather's name among the detectives involved.

'One stands out,' McGarvie informed Diamond when he turned up on Monday. 'This Florida. Protection racketeer. A hard man.'

'Can't disagree with that.'

'Jacob Blaize headed, right?'

Diamond nodded.

'With you as second in command?'

'Sidekick.'

'And Weather was a junior officer on the team, mainly on surveillance duties, but I discovered he also sat in on several interviews Blaize did with Florida.'

Tell me something new, Diamond thought.

McGarvie was showing signs of excitement. 'And we can assume Weather spent time alone with Florida when Blaize left the room, as he must have.'

'Frequently,' Diamond confirmed.

'You know that for sure?'

'Blaizy was always being caught short.'

The eyes widened, revealing more than anyone would

wish to see of the engorged blood vessels. 'Was he, by
God? That's something I didn't get from the files.'

'Well, you wouldn't.'

'It meant interruptions, did it?' He was getting as hyper
as when he had dug up the gun in the garden.

'Every ten to fifteen minutes.'

'Sounds like prostate trouble.'

'He was on a waiting list.'

Diamond was amused to see McGarvie bring his palms
together and rub them as if he was using the drying
machine in the gents: the association of ideas. 'You see
what this means? This was before we had videotaping. An
old hand like Florida would have made use of those
breaks. He'd get to work on the young officer sitting
across the table. He'd try intimidation.'

'For what? A smoke?' It was hardly enough to justify
the killing of Patsy Weather, Diamond was implying, and
McGarvie needed to do better.

But he was way ahead, compounding the plot. 'No,
he'd twist the facts of the case to make it seem he was
being set up by you and Blaize. He'd shake the young
man's confidence, doing his damnedest to turn him, you
see. He'd think he'd got him as an ally, someone who
could testify later that the interview had been improper.
When he didn't do it by persuasion, he'd use threats –
threats he really meant to carry out. He saw enough of
Weather to remember him long after. When a man like
Florida has festered in jail for twelve years—'

'Seven,' Diamond said. 'He was out after seven.'

'More than enough to turn his brain.'

'His brain didn't need turning. He hated the police. I
can see – just about – that he might have wanted revenge
on Blaizy and me. We nailed him. But Stormy Weather?
I don't think so. He was small beer.'

McGarvie was unshakeable. 'You and I don't know what

passed between them. Maybe Weather was induced to make a promise he never kept. Maybe Florida thought he could rely on Weather to save his skin.'

Maybe . . . Maybe . . . This was futile speculation, and both knew it. Nothing would be certain unless Stormy admitted he'd played along, or Florida was induced to tell all. No matter; for the present it suited Diamond if Florida was the prime suspect, leaving him free to pursue Wayne Beach. Just to get a measure of McGarvie's resolve, he asked, 'Have you given up on Dixon-Bligh, then?'

'No trace. He's holed up somewhere. Arrears of rent. The Met are working on it.' He made it sound like their problem.

Joe Florida was firmly in the frame.

Stormy Weather arrived at Bristol Temple Meads just after eleven, and Diamond met him on the platform and remembered to call him Dave. They drove directly to Sion Hill, an elegant, curving street of eighteenth-century houses built on an incline above the Gorge.

'Bit of a change from Latchmere Road,' Stormy remarked when they were parked opposite a gracious four-storey terrace with ironwork balconies, tall shutters and striped awnings.

'Envious?'

He eyed the building approvingly. 'It isn't bad for a second home. Does he own all of it?'

'That's what I heard from my snout.'

'He must have salted some money away between his prison terms.'

'More than you and I ever earned, Dave.'

They lapsed into silence, brooding on a theme familiar to policemen: the inequity between the law-enforcers and the law-breakers. 'Personally,' Stormy said after some time, 'I wouldn't choose to live in Bristol. The traffic is a pain. Always was.'

'Sounds like the voice of experience.'

'Does it? I'm only an occasional visitor.'

'Best way.'

'As a matter of fact,' Stormy said, 'I'm interested in Brunel.'

Diamond had to think before cottoning on that Stormy was speaking of the Victorian engineer. 'Top hat and big cigar?'

A nod. 'One of my heroes. I do some model-making as a hobby, and his constructions are quite an inspiration. I made an *SS Great Britain* and a Suspension Bridge.'

'From kits, you mean?'

'God, no. That's schoolboy stuff. I go there and take photos and draw up plans and build the things from my own materials.'

Weird, the things some policemen do with their spare time, Diamond thought. Keith Halliwell bred pigeons for racing and John Wigfull had a telescope and was supposed to use it to study the stars.

Stormy went on, 'So I've made quite a number of research trips, you could say. Getting here is the hardest part.'

'Ah, the one-way system is our secret weapon in the war against crime. You'd find it easier escaping from a Dunkirk beach than Bristol. If you want to visit the Brunel sites you're better off using the railway he built and walking the rest.'

Stormy agreed with that. He glanced at the house again.

'What do we do now? Go in?'

'Let's watch for the time being,' Diamond said. 'The place is probably stiff with shooters.'

'Catch him off the premises? We've tried that once.'

'This time I expect a result. So you're an admirer of old Issy Brunel?' he said, pleased to have found a topic unconnected with the tragedies in their lives. 'Have you been to Bath?'

'Not since I was a kid.'

'You ought to come. He changed the look of the city when the railway came through. The old GWR station is one of his buildings and so is the viaduct behind, but he also cut through Sydney Gardens, one of those parks the Victorians liked to strut around in their finery, and it was a neat job.'

'Yes, I'd like to see that.'

'You wouldn't.'

Stormy blinked and frowned. He may also have blushed, but on his blotchy skin it was impossible to tell. 'What do you mean? I know what I like.'

'You wouldn't *see* it – that's what I mean – unless you went right up to it. The point is that the railway is hidden from view. Really clever.'

The first person to emerge from the house, after about ten minutes, was in a red leather jacket and skirt with matching boots and a hat with a large rim that flopped. She set off down the hill with a slinky walk as if she knew her movement was being appreciated.

'Now I *am* envious,' Stormy said.

Diamond gave him a look. The remark was lightly made, the automatic reaction to a pretty woman, but to his still wounded mind it didn't come well from a recently bereaved man. He let it pass.

'I wonder if she comes with the house,' Stormy added, oblivious of Diamond's thinking.

'Visitor, I expect.'

'That's not the vibes I got.'

'You could be right. Maybe he sent her to do the shopping.'

'She doesn't look to me as if she's on her way to Tesco's.'
They waited ten minutes more.
'I reckon she's his bird,' Stormy insisted.
'Daughter, more like,' Diamond said.
'He's not that old, surely?'
'You've got to remember Fulham was fifteen years ago, Dave. Hello, we've got action.'
A dark green Range Rover had pulled up outside the house and a man in combat trousers and a khaki vest got out. He had the look of a body-builder, with heavily tattooed arms.
'That isn't Beach, is it?' Stormy said.
'Not the way I remember him,' Diamond said. 'I remember a puny guy.'
The muscleman pressed the doorbell.
'Just a caller, then.'
'Or a customer.'
'What – come to buy a gun?'
'Keep your eyes on the door, Dave. Let's see who opens it.'
Unfortunately, nobody did. The caller tried the bell twice more, looked at his watch, stood back and looked up to the balcony, and then gave up, returned to his car and drove off.
'We've wasted our time again,' Stormy said.
'No, look. Coming round the corner.'
The woman in the floppy hat and red leather had started up the hill towards the terrace, this time carrying a folded magazine.
Diamond watched, and something made him sure he'd seen her before. He couldn't tell the colour of her hair under the hat, but the face was one he knew. She wasn't Janie Forsyth, the she-cat who had attacked him, and she wasn't Danny Carpenter's wife, Celia. He needed a closer look.

Without a word to Stormy, he opened the door of the car and stepped across the street and stood outside the house.

Ten yards from him, the woman hesitated. Diamond stared, frowned and stared harder. It required a great leap of the imagination to tell that this lady in red leather was not, after all, a lady.

'Wayne?'

Wayne, if it was he, turned and started running back down the hill. Diamond pursued. His overweight, lumbering movement was about as ineffectual as his quarry's, hampered by high heels. But he kept running and managed to reach out and get a hand on a leather sleeve at the street corner and bring the chase to a skidding halt. He swung the person around and when they were face to face it was obvious he was right. This was not, after all, a woman. This was a skilfully made-up, smartly groomed, cross-dressed Wayne Beach. Prison life generally leaves its mark on an ex-con, but the result, in this case, had been unusual.

'How long have you been out, Wayne?'

The face tautened, making a mockery of the lipstick and foundation. 'What do you want? Who are you? I know you, don't I?' The voice also was at odds with the get-up, all too guttural.

Diamond showed his warrant card and reminded Beach who he was and how they'd met.

'You look different. You've changed,' Beach said.

'That's rich. What's all this nonsense, flouncing about in skirts?'

'It's a free country. I can dress how I want.'

'Is it a disguise, or what?'

'These are the clothes I choose to wear now. I don't need to justify them to you or anyone else.'

'Have you had the operation?'

'No, but I might.'

'What are you doing here in Bristol?'

'Visiting.'

'Come off it, Wayne. You live here. The house with the yellow door. Are you going to invite us in?'

'Us?' Beach looked across the street and saw Stormy Weather close the car door and step towards them. 'Beetroot face, as well? I know him. Once seen, never forgotten. What's going on?'

'Questions, that's all, if you play it right.'

'I did my time. You've got no right to persecute me.'

Stormy came over and took stock with a hyperthyroid stare. He shook his head and said, 'Well, I'll be buggered.'

'I wouldn't bank on it,' Diamond said. 'However, Wayne is going to invite us into his house for a coffee and answer our questions.'

'I don't have to,' Wayne said.

'I don't have to go to a magistrate for a warrant, but I will if I'm pressed.'

The bluff worked. Wayne felt in his shoulder-bag for a key and in so doing gave Diamond enough of a glimpse of the magazine he was holding to show it was the *Shooting Times*. They entered a hall with a crimson carpet and striped Regency wallpaper.

'Nice pad.'

'Nicer than Latchmere Road,' Stormy said.

Wayne turned. 'Listen, I only pick up the social to keep my probation officer happy.'

'Rest easy, Wayne. We're not here about your fraudulent claims.'

Beach removed the hat and hung it on a peg. He wasn't wearing a wig. He'd grown his own brown hair to a thickness any woman would have envied and had it clipped sheer at the back, twenties-style. In the kitchen – a

gleaming place of natural wood and silvery appliances –
he filled the kettle. They all sat on stools.

'What *do* you want?'

'You were released from the Scrubs when?' Diamond
asked.

'Christmas. Just before.'

'So when did you move down here?'

'Not long after.'

'Not good enough,' Stormy said. 'We're talking dates,
Wayne. You know the day you moved in.'

Beach gave a sigh and a toss of the head, playing the
harassed female to perfection. He unhooked a spiral diary
from the wall and flicked through the months. 'February
the fifth.'

'Let's see that.' Diamond was reviewing his mental
picture of that February morning in Royal Victoria Park.
What if Steph had been approached by someone she
supposed was a woman? Might that have been why her
killer got so close before firing the shots? And why Wayne
Beach got away without being noticed?

He handed the diary across. Diamond studied it. Each
day was a narrow strip where appointments could be
written in. February the fifth had the pencilled entry
'*Bristol. Keys from Homefinders 11.30.*' Various other
appointments were filled in throughout the month, some
indicated by initial letters. He looked at Tuesday the
twenty-third, the day of the murder, and it was blank.

'What about this day here?'

Beach came over to look and treated Diamond to a
whiff of some perfume heavy with musk. 'It's blank.'

'Does that mean you had a free day, or what?'

'No. If you look, you'll see each Tuesday is blank. I
keep Tuesdays clear.'

Diamond checked the rest of the diary and saw that
this was so. 'Why?'

'They're not really clear. Every Tuesday is spoken for. That's when I go to London to see Mr Dawkins.'

'Who's he?'

'My probation officer.'

'Ah.' The sound came from Diamond as if he'd taken a low punch, and that was how he felt. 'And you definitely went to London on the twenty-third?'

'I had to. Dawkins thinks I'm living in Clapham.'

'What train do you get?'

'The seven-twenty. I check in at his office at ten-thirty.'

This was beginning to look like a solid alibi. 'I'll check with him myself.'

'You wouldn't let on?' Wayne said in horror.

'What – that you're living the life of Riley here in Bristol flogging guns to any lunatic with cash in hand? Of course I'm going to let on. I'm a copper, Wayne, not your favourite uncle.'

In the act of pouring the coffee, Beach spilt some over his immaculate work surface. 'Who said anything about guns?'

'Half the criminal fraternity of Bristol. You're well known. It's a change from shooting taxi drivers in the leg. Two sugars, please.'

'Do I look like a gun dealer?'

'In your skirt and lipstick? At the risk of being misunderstood, I'd say you've got a very good front. I suppose the weapons are shipped in, up the Channel.'

'You're talking through your arse.'

'Can we look in your basement?'

Beach sighed, and dropped the pretence. 'What exactly do you want?'

'I want you to look at that calendar and tell me who bought automatic handguns in the month of February.'

'I wasn't dealing then. Honest to God. I'd only just moved in. You can't start a business from nothing.'

Diamond reached for the calendar again. 'There are letters here I recognise. DC on the twelfth, and again on the fifteenth. Would that be Danny Carpenter?'

Wayne passed a hand nervously through the shingled hair. 'Listen, you don't move into someone else's manor without a by-your-leave. I had to square it with the local chiefs, or I wouldn't last five minutes. On the days you're talking about, I wasn't dealing. I was making arrangements.'

'Dressed like this?'

He glared. 'I might be different, but I'm not stupid.'

'What brought you to Bristol?'

'I have to make a living. London was too hot to start up again. This is the next best.'

'Was there talk of a hitman coming to Bristol or Bath towards the end of February?'

'I wouldn't know. People didn't talk to me then. I was the new kid on the block. What's all this about?'

'You didn't hear? Don't you read the papers?'

Beach shook his head. 'Boring.'

'Just your gun magazines, eh?'

'That's my job.'

Diamond didn't enlighten him about the shootings. He could see nothing of use emerging. The disappointing conclusion was that they'd wasted their time on Wayne Beach. 'We're leaving now,' he said abruptly. 'You've got about twenty minutes before Bristol Police come here with an armed protection unit and knock down the door.'

'Did you believe him?' Stormy asked.

'Did you?'

'I did, oddly enough.'

'Me, too. If he'd written something in against the day Steph was shot, I'd have been suspicious. He could have done it any time. The fact that it was left blank is more convincing. I'll still check with the probation officer.'

'And will you turn him in?'

'Will I? Dave, anyone who trades in guns in scum. Whoever shot my wife and yours acquired their weapon from some flake just like him.'

He drove Stormy back to Bath, not to visit the Brunel sites, but to show him the place where Steph was killed. They parked on Royal Avenue, the road that bisected the lawns below the Crescent. Already some of the foliage had a reddish tinge and the ground under the horse chestnuts was littered with husks split by small boys in the quest for the new season's conkers. They crossed the dew-damp grass to where the body was found. He picked an empty crisp packet off the grass and crushed it in his hand.

'What's the park called?' Stormy asked.

'The Victoria. The Royal Victoria to give it its full name. This part is the Crescent Gardens.' He pointed out the advantages to the killer, the screen of bushes hiding the car park, the bandstand, the large stone vases. 'He must have waited unseen while she walked along the path and then crossed the lawn. He may not even have spoken to her.'

'And then he fired the shots and left her?'

A nod from Diamond.

'Didn't try and move her?'

Stormy wasn't being ghoulish, asking these questions. He was airing theories, and Diamond was willing to discuss them.

'Too risky. I think it was in his plan to leave her to be found.'

'Yet that wasn't the m.o. in Patsy's case.'

'I know, Dave, and I have my view on that. It's all suppo-sition, but I think it makes sense. He covered his tracks the second time. He chose an even more secluded place

to meet your wife. It could have been that little park above
the railway embankment or somewhere miles away. The
crucial thing is he tricked her into going to the place,
the same as he'd tricked Steph.'

'How?'

'Don't know. A phone call most likely. Something he
knew would bring them out. The location was written in
Steph's diary, so she knew where she was headed. She
was easily swayed by any appeal to her good nature – some
old friend in trouble. You name it.'

'Patsy, too,' Stormy said. 'She'd drop everything and
go if anyone needed her. Well, you remember what she
was like, always supporting some good cause.'

It was true. Diamond could recall her doing the rounds
of the office, collecting for this and that. 'Mary', as he
still remembered her, was always the one who bought the
present when someone was leaving. 'Well, the killer
arranged to meet Patsy on some pretext, and shot her.
He'd picked his spot and he'd picked the spot where he
would take her after the shooting. That's the added
dimension. It's one step on from the murder of Steph.'

They walked the short distance back to the car park.
It was still early and Diamond offered to show his old
colleague his present place of work. 'We'll call that probation officer, Dawkins, and check Beach's alibi.'

'And the Bristol CID, to tip them off about the gun-
dealing?'

'Specially them.'

Bath Police Station was unusually quiet. They learned that
McGarvie had gone with other senior detectives to some
location in West London after a tip-off from the Met that
Joe Florida had been sighted at a pub.

'Our last shot,' Stormy said.

'His.' In his office, Diamond got on with the business

of tipping off Bristol about Wayne Beach. He said truthfully that he'd got the information from one of his snouts. Then he called the probation service in Clapham and spoke to George Dawkins and had it confirmed that Beach had reported there on the morning of February the twenty-third.

'He's not our man,' he told Stormy.

'Wayne isn't anybody's man.'

He gave a half-smile. 'True.'

Stormy looked at his watch. 'I'd better get my train.'

'Why – have you got a cat to feed, dog to walk?'

'No, but we've finished for today, haven't we?'

'You're staying at my place tonight. Then we can start early tomorrow.'

'On what?'

'The real last shot.'

29

They brought in fish and chips and a couple of six-packs and spent much of the evening talking over old times at Fulham nick. Stormy had a better recall of those days than Diamond. You never forget your first year of policing, your first arrest, your first raid.

'I had other postings before then,' Diamond said to excuse his hazy memory. 'I signed on before you, Dave. Turned fifty this year – and don't say you wouldn't know it.'

'What did you do?'

'Do?'

'To celebrate the big five-o.'

'Oh – nothing.'

'Pity.'

'Save it, pal. It was after Steph was killed. What's a bloody birthday after something like that?'

'How long were you married?'

'Nineteen years. Why?'

'The way you talk about her, I'd have thought it was less.'

'Why? I felt the same about her as the day we met.'

Stormy nodded. 'I guess you were the kind of couple who hold hands in the street.'

A sharp look was exchanged. So far as Diamond could tell no sarcasm was intended. 'If we felt like it, we may have done.'

'There's the difference. We kept our distance. Doesn't mean we didn't care about each other. Like I told you, it wasn't rosebuds all the way for Patsy and me. I played away a few times – call me weak-willed, or oversexed – and she usually found out. But we always patched things up. Try and explain that kind of marriage to a sleuth-hound like Bowers.'

'Did you have to?'

'Not yet, but he'll be onto it soon. Friends of ours know we scrapped sometimes. They'll tell him.'

'I'm glad you told me.' Diamond appreciated the honesty. No doubt there would be suspicions that one more 'scrap' had resulted in violence and Patsy's death. The man was realistic enough to know the pattern any investigation followed. Bowers *would* dissect the relationship.

Some awkwardness remained between them. Stormy, talkative, with a tendency to blunder into trouble, wasn't the sort of man Diamond would normally strike up a friendship with, but then who was? He had almost no close companions in the police. It wasn't a job that encouraged confidences. But he was glad he'd made the gesture of welcoming him to his home. With their common cause they would make an effective team.

'Do you want vinegar with that?'

Stormy shook his head. 'What I'd really like is to find out if they nicked Joe Florida.'

Diamond said it was simple. He'd call the duty sergeant and find out.

A few minutes later he passed on the news that Florida was being questioned by McGarvie at Shepherd's Bush Police Station.

'Will he ask the right questions?'

'Who knows? They sound confident.'

'Aren't you?'

'That Florida is the killer?' Diamond looked away, at the photo of Steph he'd put in a frame on the wall-unit. 'He was never top of my list.'

'But he's a vicious bastard. You helped send him down.'

'Justly. He was bang to rights.'

'So what's the problem, Peter? He's well capable of murder.'

'I can't see the logic in it. If he hated my guts – and he probably did – then why not murder me? People like Florida live by a simple, brutal code, Dave. They demand, and they get. If they don't get, they give, and what they give is violence. We're not dealing with a chess grand master here. I don't see Joe Florida scheming and plotting in jail for years thinking when I get out I'll murder the *wives* of the coppers who banged me up, and that'll really make them suffer.'

'He'd rather kill us?'

'Of course – if he still bears a grievance. And I'm not convinced he had a reason to hate you when all you did was sit beside Blaize in the interviews.'

'I was alone with him a lot.'

'Doing what? You didn't get physical with him?'

Stormy grinned. 'Me – with Joe Florida?'

'I meant restrain him.'

'I know what you meant. He asked me things, how long I'd been on the force, if I was married, had kids. You know me by now. I can go on a bit.'

'He actually asked if you were married?'

'Yes.'

'And you told him?'

'I was trying to seem laid-back.'

'What was he after – a smoke?'

'I wouldn't have given him one. No, I thought at the time he was softening me up for something. It was scary, to be honest.'

'Softening you up for what?'

'He could see I was new in the job. He had this aura of evil. You must have sensed it, same as me.'

'What are you saying, Dave? That he psyched you out? That you did something out of order?'

Stormy was quiet for a time. Finally he sighed and said, 'I've never mentioned this to anyone.'

Diamond waited.

'He asked me to make a phone call for him, letting his girlfriend know he was nicked.'

'And did you?'

'Of course not.'

'But you promised Florida you'd do it?'

'Kind of.'

'Either you did or you didn't.'

He shrugged. 'I did, then.'

'And you think he remembers?' Diamond said in disbelief.

'I remember – and I wasn't sitting in the Scrubs staring at the walls. Things can get out of proportion, Peter.'

Diamond took a short swig of beer. 'Even if you're right, and he held a grudge as long as this, I still say he'd take it out on you, not your wife.'

About eleven, they made up an extra bed in the spare room. 'What's the agenda tomorrow?' Stormy asked.

'A trip to Guildford.'

'What for?'

'My wife's first husband, Dixon-Bligh, used to have a restaurant there. McGarvie says he's holed up somewhere, and I want to know why.'

'He's the one who could have been mentioned in the diary?'

'Right. "T" for Ted.'

'You think he's gone back to Guildford?'

'I wouldn't rule it out, but if he's covered his tracks,

as the Met seem to think, we're not going to find him that easily. We've got to go at him by a different route. I want to trace his ex-partner in the business – if possible.'

'Who is he?'

'She, actually.'

'A woman.' Stormy twitched as a dire thought struck him. 'What if he killed her?'

Diamond had thought of this a long time before. He remarked as if recalling some ancient mystery, 'It would be helpful to know.'

Stormy was still grappling with the implications. 'But there's no link between Dixon-Bligh and my wife's murder.'

'None that we know of – yet.'

After some ninety miles of Diamond's ultra-cautious driving they reached Guildford well past coffee-time and had to go looking for a place that would serve them. 'To settle my shattered nerves,' he muttered. 'I don't like the motorways.'

'You should have told me,' Stormy said. 'I could have walked in front with a red flag. We'd still have got here in the same time.'

'Cheeky sod.'

The first place they looked into after the café was a secondhand bookship. Diamond, better for the intake of caffeine, explained his thinking. There was always a shelf near the door of out-of-date guides, yearbooks and cata-logues. He picked off a 1998 restaurant guide and found the address of Dixon-Bligh's former establishment, the Top of the Town. 'See if this gets your juices going, Dave. "*The welcome is warm, the cooking classy at this easy-to-miss haven towards the top of the High Street. Edward Dixon-Bligh recently took over after a career of catering for the top brass in Royal Air Force establishments across the world. The menu reflects*

*his international pedigree, with chowders, cassoulets and pestos,
terrine of pork knuckle with foie gras, cinnamon-spiced quail
with cardomom rice and fine green beans and pan-fried salmon
with sarladaise potato and horseradish cappuccino sauce.
Desserts include Thai coconut with exotic fruit sorbets. A fine
cellar, mainly French and New World, is expertly managed by
Dixon-Bligh's partner, Fiona Appleby, who is pleased to advise."'*

'It's probably a McDonald's now,' Stormy said.

'Can't get more international than that.'

But it was no longer in business as a restaurant. They
found a body-piercing studio where the Top of the Town
had been. A window filled with tattoo-patterns and pieces
of metal designed to be inserted into flesh. The shaven-
headed, leather-clad receptionist almost fell off her stool
when the two middle-aged detectives walked in. She
thought their generation wasn't privy to the charms of
pierced nipples and navels.

Diamond confirmed the impression. He explained he
was only interested in the former owners.

'Them? They blew out of here ages ago. They split up,
didn't they?'

'What do you do with the mail?'

'It stopped coming.'

'They must have left a forwarding address.'

'The woman has a cottage at Puttenham. We used to
send stuff there.'

'Is that far?'

'Take the A31 on the Hog's Back. You'll see the sign.
It's about three miles.'

'Do you have a note of the address?'

'I remember it. Duckpond Cottage.'

'And you think she's still there?'

'Don't bank on it, mister. Are they in trouble, then?'

'It's just an enquiry. Why do you ask?'

''Cos you look like the police.'

'It's personal.'

Stormy said with a beam across his tomato-red face, 'You can't tell a book by its cover.'

Out at Puttenham they found Duckpond Cottage on its own at the end of a rutted track that Diamond refused to drive along. The place wasn't a picture-postcard cottage. It was built, probably in the nineteen-sixties, of reconstituted stone slabs that had acquired patches of green mould. But efforts had been made with the garden and the paintwork was recent. No one answered when they rang the doorbell. 'Par for the course,' Stormy said.

Through the letter box a few items of mail were visible inside.

Everyone in a village is supposed to know everyone else's business. At the nearest house a small, elderly man in a cap was standing in his doorway before they reached it.

'Who are you, then?' he piped up.

'Enquiring about your neighbour, Miss Appleby. Does she still live at Duckpond Cottage?'

'Why – has she gone missing?' He was more interested in asking questions than answering them.

It seemed she hadn't moved away.

'You're not from the council, about the drainage? Shocking, the state of that lane.'

'She doesn't appear to be at home.'

'Gone away, hasn't she?' Now there was a note of certainty in the voice, even if it ended as yet another question.

'Did she tell you?'

'I may be old, but my eyes are all right. I saw you prowling around, didn't I?'

'You did.'

'She hasn't been at home for the past three weeks.'

'As long as that?'

'Easily.'

Diamond was not entirely convinced. 'We looked through the letter box. I wouldn't say there's three weeks' junk mail on the carpet.'

'That's because someone comes in.'

'Really? Who's that – a cleaner?'

'In Puttenham? We don't have cleaners in Puttenham. Them's for fancy folk in Guildford.'

'Who could it be, then – Miss Appleby herself?'

'Nothing like her. This young lady is taller, with a good figure. She comes in a car once a week.'

'So it's a young woman we're talking about. Have you seen her yourself?'

'From a distance. I've watched her come and let herself in. Not Miss Appleby – she's different altogether. This one drives up in a fancy sports car, a red one, and leaves it where yours is, at the top of the lane. She doesn't stay long. Just goes inside for a couple of minutes and comes out carrying stuff.'

'What stuff? The post?'

'I reckon. I've seen her with a couple of bags, them plastic sacks. Pretty well filled up, they was.'

'Not just the mail, then?'

'Some of Miss Appleby's property, I expect. Clothes and things.'

'Didn't you ask her what was going on?'

The old man looked affronted. 'I'm not nosy.'

'But you don't even know who she is. Could be pinching the stuff.'

He shook his head. 'She don't act like a burglar. She lets herself in with a key in broad daylight. Must be family, wouldn't you say?'

'And always at the same time?'

'Once a week, round about two. What's today –

Wednesday? If you're willing to wait you could see her for yourselves.'

Not much fell into Diamond's lap, so he was disbelieving when it did. 'You're expecting this woman to visit the house today?'

'It's her day, isn't it?'

They moved Diamond's car to the old man's driveway. There would be under an hour to wait. Flattered by all the attention, their host offered them some of the chicken soup he was cooking for lunch, but each of them declined when they saw the state of his kitchen. In matters of hygiene the fancy folk in Guildford had the edge.

'You'll get the best view of Duckpond Cottage from my bedroom window,' the old man informed them while he dipped chunks of bread into his soup and sucked on them noisily. 'Go on up if you want.'

His bedroom promised to be no more salubrious than the kitchen, and wasn't, but they were policemen, and their work had taken them into more squalid places. They opened the window that looked out along the lane, leaned out and gulped some fresh air.

'If this woman turns up,' Diamond said, 'I think we should play this cautiously. I don't know what's going on here, but my instinct is to watch and wait and see where she goes.'

'Agreed,' Stormy said, then, after an interval, 'No offence, Peter, but if she drives off, as she probably will, and we get in your car and follow, would you mind if I took the wheel?'

A sniff from Diamond. 'Think you can do better?'

'I'm thinking of your faultless driving. We could find ourselves having to ask which way she went.'

He shrugged. 'All right.' Then added, 'I'd better warn you. I'm a nervous passenger.'

They heard the car's approach a few minutes after two,

just as the old man had predicted. It was an Alfa Romeo convertible with a fawn-coloured top, and it halted at the top of the track leading to Duckpond Cottage. The driver, a woman, youngish, with black hair teased into fine loose wisps, stepped out and touched the switch in her hand that locked the doors. She was in a turquoise sweater, black jeans and ankle-length boots.

'See what I mean about the figure?' the old man's voice piped up from behind the watching detectives. He must have finished his lunch and crept upstairs. 'Isn't that arse a peach?'

Diamond murmured, 'Haven't you got something else to do?'

'This is my time for a nap, but I can't get into bed with you here.' A strange fit of modesty.

Meanwhile the focus of all the interest was picking her way between the ruts along the track with the confidence of a regular visitor.

Diamond asked Stormy if he'd taken a note of the car's number. He had not.

'You're no better than he is, watching the floor show.'

She took a key from her pocket and entered the cottage. Diamond checked his watch.

Three minutes passed.

'Could be checking the answerphone,' he said. 'It can't take this long to pick up the mail.'

And shortly after, she emerged carrying what looked like letters in her right hand.

'We'd better get to the car,' he told Stormy. To the old man, he said, 'Siesta time.'

As the Alfa Romeo moved off in the direction of the main road to Guildford, they started up, Stormy at the wheel.

'I don't fancy our chances if she steps on the gas in that thing,' Stormy said.

'Keep your distance, and she won't have any reason to speed.'

'Which way do you reckon?'

'The A3 to London, I guess.'

Instead she turned south and immediately accelerated. 'Hope your motor is up to this, Peter,' Stormy said, putting his foot down.

Diamond braced. 'The motor may be, but don't count on the owner.'

'Got to keep her in sight. Do you think she spotted us?'

'She doesn't know us or the car. She's burning rubber for the hell of it.' He hunched down in the seat with arms folded, trying not to watch the speedometer.

They had some overtaking to do. Fortunately, the Portsmouth Road is as good as a motorway in places. Stormy drove with skill and nice judgement, getting the best out of Diamond's old Cortina, staying within sight of the Alfa Romeo without being too obvious about it. Right up the steep approach to Hindhead and the Devil's Punch Bowl the Cortina had power in reserve. 'This old heap handles well, Peter.'

'It gets good treatment – usually.'

'Who *is* this woman?'

'Never seen her before.'

'Heigh-ho, she's turning left at the lights.' Stormy jerked the car into the left lane and took the turn tightly, tyres screaming. They were now on a narrow two-way stretch through a wooded area, and she hadn't cut her speed.

'Think she's spotted us yet?' Stormy asked.

'I told you. She won't know who we are.'

'It's mutual.'

They passed more than one sign to Haslemere. 'We're still going south,' Diamond said.

'Now she's using a car-phone.'

'Bloody dangerous at this speed.'

'Maybe she noticed us.'

In another mile the brake-lights of the convertible suddenly blazed for no obvious reason. It happened twice.

'She's looking for somewhere to turn off,' Stormy said.

'Don't crowd her, then.'

When they crested the next hill the Alfa Romeo was no longer in sight.

'What the fuck . . . ?'

'Slow up, man. There's got to be a turn here,' Diamond said.

A narrow lane came up on the right, and Stormy did well to spot it and make the turn. They hadn't travelled more than sixty yards when there was a flash of metal ahead and another vehicle came fast towards them, so fast that they were forced off the hard surface onto a mud path, the wheels skidding and screeching against the wood of a low hedge. A white Mercedes with a woman at the wheel. A mop of dark hair in wisps, pale, staring face, turquoise top.

'She's switched cars.'

'Flaming hell.'

She was past, heading for the road they'd just left and there was nowhere to turn. Diamond swung around in his seat and watched the Mercedes through the rear window. 'Back up. Reverse.'

Stormy slammed into reverse and steered them back towards the road whilst Diamond strained to see which direction the Mercedes would take at the top of the lane.

'Right. She's gone right.'

'Say your prayers, then. We're going arse-out into the road.'

By a miracle nothing was passing when they did. Stormy spun the wheel again and they zoomed off in the direction the woman had taken. Two cars were on the road ahead. Neither was a white Mercedes.

'How did she do that?' Stormy shouted over the acceleration.

'Switch cars? Trying to shake us off, I suppose.'

'I didn't say *why*. I said *how*.'

'Someone must have had it ready. That phone call from the car?'

'Whatever, she's left us for dead.'

They overtook the two cars. Nothing else was in view.

'Have you thought why we're risking our bloody lives?' Diamond said as they hurtled along well in excess of the speed limit. 'We're chasing a woman who might or might not lead us to another woman who might or might not be able to tell us the whereabouts of a man who might or might not have committed murder.'

'Want to give up?'

'No. Keep going.'

And persistence paid off. Around the next bend was a sign for road works and temporary traffic lights. In a few hundred yards they joined the end of a stationary line of traffic held by a red light. Three ahead was the white Mercedes.

Back in touch.

'Is it worth getting out?'

'No. We want to know where she's going.'

The lights changed and everyone moved again. It was sedate progress behind a container lorry, which suited Diamond. He was looking at signs.

'The next place of any size is Midhurst.'

The driver of the Mercedes was getting impatient, repeatedly edging out into the oncoming lane for a chance to overtake the couple of vans and the truck ahead. Each time something appeared in view.

'She must have a death wish if she goes for it.'

'So what do we do then?'

The lorry peeled off into a layby and the vans eased towards the kerb, enabling the Mercedes to cruise past and pick up speed again. Nothing was approaching, so Stormy made the same move. Diamond cautioned him yet again to keep some distance back. They didn't have to be obvious.

Without any indication the Mercedes left the Midhurst Road at a right turn. About a hundred yards in the rear, the detectives followed, along a twisting, bumpy road through a dense wood.

'Pull over,' Diamond said suddenly. 'She's stopping.'

They slid into an overtaking bay with enough foliage around it to hide them from the road ahead.

'Think she saw us?'

'Who knows?'

'Let's get out. Don't slam the door.'

Diamond's legs felt as if he had run every yard of the trip from Puttenham, and he was mightily relieved to get his feet on the ground again. Dipping low, he trotted across a carpet of dead leaves to a place among the trees that gave reasonable cover. Stormy did the same.

They could see the Mercedes standing in a cobbled driveway in front of a large red-brick house. The woman got out, raked a hand through her hair, stretched, and stood looking along the road, probably to check that she'd shaken off her pursuers. Then she stepped towards the house. They heard a door open and close.

'So?' Stormy said.

'Let's get closer.'

There was a point where the wooded area ended and the landscaped garden began and it was surrounded by a ring fence six feet high that looked in good condition.

Diamond felt a nudge from his companion.

'What?'

Stormy was pointing at a video camera mounted on a post inside the fence and swivelling, scanning the area where they stood. They dipped out of view.

'Strong on security.'

'But you and I know that sometimes these things are just for show.'

Diamond decided on the next move. 'Give me ten minutes to size up the place,' he told Stormy. 'Better if one of us goes in first.'

Stormy said he would wait in the car.

The only way in was through the front gate, so he used it, conscious that he was likely to be picked up by a camera. The surveillance equipment looked state of the art.

He crossed the cobbles to the porch and hesitated. To his left was a large, low, mullioned window with leaded panes. It probably gave a view of one of the front rooms. He stepped closer. Inside were two large sofas and a vast coffee table with a few magazines arranged symmetrically on it. He was reminded more of a dentist's waiting room than a private home. A door stood open at the far end and he was conscious of a movement and saw someone cross the space behind. Female, he was certain, and he assumed she must be the woman they'd been following. At least she wasn't sitting in front of a CCTV monitor watching his movements.

Feeling bolder, he decided to reconnoitre the place from outside. Keeping close to the wall, he edged around the side of the building.

Straight ahead was a sunroom with metal lounging chairs and pink and green cushions. It had an exterior door that he tried and found locked.

He was totally still when he heard the scrape of a stone close by.

He spun around.

She was right behind him, the woman they'd followed from Puttenham, legs apart, leaning slightly forward, hands in front of her in a martial arts stance. There wasn't time for words. He put up a hand defensively and she grasped it with both of hers and tugged him towards her. Totally unprepared for this, he lurched forward and suddenly she executed a twist, thrust out her left leg and he crashed over her thigh and hit the ground hard.

Fortunately he'd landed on turf, or he would have broken a limb for sure. Winded and shaken, he tried to raise himself. But the combat wasn't over yet. She threw herself on him and straddled him with her thighs, forcing him face down. She grabbed his right arm and yanked it across his back. He felt something cold tighten around the wrist, like wire. Then round the other arm.

He was handcuffed.

30

The lines on Joe Florida's face gave the lie to his dark hair. They were deeply etched around his eyes and mouth and no one would mistake them for laugh-lines. He was probably past fifty. And the striplight overhead lent that hair an unlikely reddish sheen. Seated opposite Curtis McGarvie and Keith Halliwell in an interview room at Shepherd's Bush Police Station, he was well aware of his rights. The clock was ticking. They could hold him without charge for twenty-four hours and it might be extended to thirty-six by an officer of superintendent rank or above for a 'serious arrestable offence', but he was entitled to eight uninterrupted hours of rest in the twenty-four. He'd already been in custody more than eight. There had been delays. His solicitor had not been in any hurry to get there. The police themselves were slow, hampered by being a hundred miles away from their incident room.

Curtis McGarvie had thought seriously about transporting the man to Bath, but that would have added hours, and the solicitor would have raised all kinds of objections. So they were doing it here.

McGarvie wasn't discouraged. He'd watched Florida's body language. The man was uneasy each time the questioning returned to the murder of Stephanie Diamond.

'Once more, what were you doing in Bath on Tuesday, February the twenty-third?'

'Get real, will you?'

'Answer the question.'

'It's a stupid question.'

'So where were you?'

'February was months back, for Chrissake.'

'Have you visited Bath this year?'

'For the tape,' Halliwell said, 'the witness is shaking his head.'

McGarvie tried another ploy. 'And if I said we have someone who saw you that morning?'

Joe Florida twitched.

The solicitor was quick to say, 'If you do have a witness, kindly inform us. If the question is hypothetical – as I strongly suspect it may be – I'm advising Mr Florida to ignore it.'

McGarvie gave a shrug. 'It would save us all a good deal of time if Mr Florida stated where he was that morning.'

'He doesn't remember. I doubt if any of us could remember what we were doing on a precise date seven or eight months ago.'

'He does,' McGarvie said. 'It's obvious from his demeanour.'

And Florida twitched again.

She ordered Diamond to stand. Not easy when you're cuffed. Then she frisked him – expertly. She unlocked the sunroom door and prodded the small of his back. Inside, she pressed on the handcuffs and forced him to his knees.

'Face down again.'

He had no option.

The cuffs weren't the old-fashioned sort. They were steel wire loops that cut into the flesh, and they hurt. They hurt still more when she grabbed his right foot and bent the leg back and fastened it to the wrists.

'I'm going for the other one,' she said, and he realised she wasn't speaking to him. At the edge of his vision he could just make out a movement. A shoe, a trainer. He couldn't see who the wearer was.

A male voice said, 'Don't try anything.'

Some chance.

The woman was already gone. She knew about Stormy, too. The camera hadn't been for show.

He lay humiliated, in pain and confusion. It was bad enough being a loser, but to lose so pathetically was dire. The speed of the attack, its cold efficiency, had caught him off-guard. True, he wasn't in the prime of youth, but he'd always believed he'd give some account of himself in hand-to-hand combat. Joke. He'd raised one hand and been thrown and disabled by a woman half his size.

He still didn't understand why. The attack was over-reaction considering all he'd done was stroll around the outside of the house.

All he'd done? Being brutally honest, that wasn't all.

He'd tried a door handle, and that had been ill-advised. If you act like a house-breaker, you lay yourself open to attack.

Even so.

It wasn't long before he heard the door open and her voice ordering someone to get down beside him. Apparently Stormy hadn't put up much of a fight either.

Stormy started to say, 'You don't have to—' Whereupon he was dumped beside Diamond.

'She surprised me,' he told Diamond.

The big man was in too much discomfort to answer.

He heard her tell her colleague, 'I can handle this now.' To Diamond, she said, 'I'm going to release your leg. Don't get ideas. I'm armed.'

The relief was exquisite. His hands were still bound, but blood returning to the veins was bliss.

'On your feet, both of you. I'm prepared to use this gun.'

With difficulty, they obeyed, and a sorry sight they made. Stormy's nose was streaming blood and Diamond's face was heavily smeared with mud. And they were staring into the barrel of an automatic. She was using the two-hand grip recommended on all the weapons training courses.

'Who exactly are you?'

Diamond darted a glance at Stormy, trying to convey that the truth was the best option now. 'Police officers investigating a crime.'

She almost snorted at that.

'If you look in the back pocket of my trousers, you'll find my warrant card,' he told her. 'I'm Detective Superintendent Diamond, and I work out of Bath.'

'DCI Weather,' Stormy chimed in. 'Mine's in my inside jacket pocket.'

She stepped forward, still holding the gun in her left hand, took the ID from Stormy's pocket and clearly decided it was genuine. 'This beats everything. What sort of police work is this, breaking into a private house?'

Playing it straight, Diamond explained that they'd gone to the cottage at Puttenham looking for Fiona Appleby, seeking information about her ex-partner, Edward Dixon-Bligh, who was wanted for questioning in connection with two murders.

'*Murders?*'

'Right.'

'My God, you've got some explaining to do.'

'Do you want to hear about that, or shall I carry on telling you how we got here?'

'All right. You saw me go into the cottage and thought I was Fiona?'

'No. You're the one who collects the mail.'

'You knew this?'

'We found out.'

'Who from?'

'The neighbour.'

She clicked her tongue at her own carelessness.

Quick to follow up, Diamond asked, 'So do you know what's happened to Fiona?'

She ignored that. 'Let's get back to this peculiar mission of yours – how two senior detectives come all this way to interview a minor witness. A DCI and a super? What am I missing here?'

One thing was clear: this young woman was well-briefed on police procedure.

'Before I answer that, who do you work for?' Diamond asked.

'That's not for discussion. I asked you to explain yourselves.'

'You act as if you're on the side of law and order. Are you?'

She hesitated, then nodded.

'Okay,' Diamond went on. 'Did you read in the paper about the woman's body found recently beside the railway embankment near Woking?'

She had. 'The ex-policewoman?'

'Right. She was Dave's wife, Mrs Patricia Weather. My own wife was murdered in a public park in Bath last February.'

Plainly she was unprepared for this. She said nothing, but her eyes widened.

Diamond explained more, trying to sound reasonable. 'Before you ask, we're acting on our own initiative. Unofficial, in other words. We have a common cause, as husbands of the victims. The main inquiry is going its own way, and Dave and I are not involved. More to the point, we're not satisfied, so we're following an independent line.'

'I've heard of these cases, both of them,' she admitted, softening her tone. She actually lowered the gun a fraction. 'You're taking a lot on yourselves, aren't you – going out on a limb?'

'Yes. We're out of order. But that's the answer to your question – why two senior detectives are out here trying to see a minor witness.'

'And tailing me?'

'Right.'

She took time to absorb what she had heard. 'You obviously believe Dixon-Bligh is a serious suspect? On what evidence – just that he's lying low?'

Diamond explained that Dixon-Bligh had been Steph's first husband and how they were linking him to the diary entries.

'Why? What's his motive?'

'He's skint. It looks as if he was demanding money from Steph shortly before she was killed. I interviewed him in London not long after the murder. I found him unhelpful and hostile.'

She turned to Stormy. 'And is the same man linked in some way to your wife's death?'

'We're not certain,' Stormy had to admit. 'Like Peter said, we're helping each other.'

'Surely it's up to the SIO on the case to pursue these enquiries?'

'If he had, we wouldn't be here.'

She was shaking her head. 'All this is so bizarre that it might just be true. You can sit down, but I'm keeping the cuffs on you.' She waved them towards a couple of wicker armchairs.

'You asked if I have a link with the police, and I do,' she told them. 'I'm in SO10, the Witness Protection Unit. I have the rank of inspector. I'm guarding Fiona Appleby.'

'She's alive, then?' Diamond said, encouraged.

'In the next room watching television.'

'For her protection?'

'Yes. This is a police house – a safe house.'

'Who are you protecting her from?'

'Dixon-Bligh?' Stormy suggested.

She didn't answer.

'I see the answer in your eyes,' Stormy pressed her. 'You can trust Peter and me, love. Dixon-Bligh is the enemy, isn't he?'

Diamond cringed at the endearment, but to his mystification, it worked. The doughty DO10 inspector gave Stormy a look that was almost a wink.

'And others.'

She was clearly reluctant to say more, though all the aggro had disappeared.

Whatever it was that was working for them, Stormy was going to milk it. 'Listen, love, what's your first name?'

She balked at that.

'Make one up, then.'

'Gina will do.'

'Gina – that's nice. And I'm Dave. He used to call me Stormy, but he's more respectful these days.' He grinned. 'Gina, there's an "all units" out on Dixon-Bligh. Did you know that? The Met have been looking for him for the past two weeks. If you know this bozo is dangerous, don't you think there might be a tie-in with the two murders?'

She shook her head. 'There's no connection I know of.'

'Maybe we can put you right on that.'

Now Diamond chimed in. 'Hold on, Dave. Gina, you just told us Fiona Appleby is under special protection. What's special about her? I thought she was just someone who was living quietly in a Surrey village because her restaurant failed.'

'That's true. She's an innocent woman caught up in

events outside her control.' She stopped speaking, as if reminded she was giving too much away.

Diamond tried gentle persuasion. If it worked for Stormy, why not for him? 'If you could see your way, there are things we'd dearly like to ask her.'

'No chance.'

'She has vital information.'

'Do it through official channels.'

'We're not official, Gina. We're very unofficial, as I just explained. But you want to stop Dixon-Bligh from harming anyone else and so do we. This is crying out for co-operation.'

'In your dreams.'

Diamond simply didn't have his companion's charm. Stormy applied more of it. 'Gina, we have something to trade.'

The smile returned. 'Oh, yes?'

'Information no one else can give you. Think about it: this pain in the arse Dixon-Bligh was once married to Peter's wife. Peter can tell you all about his old haunts, the places he thinks of as safe, the contacts he has. Isn't that right, Peter?'

'Well—'

'Between us, we can find him, but we need to speak to Fiona.'

She looked tempted, then adamant. 'It can't be done.'

'It can, my dear, if she's only in the next room.'

'I don't have the authority.'

'You want an order from an officer of higher rank?'

She smiled faintly. 'Not you. Nor him.'

'Your guvnor.'

'How would you know who my guvnor is?' She was almost flirting with Stormy.

'Ways and means, darling, ways and means. What if your guvnor gets to hear that two old gits in a clapped-out

Cortina followed you all the way from Puttenham to your safe house?'

A muscle flexed at the edge of her mouth.

Stormy said, 'You won't forget to report it, will you?' She didn't answer.

'You don't have to, honey – so long as we keep our mouths shut. But if we boast about it to our friends, you can be sure the one person you don't want to hear the news will get it from the old bush telegraph.'

'You're not threatening me, I hope?'

'Far from it.' Diamond chipped in and raised the stakes still more. 'This is big-time for you. You caught us snooping and overpowered us. Under questioning we admitted we were senior police officers. Then you found we had significant information. Back of the net.'

Now the eyes were moving anxiously. 'You'd say that?'

'Sure – as a trade-off.' He turned to Stormy, who was nodding.

She thought in the silence. There seemed to be deeper impulses at work here, matters outside Diamond's power to persuade. Her voice shook a little as she said, 'All right. You can meet her if you wish, since you've gone to such lengths to find her.'

'Thanks.'

'Trussed up, as we are?' Stormy said, pushing the concessions as far as possible.

'I didn't say shake hands with her.'

'Gina, look at the state of us. We're a scary sight. Don't you think you should let us clean up first?'

A sigh. 'All right. There's a bathroom nearby. But don't get the idea I've caved in. I'm going to have to report all this.'

'We'll take our chances.'

'I'm the one who's taking chances.'

She had keys attached to her belt, and she unlocked

the handcuffs and escorted them to the bathroom and watched them clean up.

'Straight through the hall.' Still far from comfortable with what they had talked her into, she made sure she didn't turn her back on them. She'd slipped the gun into a holster at her waist. She was well capable of dealing with any aggression. 'Last door.'

So it was Diamond who opened the door at the end and admitted them to a sitting room where a small woman in a black tracksuit was curled on a sofa watching TV. Fiona Appleby was in her forties probably, with hair streaked with silver. She picked up the remote and switched off the power.

'Everything's OK, Fiona,' Gina said at once, and then introduced them as police officers in a way suggesting they had just driven up and called at the front door. 'They're trying to trace your ex-partner, and they have a few questions for you.'

She had the worry-lines of a woman close to breakdown. She turned up her hands in appeal. 'But I already told you, I haven't seen him in months. I've no idea where he is.'

'Do you mind if we go over familiar ground?' Diamond gently asked. 'When did you first meet him?'

'That isn't familiar ground. Nobody's asked me yet.' She closed her eyes, remembering. 'It would have been ninety-five. December.'

'Where?'

'A Christmas party at one of the City Livery companies. Mercers' Hall, I think. I was in advertising at the time and hating it. Ted was doing the catering. He's a brilliant cook.' Launched into this, she spoke with intensity, recalling the details. 'The canapés were like nothing I'd seen before. Delicious and wonderful to look at. One little pastry concoction with duck pâté and cranberry was such a gorgeous bite that I made up my mind to ask the caterer how it was done. I'm passionate about cooking. I went into the kitchen and of course Ted was charming and good-looking and promised to give me the recipe if I went out for a drink with him the next evening. I was flattered. I really hadn't thought it would lead to anything. And we clicked at once because I've always loved to cook and we spent the evening discussing all the television cooks we would shoot on sight and the cookbooks we'd throw into their coffins. He was terrific fun to be with. That was the start of our relationship.'

'You teamed up right away?'

'Not immediately. It was more gradual. We had this dream of starting our own restaurant. It was just lovers' talk at first, and yet we began to believe it. The green and white colour scheme and the two little bay trees in tubs outside the door. We talked about where it should be – somewhere just outside London in the southern commuter belt. And before the end of the year we were looking at shop premises. The place at Guildford came onto the market – to rent, that is. The flat upstairs went with it. I had some savings to equip the shop, and I can tell you we did it beautifully. The crockery, the table linen, candles – it was our dream realised. And we got in all the top restaurant guides.'

'We've seen one. They rated you.'

'So did the public. We were fully booked most evenings, and people came back. They drove in from miles around. It should have been a tremendous success.'

'So what went wrong?'

Fiona's expression switched suddenly to a penetrating frown. 'Well you know, don't you?'

'We'd rather hear it from you,' Diamond improvised. 'His habit.'

He gave a nod that was meant to be knowing, encouraging her to say more, while he reeled from the mental jolt she'd just given him.

'I didn't suspect anything when we first met,' she went on. 'He was nothing like my idea of an addict. Not that I knew the first thing about drugs. I was incredibly naïve. Ted handled the accounts, banked the takings. I trusted him. I had no idea he'd run through my savings and was putting nothing back. The money was all going to drug-dealers. And all this time he looked perfectly healthy, cooked beautifully, treated me like a goddess.'

'What was he on?'

'H,' Gina murmured.

Diamond's face registered nothing of this bombshell. Inwardly he cursed his sluggish brain for failing to think of drugs. What else could have brought a successful, artic-ulate man to the squalor of that terrace behind Paddington Station?

'But you know all about him,' Fiona said.

'Hearing it just as you tell it is so much more helpful,' he said with all the calm he could drag up from his plunging self-esteem. The case against Dixon-Bligh was red-hot now. He wanted to run through it in his head, item by item, but he had to listen. There could be more.

Fiona said, 'It came to the point where even I found out what was going on – that we had a huge overdraft and a mass of unpaid bills. It was heart-breaking. Such deceit. I found a syringe and needles hidden in a casse-role dish high up in a cupboard in the kitchen. He was full of repentance. Drug-users are when they're found out. I was stupid enough to trust him and expect him to stop. We went on for a few weeks more and the bills just mounted up. He was still buying the stuff, still injecting. We closed the restaurant and I used the rest of my savings to clear some of our debts. Ted went off to live in London and I didn't want or expect to hear from him ever again.'

'But you did?'

'Earlier this year. He knocked on my door one afternoon. I suppose it wasn't difficult to track me down. Everyone knows I live in Puttenham. Can you believe he was asking for money again? Addicts have no shame at all. He wanted a thousand pounds. Said it would be a loan and he'd pay me back at ten per cent interest. I told him in no uncertain terms that I was disgusted he had the gall to come back to me wanting more of my money. He went on arguing, saying he now had a very good job at the Dorchester Hotel.'

'The *Dorchester*?'

'Assistant chef, or something. I didn't believe him, and then he fished in his pocket for some letter on headed notepaper confirming the appointment. I still said it made no difference and I didn't have money to lend him. But he's so crafty, nosing around the cottage, spotting nice bits of furniture he'd never seen before. He soon cottoned on to the fact that my father had died the December before last and I was the main beneficiary. Once he'd got the scent of the money, he said he'd take me into his confidence because he was on the verge of making so much that he'd soon be in a position to pay me back at twenty per cent if I wanted, and he'd still have so much left he'd never bother me again. I thought he was talking about the lottery or something and I treated it all with contempt, and I suppose that just fired him up. Next thing he was telling me about these Arabs he'd met.'

Gina said quickly, 'I think you should stop there, Fiona.'

'Why?'

'They've heard enough.'

'But we haven't. We need to hear it all,' Diamond said at once. 'We know what Dixon-Bligh is like, and we're keen to stop him ruining more people's lives.' He ignored the foul look he got from Gina and said, 'Together, we'll do it.'

Fiona turned to Gina. 'You told me they were the police.'

'We are,' Stormy said.

'I can trust them, can't I? I'd like to tell it.'

Gina, outgunned, sighed and said nothing.

Fiona took up her thread again. 'Ted told me these Arabs made a deal with him. They'd offered him twenty thousand in return for inside information from the Dorchester. All he had to do was find out in advance when some prince from Kuwait was due to stay. Apparently it's all done secretly for security reasons. Nobody is supposed to know until they arrive, but of course certain people have to be told, and Ted knew who to ask. As simple as that, he said.'

'And he'd tip off the Arabs?'

'And get paid. He was ready to write me an IOU on the strength of it. He needed money now for his drugs. He couldn't wait for this payday, as he called it.'

'Did you give him any?'

'No. I wouldn't be so daft. You know that old saying? He that deceives me once, shame fall him; if he deceives me twice, shame fall me.' Fiona Appleby obviously didn't think she'd put her life at risk to preserve her self-respect. 'However, I've got to say this in Ted's favour. He wasn't lying this time. There really was some underhand arrangement going on. Whether these mysterious Arabs would pay him all that money I had no idea, but he believed it. He was going through with it, I'm positive.'

'How did you get rid of him?'

'By holding out.'

'Didn't he get violent?'

Diamond had struck a wrong note. Fiona stared at him with her large brown eyes. 'No. He's never laid a hand on me. He wouldn't.'

'Don't count on it,' he warned.

Gina murmured, 'We don't. Which is why she's here.'
'So there's more to this?'

'You can tell them,' Gina said. She was now resigned to everything being in the open.

Fiona had her hands across her stomach inside the tracksuit top. She curled her legs more tightly. 'After he'd gone, I thought about what he'd told me. All that money he was counting on. There had to be something criminal going on, and something very big. People don't pay vast sums without due cause. It troubled me. That night I couldn't sleep. All kinds of horrible ideas crept into my head. I thought of the Gulf War. It was never really resolved, was it? Suppose these Arabs he'd met were Iraqi agents planing to assassinate one of the Kuwaiti royal family? If that happened, and I knew in advance and did nothing about it, I'd have to live with the knowledge that I could have prevented a tragedy. Ted was hopelessly dependent. He wouldn't have a conscience. He didn't think past his next fix. It was up to me to do something about it. So I phoned the Foreign Office. And they took it seriously. They sent someone to see me the same day.'

· Gina cut in. 'Fiona's information prevented a serious crime. Not an assassination attempt as it turned out, but a huge scam involving diamonds. Our people laid on a stake-out at very short notice and stopped the handover, but through a combination of problems the perpetrators got away.'

'Not much of a stake-out,' Stormy commented.

'These are international terrorists. They're highly organised.'

'Unlike you and me, Stormy,' Diamond said to take the heat out of the exchange. 'So who do they work for?'

'That's secure information.'

'In short, then, Fiona needs protection now, not just

from Dixon-Bligh, but these Arab bandits as well. Do you know their names?'

'It's under investigation.'

'Meaning "no",' Stormy said.

'Do you know where Dixon-Bligh is?'

'He's in the process of being traced.'

'Another "no",' Stormy said, all too ready with the slick comment.

Diamond gave him a murderous glare. They didn't want to provoke Gina at this stage. 'Leave it out,' he said more for Gina's ears than Stormy's. 'We're as much in the dark as anyone else.'

'Sorry. I'm always shooting off at the mouth,' Stormy said, sounding genuine, and it was a pity his face wouldn't register a blush, because one was probably lurking there.

Diamond hesitated, uncertain if there was anything more of importance to be learned.

There was, and it came from the least likely source – Stormy.

'Peter, I can't clam up now. I've been listening to all this and getting more and more steamed up. My wife, my Patsy, worked with the District Drugs Unit for two or three years before she retired. It was part of her job to visit the drop-in centres in Hammersmith Road and Earls Court Road. She knew all the heroin-users in West London. That's the link, Peter. Dixon-Bligh was on her patch. She must have known him when he was living in Blyth Road, and I didn't think of it.'

31

All this came like a wake-up call to Diamond. He now remembered Stormy mentioning how Patsy Weather worked with junkies at some stage. Like much else, it had been squirreled away in his memory, unlikely to have been recovered but for this.

Gina was just as fired up as the two detectives. 'Can you be certain she knew Dixon-Bligh?'

'If he was on her patch using drugs, you can almost bank on it,' Stormy told her, eyes dilated enough to have you believe he, too, was high on something.

'Why would he want to murder her? She'd retired from the police, you said.'

'He wasn't to know that, was he? I don't know how they met again. Pure chance, I guess. Patsy was always ready to talk to someone she knew. He'd assume she was still on the strength.'

'So he put a gun to her head and shot her?' she said in a rising tone of disbelief. 'What for?'

'Fear of arrest. He thought he was nicked.'

'For petty thieving to fund his habit?'

'No, no, no,' Stormy cut in. 'He was on the run. He faced a murder rap. He'd already shot Peter's wife.'

'Ah.' She raised her hand like a tennis player who has just been served an ace. Then turned to Diamond. 'I'm not thinking straight today. When was your wife murdered?'

'February the twenty-third.'

'And your wife?' she asked Stormy.

'Disappeared on March the twelfth.'

'Two weeks after.'

'Just over.'

She was checking alternately between the two. 'Your wife was shot in a park in Bath?'

Diamond nodded. He'd cross-checked everything in his own mind, and he was as sure of the facts as Stormy, though he tried to appear calm.

'And Dixon-Bligh was once married to your wife? Why would he want to kill her?' Gina asked.

'For money, for his drugs.' Put bluntly like that, it was chilling. But every explanation he'd ever imagined was guaranteed to chill.

She kept her bright, shrewd eyes on him, inviting him to say more.

Patiently, he took her through the crucial details. 'I told you there were entries in her diary about phoning someone she knew as "T". Dixon-Bligh's name is Edward. Ted, right? That's the name you've been using yourself, I notice.'

'Right.'

He switched to a more immediate way of telling it. 'She reminds herself when I'm coming in late: "P out. Must call T." He says he needs to see her, and she promises to think it over. She gets her hair done – and that's typical of Steph, wanting to look right, even for a meeting with that berk. She calls him again – from a public phone, so the calls won't appear on our statement – and arranges this meeting in the park on the Tuesday. She says nothing to me about any of this, and Steph wasn't like that. Since reading what she wrote, I've driven myself nuts trying to understand why she set up those phone calls and meetings and kept me out of it. But now I learn he was a drug-

addict, it's all much clearer. This is the set-up. He's
pestering her for money, and she doesn't want me to
know about it. Steph is confident of handling him herself.
He's her ex, and she thinks she knows him. She may well
have been sending him small amounts of cash for some
time. She'd know my reaction.'

'Unsympathetic?'

'To put it mildly.'

'Does he possess a gun?'

Unexpectedly, Fiona Appleby spoke up. 'Yes.'

All eyes were on her.

'What sort?' Diamond asked.

'Pistol.'

'Revolver?'

'Yes. He did some shooting in the Air Force. He was
on the command team at Bisley. The gun was his own.
He kept it in the drawer beside the till. Said he'd produce
it if ever anyone tried to hold up the restaurant.'

Stormy turned up his palms as if no more needed
saying.

But Gina still required convincing. 'Why shoot her
when all he wanted was money for drugs?'

Diamond answered in a measured tone, drained of
emotion. 'He brings the gun with him intending to force
her to hand over more money than she intends, or credit
cards, maybe, instead of the small handout she offers.
She refuses. Steph was very strong-willed. He points the
gun at her head. She tries to push him away or says something that angers him and he squeezes the trigger.'

This had directness, the simplicity of cause and effect
that carried conviction.

Gina had listened impassively. She pointed a finger at
him. 'Okay. It's payback time. You said just now you knew
of places he might be hiding in. Were you bullshitting,
or can you deliver?'

In point of fact, all the bullshitting had come from Stormy, but sometimes when your bluff is called, the brain goes into overdrive. Without hesitation Diamond launched into the story Steph had once told him about the beach hut. 'At one time when he was in the Air Force and married to Steph they were based at Tangmere, in Sussex. They lived in married quarters, I think, and didn't like it much. The one good thing about it was that they were close to the sea, and on his days off they'd escape to some local beach with a peculiar name I'm trying to remember. Wittlesham?'

'Wittering?' Gina said, following this acutely. 'West Wittering isn't far from Tangmere.'

'You've got it. West Wittering. Steph told me they rented a beach hut one summer. They'd use it to change into swimming things, and brew up tea on an oil stove and so on. The point about this is that even after the rental ended, he kept a spare key, and for years he used to go back and open up the hut and use it.'

Gina was frowning. 'After it was rented to someone else?'

'People only use them a fraction of the time.'

'Sneaky.'

'That was Steph's reaction. She wouldn't join him.'

Gina was ahead of him now. 'You're thinking he might be holed up at the beach?'

'It wouldn't be a bad place to hide.'

'Out of season, too,' Stormy added support. 'Nice and quiet. You could survive pretty well in a beach hut.'

Diamond put in a note of caution. 'I don't even know if the huts are still there. Do they still have them at West Wittering?

'All the way along,' Gina said. 'I'm going to call my guvnor.'

* * *

Eleven hours in, Curtis McGarvie tried another tactic on
Joe Florida. Strictly speaking, the murder of Patricia
Weather was being handled by DCI Billy Bowers. He'd
informed Bowers of the arrest and invited him to join in
the questioning, but up to now he hadn't appeared.

'Where were you on Friday, March the twelfth?'

Florida answered casually, 'Who knows?'

'London?'

'Maybe.'

'South-west London? Your own manor?'

'What's this about?'

'A woman went missing that day.'

'Hold on, will you?' Florida said. 'Are you trying to
stick something else on me?'

'Her body wasn't found until a few days ago, on a
railway embankment in Surrey.'

'Jesus, I don't believe this,' Florida said, turning to his
brief. 'These assholes want to fit me up with a double
murder.'

The solicitor said, 'My client wasn't informed of this
at the time of his arrest.'

'Correct,' McGarvie told him without apologising. 'I
was getting ahead of myself. At this stage we're questioning him about the murder of Stephanie Diamond.'

'What does he mean – "at this stage"?' Florida
demanded. 'They can't do this to me.'

'We'll take a break,' McGarvie said. 'We've got a long
session ahead of us.'

West Wittering was less than an hour's drive from the safe
house. The long stretch of coast on the Selsey peninsula
is girdled by salt-marsh, sand dunes and fields where geese
congregate in hundreds. On summer weekends the beach
attracts large crowds, but in October is left to a few dog-
walkers, windsurfers and the occasional scavenger with a

metal detector. The land above the beach is owned by the West Wittering Estate and you enter through a coin-operated barrier. When the tide is out, as it was when the armed response team arrived, the stretch of sand is vast.

Officers in helmets and black body armour and carrying Heckler & Koch MP5s were already checking the beach huts with dogs when Diamond and Stormy Weather drove up. There was an air of confidence about the search. Apparently a local shopkeeper had been shown a picture of Dixon-Bligh and was certain he had bought food a number of times in the past two weeks.

Stormy looked at Diamond as if he was Nostradamus.

The wooden huts, about a hundred and fifty on a turf promenade above the beach, were a testimony to people's individuality. They had obviously been there long enough for some to have been replaced and others given a face-lift, so the doors and walls were decorated in a host of different styles and colours. Shuttered windows, veran-dahs and paved fronts were desirable extras. The majority were padlocked. A few of the oldest had conventional mortice locks built into the doors. It would be one of these Dixon-Bligh had illicitly used.

Diamond eyed the line of pitched roofs stretching almost to the sand dunes on the skyline at East Head, and asked the senior man how long the search would take.

'Not long, sir. The dogs will know if he's inside.'

This confident prediction was followed shortly by a result. The two springer spaniels started yelping and scratching at the door of one shabby hut towards the near end of the row. Their handlers had to haul them away.

'Game on,' the man in charge said.

Everyone took up strategic positions. Officers with sub-machine-guns crouched and took aim in the shingle below the level of the huts, watched from behind a stout wooden groyne by the others, including Diamond and Weather.

Diamond told a senior man they didn't want the suspect killed and was informed they were using soft-point rounds.

Through a loudhailer the occupant of the hut was told that armed police were outside. He was instructed to come out, hands on head.

There was no response.

Two more warnings were given. Then the order came to force an entry. A distraction device, some kind of thunderflash, was lobbed behind the hut and went off with a terrific report.

Instantly four men armed with sub-machine-guns dashed to the hut from either side. The only way in was through the front and it wouldn't take much. The wooden door was half-rotten through years of exposure to salt spray. A burst of gunfire shot away the hinges.

The door fell outwards and hit the paving stones. It had not been locked.

But no one was inside.

The anticlimax silenced everyone. There was that feeling of sheepishness – not unknown to Diamond – when the long arm of the law has reached out and missed.

Finally the man in charge said, 'Stupid bloody dogs.'

'Back to it, lads,' some other officer said. 'There's a million more fucking huts.'

The man at Diamond's side said, 'Which genius gave us this tip-off?'

Diamond said nothing, and Stormy stayed silent as well.

Interestingly the dogs were still straining at their leashes to return to the empty hut. The handlers had a problem getting them back to work.

'I know it's obvious no one is in there,' Diamond told Stormy, 'but I want a closer look.'

They stepped up to the hut and over the bits of timber that had been the door. There were definite signs of recent occupation. Just inside the doorway was a folded sleeping bag. Also a torch, a cut loaf and a carton containing canned food and beer. An *A to Z* of West Sussex and a copy of the *Sunday Express* – last week's edition. He picked up the torch and switched it on. 'What do you make of that, Dave?'

Stormy bent closer to the area of flooring caught in the beam of light.

Diamond told him, 'That's what excited the dogs.'

'Stormy wetted his finger and touched the dark patch. 'You're right. It's blood.'

After the forensic team and SOCOs arrived there was the usual hiatus. Clearly someone or some animal had shed blood in the beach hut, but it was a mystery where they had gone. The sniffer dogs took no interest in any of the other huts, or the changing rooms, toilets or café higher up the beach. With nothing else to detain them, the armed response team packed up and drove away.

'Looks like the Arabs got to him first,' Stormy said.

'Killed him, you mean? For blabbing?'

He nodded. 'Those guys don't take prisoners. Did you ever see *Lawrence of Arabia*?'

'If he's dead, I don't know where they left him.'

'Buried him on the beach, I expect. It wouldn't take long.'

'Wouldn't be long before he was found, either. Plenty of people come along here walking their dogs, even at this time of year, and when a dog gets a whiff of blood . . . And how would the Arabs have found him here?'

'They're smart operators, Peter. They escaped from the

Dorchester under the noses of one of these hotshot teams
of ninjas, so it's not beyond them to track Dixon-Bligh
to his hideout.'

'Unless.'

'Unless what?'

'Unless this is a totally unrelated incident. Remember
it was a hunch that brought us here.'

'Let's say a brainwave.'

Diamond sniffed. 'We can hope so.'

They sat on a wooden beam facing the band of grey
sea and the misty outline of the Isle of Wight. Nearer to
them, gulls and sandpipers in their hundreds had
colonised the wet sand.

'I hope this smackhead isn't dead,' Stormy said. 'I want
him put on trial.'

'Be better off dead when I catch up with him,' Diamond
muttered.

'You don't want to foul up your career for a scumbag
like that.'

'Watch me.'

'That's precisely why you and I are sidelined.'

From behind them a uniformed PC called Diamond
over to where the incident tapes kept any onlookers out
of the sterile area. 'Gentleman here wants a word, sir. He
appears to know something.'

The informant was a tall, elderly man with a white
moustache. He was wearing a windcheater and brown
corduroys tucked into green wellingtons. His red setter
started forward and licked the back of Diamond's hand.

'Something to tell me, sir?'

'Seeing all the activity here I wondered if it's anything
to do with that fellow they found on the beach yesterday.'

'What fellow?'

'Couldn't tell you who he was. I was walking the dog
as usual and saw what happened. Some windsurfers

spotted him half in, half out of the water at damned near high tide. Blood all over his shirt, but no wound that I could see. He was obviously in a bad way. Out to the world. They took him off in an ambulance.'

'Where would they have taken him?'

'Casualty, I expect. Chichester has the nearest A & E Department.'

'If my client were to make a voluntary statement about his movements on the day in question,' Joe Florida's solicitor said, 'and if he proved to your satisfaction that he had no part in the matter under investigation, would you be willing to set aside any possible prosecution on matters of a lower tariff?'

'No deals,' McGarvie told him.

'In that case, he has nothing else to say.'

Keith Halliwell leaned towards his SIO and whispered something.

McGarvie gave a petulant click of the tongue and sat back in his chair, raking both hands through his hair. Finally he said, 'If you were talking about something that happened outside our jurisdiction – we're from another force, Avon and Somerset, you understand – my colleague and I wouldn't' – he sighed, hating this – 'wouldn't necessarily be under an obligation to investigate.'

'He needs a stronger assurance than that.'

'Are you saying that after all this he remembers what he was doing on February the twenty-third?'

Joe Florida pointed to the tape recorder mounted on the wall. 'Turn that fucker off, and I'll tell you.'

'Typical breakdown in communications,' Diamond grumbled on the drive to Chichester. 'If someone is brought into hospital with blood all over him and no explanation, it's a police matter. The local CID must have been out at

that beach looking for evidence. Why didn't we hear
about it?'

'Because we were with Gina's lot,' Stormy pointed out.
'They're not exactly the local plod.'

Thanks to Stormy's driving they reached St Richard's
Hospital inside half an hour. The doctor in Accident &
Emergency took them into an office at once. A stetho-
scope hung from his neck and he fingered the sound-
receiver as he spoke. 'Yes, I was on duty yesterday when
the man was brought in from West Wittering. From the
contents of his pocket he was called Edward Dixon-Bligh,
but he hasn't been formally identified yet.'

'So he's dead?'

'On arrival.'

'Do you know the cause?'

'Loss of blood.'

'But where from?'

'His mouth. This is hard to believe, but someone cut
out his tongue.'

32

The next afternoon Diamond, back in Bath, was summoned to the top-floor suite known as the Eagle's Nest. Curtis McGarvie was there already, seated in the armchair closest to Georgina's desk. He had a half-empty mug of coffee in his fist, revealing he'd been there some time. And he was sitting at an uncomfortable angle with his knees pointing at Diamond, presumably to line himself up with the inquisition.

Georgina cleared her throat. 'Thank you for coming, Peter.' The greeting had a faintly pejorative edge, and the follow-up confirmed it. 'If you were expecting a pat on the back, think again. Just because the Yard are treating you like some footballer who scored the winning goal, it doesn't excuse your conduct here. You defied my explicit instruction to stay out of the investigation into your wife's death.'

'I did stay out, ma'am.'

'What?'

'Ask DCI McGarvie. I haven't troubled him at all. When did we last speak?'

McGarvie glared and said, 'That isn't the point.'

'You ran what amounted to a parallel investigation,' Georgina steamed on. 'You visited the crime scenes and interviewed witnesses. What's that, if it isn't interference?'

'Am I prohibited from visiting the place where my wife was murdered? No one made that clear to me.'

McGarvie said, 'You also turned up at the scene of the Patricia Weather murder – even before I did.'

'Nobody barred me from other cases.'

'Come off it, Peter. We all know it was a carbon copy of your wife's shooting.'

'We didn't know at the time. Stormy Weather is an old colleague. I was with him at Fulham. I'm allowed to have some sympathy for an old mate who goes through a similar experience, aren't I?'

Georgina said, 'This is evasion. You teamed up with DCI Weather and drove all over the south of England like . . .' She turned to McGarvie for help, and got none. '. . . like a re-run of *Starsky and Hutch.*'

'If you knew my driving, ma'am, you wouldn't make that comparison.'

'Don't mess with me. You go off on your own without any consultation, riding roughshod over sensitive lines of enquiry, blundering into this safe house where the witness was being kept.'

'That was to enquire about Ted Dixon-Bligh, ma'am.'

'And you're going to justify it on the grounds that he was the killer.'

'No, ma'am. He was family.'

'I beg your pardon?'

'My wife's ex-husband. I wanted to see him on a family matter.'

Georgina made a puffing sound of irritation.

Diamond explained, unfazed, 'DCI McGarvie told me he was holed up somewhere, and the Met couldn't find him. You'll confirm those were your words, Curtis?'

McGarvie wasn't willing to confirm anything. He stared straight ahead.

'You don't seem to remember. You'd lost all interest in Dixon-Bligh, or so it appeared to me at the time. You were getting very interested in Joe Florida. What happened about Florida?'

'Released without charge,' McGarvie said after a pained pause. 'After eleven hours, he finally decided to tell us he had an alibi.'

'What was that?'

'He was having his car tyres replaced at a garage in Hammersmith.'

'True?'

'Confirmed, yes.'

'It took eleven hours to get that out of him?'

'The old tyres left a set of prints outside a betting shop that was torched the previous evening.'

'Back on the protection game?'

'Apparently.'

Diamond gave a sigh that was almost sympathetic. 'We can't win 'em all, can we? I helped trace Dixon-Bligh, as you know, but it was too late.'

Now McGarvie waded in. 'You knew he was wanted for questioning. If you'd informed me about this beach hut at West Wittering, I would have collared him.'

'I honestly didn't think about the beach hut until I was at the safe house.'

'You're trickier than a cage of monkeys.'

Georgina continued with the tongue-lashing. 'The whole point is that your actions would have undermined a prosecution against this man. It's lucky for you he's dead.'

This time he was silent. He'd made all the points he wanted.

Georgina banged on for a few minutes more, saying she'd considered formally disciplining him and it was only because of the tragedy of Steph's murder that she chose to be compassionate.

He didn't thank her.

He was on the point of leaving when she seemed to relent a little, maybe deciding she'd taken too strong a line. 'It's brought closure, anyway, Peter.'

'What do you mean?'

'The man is dead.'

'That's closure?' he said in a flat voice.

'In the sense that we can draw a line under the investigation. I realise it doesn't put an end to your personal grief.'

He was silent.

Georgina asked, 'Did you have any suspicion Dixon-Bligh was involved with this Arab group?'

'Not till I was told, ma'am.'

'The manner of his death – removing his tongue – seems particularly brutal. I'm told it's considered a just punishment for an informer. In their society a thief has his hand cut off.'

'I've heard.'

'There's no question that it was an act of revenge by the diamond robbers?'

'That's the strong assumption.'

'They'll be out of the country by now.'

'I expect so.'

'Difficult, bringing international criminals to justice. Still, it's the Yard's problem, not ours. We're left with some tidying up of our own. It's time for some co-operation between you two. Curtis will need chapter and verse from you, every bit of evidence that seals Dixon-Bligh's guilt. It has to be written up before we can close the file. I rely on you, Peter, to pass on your findings. It will be hard for you, I appreciate, but a necessary duty.'

'Bit of a turnaround,' he commented.

'What?'

'You warn me off, tell me not to show my face in the

incident room, and now you want me to tell him how it was done. Cool.'

Not merely cool. In that atmosphere you could have preserved a mammoth for a million years.

'Well, I've got good news for you, Curtis,' Diamond filled the silence. 'You won't have to put up with those findings of mine, because they don't exist.'

'Just what do you mean by that?' Georgina asked.

'Dixon-Bligh didn't murder my wife.'

'For God's sake, Peter.'

'Will you hear me out?'

She sighed and leaned back in her chair.

Diamond said, 'I almost convinced myself he was the killer when I heard he was a junkie. It provided the selfish, blinkered, crazed motive I was looking for. But something didn't fit. I also learned yesterday that he was a chef at the Dorchester.'

Georgina took a deep, audible breath. 'We know about that.'

He nodded. 'But you didn't follow it up.'

'What do you mean – "follow it up"?'

'I did. This morning I phoned the Dorchester and asked if they happened to know if he reported for duty on February the twenty-third, the morning Steph was murdered. Yes, they said, he was in the kitchen, cooking.'

'This I refuse to believe,' McGarvie said to Georgina as if Diamond had finally flipped. 'How would anyone remember one day in February?'

'Because it was Shrove Tuesday – Pancake Day.'

'So?'

'People in the catering business remember Pancake Day. The Dorchester put on a big charity lunch hosted by the Variety Club of Great Britain. All the catering staff were there from early in the morning. It was one of the biggest lunches of the year.'

'Is this certain?'

'Dixon-Bligh was in the kitchen at the Dorchester cooking three hundred pancakes.'

'So he was definitely innocent?'

'Of murdering Steph? Yes. And almost certainly of murdering Patsy Weather. But there's no question he was involved in the diamond heist that went wrong. His fatal mistake was blabbing to his girlfriend.'

For some minutes after Diamond left Georgina's office, nothing was said. McGarvie sat in the armchair shaking his head at intervals.

Eventually, Georgina said, 'He's a loose cannon with a habit of hitting the target. A good detective. The best. I only said the things I did because I thought he'd cracked this, gone off and cracked it, and hung you out to dry.'

'I know, ma'am.'

'But he failed. We all failed. This was one of those wretched cases that beat everyone.'

33

On the first day of November, Curtis McGarvie's overtime budget was cancelled by Headquarters. Inevitably, the Stephanie Diamond inquiry was scaled down drastically, and the decision came almost as a relief to the team. They'd run through their options. Nothing new had come up. McGarvie remained in charge, with Halliwell as his deputy, assisted by three CID officers and two civilian computer operators. These days they rarely stepped outside the incident room.

Peter Diamond observed this with detachment. He'd long since lost any confidence in the murder team. He, too, was becalmed, but he promised himself it was temporary. He would never give up. He still lay awake for long stretches of the night wrestling with the big questions: why had Steph never mentioned her appointment in the park? Who was 'T'? What was the link – if any – with the shooting of Patsy Weather?

One rainy afternoon he phoned Louis Voss at Fulham. This wasn't in any way inspired, or clever. He just felt the need to talk to someone he trusted.

After they'd got through the small talk he said, 'You saw the stuff in the papers about Dixon-Bligh, I'm sure.'

'Poor sod, yes,' Louis said. 'He wasn't your man after all, then?'

'Someone else's. It gives fresh meaning to that old phrase about guarding your tongue.'

'Ho-ho. So where are you now on this investigation?'

'Nowhere.'

'I can't believe that, Peter.'

'None of the suspects measured up.'

'Square one, then?'

'Square one – which has to be Fulham nick when you and I and Stormy and Patsy were keeping crime off the streets of West London, or trying to.'

'Patsy?'

'Mary Poppins if you prefer – though I thought we'd all moved on since then.'

'You're speaking of Stormy's wife?' Louis said.

'Or wife-to-be, in those days. I'm still wondering why those two got hitched.'

'She was a good-looking woman, a knockout when she was young.'

'That's what I mean. He's a likeable guy, but let's be frank, his looks are against him.'

Louis laughed. 'Who told you that? Stormy pulled the girls like a tug-of-war team.'

Unlikely, he thought. He'd heard Stormy admit to playing away, but hadn't pictured him as quite so active. 'I can't say I noticed at the time.'

'You were a boss man. The guys at the workface knew the score, and Stormy scored more than most. Don't ask me his secret.'

Louis had no reason to exaggerate, Diamond reflected. He heard himself say something rather profound. 'Maybe women feel more confident with an ugly man. Or more confident of keeping him.'

Profound, yet hard to prove. Still, he'd watched a trained protection officer, Gina, mellowing under Stormy's charm offensive, even though it had all the subtlety of a Sherman tank. 'So did he change his ways after she married him?'

'Did he hell!'

'She put up with it?'

'At a price, no doubt.' Now it was Louis who ventured an opinion on the ways of women. 'A smart wife has her terms. Read the tabloids. There are plenty of examples.'

'Of big divorce settlements?'

'No, of wives who stay married and appear to put up with all the philandering – at a price. They come out the winners.'

'So you think she had Stormy's number?'

'Oh, yes,' Louis said. 'I watched it happen over the years. He had flings, but none of them lasted. She always reined him in.'

'Did she play around herself?'

'You're joking. She was more interested in nannying than nooky. She put her energies into chivvying us into being nice to each other – which isn't easy in our job. Well, you know what she was like. A cheery word for everyone.'

'I remember.'

'No one was better at organising a leaving party. She put on a terrific do for me when I retired. It was such a send-off I felt embarrassed coming back to the civilian job a couple of years later.'

'Yes,' Diamond said. 'She laid on a good party when I left Fulham.'

'I remember. And even after her retirement she was always coming back reminding us to organise some do or other that couldn't be ignored. We thought the world of Trish – which made it all the harder to understand why she was murdered.'

'Did you just call her Trish?' Diamond asked.

'For Patricia.'

'Is that what she was known as?'

'After the Mary Poppins joke was played out, yes.'

'Stormy calls her Patsy.'

'His privilege. She was Trish to the rest of us. Is this important?'

'I don't know,' Diamond said, but he could hear blood pumping through his head like a swan in flight. 'I'd better go, Louis. I'll talk to you again.'

He put down the phone.

The monstrous thought bombarded his brain. Could 'T' have been Trish – a woman? In the weeks immediately after the shooting he'd done his utmost to keep an open mind about the sex of Steph's murderer. But as the main suspects had lined up, all of them male, he'd drifted into thinking only a man could be the killer.

It needed a huge leap of the imagination to cast Patricia Weather as a killer. Nobody ever spoke badly of her. He remembered her as a warm, outgoing personality. She and Steph had probably met once or twice at social events, but they were never close friends. He could think of no reason for them to fix a meeting so many years after he and Steph had left Fulham and gone to live in Bath. And he knew of nothing that could have driven her to murder.

Besides, someone had murdered *her*, for God's sake.

Out of the question, then?

Not when he came at it from another direction. All along, he'd been at a loss to explain why Steph had gone to the park that morning to meet her killer. But if 'T' were Trish, sweet, caring Trish, the woman everyone regarded as Mary Poppins, and she suddenly made contact and suggested a meeting, it was possible Steph would have gone along.

Trish, being so efficient, would almost certainly have done the weapons training course in the underground range at Holborn nick. It was on offer in the eighties, and she would have wanted to prove herself as good as the men.

But that was a world away from murdering Steph.

For the millionth time, he came up against this barrier. Why should *anyone* have wanted to kill his gentle, trusting, unthreatening wife?

He reached for a pen and paper and forced himself to jot down her possible motives.

1. *She had a grudge against me.*
2. *She had a grudge against Steph.*
3. *She feared Steph knew some secret about her.*
4. *She was out of her mind.*

None of them stood out. Number 1 seemed unlikely; she was one of the few colleagues he'd never had a spat with. 2 and 3 were doubtful, considering Steph had never actually worked with the woman and scarcely knew her. And he'd heard nothing about a mental illness.

Maybe I'm wrong, he thought. Maybe they *did* know each other, and I didn't get to hear of it because Steph didn't think it important.

He picked up the phone and pressed *redial.*

'Louis? Me again. This is a long shot, but do you know anything about Trish Weather's life before she arrived at Fulham?'

'Can't say I do.'

'Could you find out?'

'That's personal data, Peter.'

'Yes, family, education, previous employment, all that stuff. Should be on her application to join the police, if that's still on file.'

'You're not listening,' Louis said. 'I can't access people's personal files.'

'But she's dead, Louis.'

The line went silent for a time.

Then Louis said, 'Couldn't you get this from Stormy?'

'I'd rather leave him out of it at this stage.'
Louis sighed.

He heard nothing back the next day. No bad thing to
mark time, he told himself. He'd leapt at the possibility
that Trish might be the 'T' in Steph's diary. Now he
needed to ponder it calmly.

And the more he pondered, the more he feared it was
another blind alley.

He'd almost abandoned the idea when Louis phoned
back.

'There isn't much, Peter. She applied for the police
straight after leaving school. Did her basic at Peel Centre
– Hendon, to you and me – and spent a year at West End
Central before she started at Fulham. It's a clean record.'

'Any firearms experience?'

'She was an AFO from nineteen eighty-seven.'

'Was she, indeed!'

'Also did courses on juveniles, driving, race relations
and drugs.'

'Is there anything on her early life?'

'Not a lot, but this might interest you. She was born
and brought up in Bath. She did her schooling at the
Royal High School. The family lived in Brock Street.'

Brock Street led to the Royal Crescent and Royal
Victoria Park. He gave a whistle that must have been
painful to hear down a phone-line. 'Spot on, Louis.'

'Does that help?'

'It's not what I was rooting for, exactly, but it may answer
one question I've sweated blood over – why they met where
they did. You see, the park where Steph was murdered
wasn't a place she would have chosen. She had her
favourite parks, but the Victoria wasn't one of them. I've
always believed her murderer suggested meeting there.'

After a pause, Louis said, 'Peter, you're not seriously putting Trish in the frame for your wife's murder?'

'Things are falling into place.'

'But she's dead. She was the second victim.'

Diamond didn't answer. His thoughts were galloping ahead.

Louis waited. 'Peter?'

'Yes?'

'I can see problems here. You want to be careful.'

'Why?'

'You know what McGarvie and Billy Bowers will think if they get wind of this theory? They'll think you went out and shot Trish Weather yourself.' After another long pause he said, 'God, I hope you didn't.'

34

A Mr and Mrs Gordon Jessel still lived in Brock Street, Bath, according to the phone directory. A check of the birth registers confirmed that they were the parents of Patricia.

Seized by the need to share the news with someone else, Diamond called Julie Hargreaves that evening and told her he had a new theory that 'T' was Patricia – or Trish – Weather. At first she refused to entertain it. But so had he, at first. Julie caught her breath when he mentioned that Trish had been an Authorised Firearms Officer.

'So what do you have here?' she said, assessing the information with the precision he valued so much. 'The name beginning with "T". The link with Fulham and the police. Experience with guns. The fact that she was brought up in Bath, so she knew where to set up the meeting with Steph. Anything else?'

'Something pretty important. Steph wouldn't have thought of Trish as threatening. She had this friendly personality everyone warmed to.'

'Then why?' Julie asked. 'What had this charming woman got against Steph?'

'Before I come to that, there's a different "why".'

'Yes?'

'Why did Steph go to the park at all?'

'It was fixed. It was in her diary.'

'Yes, but what was their reason for meeting? It's not as

if they were the best of friends. They met a couple of times when I was serving at Fulham in the eighties, but they didn't know each other well.'

'You've worked it out, haven't you?'

'It's preyed on my mind all these months, Julie, and the explanation is so bloody obvious I'm ashamed of myself. Steph gave it to me the night before she was killed and I didn't see it until today.'

'Share it, then. I want to hear it, guv.'

'You have to know the kind of person Trish Weather was. We called her Mary Poppins in the old days. She was forever chivvying us into behaving properly, doing the right thing, giving presents to anyone who left. She was the mother hen of the place.'

'There's usually one.'

'Right. I've been told that even after she quit the police to set up her temping agency, she kept dropping in at Fulham nick to look up old friends. It was as if she couldn't bear to leave.'

'It happens.'

'Now listen, Julie. On the last evening I spent with Steph she reminded me my fiftieth birthday was coming up. What's more she told me some friends had seen an article in the paper that mentioned my age and they were talking about giving me a surprise party. She wouldn't say who. You don't, do you, if it's meant to be a surprise? She was just sounding me out, confirming what she'd guessed already—'

'That you couldn't think of anything worse?'

'You know me and parties, Julie.'

'You think Trish was behind the surprise party?'

'I'd put money on it.' Immediately he was hit by a doubt. 'Don't tell me it was you.'

'I didn't even realise you had a special birthday this year.'

Relieved, he let his excitement bubble over. 'Everything

points to Trish. In the diary Steph actually notes which evenings I'm out, so she can call her and discuss it. She knew very well what my reaction would be.'

'You think Steph squashed the idea?'

'No, that wasn't her style. Softly, softly. As I say, she spoke to me first, just to be certain of my reaction. The next day – if I'm right – she meant to break the news to Trish that it wasn't such a good plan. Knowing Steph, she'd want to do it without hurting the woman's feelings.'

'She could tell her on the phone.'

'No, they fixed to meet. She'd prefer to tell her face to face.'

'Who suggested the meeting, then? Trish?'

'I think so. She'd have said it would be nice to meet anyway and she came to Bath sometimes to visit her parents. Steph was friendly, as you know. She'd have fallen in with the idea. They picked the park because that was really close to where Trish's people live. Does that sound plausible?'

Julie sidestepped. 'But why did Trish bring a gun with her?'

'She had a different agenda.'

'Obviously.'

'The surprise party was just a blind.'

'Okay,' she said with a huge note of doubt. 'So what turned her into a killer?'

'Julie, that's the big question only one person can answer now.'

'Stormy Weather.'

He didn't need to confirm it.

Julie said without prompting, 'You think Stormy shot his own wife, don't you? He found out she'd killed Steph and he put her down like a dangerous dog.'

'He's been a strong support to me,' was all he would answer.

'I haven't met the man,' she said. 'I'm just looking at it coldly. He's a Chief Inspector. You and I know what he'd face if his wife was convicted of the murder of another officer's wife. He'd be finished.'

He said indifferently, 'I'm not going to shop him.'

Julie latched on immediately. 'Exactly. What's done is done. If Stormy shot his wife, leave it to Billy Bowers to work it out.'

He started to say, 'But I have to know why—'

Julie cut in, 'Guv, I know how your mind is working. Stay away from Stormy. Don't have any more to do with him. You can only panic him.'

Speaking more to himself than Julie, he started the statement a second time, and completed it, 'I have to know why Steph was murdered and I will.'

A November storm hit the West Country that night, uprooting trees and bringing down fences. Roads right across Somerset and Wiltshire were closed by flooding. Diamond decided not to drive. He took the InterCity to Paddington, crossed London on the Bakerloo Line and completed the journey to Raynes Park by a suburban train. And at intervals, resonating with the rhythm of the wheels, he fancied he heard Julie's voice urging him to stay away from Stormy.

Fat chance.

Before doing anything else at Raynes Park, he needed to relieve himself. He found the 'Gentlemen' sign on the station platform and discovered from a smaller notice on the door that not every man in Raynes Park was gentle. '*Due to continued vandalism these toilets are locked. If you need to use the facilities please ask a member of staff for the key.*' 'I should be so lucky,' he said grimly, looking along the deserted platform. There was a similar notice on the ladies' door. He went down the steps and into the street.

A sheet of rain and a buffeting wind hit him when
he stepped out of the station. In the street, umbrellas
were being blown inside out. He never carried one. He
put up the collar of his old fawn trench coat, jammed
on his trilby more tightly and set off for Stormy's local
shops. They began almost at once, along one side of
Approach Road, and they were about as accommodating
as the station facilities. The pharmacy had ceased
trading. The fish and chip shop wasn't frying. There
were a couple of others with shutters up, covered in graffiti. There *was* a public convenience. The sign on the
door read: '*These toilets are permanently closed.*' Driven
desperate by the sound and sight of the rain, he stepped
around the back.

Feeling better, he applied his mind to other matters.
He looked for the hairdressing salon. If you want to find
out about a woman without speaking to her husband, try
her hairdresser. A shop on the corner called Streakers
had an art nouveau design, tastefully done, of running
nudes with their hair in curlers. He went in with a gust
that blew the showcards off the counter.

One of the stylists put down her scissors and came over.
She was the manager, he discovered.

'I was wondering,' he began when he'd shown his
warrant card, 'if by any chance you cut the hair of Mrs
Weather, the local woman who was shot and found dead
by the railway at Woking.' His voice was calm, but he
hoped to God he'd struck lucky. There simply wasn't time
to do the rounds of all the salons in the area.

'Trish was a client of mine, yes,' the bright-eyed, thir-
tyish manager told him – and it didn't escape him that
she used the 'T' word unprompted. She took him into
the staffroom and sent the junior there to sweep the salon
floor. 'We couldn't believe it when we heard. She was such
a sweet person.'

'You said she was your client. You personally did her hair?'

'I did.'

'For how long?'

'More than a year, once a week. After she left her job in the police she had a regular Friday morning appointment. Personal grooming was important to Trish.' She was eyeing his saturated old mac.

'You got to know the lady well, then? Did she talk about her life?'

She had, quite a bit, he learned. She had been struggling to build up the temping agency. Just when it was starting to take off, a big agency with a chain of branches opened right across the street. They spent a lot in advertising and offered better terms, so her business was hit hard.

The agency didn't interest him at all. 'Did her police work ever come up?'

'Not much.'

'It was a big part of her life. Didn't she talk about the people she worked with?'

She shook her head.

'Did she ever mention someone called Steph, or Stephanie?'

'No.'

Some of the gloss was knocked off his theory.

She told him, 'I got the impression the work was high pressure, but quite satisfying. She missed it after she left. Things got more difficult generally.'

'Not just the business, then?' He was alert to each nuance. 'Her personal life?'

She smoothed her hands down her white tabard. 'If you don't mind, I'd rather not go into that.'

'Why not? She's gone.'

'But Mr Weather hasn't.'

He told her sharply, 'This isn't about being good neighbours, ma'am. It's a murder inquiry. Did she complain
about him?'

'No more than other clients do about their husbands.
We hear it all. You get them in the chair and they tell
you all kinds of confidences.'

He waited, and getting nothing, said, 'So the marriage
was under some pressure?'

'I think being at home, Trish had more time in the
house, and got rather, well, possessive.'

'And?'

'I felt sorry for Mr Weather, to tell you the truth. You
know he slept outside in the van? If you went past in the
evening, there was often a light on inside.'

'I didn't know he has a van.'

'When I say "van", I mean a caravan thing, except it
wasn't a caravan. You could drive it.'

'A motor home?'

'Yes. That's what I mean. Big enough to live in. It used
to be on their drive.'

'It wasn't when I visited. Perhaps he moved it.'

'After Trish disappeared he moved back into the house.
He must have parked the motor home in some other
place. Or sold it.'

'You were saying you felt sorry for him,' he prompted.

'There was one time when she hurt her leg and
couldn't come here, so I went to the house to give her
the shampoo and blow-dry and I was really surprised to
find how feminine everything was, beautifully clean and
tidy, and all pink and white with swathed curtains and
ballerina pictures on the walls. Dolls and soft toys. A little
figure in a crinoline covering the spare toilet roll in the
bathroom. There was nothing of him anywhere to be
seen.'

'Except in the motor home outside?'

'I didn't go in there. I suppose her feminine side had been cramped by the police job. When she got the opportunity, she went a bit overboard.'

This made sense to him, and he was glad of the insight into Stormy's marriage. It compensated a little for his disappointment at learning nothing of Trish's feelings towards Steph.

'One more favour, and I'll let you get back to your client. Could I see your appointments book for February and March – or are you computerised?'

'No. We're far too busy to learn. Stay here and I'll send in the junior with it.'

With the book in his hands, he flicked back the pages to the months he was interested in. There was obviously a system. Regular bookings were entered by someone in a clear, neat script. The others, arranged a short time ahead, or on the day, bore the signs of being hastily inserted in a variety of styles. He soon located *Mrs P. Weather* in the tidy hand, each Friday at eleven-thirty. She'd booked for the whole of February and March.

There was something else about the system. As clients arrived for their appointments, a tick was placed beside their names. There were ticks for Trish Weather up to Friday, February the twelfth. For the nineteenth and subsequent Fridays her name was crossed through and other names had been squeezed in above.

He took the book out to the manager and showed her. 'Does this mean she didn't come in after February the twelfth?'

'That's right.'

'Did she cancel?'

'She must have done – or we wouldn't have slotted another client in.'

'In person?'

'I really can't remember that far back.'

'You must have thought about it when you heard she was murdered.'

'They didn't find her for six months. No, I didn't think it mattered. Is it important, then?'

Is it important? he thought. For crying out loud, *is it important?*

'If she cancelled, would she have called you personally?'

'Any of the staff could have taken the message. It's a matter of who's free to pick up the phone.'

Clearly, she had no memory of speaking to Trish.

'If someone cancels, don't they normally make another appointment?'

'Unless they say they'll get in touch later. If they're ill, somebody might cancel for them.'

'The husband?'

'Anyone.'

'And if you don't hear from the client after that?'

'We don't chase them up, if that's what you mean. If they don't get in touch again, that's the end of it.'

And it was, for Trish Weather, he thought.

He left the salon to walk to the Forester, the local he'd visited before. There was a fair chance that by this time, eleven-thirty, Stormy would be installed there.

The downpour was so heavy by now that everyone else was sheltering in shopfronts and under awnings. Peter Diamond strode through the rain without caring, his thoughts ten months in the past and a hundred miles away, picturing Steph's meeting with the person who was armed and ready to execute her.

From that day to this the question uppermost in Diamond's mind had been 'Why?' Elusive, maddening, paining, it had always been the key. He'd been certain he would find Steph's killer when he understood. He'd not wavered, tortuous as the route had been.

Finally, he knew.

The motive wasn't rage or passion or revenge or greed. It wasn't malice. It was more appalling than any of those: a decision made in cold blood and carried out impassively. Steph had died for no better reason than that she had made a phone call that – unknown to her – undermined a killer's alibi.

He understood enough about the tunnel vision of the murdering mind to know that her life, her individuality, the precious, warm, vital person she was, had not come into the reckoning. She was a risk, so she was eliminated.

Sheer, bloody-minded persistence had got him to the truth. No inspiration, no shaft of light, just his refusal to give in.

The saloon bar of the Forester was almost empty. Stormy was in there, seated at a table with his back to the door. Inconveniently, someone else was with him, a woman. Dark-haired, well made-up, probably around forty, she was in a backless peacock blue dress you wouldn't have expected to see outside a nightclub.

Diamond marched up to the table and said, 'Can we have words?'

Stormy turned in his seat. 'Peter?' He tried to make it sound like a greeting, and didn't convince. 'What brings you out here? You're drenched, man. Get that coat off and let's line up a drink for you.'

'Don't bother.'

A frown threatened Stormy's face momentarily, and then he recovered to say, 'This is Norma – as charming a lady as you'd meet anywhere. Norma, say hello one of my old workmates, Peter Diamond.'

Diamond said to the woman, 'Leave us alone, would you? We have things to discuss.'

She looked to Stormy – who leaned towards her and whispered in her ear. She picked up her coat and walked out of the bar, leaving her drink half-finished.

'What's up?' Stormy asked when Diamond was seated opposite him.

'You want to know what's up?' Diamond said in a hard, tight voice. 'Everything's up – for you. I came here not wanting to believe you murdered your wife.'

He stared back. 'You're not making sense, Peter.'

'Did you ever love her?'

'Patsy?'

'Trish. She liked to be known as Trish.'

Stormy gripped the tankard in front of him with both hands. 'Of course I loved her. Haven't I made that clear?'

'The story I got is that she wouldn't let you in the house.'

'I told you we had arguments sometimes. I made no secret of that.'

'You slept outside in a motor home.'

'Have you been talking to my neighbours?'

'Is it true, then?'

'Sometimes,' Stormy admitted. 'Model-making is my hobby. We spoke of this, didn't we? I keep my materials in the motor home. I can make a mess in there and nobody bothers, and if I want to work late I can.'

'So that's all it was?' Diamond said without irony, as if he was reassured. 'Your marriage was okay?'

'Absolutely.'

'And you got on all right with the in-laws?'

'I got on fine. I still do.'

'Visited them from time to time?'

'Often.'

'Strange,' Diamond said in a voice as dry as last week's bread, 'because when we were sitting in the car on Sion Hill in Bristol you told me you didn't know Bath at all – and it turns out Trish's people live in Brock Street.'

For a moment it seemed Stormy Weather hadn't taken

in the point. He was still coming to terms with the realisation that his background had been investigated. 'In the car we were talking about the Brunel sites. All I said was I haven't seen them.'

'No. I asked if you'd been to Bath and you said not since you were a kid. That was a lie.'

Stormy didn't deny it.

For Diamond, these were pivotal admissions. The molten rage inside him threatened to erupt any second, yet he had to contain it to get the truth. 'What was the problem in your marriage? Was it the fact that you had no children?'

'Plenty of people don't have kids,' Stormy pointed out, rashly adding, 'You don't.'

Don't rise to it, Diamond told himself, don't rise to it. Keep the focus on him. 'You admitted to having affairs. Had Trish given up on sex?'

'I don't see where this is leading.'

'This Norma I just met. How long have you known her?'

'Leave Norma out of it.'

'I can ask the barman or anyone else. I get the impression you're regulars here. Does she want to marry you?'

His silence was as good as a nod.

'But Trish wouldn't let you go, would she?' Diamond pressed on. 'She had things sorted as neat as a knitting pattern. The house to herself, all frills and pink wallpaper and nothing out of place. A good pension. A nice welcome any time she wanted to look up old friends at the nick. And this Mary Poppins image of a perfectly managed existence. No, she didn't want a divorce fouling up her tidy life.'

Stormy took a long sip of beer, transparently trying to appear calm.

'Your life was bleak, sleeping in the motor home and

only allowed into your own house on sufferance. She wouldn't let go, and Norma wanted something more permanent. The pressure got to you.'

The calm was ebbing away.

'Like me, you knocked off a police weapon in those Fulham days when old Robbo was mismanaging the armoury. Piece of cake. No big deal. Like me, you tucked the shooter away and almost forgot about it, right?'

'Who told you this?'

'You planned it well. Some time between February the twelfth and the nineteenth you took out your gun and put two bullets into Trish's head.'

Now Stormy decided a show of outrage was wanted. 'I don't have to listen to this crap.'

'You do. You don't know who's waiting outside,' Diamond bluffed.

Stormy glanced at the door.

'The timing of the murder is absolutely crucial – because she wasn't killed a couple of weeks after Steph was shot, but *before.*'

He swayed back, squeezing his eyes shut as if it were a physical blow. 'You can't say that.'

'I know it. Trish missed her appointment on the nineteenth.'

The eyes shot open and real panic flashed in them. 'What appointment?'

'The hairdo.'

He stared blankly back.

'The shampoo and blow-dry. You were so cut off from her life you didn't know she went to Streakers every Friday. I've been to the shop and seen the book. She missed the next appointment on the twenty-sixth as well, when she was still alive according to you. And the one after.' They were hammer blows and Stormy was reeling from them.

Like any good fighter sensing the end, Diamond didn't relent. 'You're a detective. You've seen plenty of killers fail because someone discovered the body. You thought of a very good place where nobody walked their dogs. After shooting her, you drove the body to Woking and dumped it on the railway embankment where it wouldn't be found for months, if not years. Went home with the idea of waiting a couple of weeks before you reported her missing. Devious, that was – to confuse everyone over the date she disappeared, just in case they investigated your movements on the day of the murder.'

Stormy grasped the arms of his chair to get up, but Diamond grabbed his shirt-front and held him where he was. 'Don't even think about it.'

'Free country,' he said in a rasp.

'Not any more it isn't – not for you. You thought you'd got it all sussed after you disposed of Trish. You were sitting at home – back in the house you owned – when the phone rang and it was Steph, my wife, expecting to speak to Trish. Awkward. You said she was out and offered to take a message and it soon became obvious they'd arranged to meet in Bath to discuss the surprise party Trish wanted to arrange for my fiftieth. Man, oh man, that threw you, didn't it? Your plan was in ruins. You'd meant to wait another two weeks before doing your worried husband act and reporting your wife missing. But Steph would kibosh that. She'd say it was you she spoke to on the phone, not Trish. She'd say Trish didn't turn up for their meeting. She was trouble.'

A strange thing was happening to Stormy's face. The red blotches were standing out like a leopard's spots, separated by patches of dead white skin. His lips, too, were drained of blood. They didn't move.

Diamond leaned closer, still holding him by the shirt, his voice cracking with emotion. 'You decided to kill my

wife, you sick fuck, simply because she got in the way of
your plan. You'd killed once and it was easy, so you'd do
it again. Am I right?'

Not a flicker.

'This wasn't done in the heat of the moment. This was
premeditated, cold-blooded murder. You thought it
through. When you'd worked out what to say you phoned
back and told her you'd spoken to Trish and she'd asked
you to confirm the time and place of their meeting. It
was to be the Crescent Gardens, opposite the old bandstand, at ten. You drove to Bath and waited in the park.
When Steph arrived, expecting to meet Trish, you walked
up to her and took out the gun and shot her twice in the
head. Then you got in your car and drove home.'

The eyes confirmed it, even if the voice was silent.

'By killing her, you kept your trump card, the chance
to mislead everyone about the date of your own wife's
death. You waited another two weeks before reporting that
Trish was missing. And ever since, you've been doing your
damnedest to lay false trails, insisting on calling her Patsy,
putting in the frame every villain we ever crossed, sending
me every bloody way but here. I took you for a friend and
you're a bloody Judas, the worst enemy I could have had.'

The man had nothing to say. His eyes were opaque.
He seemed indifferent, passive. But it was a trick.

Abruptly his two hands reached up and smashed down
on Diamond's wrist, wrenching it away from the shirt. He
stood, wheeled around and made a dash for a door at
the back.

Diamond's reaction was slower than it should have
been, partly because of where he was seated. The table
tipped over and the glasses crashed as he shoved them
aside and stepped out. Unfortunately he blundered into
a bar-stool and stumbled to his knees. The door had
slammed before he was on his feet again.

He charged across and yanked it open. He was looking out at the car park, and Stormy Weather was already climbing into the passenger seat of a white motor home driven by the woman in the blue dress. He must have given her the order to wait with the engine running.

Diamond sprinted.

The vehicle had revved and powered away before he made a grab for the door. He grasped the handle and had his right arm tugged almost out of its socket. Acting on impulse and anger alone, he held on, taking huge strides beside the cab, and jerked the door fully open.

A mistake.

He was staring at imminent death, into the muzzle of a gun. Stormy Weather, eyes wild with panic, took aim.

The bullet hit Diamond like a sledgehammer and he fell backwards and knew no more.

'Peter.'
  'Mm?'
'How are you doing?'
'Steph?' He tried to rise and felt a searing pain in his chest.
'Stay still, love. Don't fight it.'
'Fight what?'
'You can relax. The job's done. You're a brave man.'
'Is it really you, Steph?'
No answer.
'Am I dead?'
'Not dead. You'll survive this time. lucky you.'
'Love you, too.'
'You, too . . . You, too . . . You, too . . .'
She was fading and another voice, not Steph's, was saying, 'He's coming round, I think.'
He succeeded in opening his eyes and was conscious of someone above him. Devastated, he saw she was not Steph, but a much younger woman in nurse's uniform. He asked, 'Where did she go?'
'Who do you mean?'
'Steph was here.'
'You must have heard Sister speaking.'
'Her sister went back to Liverpool. Where am I?'
'Kingston Hospital. Listen, you're a little woozy from the injection, and you will be for some time to come, but

you're going to be all right, as Sister was trying to tell you.'

'Hospital?'

'You were shot in the shoulder. Don't try to move it. The back of your head hit the ground hard, but there doesn't seem to be any damage to the skull. You've got visitors, by the way.'

'Steph?'

'Who's this Steph you keep on about?' She spoke to someone else. 'He's still bosky, poor bloke. Maybe it's better if he rests for a while.'

When he came round again, he was clearer in the head, and sadder. The visitors were seated by the bed. They were a youngish man whose face he couldn't put a name to, and another he'd never seen in his life.

'Bowers. Billy Bowers,' the first man said when it was obvious Diamond was at a loss. 'Woking CID, investigating the death of Patricia Weather. Remember?'

'Now I do.'

'And this is Sergeant Sims. He was on the search party, but I don't think you met him that day. How are you feeling?'

'Sore.'

'Clear-headed?'

'Better than I was. I expect you want to know who shot me.'

'Dave Weather. He's in custody.'

He flexed and gave himself a stab of pain. 'You nicked him? Brilliant!'

'Thanks to the tip-off we got from your friend DI Hargreaves.'

He was talking about Julie. What did Julie know about it? With an effort, Diamond recollected his last conversation with her. He'd told her on the phone he was going after Stormy.

'Pity we didn't collar him before he shot you. If only you'd told us—'

'If I'd told you, I wouldn't have been allowed within a mile of him.'

'You've got a point there,' Bowers admitted with a grin. 'We had the tactical firearms unit waiting outside the house. When the shot was fired in the pub car park, they got round fast. Those motor homes aren't built for easy getaways.'

'Was there a shoot-out?'

'No, they gave themselves up. We'll release the woman without charge later on, but Weather won't be joining her. He thinks we know the lot, and of course we don't – yet. What I need is your account of what happened.'

Later in the day, he was seen by a doctor who told him the bullet had ripped through the deltoid muscle and pierced the scapula. There was some splintering of the bone and he would be kept overnight for some more 'hoovering' under anaesthetic. Apart from the scar, there would be no permanent damage.

'You're lucky.'

'Oh, yes?'

'Or were you looking for early retirement?'

'A living death? No thanks.'

Keith Halliwell came to visit later in the day, a call Diamond appreciated. He brought with him a bottle of malt whisky and a Get Well card signed by everyone on the Bath murder squad.

'You should have been in the incident room when the news came through, guv. Mr McGarvie's face had to be seen to be believed. Not only did he screw up, but you got your man and Bill Bowers gets the collar. He's not a happy bunny.'

'If I could move my arm I'd wipe away a tear, Keith.'

'All I can say is it's lucky for Weather he isn't in our nick. What a weasel, cosying up to you when he'd murdered your wife. How could he do that?'

'It suited him nicely, Keith. When I first offered to work with him he back-pedalled a little, but after he thought about it, being with me he was beautifully placed to foul up the works. Any time another suspect was in the frame, whether it was Joe Florida or Wayne Beach or Dixon-Bligh, he said just enough to point the finger their way.'

'You must hate the man.'

'Hate is too good a word.'

'At least you got satisfaction.'

Later, after Halliwell was gone, he thought about that word 'satisfaction'. In earlier times a duellist was said to demand satisfaction for some offence. There had been none in catching Weather, nor would there be when he was sent down for life. It had mattered that he was caught. The law of the land would be upheld.

Satisfaction?

No.

Yet he felt less gloomy than he had at the lowest point. He would never admit to anyone that he believed in the supernatural. The words he'd attributed to Steph when he was lying in the hospital bed must have been spoken by one of the nursing staff. Must have. He'd been drowsy from some pain killer, hadn't he?

At the time, he'd believed every word.

Well, someone sounding very like Steph had said the job was done. He was comforted by that, whatever the explanation. In this savage world any comfort is worth holding onto.